THE TALISMAN

LYNDA LA PLANTE
THE TALISMAN

**SIMON &
SCHUSTER**

London · New York · Sydney · Toronto · New Delhi

A CBS COMPANY

First published in Great Britain by Sidgwick & Jackson, 1987
First published by Simon & Schuster UK Ltd, 2013
This hardback edition published by Simon & Schuster UK Ltd, 2018
A CBS COMPANY

1 3 5 7 9 10 8 6 4 2

Simon & Schuster UK Ltd
1st Floor
222 Gray's Inn Road
London WC1X 8HB

Simon & Schuster Australia, Sydney
Simon & Schuster India, New Delhi

www.simonandschuster.co.uk
www.simonandschuster.com.au
www.simonandschuster.co.in

A CIP catalogue record for this book
is available from the British Library

Hardback ISBN: 978-1-4711-7586-2
Trade Paperback ISBN: 978-1-4711-7625-8
eBook ISBN: 978-1-4711-3082-3

Typeset in Bembo by M Rules
Printed and bound by CPI Group (UK) Ltd, Croydon, CR0 4YY

Simon & Schuster UK Ltd are committed to sourcing paper
that is made from wood grown in sustainable forests and support the Forest
Stewardship Council, the leading international forest certification organisation.
Our books displaying the FSC logo are printed on FSC certified paper.

Dedicated to my beloved sister
Gilly Titchmarsh

Acknowledgements

My sincere thanks to Suzanne Baboneau and Ian Chapman for their constant support and encouragement over the many years we have worked together. I am so thrilled that Simon & Schuster are publishing *The Talisman* as it will breathe new life into the novel that is closest to my heart. It seems a long time ago when I first began to research the characters, and was led into the Romany world by some very special people.

Jake 'The rake' Woodly, his manushi Eda, his docha Tina and his stories and dreams, made the writing an exciting journey. So much so, that I found it hard to finish the book as I literally fell in love with the characters and their lives – they became like family to me. I recall how their deaths affected me emotionally, as sometimes you reach into real events and release the words that you should have said long ago, but the timing never seemed right.

The Legacy and *The Talisman* were the beginning of my writing career and to have Suzanne Baboneau, who along with the late Susan Hill, was so supportive throughout my early career as a novelist, I think was more than fortunate. I am sincerely grateful for my on-going relationship with Suzanne who remains enthusiastic and encouraging and a dear, treasured friend.

ROMANY CURSE

He must lie with his treasures, be they tin or gold.
Resting in finery, his back to the soil.
One wheel of his vargon must light up with fire.
In the flame is the evil, his pain and his soul.
But beware of his talisman, carved out of stone.
If not in his palm, then a curse is foretold.

For who steals the charm of a dukkerin's son,
Will walk in his shadow, bleed with his blood,
Cry loud with his anguish and suffer his pain.
His unquiet spirit will rise up again,
His footsteps will echo unseen on the ground
Until the curse is fulfilled, the talisman found.

Prologue

During the Second World War Blitz on the East End of London, Freedom Stubbs, the Romany ex-British Heavyweight Boxing Champion, was killed by his eldest son, Edward. Edward had just received confirmation that he had won a scholarship to Cambridge University, the fulfilment of a long-held dream of his mother's. To enable him to continue his studies, his younger brother, Alex, agreed to confess to the killing of their father.

The two brothers were parted: Alex going to jail to await sentence and Edward to university. Neither of them went to their father's burial, but many East Enders showed their respect, saying farewell to their gentle champion by walking silently behind the hearse. The mourners were joined by gypsies who came from all parts of England. Freedom had been not only their champion, but also the son of a dukkerin, and a prince of royal Romany blood.

In the past, Romanies of high rank were buried with their most valuable possessions. All their other belongings were burnt to ensure that the soul of the dead would rest in peace and not haunt the living. Freedom was buried in his best and only suit. During his life he had become a kairengo, a house-dweller, so there was no vargon or caravan wheel to burn, but, ironically, his house had burned down in the Blitz. His wife,

Evelyne, left alone with the gypsies by her husband's grave, was asked if a talisman could be buried with Freedom, as was their custom. It should be something gold, and honoured by the dead man.

Freedom had no talisman, but Evelyne promised that she would return to place in his grave the one item of value the family still had. This was a gold necklace, and was accepted by the gypsies as appropriate for their royal prince.

Freedom Stubbs had given the necklace to his wife, given it with pride and love when he was the British Heavyweight champion, when the long-awaited World Championship was to be his next fight. The necklace represented his success, and even when he lost the title, along with his winnings, even when the family had sunk into poverty, it was never sold. The gypsies were right; it was Freedom's talisman, and with it in the palm of his hand it could be seen that he had once achieved something, he had been somebody. So it was right that he should lie in his grave with the gold that he had fought so hard for; it was right he should be given the dream that was so very nearly his.

The promise was made in good faith, but the forthcoming trial of Evelyne's younger son, Alex, made it appear wasteful, even sinful, to bury such a valuable possession in a grave. Evelyne felt that when Alex was released from jail they would need the financial security the necklace could bring them.

The unquiet soul of Freedom began to weep, reaching out to the son who had inherited the powers of the dukkerin. The restless spirit with soundless footsteps began to haunt the living . . .

Book One

Chapter One

Two weeks after the burial of his father, Alex Stubbs was sent to a remand home, Rochester House, a large Victorian building with a six-foot wall and another six feet of barbed wire on top. Not exactly a prison, yet it still had the feel of one, and for those boys sent there Rochester House was anything but homely. They all wore grey shorts and socks, with navy blue pullovers over white vests, and black plimsolls. There were strict rules and regulations. Rochester was an assessment point, a halfway house until the boys went before the 'beak' to be sentenced for their crimes. It was therefore imperative that they obey the strict regime. Many of them would, after assessment, be released, but those with a past record would be sentenced and transferred to the reform schools.

The boys' hair was cut short to avoid nits spreading, and they all smelt of carbolic from the showers, and of mothballs from their institutional sweaters. Their ages ranged from ten to sixteen. Alex, being fifteen, was placed in a dormitory with the older boys, all of whom were already hardened to reform school life, having been in and out of institutions since they were ten.

Alex was terrified, but he never showed it. His fear made him silent, a loner. His manners, his gentleness and his obvious intelligence set him apart. He was a grammar-school boy, and that was something in itself. During classes, Alex soon learned not to answer all the questions put to them by the teacher. Any boy standing out as 'different' or 'special' would be tormented. He learned fast, even going so far as to make deliberate spelling mistakes in his essays. At grammar school he had been at the top of his class in maths, but at Rochester House he made sure he achieved only average marks.

The boys had little or no privacy. Throughout their waking hours they were watched and monitored by the warders. The head warder of the school, Major Kelly, was a threat to all the boys living under him. If they didn't behave, the staff would report them to 'The Major', whose name was enough to instil order.

Even at night Alex could find no comfort in sleep. He tried to blank out from his mind the terrible pictures of his dying father wrapped in his mother's arms, tried not to hear the sounds of his mother's weeping. He willed himself once more to conjure the dream he had dreamed when he had first been held in jail. The dream that had given him peace, had comforted and cleansed him.

In the dream Alex had been running up a mountain bathed in sunlight, lush green grass beneath his feet, and above him a brilliant blue sky. It was surreal and yet tangible, and running he had felt free, heading towards the very peak of the towering, magnificent mountain. Then he heard the thunder of hooves, ringing and echoing around the mountainside. Still he ran on, filled with joy, breathing the sweet, clean air . . . and then he saw, breaking through the clouds with his raised hooves, a black, shining stallion galloping towards him. Astride the horse sat a man with flowing, blue-black hair, at one with the beast. Alex lifted his arms to the man, calling to him as if he represented his own free spirit. The rider was his father, he was Freedom . . . 'Don't go, don't go,' Alex cried. But the rider had passed by, into the clouds, which closed like a grey curtain behind him.

Alex had recaptured his dream, but now it turned into a nightmare. There was no rider, no stallion, just the suffocating, grey cloud enveloping him. He was awakened by his own cry, his body drenched in sweat. He pulled the rough blanket around him, shivering now, afraid his cry had been heard by the other boys in the dormitory. He was not alone. Around him he could hear the muffled sobs of boys as frightened as himself hiding beneath their sheets, all of them afraid of tomorrow.

Fights broke out in class, and in the yard at recreation time. Bullies, already hardened to the system, took delight in tormenting first offenders.

Alex watched closely and remained apart, ignoring taunts, ignoring any incitements to argument. He had heard the whispers behind his back. Somehow the boys had learned why he was there, that he had committed murder. This gave him some standing among them, and a slight aura of menace.

Wally Simpson was the same age as Alex but only half his size, which earned him the nickname 'the Shrimp'. He had the next bed to Alex. A cheeky, cocky little chap, he took a lot of beatings from the bigger boys, but he always fought back, if not with his fists then with his sharp wits.

Often during the long, lonely nights Wally would try to make contact with Alex. 'Psssst, hey, Alex, can yer 'ear me, mate? Yer got anyone visitin' yer? Psssst . . .'

Alex feigned sleep, facing the wall, glad he was in the last bed.

'Is it true what they say? You in fer murder? Alex . . .?'

With one eye on the door, Wally slipped out of his bed, crept over to Alex's and tapped him on the shoulder. Alex whipped round, and Wally stepped back sharply.

'Stay away from me, stay away.'

'All right, mate, only offerin' ter be friendly – sod ya!'

Alex drew his blanket over his head and snuggled down. He wished his brother, Edward, was with him, wished it was all a nightmare, but the stink of the blanket brought it home to him that this was reality. No matter how hard it was, he would do just as his mother had told him.

Alex's mother, Evelyne, had come to the police station on the morning after Freedom's death. Only twenty-four hours had passed since the murder, and yet she seemed to have aged. Her son was deeply shocked by the change in her. Evelyne had always been thin, but her tall, angular frame had never stooped before. She had always stood upright, her big-boned hands strong, a firmness and strength to her that had set her apart from an early age, even in the small Welsh mining village where she had been born. She had never been known as a beautiful woman; her cheekbones were too prominent, her face appeared carved rather than moulded, and her face had always lacked youthfulness. But her dark green eyes, set off by wild red hair – her 'crowning glory' as her mother used to say – made one turn to look again. She was striking, and with that hair one knew she had a fiery temper. She could be disdainful, even arrogant, when she wanted, but when she smiled that fierceness disappeared, and then she was simply lovely.

It was this picture of her that Alex had held in his mind since the murder, the face he loved so much and was so desperate to see again.

The twenty-four hours since Freedom's death were etched in her face. The brightness was gone from her eyes, her shoulders were bent and her hands constantly fumbled with the strap of her worn handbag. He reached out to hold her, but she stepped back, hugging the bag to her chest. There was no colour to her, she was drab and empty, and even her lovely, lilting voice had changed. When she spoke she sounded hoarse ... he could hardly believe that this was his mother; all her strength had seeped away.

'I've a lawyer. He says for you to tell him everything. They'll send you to Rochester House. You'll be evaluated there, so it will be up to you, son. Do whatever they tell you, and don't mix with the other boys – keep yourself apart. When it's over we'll start afresh, you and me – when you come out.'

Although distraught with worry for her, he was so upset himself he couldn't think how to comfort her. She continued to hug her handbag, hunched in the chair.

'I'll visit. I know the truth, I know it was Edward, I know, but you tell the lawyers what you have to.'

Alex bit his lip so hard he almost drew blood. 'How's Edward, Ma? How's he taking it?'

Her face twisted, her mouth turned down. 'It's just you and me now, Alex, just you and me. Don't ever mention his name, not yet. I can't stand the sound of his name.'

He choked back the tears and his lips trembled. There was an awful, heartbreaking silence, then he remembered his beloved dog, Rex. His father had bought him the puppy one Christmas. He leaned forward. 'Will you take care of Rex for me, Ma? Tell him I'll be home soon to take him for walks.'

Evelyne shook her head and made a strange, small moaning sound. Then she pushed her chair back and walked away, without touching him, without kissing him. When she finally spoke, there was the strange hoarseness in her voice again.

'Rex followed the ambulance, after your Da, followed it until he dropped. They said his paws were bloody. God knows how many miles he must have followed ... He loved him so, he loved ... He's not come home, nobody's at home.'

The warder opened the door to let her out, and Alex knew she was crying. He shouted after her.

'Mum! Mama! I'm sorry ... I'm sorry!'

The warder had to prise Alex away from the door. He was as gentle as possible; the boy seemed so young, so distraught.

'Your Ma's gone now, lad. Now quieten down, don't go making a fuss.'

Alex flung himself down on his bunk and cried his heart out. He cried for his father, he wept for his beloved dog, and he sobbed for his mother until he lay, face down, head buried in the pillow, exhausted. Then he whispered over and over, 'Eddie ... Eddie? Why did you do it, Eddie? Why?'

At weekends the boys had more recreation time. They could play football games in the yard, and billiards in the main hall. Parents arrived to visit their sons in shifts, as they could not all be accommodated at once. They were led into the dining hall, which doubled as the visiting room. The boys sat on one side of the long row of tables, parents on the other.

'Alex Stubbs to the dining hall!'

Alex ran from the yard into the hall. He had to search almost the entire row of parents before he found his mother near the far end. She wore her best brown coat and hat, and sat erect with her usual handbag and a paper carrier bag on her lap.

'Hello, Ma, everything all right, is it?'

She held out her hand and gripped his tight, lifted it to her lips and kissed it. Alex looked covertly around, not wanting the other lads to see.

'You're eating all right, are you? I've brought a bag of fruit and nuts for you.' She passed him the bag in which she'd also put a chocolate bar and a few shillings in case he needed them. She sighed and told him that Mrs Harris' youngest, Dora, was giving her a terrible time, getting up to all sorts of tricks. 'She's out all hours in high heels and little else, according to her mother. She's been nothing but trouble, that one.'

Alex enjoyed her gossip, not wanting to talk about anything serious.

'I'll be here next weekend. You behave yourself and there'll be no reform school – that's what the social worker said – so be a good boy. They're just assessing you in here, that's all, then they'll let you come home!'

Alex murmured that he always behaved himself, and had no intention of doing anything else. The bell rang for the end of the visit, and Alex asked quickly if Evelyne had heard from Edward. She flushed and pulled at her hat. He knew she was trying not to let him see the tears in her eyes.

'Edward's just fine, thanks to you, and he knows he's got to make this up to you, he knows.'

Alex wanted to ask her if he could write to his brother, but the warders were already ordering the boys out of the hall. He stood up and gave Evelyne a wink, then stuffed his hands in his pockets and strolled out, head high. He kept it up right to the door, then turned; she could see the tears on his cheeks before he hurried out.

Evelyne tried to stand, but had to sit down again. It had been so hard, so hard not to wrap him in her arms. He had looked so tall, so thin, and his knees were red raw. He had just got into long trousers at grammar school, and now they had put him back into shorts. If he was suffering, he made no mention of it, only in his beautiful blue eyes could she see her son's fear. She almost decided to go to the police and tell the truth, but then if it wasn't Alex behind bars it would be Edward. At least for Alex it wouldn't be long, she told herself.

Later that night, Alex was sitting in a corner of the games room reading a book. A snooker match was in progress, and a group of rowdy lads was arguing about whose turn it was. Kenny Baker, a big sixteen-year-old and the self-appointed 'guv'nor' of Rochester House, sauntered in. As he passed the snooker table he picked up one of the balls 'the Shrimp' was just about to take a shot at. He tossed the ball in the air, caught it, and held it just out of Wally's reach. He turned to Alex. 'Hey, you, skinny Jim, wanna game of snooker wiv me?'

'You give us the ball back, Kenny, or I'll stick this cue up your arse. Way I hears it, that's just what yer like.' With three boys grouped around him, Wally was full of bravado, but he shrank as they moved quickly to avoid trouble.

'Well, ain't yer got a big gob on yer fer a shrimp? Wanna say that again, eh? You wanna say it again?'

Wally sprang around the table, and tried to wheedle his way out of it. 'I were just jokin', Kenny, honest!'

Whack! The cue came down across Wally's shoulders. Next minute Kenny had him lying across the table, and was pushing him down, trying to stuff a billiard ball into Wally's mouth. None of the other boys did anything to help. Alex watched for a moment, then went back to reading his book. The screams and scuffles got louder as Wally struggled.

'Leave him alone.'

Kenny turned round and gave Alex a nasty, sickly smile. 'Well, well, the beanpole can talk! Well I never, yer got yerself a champion, Wally . . .'

Wally slunk away from the table and closer to Alex. Kenny leered at the boys behind him, keeping a watch on the doors. 'You fink yer boss around 'ere, do yer, Stubbs?'

The printed page blurred before Alex's eyes, but he refused to look up, pretending to continue reading. The next moment the billiard cue cracked down on his knee. Slowly, he closed his book and stood up, as Wally danced around, his little fists up. 'Come on, Alex, we can take 'im. He finks 'e's so bleedin' tough, we all know he's only in 'ere fer nickin' shillings from 'is granny's gas meter . . .'

Alex stepped behind Wally, heading for the door. The boys on guard promptly shut it and stood in his way, arms folded. Pushing Wally aside, Kenny faced Alex, grabbing him by the arm. 'Least I didn't knife me old man,' Kenny sneered. 'That's what you done, ain't it, Stubbs? We all taken a beatin' from our Dads, ain't we, lads, but knockin' off yer old man . . .'

Alex could feel the fury building inside him, and he spoke through clenched teeth, 'Will you get away from the doors?'

He felt a blow on the back of his neck, and saw stars. He knew he couldn't take Kenny on, he was so much bigger, so he had to get out. He tried to reach for the door handle, and one of the boys on guard pushed him. He sprawled backwards on the floor. Kenny kicked him hard in the ribs, so hard his breath caught and he coughed and spluttered.

Laughing, Kenny picked up Alex's book and tossed it aside, then saw the brown paper bag. He tore it open and held the chocolate bar aloft. 'Gor blimey, what else yer got in 'ere, Stubbs?'

Alex picked up the pool cue and brought it crashing down on Kenny's head, then held it crosswise and hit him in the throat. He was caught red-handed with the cue by the warders as they burst into the games room and saw Kenny screaming and clutching his throat.

'Right, who started this? I want the truth, which boy started this?'

Kenny, Wally and the other witnesses remained silent. The Major rose to his feet behind his desk. He was a massive man, with a vast barrel chest and a waxed, grey moustache. His left arm was stiff, pressed to his side, and a brown leather glove covered his false steel hand. 'Put them in the detention block . . . all of them. You'll be a damned sight sorrier in there. Go on, get out of my sight.'

The warder ushered the boys out and returned to the office. The Major was standing at his desk, holding Alex's report file. He flipped it open. 'Keep your eye on Stubbs – not like the rest of 'em, he's a grammar-school boy, and cocky with it. When his mother comes next visit, ask her to see me, would you?'

The warden nodded and took out his notebook. He asked what Stubbs was in for, and the Major pursed his lips, then handed the file over. 'As I said, he's different. Stubbs knifed his own father. Dear God, what is the world coming to . . .'

Evelyne was dumbfounded when she was led to the Major's office, and even more shocked when she was told of Alex's behaviour. She told the Major over and over that it was very unlike Alex, he was always quiet, and when he showed her Alex's school reports she was stunned. They were bad; although he wasn't at the bottom of the class he was still well below his average at grammar school.

Although he felt sorry for Mrs Stubbs, the Major told her that as Alex had been causing trouble in the detention centre, he was denied future visiting privileges.

The next time Evelyne saw Alex was when he was led before the judge to hear what his fate would be.

'Well, Stubbs,' said the Beak, 'you don't appear to have learned your lesson. On three occasions you were warned to behave yourself. I therefore have no alternative but to send you to reform school for two years.'

Alex stood in the dock, white-faced, and could not bear to look at his mother. He could not believe his ears. Evelyne wept and hung her head, wiping her face with her handkerchief.

Letting herself into the empty house, Evelyne set her gas mask on the kitchen table and, too tired to build the fire, sat alone, sipping a cup of strong, sweet tea. The broken windows had been boarded up, and a large tarpaulin covered the bomb-damaged roof. She had always been a fighter, but now she was giving in. Overwhelmed with tiredness, she sat in the chair. She couldn't bear to think of Edward, and now Alex had failed her, too.

The train thundered through the black tunnel, and Alex sat opposite Major Kelly, his haversack on his knee. The Major snored, his steel hand hanging limply at his side. Eventually the train pulled into Brighton.

Oakwood Hall was a gothic monster set in large grounds a few miles outside Brighton. Alex half-expected the place to be surrounded with barbed wire, but the manor house looked more like a grand hotel. As the taxi entered the gates, he stared around at the grassy fields and woods.

The hall was oak-beamed, Tudor style, with highly polished oak floors. They waited in the hall as a plump woman, wearing a starched white apron, came down the wide staircase. Alex was ushered in to meet his housemaster, Mr Taylor. He had a thick thatch of straw-coloured hair with a reddish tinge. His eyes were blue, piercing and icy, framed by round wire glasses. Alex could see that he was actually rather a handsome man, with full, red lips and wide cheekbones, very fresh-faced. When he rose from behind the desk he stood at least five foot eleven, well built with broad shoulders. He wore a crumpled tweed jacket and the fashionable, baggy grey flannels. They were held at the waist by a tie, which Alex was later informed was from Eton, where Mr Taylor had been educated.

Taylor gave Alex a quick, sharp lecture, a stamped envelope

for his weekly letter home, and, just as Alex reached the office door, he snapped, 'I run a tight ship, Stubbs. Just do as you're told and we'll get along. I'll have a chat with you at a later date, run along.'

Lounging outside Mr Taylor's office was Sidney Green. Dapper in his uniform, his hair slicked back with grease, he possessed a natural sharpness. 'Well, that was short an' sweet, must be yer lucky day. Name's Sid, just follow me, I'm ter show yer the ropes . . . got all yer kit? Let's get this over wiv, got a game of football. You play footer, do yer?'

Alex trailed behind Sid down endless corridors, until they came to a long dormitory. Sid barely paused for breath, keeping up a steady flow of chatter. He pointed out a small bed, a locker, and then sat swinging his legs impatiently while Alex unpacked. 'Take yer gear, stick us in this ruddy uniform, makes yer sick. I got meself a nice suit just before they copped me – nice double-breasted with a crease in the pants yer could cut yer 'and on, very tasty – got one of them new skinny-rib ties what's all the fashion . . .'

Sid continued to talk all through the tour of Oakwood Hall, making rude remarks about every room, every teacher, until his black humour had Alex smiling. 'Yer fink I'm jokin', mate, but wait, just wait. You'll see all I'm talkin' is God's truth. This place comes wiv the ark, no kiddin'.'

Alex never really chose Sid as his friend, Sid simply latched on. He was very glad in the end as Sid was so popular, forever joking, always ready with the hottest rumours. Oakwood Hall was a far cry from Rochester House, and Alex settled in fast. Lessons were treated seriously, though not by Sid. The only thing he really worked at was his football. On the pitch he could dribble the ball so fast he was at the far end and back again with no one to touch him. They became even more inseparable when Sid saw how fast Alex could run. 'Hey, you an' me, yer know, we could make it on the professional circuit – did I tell yer me Dad's a professional? Yeah, he's one hell of a football player. Soon's I'm out, an' the war's over, I'm gonna try out fer Fulham.'

Evelyne's weekend visits left Alex increasingly anxious about her. She seemed thinner and unnaturally quiet, but she always brought him a bagful of fruit and a chocolate bar. She gave him a half-crown to slip in his pocket and told him it might be difficult for her to come every week as it was such a long way from home. 'You look well, son, it must be the sea air. Do you get out on to the beach at all?'

Alex told her they went for long walks every other day, and one of the masters took them on country rambles. He did look well, and he was filling out. He was taller, and his long trousers made him look very grown-up. To Alex, his mother seemed vacant, and her big, worn hands fiddled nervously with her handbag strap all the time.

'You heard from our Eddie, then, Ma?'

Evelyne frowned slightly and said he'd written, but he was very probably busy with his studies. 'I asked Mr Taylor and he said you were doing well here. So stay that way and I'll have you home soon. That will be nice, just the two of us.'

Alex gave her a soft, shy smile, and she reached over and gently touched his face. She noticed his quick, embarrassed glance to see if any of the other lads were watching.

'You've not been getting into any fights, the way you did at Rochester House?'

'No, it's not bad here, and I'm working well. They tell you I was top in maths? And then there's the sports. I play a lot of football.'

She smiled, pleased, and he slid his hand across the table to hold hers. 'I love you, Ma . . . love you with all my heart, I do.'

'I know, son, I know . . . I never told you much about your grandfather, but, well, you've got more of a look of him than ever. It's the dimple in your chin.'

Alex had rarely, if ever, heard her mention his grandfather. He couldn't know that Evelyne had her reasons, deep, hidden reasons, and there was also the fact that there had never been a legal form of marriage between herself and Freedom.

The wardens began to open the doors, at any moment the bell would ring. 'I'll write to you, Mum.'

Evelyne appeared to be miles away, staring into space.

'Mum, I know it's hard for you to come and see me, so don't put yourself out too much.'

Alex always had so much more to say when the bell rang. There was that emotional surge when he first saw her that made him go dumb. Then, just as he relaxed, it was time for her to go.

The wardens called 'Time up', and the boys had to file out before their parents left. Evelyne noticed that Alex had a manly swagger to him now. He was growing away from her and it tore her heart. When he turned and gave her that smile of his at the door, she fought to put on a brave face, giving him a little wave of her hand. Today more than ever she saw Hugh, her father, in her son – his curly hair, his blue eyes – then the pain swept over her and she could see Edward's face, Edward her first-born, Freedom's mirror, and by the time she boarded the train home she was drained, a terrible empty feeling inside her. She felt cut off, and desperately alone, the confusion of faces dead and gone haunting her . . .

Like all the boys at Oakwood, Alex felt deeply depressed after these visits. He jogged out to the football field in search of Sid, who appeared never to receive either letters or visitors. Seeing two younger boys kicking a ball around, he asked after Sid.

'Matron took 'im up to the sickroom, he's had one of his turns.'

It was not until they were getting ready for bed that Alex saw Sid again. The matron brought him in, looking pale and drawn, and she had to help him into bed. The young lad next to Alex whispered, 'They give 'im somefink ter quiet 'im down, drug 'im . . .'

'Why does his Dad never visit?'

The boy sniggered, 'You don't believe 'is stories, do yer? He ain't got no Dad, that's why they keep bringin' 'im back 'ere – he got no place else.'

Alex lay back. He couldn't believe it – why had Sid lied to him about his father? He looked over at the still figure of his usually buoyant friend and was angry at Sid for making such a fool of him.

At breakfast next morning Sid was as lively as ever, fooling around and spilling sugar on the floor. Eventually Mr Taylor yelled at him.

'Hey, Alex, want a quick game at break? Alex ...? Whassamatter wiv yer?'

'You should have told me, Sid, why'd you lie? What you lie to me for?'

Sid sniffed and shrugged, looked down at his shoes. 'Why don't yer mind yer own friggin' business ... you want ter play or not?'

'No, I gotta see Taylor ...'

Sid stuffed his hands in his pockets, gave Alex a peculiar smile. 'Taylor asked to see yer, 'as he? I wondered 'ow long he'd take to get round yer ... Well sod ya, I'll play on me own.'

Sid went to move away and Alex caught him by the arm. 'Sid, is it true yer don't 'ave a Dad?'

'Look, I ain't got nobody, so I make 'em up in me 'ead – is that such a terrible fing? I don't hurt nobody ... But you try it sometimes, everybody comin' in wiv fings what they been given. I don't even get a friggin' letter.'

Alex put an arm around him, pulled him towards the lockers. 'All right then, from now on what I get, we halve ... here you go, fruit, chocolate ...'

Sid slipped an arm around Alex's shoulder, grinning from ear to ear, then he glanced at the door and whispered, 'Watch out for Taylor, he's a bastard – know what I mean?'

Alex shook his head.

'Gawd 'elp us, you are green, yer know that ... Look, this is what yer say when he asks ...'

Before Sid could elaborate, Alex was called by a junior to get a move on, as Taylor was waiting for him.

'Tell me later ... We'll have a game after tea, okay?'

Sid watched Alex hurry off. He snapped the bar of chocolate in two and ate a square. Alex grinned from the door, and Sid gave him the thumbs-up sign. No older than Alex, Sid was streetwise. Alex was such a good-looking boy, skinny maybe, but a real looker. 'Well, son, you're gonna learn the 'ard way, that's fer sure.'

Mr Taylor was sitting at his desk marking exercise books, his pebble glasses stuck on the end of his nose. He looked up, smiled at Alex and told him to sit down, he would be with him in a moment.

Mr Taylor continued to work, ignoring Alex, who sat and looked around the comfortable office. The bookcases were crammed, in fact the whole room seemed to bulge at the seams with books on every available surface. There was an old couch close to the window which overlooked the play-ground. On the mantel a big, white-faced wooden clock ticked loudly. The scratching of Taylor's pen continued as the minutes ticked on and on. Alex shuffled his feet and looked at the thick crop of hair bent over the books. Taylor finished his work, carefully replaced the cap on his pen, and stood up. He yawned and stretched, took off his glasses and set them down. Then he walked to the office door and locked it. Leaning against the door he smiled again, and rubbed his hands through his hair.

'Going to ask a few questions, Stubbs, and I want you to answer them clearly and truthfully, understood?'

Alex nodded his head, and watched as Taylor returned to his desk and picked up a steel-edged ruler. He wondered why Mr Taylor had locked the door, but he straightened up and tightened his tie.

'Right then, tell me if you have had any sexual relations to date?'

Alex gasped, he didn't know what to say, and he blinked at his housemaster, who moved closer. Alex shook his head and shrugged his shoulders.

'What kind of an answer is that?'

Alex felt the stinging blow of the flat end of the ruler on the top of his head. Taylor repeated his question, and Alex ducked another blow.

'I haven't had any, sir.'

Taylor gave a weird, high-pitched laugh, and he stood in front of Alex, smirking into his face. 'Don't joke with me, sonny, it won't wash. I want every detail and you'd better tell me – big boy like you, never had a woman, that right? That what you are trying to tell me?'

Alex looked nervously towards the door, and his head was jerked back by the hair as Taylor leered down at him. Alex couldn't believe what he was hearing. Taylor went on about how he knew Alex was having an affair with Miss Walters, how he had seen Alex looking at her. He knew Alex fancied her and suspected that Alex had put his hand up Miss Walters' skirt.

'No sir, I swear, sir, I never.'

Taylor patted Alex's cheek so hard that it hurt, patted it with the flat of the ruler. He pushed his face close, until Alex could smell his breath, then he hauled Alex to his feet by the back of his shirt collar. 'So it's not Miss Walters, all right then, which boy, come on, you'd better tell me, which boy have you been with?'

Alex tried to squirm away from Taylor's grip, but Taylor kneed him from behind and he fell to the floor. He tried to crawl under the desk, but Taylor yanked him back and kicked hard so he curled up with a howl of pain.

'What experiences have you had with men, Stubbs?'

Alex looked up from the floor and he could see the bulge in Taylor's trousers as he stood with the ruler in one hand, the other buried deep in his trouser pocket. 'Get up on your feet and sit over there, come on, get up, up.'

Alex huddled on the sofa, hugging his knees. He said he had had no sexual experience with men, but he had hardly finished the sentence when Taylor struck him again and sent him sprawling back on to the sofa. 'You lying little bastard, if you don't tell me the truth I'll beat it out of you, so help me I will.'

This time Alex retaliated, putting his fists up to block the next punch, which seemed to infuriate Taylor even more. He lashed out at Alex again, knocking him to the floor. Alex felt his nose snap, and blood gushed on to the carpet, but try as he might he could not get up. Taylor sat astride him as though he were riding a horse.

'You want to fight, do you, sonny lad? Well, fuck you, I'll teach you not to answer me back, I'll teach you.'

He rained blow after blow on Alex's head until Alex thought he would pass out. He began to plead for Taylor to stop. Taylor was rubbing his bulging crotch up and down Alex's back, his hands everywhere, his voice thick and hoarse. 'Tell me, tell me what happened, I want to know what happened, what did he do to you?'

Alex was crying, and he blurted out that once, when he and his brother had been in bed together, they had played with each other. That was all, there had never been anyone else. Taylor rode him maniacally, demanding that Alex give him a full description of his brother and what they did together. Alex, his face pressed against the carpet, breathing in the dust and his own blood, was helpless. 'I've never had any other experiences, sir, I swear it on my life . . . just with Eddie, my brother Eddie, that's all, honest, sir.'

Taylor got off Alex's back and bent to help him to his feet, took out a handkerchief and dipped it in a bowl of water, wiped Alex's bloody nose. 'Come on lad, stop crying, wipe your face, come along now.'

Alex was utterly confused about who was right and who was wrong. He believed he was in the wrong, he shouldn't have fondled his brother and was being punished for it. Taylor led him to the couch and began to undo his shirt, gradually stripping him naked. Alex shivered from the cold and lay, terrified, doing nothing to stop Taylor, not knowing what to do.

'Just have to examine you now, this is all part of the interview, now turn over, there's a good boy.'

Alex could feel the hands caressing him, saw Taylor's clothes dropping to the floor. Then Taylor lay on top of him, his hands everywhere, kissing and sucking Alex's ears, his neck. Alex bit his lips to stop himself crying out. Taylor masturbated him, rolled him over and kissed his body, pushing his legs apart, kissing and sucking his penis. Alex wept, the tears running down his face, even when Taylor forced his own penis into the boy's mouth.

Taylor leaned back, moaning with satisfaction, and suddenly Alex went crazy. Grabbing Taylor's erect member, he wrenched with all his strength. Taylor screamed, and Alex brought his fist crashing down into the open mouth. He felt Taylor's teeth cutting into his knuckles, but he brought his fist down time and time again, until he saw that his hands were covered with blood. He pushed Taylor's unconscious body from him and watched as he crashed to the floor. Then he collected his clothes and dressed as fast as he could. He didn't know if Taylor was alive or dead, and didn't care. He quickly wiped his face and unlocked the door, locked it again behind him, threw the key away and ran to the dormitory.

He stuffed his few possessions into his haversack. A couple of other boys had seen him come in, but they turned away and went back to their game of draughts. As he ran to the door he collided with Sid, and shoved him against the wall, calling him a shit. He must have known what would happen. Sid laughed, but his face straightened when he saw the haversack.

'I tried, Alex, but you wasn't listenin' ... Hey, where you goin'? You doin' a bunk, are yer? Well, wait fer me.'

It was so easy. They simply walked out of the main gate, crossed the gardens, hopped over a wall and thumbed a lift into town. By this time Alex had told Sid that he might have killed Mr Taylor, Sid might be better off going back. But Sid wouldn't hear of it, and flung an arm around his mate. He admired Alex. Like all the other boys at Oakwood, he had at one time endured an 'examination' at Mr Taylor's hands. No one had dared say anything about it, they suffered in silence. But Sid was happy, at long last the pervert had got what he asked for.

They took the train to London, and from there a bus to Hackney, where Sid had friends. 'You'd best not show yer face near 'ome, Alex, or they'll pick yer up. That'll be the first place they look. We'll stay under cover for a couple o' weeks until the heat dies down, then we'll travel the world.'

Sid's excitement kept the pair of them going, and Alex was thankful that he'd made up his mind to leave.

They threaded their way through the bombed-out buildings to a boarded-up house that had been severely shelled. No one occupied it now. Sid pulled back the corrugated iron door and led Alex down into the dark basement. His friends were not around, but there were mattresses scattered about and a pile of tinned food. The place stank to high heaven as the drains were open, and they crawled along the filthy hallway into a back room.

'This'll be fine when we do it up, Alex. It's dry, and it's not too cold. No one'll find us here.'

Sid fetched blankets from the other room and dragged in one of the dirty mattresses. They huddled together and made elaborate plans for what they would do the following day with their new-found freedom.

Later, Sid slept like a baby, but Alex lay staring into the darkness, seeing his mother's face when she learned what he had done. He didn't cry, he couldn't, and he knew he wouldn't go back to the school, not ever.

In the morning they were woken by the sound of the corrugated iron being dragged back. They listened as voices echoed around the empty house.

Johnny Mask looked into the room and snorted, called to his mates that there was no panic, just a couple of kids.

'It's me, Johnny, it's Sid, we just come over the wall – the pair of us – last night. I said it'd be all right to doss down here for a few days until the heat dies down.'

Johnny laughed, and handed the boys the greasy remains of

his fish and chips to finish. His two friends came through the doorway behind him. They were much older, and looked pretty tough.

'It's young Sid, lads, remember we used him as lookout on the dairy job? Well, well, who's your mate then, Sid?'

Alex, wolfing the chips, introduced himself.

'Johnny, it's okay for us to doss down 'ere, ain't it?'

On closer inspection, Johnny was much better dressed than his mates. His tell-tale coal-black hair, greased and swept back from his face, and his dark eyes, gave away his origins. Johnny Mask was a gypsy.

Freedom's path had already begun to cross his son's. It would pass unseen, unfelt and unknown. If discovered, it could be said that it was just a coincidence. But for Alex it had begun with Johnny Mask, because he was linked to Freedom. Not just because he was a gypsy but because he was the illegitimate son of an old friend, Jesse Evans. It was Jesse who had stood by the champion's grave and warned Evelyne to give him the talisman. A life-long friend, Jesse had been a member of Freedom's clan. He had fathered many illegitimate children, but Johnny had been his first. And young Johnny had been given the name 'Mask' because no matter how many times he had been beaten for thieving, he always smiled. No one ever really knew what he was thinking.

His white teeth gleamed, his one gold cap sparkled – he seemed to find the boys amusing. In some ways they reminded him of himself; he had absconded from more juvenile homes than he could count. He had not the slightest inkling that Alex, the big, raw-boned kid, had any Romany blood in him, let alone that of a royal prince. But the curse had begun.

Sid sidled up to his hero, asking, 'You know of any jobs we could get in on, Johnny? Just that me an' me mate are short of the readies.'

Johnny took out a nail file and began to clean his nails. He gave Alex the once-over and asked him why they'd run. Alex couldn't meet Johnny's eyes, black eyes with thick, long lashes.

He stammered a few words about trouble with his housemaster, but Sid interrupted. 'Bastard was a faggot, Johnny, after 'is arse. He'd done it to all the kids in Oakwood. Alex gave him one hell of a thrashin', so we done a runner.'

Alex flushed with embarrassment, half-expecting Johnny to laugh, but instead he yelled to his mates to go out and get some coffee. He still lounged in the broken-down doorway, filing his nails. 'What you say your name was?'

Again Sid interrupted before Alex could speak, and Johnny clipped Sid round the ear. 'Shut up, I'm not talkin' to you . . . Come here, Alex, an' you, blabbermouth, get into the other room and clean it up.'

Left alone with Johnny, Alex stood with his head bowed. Johnny moved closer, and Alex could smell his cologne, a heavy, sweet smell. When he spoke his voice was soft and gentle. 'You do him in good, did ya? Eh, look at me when I'm talkin' to you.' He took Alex's chin and turned his face to the light, then ruffled his hair, leaving his hand resting on Alex's neck. He was shorter than Alex and had to look up into his face. 'Those shits always go for the lookers. I know, believe me, I know . . . You forget it, I'll find you and Sid a little money earner, all right? Big lad like you would be useful. Now go and give the little squirt a hand, wanna get the place cleaned up.'

Johnny watched Alex leave the room as one of his mates came in. He looked at Alex's retreating back. 'What you want those kids hangin' around for, Johnny?'

Johnny shrugged and didn't answer. In fact, he didn't really know what he could do with them. But there had been something in the big blond boy's face, his pained eyes. Johnny knew exactly what Alex was feeling; he hadn't been home since the age of ten himself. Maybe it was the scars of his own rape that had made him reach out and touch Alex. But whatever it was, Johnny had felt an immediate bond between himself and the tall, skinny boy. He laughed, then took out a greasy comb and ran it through his thick black hair. 'Nice-lookin' kid, may be useful, an' we've got a lot to do before we get this place workin'. I got the beds comin' in and all the girls standing by. Get 'em white-washin' the walls.'

Evelyne sat in Mrs Harris' house, worried half to death. Her oldest friend, Mrs Harris, had helped deliver Edward. She was a big, motherly woman, very overweight, and had in many ways been a surrogate mother to Evelyne when she had arrived in London.

Although many years younger than her friend, Evelyne now seemed just as old and worn out, and her constant fiddling with her handbag strap was getting on Mrs Harris' nerves. The change in Evelyne could not be missed; but they didn't discuss it, just as Evelyne's real feelings, deep down, were not expressed. Sometimes her eyes were so vacant, her expression so distant, that Mrs Harris feared for her sanity, but then she would come round and talk about her problems with Alex. Then she would be the old Evie again, but those dream-like lapses were unnerving, and her constant fiddling drove Mrs Harris spare.

'Did I tell you the police were round again today? Yes, they came again today.'

Mrs Harris nodded. Evelyne had told her this piece of news three times, and everyone in the street knew the police were looking for Alex since he had run away from the reform school.

Evelyne lifted the cracked tea cup to her lips, but did not drink. She sat staring into space.

'Oh, God help me, she's going off again,' thought Mrs Harris. She coughed. 'Evie? Evie love, can you hear me?'

Evelyne turned, surprised, and gave a beautiful smile, just like her old self. 'What are you shouting for? You're the one that's gone deaf, not me.'

'Well, you get so far away sometimes . . . What I was going to say was, it fair surprised me about your Alex. He was always the quiet one, and you said he was getting on so well.'

'It just doesn't make sense, I know, but then there's always two sides to a story. Maybe something happened.'

Mrs Harris nodded. 'Yes, you're right. But then, he and Edward was always together, like peas in a pod. They was always side by side.'

Evelyne's whole being tensed at the mention of Edward's name. Her foot began to tap. Suddenly she said, quite loudly, 'You know, if I had my time over again I'd not have children. If I had my time again I'd be with him. Wherever he wanted me to go I'd go, because when all the learning's over, when all the education's done, it can't warm you when you're cold, it can't hold you when you need to be held, and it can't kiss you awake in the morning.'

Mrs Harris could not quite follow her, particularly as Evelyne had always gone to such lengths to educate her boys. 'You sayin', ducks, that you wish you'd not educated the lads so much? You think that's where it went wrong?'

Evelyne laughed. It was strange, because it sounded so alien, even to herself. She shook her head. 'No, I think what I'm trying to say is – I didn't know until he'd gone what it was to have such a gentle soul love me. I miss him with every breath I take, I look for him down every street. Sometimes I think I hear his voice and my heart lifts, because I can remember now what it was like to run into his arms, run to him and have him sweep me off my feet ... I can remember so much I had forgotten while he was alive, and it's all that keeps me going. I'm scared, though, scared of when I run out of these memories, so scared ...'

'Well, love, that's when the grieving's over ...'

'Ah, that will be when I die, then.'

Mrs Harris sighed. Nothing really made sense to her any more. She was sorry for Evelyne, but everyone had their problems and she was sure the boy would turn up.

'He almost killed his teacher, the man's in hospital. Why he would do a thing like that I just don't understand.'

Mrs Harris couldn't provide any answers, she just nodded and made soothing noises. Alex sounded like a bad lot to her and she was afraid her friend would have nothing but trouble. It seemed so unfair to have one son at Cambridge, doing well, and the other on the run from the law, but that was life.

Dora, Mrs Harris' youngest, swept in with her bleached blonde hair and scarlet-painted nails, teetering in heels so high that Mrs Harris didn't know how she could walk. She was wearing a new dress, and was in high spirits as usual. She had brought a huge bunch of flowers and a box of chocolates. ''Ello, Mum, these are for you ... Hello, Mrs Stubbs, how you doin', all right, are you? I'd love a cuppa, Mum.'

Both the older women knew what Dora was up to, you could tell with one look. She even carried her gas mask in a special embroidered bag. She tucked a bundle of pound notes under the tin on the mantel and gave Evelyne a wink.

'You can take that money back, Dora, I won't have it.'

'Don't look a gift horse in the mouth, Mum ... an' I got some chewing gum for the kids, here, from their Auntie Dora.'

Evelyne sipped her tea and murmured that she really should be going, but the warmth of the kitchen and Dora's cheerful chatter made her forget her troubles. 'So how's things, Mrs Stubbs? Your two boys doing well, are they? Mum says you got one at university, that's somethin', ain't it? I always said education was worth the trouble, but there again it's no good tryin' for it if you've not got what it takes. Me? Well, I was never good at nuffink at school. Me fortune's in me face, isn't that right, Mum? Gawd 'elp us, is that the time? I gotta rush.'

Dora was up and out before Mrs Harris could say a word. As the door closed behind her, her mother banged on the table with the flat of her hand. 'I know what she's doin', Evie, an' I know no amount of tryin' will stop her. She's with the American airmen, an' it's a different one every night. It's breaking my heart. If her father knew he'd turn in his grave.'

Evelyne stared vacantly ahead, remembering how she had bathed Dora when she was just a baby. That had been the time when she was pregnant with Edward, living with the Harrises. The years had passed so quickly, and now Dora was a woman –

and, by the look of her, a very knowing one, most certainly up to no good.

Both women, wrapped in their own thoughts, sighed, and dipped Dora's black-market biscuits into their tepid tea.

Dora giggled as she was helped over the corrugated iron fence. She swiped at Johnny with her handbag, and said that she'd been in some dives before, but this had to be the worst. Johnny carried her over a puddle and put her down in the passageway. The red bulb cast a warm glow over the dank, whitewashed corridor. 'Difference is, Dora, this is my place, an' wait 'til you see the rooms. I got them all done up fine, all we need now are the customers, an' that's your job. Come on love, let me show you.'

Dora had to admit Johnny was a fast worker, and she loved him more than ever. She agreed to contact the girls she knew at the airbases, and put them in touch with him. Here they would have free beds, free drinks, and would pay the management a percentage of their fees.

Sid and Alex were put to work on three more of Johnny's establishments. The two boys worked hard, and Johnny gave them a 'tenner' a week. He had to admit the kids really put their backs into the painting, and they were always ready and willing to do anything he asked. Alex was particularly good, and one day when he helped to cash up the evening's takings, Johnny was amazed at how fast the boy could handle figures. 'Eh, son, how old are you?'

Alex lied and said he was eighteen, and Johnny gave him an extra couple of quid, saying he might be useful when it came to doing the books. The following week he took Alex with him on his Friday round-up, and was very impressed. The boy was as sharp as a tack with money, even suggesting a couple of ways for Johnny to make extra cash. For instance, he and Sid could make up a few sandwiches, deliver them to the brothels, and they could charge a ridiculous amount to the girls and their clients.

So Sid and Alex added a string to their bow, and business was good enough to buy them new suits and shoes, and flash ties and fedoras like their idol, Johnny.

One of Johnny's bouncers at the Angel club had taken Alex under his wing, and they would work out at the local gym. Alex's skinny body filled out with weight training, and his personality changed with it. He liked the look of his body now, the frame tight and muscular.

He and Sid had been up to the West End to 'kit themselves up', as Sid put it. They had visited all the menswear stores, and had even been down Jermyn Street. Sid couldn't believe the way Alex lingered outside one of the posh tailors in Jermyn Street. 'Do us a favour, yer don't want nuffink like that! I mean, it's like old-fashioned, ain't it? An' look at the price, just look what they got a nerve askin' fer a ordinary suit what you wouldn't be seen dead in.'

Alex liked the suit, liked the plain styling of it. But his money wouldn't run to the navy pin-stripe. He recognized the difference in the cloth, never mind the cut, when they paraded in front of Tooley's Menswear's window and saw a brown suit. He wished he had stuck to the dark blue, but Sid had been so persuasive, insisting the brown suited him. 'Well, what yer fink? Couple o' smarties, eh?'

'I should 'ave got the blue.'

'Bleedin' hell, I never known a man go on more about 'is gear than you, Alex. The brown's very nice, an' yer can't see yerself from the back. It's a lovely cut, an' the Slim Jim tie's fantastic.'

Unlike Sid, he had chosen plain shirts, one white and one cream. He alternated them, inspecting them each time they came back from the laundry. Sid had offered him a pair of cufflinks, the sort Johnny would wear. They were theatrical masks with red chips of glass for eyes. Sid thought they were real class, but Alex refused them. Instead he bought a pair from Woolworth's. They were plain rolled gold, and he was very careful not to get them wet in case they went green.

Sid watched Alex as he carefully tied a tea towel around his waist and rolled up his shirtsleeves before cutting the sandwiches for the club. He sliced the bread carefully. 'You just gonna look at me workin' then, Sid? Ain't you got the butter ready yet?'

Sid set to work, managing to get margarine on his sleeve as he slapped it on the bread. Alex had finished cutting bread and while he waited for Sid, he combed his hair and studied his face in the mirror.

'Alex, what was you in Oakwood fer? Was it thievin' like the rest of us? Yer never tell me when I ask, but what was yer in fer?'

Alex had learned fast how to impress. 'Murder – I killed a bloke. Now, you got those sandwiches ready?'

Sid's jaw dropped and he hurriedly packed up the food. 'Christ, if old man Taylor snuffed it, you'd better stay well clear of the cops. Won't be no reform school next time fer you, Alex, you'll do time, real time, in prison.'

When Sid delivered the sandwiches, wanting to impress Johnny he told him what Alex had said. Johnny feigned indifference. 'That right, Sid? Well, I always said the boy had somethin'. Maybe he should start looking out for me instead of that boozed-up Harry – I'll talk to him.'

That night Johnny approached Alex with a proposition. Now they were making the rounds together every Friday, he wondered if Alex would like to start working even closer, on a day-to-day basis. He needed people he could trust. Alex was quick to agree.

Alex's education gained a great deal as he went from house to house with Johnny, meeting all the girls Johnny and his gang controlled. They were all shapes and sizes, even, to Alex's amazement, a black girl and two Chinese. They all seemed to dote on Johnny. Alex was seventeen years old and still a virgin, but no one would know it.

Sid was growing jealous of Alex. He was still making the sandwiches and running small errands for Johnny. When he complained, Johnny grinned and said if he wanted to do something more ambitious there might just be something suitable. 'I need a lookout, little warehouse we're gonna knock off, so stand by and I'll give you the nod when I need you.'

Sid couldn't wait to tell Alex, implying that Johnny had been keeping him under wraps for bigger things. Alex polished his two-tone shoes and listened, then said quietly, 'I wouldn't do it, Sid. Collecting cash from the girls is one thing, but getting involved in robbery is another.'

'You mind yer own friggin' business, Mister Big Shot, Mister Know-It-All . . . Johnny dropped me the wink that I might end up a partner in the business, so you just keep yer nose out of it. You do your job an' I'll do mine.'

Alex slipped his shoes on, saying nothing. He had outgrown Sid and he knew it. At the same time, he knew he owed Sid a lot. Without him he would never have met Johnny.

Alex took the takings to Johnny, forgot to knock on the door, and apologized when he saw that Johnny was in bed with a girl. 'Sorry, Johnny, I'll come back later.'

'Not with my money you won't, get yer arse in 'ere, help yer-self to a drink an' I'll get me trousers on.' Johnny wandered around stark-naked, and Alex flicked an embarrassed glance at the bed. Dora lolled back and yawned. Alex poured himself an orange juice.

'Now, that's what I like to see, dedicated – see, Dora, offer the lad a drink an' 'e takes an orange juice! Good on yer, son. Alex, say hello to Dora.'

Alex knew who she was, Mrs Harris' girl, but he flushed at her nakedness and looked down at his shoes.

'Aw, bashful, ain't 'e?'

Dora hadn't the slightest idea who Alex was, it had been ten years since she had seen him. His face had altered, anyway, his broken nose had been flattened in the fight with Mr Taylor.

'Put something round yer tits, Dora, can't yer see you're embarrassin' the lad?'

Hot under the collar, Alex still tried to avert his eyes, but felt himself drawn to Dora's perfect breasts. Johnny laughed, and immediately knew it was a mistake. He saw Alex tighten, clench his fists. 'Can I talk in front of her, Johnny?'

Johnny nodded as he pulled his socks on.

'You really think it's a good idea to use Sid on this caper next week? He's only a kid, you know.'

Johnny stamped into his shoe. 'Nobody's makin' him do it, Alex, it's his choice, unless you want the job, do yer?'

'No way, I'm nobody's lookout, Johnny ... here you go, fivers one packet, tenners the next, the ones in the big pack.'

Johnny caught the packets of money. 'You're a strange one, Alex, you know that? You got brains. What you after, eh? Somethin' bigger? More'n a few cases of booze, yeah?'

Alex gasped as Dora casually flung off the bedclothes and wrapped a silk dressing gown around herself. He knew he was flushing bright pink so he made a hasty exit, saying he'd see Johnny later.

'Where'd you find him, Johnny? He's a good-lookin' kid.'

Johnny was checking the accounts. As usual, Alex had done them in meticulous detail and he wasn't ripping Johnny off, which made a change. 'Never mind the kid, get yerself dolled up, Dora, and sharpish, I got a party of Yanks comin' in ternight.'

He splashed cologne on his face and straightened his tie, and she threw off her gown and walked into the bathroom. She could see there was no point talking to him any more now, it was back to business. She ran water into the cracked washbasin and sighed; she wished Johnny didn't make her work every night.

'I'm off, sweetheart, clean yerself up, ta-ra!'

Dora stared at her lovely face in the fly-specked mirror, then rinsed out the face cloth and washed herself.

She was dressed up to the nines when she went to the basement club in Hackney. The place had been really smartened up, not like most of Johnny's dives. This one had had real money spent on it, and there were quite a few punters already coming into the small bar. She saw Alex again, and smiled, asked if he'd like to join her for a drink before business started. He said he couldn't, he had to go and collect from one of the other places.

'Another time then, okay?' Somewhere in the recesses of her mind she had a vague idea that she knew him from somewhere, but she forgot about it as the air-raid sirens sounded and the lights dimmed. They all waited to see if they would have to go to the shelter, but the all clear sounded quickly and the party-ing began.

Alex made the rounds. Everything Johnny was involved in was makeshift, all his properties were derelict, even the small office was a temporary affair. He lived in a small bedsitter next to the office. After his daily collections, Alex would go to Johnny's office and work on the accounts. He had his own key and came and went as he chose. One afternoon he had just closed the door when he heard a voice from the bedroom. 'That you, Johnny?'

Alex flushed as Dora appeared, wearing only a bra and panties. She was smoking as usual, and her hair was hanging loose like Veronica Lake's. She looked around for an ashtray and Alex dived across the room to hand her one.

'Well, ain't you the gent, thanks. Why don't you come an' sit with me, it's hours before I gotta work. Come on, you ain't shy, are you?' She smiled at him, puzzled. 'I know you from some-where, an' I just can't put me finger on it. You ever met me before?'

Alex knew exactly who she was, but he shook his head. She got up from the bed and came over to him, standing there in her brief underwear with her hands on her hips. She had the palest skin, unblemished, pink, and he wanted to touch it. But he kept his eyes lowered, staring at the tips of his polished, two-tone shoes. She started to laugh, but he wouldn't look up, and suddenly she sat on his knee, simply sat down astride him, and held his face. 'I've been wanting to do this since the first time I saw you.'

She cupped his face in both hands and kissed him, lightly and swiftly, and it took his breath away. He could smell her perfume and face powder. 'Why don't we move three paces across the room to the bed?' she said.

Alex could hardly form the words, he coughed and said something about Johnny – what if he was to walk in? Dora hopped off his knee and locked the door. She strolled over to the bed and unhooked her bra. Standing with her back to him, she tossed it aside and lay on the bed, lifting her arms to him invitingly.

'I can't, I can't.' He went to the door and reached for the lock, but instead he flipped off the light and stood in the dark waiting until he could make out her shape clearly.

'I've never been with a woman, Dora, I don't know what to do.'

Dora took his hand and began to undress him. He moaned, but he didn't know what to do with his hands, they hung at his sides. She unbuttoned his shirt, loosened his tie, and whispered that he didn't have to do anything, just relax and she would teach him everything he needed to know.

She took a long time removing each item of his clothing, laying them down carefully while he stood frozen, unable to speak. His chest was now bare, and she kissed each nipple until he felt he would scream out, then she began to unbutton his flies, and slowly got down on her knees to kiss him. He gripped her shoulders tight. 'No, don't do that, don't.'

Dora eased herself up and pulled him close, whispering that he would like it, like what she was going to do – but she could feel his strong arms picking her up. 'I thought I was supposed to be teaching you.'

He laid her on the bed and removed his trousers, kicked off his shoes. He had lost his erection, and he sat on the side of the bed, unsure of himself, but she held him and began to kiss his neck softly, licking inside his ears. Her hands fluttered slowly over his body, and his heart began to thump. He lay down and closed his eyes.

She eased herself on top of him, held his face. Although he

tried to reach her lips, she didn't kiss him, not once, she didn't want him to kiss her lips. She played with him for so long he thought he would die, and she whispered to him to let it go, let it go, and without ever having been inside her he climaxed. He lay in confusion, not knowing what to do or say.

'Now then, let's start all over again, an' you hold on, understand me, hold on until I say so.' Dora was an expert, she worked on him, caressed him until he reached screaming point. She liked virgins, enjoyed them, liked the power games, and it was hours before she allowed him to enter her and make love to her. Still she wouldn't kiss him, every time he tried she bit him so hard it hurt, so he contented himself with sucking and kissing her nipples.

He was exhausted, but happy, and she slept in his arms. He felt so good, and he smiled to himself. Eventually she stirred and muttered that they must get up, but he wouldn't let her, he held her tightly as if he never wanted to let her go.

'Alex, come on, I got to work, and Johnny will be back . . . Hey, come on, we can do this again.'

Sid and four of Johnny's men were picked up by the police as they attempted the warehouse robbery. They were taken to the police station and Sid, terrified, tried to save his own skin by telling them everything he knew. What frightened him most was that he might be named an accomplice to the attack on Taylor. He gave Alex's name to the police.

Alex was arrested as he left the basement. He ran straight into the arms of two police officers, and was thrown into a Black Maria with three other men and two girls. At Hackney police station he was put in a cell, but was soon led into the chief inspector's office, where a sergeant read out a report. 'Alex Stubbs, absconded from Brighton. They picked him up at one of Johnny Mask's brothels.'

The chief inspector turned, expecting to see a young, seventeen-year-old boy, and was taken aback when Alex swaggered in, looking taller than ever in his pin-striped suit. His hands were stuffed in his pockets, and when he was told to sit he slouched in the chair and crossed his legs.

The chief was disgusted. His own son, not two years older, was fighting for his country and this bloody delinquent, with his slicked-back hair and cocky manner, appalled him. 'You're going to be taught a lesson, son, but first, do you want to tell us about Johnny Mask?'

Alex stared, blank-eyed, at the chief inspector.

'Let's try one more time, son. We want to know where Johnny Mask is. We know all about you, we know you've been working for him, so why not help yourself? We'll make it easier for you if you co-operate.'

Alex remained silent, staring straight ahead. He got a sudden, stinging blow on the back of his head. The chief inspector leaned forward, his face close. 'That bastard Mask, that stinking gyppo, would sell you, and anyone else who worked for him, for a ten-bob note, and you're too dumb to know it. But your pal Sid isn't ... He's been very helpful – how do you think we picked you up? Now, you've had time to think about it, so talk if you know what's good for you.' He slapped Alex's face, first one side, then the other. The ice-blue eyes never flickered, and there was a slight hint of a smile on his face.

'Get him out of here. You're going to the Scrubs this time, son, that'll teach yer. See how long the smile stays on your face in there. Go on, get him out of my sight.'

Evelyne had to fight to keep herself from weeping openly. Alex had changed, she hardly recognized him. His broken nose had healed crooked, and his hair was combed back from his fore-head, the blond curls flattened with grease. The two warders stopped at the door of the visiting-room and Alex walked for-ward. He put his hand out to her and one of the warders motioned him back. Evelyne was shocked at the coarseness in his voice when he turned on the warder. 'I just wanna hold 'er 'and, fer Chrissakes.'

Evelyne withdrew her hand sharply. She was afraid to ask what he had been up to while on the run. He had not made contact with her, and now he sat there like a stranger. She couldn't speak, and began to wonder if all the terrible things she had been told about him were true.

Alex's bravado began to slip. She was so frail, so helpless, and her desperate, pleading eyes made him want to weep. His voice was softer. 'I love you, Ma, I love you ... Don't worry about me. Don't come to court – fings'll be all right, you'll see.'

Their time was up, and the warders led him out. He didn't look back, he didn't have to, he could hear her sobbing. Alone in his cell he felt full of remorse, and he vowed he would make it up to her, somehow.

The lawyer Evelyne had hired for Alex came to visit him. Alex told him exactly why he had attacked Taylor, and watched him write copious notes. He listened to everything Alex told him, and spoke reassuringly. He would see what he could do.

Alex did not see Evelyne as he was led into court. She sat alone in the gallery, hands tightly clasped. The lawyer had told her that, under the circumstances, he felt sure Alex would be sent to a borstal for young offenders. He chose his words carefully as he explained her son's reason for running away from Oakwood Hall, and told her a full statement had been handed to the court and the education authorities.

Alex's case was heard in fifteen minutes flat. The judge, known for his harshness, dismissed the lawyer's plea for Alex to be returned to reform school. He sentenced Alex to four years in Wormwood Scrubs, one of the country's toughest prisons, which had a section for hardened juvenile offenders.

The judge's voice grated in Alex's ears. He clenched his hands violently. So much for that sweet-talking bastard lawyer, so much for justice. As he was led down from the dock, he knew his mother was there, and he stared frantically around the court-room as the warders pulled at his handcuffs to drag him out. He caught sight of her in the gallery and forced a smile, looking up at her ... But all his cocksure manner had gone, he was just a boy and very frightened. 'Mum! Mum!'

They hauled him out, but she could still hear him calling for her, his terrible screams, and she could do nothing. She was still sitting in the gallery an hour later when one of the clerks told her gently that she would have to leave, the court session was over.

Chapter Two

If Edward Stubbs felt any remorse for the murder of his father, he never showed it. Even immediately after the killing all he had felt was relief, that Alex had agreed to say that he'd done it.

He adapted quickly to his new life, putting the past behind him, including his brother. He refused to think about Alex, and was capable of behaving as if he had never existed.

Edward walked out of the local Post Office in Cambridge and paused, frowning. He had miscalculated and was running very low on funds, lower than he had anticipated. He sighed as he put his Post Office book away, wondering if he could touch his mother for a few more shillings a week. He was on such a tight budget he hardly ever had so much as a spare penny in his pocket. Evelyne had calculated the costs of his gown, his books, all his accessories, down to the last penny, and he could see no way round the situation. He shifted his weighty books on to his other hip and worked it out in his mind. If he left the hall of residence, moved into digs, it would be cheaper. Then he could get a bike so he could ride to college and that would save his bus fares.

The sun was shining, it was a beautiful clear day, and here in Cambridge there was little sign of the continuing war, apart from the odd pile of sandbags propped around the doorways of the colleges. Edward walked to the river bank and sat down, going over his money once again. His mother had certainly got him living on a shoestring, and it annoyed him. He had his meals in hall, which was cheaper than eating out, but it meant his social life was a void. He couldn't really join the crowd in the pubs in case he got stuck for a round, that could wipe him out for a whole week. No one else was really aware of Edward's financial situation, no one really cared, they put him down to being a bit of a loner. His thick cockney accent amused some of them, but it set him apart from the jet-setters.

He had tried hard to be part of the crowd, even rubbing his new grey trousers so that they looked worn, scuffing his shoes and rolling his gown in the road so it didn't look so shiny and new. Most of the students wore baggy cord trousers with white cricketing sweaters, their shirt collars undone and ties hanging loose on their chests, ready to be tightened up fast if they saw their tutors. Edward only had an old, grey sweater Freda had knitted for him, and he wanted a white Cambridge one and dark green cord trousers, wanted them so much and was so frustrated – he couldn't even afford an extra pint of beer after classes.

The first months had been the hardest, as he had had to adjust to his new life. He found his background such a hindrance that he quickly covered it up as much as possible. All his books had been second-hand, and those he couldn't afford he borrowed from the university library, like all the students who couldn't buy their own. Edward was well aware that many students were in a similar financial position, but they were not of the same class. There were very few working-class boys, most of them were middle or upper class, and he was therefore an oddity, knew it and hated it.

During his first few days he had overheard one of the students talking outside his window. 'Thing is, according to my old man, never make friends in the first term, means you are stuck with them for the rest of your time here. You can get some frightful bores, you know, dreadful fellows, but first-termers are so nervous and desperate for pals that they latch on to quite the wrong sort of chap. I never spoke to anyone in my first term, jolly glad too.'

Edward said 'jolly glad too' to himself, using a high-pitched, plummy voice. He took what the idiot had said to heart, and during his first term he watched, listened, and worked like hell. He was reading geology, and his tutors were helpful. He was learning fast, and he didn't want to appear vulnerable to the other students.

His tutor, Professor Huston, detected Edward's discomfort with his own background from the word go. He tried to assure Edward that, contrary to being ashamed of his roots, he should be proud. However, his advice fell on deaf ears, and he watched with interest as Edward kept himself to himself. He could not help but notice that the boy was gradually losing his accent.

The process was by no means easy. Night after night Edward sat in front of his mirror, practising the vowels over and over again, gradually interspersing his conversation with 'Oh, I say', 'Jolly good man' and 'Whizz-o'. He had no idea that his attempts at aping the upper classes were mimicked and ridiculed by the rest of the students in his tutorials. He was the source of many a night's entertainment as they copied his broad cockney voice and followed it with 'Oh, holly hood, old bean.'

Edward had walked all the way across Cambridge to look at his new lodgings. He was very dispirited that they were in a large, Victorian house where the rest of the rooms were let to travelling salesmen, chefs and domestics from the colleges.

All students 'living in' bought any furnishings and fittings left by the previous tenant. Edward's room contained nothing but a small bed, a chair and a desk. The previous occupant did not even bother to ask for payment. Edward brought nothing other than his books to his room. He hung no posters on the walls, it was as bare as the day he moved in. He reckoned that even with his scholarship he needed at least forty-five pounds a term, and that was cutting it fine. He hadn't joined any clubs or organizations, he didn't take part in any of the sporting events. He had never played rugby at his school, only football, and he had never been keen on cricket so he didn't bother with sports at all. He made careful notes in his book, initial expenses, university fees, college fees, board and lodging, personal expenses, and a few possible additions. His mother had bought his cap and gown, had it made up by a Jewish tailor in the East End, and had also bought him two shirts and two pairs of trousers. He hated everything he wore. He wanted a sports jacket in brown, the fashionable colour that year, but all he had was an old black jacket of his father's and a raincoat.

He lay back on the river bank and closed his eyes. He was free for the afternoon, he had no lectures until the following morning. The sound of someone sobbing made him sit up and look around. He couldn't see anyone, but the sound continued and he got to his feet and searched around, eventually finding a pair of green cord trousers sticking out from beneath some bushes.

'You okay? Hello . . . you okay?'

The trousers wriggled and the bushes parted, and he recognized the chap from lectures, but realized he had no idea of his name. He was small-boned, with delicate features and big, china-blue eyes, red-rimmed from weeping. The boy blushed at being caught. 'Oh God, I didn't think anyone would be around here.' He spoke with a very refined, upper-class accent, and took a small, crumpled linen handkerchief out of his pocket to blow his nose. This seemed only to start his crying all over again, and he flopped back into the bushes. 'I'm so sorry, but I've had dreadful news, I can't cope at all.'

Unsure what to do with the boy, Edward hovered by the bushes.

'I'll be all right in a while, really, it's just . . . Oh God! This is so embarrassing.' He wiped his eyes and sniffed, but for all his apologizing he seemed quite unconcerned at being caught weeping, hidden in the bushes. 'I say, do I know you? Think I've seen you around, haven't I?'

Edward sat down beside him and introduced himself, and the boy held out a slender, delicate white hand and shook Edward's big paw. 'I'm Charles Collins, everyone calls me Charlie. You're the frightfully keen chap, aren't you? Where do you hide yourself, you never go to the clubs.' He sighed again and stared into the river, picked up a stick and began ripping little twigs off it, throwing them into the water. 'Just got the old telegram, my brother missing in action, they don't hold out much hope of finding him, judging by Ma's letter. Oh God, I'm sorry, I'm going to start again.'

Much to his surprise, Edward found himself putting an arm around the boy's shaking shoulders. Charlie was easy to be with, and so unembarrassed by his sobs.

'Have you been up before the conscription board?'

'I'm on the waiting list along with everyone else. Frightful, isn't it, putting me dreadfully behind with my study programme. Mind you, what's the point if they're going to tog you up in the old khaki, what?'

Edward realized that Charlie, even though he didn't look it, must be a couple of years older than himself.

'All my pals are on tenterhooks, absolute tenterhooks, I mean, they're whisking them off willy-nilly, clutching their rifles, poor souls. I say, do you know Edgar Willard? Well, he went before the board four months ago, got such jolly good marks in everything that they told him to stand by for officer training. Anyway, the adjutant told him he could be called up but he was to take his exams, it's not on . . . I say, you don't know Henry Fullerton, do you? He's waited so long that his plans have been changed goodness knows how many times now. He lives from day to day, lecture to lecture, very firm believer in kismet. Fabulous fellow, nothing worries him, he says he's resigned to whatever happens, whether it's Aldershot, the Tripos, the Maginot Line or, worst of all, his college bills.'

Edward listened, fascinated. He had never heard of any of Charlie's friends, but Charlie seemed not in the slightest bit interested in whether he had or not, keeping up such a fast, steady flow of chatter that Edward's brain reeled.

They walked along the river bank, but Edward had to go

back to retrieve Charlie's jacket from the bushes. He noticed it was of very fine quality, like the rest of Charlie's clothes. Charlie chattered on and threw sticks into the water, and then he started to cry again because he suddenly remembered his brother, Clarence, and threw his arms around Edward.

'Actually, that is only part of my troubles, one of many, dear chap. You see, I have been so preoccupied with all this war effort that my studies have taken a turn for the worse, and my tutor really hauled me over the coals last Monday. I'm not even going to take the exams, they don't think I'm up to it. Father will have a fit, not that it would be anything new, he's been having them since the day I was born. It's Ma that's my real trouble, she'll throw such a tantrum ... You see, she adored Clarence, and with him gone all her bloody-mindedness will be directed at me. God, what am I going to do?'

They had walked all the way back into town along the river bank, and Charlie had not stopped talking for one moment. As they passed people they all called out his name, everyone seemed to know him, and the gatekeeper laughed and made a joke as they entered the gate to the hall of residence.

'You want to have some tea, Edgar, you've taken such good care of me? Do come along, I'm top floor, number eighteen, say about four-fifteen? Super ... cheerio.'

Edward hadn't liked to point out that Charlie had got his name wrong, and he was in no hurry to go up to number eighteen for tea. He went to the main hall for his tea instead, and then regretted it when he saw Walter Miller approaching him. The boy wore such thick glasses that he looked Chinese, and he suffered from appalling acne. He had latched on to Edward almost from their first lecture. Walter was extremely clever, working diligently all the time, and when he wasn't studying he went to the pictures. He sat down and asked Edward if he had seen the new W. C. Fields comedy at the local picture house. In his broad Lancashire accent he told Edward all about the film. 'It's very funny, Eddie, he's got such a bucolic humour he has you splittin' yer sides, lot better than that ruddy Gunga Din at the Rex.'

Edward hated to be called Eddie, and loathed the way Walter latched on to him. Walter loaded jam on to his bread and made slurping noises as he ate. He talked about wanting to see *The Return of the Scarlet Pimpernel*, it was part of a double feature at the Cosmopolitan. Edward listened with only half an ear to Walter's theory that Hitler had ordered Leslie Howard's plane shot down because, in his portrayal of the Scarlet Pimpernel, there was a definite insult to the Third Reich. Walter squinted as Edward suddenly pushed his chair back and stood up. 'You want to come, I'll pay for you, Eddie, I don't mind, really I don't.'

Edward looked for a moment as if he would hit Walter, then he turned on his heel and strode out of the hall. He was angry because he had used Walter a few times, used him because he couldn't afford to go to the pictures, and now he regretted it. Walter only hung around him all the more.

Edward made his way to number eighteen, even though he told himself he didn't want to bother with fools like Charlie. The door was ajar, and music thudded out from a gramophone, but he thought he could hear Charlie's high-pitched sobbing and gasping despite the music. When Edward pushed the door open it was his turn to gasp. Even though it was light outside, the blackout curtains had been drawn, not only across the windows but also from the ceiling, making the room look like a tent. There were candles on every available surface, and on a long monk's refectory table were massive, dripping silver candlesticks holding huge, gothic monastery-type candles. The table top was a sea of wax.

Tears were running down Charlie's cheeks, but he wasn't crying, he was helpless with laughter and surrounded by a group of very pissed friends. He waved to Edward and shouted to everyone to welcome 'Edgar', then continued with his story, laughing so hard himself that it made everyone around him laugh, even though they didn't know why.

Edward slipped into the room and sat to one side, picked up a silver goblet and poured himself some wine. He had never seen such an untidy room, there were clothes strewn everywhere, books and papers tumbled on the floor, all over the unmade bed. An old gentleman pottered around trying to empty ashtrays and wipe the debris of toasted teacakes, wine and jam from the table and every other flat surface. Charlie held everyone in rapt attention as he acted out his date the previous day with Gloria, from the local ladies' lingerie shop, pulling hysterically funny faces as he did so.

'When I asked for a pair of knickers she replied, "What size?" and I, looking her over very carefully of course, as you all know is my way, I said, "Your size will do, my darling," and she wrapped them up and I made the grand gesture and said, "My dear, they are for you, on condition that we have a date."'

Charlie went into such peals of laughter that he fell across the table. He took another gulp of wine, filled his goblet again and swung his arm, spraying everyone close to him with red drops. 'No, wait for the punch line, chaps . . . Later that night, back at her flat – have I told you how well stacked she was? My dears, a good thirty-eight C cup if ever I've had my hands round . . . Anyway, when I stripped her she was wearing the damned things, still had the price on them, and I have to say that was the best fifteen-and-sixpence I have ever spent.' He swung back in his chair as everyone hooted with laughter and thumped the table with glee.

Everyone wanted to get their stories in about who had done what to whom, and in the rowdy room no one noticed Edward beating a hasty retreat. As he left, Charlie was launching into a detailed description of how he was working his way through all the counters in Woolworth's. He was now past the cosmetics and on the record section. 'I aim, before the term is out, chaps, to have had every single woman in Woolies.'

Edward returned to his rooms and lay on the bed. He found their tales of sexual prowess faintly ridiculous. He had not seen one woman in Cambridge he would bother to speak to, let alone have sex with. Not that he had been inundated with offers – far from it.

He awoke to hear shouting from below in the courtyard and looked out of the window to see Charlie, so drunk he could hardly stand up without help. He was attempting to climb up the side of the building, holding what looked like a rag doll. The place was in darkness because of the blackout, and Edward had to squint to see what was going on. Charlie was standing on Freddy's shoulders, clinging on to a window-ledge. Edward swore at his foolishness, grabbed his dressing gown and made his way down the inky-black staircase to the courtyard. Charlie was now up to the second window-ledge and stood, weaving, one hand holding on to the window and the other still clutching the rag doll.

'Get him to come down, the idiot, he'll hurt himself.'

Freddy smirked and waved his arms for Edward to follow Charlie up if he was so clever. From the main gate voices echoed, a torch flickered, and Charlie's friends all ran like hell, knowing they would be in for it if they were caught.

Edward climbed up and grabbed Charlie's legs, hauled him down, and they both crashed to the ground. The torchlight moved closer. Edward heaved Charlie over his shoulder and moved back into the shadows.

'This is very decent of you, old boy, but if you don't put me down I'll vomit all over your dressing gown.'

Edward put his hand across Charlie's mouth as the two porters searched the courtyard. 'Bloody war on, you'd think these lads would have better things to do than play silly buggers.'

The porters departed with the rag doll and Edward released his hold on Charlie's mouth. The next moment Charlie had passed out in his arms. Edward carried him back to his quarters, all the way up the stairs, opened the door and dumped the drunken boy on the bed.

'Thanks awfully.' Charlie fell immediately into a deep, drunken sleep, and Edward stripped him and put him to bed. The room was a shambles, the remains of tea still all over the table. Edward stared around the room, at the closet full of clothes, rows of shoes, every drawer half open. He crossed the room to blow out a guttering candle.

He couldn't help but see the stacks of papers stuffed into a desk drawer, and he carefully inched one out. There were shoals of bills – unpaid bills – from tailors, bakers, wine merchants, clubs and restaurants. Edward left his sleeping friend and closed the door silently behind him.

The following morning Charlie did not appear at the lecture, which was not unusual, but this time Edward was looking out for him, had even kept a space for him.

After lunch Edward went to see Professor Emmott to ask his permission to move out of the hall of residence into lodgings. He tapped on the study door and a high-pitched voice bade him enter. Emmott was sitting at his desk, elbow-deep in papers. He was a strange-looking man in his late forties, and his thick black hair had receded to the halfway point, making his domed fore-head look even larger above his thick, round, black-rimmed glasses. He also had an unfortunate humped back that forced him to bend almost double to walk. Sitting down, however, he was a chilling spectacle, and he looked over the top of his glasses with strange, clear eyes.

'Ah, Stubbs, come in, come in, wanted to have a chat with you. Take a seat. I have been looking over your half-term's work, excellent, excellent. What was it you wanted to speak to me about?'

Edward tried not to sound desperate, he just said that he felt it would be more convenient if he moved into lodgings.

'Finding it a tight squeeze, are you, old chap? You do know that there are certain extra scholarships, exhibitions, sizarships, sub-sizarships and what have you, grants for those in special need? Those eligible for, shall we say, "poor student grants" are usually restricted to divinity students, a lot of conditions, of course, City companies and so forth, but if you would like me to put forward an application . . .?'

Edward flushed. It was the 'poor student' line that really got to him, and he assured Emmott that it would not be necessary. In truth he hated the mere mention of 'poor', and wouldn't even stay to listen to the pros and cons of applying to a company to supplement the scholarship he had already won.

'I'll be able to manage quite well, sir, you see, I can save a little by taking lodgings instead of remaining in residence.'

'As you will, as you will. Got your notes here, good work in the laboratories, Stubbs. Like your essay on petrology, good identification, chemical analysis faultless . . . got a few books of my own, maybe you'd like to take them away with you?'

Edward smiled his thanks. He wanted to leave the hot, stuffy study, the fumes from the gas fire were drying his mouth.

'All work and no play, not always a good thing, you know, Stubbs. I notice you do not take part in any form of sport, any reason? Good to socialize a bit – not too much, I grant you – but from what I have seen you are working harder than any other student I have this term. Takes me all my time to keep up with you.'

Edward heard a weird, high-pitched cackle and realized it was a laugh, the strange little man was laughing. 'Remind me of myself when I was your age, but then, well, I'd say it was slightly different with me! Thought of joining any debating societies? Good to come out of yourself, you know, get up on the plat-form and spout a few illogical things, always good for the future. You a member of any of the societies?'

There were two reasons why Edward did not belong to any of the clubs. One was financial and the other was embarrassment at not being sure exactly what to do.

'Fine chap like you should perhaps try for the boating crew, you are fit, I presume? Fit, yes?'

Edward was quite obviously fit. He stood six feet two and a half inches tall, but his body was slender, not yet filled out. He was deeply embarrassed by Emmott's enquiries and looked down at his shoes. Eventually Emmott got round to his reason for wanting to speak to Edward; his name would be going before the board, and he could quite easily be called up to the army.

'You'll have to go before them in a few months' time. If you are fit, which you obviously are, you will stand in line like the majority of students this term. I have already made my feelings felt on this matter. You are one of my best students and I would be loath to lose you, very loath, but there is a war on, and . . . you see all right, do you? No problem with your eyesight? Not deaf either? In certain cases the medical is pretty rigorous, there again, occasionally not, flat feet is a certain let-out . . . I just wondered, as you have not joined any of the sports societies, if perhaps you are flat-footed . . .' Edward was still slightly unsure of what Professor Emmott had been hinting at, but he thought that if he had read the old boy right he was tipping Edward off before he went for his medical. The last thing Edward wanted was to be conscripted, having got this far, and if he joined up it could be years before he came back to college, if ever.

As Edward left the study Emmott was already sitting back at his paper-strewn desk and, without looking up, he suggested that if Edward wanted to make a few bob, the radio factory just out of town was looking for people to do shift work, perhaps he should look into it.

Edward smiled his thanks, and Emmott gave him a direct look, then returned to his studies. He believed Edward to be academically brilliant, with a great future ahead of him. It was rare to find a student who was so diligent, but Emmott's uppermost thought was that Edward was the first student he had ever come across who touched on his own obsessive interests. Emmott's life centred on study, stretching his mind inside that domed forehead. Edward had the same yearning, Emmott recognized his hunger for knowledge and would have liked to express it in words. He didn't, however; not many virile young men wanted to be told they were akin to a bent cripple.

Edward went to the radio factory, where they offered him three shillings a night on the late shift. He had to sort and examine plastic washers, a boring, tedious job, but he needed the extra money for the sports jacket he was saving for.

He had to get permission from the college to work, but of course Emmott gave it, so Edward had a special pass for the three nights a week. His good looks made him very popular with all the factory women, and some of them hovered around his table with cups of tea and home-made biscuits. They were all after him, but he found them coarse and he hated the way they giggled behind their dirty hands. They wore headscarves knotted at the front, and it made them all seem unattractive, but most of them came from the farms around Cambridge where they could lay their hands on butter, eggs and milk, and so he charmed them and played them along.

The digs were the pits, but he bore with them because they saved him money. One night he was working in his room when he heard the 'toot-toot' of Charlie's car horn below. He burst into Edward's room, then stopped and sniffed. 'Good Lord, place stinks of cabbage, or cat's piss. Listen, old chap, you fancy coming for a spin? Not seen you about.'

Edward refused, saying he wanted to finish an essay.

'Why not show your face at the rugger match, Sat'day, should be a good game . . . won't change your mind, eh? Few jars at the Duck and Feather?'

Edward shook his head and Charlie bounded out. Edward looked out of his window as Charlie hopped into his MG. There he was with a strapping blonde sitting beside him. He waved to Edward and careered off. Edward sighed, Charlie never seemed to worry about anything, least of all finances, and although petrol was rationed Charlie was never short. Edward had heard he got all the boys' petrol rations in exchange for alcohol.

When Edward went to collect his mail from residence, he found a letter from his mother. He hated her letters, they always depressed him. There was little mention of Alex, only a paragraph to say his brother had got into trouble, but there were no details. Whenever Edward saw his brother's name in his mother's writing he felt a certain amount of guilt, but he always assured himself that he was doing what they had both wanted, therefore it was all right. Evelyne mentioned that she had not been feeling too well, but she hoped he was fit, and working hard. She would write again soon. There was no mention of the extra money he had written to ask her for and, angry, he ripped the letter into shreds. He was sick and tired of working at the radio factory with those stupid bitches tittering and nudging each other every time he inadvertently touched them. He had now taken on another part-time job, one school-kids usually did, sitting watching for incendiary bombs for three shillings a night. He would sit by the sandbags with a torch hidden under a blanket and do his reading.

Edward hated being poor, and began to resent the sight of Charlie and his crowd as they steamed around town, in and out of the dance clubs, their days seemingly revolving round a desperate search for pleasure. They all suffered from hangovers, and several times Edward had seen Charlie staggering across the quad, wearing his pyjamas under his cords and jacket, on his way to the Dot to join his ever-increasing circle of friends. They danced and drank, their eyes always open for new girls, and then they would go on to Leo's where they would down Pimm's or whisky. They were known to be in a permanent alcoholic haze, always hunting out the women in Woolworth's or Boots, wheeling around the town laughing too loudly and propping each other up as they made their way unsteadily back to college during the blackouts.

Edward worked all the hours that God gave him, and yet was never late for a single lecture. Charlie, on the other hand, played hard all night and caught up on his sleep during lectures. Edward presumed that Charlie spent most of his days sleeping off the booze, until one afternoon he passed the rugby pitch. He stared in amazement at the game, which he couldn't begin to understand. The boys, covered in mud, hurled an odd-shaped ball backwards and forwards, while rows of men stood on the touchline, waving bottles of beer. He had been impressed by Charlie, however. Small as he was he was a little demon on the pitch, zigzagging through the larger men like an eel. He was so obviously popular that it needled Edward, and he stayed to watch. He started to laugh when he saw Charlie in the centre of the scrum, and joined the cheering when it seemed that Charlie's team was ahead. He watched Charlie fighting at the side of the pitch, yelling and striking out at the linesman, which was greeted with cheers and shouts from those on the touchline.

When the match was over Edward followed the crowd into the local pub, and there was Charlie with his hair plastered down after his shower, ordering beer all around, and as always the centre of attention. 'Eddie, my boy, come over and meet the team; everyone, this is Big Eddie, we should rope him in, look at his shoulders . . . come on Eddie, have a beer.'

Although it upset him to be called 'Eddie', Edward accepted the beer, and afterwards it seemed only natural to go with them all to the restaurant for a booze-up. The food kept on coming, even though rationing was in force, and it was good. The pro-prietor obviously knew Charlie and was bowing and scraping and allowing them to sing at the tops of their voices.

Edward began to get a little uneasy as the drinking got heav-ier, the coffee had been and gone and he wondered how the bill was to be paid. He was in a very difficult situation. He had to admit he was enjoying himself, but he kept one eye on the wait-ers as they began adding up the cost of the food and the drinks. 'Okay, everyone, it's twenty-five bob a head, and I think that's jolly reasonable, so let's have a cheer for Angelo! All together now – For he's a jolly good fellow, for he's a jolly good fellow . . .'

Charlie was prone on the floor, and his pal Freddy took out a wad of notes and shouted that he'd take care of Charlie's share. Two other players passed their hats round the table. Edward was tight-lipped, angry because he had allowed himself to be drawn into the binge. Now he had to pay for it, and pay for it dearly. This meant that he would have no cash for the rest of the week.

He made it look as if twenty-five shillings was nothing, but considering he could get a three-course meal for three shillings and sixpence it was an outrageous amount of money. He dropped his share into the cap, picked up his coat and walked out. That would be the end of his mixing with Charlie and his pals.

Edward worked late at the radio factory, doing double time and hating every minute of it. By the time he got home it was after twelve. The landlady warned him that she would have to report him, he was supposed to be in by ten-thirty. He wanted to hit her, but he controlled his temper and smiled, and told her there had been a bomb scare at the factory, so he had had to stay later than normal.

Charlie breezed into the lecture the following afternoon and squeezed in beside Edward. He pressed up close and whispered, but Edward couldn't hear. 'Can you help me out, I've got nothing done, not had the time, just fill in a few pages for me?'

Edward obliged, and the lecture continued with Edward writing down the notes for Charlie that were to be handed in the following day. Charlie was very grateful, and waited for Edward as he came out of the lecture. Slinging his arm around Edward's shoulders, he walked with him to the hall for lunch. They were coming up to the end of term, and Charlie, with his mouth full, asked Edward what his plans were. Edward shrugged and said he would be going back to London, and Charlie asked if perhaps Edward would like to spend the long vacation with him. 'There's a bit of a catch, see. If Ma finds out the condition I'm in this term all hell will break loose, know what I mean, old thing? On the other hand, if you were to stay for the summer vac, as a house guest, she wouldn't go out and grab Emmott or some other cripple to get me working all summer. You and I could do a bit of swotting, help me along, what d'you say?'

Edward wanted to say yes, but he thought of money as always. Charlie grinned, as if reading his friend's mind, and said it would cost his Ma about ten shillings an hour to pay a tutor and he, Charlie, would hand it over to Edward instead, then he would have his full board and lodgings plus a hell of a good time.

Edward wrote to his mother to say he would not be able to return home for the summer, as he was taking a special course in Wales. She did not have to worry about money as he would have all his costs paid. He would write to her when he got there. He wrote the note on a picture postcard of Cambridge town centre, knowing she would like to show it to her friends.

Edward packed his case into the back of Charlie's MG, and was amazed at how much luggage Charlie had – two trunks and three cases. Edward's small, cheap case looked embarrassing.

'You travel light, don't you? Well, come on, hop in, we've got a long drive. You ever been to Wales? We've got a pile of rubble there we use for hols.'

They drove fast, and Edward was again astonished that Charlie never seemed concerned about petrol, just as he seemed unconcerned about everything in his life.

They headed for Cardiff, and Edward looked around the countryside. It was so different from bombed, scarred London – as if war were far removed from this part of Britain. The sun shone, they passed farms where cattle grazed, it was idyllic and Edward started to relax. He had worked hard all term, and he looked forward to days with nothing to do. As usual, Charlie talked incessantly throughout the journey, gossiped about his pals, who they had been out with, the abortion they had fixed up for the redhead from the cosmetic counter at Woolies, the barmaid with the big tits from the Old Boar.

They drove through Cardiff town centre, shooting through red lights while Charlie yelled to Edward that he should look at this or that sight. As he never stopped, Edward was forced constantly to swivel round in his seat. The town disappeared behind them and they drove along twisting country lanes.

Charlie stopped and went behind a hedge to pee. He shouted to Edward that they were nearly there. When he got back in the car his mood had changed, suddenly he was quiet and he drove more slowly, and he spoke more calmly. 'Look, there might be a bit of an atmosphere at home, with Clarence getting it. Ma might be a bit down. But she'll be all right, there's lots of friends coming up, so we won't get too bored.'

They travelled on in silence, and Edward looking sidelong at Charlie who was chewing his lips and seemed edgy. They went on for another ten miles before Charlie spoke again. 'You'll find my old man a bit strange. Just ignore him, something happened to him in the war so he's a little daffy.'

Edward asked which war, and Charlie chortled, said the first one, but he doubted if his father even knew what day it was so he might think he was fighting in the present war.

The car bounced along a dirt track and across a field, which Charlie said was a short cut. He waved to a farmer, who shook his fist at them, and then doffed his cap. They emerged on to a man-made road, wide enough for one car only. The hedges were thick on both sides so Edward could not see what went on. Suddenly they ground to a halt before a wall in which were set two huge iron gateposts, the gates missing. Charlie eased the car over the cattle-grid, bumping and thudding, then put on speed again. The path was edged with rhododendrons in full bloom, some of them overblown, the pink petals littering the ground. The drive seemed to go on for ever, but then they were among gardens and long, sweeping lawns which needed trimming, but were thick and lush. The car rounded one more curve and Edward gasped, 'It's a castle, Charlie, it's a castle, you never said you lived in a castle.'

Charlie snorted and said again that it was just a pile of rubble, they could only use it in the summer as the place froze every-one to death in winter. 'We only use one wing, the rest is falling down. We were lucky – my uncle, oddball fellow, died without any heirs, so he left it to Ma, there she is ... Ma! Maaaa!'

Edward looked in the direction Charlie was waving, and he could see a figure in a picture hat, cutting roses. She carried a large basket on one arm and wore a man's gardening glove on the other hand. She waved frantically and put the basket down, running towards the car.

The car skidded to a halt and Charlie jumped out, not bothering to open the door, and ran to her. She was shouting and waving as she ran, and Charlie caught her up in his arms and twirled her around, kissing her. Edward had still not seen her face beneath the hat, she was kissing Charlie and holding him at arm's length, cooing that he looked just wonderful. Edward detected the same plummy accent, just like Charlie's. He remained sitting self-consciously in the car as Charlie pulled his mother by the hand towards him. 'Eddie, this is Ma; Ma, Eddie's staying for the vacation, his family was bombed out so he had nowhere to go.'

The lie came out without Charlie batting an eyelid, and Edward tried to get out of the car and shake hands at the same time.

Lady Primrose Collins was furious with Charlie for not warning her or asking her permission to bring Edward, but Edward couldn't detect anything but a rather cool welcome. She took off her hat and removed the gardening glove. 'How do you do, please come into the house, Humphrey will see to your luggage.' She linked hands with her son and walked up the big, crumbling steps into the castle. Edward hung back slightly, then followed them. He had been taken aback slightly at Lady Primrose's age, thinking at first that she was very young. It was the way she moved, but close up he could see that she must be in her fifties. Charlie had inherited her pale blue eyes and snub nose. Even though she was gardening she was perfectly made up.

Edward's initial reaction was disconcerting; a shadow seemed to pass over his heart and he felt his entire body shake in a strong sensation of déjà vu. Yet he knew he had never met Lady Primrose before.

Perhaps not, but his father had known Lady Primrose Collins. And his mother, Evelyne, knew this pretty woman very well. If Lady Primrose had looked closely at Edward she, too, would have felt the powerful hand begin to manipulate from the grave.

Edward strongly resembled his father, although he was not as tall, or as wild. His dark hair was cut fashionably short, but the young man's face was almost a mirror image of the gypsy fighter's.

Lady Primrose did not feel the past catching up with her, not yet. She simply welcomed into her home a young friend of her son's, that was all.

The huge, baronial hall with its stone walls and massive, open fireplace was, as Charlie had said, cold, even though the sun was shining outside. There were suits of armour, shields and animal skins everywhere, very masculine, and the stone floor echoed their footsteps. Humphrey, in his butler's uniform, walked past them to collect their luggage, while Charlie chattered away to his mother, telling her about the journey down and how well he had been doing.

'Eddie, is it? Would you like to go into the drawing room, I will have to see about getting a room ready for you . . . Charlie, come up and say hello to Daddy.'

Edward stood, not sure which door led into the drawing room, and watched the pair walk upstairs. The sun shone on the carpeted steps and he could see threadbare patches. Humphrey returned with Charlie's big trunk, staggering slightly, but he frowned when Edward went to give him a hand, preferring to stagger on alone. 'The drawing room, sir, is to your right. Tea will be served at four-fifteen.'

Edward pushed open the thick oak door and walked into the sunny room, with its oriental rugs covering most of the wooden floorboards, large, squashy, flower-printed sofas, and cushions thrown all over the floor and heaped up by the inglenook fire-place. The room was cluttered and friendly. There was a polished table filled with books and a large bowl of fresh roses, their perfume filling the air.

Edward wandered around the room, smelling the roses and picking up a few of the books. From the window he could see Humphrey carrying in more of Charlie's bags. He opened the window and looked out across the tangled garden.

Hearing someone approaching, he closed the window and walked back to the fireplace. Charlie breezed in and clapped his hands, said he was gasping for a cup of tea, but would Edward like to be shown round before tea was brought in?

They wandered through the old, ruined areas, Charlie pointing out the rotten floors and warning Edward to be careful. He then led him out to the back of the castle.

There was an enormous swimming pool, Grecian in style, and it looked as if it had been added by someone without much artistic sense. It was an eyesore, completely out of keeping with the castle. Charlie whistled, his hands stuck in his pockets. Suddenly he burst into giggles.

'Clarence was such a hoot, he had some crammer staying during one vacation who was terribly shortsighted. Clarence brought him out here, keeping him talking, telling him to go up on the diving board and jump straight in. Chap was actually on the board, teetering right on the edge, when he looked down.' Charlie bent over, laughing until the tears came into his eyes. 'Pool was absolutely covered in millions of wasps, wasp nest had been built close by, millions of them all floating on the surface ... Oh God, it was funny seeing that chap doing a Charlie Chaplin on the end of the board.'

Edward didn't think it funny at all, and he asked Charlie if the fellow had fallen in.

'Course he did, stung all over. Do you swim? Be jolly nice when the weather warms up. It needs cleaning, but it's a jolly good length ... oh, don't look so squeamish, no wasps now, old fellah! Come on, let's go in for a cuppa, I'm parched, what about you, Eddie?'

As Charlie was about to walk back indoors, Edward told him quietly that he preferred to be called 'Edward', not 'Eddie'. Charlie shrugged and said if that was what he wanted then so be it; he was edgy again, Edward could feel it, and his uneasiness manifested itself when they returned to the drawing room. 'Why are there four cups laid out, who else is coming?'

Lady Primrose entered with a plate of buttered scones, which she placed on a large warmer. 'Your father is joining us, have you mentioned him to your friend?'

Charlie muttered that he had, and sat down. Without offering anything to Edward he picked up a sandwich.

'Good heavens, I hadn't realized how tall you were, Eddie . . . please help yourself.'

Charlie laughed and told his mother that his friend didn't like to be called Eddie. She seemed flustered, then apologized. Tea was poured and handed round, Charlie devouring everything with such speed that Lady Primrose gave him a cold stare.

The door opened and David Collins appeared, wearing a velvet smoking jacket and using a silver-topped cane. Edward was taken aback by his handsome features, Charlie paled beside him. He looked delicate, his face had a fine paleness, and very few wrinkles creased his skin. Charlie sprang up. 'Hello, Pa, want you to meet a friend of mine, Edward Stubbs, Edward, this is my father, Captain Collins.'

Captain Collins paid no attention whatsoever, as if he had either not heard Charlie or didn't wish to meet his friend. Charlie gave Edward a wink, and they both watched as David made an elaborate, slow manoeuvre around the winged fireside chair. He sat down, placed his feet very carefully together, and seemed to be fascinated by the gold monogram on his velvet slippers.

Lady Primrose was fussing with the tea tray. 'Would you like tea, David? Darling, tea? It's just brewed, tea?'

David gave her a vacant stare, then a puzzled frown. 'I haven't had tea, have I?'

Charlie gave a short, quiet giggle and turned his back.

'No, you haven't had tea yet, I'm asking you if you want a cup?'

'Well, if I haven't had tea, then yes, please, I would, thank you, darling.' He took out a silk handkerchief and laid it on his knee in preparation for his plate, and his teacup was put on a small table next to his armchair. He ate his cake with his delicate hands, carefully picked up every crumb and popped it into his mouth.

Charlie winked at Edward, who was trying hard not to stare at the older man. He actually seemed to be getting older by the minute, every gesture was ageing him. He was as fussy as an old maid. As Lady Primrose rang a bell beside the fireplace, David leaned forward and goosed her. She jumped, and he sat back as though he hadn't moved. Charlie tittered and Lady Primrose gave him an arch look, but Edward could see she was as amused as Charlie.

Humphrey came in to clear the tea things, and Lady Primrose fetched a plaid rug from the windowseat and carried it across to David. She unfolded it and gently wrapped it around his knees. As she bent forward, David's eyes gleamed. 'Had a flash of your titties then!'

Charlie had to put his hand over his mouth. Primrose turned and made exactly the same gesture, cupping her hands over her lips. The pair of them were like naughty schoolchildren, their giggles getting completely out of hand. They ran out of the room.

Without batting an eyelid at the extraordinary behaviour of the lady of the house, Humphrey bowed formally to David and backed out of the room with the tea tray, inviting Edward to follow him and be shown to his room. Charlie and Lady Primrose were laughing in the hall, Charlie mimicking his father's voice. 'Ohhh, I saw your titties ...'

Edward's room was some kind of nursery, with a heap of broken toys thrown into one corner, and a rocking horse surrounded by tin soldiers in worn boxes. A bookcase was filled with children's fairy stories, and a large cardboard box contained school exercise books. Also, the bed was about six inches too short for Edward.

He unpacked and hung his clothes in the blue-painted wardrobe with the transfers stuck all over it, and then, having nothing further to do, he picked up one of the exercise books which had the name 'Clarence Collins' scrawled across it. The name was everywhere he looked, scratched into the headboard of the bed, on the walls ... it made Edward feel ill at ease, as if a ghost inhabited the room. The strange feeling persisted, making the small hairs at the back of his neck prickle, and he picked up a small tin soldier, holding it in the palm of his hand as though to conjure up a picture of the dead boy.

Clarence had been a tiny child when Edward's mother had first seen him. She had paid a call on Captain David Collins, Lady Primrose's husband. These people had all been linked to his father's past, a past Edward knew nothing about. The curse now touched Edward; the shadow had already entered his heart.

Captain David Collins had been the leading light of the society set in Cardiff, people far removed from the lives of a poor young village girl and a gypsy fighter. Freedom Stubbs was a booth boxer, travelling with his people from fairground to fairground. And the lives of all three had crossed when David had taken Evelyne to see Freedom fight. It was a night all of them would remember; a young gypsy girl had been raped and beaten by four young miners. Over a period of three years all four had been found brutally murdered; their hands tied behind their backs, their throats slit from right to left, and on each boy's forehead a curse was written in his own blood. The murders became known as the 'gypsy revenge killings', and Freedom Stubbs had been charged with all four murders.

Edward replaced the tin soldier. He smoothed the back of his neck with his palm, and when he looked at it he could still see the imprint from the toy, like a red stain. The strange mark disappeared as he stared, and he jumped, startled, as Charlie burst in and bellowed that the bathroom on this floor was dodgy. Edward could use his on the floor below. 'Want a drive around the country before dinner? A few folks coming over, just old family friends, no doubt Father will keep them amused with his repartee, quite a jolly fellow, isn't he, what?'

Edward was nonplussed, he didn't know how to take Charlie's jokes about his father, and he simply smiled. He asked tentatively if they would be dressing for dinner. Charlie mimicked Edward's cockney accent, and with a grin said that of course they would be 'dressin' fer dinnah'. He saw Edward's mouth tighten and knew he shouldn't poke fun at him, but sometimes he was such a big oaf.

'I'm not hungry, you go for a drive, I'll just stay here, have a lie-down.'

Charlie shrugged and went out whistling. Edward could hear him banging down the corridor, then he heard the footsteps coming back. Charlie burst in again, walked over to the wardrobe and swung the door open, then slammed it shut and turned to Edward. 'You liar, you just haven't got your kit with you, won't get out of it that way, old man. I'll have a word with Ma, get you kitted out.'

Lady Primrose tapped on the door and entered. She was so like Charlie that Edward found it unnerving. She crooked her finger at Edward to follow her. They walked along the corridor and down to the next landing, and she opened a door, putting her finger to her lips for Edward to keep silent. She tiptoed into the room and closed the door after Edward. 'This was Clarence's room, I don't want David to hear us in here, he may get confused and think it's ghosts. Come along, follow me, but quietly does it.'

They tiptoed over to the adjoining dressing room, where there were rows of wardrobe doors, each mirrored, and she opened each one, searching, then in the end she turned to Edward. 'He was a little shorter than you, but I'm sure everything will fit, much too big for Charlie. Please just take what you need, but do it quietly.'

She walked back into the bedroom and left Edward gazing into the immaculate wardrobe. There were rows of suits, racks of shirts, ties, shoes . . . he had never seen so many clothes outside a shop in his life. He didn't know where to begin, and he went back to the bedroom. She was still there, standing with her back to him by the side of the bed, holding a photograph in her hand. She was crying softly. 'I can't take these things, really, it's ever so kind of you.'

She put the photograph down and turned to him, her face, even with the tears on it, set and hard. She kept her voice low, but it was fierce. 'I am sure it is "ever so kind", but if you don't they'll only be eaten by moths, please just take whatever, take them and leave the room.'

She went out, and Edward returned to the closet. He began to sort through the clothes, feeling each piece of fabric, his heart thudding with excitement. He could get his whole year's wardrobe out of this. Never mind just a dinner jacket, there were coats and cord trousers, the very ones he'd been saving for. He carried the things back up the stairs to the nursery, laid them on the bed and then carefully dressed, inspecting each item with care. The sleeves were slightly short, as were the trousers, but if he pulled the waist down on to his hips they looked perfect. He had sweaters and shirts, and after a while he made another trip, wondering if he and Clarence had had the same shoe size.

They pinched like hell, but they would stretch, he kept on telling himself they would, and even if they didn't he'd still wear them.

Dressed from head to toe in Clarence's clothes, Edward returned to his own room. He opened the child-size wardrobe, bent low to see himself in the mirror, and studied his reflection. For a moment he felt it again, the strange sensation that made his body tingle. He gasped – he was sure he had seen his father in the mirror, wearing an immaculate dinner jacket. He shook his head, smiling to himself. He had never seen his father dressed in anything but worn working clothes. Again he peered into the mirror, struggling unsuccessfully with his bow tie.

Charlie appeared flushed and wearing a dinner jacket. He laughed at Edward because he was purple in the face from trying to do up the bow tie. In the end Charlie made him practise it so many times he could do it blindfolded. Then Charlie held him at arm's length and nodded his approval, grinned and said that he looked like a million dollars. If he didn't drop too many 'aitches', anyone would take him for a gent. Then he backed off, his hands up. 'Just a joke, it's a joke – when you get that frosty look on your face it sends shivers up me. Right then, you set for a cocktail?'

They walked down the broad stone stairs covered in the threadbare carpet and entered the drawing room together. A fire had been lit, even though it was summer, because the castle walls were damp and cold, but the fire brightened up the room. Charlie began mixing Pimm's for them. 'Better fill you in on the guests, Lord and Lady Carlton, Ma's oldest friends. She's a dreadful, hatchet-faced woman and he's a spellbinding chap, real bore of the first order, then there's the "Hons", their daughters, take after their mother and are frightfully ugly, but they are sooooo rich ... Here you go, get this down you.'

Edward sipped his drink and liked it. He asked if Charlie was rich, judging by the looks of the place he thought they must be pretty well off. Charlie sniggered and said they were all broke, but there was a trust set up by his uncle, his mother's cousin, he was the chap who had left them the castle. From what Edward could gather it was his money they were living on. 'My father, as you may be able to tell by his amazing, zestful, energetic, athletic appearance, never earned a penny in his life. Mother believes she married beneath herself. Must be obvious he's round the bend, got well and truly lumbered with the old boy. Well, here's to us, chin chin.'

Lady Primrose entered, wearing a long, dark rose-coloured evening dress with padded shoulders that accentuated her slimness. She looked very elegant. 'My, Charlie, your friend does look smart. Turn around, Edward, yes, frightfully good, sleeves a trifle on the short side, but ... oh, let me see ... cufflinks, Charlie, go and get a pair of ... there must be lots of cufflinks upstairs.'

Charlie moaned but departed, and as Lady Primrose helped herself to a cocktail she turned to Edward and gestured with her hand, a small fluttering motion.

'I like a gin and it before dinner, just so you know, this much gin and this much . . . it . . . and no ice, but I do like a cherry.'

She giggled, and Edward stood like a sentry as she moved closer. Her perfume swamped him, 'Tea Rose', a bitter-sweet tea rose. She had to look up into his face, he was so tall. 'Where do you come from? Foreign blood in you, I can see it. You are very dark, and my goodness, what long eyelashes you have, well, where are you from?'

Edward looked down at her, she was standing too close for comfort, but he didn't like to back off in case it was rude. But she was very close, so close he could see the fine wrinkles around her eyes, and tiny, tell-tale lines around her mouth.

'I'm from London, the East End.'

'Ho, the East End? Well, well! Oi, Charlie, yer should 'ave told me he is from da East End, lord love yer! Now then, Charlie Collins, don't you splash the drinks around, it is rationed, yer know! Oi, is dat their car?'

She enjoyed herself with her appalling impression of an East End accent. Charlie gave her a stern look and winked at Edward, then poured himself a very large gin. He inched the blackout curtains up a fraction. 'Yep, they've arrived . . . all four of them. Can't you hear the gravel crunching under their deli-cate feet?' He slipped over to Edward's side and nudged him. 'Come on, she was only joking. Lighten up, old man. Here's Clarry's best cufflinks – all yours. Oh, God, here they come.'

Lady Primrose laughed as Lord Freddy entered the drawing room unannounced. He strode across the room, beaming, hand outstretched. 'Charlie, Charlie, good to see you . . . looking handsome as ever, Primmy, how are you, darling one?'

Lord Carlton kissed Lady Primrose's hand. She giggled girl-ishly, and introduced Edward as a friend of Charlie's staying for the vacation. Lord Freddy hardly gave him a look, he was already pouring himself a drink, completely at home in the castle.

'Where are the girls, darling?'

As if on cue, and with a shuddering of the floor, Lord

Carlton's wife appeared. Lady Heather was a thickset woman, her short, stocky legs set rather wide apart to support her weight. She wore a terrible, moth-eaten silver fox cape, the head of the fox jumping up and down on her ample bosom.

She wore her greying hair in an unflattering wartime style, rolled around her head. 'Charlie, you're home, jolly good ... How are you, Primrose? Good God, you've got a fire at this time of year? Aren't you hot? It's frightfully hot in here, isn't it?'

No one introduced Edward, and Lady Carlton showed no interest in him. Her husband handed her a large gin and tonic as their daughters appeared, standing shyly at the door. 'Now, gels, let me introduce you to a lovely, eligible young man, bound to need partners for all the summer dances, this is Edward ... Charlie you both know, of course, and ... oh, one martini, Edward, and one gin and it.'

Edward had not said a single word. Charlie, in fine form, had already taken Lady Carlton's fox fur, and was doing impressions with his hand inside the fox's mouth. Humphrey announced dinner, and the next moment Charlie leapt on the two girls with the fox.

'Charlie, that will do, don't have any more to drink. Edward, make sure he doesn't drink too much, he gets out of control.'

The dining room was even more medieval in style than the sitting room, with a long refectory table and heavy, carved chairs, a throne covered in worn red velvet at one end. The walls were decorated with shields and ancient guns, and deer heads leered down at them. On the far wall was what looked like an African shield with two spears. The main source of light was an iron chandelier, with more candles scattered along the table. Lady Primrose told everyone to sit where they liked, and she herself sat to the right of the throne with Lord Freddy opposite and his wife at his side. The party did not fill the table and Edward noticed that the far end of it was unoccupied and rather dusty.

'I'm afraid the dinner will be the usual hotch-potch ... Oh, darling! There you are!'

Captain Collins, wearing an immaculate dinner jacket with a rose in the buttonhole, walked slowly down the room, using his silver-topped cane. He didn't even acknowledge his guests, but seated himself on the throne, which Humphrey moved closer to the table. Out came a clean silk handkerchief, and he carefully picked up each piece of cutlery at his place and cleaned it. Each prong of the fork was treated to a careful inspection as he slid the handkerchief between them. That done, he wiped the table carefully around where he sat – fussy, tidy movements, without saying a single word. No one paid him any attention, apart from Edward, who watched, fascinated, until he got a nudge from Charlie, who twiddled his finger at his head to show that his father was 'up the wall'.

The first course was a thin, gravy-like soup, and it wasn't very warm, but no one seemed to mind. The clatter of spoons as they ate covered any embarrassment.

'Eddie, old chap, I think you've just eaten my bread roll.'

Edward had forgotten his side plate was to his left, and he had indeed eaten Charlie's roll. He offered Charlie the other one, apologetically.

'Well, I don't want it now you've had your sticky fingers all over it, chuck it away . . . here, give it to me.'

Charlie hurled the bread roll down the table. It hit Captain Collins and bounced off. He appeared not to notice. The conversation continued.

After that, Edward did not eat anything until he had seen which plates and cutlery everyone else used. He sat quietly, listening. Charlie started a general conversation when he denounced Somerset Maugham as a futile, irrelevant writer, and gradually they all joined in. Lord Freddy disagreed, and his wife nodded her head in agreement with him. Lady Primrose told Charlie he was being ridiculous.

'I say he's very competent, I give him that, and don't suppose I am actually criticizing him. Ma, good God, I am far too conscious of the difficulty of constructing even the most simple paragraph myself . . . I simply said that I do not think he is a writer of great importance because he doesn't have anything of importance to say.'

Lady Primrose laughed and said that now he was backtracking, and they began to discuss authors they liked and disliked. Lord Carlton pounded the table as he talked about Lockhart's *Life of Scott*; he had found it invigorating. Lady Carlton turned to Charlie and asked if he enjoyed Byron, and this was greeted with a typical Charlie-type yawning howl. 'Enjoy? Enjoy? The cumulative effect of that cripple's style is stupefying.'

Lady Carlton turned to Edward. 'Are you reading the same subjects as Charlie?'

Edward's mouth was full and so Charlie answered, saying that he was a brilliant scholar. The girls tried to continue the literary conversation, asking if Edward had read *Amurath to Amurath* by Gertrude Bell. It was exceedingly interesting, about travel and archaeology in Asiatic Turkey.

'Sounds utterly boring to me, what on earth are you reading garbage like that for, dear gel?' asked Charlie. 'You should be buried in Virginia Woolf, much more your type, and such a life! Did I tell you she was a lesbian?'

Lady Primrose threw her bread roll at Charlie, and he thanked her because Edward had eaten his.

Throughout the meal David Collins ate like a bird, chewing each mouthful carefully, wiping his mouth after every swallow. He sipped a watery, milky-coloured drink that Humphrey topped up from a decanter kept separate from the other bottles. He seemed unconcerned with anything at the table, and paid no one the slightest attention, keeping his eyes on his plate.

Charlie launched into another anecdote. 'Did I tell you, Ma, the bomber pilot brought down near Cambridge is supposed to have been a German ex-undergraduate, jolly good example of those bastards' thoroughness.'

Lady Primrose looked puzzled and turned to Lord Freddy for assistance.

'Mother, you really are unbelievable. No need for sir to deliberate, bugger tried to pass himself off as one of us.'

Suddenly the whole table went quiet as David Collins spoke. 'I hate the place, caught a devastating cold there.'

Charlie had to put his hand over his mouth to stop himself bursting into a fit of giggles, and Edward noticed his mother doing the same.

'Are you referring to Germany or Cambridge, old chap?'

David looked blankly along the table as if he hadn't spoken and sipped his cloudy drink.

They were about to leave the dining room when David did it again. His voice was clear as a bell, but this time he was pointing at Edward. 'Why is that fellow wearing Clarence's cufflinks?'

Everyone turned to Edward and then back to David. He seemed very lucid, and his pale blue eyes were staring hard at Edward. He pointed again, and his face was tight and angry.

'You must be mistaken, darling, now come along, we are all going into the drawing room, and it's time you went to bed, come along everyone, Edward, Charlie.'

They trooped out, leaving David sitting at the table. Lady Primrose was the last to leave, and she turned when she reached the door. 'Go to bed, David, you're tired.'

As the party crossed the hall they couldn't help but overhear the high-pitched, bell-like voice rising in anger. 'That chap's got Clarence's cufflinks on, I bought them for his twenty-first, I would know them anywhere. He's a ruddy thief, I want the police called. Primmy, please don't walk away when I'm talking to you. Who is that fella, and where is Clarence? He won't like it, I am going to do something about this.'

Charlie closed the sitting-room door with a wink to Edward and began to pour port and brandy, spilling it as he was already rather drunk. The raised voices continued out in the hall, and Charlie grabbed hold of Edward's cuffs, swearing and trying to take out the cufflinks.

'Better get 'em off, old chap, he's liable to get into such a state. Here, give them over.'

Lord Carlton looked on and the girls sat eagle-eyed on the settee as Charlie ran from the room. He left the door ajar, and they could all see the irate David standing with his cane in the hall.

'Here, Father, take them, put them away safely so no one can take them, here, these are what you want, aren't they?'

Lady Primrose hovered at the door and gave Edward an apologetic shrug of the shoulders. The high-pitched voice continued, and now Humphrey could be seen trying to cajole David up the stairs, holding a cloudy drink out for him like a carrot to a donkey.

'All I'm saying is, that chap has no right to be wearing Clarry's cufflinks. When he comes back he'll play hell, don't like this sort of carry-on at all, not nice, throw the beggar out on his ear.'

At last the door was shut, and everyone tried to cover up their embarrassment by talking at once. Edward sat with his sleeves flapping and his feet, in Clarence's patent-leather shoes, hurting. At the first opportunity he excused himself, pleading a headache.

He stood outside the door and knew they were talking about him. He hated the feelings churning inside him, hated being laughed at, but more than that he hated being the outsider. Edward had only just undone his tie and hung it on the doorknob when Charlie knocked and walked into the bedroom.

'Look, sorry about all the carry-on down there, but the old man is out of it, been that way as long as I can remember.'

'Just so long as he doesn't undress me next time. You want Clarry's suit back? Tie? Shirt?'

Charlie thumped him on the shoulder and then sprawled on the bed. 'You know Freddy was engaged to my mother when they were young, and then she ditched him for old loonydrawers ... Apparently Freddy is still getting the old leg over her, and I can't really say I blame him – or her, for that matter. Neither of them have what one could describe as perfect partners. Lord Freddy was married for his title – the little hairy woman is *très riche*, but poor Ma married for love.'

Edward was unbuttoning his shirt. 'What happened to your father?'

'Well, it's all cloaked in mystery, something like shell-shock. He was getting better for a while, then this scandal blew up . . . Well, that's what Ma says put the lid on him.'

Edward sat next to Charlie, cocking his head to one side. 'Well, don't stop there, you've got me hooked now . . .'

Charlie's face puckered, and then he stuffed his hands in his pockets. 'I don't know all the facts, but I had an uncle – he was a boxing promoter. You know the kind – "Gentleman Jim" – with more money than he knew what to do with. Well, Pop took some tart to a boxing match – you know, bare-knuckle job. What the hell he was doing there I don't know. But then he was a bit of a social climber, ya know, maybe thought it was infra dig. But he dragged poor old Freddy with him, and a bunch of debs too – not, I hasten to add, my dear mother, she'd never have been seen dead at a boxing match.'

Edward could feel the hairs on the back of his neck prickling again, and he started to feel cold, icy cold.

'Well, go on,' he said.

Charlie continued, 'Well, it all got out of hand and some blokes raped a gypsy girl. Then this tart tried to make Pa take her home. Well, he paid her off, and all of a sudden these horrific murders started, they called them the revenge murders . . . the gypsy revenge murders. Seems the lads who raped the girl were found bound and gagged, throats slit. Oh, yes . . . and some weird markings on their forehead, or so the story goes.'

Edward stared at his tie. It was hanging down the door like a noose, a hangman's noose.

Charlie yawned and sat up, rubbing his head. 'Next thing, this whore reappears, saying she's going to stand as a defence witness for this gyppo, who was charged with the murders, and she wants Pa and Freddy to act as witnesses because they were at the fight. I think she wanted them as character witnesses, not for the gyppo but for herself, so you can imagine what a scandal that would start up . . . so they refused. Then Gentleman Jim, Uncle Charlie, swashbuckles his way into town. He wants this gyppo for his boxing stable, so he organizes all the legal buffs, and gets poor old Pa into such a state that he agrees to appear. He also gets Lord Freddy to stand up for this dreadful woman.'

'What was she called?'

'Dear God, I haven't the slightest. You've no idea how tough it was trying to get that much out of Freddy, and he was pretty tight so I've no idea how much of that was true. Ma won't even discuss it, says that if that tart hadn't made such a fuss, Pa would never have had a relapse.'

'What happened to the fighter?'

'No idea. I was just getting to the nitty gritty when Freddy got all tearful ... Apparently, this old bastard uncle, the gent I owe my name to ... well, apparently he was a tough negotiator, blackmailed Freddy and Pa ...'

Edward interrupted. 'How? What did he have on them?'

Charlie stared at Edward, finding his interest a little distasteful. 'Freddy never said what made them step forward, but ... Look, what's it to you?'

'But what?'

Charlie's face tightened, then he shrugged. 'Maybe it's just deserts.'

'I don't follow?'

'I didn't really intend you to, old boy ... It's not something one likes to broadcast, but Clarry knew. Maybe that was why he couldn't wait to get to the front, get himself shot in a decent hero's death.' He ran his hand along the name scratched on the bedpost, tracing the childish letters over and over with his fingers. Then he stuffed his hands back into his pockets, no longer joking; Edward felt that he was ashamed.

'The old man, Edward, turned custard yellow and fled. He left his entire regiment to be hacked to death, that's why he's loony. He can't face the past, can't face the truth ... *C'est la vie*, huh?'

Edward knew who the fighter was, knew the woman Charlie had referred to as a 'tart' was his mother, but he showed no sign that anything Charlie had said had affected him personally. He

spoke flippantly, hoping to get more information. 'So what happened to the tart and the fighter?' he asked.

Bored by the subject now, Charlie picked his nose, then
lurched to his feet, dismissively. 'God only knows. No doubt
they lived happily ever after – luck of the gyppos, I suppose. And
I've said too much, always do when I've been on the gin. Well,
g'night, I'm falling asleep on my feet. See you on the morrow,
old chum.'

He sauntered out, and Edward relaxed, stretching his hands,
his fingers ... Then he undressed and lay, naked, on the small
bed. He was sure Charlie had no inkling of his background, it
had been sheer coincidence. Freedom Stubbs and Edward were
too far apart, worlds apart now, and no one could link him with
the gypsy and the 'whore', as Charlie had called her. He turned
to lie on his belly. He would make sure no one else would make
the connection.

Softly, he practised his speech over and over again, listening
to his voice, modulating the accent Lady Primrose had mimicked so poorly, flushing as he remembered. He knew she would
have been horrendous to his mother, and he would have liked
to shove the cufflinks down the old fool's throat. He found himself wondering if his mother had been David Collins' girlfriend,
and why a man as well connected as the captain would have
been involved with a girl like her. He would have liked to get
up and leave there and then, but he was stuck without enough
cash to walk away. Anyway, something held him here, held him
to this dead boy's room, to these half-dead people. Somehow he
knew that by the end of the summer he would change.

Eventually he slept, while the noose he had made out of his
tie slid slowly from the door to lie on the floor.

The following morning, Edward borrowed a bicycle and rode
into the nearest town. He spent four hours in the public library,
looking over the old newspaper cuttings of the trial of Freedom
Stubbs. His mother had never mentioned her past, her life in the
valleys or the murder trial.

His father, the man Edward had knifed to death, had himself been charged with four murders. Again and again Edward turned the pages to look at the black-and-white photograph of Freedom. The strange, youthful face glared back. In one shot, his long hair swirled around his shoulders as if daring the photographer to take his image. There were also several photographs of his mother, often blurred, out of focus, but it was Evelyne, haughty yet shy, arrogant yet so innocent. The photograph touched a chord inside him that made him ache to see her.

He read the articles over and over; how she had become a heroine, standing as a witness for a man she barely knew because she believed in justice. There was an account of how she had been asked, before the jury, if she had had any kind of sexual relationship with the accused, and she had replied that she had not, she was there simply to see that an innocent man did not hang. She had been with the gypsy on the night of the last murder and knew he could not have committed it. The lawyers were able to prove him innocent of all charges, and he was freed.

Edward wondered if her story was true. It certainly read so, yet his mother had eventually married Freedom. There was so much he wanted to ask her, so much he wanted to know, but he knew he now had no right ever to ask. He had killed the man she had saved from the rope, killed his own father – he even mused over the fact that it was possible his father had been a murderer. He read of the way the gypsy had caught the press's imagination with his handsome looks, much like the film star, Valentino. With a sense of foreboding he read of the curse sign on each of the four young miners' foreheads. So much he had no knowledge of, so much of his father he had never known. And the more he read the surer he was that he did not want it known, the more he reconciled himself to moving further and further away from his roots. He wanted no part of this past, no whispers attached to him of his gypsy father; yet carefully, surreptitiously, he cut out as many of the newspaper photographs as possible. Then he returned to the castle.

*

The days passed by, and although Edward spent two or three hours in the early mornings reading and revising, Charlie made no effort to study. He was out shooting rabbits for food, or chasing the farm girls for other reasons. Charlie was a walking time bomb, full of energy.

One morning, after Edward had been at the castle for three weeks, he went as usual to the breakfast room. The housekeeper shuffled around, carrying dishes and muttering about everything being 'short'. Yet there never seemed to be a lack of food. It was never cooked well, but no one went hungry. The feeling that the war was far away was more prevalent here in the country.

Edward sat between Lady Primrose and Charlie as they argued about money, and was astonished yet again by Charlie's total unconcern. He talked to his mother as if she were one of the girls from Woolworth's, at the same time wolfing down his breakfast as though he had a train to catch.

'You'll just have to find the money yourself. Two hundred pounds, Charlie, how could you?'

Charlie munched on his toast and shrugged, then he scraped out the marmalade jar and kicked Edward under the table.

'You've got the cash, Ma, I know it, all the booty you got from Uncle Charlie – you've just become a miser in your old age.'

Lady Primrose turned to Edward for help, and told him his cousin Charlie had been dead for nearly twenty years. 'He just doesn't know the meaning of money, Edward, but he's going to learn, I'm not going to pay this time. Last term how much did you owe? Three hundred, and you promised me, you promised me faithfully.'

Charlie laughed. He knew if he encouraged his mother to talk about Uncle Charlie, his namesake, she would forget about the bills. Lady Primrose sighed. She wandered around the room while she told Edward about Sir Charles Wheeler. 'I don't suppose you know anything about boxing, do you, Edward? Well, Charlie was a promoter – you know, he used to find boxers and then take them all over the world – he was such a sportsman, everyone knew him. He died in a plane crash in Nevada, or was it Florida, I don't really remember – anyway he never married, and his money went to the trustees of his estate, and they are so mean, really awful. You see, we are the only heirs, and it should all be ours.'

As Lady Primrose talked on and on, Edward felt as if a ghost were walking across his grave.

'I say, are you all right? Gone a paler shade of yellow, you should come out shooting with me, get some colour into your dark cheeks.'

Edward smiled and drank the dregs of his cold tea. Lady Primrose was called to the telephone, and Charlie stuffed the bills away in a drawer with a bow.

They walked for miles, and Charlie showed Edward how to use his shotgun. As they walked, Edward turned the conversation to their studies, asking when Charlie was prepared to begin work. 'And you did mention paying me for my time here, sorry to bring it up, but I would have got a job during the vacation. Unlike you, Charlie, I don't have a rich mother, so when do we start?'

They began, in a haphazard way, to set aside a few hours a day for work, and Edward began to realize that his pupil was way below himself in his studies. It was something of a shock, how on earth had he got himself into Cambridge? 'Look, why don't we start at the first lecture and work our way through, Charlie? You don't have the foggiest notion of what I'm talking about.'

Charlie admitted it, saying he had actually wanted to read English literature, but as his brother had done that he chose geology. He hadn't the slightest interest in rocks or anything to do with mineralogy or petrology, and to prove it he began to hurl his books across the room. 'I want to live, Eddie, really live, you know, enjoy life. What's the point of being cooped up in those ruddy lectures, those interminable centrifuges? I am so fucking bored all the time. My mind's petrifying like your bloody rocks.'

Edward had never seen Charlie so 'real', this was what he was really like, and all the laughs and the madcap antics were out of frustration.

'Clarence was the clever one, you see, always Clarence, and he went and got himself shot to pieces. So I have to go to Cambridge, I have to emulate the "Boy Wonder" ... Well, I can't, I simply can't. Added to that I've got this wretched farm girl up the spout and she's chasing me all over the place with a pitchfork.' Charlie's face tightened and he chewed his lip. 'Look, I'm going off for a while, see a few old friends, you won't mind being on your tod, will you? Only I'm sure they'd all bore the pants off you ...'

Charlie didn't wait for a reply, he just turned and marched off, leaving Edward feeling like a spare part. He somehow knew Charlie didn't want him to meet his friends.

Edward sat at the small nursery desk for a few hours, studying, until he heard a car outside on the gravel. He looked out of the window to see Lord Carlton in his car. He opened the door and Lady Primrose ran to join him. They drove off, and Edward could see her kissing Freddy's neck as they disappeared from view. He felt slightly disgusted – Lady Primrose had to be in her early fifties, yet she was acting like a teenager, and a naughty one at that.

By mid-afternoon the sun was hot enough to crack the flagstones so Edward crept into the dead Clarence's room and found himself a pair of swimming trunks. The water was icy cold, and the surface of the pool was covered with leaves. He nervously lowered himself into the water. Clinging to the edge, he dog-paddled, never having swum in his life. He tried a few strokes, and made it from one side of the pool to the other. Then he got out of the water and sunbathed, lying on the marble side of the pool. He had still not been paid, and it was beginning to irritate him. So Charlie was in a mess, that didn't mean Edward had to follow in his tracks. He was going to succeed, even, perhaps, one day, live in a place like this. He liked the old furniture, its weight. 'Yes,' he thought, 'one day I'll have a place like this.'

He began to burn from the heat of the sun, so he returned to his room. He had a long bath, then changed for dinner. He was always a little wary of going to the drawing room before the dinner gong sounded, as he felt such an intruder.

At last the gong boomed, and Edward made his way downstairs. He was starving from his walk and his swim. Charlie thumped him one from behind as he moved down the stairs. He was in full evening dress, a white silk scarf wrapped around his neck. 'Just out for the evening, you don't mind. Oh, Ma, Ma ... the Henleys want you to call them, I said you'd see them at their fête.'

Edward hung back slightly as Lady Primrose stood at the open doors waving Charlie off, calling to him to enjoy himself. Edward stood in the hall, uncertain what to do.

'Well dear, it's just you and me. God knows what Mrs Forbes has come up with tonight ... now, I insist you sit in the throne, David won't be down. Do help yourself to wine ...'

'Thank you, er ... where's Charlie gone, Lady Primrose?'

Lips puckered, she picked at the dreadful mess on her plate, then jabbed at it with her fork. 'Oh, he'll be with Lorna ... they've come for a few weeks, all staying at the Waverleys' ... Humphrey, what on earth is this? It's like dead frog.'

Edward ate in silence while she chattered away, hardly touching her food, but the wine decanter was refilled by Humphrey and they both drank liberally. 'She's such a darling, awfully pretty gel, poor darling child was so in love with Clarry.'

Edward found it difficult to follow her train of thought. When she mentioned her dead son she stared into space. 'Lorna is so patient. Charlie's supposed to be engaged to her, you know, but he won't name the date. This is dreadful, I can't eat another mouthful. Why don't we have some coffee in the drawing room ... come along.'

Edward, still hungry enough to eat anything and light-headed from having consumed nearly a bottle of wine by himself, dutifully followed her into the drawing room. She offered him brandy and he accepted. He had never had it before and found it a harsh, burning liquid, but he liked it, it relaxed him. He even accepted the proffered cigar.

The fire blazed, the room was hot and stuffy, and the brandy and cigar made Edward feel a little dizzy, but he liked the feeling. He asked Primrose if she would mind if he loosened his tie, and she laughed, crossed over to him and, with one deft finger, unhooked the tie, then loosened his collar. He averted his face, ashamed. Lady Primrose misconstrued his look. He was certainly a very handsome young man, much better-looking than any of the other students Charlie had landed her with. 'Shall we play some music, sort out something from that pile of records over there – not that other stack, they were Clarence's.'

She watched him standing over the record-player. He hadn't refused, hadn't made an excuse to go to his room. Perhaps he rather liked her. She leaned back and sighed, that would be nice, to have a young man in love with her. She lolled against the cushions and closed her eyes in what she thought was a provocative pose.

Edward had no idea what record was what, and he looked through them at a loss. He chose one at random, placing it on the turntable and winding the handle energetically. 'The Moonlight Serenade' drifted out, slightly cracked and at a rather slow tempo as he had not wound the phonograph up properly.

'I've had a disastrous afternoon.'

Edward wound the handle. 'Pardon?'

'Shall I tell you something, something naughty? I have been having an affair with Lord Carlton for more years than I care to remember. It's not as shocking as it sounds, his wife knows, she's known for about as long . . . she just turns a blind eye. But it's no good when it's sort of accepted, is it?'

'I wouldn't know.'

She laughed, held out her glass. 'Be a sweet boy and give me a refill, would you, make it a large one. Thank you, sweetie.'

Edward took her glass to the cabinet and filled it, took it back to her and turned the phonograph off as he went. He handed her the glass.

'Well, chin chin, aren't you going to join me ... oh do! Go on, help yourself.'

Edward shrugged and refilled his glass.

'He's impotent, well, he has been for the past four months ... I put it down – haw, haw, haw! That was a slip of the tongue – his factory, or his wife's factory, is being closed down, not many people are really all that interested in toffee when there's a war on ... Come and sit beside me.'

Edward moved closer, but did not sit beside her. He sipped his brandy and stared into the fire. He felt Primrose's hand touch his head, stroking his hair.

'You're very quiet, what are you thinking about?'

'Oh Christ,' he thought, 'she's making a play for me.' Aloud, he said, 'I think I'll go up and do some work, do you mind?'

'I've got a super record somewhere, better than that creepy slow stuff, we'll have something bright and lively.' Her whole body broke into a flush as she looked at him. He was so tall, so lean, and his hair coal black. It had grown longer over the summer and it suited him. He was quite the most beautiful boy she had ever seen in her life. There was a quality to him that she found so overtly sexual, even on their first meeting she had noticed it – a strange, animal quality, the way he moved, so guarded, so watchful, his eyes brooding.

Edward turned as she laughed. 'I was just talking to myself, in my mind, thinking what a handsome boy you are. My thoughts were like those cheap penny-dreadfuls; "animal quality", you know the sort of thing, "He paced the room like a wild beast, his broad shoulders, his dark, handsome looks."'

When he looked at her, she couldn't tell from his expression what he was thinking, and she didn't care if it did sound like a cheap novel, his eyes were as unfathomable as ... somewhere, somewhere she had seen eyes like these before, perhaps in the picture house, some long-forgotten film ... she got up and went to the gramophone. Edward watched her tossing records about, and downed his drink. He shouldn't have mixed them. 'I don't dance, and I'm a bit drunk, actually, I really think I should go up to my room.'

'I'll teach you, this is a tango, come on, up you get, on to those long legs of yours.' Lady Primrose began to dance, and she swayed across the room as the music crackled from the old gramophone. She was still slim, still able to move like a young girl, and she began to tango. She tugged a shawl from the table, almost overturning the bowl of flowers. 'Come on, dance with me, dance, hold your arms up, that's it. Now stamp your feet, as if you were a bullfighter ... wonderful, da-da, darumrum-rum da ... da rumpupup daaa.'

Suddenly she threw herself into his arms and clung to him. The sunburn on his back was painful, and he tried to push her away, but she hung on. 'Please, oh please don't push me from you, hold me, hold me tight.'

The record stuck, but she didn't seem to hear it. She hid her face in his shoulder and ran her hands up his arms, murmuring, moaning, 'You have such a body, such a body, so firm, so young, make love to me, please, please make love to me.'

Primrose grabbed the decanter and pulled him by the hand towards the door. She was drunk and she knew it, but she wanted him, wanted him naked beside her.

Edward allowed himself to be dragged up the stairs, along the corridor and up to his nursery room, where she shut the door and pressed her back against it. She drank from the decanter itself, then swung it in her hand. Edward took off his jacket and hung it neatly on the small child's chair.

He looked at her through the mirror, her face flushed, and in the dark he could make believe she was young, or youngish, but as she stepped out of her dress he had to turn away, disgusted. She was Charlie's mother, for God's sake.

She lay on the bed and held out her arms to him, begging him now, pleading, and it sickened him. He picked up the decanter and took a heavy swig, feeling the brandy hit the back of his throat, then he stood by the bed, looking down at her, and found her pitiful as she writhed in front of him.

'I have no money, I need money, I don't have a cent with me, not a penny, Lady Primrose.'

She stared at him, suddenly cold. She pulled the sheet around her naked body, ashamed, and turned her back on him. He slowly rubbed her shoulder, softly, gently.

'How much do you want?'

'God,' she thought, 'was that my voice, asking how much?'

Edward began to unbutton his shirt, pulling it out of his pants, and he smiled down at her, bent to kiss the side of her head.

'Ten pounds, I want ten pounds.'

Primrose lay back in his arms and sighed. He had been worth every penny, and she kissed him. The fact that she was paying for it somehow heightened her enjoyment. He looked down into her face, patted her bottom and said that was all she was getting for a tenner. She laughed, searched around for her underwear, and as she gathered it up in her arms she bent over him, over the small bed, to kiss him goodnight. The childish, scrawled writing of her dead son confronted her, and she blushed with shame.

The next few weeks Edward rarely saw Charlie. He was always driving off to visit 'friends', seldom back until the early hours, sometimes not appearing at all. Edward spent his days working, walking and practising swimming. The evening began to take on a pattern; if Lady Primrose was home, she invariably came to his room, often the worse for drink, and always clutching her ten-pound note.

One night, Charlie arrived home unexpectedly. Edward and Lady Primrose were in the small child's bed when they heard him calling. Lady Primrose hastily wrapped her dressing gown around her and was just reaching the door when Charlie burst in. 'Oh, hello, darling, I just brought poor Edward an aspirin, he's not feeling at all well . . .'

Edward lay on the bed, naked apart from a sheet draped over him. He had tanned to a dark brown from his sunbathing, and Charlie was quick to take in the situation. He lolled at the door. 'Just thought you should know, Ma, I've sort of said we'll throw a dance before I go back up ...'

Lady Primrose covered her embarrassment fast, clapping her hands with delight and telling Charlie it was a wonderful idea. She then beat a hasty retreat. Charlie remained at the open bedroom door. 'You got a cigarette, old chap?'

Edward sat up, reached for his trousers and tossed a packet of Craven 'A' cigarettes to Charlie.

'What was she doing up here? Trying to grope you?' Charlie lit the cigarette, tossing the match aside. He had a smirk on his face. Edward shrugged his shoulders. 'I've got a headache.'

'Too much study, old fella, not enough play ...'

'Look, Charlie, you owe me, you know. I could have got a job – you said ten bob a week. I'm not one of your fancy friends, I need the cash.'

Charlie wandered about the room, puffing at the cigarette. 'I'll pay, for Chrissakes ...'

'You should have done some work, you know. Emmott'll haul you over the coals next term.'

'I think it should be fancy dress. We've got loads of costumes up in the attic, should be great fun ... You could wrap a few sheets around you, come as Rudy Valentino ... You okay? What's up?'

Edward broke out in a sweat. He could see himself, sitting at the kitchen table with Alex, his mother, and the scrapbook. Freedom's face, the programmes, the boxing pictures. He could hear his mother laughing, 'They used to say your Dad was the image of the film star, Rudolph Valentino ... see, look at this picture. Look, Eddie, here's another. This was in Miami ...'

'Eddie, you all right?' Charlie moved closer to the bed and Edward shrank back from him.

'What's the matter?'

'Nothing, nothing, just ... You mind leaving me alone?'

Charlie stubbed out his cigarette and wandered out. Edward opened the window. He was panting, nausea swept over him. He couldn't get the picture of his father out of his mind. He began to pace up and down the room, feeling the walls closing in on him. He dressed, crept downstairs and out into the garden. It was a clear summer night and he slowly began to shake the panic inside him. He sat on a bench, leaned back and closed his eyes.

'Hello . . . I saw you out here. Did Charlie suspect anything?'

The last person he wanted to see was Lady Primrose, wrapped in her floating pink negligée. He sighed, gritted his teeth. She put her arms around his neck.

Standing up at an unlit window, overlooking the gardens, was David Collins. He could see his wife fawning over some fellow who, to his mind, looked like a bloody gypsy. He sipped his medicine, his mind as clouded as his drink, then turned away from the window, missing the sight of Edward pushing Lady Primrose roughly away.

'Oh, you brute, that's what you are, a brute . . . let's go inside, I want you, darling, I want you.'

Edward gripped her arms and pushed her away again, making her stumble backwards. She began to be afraid of him. 'Eddie, is something wrong, Eddie darling?'

He wanted to slap her over-made-up face, felt his hands clenching and unclenching. If she tried to hold him one more time, he didn't think he would be able to control himself. 'I don't like being called Eddie. My name is Edward, for Chrissakes, Edward.'

Lady Primrose, with all the confidence she could muster, told him that she knew who he was, there was no need to be cruel.

'You don't know me, none of you know me. If you must know, you disgust me, disgust me as much as my own pitiful circumstances do. Now leave me alone.'

She made the mistake of putting her arms around him as he walked away from her. He turned and slapped her so hard with one hand that she fell on to the gravel path. 'Get off me, you old hag, for God's sake get away from me.'

She started to cry, her make-up running, begging him not to call her old. He had said she was beautiful, said she was beautiful . . .

'I'll say anything if I'm paid for it, darlin', now get lost, hear me, fuck off.' The cockney accent, so carefully disguised, burst out of him, and he walked away cursing himself for letting it slip. He wasn't worried that he had struck her, hurt her, only angry that he had let his accent slip.

The fancy-dress dance never materialized. The following morning Edward found Charlie sitting at the breakfast table. He looked up with a glum smile as Edward joined him. 'Look, old chap, I think we should beat a hasty retreat, get the hell out of here . . . About this cash I owe you – I feel really rotten about it so if you agree, there's a whole load of stuff up in the attic. You sort through it, take what you want, sort of payment in kind. Then we'll be on the road . . .'

'Fine by me – what's up, the wedding off?'

Charlie shrugged, poured himself more coffee. 'Not much point, really . . . I'll explain when we're on the road. Just think we should make preparations to leave.'

Edward didn't argue, and was left eating alone. He wondered if Charlie knew about Lady Primrose and himself. Something was up, that was for sure. He finished his breakfast and went upstairs to his room to pack.

Charlie popped his head round the door. 'Look, I've got my gear in the motor. You go upstairs to the attic and take what you want. I'll be outside waiting. Really, just take anything that takes your fancy . . .'

'Charlie? Charlie, what's wrong? What's happened?'

'Tell you later. Get a move on, I'll have to go and see Ma.'

Edward searched the musty, dust-filled attic of the castle. He found three oil paintings, two embroidered velvet curtains, vases and candlesticks. He would have taken more but he felt there wouldn't be enough room in the car. He carried everything downstairs and piled the boot high with his luggage first – all his

new clothes, courtesy of the dead Clarence. Somehow he managed to fit all his pieces of furniture in. As he was coming down
the stairs on his final trip, the drawing-room door was open.
Lady Primrose sat on the sofa, weeping, with Charlie next to
her, holding her hand. Edward stood outside by the car, unsure
whether or not he should disturb them. At long last Charlie
came out.

'Don't you think I should say goodbye to your mother,
Charlie?'

Charlie hopped into the driving seat, searched his key-ring
for the car key and said nonchalantly, 'No . . . Besides, I have a
feeling your goodbye would take longer than a peck on the
powdered cheek.'

Edward flushed at the insinuation. So Charlie had known
about himself and Lady Primrose. Charlie laughed, 'Write her
a note. She's a bit upset . . . come on, let's get cracking. Good
God, it looks like a removal van.'

Edward went even redder. 'Well, you told me to choose . . .'

'I was joking. I suspect you've earned every stick of it. Now
get in and stop rabbiting. It doesn't bother me in the slightest,
more than likely it gave the old boiler a new lease of life.' He
revved the MG and slammed it into gear. They shot off down
the gravel path as Lady Primrose opened the door, just in time
to see the bright red car career out of sight. She leaned on the
door and sobbed.

From his bedroom window, David Collins looked out. It was
a beautiful, sunny day. He presumed they were off on a picnic.
'Pity,' he thought. 'They should have asked me along. Nice day
for a picnic.'

Charlie drove fast, bumping over cattle-grids, and Edward had
to reach over the back to secure one of his paintings. The car
skidded around a narrow bend and they almost ended up in a
hedge.

'For Christ's sake, Charlie, there's no need to kill us both.'

Charlie brought the car screeching to a halt, and rested his head on the driving wheel. 'Oh, shit, shit, shit ...' When he looked up, his eyes were brimming with tears. 'Got the old papers, bloody awful ... You know, I wanted to go so badly, but now I am, well, it's just so ruddy inconvenient.'

Edward was not sure what Charlie was talking about.

'I'll be in uniform, old bean, off to fight the ruddy Germans. I'm joining my regiment as soon as I report back to college. Ask me, it's bloody Emmott's fault. He couldn't wait to get rid of me.'

Edward was stunned, but Charlie shrugged it off in his usual manner. 'Will you do me a favour, sort of keep in touch with Ma? She's taken it awfully badly – Clarence, you know. The old man's no use to her, he's completely whacko. She liked you, so drop her a note.'

Edward slipped his arm around Charlie and gave him a hug.

'You're an odd chap, Eddie. Underneath all your brooding, you're all right. Tell you what, why don't you take over my old rooms? I dare say a lot of my stuff I won't need where I'm going.'

Edward smiled his thanks, and they started the drive back to Cambridge. Charlie began to whistle, as if he didn't have a care in the world.

Edward took over Charlie's rooms, and now he had his own bathroom, study and bedroom, plus a small area for cooking if he wished. Additionally, he had the services of a bedmaker and cleaner, and, with all his acquisitions from the castle, he made the rooms look very classy. He sat and surveyed his handiwork, well pleased. He had his own castle now, and a wardrobe that was more than suitable. Even better, he had cash in his pocket.

Edward hung the oil paintings and threw all Charlie's outrageous black sheets into a corner. He preferred the room more austere and, with the heavy curtains he had taken from the attic of the castle, he didn't need the sheets as blackouts. Pleased with himself, he lay in his bed, surveying the room. Sleep was hard to come by, and when he eventually dozed off it was only to wake again, sweating. He looked at the alarm clock Charlie had left behind and saw that it was only two o'clock. He tossed and turned, and couldn't tell if he was awake or dreaming. He saw boats, hundreds and hundreds of boats of all shapes and sizes, landing on a long beach. Men were running, screaming . . . a small group of soldiers was rushing to the water's edge, carrying a soldier in their arms . . . Edward sat bolt upright. The boy was Charlie, bleeding, his head blown away on one side . . . 'Charlieeee . . .!'

Edward ran to the gates. They were locked and bolted, and the night porter came to the door asking what the hell Edward thought he was doing. If he was drunk, he would be reported; if not, he should go back to his rooms immediately. Edward climbed the stone steps and returned to his rooms, telling himself he was just being stupid, he was crazy . . . It was just a dream, a nightmare. Old Charlie would be all right.

Edward's premonition of Charlie Collins' death became a reality. He died in action six months later in the arms of two young officers as they carried him towards a waiting ambulance. Shrapnel was embedded in the left side of Charlie's skull and his face was horribly disfigured. When Lady Primrose received the news, she arranged for her husband to be committed to a nursing home. She returned to the castle and dressed herself in a full-length, floating, pink evening gown. At the inquest, her butler said he had heard the gramophone playing in her room, so he had not disturbed her. The following morning her body was found in the swimming pool. The remains of a note were found. It was addressed simply to 'Edward'. She had begun the letter and been unable to send it as she could not remember his surname. The torn fragments were pieced together from the waste-paper basket. It contained no reason for her suicide.

David Collins lived contentedly in the nursing home, in a world of his own, until he died alone, ten years later.

Chapter Three

Alex Stubbs became prisoner number 4566. He occupied a cell with four bunks in the juvenile section of Wormwood Scrubs. They were separated from the prisoners in the main block, the old lags. But the boys in the juvenile section were hardened offenders, most having had one or two stays in the more lenient borstals. The Scrubs differed greatly from the borstals and remand homes, as it was run on similar lines to the main prison.

Alex was quite pleased that he was allocated a cell with a friendly faced cockney boy. Some of the men he had seen looked like real criminals, at least Dick was around his own age. As they prepared their beds two more inmates appeared. They were tough-looking, and already on friendly terms. Tom Donaldson had red hair and a freckled face, and he chucked his sheet on to the top bunk opposite Alex. 'You take the lower deck, Joe.'

Joe, a fat boy with hair so short it stuck up on end, complained about always getting the bottom bunk, and Tom flicked his towel at him. 'I don't want that arse comin' down on me at night, so you git the bottom whether you like it or not, okay, fat man?'

Alex checked the washing facilities. There were four enamel bowls and jugs on three scrubbed corner tables, some nail brushes and four plastic mugs. On the floor were four chamber pots.

Tom swung himself up on to the top bunk and dangled his legs, looking down at Dick and Alex. Dick grinned and said he was in for armed robbery, and Tom smiled and shook his hand, saying he was in for 'aggravated burglary'. 'Bleedin' aggravated, all right. They copped me, that's all I know. Joe down there's in for shoplifting, what yer say you were in for, Alex? Alex, is it?'

They all looked questioningly at Alex, who busied himself clearing a space on the corner table. 'Murder . . . Okay, that's my place.'

The effect was just as he'd hoped, just as it had been on Sid, even Johnny. He could see their reactions and it amused him, suddenly he was the big shot.

Tom, impressed, jumped down to stand by Alex, and picked up his chamber pot. He asked if Alex had done time before, knowing he hadn't by the way Alex examined everything in the cell. 'Right, then, lemme give you a piece of advice. It's kid's stuff in 'ere, but yer gotta remember the golden rule. Make sure you have a shit before you're banged up for the night, otherwise it's terrible sleeping wiv yer own stink, even worse wiv some-one else's . . . If yer caught short in the night, then chuck it out the winder, wrap it in paper an' chuck it. I mean it, yer think it's funny but you take a look outta any nick's windows and yer see the bombs chucked out in the night.'

The spyhole in the door was moved aside, and they turned to see an eye staring in at them. 'Lights out!'

The lights went off and the small, claustrophobic cell went quiet. Joe let rip with a fart and laughed. Tom belted him one, but was laughing too. They settled down for the night.

They lined up for their breakfast, grabbing trays and moving along as the food was served. The enamel trays were just large enough for a bowl, a cup, and a knife and fork. They had 'skilly', a very thin porridge, an egg and a couple of slices of bread. Weak tea was poured from a vast pot at the end of the line. They carried it all the way back to their cages and ate hurriedly, because when the next bell rang they had to clean up the cell. The bunks had to be stripped and the sheets and blankets folded box-style. The washing bowls had to be cleaned and the clothes and towels folded, everything neat and orderly, ready for the screws to inspect.

The first morning was to be like every other. There were no classes here as there had been in the reform schools. They waited to hear where they would be put to work – some would be assigned to cleaning, some to sewing mail sacks, others to the radio repair shop. They worked from eight-thirty in the morning until twelve-thirty. Alex was pleased to be taken to the radio shop, it was considered a good job. But he soon found out that it was very boring, mundane work. He had to take old radios apart for scrap metal, and it took no brains whatsoever, a child could have done it.

The exercise periods were heavily patrolled by screws, as this was when fights usually broke out or attempts were made at escaping. Although the borstal boys were separated from the older prisoners, they would occasionally see a 'trusty' with a blue armband circulating the library trolley, or washing down the corridors. After exercise came tea, and then they were locked in their cells until the recreation period at six o'clock. It was a rowdy time and they played table tennis, draughts and chess.

Sid was the first person Alex saw, laughing loudly as he knocked a table-tennis ball back and forth. Alex walked slowly around the table, pushed Sid's opponent away and took up the bat. Sid's jaw dropped, he turned around, scared, and Alex bounced the ball up and down. 'My serve . . . All right, Sid?'

'Sure, Alex, ready when you are.'

Alex looked at his cell-mates, nodded to the recreation-room doors for them to keep watch. All the boys knew something was about to happen, and the room went silent.

Alex moved fast around the table and the bat crashed down on Sid's head. Alex gripped him tightly. 'What you tell the law on me for, Sid? Why'd you rat on me?'

Sid tried to wriggle free, but Alex was far bigger and stronger. 'You know what you done to me? My mum hadda come an' sit in the court, you know what that done to her, do you? Do you?'

Suddenly, Alex went crazy, hammering Sid over the head with the table-tennis bat. Tom yelled from the door that the screws were on the way running down the corridor. They burst into the games room. 'Right, you – Stubbs ... Come on, let him go ... Stubbs!'

Alex threw the bat at one of the screws, and the next moment he was down on the ground and they were kicking the daylights out of him.

When he woke up in the hospital, Alex's face was puffy from the beating. He had lost a front tooth, and one ear had been stitched badly, making the lobe lumpy and extremely unattractive. Alex was examined and given the all clear and two weeks' solitary confinement on bread and water.

A naked light bulb was kept on in the cell at all times. The only way Alex could sleep was face downwards.

During the second week, the diet of bread and water making him feel shaky, he didn't even get up from his bunk. He lay and stared at the light bulb, and stared ... he began to hallucinate, shadows on the walls took on weird shapes. Suddenly it started again, the dream, the mountain, the green grass, the fragrant smell of fresh, clean air. Alex began to breathe deeply, filling his lungs, willing himself to hear once more the horse's hooves galloping ... Now he was running, running, wanting to see the man he knew was his father. The pounding became more and more insistent, he couldn't tell whether he was awake or dreaming ... He was awake, the screws were unlocking his cell to take him back to the prison. He didn't want to go, he wanted to stay by himself, alone. The screws thought he was being difficult and dragged him out, shouting that if he didn't behave he'd be back in solitary.

When he returned to his cell he was greeted as a hero. There were three letters waiting for him from his mother. The lads backed off, letter-reading was private, and they picked up their magazines as Alex slowly opened his letters, one by one, savouring the contact with the outside world.

Evelyne's letters always managed to upset him. He knew she was trying to sound cheerful, but it only made things worse.

The bell rang for recreation and their cell was unlocked. The boys left Alex sitting on his bunk, reading.

The third letter made Alex even more depressed; she was to go into hospital, she had underlined that it was nothing serious and he was not to worry. Alex wanted to cry, he felt so helpless. There was his poor old mum, no one with her, dependent on neighbours. She did not mention Edward, and Alex swore, hitting the wall with his fists. 'Bastard, didn't even go an' see her in 'is 'olidays.'

A warder knocked on the cell door with his baton. 'Hey, Stubbs, what you think we're runnin', a post office? This come fer you, an' Stubbs, there's a message inside, all right?'

Alex took the open brown-paper parcel. Evelyne had sent him the only two leather-bound books she had left. They still bore tell-tale marks of the fire. They were Christina Rossetti's poems and a thin volume of plays by Strindberg.

Alex was so emotionally disturbed by the books, the feel of them, the memories flooding through him, that it was a while before he even opened them. Tucked into the centre of the book was a sheet of cheap, lined notepaper. Opening it, Alex knew immediately that his mother had not written it. The writing was that of a child.

'Frankie Warrs wants a meet, breakfast, Monday.'

Frankie Warrs was the baron of the main prison. He offered Alex the borstal section to run on his behalf. It was an offer Alex couldn't refuse. Frankie Warrs was an old friend of Johnny Mask, and Johnny was making sure Alex was being taken care of, as a 'thank you' for not grassing on him.

The barons operated food, drink and cigarette rackets, and could get you anything you wanted provided you could pay the price. Alex was given careful instructions on how to proceed. The commonest weakness in prison was smoking. The men were given their cash on Friday and they shelled it straight out on tobacco. By the next day it would be gone. They would then have to buy from the barons, whether a single roll-up or a larger quantity. They had to pay three times the proper price, so they were always in the red. The barons' paid runners took money to relatives to buy goods outside and smuggle them in. Prisoners often saved themselves a beating by getting their families to bring in the cash they owed, but the less fortunate would have to perform sexual favours. They even got cut up with knives that were smuggled in somehow. No one dared rat on their attackers for fear of further harassment.

As a baron, Alex even had two screws in his employ, who brought him whisky, for which he paid three times the market price. Tom, Joe and little Dick became his runners. Above all, Alex was a very popular boy, so that when his eighteenth birthday came round they threw a party for him in the recreation hall. Evelyne had been allowed to send him a gift, cakes and biscuits, and even the screws sang 'Happy Birthday'. But the best gift Alex had was a short letter from Dora. He had written to her, not really expecting a reply, and was tickled pink when he got her funny, misspelt letter. She asked if he was okay, and said she was doing fine, but that Johnny Mask had been arrested shortly after Alex and was in Brixton Prison. She added a footnote that she would try to come and see him one visiting day. She didn't say when, but Alex lived in hope. She had also sent him a photograph of herself, and Alex had pinned it on the cell wall. All the lads thought she was the best-looking 'bird' they had ever seen, and Alex gained even more glory through her. He seemed to have everything, and they stared hungrily at Dora's smiling face as they drifted off into their wet dreams.

Alex was counting his weekly take from the tobacco sales when Tom hurtled into the cell. He could hardly speak, he was so excited, and he gasped out that Alex had a visitor. It wasn't his ma, he'd seen her arrive and all the lads were trying to get a look at her. It was her, the girl in the picture.

She was looking wonderful, her lipstick red and glossy, her nails scarlet. She waved, and Alex felt his heart thudding as the screws made snide remarks about his girlfriend. He could hardly speak for nervousness, and Dora giggled, saying he looked even bigger than when she had last seen him. He had grown – he was now six feet two inches tall, and had filled out because of all the work-outs he did in the gym. He cracked his knuckles, showing off the muscles in his arms, and she giggled again. 'I got a few things from your ma – she don't know I know you, I never said – but remember me once sayin' I thought we'd met? Well, you could 'ave knocked me down with a feather when I realized who you was. Anyways, she told me to give you these. It's just some fruit – things are hard to come by with the war an' all . . . How do you do in 'ere when the sirens go? Bet they can't let you all out into a shelter, can they?'

Alex asked if Johnny knew about him and Dora, and she laughed. She didn't really think there was anything to know. When Alex leaned forward he could smell her perfume. 'You know how I feel about you, you know it . . . Open your blouse for me, go on, just a bit – lemme see them.' Dora looked around, then slowly unbuttoned her blouse and let him peek at her lace bra, running her tongue round her red-painted lips. Alex rubbed at his erect penis and squashed his legs together until his balls burnt him. She was still talking away, telling him how bad her mother was and how her legs were swollen up like balloons. 'I said to your mum that if she couldn't come next visitin' day I'd like to come again, would you like that?'

Alex was puzzled – what did Dora mean his mother couldn't come? She looked at him in amazement. 'Haven't you been told?' she asked. Then she looked at the screws and frowned. 'Bastards never told you, she had to go in for an operation. They say she's all right but she's ever so weak, maybe she just didn't want to bother you.'

The bell clanged and it was over. Alex was led back to his cell. On the way he asked the screws if they could check on his mother – that he had just heard she was ill.

He couldn't sleep that night for worrying about Evelyne. The lads in their bunks could hear him tossing and turning, and presumed it was because of his lady love. In the morning he requested an interview with the Governor.

He had to wait a whole week before he was taken to the Governor's office. 'I want someone to check on me ma, she's ill, and she's got no one ter look after her.'

Predictably, he was told that perhaps he should have thought of that before he got himself into trouble. He was so angry that he slammed his fist on the desk and demanded that someone go to see his mother. The wheels were put in motion, and various letters were written to social workers to check up on Mrs Stubbs, but no one seemed particularly concerned.

Edward collected his mail from his pigeon-hole. He recognized his mother's letter immediately, but was confused by the large manila envelope. He had no idea who it could be from.

He was going to be late for a lecture, so he stuffed the letters in with his books and crossed the quad.

It wasn't until he got back to his rooms to study that he remembered the letters. He picked them up and sighed – he hated reading Evelyne's letters, they depressed him so much. But he deftly slit the first cheap envelope with a paperknife. He gave the letter a cursory glance – the usual chatter about the neighbours. Mrs Harris' daughter again – Edward sighed, and was just about to toss the letter in the waste-paper basket when he noticed there was a postscript. He put the kettle on the small stove to make his cocoa, helped himself to a biscuit and carried it back to his desk, munching while he continued to read. Evelyne wrote that the operation had been successful but she would be in for a few more days. She was feeling much better, but had been worrying about certain financial matters that Edward should be aware of.

Edward's hand shook when he read that Alex was in Wormwood Scrubs – in the circumstances Evelyne had made a will, leaving everything to Edward. She had signed the letter, as usual, 'Your Mother'; no love. It was a single sheet of cheap paper. He turned it over. Scrawled on the back was one sentence, underlined, 'Whatever the outcome, you must take care of your brother, you have a debt you must never forget.'

Edward felt sick, his stomach churning. She had made no mention of why she had had an operation, or why Alex was in Wormwood Scrubs. He crumpled the letter into a ball and hurled it across the room. 'Stupid bitch, stupid bitch.'

A sob caught in his throat and he retrieved the letter, pressing out the creases. He ran from his room, down the stone stairs three at a time to the telephone booth by the main hall. As he hurried across the quad Walter waved and joined him. 'I'm just going to see the new Carole Lombard flick at the local, there's a double feature, Greta Garbo, you want to come? I'll pay for your ticket.'

'I've got to make a phone call.'

'You'll be lucky, all the lines are down, didn't you hear the blast last night? Do you want to come? Have to get a move on, film starts in five minutes.'

In the small, dark picture house, Edward sat with his eyes closed. The letter felt as though it was burning in his pocket. He took it out and then leant forward and stuffed it in the ashtray. On the screen Greta Garbo portrayed the dying Camille. She held her arms out to her lover, saying over and over in her deep, throaty voice, 'I love you, I love you, I knew you would come to see me, my love.'

Walter sighed, his thick glasses had steamed up. He was about to dig Edward in the ribs to see if he wanted a choc-ice in the interval when he realized that he was staring at the screen, tears streaming down his cheeks. Walter was surprised, he'd never seen Edward show any emotion at the pictures before. He looked up at the screen; Greta was dead, lying on a bed covered with gardenias, one clasped to her bosom.

It was a month later that the Governor got the word that Alex's mother was indeed seriously ill. She had already been operated on for cancer, but had been released from hospital. Alex was called and told the news. He was shattered, and had to be helped into a chair.

'I've put in for a special visit, Alex, but the Home Office have to agree – so get back to your cell and as soon as we have news I'll let you know.'

Alex was in such a black mood when he returned to his cell that the lads were half-afraid to speak to him. Tom climbed up into Alex's bunk as soon as the lights went out, and held him close. He knew Alex was worrying about his mother. Alex smiled at his pal, and tried to explain what his mother was like – how she was such a fighter, how she had fought all her life to better herself and her sons, even her husband. 'She always said that you can only climb out of the shit by yer brains, Tom, not yer fists. Always was a stickler for books an' reading. Since I can remember she was always at the kitchen table wiv a book ready and waitin', and the way she'd read to us when we were kids . . .'

Tom had never heard Alex speak of his brother, and he was puzzled for a moment. 'Eh, you didn't tell me – you got sisters an' all, Alex?'

Alex shook his head, his voice so quiet Tom had to lean close to hear him. 'I just got a brother, just one, his name's Edward.'

Tom knew for a fact that Alex had never received a letter from a brother, and he was surprised. The fact that Alex never spoke about him made it even stranger. 'Don't you two get on, then? I mean, you don't ever talk about him? What's he up to, doin' time, is he? Where is 'e, then?' Tom laughed and Alex cuffed him, then stared blankly at the wall. After a while he told Tom that Edward was at Cambridge. Tom giggled, nudged Alex and said there was a good open prison near Cambridge. Alex didn't laugh, he got down from his bunk. 'He's not in prison, he's at university.'

Still Tom laughed, letting his head loll over the edge of the bunk. 'Go on, yer 'avin' us on – you ain't got no bruvver, do us a favour.' Tom could have bitten his tongue out, his hero seemed so helpless, so vulnerable, and he wanted to reach out and hug him. Whatever emotion Tom saw disappeared in the fraction of a second, and Alex laughed, tugging Tom's hair good-naturedly. 'You're right, mate, I ain't got no friggin' brother . . . I was just 'aving you on. Yer think the likes of me would have a nob at Cambridge? You lot'd believe anything I say.'

They all laughed and Alex swung himself up into his bunk. He flicked open a well-thumbed American movie magazine, pretending to read. None of them heard a murmur, they all went back to their comics. Alex had to grit his teeth so hard, staring at Carole Lombard's glossy red lips, her gold lamé swimsuit and all the time hearing Eddie's voice – the voice he hadn't heard for so long – yelling at the kids in the street, 'We are brothers – take 'im on, yer take me . . .'

Alex wouldn't release the tears. He ground his teeth and flipped the page over. It was true, he had no brother, not any more, and if he did see him, after all this time, he would knock his teeth down his throat.

He slipped his hand under his pillow to the two small, leather-bound books. Holding them brought his mother closer. He tried to remember the poem she loved so much, the one she could recite from memory, 'Remember me when I am gone away, Gone far away into the silent land . . .'

He closed his eyes, holding the book close to his chest. He wanted his dream so badly – the mountain, the horseman, the clean, sweet air . . . 'freedom'.

Chapter Four

Mrs Harris shuffled down the hospital corridor stopping constantly to catch her breath. She asked a passing nurse the way to Keats Ward, and was directed to a lift. It was on the third floor.

She looked down the long row of beds and noted that they had moved Evelyne again. She was even further along than she had been on the last visit. She was watching out for Mrs Harris, her face pale, and she waved. It broke Mrs Harris' heart. Evelyne's arm was so thin and she looked so fragile. Mrs Harris put on a brave smile.

'Well, ducks, nice to see you looking perkier today. My God, the bus was stopped five times – more rubble in the streets – and as fast as they get it away another attack comes, poor Mrs Smith blown right off her feet she was, an' her two kids with her – it was a sight to be seen, so I was told, legs up in the air an' her bloomers showing for all the world.' She kept up a steady flow of chatter as she took a washbag out of the cabinet, wiped Evelyne's face and then unbraided her long hair and brushed it slowly. She knew it soothed Evelyne, and that she liked to look neat and tidy.

'My God, what a length it is, what a length, you could make a few shillings on this, you know. I tell you about Mrs Walter's youngest, well she was sitting on the bus on the way home from school, and you know she had hair right down to the back of her knees ... Well, she didn't even feel a thing, didn't even hear anything, but my God, Evie! She got off the bus with a bob! No kiddin', some bugger had cut off her hair, somebody sitting behind her, her mother had a fit!'

Evelyne closed her eyes. She liked Mrs Harris' chatter, and the gentle strokes of the hairbrush soothed her. 'I wrote to Edward, and the lawyers, but I've not heard back.'

Mrs Harris told her, pursing her lips. She tutted and had to apologize for giving Evelyne's hair a tug.

'I know I said I'd keep my mouth shut, but don't you think he should have written by now, I mean, you've been in here right the way over Christmas with not even a card, just that one with the Cambridge school on it, I think he should get a rap over the knuckles, that lad, I do, he should have been home and here with you, looking after you. I dunno, one lad gallivantin' all round and the other behind bars, it's a dreadful thing, Evie, it really is.'

Mrs Harris wished she had kept quiet when she saw Evelyne close her eyes, and she began to braid the hair, saying that she would write to them both and give them a piece of her mind, that's what she would do.

'No, no, don't, best not ... will you pass me my bag, it's on the side there?'

Mrs Harris handed Evelyne her old brown leather handbag, and had to help her into a sitting position. As she spoke, she put her arms around Evelyne and felt her thin, frail body. She couldn't help herself – she burst into tears. Evelyne raised her hands in a futile gesture, 'Now you just stop that – you know you'll have me in tears if you carry on like this. Now then, look in my handbag there. Take out that leather case – I want you to take it away with you. There's so much coming and going in here, I don't think it's safe to be left. You never know who might take it in the night. They give me pills to make me sleep and I'm out for the count by nine. Here, now you keep it safe until I come home.'

Mrs Harris took the small leather case, opened it and gasped. It was the pearl necklace with the gold beads and fine, detailed work, the pearl drop earrings to match.

'I'm going to ask you to do something for me, and you must promise me to do it – it's very important. I want you to bury the necklace with me, with me and Freedom. They told me I should have put it in his grave when he died, but what with one thing and another I just never got around to doing it. But it's very important, it's his talisman and it must lie with him. Promise me?'

Mrs Harris put the leather case on the bed and grabbed Evelyne's hand. 'I'll not listen to that talk. You're coming out, of course you are, and I'll have you at my place while you get your strength back. Now, no more of this.'

Evelyne grasped the big, raw hand tightly, lifted it to her lips and kissed it. Then, as if even that had taken all her strength from her, she let her hands fall back on to the covers. 'No more games, you know as well as I do that I'm going. Now don't you start the tears, just listen to me. The bell will be ringing any time and there are a few things I want to say to you.'

Mrs Harris was sweating, her mouth dry, and she was trying so hard to stop herself crying that she wanted to go to the lavatory.

'I want to be buried with him, you'll make sure of that, won't you? It's all arranged and it's all paid for. Mr Georgeson's the man you ask for at the funeral parlour, he has everything ready for me. I don't want flowers or anything like that, the money would be wasted. Once, a long time ago, when we were parted, he said that while I'd been away from him he'd been dying, little by little . . . Well, I know now what he meant. Since he's been gone I've not had the will, somehow – not the strength I used to have – and I'm not going to fight any more. You see, I miss him so much, I just can't go on without him. I'm not frightened, I'm going to be with him, where I should be. We weren't like ordinary folk, we were closer, we were blood to blood.'

The bell rang, and Evelyne smiled so peacefully that Mrs Harris felt her heart break. She stood up and had to hold on to the bed to get her balance. 'I'll be here next Wednesday, lovey, and I'll take care of your necklace, now I'd best be going.'

Evelyne looked like a young girl in her white nightgown, her long hair braided in plaits on each side of her head, her strange, dark, greenish eyes so large in her pinched face that it added to the childlike effect. Mrs Harris picked up her shopping bag to leave. She couldn't even bring herself to kiss Evelyne, she knew she would break down and sob, so she bustled around and chatted about the bus she would more than likely miss.

'Go on with you, and give my love to Dora. Don't look back, don't look back, it's unlucky. Don't look back . . .' But when Mrs Harris reached the double doors leading into the corridor, she couldn't help but turn. Evelyne had raised her skinny arms above her head, both hands waving goodbye, and she was smiling. She looked so happy, so at peace with the world. The tears rolled down Mrs Harris' fat cheeks as she mouthed, 'Goodbye, Evie, goodbye my love.'

'Stubbs 4566, to the Governor's office.'

Alex brushed his hair and Tom instructed him to ask for permission to wear his own togs, he didn't want his ma seeing him in prison overalls at the hospital.

The Governor was sitting at his desk as Alex was led in by the screws.

'Prisoner 4566, Stubbs, Alex, sir.'

The Governor looked up, removed his glasses and indicated a chair beside his desk. He waited until Alex had sat down before he carefully laid his glasses on the desk and gave a warning look to the two warders. He coughed, hesitating before he spoke. 'I'm afraid, Stubbs, I have some very sad news for you – your mother died last night.'

Alex never moved a muscle, but he stared at the Governor as if he hadn't heard.

'I am deeply sorry, even more so as it took so long for permission to be granted for you to visit her, but these things cannot be helped. It is most unfortunate.'

Alex sprang over the desk and had the Governor by the throat before either of the guards could stop him. He was like a man possessed. The Governor screamed as he felt the air being squeezed out of his throat, and his head shook as though he were a rag doll. The guards couldn't get Alex away, he was pressing his thumbs harder and harder into the Governor's scrawny neck. One guard pulled at his hair and another kicked him in the groin as the alarm bell sounded.

Three more guards and half an hour later, Alex was handcuffed. With blood streaming from his head where he had been beaten he was led into solitary confinement. The Governor was rushed to hospital but was released the following day, and the whole prison was agog at what had happened. The number of guards Alex had taken out tripled and the stories so embroidered that his name was on everyone's lips. He had eighteen stitches in his head, another twenty in his face and cheek, and his already broken nose was cracked again.

Alex smashed his fists against the wall until they bled. His bread and water were pushed through a hatch in the cell door, and even that he hurled at the walls. The Governor, when informed, remarked that if he carried on that way he would remain in solitary until he was controllable. 'If he behaves like a wild animal, we shall treat him as one, and until he quietens down, leave him.'

In the fifth week a doctor was called in. He treated Alex's hands, which were badly infected, and made notes that the man was deeply distressed. He prescribed sedatives and said the prisoner must be properly fed, force-fed if necessary. He requested an immediate visit from a psychiatrist.

The food was refused, and Dr Gordon was called in again. No psychiatrist had been to see Alex, who just sat very quietly in his own excrement, staring vacantly at the wall in a drugged, semi-catatonic state.

They should have been suspicious when Alex meekly held out his hands to be rebandaged. As Dr Gordon cut through the plasters, Alex punched him in the face and got hold of the scissors, held them at the doctor's neck and demanded to be released. If he wasn't, he would slit his throat. The warders stood by helplessly and Dr Gordon ordered them out of the cell, then still with his arm twisted behind his back but with no sign of fear he talked quietly to Alex. He asked Alex what he wanted. He would do his utmost to help, but what Alex was doing was an act of madness.

Alex wanted to go to his mother's funeral. Time appeared to have stood still for him, he didn't realize how long he had been in solitary confinement.

'Alex, you know that's not possible, now lad, you know that, why don't you release me and I'll do what I can? I give you my word, but what you are doing now will only add to your troubles.'

Alex stood at the open door of his cell, the screws in a row in front of him. He knew it was pointless, and he suddenly dropped his arm and threw the scissors aside. He turned to walk back into the cell and the screws moved, surrounding him as the doctor begged them to stay clear, even tried to physically pull them away from the prisoner. They threw Alex against his bed and out came the truncheons.

In a fury Dr Gordon went to the Governor, demanding that Alex be removed from solitary and treated.

'There's a war on, men are dying every minute of the day, and you want everything here to revolve around a prisoner who has blatantly and consistently fought the rules of this establishment? He's only got himself to blame. If I allowed every man to behave as he has and get away with it, my position would be intolerable. We are overcrowded, understaffed – the man attacked me, for Chrissake, what do you expect me to do with him?'

Stony-faced, Dr Gordon sat and told the Governor quietly that the boy was grieving, he needed time. He needed help to face up to the fact that his mother was dead.

'That boy, as you call him, Doctor, murdered his own father! You have his records, why don't you read them?'

Dr Gordon said of course he had read Stubbs' reports. He was the prison doctor, and his request for a psychiatrist had been ignored.

'If there was one available, he would have been brought to the prisoner. As I have said, Doctor, there is a war on, and we are seriously understaffed and overworked. Right now, Stubbs is a hero to the rest of the men. If he goes unpunished, we will not be able to maintain any kind of discipline.'

Alex was removed to the hospital wing and remained there for another five weeks. He was drugged to keep him subdued, and the doctor used every power he had to get him transferred to a rehabilitation programme. He had spent a long time going over Alex's records, and found them disturbing.

Due to Dr Gordon's persistent efforts, a psychiatrist was eventually found and, after discussing Alex with the doctor, he agreed to take on his case.

Alex would not co-operate. He didn't want any 'nut doc', he wanted to go back to his cell. Dr Gordon went in to see him, in his own time and purely because he wanted to help Alex. 'Alex, if you want to get out, lead a normal life, you have to help yourself. First, you will have to go before the prison authorities. You've got a list of charges as long as your arm, and even with mitigating circumstances you could get another God knows how many years on your sentence ... Talk to the man, he only wants to help you, that's all. Maybe we can do something for you.'

'There's fuck all wrong with me – I just want to get out an' see me mother. Bastards, keeping me penned up in here. I just want out.'

'Well, you're going about it the wrong way. If I try to get permission for you to go to her grave, acting up like this will make them refuse to even consider it ... Now, talk with the psychiatrist, just talk things through. Is that too much to ask? Can't you do that for me?'

After a long pause Alex slowly nodded his head. Dr Gordon patted his shoulder. 'Good lad ... I'll keep on coming, all right?'

Alex shook his hand and held it a fraction longer, as if he needed some sort of contact. He gave a strange, shy smile. 'Thank you.'

Frank Nathan closed the cell door and winked at Alex as the key turned in the lock. He was not at all what Alex expected – his short, squat body was muscular, and the black hairs sprouting on his barrel chest were visible even though he was wearing a shirt and tie. Nathan was like a chimp, his big hands fuzzy with thick, black hair. Stubble seemed to appear on his chin as you watched him. He had a pug nose, as if he had been in the ring at one time, and a wonderful, raucous, rumbling laugh. He jerked his thumb at the cell door. 'Looks like they don't fuckin' trust me, neither . . . Right, you an' me are going to thrash a few things out. I'm here to listen. Sometimes I'll ask you a few things, but on the whole I'm a bloody good listener. You smoke . . .? Here.'

Frank lit his cigarette and his powerful body made the chair creak alarmingly as he sat down. He folded his chubby hands over his belly and leaned forward. 'My time's valuable, so if you want to act like a prick, go ahead. I'll just cross you off. There's fellas who need me, an' if you think you don't, sod ya. If you don't want to help yourself, then if you don't mind my sayin' so, you are well and truly fucked . . .'

Alex was taken off guard, not only by Nathan's presence but by his gruffness, yet he liked him. There was something powerful and, more important, genuine, about the man.

'Let's start off with why you knocked the Guv'nor's front teeth out.' Nathan puffed on his cigarette and waited. Alex hesitated, and Nathan prompted him, 'What is it, son? What do you want to say – best to get it off your chest . . .?'

Alex clasped and unclasped his hands, refusing to look up. His voice was quiet and strained, 'She's dead. Some way I've been thinking, maybe, just maybe, she's still alive an' you was all doing this to me to get at me. Like even you was tryin' to deceive me.'

'No, Alex, your mother is dead, and nobody has tried to deceive you in any way. It was just unfortunate that you couldn't see her in hospital. No one realized how ill she was until it was too late.'

'Aye, well, she was never one to complain – she was that sort of woman. She was a wonderful ...' He pressed his hands together until the knuckles were white.

'Alex, it's not wrong to cry for her. It'd be a release, don't try to stop it. No one's here to see you but me ... Come on, son, cry for her, get it out of your system.'

Nathan watched Alex struggle to regain control of his emotions. He took Alex off guard with his next question. 'Did you cry for your dad when he died?' He could see the barrier – the feeling in the boy's eyes was breaking him up, it was so desperate. Still Alex's hands opened and closed spasmodically. Nathan kept up the pressure. 'Did they love each other, your mum and dad?'

Unable to speak, Alex just nodded his head. His eyes never left Nathan's face now, as if mesmerized by him.

'They love you?'

Nathan could see the marks on Alex's hands where he was inflicting pain on himself to control his emotions. Alex made a strangled, guttural sound. He wanted to tell Nathan they had loved him.

'I didn't hear you. You say they loved you or they didn't?'

Alex's voice was alien to him, childlike. He gasped out, 'They loved me.'

'What about your brother? You've got an older brother, haven't you?'

There it was – Nathan saw it, the boy's whole body altered. One moment he was helpless, a child in need, and the next the body was tight, the face set, the highly charged emotions under control. It was as if someone had stopped a dam bursting. The transformation fascinated Nathan. He knew he wasn't dealing with a schizoid or a psychopath, as the prison had hinted. He also knew that to unlock the boy's trauma would take time, time he didn't have, wouldn't be allowed.

'I read about your dad. He almost made heavyweight champion

of the world, didn't he? Used to box meself, tell by me hooter. You box, Alex?'

The blue eyes met Nathan's. The barrier was still there. Nathan tried again. 'Did you want to follow in his footsteps? Eh? Big lad like you could fill out, maybe go on the heavy-weight circuits – good set of shoulders on you. Mind you, you'd have to put on quite a few pounds. What are you, six-two, six-three? Your dad now, lemme see, I was readin' up on him – six-four, wasn't he, Alex?'

Rising from the bunk, Alex walked to the wall, leaned against it. Nathan showed no fear of him, just lit another cigarette. He hated having to cut corners, hated the pressure he was under. He had reached retirement age, but being wartime he had been roped in. But more than anything he hated knowing that time was against him. If he didn't crack Alex fast, he wouldn't get another chance. He also knew that if Alex didn't get help, and fast, they would have a potentially lethal young man on their hands. 'He ever hit you? That what made you go for him? Your dad a violent man, was he?'

That guttural sound again, the low moan, the hands moving rapidly.

'Sit down, son . . . come on now.'

But Alex turned his face to the wall, and when he spoke his voice was strained, close to breaking. 'He was gentle . . . I had a dog, he give me a dog. He never hit none of us.'

'What about your ma?'

The fist slammed into the brick wall and Alex turned on him, eyes blazing. 'No!'

'All right, all right . . . what about your brother?'

There it was again. At the mention of the word 'brother', Alex recoiled. Nathan knew he had put his finger on it, but he had to get Alex sitting, had to calm him. But he knew his time was up, although he hadn't looked at his watch once. At any moment the screws would bang on the door, and there were a lot more patients to see. 'I am trying to arrange for you to visit your mother's grave. You'd like that, wouldn't you . . .? Maybe get some flowers ... We'll take it stage by stage, all right? And I'll come and ...'

Alex put his head in his hands and wept. He slumped on to the bunk, mumbling over and over that he wanted to see her, see his mother. Nathan stubbed out his cigarette and then put his hands on Alex's head in a comforting, fatherly gesture. He had to go, and he felt badly about it, he could feel that the boy was ready to open up.

'I can't find my dream no more, I don't seem to be able to lose myself anywhere no more.'

'Maybe, son, that's what the problem is, you've been trying to lose yourself. But we'll find you, and we'll do it together, okay? I'll pull every string I can, I'll get you out of here. You'll say goodbye to your mum first, then – well, we'll set about putting you together. You'll have to take the punishment doled out to you, son, for the little fracas with the Guv'nor, but don't let it get to you. I'm on your side, I give you my word ...'

Later that night, Nathan sat in a pub with Dr Jim Gordon. He had already put away a few Scotches, and his pug face was flushed. Both men were depressed as Alex had had five years added to his sentence. The Governor, however, had promised that Alex would be allowed to visit his mother's grave.

'I need time. You can't help a kid with his kind of problems in a few hours ... I feel sorry for the bastard. Any chance we can get him out of the Scrubs, somewhere he can pick up his education? The lad's clever, that's one of his problems. If they keep him banged up in a cell, when he gets out you'll have a fucking killer on the loose. The key to Stubbs lies with his brother, I'd put money on it. You know if there's any way I can get to him?'

The sirens sounded, and everyone in the pub had to run like hell as the bombs began to drop. The two men lost each other in the confusion. Nathan never made it to the shelter – he was killed by a second bomb one hour later – and Dr Gordon worked through the night, helping the injured. Prisoner Stubbs was forgotten.

*

Evelyne was buried in as neat and orderly a fashion as she had lived, with only Mrs Harris and a few other neighbours attending. There was no great fuss, no weeping, and no high tea afterwards. Mrs Harris, exhausted from the effort of standing by the grave, went home alone. She had shed her tears, and even when she went into number twelve the next day, to collect Evelyne's things, she didn't cry. She crept around the silent house, then locked up and took the key to the lawyers as requested.

Later that night the house took a direct hit. The blaze lit the sky, and Mrs Harris watched it from her bedroom window. 'Dear God, there's nothing left there now. Almost the whole street gone, and neither of those boys around to give a helping hand.'

Mrs Harris remembered then, and went to her dressing table. She took out the leather case containing the gold and pearl necklace and stared at it as Dora moved away from the window.

'Well, that's them finished, it's as if they never existed. Sometimes it makes you wonder what life is all about.'

'She wanted me to bury this with her, and I promised.'

'What is it? Let's have a look.'

'It's her necklace. She said it was like his talisman, that it had to be buried with them, and I promised . . .'

'Bloody 'ell, Mum, this is real gold, an' these are pearls. This must be worth a packet.'

Dora danced over to the mirror and slipped the necklace around her neck. 'Oh, Mum, isn't it beautiful? It's so beautiful.'

'Well, you can't have it. It belongs to her sons.'

Dora put the earrings on and admired herself. 'Yeah? Well, they don't deserve nothing, them two, and what they don't know you got they won't miss.'

'Dora, you put that back now. It's unlucky, don't wear it, you can't have it.'

'Why not? You think about all the years she stayed with you, the way you was the only one to see her at the end. You've got a right to it, so I'm keeping it. Besides, who's paying the rent and feeding you? You gotta let me keep it, Mum ...'

Mrs Harris shrugged. She knew it was pointless to argue with Dora when she wanted something.

Mrs Harris took a long time to decide exactly what to write. Dora had promised to copy it out neatly for her, as her eyesight was none too good, let alone her spelling. Dora would do anything for her mother right now, since the pearl and gold necklace and matching earrings had been given to her.

Mrs Harris had found Edward's last letter to his mother with her other things at the hospital, and she was so furious at his request for money from the poor, sick woman that she crumpled it up and threw it in the fire. Dora had told her off, because now they didn't have Edward's address so how could they tell him about the funeral? In the end they had written to Edward care of Cambridge University, hoping it would reach him, and in the meantime Mrs Harris had gone to the funeral directors and found that Evelyne had organized every last detail. She had forgotten nothing; the casket had been chosen, the cross and the exact wording for Evelyne and her husband. And everything had been paid for.

Edward stared at the strange, scrawled writing on the cheap pink envelope. He hadn't the slightest idea who it was from. He opened it and read the badly spelt letter as he walked across the quad.

'... I am sorry to inform you that your mother died last Wednesday and was buried Friday. We had tried to contact you and hope you will understand why everything went ahead as your mother had arranged everything. Please call on us when you come to London as we would like to tell you about everything then, also that the lawyers have the keys to your house as your mother instructed us to leave them there. I am writing this on behalf of my mother as she cannot see too good, and is still very upset as she loved your mother very much as did everyone else in these parts. Yours sincerely, Dora Harris.'

In the privacy of his room, Edward read and reread the letter. He was ashamed that he couldn't cry, could feel nothing. He tore the letter into shreds and burnt it, then lay on his bed for hours, staring at the ceiling. His body felt light, alien to him, and he tried to feel some kind of emotion, tried to recall his mother's face.

Walter found him still lying there, fully dressed, the next morning, staring into space. He offered to call a doctor, thinking he was ill. 'There's a big bash tonight, Teddy Kingly's departing for the army, it's over at King's, you going?'

Edward stared vacantly at Walter and asked him to get his dinner jacket out, it would need cleaning.

Walter did as Edward asked, then turned and asked again if he was all right.

'I'm fine. Look, can you do me a favour? I need a weekend leave, I used mine up going to that party at Cynthia's. You don't need yours, do you?'

Walter hesitated. 'Nothing wrong, is there?'

'No, old chap, I just got an invite to a dinner party in London. Can you fix it for me?'

Although he had been thinking of going to see his parents, Walter gave in to Edward as usual. The next weekend Edward returned to the East End for the first time since he had left for college.

He walked among the bomb sites, turned into the old street and stood at the top of the road, stunned. Hardly a house was left standing, and he could see that number twelve was no more than a piece of waste ground. He walked slowly to the site of his old home and stood where the doorstep had been. He felt nothing, just as he had been unable to feel anything when he learned of Evelyne's death.

Side-stepping puddles and piles of rubble he walked on, trying to remember where Mrs Harris used to live. As he turned into a narrow alley the sirens started screaming overhead. A warden ran along the alley towards him and yelled for him to take cover as they were coming this way. Edward asked for the nearest shelter and ran for the railway sidings.

He had forgotten the voices, the accents, and he stood huddled against the wall, remembering, as more and more people crowded under the railway arches. The planes passed overhead and as they heard the bombs dropping they were all looking skywards.

'Bleedin' bastard Jerries, sons of bitches, go on ya buggers, get out of it.'

The all clear sounded, and they made their way out, carrying their gas-mask cases. Edward asked a couple of people if they knew a Mrs Harris, and he was eventually directed to a rundown block of flats. The smell of cabbage and the stench of urine swamped him as he went up the stone steps – obviously many people used the stairs to live on – and he shuddered. Most of the windows were boarded up, and the flats had evidently been hit more than once, as there were holes in the roofs.

'All right, I'm comin', for Chrissake 'ang on, no need to ring on an' on.' Dora Harris opened the door and stepped back, surprised. She didn't recognize Edward, saw only a well-dressed gent who, when he spoke, sounded posh, upper crust.

'Mrs Harris?'

Dora tried to close the door, thinking he might be the law, but Edward put his foot between door and post.

'What you want 'er for? She's busy right now, if it's the rent then you'll have to come back, but you ain't the usual rent man, is you?'

Mrs Harris shuffled out of the kitchen and asked what all the racket was about. She squinted past her daughter and stared.

'Are you Mrs Harris? It's Edward, Edward Stubbs.'

She stared at him then after a moment nodded to Dora to let him in. Dora went towards the lounge, but Mrs Harris moved back into the kitchen. Dora wore only a thin wraparound and fluffy slippers, her hair in curlers. She watched the smart gent as he passed by her into the stuffy, smelly kitchen.

'I'll be gettin' changed, Ma, won't be a tick.'

Mrs Harris lowered her bulk into the easy chair and looked into the fire. She was sweating with the effort, and her heart thudded in her chest. 'So you've come. You took your time – well, sit down, lad, sit down.'

Uneasy, Edward sat down and wished he hadn't bothered, the place reminded him of his old home and he felt sick.

'You look all done up like a dog's dinner, what you up to, then?'

Edward explained that he had not received her letter until too late, and thanked her for taking care of his mother.

'I never did nothing, boy, she took care of herself, that one, even arranged her own funeral down to the cross, have you seen the grave? No, didn't think you would have done. What about your brother, been to see him, have you? Our Dora used to go, but they moved 'im, did you know that? You want a cup of something?'

Edward shook his head and stood up, he had nothing to say, he should never have come. Mrs Harris looked at him in his smart clothes. 'She was ill, you know, cancer, but she never let on, not to me even. Yer brother took it hard, is he all right?'

Before Edward could answer, Dora swung into the kitchen, wearing a cheap perfume that filled the room, and bright red, high-heeled shoes. Her breasts were pushed up into a new type of bra, and her flowered blouse was open at the neck to display her cleavage. Her blonde hair was fluffed out into the latest fashion, and she was wearing the full war paint.

'You off, are you? Don't suppose you're going up west are you, only I could do with a lift?'

Edward buttoned his coat, eager to be gone, and shook his head. Dora kissed her mother's balding head and then opened a drawer in the untidy sideboard. 'So you're Eddie. Well I never, you grown up a real dandy, that's for sure. Looks ever so nice, don't he, Ma? Hang on, I'll walk wiv ya. I'm almost ready.'

Edward watched her open a leather box, take out his mother's gold and pearl necklace and clasp it around her neck, looking into the mirror above the fire. While she fixed the earrings she caught him looking at her, and she flicked her tongue over her painted lips, smiled at him with a coy, sexy pout. 'You recognize this, do you? It was yer mother's, she left it to me in her will, didn't she Ma? I never have it off, do I? It's just lovely.'

Edward's stomach churned. Emotions he had thought himself incapable of feeling were beginning to surface and he had to get out. But Dora wasn't letting him off the hook that easily – she caught his arm and teetered on her heels, clip-clopping beside him down the concrete stairs. 'Stinks here, don't it? Terrible, I'm only here 'cause of Ma, otherwise I'd be in my own place, I got enough put by for a nice flat, but until she pops off I have to stay. Only fair really, all the others are married now, with kids, and they got their own problems . . . You got a girl, have you, Eddie? I bet you have, nice-looking boy like you, and yer ever so tall, taller than yer brother by a couple of inches. Oh, he's been ever so hard done by, did me mum tell you? Poor bugger, just one of those types, isn't he? Walks into trouble.'

Having nothing better to do, Edward went all the way into the West End with Dora. She kept up a steady flow of chatter, and as they neared Mayfair she asked Edward if he would like to have a drink at the club where she worked. 'It's ever so nice, and very exclusive, lots of Yanks in there, but they are really nice blokes, you know, not just servicemen but officers.'

Edward found himself sitting at a small, seedy bar in a drinking club close to Berkeley Square. The club had only one main room, fitted out with tiny, two-seater tables and a couple of booths. There was a dance floor the size of a postage stamp, and crammed into a corner was a three-piece band. Dora seemed to be the 'head girl', all the other 'hostesses' were younger by a few years. Edward watched her circulating among the tables, chatting with everyone and ordering champagne. He could see the girls were hookers, but he reckoned they were reasonably expensive ones, since they were all well dressed. Dora herself had changed into a slinky evening gown which was cut very low at the neck, and it showed off his mother's necklace very well. She constantly checked her lipstick in the wall-to-wall mirrors.

After a couple of drinks Edward decided to call it a night. He was bored and the music annoyed him. He was just about to leave when Dora sat down with a glass of what looked like champagne. She leaned over and whispered that she was drinking ginger beer, although nobody knew it, but she had to keep sober for the clients. A swarthy gent in a flash tuxedo with red cummerbund joined them, and Dora introduced him as her manager.

Johnny Mask took a good look at Edward and smiled his flashy smile, showing two gold-capped teeth. Edward seemed familiar to Mask and he asked if they had met before, but the upper-class twang to Edward's voice confused him.

Edward wanted to get out now, the seedy little club was beginning to grate unbearably on his nerves, and he was wary of the sly-faced Johnny Mask. Dora walked him to the exit and clung to his arm, her sickly-sweet perfume becoming even more cloying. 'Why don't you come back later, Eddie, place doesn't liven up until two or three in the morning. These are just a few regulars, we get all sorts later on – types you'd more'n likely mix with these days – you know, high-class . . . An' out at the back, through the mirrored doors just by the bar, there's a private card game goes on. You come back, lovey, you'll like it, I could show you a nice time.'

Edward had to unwrap her fingers from his arm. She disgusted him, and yet he couldn't help but find her attractive. She had a beautiful figure, and even though she was no longer a young girl she was still very pretty in a common way.

He buttoned his coat and asked her how much she charged, saw the hurt look on her face and smiled. But she tossed back her head and said that if he was a real nice gent she might give him one for nothing. He may look posh, but he shouldn't forget that she knew where he came from, and more'n likely he couldn't afford her anyway.

Edward cocked his head to one side, then pulled her close and whispered, 'Nothing is free, sweetheart. Get your coat.'

Dora wanted him, not like a 'punter' – she wanted him, so she went over to Johnny Mask and took him aside. 'Listen, this toff, he could be useful – you know, bring in his friends? You want me to make him a happy boy?'

Johnny looked over at Edward and gave Dora's arse a slap. 'Go to it – tell him he'll get a special membership price if he helps with the cash flow down here . . .'

Johnny Mask's flat was a monument to bad taste – full of glass and Formica, the new rage. The furniture was Art Deco – there were dreadful satin drapes and bowls of wax fruit everywhere, a grubby white carpet and a huge radio.

Dora danced over and switched the radio on. She smiled at Edward. 'You like jazz, Eddie? I like the soft, quiet kind, not all those bleedin' trumpets. Come on through, it's fantastic, isn't it?'

The bedroom was even worse, with purple drapes around the bed, which was flanked by statues, and behind the drapes a mirror. Dora lay back on the bed and pulled a cord. 'See, isn't it something? And guess what – you gotta promise me that you won't let on I told you – the mirror, well, it's two-way glass. He gets people here, huddled behind it, watching the sessions.'

Edward walked around the room, its seediness and decadence exciting him. Dora giggled and began doing a striptease in time to music, throwing each item across the room as she removed it. Naked, she lay back and stretched, then sat up and leant on her elbows, her face sweet and childlike. 'Well, come on, if you're coming . . . I've not got all night, and Johnny don't like me doin' too much "voluntary work". I just said you was an old friend, that you'd bring us a lot of business. Johnny wants new cus-tomers, you know, with class and cash. They're always easy for us. Only trouble is the bleedin' poor ones, they always cause problems.'

Edward folded his clothes neatly on the satin-covered chair and leaned, naked, against the bed.

'Oh, I knew you were lovely but not this good, yer got a body on yer that's just perfect, just beautiful. Come here, I'm going to enjoy this one.'

Slowly, he lay against her soft, pink body, and had reached for her before he realized that she was still wearing his mother's necklace. He shut his eyes, clenched his teeth, feeling sick, and his head throbbed.

'What's the matter, lovey? What's the matter, darlin' – you're not gonna pass out on me, are yer? Come here, come an' let me hold you, just don't be sick, not on this nice bed.'

Instead of Dora he could see his mother, hear her, the way she would hold him and rock him in her arms. He didn't know what to do, he could feel it all churning up inside, and he wanted her to shut up. But she kept talking, talking ... He grabbed the necklace and tore it from her neck, rolling off the bed. 'You don't deserve to wear this, you cheap tart, you slut – give me the earrings, give me ... Give!'

She wriggled away, cramming herself against the headboard, hands to her ears. 'Ah, no! What you doin', what you doin'? It's mine, I was give it, yer mother give it us, it's the truth, Eddie – I swear it, yer mother give it to me!'

He crawled up the bed and grabbed her, close to him, snatched off one earring then the other.

'You bastard, they're mine, I'll have you for this – I will, I'll bleedin' have you, you bastard!' She slid off the bed, grabbed one of her high-heeled shoes and went for him. He slapped her so hard she fell across the room. Her mouth bleeding, she was up like a little tigress, screaming at the top of her voice. He caught her and slapped her face, first one way, then the other, until she was crying, begging for him to stop. Weeping as he punched her, he banged her head against the headboard until she nearly blacked out. She was convinced he was going to kill her, and she held her hands over her face to protect it, but the next moment he gathered her gently in his arms and was kissing her, lovingly, and she stopped crying. 'Don't hurt me, Eddie, please don't, please don't, I'll make it right for you, you'll see, you'll see.'

He made love to her and she played along, pretending, kissing his shoulders, his neck, his ears ... Suddenly she wasn't acting, it was for real, and she could feel it. To be excited was, for her, something new. She could turn any man on, do any amount of tricks, but she had learned to block it out of her mind. But she lost that with Edward, for the first time in years, years of being screwed by so many men she couldn't even remember how many, let alone their names. This boy made her feel clean, unused and fresh, and she lay in his arms crying her heart out.

Exhausted, they curled around each other, and he rested his head on her belly.

'Eddie, you believe me if I tell you that was special, honest it was. I got so used to doin' it, it's like makin' a cup of tea, I got so I don't feel nothin', but you've just changed all that. Will you kiss me? On the lips, like you was my boyfriend?'

He held her head in both hands and kissed her lips, looking into her eyes, and she reached for him, pulled his head down and kissed him over and over again. 'I don't kiss, ever, I never let 'em kiss me, that sound weird? They don't mind, yer know. I say, "You can kiss me fanny, me arse, but me lips are me own" . . . you want that necklace, them earrings? Take 'em, it was worth it.'

He was up and out of the bed, dragging his trousers on, and as he looked at her his eyes were so blank and unemotional he frightened her all over again.

'You angry? What's the matter with yer?'

Edward pulled his shirt on, grabbed his jacket, and at the same time he shoved his bare feet into his shoes, put his socks into his pocket. He had been paid by Lady Primrose and now a tart was paying him – he hated it, and he had to get out before he really hurt her.

'What did I say? You want your mother's necklace, don't you? Eddie? Eddie, why don't you say something to me?'

He picked up the necklace and put it in his pocket, and she drew the satin sheet up around herself. She tried to touch him, but he moved away.

'Eddie, will I see you again – you're comin' back, aren't you? Tell me it wasn't just a one-night stand, I wasn't just that, was I?'

He was at the door, yanked it open and then changed his

mind. He turned to look at her, still draped in her sheet. 'How much do you pay Johnny Mask?'

Dora stammered out that she gave him twenty-five per cent, but there was more to it than that, she earned from the club, she was more than just one of the girls. 'I'm not just a tart, Eddie, I own part of the place. Johnny's my manager.'

Edward smiled and walked out, and Dora slumped on the bed and curled up like a baby. Johnny found her there two hours later and hit the roof – he'd had God knows how many customers asking for her, and here she was, kipping. She had all day to sleep. He slapped her around, and she took it, picked up her clothes and walked towards the bathroom. 'Is it that swish fella, the one with the face like a gyppo that you bin half the night with?' he yelled to her retreating back. 'Gawd 'elp us, anyone can see what's he's worth – fuck all – he's just a punk that's learned to speak with a posh voice. You stupid?'

Dora went into the bathroom without answering. She knew she was stupid, but she also knew that Eddie would be back – she knew it.

Edward caught a tram to the East End, with his mother's necklace and earrings in his overcoat pocket. The guilt clung to him; he wanted to see her grave. He swallowed constantly, using all his self-control to block out the grief that was building up inside him. The closer he got to the cemetery, the worse it was.

When Alex was informed that Nathan, 'the Chimp', had been killed in the Blitz, he shook his head in despair. Why was it that every time he trusted anyone, felt for anyone, they were taken from him? Dr Gordon had given him the news, half expecting trouble, while the two warders watched at the open cell door. Over the weeks they had grown fond of Alex, had come to sympathize with him, and he had given them no trouble. This, along with the doctor's report, persuaded the authorities to allow Alex to be taken, at long last, to see his mother's grave.

*

Dr Gordon repeated over and over that they were trusting Alex to behave. The two guards that Alex had grown used to accompanied them.

The green security van with the tiny slit windows drove slowly across London in the early dawn. Alex stared through the small aperture like a child. He was scared – everything looked so different.

Twice they were held up by workmen redirecting traffic around huge bomb craters in the road. Alex took everything in, and his realization that a war was raging while he was incarcerated shamed him.

At the cemetery Edward paid off the cab driver, refusing his offer to wait, and watched him drive away. He wandered among the tombstones for quite a long time, looking for his mother's grave. Then he stood still, closed his eyes and, when he opened them, he walked directly to her, sensing where she was buried.

The necklace felt as though it was burning in his pocket. No one had told him what to do, he just seemed to know, as he slumped to his knees and began to dig with his bare hands at the soil to the edge of the white cross. He dug a deep, narrow hole, blackening his hands and nails with the soil. His breath heaved in his chest as he took from his pocket the gold necklace and tiny earrings. He wrapped them in a clean white handkerchief, knotted it, then placed it in the earth and filled the hole.

He could hear his own voice, as though someone else was speaking aloud, 'Don't haunt me, Mama. Rest, sleep in peace with him – and forgive me.' He bowed his head and wept, the tears that had refused to come before falling now.

The release was immediate; his body felt cleansed, and he was free. But in his grief he could not stop shaking. He remained on his knees beside the small white cross, then bent his head until it almost touched the centre of the cross.

'I'll make you proud of me, I swear to you. I'll be rich one day, Mama, I'll be everything you ever dreamed of for me. I love you, Ma. I love you.'

As the prison van pulled up at the cemetery gates, the doctor draped an overcoat around Alex's shoulders. It was winter, and the rain was lashing down. The strange group stepped out of the van and Dr Gordon reminded Alex of his promise to behave.

At the gate an old woman sat on a beer crate, offering a few bedraggled flowers for sale. The doctor bought a bunch and handed them to Alex, who waited with a warder on each side of him. The overcoat hid the fact that he was handcuffed to one of them.

Edward's knees were wet from the muddy ground, but he still knelt. There was more, much more he had to say, but he couldn't form the words. His father Freedom lay with her, but even here he couldn't say that name, ask for forgiveness for what he had done . . . He found himself trembling violently, and the hairs on the back of his neck stood up. The steady rain gave way to a torrential downpour, and he got to his feet, pulling his collar up around his ears. It wasn't the rain that was making him feel this way, it was something else. His heart was thudding and he was flushing hot, then cold. 'Jesus,' he thought, 'what the hell's the matter with me?' He turned to walk away from the grave.

A group of four men headed towards him from the entrance. He turned away from them and walked to the lee of a large tomb surmounted by a six-foot-high stone angel, kneeling with clasped hands. He was sweating so his shirt stuck to him, despite the chill rain. Apparently unnoticed, he watched the four men approach his parents' grave.

Dr Gordon had visited the cemetery previously to be sure he knew exactly where Evelyne Jones was buried. He was thankful for that as he guided the little party through the downpour – he didn't want the boy to have to search for her. They threaded their way along the narrow path, the handcuffs forcing Alex and the screw to walk very close together. Before the doctor could indicate the grave, Alex stopped and pulled at the handcuffs – he knew instinctively.

The grave seemed small, and its white cross had just enough room for the two names and short inscription: Freedom Stubbs, Evelyne Stubbs. Heart to heart – Camipen-lil, manushi.

Alex laid the flowers gently on top of the cross and bowed his head. He stood as if frozen, making no sound, but the tears streamed down his pale cheeks. It came as a shock when he finally spoke, 'They left no room for us, no room, as if she didn't want us buried wiv 'em. My Dad was a Romany, yer know. In the old days, when a Romany of high-ranking blood – like my father, he was a Tatchey Romany, pure-blooded – well, when they died they destroyed everyfing they owned, 'cept money, of course. Everyfing they could burn was set on fire, an' their crockery, pots an' stuff were broken or thrown in the nearest river. They even destroyed jewellery, an' if there was a horse it'd be shot. They said it 'ad to be done or the dead person'd haunt yer. Gypsies believe the ghost hovers near its possessions after death, so it 'ad to be done.'

Edward had not recognized Alex at first. He leaned against the praying angel and watched. Alex was so tall now, so terribly thin. His face was gaunt and his blond, curly hair was cut close to his head. What shocked Edward most was his brother's face. With his flattened nose this once-beautiful little brother looked like the thugs Edward had seen in the movies. They were so close he could hear their voices, and yet he could not move those few steps to reveal himself. He had seen the handcuff on Alex's wrist as he had laid the flowers on the grave. He knew what he had done, knew that those handcuffs should be around his own wrist, but still he could not move. The rain had eased a bit, and he could hear every word they were saying, as if he were standing beside them.

It was time for Alex to leave. Dr Gordon nodded briefly to one of the warders, who tapped Alex on the shoulder. 'We've got to get back now, son, I'm sorry. You all right? Come on, stand up, lemme give you a hand.'

Alex had been kneeling in exactly the same spot Edward had vacated moments before they arrived. He reached out and touched the disturbed earth close to the cross. He could tell it had been freshly turned, despite the fact that the soil was sodden with rain. The warder jerked slightly on the handcuff, and Alex looked up. 'Sorry,' he said.

The doctor began to talk quietly as he helped Alex to his feet, mainly to distract the boy as they left. 'Do you believe those stories, son? Do you think your mother's ghost is at rest?'

Alex laughed softly, unnerving them all. 'She was no Romany. He was, Freedom, and he'll not rest, he'll haunt 'im all right. He 'as to live with what he did, not me. You see, Doc, I know it's too late to do anyfing about it now, but I never killed 'im. My brother did it. The ghost'll be on 'is shoulder, not mine.'

The doctor walked back to the van in silence. He couldn't take in what Alex had just told him – could not believe that Alex was in prison by his own choice for a murder he did not commit.

The prison van was out of sight before Edward could move. He averted his face as he passed the grave. If he had been determined before, it was now an obsession with him to succeed in life. His guilt on seeing what his brother had become had sickened him. But Alex was a millstone around his neck from which he would never be free, and he wished him dead. The realization that he hated Alex released him from all ties. He would repay Alex, but that would be the end of it. From now on, Edward was alone.

Book Two

Chapter Five

Edward's renewed determination to succeed was defeated on his return to Cambridge. The dreaded summons to appear before the Army Recruitment Board was waiting for him. He slumped down in the chair in his study.

Walter appeared within moments. 'You want to come along to the Marlowe Society, do you? It's next week, should be good fun. I'll pay for your membership, what do you say, Edward? It's a jolly good society, they do plays. I wondered if I could get a part, what do you think, Edward?'

'They've got me, the bastards, I've got to go before the ruddy board, could get called up. Shit, this is all I need right now, with exams coming up.'

Walter told Edward he wouldn't have that problem, not with his eyesight. Suddenly Edward became very interested in Walter's vision, asking if he was long- or short-sighted, how much he could and couldn't see, and Walter, who was rarely asked anything personal, launched into a long, boring speech about his myopia.

Edward leaned back, smiling. Old Emmott had given him the hint and now he would take it. He wasn't going to be called up by anybody, he was going to make damned sure of that. He dismissed Walter with a wave of his hand and as soon as he had left, Edward began practising a convincing myopic squint. Later, he paid Walter an unexpected call, having rarely bothered to visit him before. Walter's desk was a mess of papers and documents, but Walter's spare pair of glasses also lay there.

Edward walked into his interview with the Recruiting Board wearing Walter's glasses. The Marlowe Society would have been astonished at his performance, as none of the board members were fools, having seen every trick in the book pulled by under-graduates reluctant to join up. Edward was a first-class student, one they would have shipped into the intelligence offices where he would have spent his time deciphering codes and developing new ones. Many students had been used in this section, partic-ularly those in Edward's field.

He had sat up for a whole week, his eyes red-rimmed, paying close attention to the way Walter used his glasses, and particu-larly the problems associated with shortsightedness. They could not fault him, although the medical officer gave him stringent tests. He examined Edward's eyes, but did not give a very detailed report. Edward sighed with relief when he was passed over, but he would have to continue wearing glasses. He paid a visit to a local optician and bought a pair with plain glass lenses.

Although he joined the Marlowe Society, Edward felt ill at ease. He wasn't exactly ignored, but there were so many strong personalities that he paled beside them. He was asked if he wanted to act, in which case he would have to audition before being accepted, or if he wanted to submit script ideas for the forthcoming 'Footlights' revue. Walter introduced him to the other members, but he only half listened. He was thinking he wouldn't bother coming to any more meetings, and would have left immediately if Allard Simpson hadn't made an appearance. Allard was the star of the company, outrageous and brilliantly funny. He came sweeping in, wearing an opera cloak and jodh-purs with high brown boots. He told them that they must have new material, they were running dry, and if they had to give any more concerts with that idiot trombone player they would fall apart. All the members were set to work to find new pieces,

Edward among them. Not that he had any intention of wasting his valuable time. He dismissed it from his mind and continued to study.

One morning Edward's bedmaker handed him a folder of papers he had found beneath the mattress, and Edward flipped it open to find numerous essays in Charlie's handwriting. He found himself laughing as he read page after page of notes and drawings, done for Charlie's own amusement. It gave him an idea. He copied all the papers and gave some to the society as if they were his own work.

Allard called on him to say the pieces were wonderful, and he wanted to put two into the latest Footlights offering. He wandered around Edward's room remarking on the paintings, then stopped in front of a portrait of an army officer and tapped it. 'This your father?'

Edward told him it was an uncle, and the others were assorted members of his family. In response to Allard's enquiry about where he lived, Edward invented a house in Kensington.

'You must come over to my place during the vacation,' said Allard, wandering around Edward's study, picking up objects and setting them down. He slumped into a chair. 'Very impressed with the decor. My old man wouldn't give me a pot to piss in, he's so tight-fisted. Old boy's a judge. They've got me studying law to follow in his wake. I hate it all, only reason I'm here is the Marlowe Society. If I weren't so good, they'd have sent me down. Have you been before the Recruitment Board yet? I'm lucky, following in Pa's footsteps in more ways than one – I've inherited his flat feet.' Lounging in the chair, he asked if there was anything to drink, then invited Edward to join him for Sunday lunch – a few friends would be driving down from London to join him.

Allard was a strange-looking boy, very tall and pale with a thick mop of bright red curls. His eyes were slanting and very blue, and, although his hooked nose and small mouth were not good features on their own, together they made Allard very striking. He wore outrageous clothes, always with a flower in his buttonhole, and a sweet perfume wafted around him at all times.

As Edward had no drinks to offer, Allard uncurled his long legs and made for the door. 'We'll have to work a bit together on your material, so get a few bottles of plonk in. I like to wet the whistle . . . see you Sunday.'

Edward smiled to himself. 'Mr Popular' would be very useful and, apart from that, Edward liked him.

The Sunday lunch proved to be an eye-opener for Edward in more ways than one. He arrived promptly at one o'clock, and Allard appeared in his dressing gown, swearing that he had no idea it was so late. He opened his wallet and sent Edward to collect the champagne he had ordered for the luncheon, and Edward went hastily, angry with himself for not realizing, as usual, that this crowd didn't behave as if they were at school, doing everything promptly by the clock.

When he returned with the champagne, he could hear Allard's angry, high-pitched voice. 'I promise you he's just the writer, for God's sake, there's no need to get hysterical – I hardly know him, he's just early for luncheon, that's all. You really are so stupid! You know how I feel about you, why always ruin everything by being obsessively jealous? It's too tiresome . . . you'd better go and change.'

The reaction to Allard's tirade was an outburst of sobbing, so Edward decided on a strategic retreat. When he was halfway down the stairs, he heard a door slam, then running footsteps. The Honourable Henry Blackwell, head of the union and 'Mister Snob' himself, ran past Edward in tears.

When Edward entered the room, he found Allard, dressed in a plum velvet smoking jacket, instructing his porter on how to set the table. It was after three o'clock by the time the lunch began, by which time eight more people had arrived, carrying more champagne, home-brewed wine and caviar. They all got so drunk that the lunch became a shouting match. Edward made a mental note of everyone's names, and watched his speech to make sure he didn't drop any aitches. He made himself useful, helping to serve and being very much a part of Allard's team. All the girls were titled, very young with high-pitched voices, and the girl next to Edward passed him her card and insisted that he look her up when he got to town. They all showered Edward with their cards, and Allard roared with laughter. 'All after that lean body of yours, Edward old chap. Ahhhh ... Henry, come in, come in, you're very late.'

Henry Blackwell entered, his arms full of flowers. He knelt at the feet of one of the debs and kissed her. It appeared that this was his fiancée. The girl blushed and kissed him back, looking at him with adoration in her eyes. Edward watched the play between Allard and Henry – they were very friendly, but they sat at opposite ends of the table. Edward knew that no one would believe what he had overheard, yet he detected a slight frostiness emanating from the Honourable Henry. He knew why, but he said nothing, knowing intuitively the value of his secret.

Cambridge University was well known for its revues, but the most prestigious of all was the Footlights. Some of its members actually went into the theatre after gaining their degrees. The shows were very professional, and many West End managements paid visits, talent-spotting. This year's show was one of their best yet, and Edward's comic monologues were the hit of the night, thanks to Charlie.

Edward had been slightly wary, wondering if Charlie had ever shown any of his work to his friends, but it became obvious he hadn't. As Edward supplied more and more of Charlie's monologues, he became quite a star attraction himself, and no one was aware that he had stolen his new-found fame. His mantelpiece was filled with embossed invitation cards for the forthcoming vacation, and he was very careful not to answer any of them, hedging his bets. Now he was accepted as part of the crowd he intended to stay in with them. Walter asked if he would like to spend the vacation with his family in Manchester and was laughed at for his pains. Edward had dropped Walter since he had become friendly with Allard, and no longer accepted the offers of free trips to the pictures. 'Why don't you find yourself a girl, Walter? You shouldn't want to take me with you every-where you go, doesn't look too good. You ever had a girl, Walter?'

Poor Walter blushed and polished his glasses, and stuttered painfully that he had known lots of girls, he just didn't talk about them too much. He had become editor of a varsity magazine called *Cambridge Front*, and offered to let Edward write for it. 'I've got some great people contributing, Dylan Thomas, Vladimir Mayakowsky and Raj Anand. Would you write one of your monologues for me, Edward?'

Edward's store of Charlie's work was running low, but he promised to come up with something for poor Walter.

Allard, who never knocked, just breezed in, his hair standing on end. He started talking before he'd even closed the door. 'Edward, old chap, it's about this piece on the ballet dancer, I think it would be perfection if I had a rugby forward with me who changed into a tutu halfway through; it'd be hysterically funny, don't you think?' He pranced around the room, pro-claiming the monologue about the male ballet-dancer's position in the world of dancing. 'Okay, now when I get to this bit ...' He took up a balletic pose and continued in a high-pitched, camp voice, 'The main problem with the public is that they believe that dancing is for women, and any boy taking it up as a career could be termed a cissy ... Now then, when I go on about Nijinsky, I think I should prance around doing the "golden slave" routine from *Scheherazade*, the costume would be funnier, don't you think, than what you've suggested – the "Spectre de la Rose". So instead of knocking Nijinsky I'm going to be that other fella, you know, whatsit, Stanislas Idzikovsky, much funnier name, that all right?'

Edward had to cover because he'd never heard of Idzikovsky. Allard took his silence for disapproval. He put his hands on his hips and sighed. 'Oh, come on, it's much better. Sometimes you are so earnest . . . Do I change it or not?'

Edward nodded and Allard beamed. He could snap so fast – one moment all laughs and smiles, the next acting like a bitchy woman. Edward also began to detect how Allard's voice switched with his moods. One moment he would be dead straight, the next he would be speaking with a camp lisp, savouring his words with that twinkle in his eye. Allard opened the door with a sweeping gesture.

'For Chrissake, Allard, can't you even open a door without making a performance of it?'

Allard primped, hands on hips. 'Listen, who do you think you are, Noel Coward?'

Edward attended the rehearsal, but soon decided he had seen enough and went for a late stroll along the river. He walked on to the small bridge and leaned on the parapet, watching a few students in punts messing about and making fools of themselves. Continuing over the bridge, he cut down the steps to the river bank. He recognized Walter in one of the punts, and couldn't help but laugh. Walter was obviously extremely drunk. His glasses were askew, and he was clinging on for dear life to the punt pole. Edward had not seen Walter for a few weeks because of his new friends, and he knew Walter was upset about it. He also knew that if Walter and the others were caught on the river at this time of night they would be up before the provost.

Edward walked on but, hearing the hilarity increase, he turned back in time to see Walter flying head-first into the river. The girls thought it was all very funny and smashed their poles into the water close to him as he thrashed around, yelling that he had lost his glasses. The other boys clung to the side of the overturned punt, and one of them called to the girls to lend a hand. They manoeuvred themselves closer. Edward could see it was going to happen and shouted, but he was too late. The two girls were tipped into the water. There was so much splashing that Edward couldn't see Walter, but he did see one of the girls go under. She came up gasping for air, and he could tell by her terrified screams that she couldn't swim.

Edward dived in and dragged the girl to the bank. She was near collapse and he turned her over, pumped at her lungs. All around him was pandemonium in the darkness as the boys crawled on to the banks, and Edward shouted again for Walter without success. The girl sat up, coughing and spluttering, and Edward waded back into the water, calling for his crazy friend. Suddenly he spotted him, a little way up the river, floating face down. Edward swam to him, grabbed his inert body and doggy-paddled to the bank, doing his best to keep Walter's head above water. He shouted to the boys for help as they ran back towards the boathouse, but he could see torchlights approaching. He knew if they were caught they would all have to go before Emmott, and would be in serious trouble. He held Walter for grim death as the torches came closer and closer, scanning the river for the culprits as the two overturned punts gradually sank.

Walter began to cough and choke, and Edward dragged him to the river bank, where he spewed up the water he had swallowed. Walter's teeth chattered all the way back to the college, and they had to stop occasionally while he vomited. Edward despatched him to his rooms with orders to get a hot drink inside him and to keep his mouth shut about the night's events.

Back in his own rooms Edward took off his wet clothes, and had only just got into bed when there was a tap on the door. Walter stood there, ashen and shaking, the tears running down his face. 'Edward, something terrible's happened,' he sobbed. 'It's Cordelia, you know, she was with us in the punt, she's ... oh God, Edward, she's drowned! Jasper and George came up to my rooms to tell me. What on earth are we going to do? We'll have to go and see the provost, there's all hell let loose.'

Edward had to slap Walter's face to calm him. 'Listen to me. If none of you wants to be sent down, get them all to keep quiet, hear me? None of you must admit to being there. Now get out, or you'll make me a bloody accessory.'

Walter stumbled to the door, still crying. He stammered out his thanks and left.

Whatever the tragedy meant to those involved, they all kept silent. As no one came forward at the inquest to admit to being with poor Cordelia that night it soon blew over, and the matter was kept out of the press. There were questions asked at the college, of course, but everyone had been so drunk that no one could remember anything. A few wits remarked that she should have been called Ophelia, and the incident was held up as an example to students not to go boating in the middle of the night. The end of term loomed, and college life reverted to normal.

After persistent recommendation from Dr Gordon, Alex Stubbs was transferred to an open borstal in Southport, in the north of England. Although he had received a further sentence for his attack on the Governor of Wormwood Scrubs, Dr Gordon had insisted upon mitigating circumstances. Alex had been assured that if he behaved himself and showed progress, his stay in Southport might be no longer than eighteen months.

The open borstal, Hamilton Lodge, was run on similar lines to Oakwood Hall, but the inmates were given much more freedom. Among Hamilton's methods of rehabilitation, education rated high.

The group of warders and officers sat drinking tea in their common room. They held staff meetings every week to discuss the prisoners. The English teacher, Captain Barker, known as 'Hopalong' because of a pronounced limp, listened as each prisoner's notes were reviewed, their progress at the open prison determined. When they reached Alex's name, the psychologist observed that Stubbs was very much a loner. He did not mix with the others, and did not take part in any of the recreational activities. Alex, he felt, had adjusted to life at Hamilton, but he recommended that he still be watched closely, as he had often resorted to violence.

Captain Barker gave a detailed report. He thought it possible that Stubbs was keeping himself apart from the rest of the inhabitants as a means of survival. Judging from his records, being enclosed with other prisoners had, if anything, destroyed his chances of being released. The consensus was that Alex should be encouraged to take part in the activities offered, and to become part of the community.

Although they had tried to get Alex interested in sports, he had declined. He studied obsessively, becoming totally immersed in order to make up for the lost years. His progress was good, and he took the jibes for being a swot in his stride.

Captain Barker found Alex interesting. He was impressed by the meticulous work Alex always handed in. He had also looked through Alex's bedside locker, and was intrigued to find the two leather-bound books his mother had given him. He stood watching Alex as he sat alone in the main study hall. When he approached, Alex jumped in shock – he had been so busy working he had not even heard Barker's distinctive step.

'Mind if I join you, Stubbs, have a little chat?'

'No, sir.'

Barker noted Alex's good manners, the way he rose from his seat while Barker seated himself and eased his bad leg into a comfortable position. 'You reading?'

'No, sir, I was just going over some of the algebra equations, not up to scratch on those yet.'

'Your English marks were good, very good – can't expect to do everything at once, you know. You were a grammar-school boy, that correct?'

Alex gave him a slight smile, and nodded. He knew the system – Barker would have all his previous records.

'So what's all this interest in maths, then? You're not too behind, are you?'

'No, sir, it's just that ... well, I'm thinking about when I leave, what I want to do. Mr Thomas, my maths teacher, said that accountancy is a good profession, good earner.'

'Yes it is, it is. Everybody needs one if they make a few bob.

I know I need one. All those tax forms certainly confuse me. Mind you, I've a terrible head for figures, not my line at all. Sure it's yours?'

'Yes, sir, I quite like it – you know, figuring how things will come out. I like working them out in my head.'

'Ah, well, each to his own. But you know, all work and no play makes . . . some stupid saying or other. What about going in for one of the sports programmes? You could do with putting a bit of weight on, get some fresh air.'

Alex did not reply, but twiddled his pencil. He seemed, if anything, uneasy.

'There's cricket, tennis, football . . .'

'Running.'

'What?'

'I like to run, sir.'

Barker smiled and struggled to get up. Alex promptly rose to help him.

'I'll have a talk to the sports master and see if we can get you some running togs, all right? Might even hobble out to see you myself.'

Alex gave him a shy smile. 'Thank you, sir.'

Running became a release for all his pent-up frustrations. Only in this way could Alex escape the confines of the school. The most trusted prisoners were allowed to go out on weekend runs. Alex received his reward for hours of training when he was granted the privilege of going on a long-distance run on the beach at Southport. The green van took the runners, together with the sports master and two warders, to Ainsdale Beach.

In winter, with the tide out, Ainsdale Beach was like a grey desert, with Southport pier looming in the distance. They had a five-mile run, and those who wished to, and still had enough wind, could turn round and run back, making a ten-mile circuit in all. The wind was blowing, the tide was out, the pier and the glass-domed swimming pool were grey and empty. The prisoners behaved like children, whooping and shouting to each other as they took off their tracksuits. The sports master lined them up and waved them off, then hopped into the van and drove alongside, shouting advice and encouraging them. He kept one eye on the running lads and the other on his stop-watch. It would be a real coup if he could find one lad to enter the Inter-Counties Cross-Country race.

Alex was as happy and excited as the rest. He ran until he felt his lungs would burst, wanting to run for ever. His legs began to hurt but he pushed himself on until he felt light-headed, run-ning in perfect rhythm – long strides, head up – feeling the sea breeze and smelling the sea, which was so far out it was a grey line on the horizon. He was unaware that he had overtaken the rest of the lads. He turned at the five-mile flags and ran back. Behind him the van picked up exhausted boys who climbed aboard and flopped on the cushions in the back, leaving only four runners on the beach.

Alex romped home, and stood by the finishing flag, shading his eyes and gazing towards the pier. He could have gone on, he knew, but he was obeying the rules. His lungs felt as though they had been cleansed, his head was clear, and he laughed, threw his arms up in the air and laughed out loud. The next runner came in and bent double, gasping for breath, closely followed by the last two, who flung themselves down on the beach, exhausted. The teacher had to look twice at his stopwatch, but he said nothing, just gave the order to get back into the van and they returned to base.

The lads ran into the showers, shouting, and were watched with envy by some of the others for having been allowed beyond the gates.

The sports master barged into the teachers' common room so excited he could hardly speak. 'We've got a champion, I've never seen anything like it. Christ, he's bloody magnificent, a ten-mile run and the lad wasn't even winded! I swear he could have done it again – he could have lapped himself – and the time! I had to keep looking at the stopwatch – he's cleared the record here by two and a half minutes. Would you believe it, two and a half ruddy minutes!'

Barker, lighting the gas stove, grinned, saying that Vic Morgan was pretty good on the football field, so he had heard.

'I'm not talking about that pig-headed bully Morgan – it's Stubbs, the boy's like lightning. You realize what it would mean for this place if we came up with a champion? Just in morale alone. I'm going to push Stubbs and see how much he can take, and if I'm right we can enter him in the Inter-Counties Cross-Country.'

Alex was rubbing down his legs in the shower. He ached all over but he didn't mind, it had been worth it.

'Hey, Stubbs, swot-face, I wanna talk wiv you, yer listenin', Stubbs?'

Alex swished back the shower curtain and found Vic Morgan lounging in the doorway, his wet towel in his hand. He flicked it hard, and it lashed Alex's back. It hurt. Alex went to pull the curtain across but Morgan yanked it back, flicked the towel again. Alex grabbed it.

'Think yer somethin', don't yer, Stubby boy? Swot! Special education one minute, the next taking over my sport. Well, I don't like it, understand, makin' meself clear? So if you know what's good for you, you'll just get back to yer swottin' like a good girl and leave my sport to me, understood?' Morgan yanked his towel from Alex's grasp and Alex overbalanced, slipped on the soap in the bottom of the shower and fell heavily, cracking the side of his head on the tiles. Morgan laughed and walked away, and Alex got up, shook his head and stepped out to fetch a dry towel. His own was lying, sodden, at the bottom of the shower.

Morgan's friends were lined up in the corner of the shower room, sneering at him and telling each other what a well-endowed poofter he was.

'Here you go, Alex, use mine, it's almost dry.' Eric Motley, a small, skinny lad, handed Alex his towel, and with his back to

Morgan and his friends whispered that Alex should ignore them, they would only cause trouble.

Alex gave the funny little Eric a wink, towelling himself dry. 'I can take care of meself, Eric, but thanks anyway. Good to know I got someone tough on my side.'

Eric beamed with pride. He was a runt, and jokes were always directed at his misshapen body and his inability to play any sport. Now his face shone – he had a pal, his hero.

Due to all the excitement over Alex's astonishing performance, the head gave permission for everyone on the running teams to attend the official record run. This was to take place on the track in their own grounds, not on the beach. Morgan was seething, but he and two others were delegated to run alongside Alex to act as pacers.

'I'll fucking pace him, the son of a bitch, it should be me out there. You know what he's doing, don't yer, he's butterin' up that ponce of a teacher. Well, I'll show the friggin' bastard, I'll pace him right off the fuckin' track.'

Saturday was a good, clear day. The Governor's wife came to watch the race and all the inmates were told they could watch. This made Alex quite a hero, as any excuse for not doing their mundane jobs was cause for celebration.

Alex concentrated on keeping calm and blocked out everything else around him. He didn't want anything to throw him – this was one of the best moments of his life.

'Okay, Stubbs, let's have you. And keep on the run, there's a nip in the air. Get yourself warmed up . . . and you, Morgan – come on, move it. No foul language – just keep your mouths shut and let's see if we can make Stubbs a champion.'

Alex ran on to the track, his breath steaming in the chilly air, and was greeted with a cheer from the spectators. He began doing press-ups to warm his muscles.

'Okay, come on, let's get you in line, check your shoes, and get into the traps . . . come on, Morgan, stop talking.'

Morgan was whispering in Alex's ear, 'Watch your heels, Stubby boy, because I'll be right on 'em, an' I'm gonna fuck you over.'

They lined up, with Alex on the inside lane. He bent down to fit his left foot into the running trap. His trainer knelt in front of him, telling him to pace himself. When the flag waved for the finish he wanted Alex to take off and keep on running, just as a tester. They were only interested in the record for today, but he wanted to see how far Alex could go it alone. It was a chance and he wanted Alex to take it. 'The prison record's one thing, let's see if you can take the long-distance one at the same time?'

Alex could hardly hear him, he was blocking out all distractions. He could hear nothing, and all he could see was the track ahead of him.

The starting pistol cracked and they were off, Alex pacing himself and hugging the inside lane. At the first bend they were all lined up behind him, very close, and Morgan was too close. Alex put on a spurt of speed and Morgan followed, right on his heels again.

'What the hell is Morgan doing, he's pushing him too hard too early, the stupid bastard.'

The runners had reached the farthest point of the track, a linesman waved a flag and they were heading down towards the starting line again. Now Morgan was virtually treading on Alex's heels. The trainer swore, then clocked the stopwatch. They were already ahead of time on the first lap.

Alex felt the studs rip into his ankle and overbalanced, then righted himself, but Morgan moved up ahead. A cheer went up as he took first place, and Alex was being elbowed by the second man. He put on speed again and crept closer to Morgan. He could actually get heel to toe, but instead he gave Morgan a wide berth and moved again into the first position.

'That just lost him a second, he's crazy, and I'll crack Morgan's head when he comes in.'

The trainer was running, yelling, along the side of the track, but Alex didn't hear him. They were on the third lap, with three more to go, and Morgan was still pushing Alex from behind. By trying to bring Alex down he was driving him far harder than he should have, and Alex was taking it. One runner dropped out and collapsed on the grass, heaving for breath. He sat up in time to see the field split in two – Alex and Morgan in the lead, the other two way behind. As the leaders went into lap four, the stragglers dropped out, leaving just the two of them.

Eric was on the sidelines with his cheap Woolworth's watch, trying to time them. He was beside himself, shouting and cheering his hero on. Round they came, and Morgan was tiring, but both were coming in under the record for the fifth lap. The trainer was jumping up and down. Morgan was neck and neck with Alex, he had two possible contenders, not just one . . .

The final lap, and they moved into a last-minute sprint. Alex's heel was streaming blood from Morgan's studs, but nothing was going to stop him. They crossed the line, both inside the record, and Morgan caved in, fell on the track and lay gasping, snorting for breath. But the cheers had stopped, and he looked up, expecting to see Alex close by, only to stare in disbelief. Alex was still running, and running at a crazy pace. Morgan's moment of glory passed, he was hauled unceremoniously off the track as everyone watched the lone runner continue.

'If you put your mind to something, son, you can do it, it's all a question of will . . . and now, ladies and gentlemen, I'd like you to give a warm round of applause for the ex-British Heavyweight Boxing Champion, Freedom Stubbs!'

Alex ran on, still hearing the applause on the day his father had walked with such pride on to the grammar-school platform. He could hear his mother's voice, urging him on and on, her arms open, and he just couldn't get to them, couldn't reach her. She was standing by the white cross, wearing her old brown coat, her flat leather handbag over her arm, and her beautiful hair was braided around her head. She smiled at him. 'Come on, my love, you can do it, you can be anyone if you want. Put everything you've got into it, my son, my own love.'

The trainer stared at Alex, back at his watch, then back at the track. The lad wouldn't be stopped, round he went again and again, never letting up his pace. The crowd waited quietly as they watched the lone runner, and even when the trainer waved the flag for Alex to stop, he continued to run. They couldn't cheer, and no one knew exactly what to do. They could see as he passed that his face was like a mask, set, his eyes staring vacantly ahead, his limbs working by themselves.

'He's going to run himself to death. For God's sake, somebody stop him.'

The trainer took off, running at top speed along the track, but it took him all he had to catch up with Alex. He shouted that it was over, Alex had done it. 'It's over, Alex! It's over . . . Alex!'

Alex collapsed in a heap and lay face down, his chest heaving, his hands clawing at the gravel. He felt his head being rubbed, and a voice told him it was all right, it was over, he had done it, he had done it.

The matron bathed his feet and put disinfectant on his cut heel, bandaged it very carefully, and checked his pulse. He was lying with his eyes closed, still, and she pulled up a chair and sat close to him.

Down in the canteen the group of boys whispered, and Morgan, his nose out of joint because he realized he was losing his position as the 'Guv'nor', knew he had to do something to reinstate himself. Drinking his cocoa he rolled a thin cigarette, clicked his fingers for one of the lads to snap to with a match. 'I'm gonna have ta show that creep Stubbs, wipe him out, he won't make that run, I'll bloody see he doesn't.'

'Pssst, Alex, Alex, a few of the lads thought you might fancy half a Mars Bar . . . You okay?' Eric's sweating face was close to Alex, his bad breath swamping him. Alex propped himself on his elbows and gave the thumbs-up sign. He accepted the half Mars Bar and a packet of five cigarettes. Two more boys crept in and whispered, 'We're all gunnin' for yer, Alex, an' we got a few suggestions, like. If the Chief, the boss man like, asks yer if yer want anyfink – we all bin discussin' it – we wanna learn how ter dance, like. Yer know, ballroom stuff. Will yer suggest it? We're serious, like, all of us wanna dance, so will yer put it ter the Chief, Alex?'

Alex thought they were joking, but they insisted they were serious, so he gave them his word that should the Chief offer him any perks he would ask for a gramophone and a dancing instructor.

The Governor did appear the following morning, in high spirits, and wanting detailed medical reports on his prized boy. The matron assured him Stubbs would be up and about in a day or so. Alex watched the man stride down the row of empty beds, wearing suede boots, his Merchant Taylors' old school tie, blue shirt with stiff white collar, the creases in his trousers like razors. 'Well, you gave us all a good day, I must say, never seen anything like it, congratulations! You know we had the clock on you, Stubbs, bloody marvellous.'

The Governor wandered around the ward, coughing and picking his nose, then stared out of the window. 'Inter-Counties race, what you reckon on your chances, Stubbs?'

Alex shrugged, he had no idea of the times set by other runners.

'The other schools happen to have some of the best running clubs, son, Merchant Taylors' best, and the Harriers . . . I think you can take them on, all of them.' He moved around the bed and sat down, took out a packet of cigarettes. He lit one and blew a smoke ring. 'Thing is, to date we've not had a chap good enough or trustworthy enough to try for a place.'

Alex sat up and hugged his knees, saying that no matter what, they could trust him. He gave his word, which was greeted with a hearty slap on his shoulder. The Governor had reached the door before he turned to ask if there was anything Alex wanted.

'There is something, sir. The lads I've been training with, they sort of asked if I'd put in a word . . .'

When Alex mentioned ballroom dancing the Governor almost keeled over. 'Ballroom dancing? You serious, Stubbs? You any idea what the rest of the lads'll do if they hear about it? Good God, I've been asked for some odd things in my time, but this takes the medal. Ballroom dancing? How many lads want to do this fancy footwork, then?'

Alex shrugged and said about eight of them, with a gramophone.

'You'll take a hell of a ribbing, you know that? But if it's what you want then I'll see what I can arrange.'

Vic Morgan roared with laughter – friggin' ballroom dancing! Ponces headed by friggin' 'Goody-Two-Shoes' Stubbs. This he had to see to believe. Stubbs' popularity was eclipsing Morgan's, and his hatred was intensified when he discovered that three members of his inner circle had joined the 'fairies'.

Fully recovered, Alex returned to classes a hero. Along with eight other boys, all serving long sentences, he was called into the Governor's office.

He had kept his word, they were to have the use of a gramophone two nights a week between tea-break and dinner, and there were four records – a waltz, a foxtrot, a rumba and a tango. They would be taught by the Governor's wife. Mrs Dennis stood by her husband's desk, a pleasant, plain-looking woman in lisle stockings and brogues. 'You will start with the waltz, and work your way through the other routines. But any boy abusing this special privilege will ruin it for the others.'

The sarcastic references to the 'pansies' special brigade' were ignored, and twice a week the ballroom-dancing lessons took place in the drill hall. But before long the other lads began to envy the group as they marched across the quad to the hall and the sound of the Joe Loss Orchestra belted out. Mrs Dennis' strident voice was heard, 'One, two three, one, two three, one, two three . . . No, no, you must walk backwards . . . One, two three and fishtail, one, two three . . .'

The eight members of the formation dancing team became friends. They laughed as they partnered each other, but they were obviously dedicated to learning. Ted Smith took it upon himself to divide the group into male and female so they could learn to move backwards as well as forwards. Alex, being so tall, rarely had to be the lady. Ted, a small-time spiv, was mastering the tango, and encouraging the others. 'When ya get out, all of yer, yer gonna need ta know how to move on the floor, best way of pickin' up girls, right? Yer come out not knowin' one move from the next an' yer sunk. We gotta learn, only way yer can pick up the chicks, I'm tellin' ya . . .'

The lads laughed a lot, especially at poor Eric, who tangoed across the floor on his own.

More and more, Alex was becoming the hero, and Vic Morgan slunk around trying to find any way he could to sabotage Alex. He managed to steal a small file from woodwork class, and every night he worked on carefully sharpening the spikes on his running shoes. He cajoled and threatened one of the lads in the mailbag section to get some thick cotton and a strong needle without saying what he wanted them for.

The news came through that Alex had been accepted for trials, and he was called to the Governor's office to fill in an application form. This was the first time any borstal lad had been allowed to take part in the Inter-Counties Cross-Country race. Mr Dennis checked the form and clapped his hands, smiled his satisfaction and asked how the dancing was coming along.

'It's very good, sir, thank you very much. We're on to the rumba now.'

The Governor was surprised and impressed at the way the lads had conducted themselves. He knew the other prisoners had been merciless, but they had kept themselves to themselves and there had been no fighting. His wife told him the lads were always on their best behaviour and really did want to learn to dance.

'Tell the others that next Saturday night they'll be allowed to wear their own clothes. I'll rope in a few girls, give you a small dance – no alcohol, mind, just fruit juices, but it's about time you had female partners.'

The news spread like wildfire, and those who had done nothing but send up the dancers were green with envy. Allowed to wear his own suit, Ted Smith oiled back his hair and even let two of the lads have a small dab of his Brylcreem.

Eric was happy, and his twisted back seemed straighter. Either that or Ted's padded sports jacket, on loan for one-and-six, disguised his curved spine. Watched enviously from the windows by the other prisoners, dolled up and reeking of aftershave, they walked across to the drill hall. Mrs Dennis had been seen taking cakes and sandwiches over, and the others were thoroughly disgruntled.

Mrs Dennis had had quite a time finding eight suitable girls. They included her own daughter, two of her school friends and a couple of aunts. They were all gathered in the office.

'Now, these boys are juvenile offenders, but they are offenders, and they are serving time. Please treat them kindly. This is a very special treat for them, and they have been looking forward to it for a long time.'

The women stood silent as Mrs Dennis tried to put her next point as delicately as possible. 'If any of them makes any kind of move that is distasteful, approaches you other than to dance, you must inform me immediately and we will cancel the dance there and then. You are invited as dance partners, to put into practice what they have learned. There'll be a few sore feet at the end of the evening, but I am sure you are all aware that this is in a very good cause, some of the boys come from dreadfully deprived backgrounds . . .'

Extremely nervous by now, the women made their way across the quad to the drill hall. Every available window was filled with faces, and the odd lewd remark was heard, quickly silenced as Mrs Dennis frowned up at the offenders.

In their cheap suits and with their slicked-back hair, the boys sat at one end of the drill hall, close to the table where the food and lemonade was laid out. The gramophone with the worn records was on the stage. The sight of the women drew veiled looks and nudges, and Ted whispered that there was only one worth attempting to pull, the rest were old ponies.

'Now, boys, the first dance is a waltz, please take your partners.'

The boys stood in a solemn line, no one having the guts to make the first move. The women, standing on the opposite side, were equally embarrassed, and after Mrs Dennis' warnings they were beginning to think they should never have agreed to come.

'I'm going for the Old Man's daughter, all right, lads? Here goes.' Ted sashayed across the floor in his brothel-creeper shoes, his skinny tie only an inch wide, his spivvy suit shiny at the bum and showing the lines where the trousers had been let down. But to the rest of the lads he was Clark Gable showing them how it should be done.

'Er, you want to dance, love?' The Governor's daughter blushed at being the first on the floor. Guided by Ted's firm hand at her waist, they moved into a waltz.

Eric gaped, mightily impressed. 'Gawd, he looks like Fred Astaire, he's got the fishtail down all right, ain't he? Gawd, I'm gonna have a hell of a time, I've always been the bleedin' woman, I can't go forwards.'

Slowly the boys summoned their courage and asked the women to dance, and one by one they moved their partners on to the floor.

The drill hall resounded to the rumba, and the envious listeners at the windows groaned, 'Not again.' Later, they watched the ladies leaving, the boys walking back to their dormitories. They were all agog, wanting to know if anyone had 'pulled a bird', but Matron was patrolling and ordered those not in bed to get in, it was lights out.

Morgan watched two of the boys enter his dormitory, laughing together and telling stories about how Ted Smith had been the first on the floor, and that he had vowed to date the blonde with the big knockers as soon as he was released. Alex, with two more of the lads, passed the dormitory and gave the thumbs up. From the bed nearest the door he heard a voice whisper, 'Eh, Alex, is it true you gave Mrs Dennis one?'

Chuckling, Alex moved on towards his own dorm. He got into his pyjamas and hopped into bed. The door creaked open and he heard whispering. Then Eric and Ted, followed by the other formation team lads, crept into the dorm. Eric whispered hoarsely, 'One, two, three . . .' They each struck a match in unison, held them up and sang, 'For he's a jolly good fellow, for he's a jolly good fellow, for he's a jolly good fellow, and so say all of us.'

Unceremoniously they dumped their token gifts on Alex's bed and scuttled out, embarrassed. Alex now owned half a tin of Brylcreem, a comb, five cigarettes and a skinny-jim tie. He snuggled down and, happier than he had been in years, he whispered, 'Going to be a champion, Ma . . .'

Chapter Six

Edward packed up his belongings to take to London, and made arrangements to keep his rooms for the following term. He had taken up Allard's offer to spend the Christmas vacation at his family's country house.

With so many trains commandeered to ferry soldiers around, there were long delays on the passenger trains, and it was late when they arrived in London. A chauffeur-driven Rolls-Royce was waiting for them at Paddington Station, and Edward and Allard were driven across the park to Kensington. The house was in a very exclusive area, the Boltons, and had large gardens with high, wrought iron gates.

Allard's parents were already in the family's country house, and there was only a housekeeper waiting for them. Allard, with little pretence at being a good host, muttered that he was tired out. Edward was flippantly introduced and shown to a large double bedroom with a bathroom adjoining. He was impressed, and pleased that he had made the decision to take up Allard's invitation. If the family's town house was anything to go by, he reckoned their country place would be even better.

'Alleyyyyy! Yooo-hooo! Alleyyyyy, where are you?'

Edward's bedroom door was flung open by a very tall girl

with a thick mop of red hair very like Allard's. 'Oh gosh, sorry! I was looking for my brother, who are you?'

Edward shook hands with the long-legged girl, who said her name was Harriet. She stood back and grinned.

'Well, you look better than the weakling he dragged back last vac. Do you play table tennis?'

As Edward was admitting he didn't but was willing to try, Allard came in and caught the girl up in his arms, swinging her around. She squealed with delight, then went into a boxing stance, trying to get a punch at her brother.

'Don't they teach you anything at your posh finishing school, brat-face? Look at you – my God, you're filthy, and your neck looks as if it hasn't been washed for years. You dirty, scruffy gel, you nasty, dirty little fink rat!'

Brother and sister chased each other around Edward's bedroom and fought on the bed, bashing the hell out of Edward's pillows. Harriet, with her skirt up round her waist, was a real tomboy, and the noisiest girl Edward had ever come across. She never walked, but hurled herself around like a human tornado, causing anything within her range, ornaments especially, to fall to the ground. Her laugh rang out like a schoolboy's, and she shouted at the top of her voice. She was so tall, and Edward could see the nipples of her small breasts, formed like two tiny hills, showing through her school shirt.

'How old are you?' Edward asked her. He took her to be about seventeen.

Harriet looked at him and told him to mind his own business, and if he didn't shut up she would belt him one in his smarmy face. Allard stood in the doorway and laughed. He turned to Edward and told him he had permission to sock his sister at any time. 'She's fourteen and a half, and I would say by the time she reaches eligibility she will be so tall no man will be able to look her in the face.'

'Oh, shut up, you. What time are we leaving in the morning? Does Mother know you've got someone else coming? She'll hit the roof, you know. We've got bloody BB and Auntie Sylvia …'

Allard dragged her out by the scruff of her neck. Edward could hear them bickering and Harriet's boisterous laughs and squeals as Allard threatened to leave her behind.

The threesome left for King's Cross the following morning, brother and sister still apparently at loggerheads. At the station, Harriet disappeared, to Allard's fury, but soon came bouncing back with a large sandwich. She wore what looked like a pair of Allard's old trousers, tied up with string, and her grubby school shirt. Her overcoat belonged, Edward presumed, to someone considerably larger. The sleeves flapped and the hem dangled around her ankles. Allard was no better dressed, wearing the same clothes as he had the previous day, but more crumpled. They each carried battered, dog-eared suitcases, and they marched around the station demanding to know from porters which platform the York train went from.

At last they were settled in a first-class compartment, and Allard sorted out who owed what for the tickets. Edward began to think he should have taken up one of his other invitations as he ended up forking out fifteen shillings. He was running low on funds, and sat, tight-lipped, gazing out of the window. The journey was not without delays – lines up, faulty signals – and Allard began to get restless, pacing up and down the corridor.

Edward had a moment's peace when Harriet departed to the Ladies'. He wondered what Mrs Simpson looked like, and smiled, thinking it could be useful if she suffered from the Lady Primrose syndrome.

'Next stop, get the cases,' said Allard. 'Christ, where is she now? Well, we'll get off and leave her on the train, serves her right.'

Edward looked at the sign on the station platform – Thirsk. So this was Yorkshire. Not that he had much time to take in the scenery as Allard steamed along the platform with Harriet bounding in front of him. A black, highly polished Bentley was waiting outside the station and a chauffeur, cap in hand, sprang to attention. He took their cases, stacking them in the open boot.

'Gosh, you look good, Fred, *très* smart ... Come on, Edward, get in.'

In fact, on closer inspection, Fred was rather frayed around the edges. His uniform was ill fitting and his florid complexion went well with his broad northern accent. 'My, yer growin' oop, Miss H, we'll have yer out an' int' saddle in no time. Yon boy's grown oop an' all, got a coat that's better'nt' polish ont' motor ... Reet, we all settled? Then let's be getting on.'

Fred put on his chauffeur's hat, which was so large that he was in danger of being blinded by the peak. That was not the only danger, however; Fred's driving was a wonder to behold. The grinding of gears, the revving and the hopalong jerks gave them all a bumpy ride. Allard sighed. 'I say, Fred old chap, the motor does have two more gears, you know.'

Harriet, sitting next to Edward, chortled, 'He's never going to make it up the hill – it's three in one, he'll never do it.'

They could see the village of Helmsley, snuggled in a dip, with its cobbled village square. They passed over a bridge, through the village and out into open countryside. They drove for an hour and a half before turning in at the gates of Haverley Hall. There was a small lodge to one side, and Fred gave a loud toot on the horn as the car jolted up the drive.

Haverley Hall had seen better days, but it was obvious it had been magnificent at one time. The Georgian Hall was vast, white stucco fronted and surrounded by rather dilapidated stables and outhouses. The gardens were overgrown and the orchard ran wild, but the overall impression was that the Hall was held in suspension – very much in need of repair, but still standing proud.

As the Bentley drew up with another crash of gears, a bulldog hurtled out of the open front door. Harriet clambered out and ran towards the enormously fat dog. 'Buster, Buster ... Hello, my darling ... Come and say hello.'

Allard opened the boot to take out the cases and the huge

animal wobbled around them, snuffling and barking. He had no tail and his bottom wagged from side to side.

'I wouldn't go too near him, Edward. He's not vicious, but his farts are deadly.'

A woman emerged from the Hall as Allard spoke. 'I heard that, Allard. It appears Cambridge has done nothing for your command of the English language.'

Mrs Simpson was an imposing, hawk-faced woman with iron-grey hair and steely blue eyes, far from the Lady Primrose type. She wore a tweed skirt and heavy brogues, and was very tall with a harsh, loud, upper-crust voice. She stared at Edward and then turned, nonplussed, to Allard.

'Edward, this is my mother. He's staying with us for the vac, Ma. Pop inside, is he?'

Mrs Simpson fixed her steely gaze on Edward and told him crisply that he was most welcome, then she turned on her heel and followed Allard into the Hall.

Harriet yanked at her case, telling Fred not to bother taking them inside, but to get her horse saddled up. She grinned at Edward and told him to follow her. The interior of the Hall was vast, with a predictably run-down feel to it. Everywhere the eye fell, there were antiques and paintings, while a profusion of wellington boots and riding boots littered the floor. Edward stood abandoned, not knowing where Harriet had disappeared to, and couldn't help overhearing Mrs Simpson's voice somewhere behind him.

'You might at least have warned us. There is a war on, you know, and we're bursting at the seams as it is. Daddy won't be pleased.'

The wide sweeping staircase had numerous portrait paintings. None very special or very old, however one was rather amusing of a judge in wig and robes. Someone, no doubt Harriet, had drawn a black fly on the end of his nose. As far as Edward could see there were endless rooms. A chandelier with hundreds of crystal drops, a few having dropped off completely, was suspended from the centre of the remote ceiling far above him. As

Edward looked up, Harriet's head appeared from the landing above. 'Come on up. Do you want to know which room Mother's given you? Ma . . . Ma, which room is Edward in? Ma?'

Mrs Simpson came into the hall. 'Harriet, please don't shout, how many times do I have to tell you? Now – Edward, isn't it? Get Harriet to show you to the room on the top floor, then it will be time for dinner. Usually we're very casual . . . Oh, there you are, darling. This is a young friend of Allard's who's staying for the hols.'

Judge Simpson walked into the hall, carrying a shotgun. He tossed his cap towards the hat stand, missing it by several feet. He was stout and muscular, but a few inches shorter than his wife. He had grey hair and a stern, strong face. Edward felt as if he was being scrutinized from head to toe.

'Well, welcome aboard . . . Any hope of a cup of tea?' The Judge strode into a room on the other side of the hall and closed the door behind him. Allard could be heard somewhere, speaking on the telephone, and still Edward stood, not knowing where he should go, feeling very much the uninvited guest.

'Ma . . . there's no sheets on my bed.' Harriet's voice echoed down the stairwell, and Mrs Simpson sighed, then forced a smile.

'You'd better go up, Edward. I'll see to that wretched child later. I have to get the other rooms ready.'

Beginning to get angry, Edward picked up his case. He thought to himself that he was being shoved in the bloody nursery again. But far from being a nursery, Edward's room was enormous. The four-poster was canopied and draped in dark-navy velvet. The room smelt of mildew, but it was, or had once been, very ornate.

Harriet appeared, her arms full of sheets and blankets. 'Come on, I'll help you make up your bed. Sorry about this, but you'll get used to it.'

As they removed the counterpane, Edward couldn't help but notice the clouds of dust. The linen sheets were clean, though, and with Harriet's help he made up the bed. She flopped down on it, lying flat out. 'Right, I'll give you a few tips. If you want a hot bath, be sure to get up early, otherwise you'll never get one. Don't use the lavatory on this floor because it doesn't flush. Use the one on the second floor ... Do you ride? We've got five horses – three hunters and two geldings. Dreadful thing to do to anyone, isn't it? I always think they shouldn't do it. Have you ever seen a stallion's donger?'

Edward started unpacking, opening a Jacobean chest of drawers lined with yellowing newspapers and reeking of mothballs.

'Only, if you don't ride,' Harriet continued, 'you'll find it ever so boring here. How tall are you?'

Edward laughed, and Harriet cocked her head to one side.

'Do you always ask questions and then not wait for an answer?'

She chortled, wrinkling her nose. 'It's habit. No one here ever listens to anyone else. Where are you from?'

Edward pointed to the front of her trousers. 'Your flies are undone.'

She looked down and, without any shame, buttoned up her old, baggy trousers. Edward finished unpacking and stood in front of the dressing table, combing his hair. Harriet hovered behind him, standing first on one leg, then the other. 'You look a bit foreign – you know, like an Italian.'

Edward smiled at her through the mirror. She looked like a boy, but she was sucking her thumb. 'You'll get buck teeth,' he told her.

Harriet blushed and quickly withdrew her thumb from her mouth. She marched to the door, all skinny arms and legs. 'I'm going for a ride, do you want to come with me?'

Allard appeared and interrupted, 'No, he doesn't. Go on, hop it, pest, and stop hanging around Edward. Go on.' He shoved his sister out, then closed the door. 'Listen, I'm just going to shoot off for a while. It's a coincidence, really – do you know Henry Blackwell? Well, he is staying with friends a couple of miles away. I'm just going to trot over for a drink, might ask him over. Won't be long – see you later.'

· Edward sat on the bed, the smell of dusty curtains in his nostrils. He swung his fist and punched one. He knew Allard was using him to cover up his so-called friendship with Lord Henry. He muttered angrily, 'I've got to get out of this dump ...'

When the gong for dinner rang with a strange, clanging sound, ending with a clatter as it fell off its stand, Edward heard Harriet yelling down the stairwell that she would be two minutes. Edward checked his appearance in the mirror and went down to dine with the Simpson family.

Later the doorbell rang, and they could hear the thunder of Buster's paws along the hall as he raced to the front door. They heard the butler shouting to the person outside to push hard on the door as the dog was on guard.

'We expecting anyone, dearest?' Mrs Simpson asked her husband.

Allard jumped to his feet and told his mother that it would be Henry. As he rushed to the door he turned to Edward. 'We'll all go and gate-crash a few parties.'

Henry appeared at the door in his evening dress and waved to Mrs Simpson. A rather chinless young man, Robert D'Arcy, waited as Allard, behind him, booted Buster up the bum. 'Go on, get out of it. Come on Robert, Edward. Let's get going.'

Harriet, not included in the invitation, paid not the slightest attention to anyone. She sat curled up on the sofa, reading *Horse and Hound*.

Although Edward didn't have much inclination to 'party', he departed with the three boys. They were in high spirits. Allard drove the Bentley, and they went on a round of gate-crashing, except that there was a shortage of young, eligible men, so they were made welcome wherever they went. At first, Edward was very much on the outside, not knowing any of the people, but in one night he got a clear idea of the English social scene. He was half amused, now able to assess the social strata of the Simpson family. They were really upper-middle-class social climbers, with as many aspirations as Edward. He now saw the other side of the country set in a series of parties in ever more splendid homes. The smell of money, old money, was intoxicating, and he took it all in. In those few hours he met more titles than he had in his entire time at Cambridge.

Edward was accepted as part of the group. He looked right, spoke well, and his costume fitted the play. He started to relax. Being by far the most handsome of the four young men, he was soon the centre of attention. He was no fool, and knew not to make the first move himself. Accepting Allard's invitation had not, it was now clear, been a mistake. Somewhere among this horde of society people he would find one to act as a rung to help him climb onwards and upwards. But he had plenty of time, he would only make his move when he was sure he had made the right connection – one with money. The debutantes twittered and giggled around him, flattering him and making advances. He charmed them, smiling shyly. If they had known what thoughts were running through his mind, they would have blushed.

As he listened and laughed on cue, he amused himself by making each girl believe he was enamoured of her. When he danced he held his partner just that little bit closer than was entirely polite, and he knew he had them creaming their little silk drawers. Nor did he stop with the debs. He made himself equally charming to their parents. He asked them seemingly innocent questions, wanting to be very sure precisely who they were.

He had no thought of marriage, nothing could have been further from his mind. He wanted finance, connections. His intention was to make enough money by the end of the holiday to see him through his final term. He was introduced to mothers, and was astute enough to create just the right air of formality. The invitations flooded in. Everyone agreed Henry's friend from Cambridge was adorable.

Allard watched Edward 'work the room' and nudged Henry and Robert slyly. 'He's going to be a great asset this vac, very useful, wouldn't you say? I reckon we'll be invited to every "do" in Yorkshire.'

Robert disappeared, and Allard and Henry departed together, making it obvious to Edward that they didn't want him along. He was assured of a lift back to the Hall, so it took little persuasion for him to stay. Indeed, he had no intention of leaving, the ground was too thick with rich pickings.

It was after midnight when Edward was finally driven home by Lady Summercorn, her two daughters flanking him in the back of the car. She was swathed in mink, an attractive woman in her late forties. She gave him dazzling smiles in the rearview mirror, and when they reached the Hall she turned to him, resting her arm on the back of the driving seat. 'I'm sure we'll be seeing a lot of you. Please do call.' As she handed Edward a card he noted the square diamond solitaire ring, and the veiled look in her eyes. The Lady Primrose syndrome again – he had received several of these 'come hither' looks during the evening. These women were more rampant than ever, due to the number of absentee husbands who had gone off to war.

Edward watched the Rolls-Royce glide away as he placed Lady Summercorn's card carefully in his wallet. He now had seven cards and two scraps of paper with phone numbers scribbled on them, all of which had been discreetly slipped into his pocket.

Harriet heard the tiny stones rattle against her window and leapt out of bed. Looking down into the garden, she waved, then tiptoed downstairs to let Edward in. She put a finger to her lips and whispered so loudly he thought she would wake everyone in the house. 'Don't make a sound or Buster will head straight for the front door.'

They crept to her bedroom, and Edward trod on a teddy bear that squeaked, causing Harriet to titter and put her hands over her mouth. 'Have you been having it away, like Allard?'

Edward looked back at her, standing there in her child's nightie, and grinned. 'Not quite.'

'Oh, tell me what you've been doing, go on. It's only fair, I've let you in.'

Edward tapped her snub nose and whispered that he had been screwing the knickers off a tart. Harriet stared, round-eyed, then crept to his side. 'Did you pay for it? How much did she cost?'

He pinched her and pulled her chin towards him, looking down into her outrageously cheeky face. 'She gave it me for free because I have such a big cock, bigger than Allard's.'

Harriet mimed a faint, her face lit up with glee. She would have liked to keep him there, but he had already slipped out of the room. She flung her tall body on to the bed, her thick red curls covering her flushed face. 'I wish he'd stick it in me,' she whispered. Then she giggled so much she had to put the pillow over her head to muffle the noise, and in her imagination it turned into Edward, and she hugged it close to her. 'I love you, Edward, I do – I really love you.'

Alex had been in training, working daily with the sports master. He had been accepted as a candidate for the Inter-Counties Cross-Country race – no easy accomplishment. Many people were against allowing a borstal boy to run in the competition. On his back rode the reputation of the borstal and, above all, the trust placed in him to mix with the other runners, the chance to run freely in open country with easy access to public transport.

Alex had also continued his studies, showing remarkable progress considering the pressure he was under. He had changed radically, from a shy, introverted boy into an outgoing, well-liked lad. He was popular, a hero to the other borstal boys. He was proud of his new status and took care of his new-found image. He was an example to the younger boys, showing them it was possible to succeed even within the boundaries of a reform school.

On the morning of the race, Alex was up at five o'clock, tingling with excitement. The sports master found him in the gym, working out at a gentle pace. 'It's cold, and there's a frost.

Ground'll be hard going, could be snow later, it's forecast. How you feeling, lad?'

'Feeling good, sir. Ready to go.'

The whole school wore an air of excitement. At breakfast, Alex was patted on the back, and shouts of 'Good luck!' echoed around the hall. Alex was fit, his body in great shape with not an ounce of fat, his legs muscular but still slender. His eyes sparkled with health and vitality. Eric, his shadow, was ecstatic, saving Alex's place for him at table. He beamed up at his hero and gave him a wink.

'Right, Stubbs, this is it. Get your gear, the van's waiting. Calm down, lads ...' Even the sports master was showing excitement, bouncing around dressed in tracksuit and plimsolls. He raised his hand for silence, and indicated the package he carried under his arm. 'All right, come on, settle down. Stubbs, this is for you. The staff had a whip-round, so get into it on the double.'

The boys clustered around as Alex opened the parcel to reveal a new, pale blue tracksuit. They cheered, but Alex was so overcome he didn't know what to say. Eric hugged him, jumping up and down at the same time. 'I'll get yer shoes an' fings, all right?'

Mobbed by well-wishers, Alex made his way towards the lockers. He looked like a real 'golden boy', head and shoulders taller than most of the others, straightbacked, with his long, curly blond hair. Had it not been for the broken nose he might have been called handsome.

He turned the corner into the corridor. Eric shot out of the locker room, Alex's running gear under his arm. He was red in the face, panting and terrified. Something was wrong, Eric was shaking. 'Don't go inter the lockers, fer Chrissake. They're waitin' for yer, Vic Morgan an' 'is mates. He's got a runnin' shoe wiv spikes an' he's goin' ter mark yer. Take yer gear an' get out before they find out I told yer. Go on, get out. I had ter sneak in – the bastards want you to lose.'

Alex hesitated, then grabbed his gear. 'Thanks, mate.'

'Hey, Alex ... win fer me, will ya?'

Alex laughed and cuffed his friend lightly, saying that if he won the cup, Eric could keep it on his locker.

In the locker room, Morgan's lookout banged open the toilet door. 'That shit-head, Eric, gone an' warned 'im off. He's gone, yer'll never get 'im now.'

Morgan swore and kicked at the tiles. Wound around his fist was a running shoe, sewn together heel to toe, like a knuckle-duster. Each spike had been filed to a razor-sharp point. From the window they watched the van drive out of the gates, and Morgan screamed obscenities. In a rage, he turned and shouted that he wanted that little shit, Eric, brought to him. He was going to teach the dirty squealer a lesson.

Alex looked splendid in his new tracksuit. He shook each leg in turn, then bent double to rub his thighs, while the sports master talked quietly to him. 'Just pace yourself, lad. Don't push, you got a lot of miles ahead of you. Don't let the front runners set the pace. A lot'll drop out. You run like you've trained, conserve your energy . . .'

Hundreds of spectators with a good sprinkling of sports reporters lined the starting point. The runners gathered in a pen and were given their numbers. Alex was the last to join them, and he felt self-conscious, wondering if they all knew where he was from.

The runners were called to the starting line. They were all jogging on the spot, trying to keep themselves warm, Alex among them. Captain Barker and the sports master looked on, watching as he shook his head, eased his neck muscles. This had become a familiar sight. They could see his lips moving.

Alex was setting himself apart, talking to himself, oblivious to the rest of the field. He was standing, hands on hips, shaking out each foot in turn. Out of the corner of his eye he could see the starting pistol being loaded. He panted, sniffed the air deeply into his lungs, shaking his head from side to side, and all the time he talked to himself under his breath. 'This is it, go for it. You're going to take it, take it, take the son of a bitch. Go for it, Alex. Nobody can touch you, nobody.'

Bang! They were off. Alex found his place with a tight group, taking easy, long strides, not pushing it. They had five miles of road before they hit the open country, and the going was tough because of the ice and the thin film of snow that was beginning to lie on it. The runners' breath steamed in front of them – it was going to be a tough, gruelling race.

Four hours later the runners were far apart, many having dropped out. Alex began to push himself through the pain barrier. He was well out in front, with only eight runners ahead of him, and he was pacing himself well.

Captain Barker held his stopwatch tight as the van jolted and rolled along the country lanes. 'There he is – by Christ, he's going well. How's his time?'

'Bloody marvellous. If he keeps this pace up, he'll break the record. The ruddy snow's not helping, though.'

The snow was falling thick and fast now, and they watched their boy overtake two more runners. 'Not so fast, son, don't overdo it. Take your time.' Barker, suddenly an authority on cross-country running, was banging his stick on the dashboard as he spoke.

Alex was now in fourth place with one mile to go. His legs were agony, his breath heaved and the sweat dripped down his back. Far ahead he could see the faint blue line, the small dots that were spectators gathered for the finish. He was still talking to himself. 'Take it, Alex, take the motherfucker. Go, go, don't let no bastard in front of you. Take it, it's yours . . .' Suddenly he was aware of a runner coming up behind him, and he pushed himself even harder. 'Bastard, that bastard, he took everyfing . . . Bastard's right on yer heels, Alex, he's going to take it from yer like he took everyfing . . . Eddie, you bastard, you're not taking this – this is mine, this is mine, mine, mine, mine . . .'

The last stage of the race was suspense all the way. The two of them overtook the first three, jostling for the lead. Alex was losing headway, the boy trying to take him on the inside, but Alex's elbows kept him back. His heart was bursting, his brains about to explode. He had no energy left, he had used his final reserves on that last push . . . He could almost feel the breath of the runner behind him, the thud of the boy's feet almost on his heels . . . 'Bastard motherfucking bastard . . .'

Barker was shouting, banging on the dashboard, 'Run, Stubbs, you're there . . . Run!'

The sports master was panting as if he had run the race himself. He had a sickening feeling that their boy was going to be pipped at the post. 'He's not going to make it, he's run himself out.'

The blue line was blurring, so near and yet so far. Alex felt the runner's arms brush him, trying yet again to pass him. With a superhuman surge Alex moved through the barriers of pain and exhaustion. Through it and out the other side. He was on top of the mountain, he was free, he was flying. He lifted his arms above his head as he hit the blue ribbon, trailing it, streaming out behind him . . .

He turned and jogged back to his trainer, to Captain Barker, who was punching the air with his fists. For a moment the two men were so emotional they could have wept. Their golden boy, their champion, had beaten the record. 'Beaten' was hardly the word – he had pulverized it, knocking off over four minutes.

The canteen was in uproar. Everyone banged their plates, shouting in unison, 'Champion, champion . . .'

Alex, now even more the hero, saluted with his fist in the air, and the room erupted into screams and cheers. He didn't want the day to end, he was happier than he had ever been in his whole life. He had a big silver cup and a shield he could keep for ever. The cup had to be handed back after a year, but for the time being it would take pride of place in the assembly room. Alex paused, looked around. 'Where's Eric? Where's the runt?'

The boys nearby went quiet, sheepish. Eventually, Ted summoned the courage to tell Alex. Eric had got himself into a bit of trouble and was up in Medical. 'You can't see him, they won't let you. You'll get into trouble if you go up there without permission.'

Alex grinned and pointed to himself. 'Who, me? Do me a favour! After what I done for the school today, you fink they'd haul me over the coals for a little misdemeanour like goin' ter see me mate?'

Alex slipped out of the dorm and up the stairs. It was past lights out, so the corridors were dark. He edged his way up three floors, dodging the night patrol, and up to the infirmary. It was on the top floor of the wing, next to the matron's office. Her half-glass door looked out on to the corridor. It was strictly forbidden for any boy to be in the infirmary without permission. He bent double and sneaked past the office.

The beds were all empty but one, and Alex smiled when he saw the small mound in the nearest bed. Eric's little body was no bigger than a ten-year-old's. He crept to the bedside and whispered, 'Hey, what's this? I win the race for yer an' yer not even around ter congratulate me! Hey, you awake?'

The mound shifted and Alex had to creep right around the bed. He squatted on his heels and held out his running shield. 'Look, I won.'

Peering closer in the gloom, Alex could see that Eric's face was in a terrible state. His lips were puffy and bruised, and both eyes were blackened. Eric tried to smile, but his eyes filled with tears.

'Christ, what happened?'

Fighting his tears, Eric whispered that Morgan and his crowd had set on him for tipping Alex off about the running shoe. Gently, Alex patted Eric's greasy, spiky hair and tucked the shield into the bed beside him.

'It's me back playin' up,' Eric whimpered. 'They kicked me hump.'

Alex leaned close and whispered, 'They'll be sorry. Gimme their names, I'll get 'em.'

'Don't do nuffink, Alex. Best ter forget it. You'll be out soon what wiv winnin' the race an' all, you'll get remission.'

'Sod that. Besides, I ain't goin' no place wivout you.'

Eric held Alex's shield in his small fist. He looked so pitiful that Alex sighed.

'I'll be in fer a long time, Alex. You just go back ter bed.'

'What you in for, Eric? Not the infirmary, here, in the Hall?

'I got a bit of a problem . . . arson . . .'

Alex couldn't help but smile. He leaned close to Eric's ear. 'Well, there'll be a bit of a bonfire tonight . . .'

'I love you, Alex – I know it sounds soppy, but I do . . . Not like a queer, nuffink like that – like you was my bruvver.'

Eric felt Alex's soft kiss on his forehead. He clutched his hero's shield. Alex was gone as silently as he had crept in.

But Alex didn't go straight to bed. He made his way to the locker room and prised open Vic Morgan's locker before returning to his dormitory.

The following morning Alex took his ballroom-dancing cronies aside. 'You all owe me, right? I want Morgan's gang, but I want 'em one by one. Bring them into the locker room . . . Any of you open yer mouths about this an' you'll be for it. Leave Morgan until last.'

Ted organized it, making up a story that they had got some booze stashed away in lockers, but only one could come along at a time. Morgan agreed to exchange his brothel-creepers for some of the booze.

Alex scared each one of the gang witless, sitting like a king in the end toilet with the lethal running shoe curled in his hand. 'You won't be hurt. All I want is ter know which one of yer worked Eric over. You can't get out of 'ere, my lads are on the door, so you might as well talk.'

Without their leader, the gang members crumbled. They offered bribes to be let off, and with only a little pressure Alex discovered that Morgan himself had punched Eric's face in, and his 'sergeant' had applied the boot. Vic's sergeant was a loud-mouthed, fat boy who thought he was going to be hanged when he was brought face to face with Alex. They tied him up, pulled his trousers off and hung him upside-down in the end toilet with an old sock stuffed in his mouth. He was sobbing in terror.

'Okay, now all of you get out. Just bring Morgan.'

Ted chattered away to Morgan as he led him to the locker room. As they arrived, one of the other lads yelled to Ted that a master wanted to see him urgently. 'The booze is in the end lav, Vic. I'll try the shoes on an' we can talk about it when I get back.'

Morgan strolled along the row of toilets, pushed open the door at the far end and found his half-naked sidekick trussed up. 'What the fuck is this?' He backed out of the toilet, almost bumping into Alex.

'You got nobody to 'elp yer this time, Morgan. It's just you an' me.'

'Hey, come on, Stubbs . . . Look, I know we ain't exactly been friends, but we can sort this one out. What you want, you name it?'

Alex was amazed how easy it was – the smell of fear gave him a strange sense of power. He could see the terror in Morgan's eyes, and it made him feel even better. 'This is for Eric.'

The shoe's razor-sharp spikes slashed into Morgan's face. The boy screamed and tried to push Alex off, but he was cornered. He fought desperately, but the spikes kept on coming. Blood streaming down his face, he fell to his knees, begging for mercy. The more he cowered the more rage Alex felt. It wasn't Morgan any more, it was Eddie – Eddie, crying for him to stop, scream-ing at Alex not to hurt him any more.

'Jesus Christ, he's killin' him – somebody get him off.'

Ted was terrified. Beating Morgan up was one thing, but Alex had gone crazy. Captain Barker heard the screams and he ordered the boys away from the locker-room door, forcing them aside with his stick. He limped to the far end of the toilets, unable to believe his eyes. The 'golden boy' was splattered with blood, and he scarcely recognized Morgan, who was moaning in terror and covered in blood. Hanging from the cistern in the last closet was another lad, half-naked and weeping.

'Get back against the wall, Stubbs . . . Stubbs!'

Alex turned on him, fists raised. He would have taken on Barker as well if the walking stick hadn't come crashing down on his head.

Two warders led the handcuffed, struggling Alex to a padded cell. He was kicking and yelling obscenities, and it took all their strength to hold him down. Alex was crazed, spitting, lunging at his captors and trying to head butt them. They paid no attention to the words he was screaming, being too intent on getting him into the cell. 'I didn't do it, he killed him, he killed him . . . Eddie! Eddie . . . bastard, fucking cunt, bastard.'

Captain Barker was stunned into silence. The sports master turned helplessly to him, close to tears. 'Dear God, why? Why? Why did he do it?'

The fall of the hero hit everyone hard. Barker was as distressed by the incident as anyone else. Quietly and sadly, he took out Stubbs' record. There it was, in black and white: 'potentially dangerous'. Something had sparked off his violence, but what it was they would never discover.

Matron came into the teachers' common room to report on Alex. She was very depressed. 'He's quiet. I've given him a seda-tive, but I think it's best to leave him in the strait-jacket. He doesn't seem to understand what is going on. It's pitiful, he's call-ing for someone called Rex. Is there anything in his report about a Rex?'

Barker shook his head and told her the only living relative was a brother, but they had no address for him. He turned to the sports master. 'I found this in Eric's bed after they took him to the hospital,' he said, handing him Alex's shield. 'Who knows, that might have started it. You think little Eric stole it from him?'

The sports master took the shield, held it for a moment then put it down on the table. He shrugged, a helpless gesture. 'He could have been a British champion . . . He was magnificent.'

Chapter Seven

Edward could hear the Judge's loud voice in the stable yard, talking to Harriet. The stable lads were saddling up and the Judge gestured with his riding crop as he talked. 'Any hunter unable to control his horse and hounds should be shot. Some of 'em think they can clear a fence without a thought for the dawgs. They end up clearing nothing. Master of Frogmorton is an absolute bastard. Saw him kick a hound once – frightful incident.'

Edward had heard nothing but horses and hounds throughout breakfast, luncheon and dinner. He was heartily sick of it – especially as he had never even sat on a horse, let alone ridden one. Not that any member of the Simpson family appeared to notice his silence on the subject, and he had managed to excuse himself from morning rides by pleading his studies. He was also socializing, however, and enjoying his vacation, although the hunt seemed to be uppermost in everyone's minds, including his new-found friends. Everyone presumed he would ride to hounds, and Edward was beginning to wonder how he was going to get out of it.

When he looked up again, Harriet was cantering across a field beyond the stables. She was a joy to watch; the winter sun shone on her hair, her curls bounced as she pulled the horse in to a trot, and her cheeks were like two red apples. She wore only jodhpurs, black riding boots and an old white school shirt, and Edward thought she must be freezing. Horse and rider were fluid, like a single being, and he was fascinated. Usually Harriet was so ungainly, and yet she looked as graceful as a ballet dancer out there in the fields. He saw the Judge, dressed in an ancient jacket and jodhpurs, join his daughter, riding a seventeen- or eighteen-hand chestnut with a sheen that glinted like Harriet's hair.

Assuming that the whole family were out, Edward decided he would take the opportunity to have a bath. He opened the bathroom door to find Allard just jumping out of the big tub. 'Morning, come in, come in.'

His teeth chattering, Allard proceeded to rub his pale, freckled body dry with his once-white towel, now a dirty grey colour. In two seconds flat he was dressed, his sweater, shirt and vest having been left one inside the other, as were his underpants and trousers. In one swift move he had his top layer on, and in another his trousers followed. 'Learnt this at Harrow – we had to crack the ice on the tubs there. It's quite easy when you know how. It's taking the garments off that's the trick, making sure they come off in one move ready for the following morning.' He padded out with his sodden towel, forgetting to brush his teeth, and told Edward there was no hot water. He would have to get up at the crack of dawn if he wanted that luxury. As he wandered off down the corridor, he called out that he was going to drive into town and would no doubt see Edward later.

Edward had seen very little of Allard, and as he had no transport of his own he was dependent on his newly acquired friends sending their chauffeurs to collect him. He had made no move on any of his prey, but he was lining them up in his mind, and Lady Summercorn was high on his list.

Walking into the kitchen, Edward found the back door wide open. He could see the Judge and Harriet kicking off their riding boots. The Judge was arguing with Harriet about which packs were the best in the country. 'I would say without a doubt, Brocklesby. But one has to look at knees and ankles . . . On the other hand – let me speak, Harriet, shut up – I would say that the Belvoir's are beautiful animals . . .'

Harriet wrinkled her nose and said something inaudible. Her father turned on her, pointing at her with his crop. 'Remember that time with old man Burton? This gel, Edward, only hal-looed, shouting that she'd seen a fox. I galloped up on – what was I riding then, dear? Oh, never mind – anyway, Edward, I get up to the gel and she's hysterical, jumping up and down in the saddle, and I said, what on earth did you halloo for?'

Harriet muttered that she was sure Edward wasn't interested in something she had done when she was eight years old. The Judge roared with laughter and carried on with his tale, regard-less. '"A fox, Daddy, it was a fox, and he was so dirty and covered in mud . . ." Mud be buggered, I said, what on earth did you halloo everyone out for? A mangy fox, the hounds won't run to that.'

Harriet flew into a rage, shouting that she was sick and tired of her father always bringing up that old, motheaten story. Edward turned to the Judge. 'What is a mangy fox, sir?' He knew immediately that he should have kept his mouth shut.

The judge gave a snort. 'Good God, doesn't this chap Allard's lumbered us with hunt? Doesn't he know what a mangy fox is? Well, he won't be out with us, that's for sure! Now, dearest, coffee please, and I'll have a nap.'

Harriet looked at Edward's embarrassed face and moved round the kitchen table to sit next to him, resting her chin on her hands. 'A mangy fox, Edward, is one not worth hunting. The hounds can't pick up the scent – the gamekeepers are usu-ally sent out to shoot them, if they can find them.'

Buster, who had been dozing in a corner, stood up and padded out, delivering a raspberry as he went that echoed around the kitchen. Harriet closed the door and leaned on it, smiling sweetly at Edward. She trailed her hand along the backs of the chairs as she returned to his side. 'You can't ride, can you? Oh, don't fib, I know you can't.'

Edward felt himself blushing. He coughed and said no, actually, he didn't ride. Of course, his family had horses, but he had never had the inclination to learn. Harriet turned with a devilish grin and giggled, and Edward smiled back. She knew he was lying. He leaned back in his chair and admitted that he was, in fact, scared of horses. He almost told her about running to the docks to see if his father was working, and how the mounted police had pushed the desperate workers back, but he managed to stop himself. He remembered Alex holding out a lump of sugar to one of the horses and getting a sharp kick from the policeman ... He was miles away, wrapped in his memories, when Harriet called him back to the present. 'Well, I can teach you if you like. I ride every morning, and I would be happy to teach you, what do you say? It's all very simple, really, most important thing is that you convey to your horse exactly what you want him to do, they know when they have someone unsure of themselves on their backs. You must always judge the speed that'll carry you over the jumps, you mustn't lose confidence because the horse will know. The most crucial moment is the last few strides ... you listening? Edward?'

Edward shrugged, saying that he doubted he could learn fast enough to take jumps, and she slipped her arms round his neck and promised him he would. She smelt of fresh air and horses, and he couldn't help but give her a quick, light kiss on the cheek. She galloped off to the door like an unruly animal – she never seemed to walk, but loped, her arms swinging. She banged open the door, winked and told him she would wake him at five-thirty.

She was true to her word, and early the next morning Edward felt himself being shaken. He started and sprang up, and Harriet flung herself down on the edge of his bed to give him his instructions, waggling her crop in front of his nose. If he didn't have boots, he would find rows of them at the side of the kitchen door, and he should put on a warm sweater and a vest. She would meet him at the stables.

Edward had no jodhpurs, so he tucked his trousers into the tops of the boots and went to the stables. She was saddling up a very frisky mount, while the stableboy held the reins of the enormous gelding. 'He looks more frightening than he is. He's Ma's nag, and he's a big softie. Stan, help Mr Edward up, show him how to put his feet into the stirrups and not to fall arse over tit. I'll just have to get Kentucky out, he's very jumpy this morning.'

Edward didn't want her to leave him. He was terrified and had great difficulty mounting. The stableboy hitched him up three times before he was in the saddle. He then took for ever to adjust the stirrup length to suit Edward. Harriet came cantering back, clattering on the cobbles. She took Edward's reins and walked his horse back through the archway towards an open field. Edward held on tight, leaning forward. The ground looked very far away and he was sweating with nerves.

Harriet's patience and encouragement were endearing, and by nine o'clock he was feeling more secure. She never pushed him too fast or too soon, making him walk round and round the field until he felt comfortable on the mount. She made him grip with his knees, and instructed him to get to know the horse, talk to him and encourage the animal as much as she was encouraging him.

'He's got no balls, but that doesn't make him a dunce. He's a sharp old boy and he likes attention, bit like Pop – maybe Ma had him gelded.'

The following morning Edward felt as if he had a tea trolley between his legs, his body was so stiff, and he almost called it off. But Harriet was there, waiting for him, at five-thirty. This time they trotted, and Edward at first bounced all over the horse's back until she pulled him in and, sitting astride her own horse, demonstrated the proper rhythm. It took a while, but then it came to him and he was trotting round and round the field, delighted with himself. By the end of the third day's lesson he was cantering and galloping. He no longer needed Harriet to wake him up, he was up and dressed and waiting at the stables for her. He learned to saddle up, how to groom, and Harriet insisted that he must know everything, including how to muck out. There was a way to do it, a correct way, and to do it any other way meant he would be immediately spotted for a 'townie'.

More than anything he remembered, Edward looked forward to his morning rides. He was so keen that he asked if Harriet would also ride with him in the afternoons. She grinned and said he would soon be ready to take the jumps if he went on at this pace, but after lunch she was ready and waiting.

'Tomorrow, Edward, want to go across country with me? We can take a picnic and really have a good ride over to the woods. They're about eight miles to the north, give you an idea about cross-country riding.'

Edward shaded his eyes, smiled at her and agreed, then heeled his horse into a gallop. Harriet watched him and yelled at the top of her voice.

'Your bum! Sit, sit on the horse!'

The house was getting 'a thorough clean' in preparation for the arrival of guests. Edna Simpson's efforts at flower arranging with sticks and dusty willows appeared all over the house. Invitations began to arrive for the season's social events, and were lined up on the mantelpiece with the Christmas cards, to be discussed at breakfast. Edward read them all but knew no one. But titles abounded.

'We've cracked it, Ma, look at this invite, all your Red Cross activities have paid off.'

Mrs Simpson turned it over and beamed, then placed the crested invitation in the centre of the row of cards, stood back to admire it. 'Daddy will be pleased, this'll be the first season we've had a royal invite ... Fred! Someone get Fred.'

While Edward drank his tea at the table he listened to the instructions for the Judge's formal attire to be taken out of mothballs. Mrs Simpson sang, off key, but cheerfully so. Then the rumble of the plumbing rattled down the array of pipes and she charged out. 'Allard, get the hammer and hit the bathroom pipes, Daddy's overrun the bath again. The place will be flooded.'

Harriet appeared with a straw bag slung over her shoulder, impatient to be off for their picnic. She looked at the mantel and picked up the invitation, turned it over. 'I say, we're really in with the in crowd this season. Pa will be pleased, we've been trying to crack this set for years ... you almost ready?'

Edward downed his tea and took a sneaky look at the invitation crested with the small gold crown on his way out. The Judge appeared, clutching a large hammer, looked over Edward's shoulder and grunted. He went through to the scullery, from whence loud clanking and banging noises issued as he belted the pipes. Allard strode in holding two white envelopes. He tossed one on the table, telling Edward it was for him, end-of-term results, and opened the other with a marmalade-covered knife, at the same time enquiring how the riding was coming along. The knife left a thick ridge of marmalade on his envelope and he sat down to read the contents. 'You want any washing done, chuck it in the laundry basket in my bathroom, and leave your DJ out for pressing – looks like we've got quite a social time ahead of us. 'Bout time things picked up, getting bored out of my mind ... oh, shit, shit, shit.'

Edward opened his results and flushed a deep red, looked at Allard, who was turning his pages over and over in a fury. 'How did you do, old chap?'

Edward shrugged and pocketed the papers. Allard seemed relieved, said he had just scraped through, or rather crawled. 'Old boy'll have a fit, I'll have to have a private chat with Ma, see if she can get me some extra tuition next term ... What did you get?'

Sighing, Edward told him that he would more than likely

have to do the same thing, and Allard patted his shoulder, asking him to keep mum about the results. He would find the right time to discuss it with his father.

Edward had got a first in everything – a remarkable achievement. There was even an added footnote of personal congratulations from Emmott himself. As he strode out to the stables, Edward whistled, did a small hop and skip, and patted the precious exam results in his pocket. The horses were being groomed, the stables mucked out, the tack being brought out to be cleaned and polished. Harriet was waiting impatiently, with the two horses already saddled. 'You took your time – come on or Pa will make me stay to help out here, there's a lot to be done . . . you look very chipper . . . No! Wrong foot, how many times do I have to tell you to mount the other way round, idiot!'

They trotted out of the stables into watery sunshine. It had rained heavily in the night, but now the clouds were high and far apart.

'Right, let's go. Follow me – we cut across the road and head through the fields, then it's a free ride for about six miles with some good jumps . . . By the way, don't you have a hacking jacket? You really should get one, you know – look like a dreadful townie in that thing you've got on.'

They galloped across the fields and Harriet took the jump with ease, but when Edward heeled his horse forward it pulled up short, and Edward was pitched over its neck to land in a muddy ditch. Harriet's head appeared against the bright sky and yelled down at him that he was a stupid bugger, what had she told him? 'If you don't pace him, how in God's name is he going to jump? Now go back and try again.'

Edward picked himself up and remounted, trotted back again for about twenty yards and took the jump. Harriet, waiting on the other side, gave him the thumbs up and cantered on. She was going at full gallop when her horse pulled up short and she rolled to one side, slipping off the saddle. Edward joined her and looked down at her as she lay on the ground with one foot in the stirrup. 'Having problems, old thing?'

Harriet wrenched a thistle bush out of the ground and held it up as a warning. 'Most horses hate thistles and will veer away from them, so be warned.' She was up and giving chase to Edward, the straw bag bouncing on her back as she passed him. 'See the gate ahead? When you're on a hunt, if the pack veers off giving you a leading position, never take a gate, always open it, remember that even if the horses can jump it, the hounds might not and you'll be given hell if they start ripping their bodies trying to get through hedges. Keep on a straight line now, head towards that thicket and then we go into the woods – be good exercise, see how you cope with trees and branches.'

Edward was enjoying the damp morning air and the sun. He was also elated, the prized results burning in his pocket. He overtook Harriet and looked back, laughing, and she came to his side as they pulled their mounts in and headed for the thicket. 'You hardly ever laugh, you know that?' Her red hair bobbing and shining in the sun, cheeks flushed, sweat dripping down the back of her shirt, Harriet swiped at the branches with her crop, looking back and urging Edward on. She shouted to him to make sure his mount had a clear path at all times, horses don't like being whacked in the face by branches any more than their riders.

The bushes grew thicker and they slowed to a walk, finally emerging into a clearing. It seemed darker, and they looked up between the trees to the sky. Black clouds had gathered above them, and Harriet cried, 'Oh pisspots, it's going to rain.' They mounted and trotted up a small bank towards a wood.

'Keep on talking to him, tell him he's doing well, he's getting to know you now . . . we'll head for the woods, I'm taking you to the special place I know where we can shelter.'

Edward patted the neck of his sweating horse and whispered 'good boy' and 'good chap'. Harriet disappeared into the woods about eight yards ahead of him, and he thrashed at the branches with his crop.

The sky grew darker and a cold wind began to chill them. Fierce rain lashed down, and the ground quickly became slithery with mud as the horses picked their way over the uneven grass.

'We'll have to get off, walk the rest of the way, it's too dangerous. The stream up ahead must have burst its banks. You okay? Just lead him on.'

Within a matter of minutes Edward was soaked to the skin. He pulled at the horse's reins and followed Harriet, twice losing his footing, the mud oozing around his boots. 'Harriet, Harriet, we should go back . . .'

She was way up ahead, dragging her horse beside her, and she pointed off to the left. 'Just a few yards . . .'

The tiny chapel was dilapidated, the roof had partly fallen in and one wall was crumbling. In the old arched doorway two heavy oak doors hung off their hinges. Harriet tethered her horse to some branches and nuzzled him. 'Get his saddle off and take it inside.'

Edward obeyed, wiping his face as the rain was blinding him, and pulled his horse towards the arch to give him some shelter. Heaving off the saddle, he carried it into the chapel.

Inside, it was a mass of fallen debris and overturned pews, and the font was cracked in two. The stained glass window was shattered, broken glass littered the small stone altar.

Harriet's voice echoed as she pulled off her boots, rubbing her cold feet. She sat on a pew and turned to grin at him. 'This is my secret place, you like it? Used to come here when I was little – course, it wasn't all tumbled down then. I was christened here, it belongs to the family. Some of my father's family are buried here. His father was a curate, not that he likes to broadcast that too much.'

Edward removed his soaking jacket, rubbed his wet hair and sat in a pew opposite Harriet. She shook her hair and unwound the ribbon that held it at the nape of her neck. She grinned at him. 'You hungry? Open up the bag, I'm starved.'

She wandered around the chapel as Edward unloaded the picnic, telling him that her father had always kept his origins quiet. Being a judge he liked everyone to think he was somebody, but really he was just a vicar's son. The family had bought the old manor house, they didn't inherit it. 'I think Pa married the old lady for her cash. I mean, have you seen some of the old photographs of her when she was young? Frightfully ugly, but he was quite good-looking.'

Throwing herself down beside him she searched the contents of the bag, opened a neat packet of sandwiches and munched hungrily, still shaking the water out of her hair.

'I didn't know you had such long hair.'

Harriet told him she had cut the fringe herself, and if she'd had long enough she would have cut the back as well, but the needlework teacher had taken the scissors away. 'Shall we light a fire? I'm frozen, we could light one on the altar, it wouldn't be sacrilegious, I mean nobody uses this place now.'

Edward shrugged his shoulders and began picking up dry sticks from the floor of the chapel.

Edna Simpson's sister and her family, the Van der Burges, arrived to find no member of the family there to greet them. They sat in the warm spot in the house – the kitchen, Sylvia still wearing her mink coat. She surveyed the cards and invitations, assuring her husband they were going to have a pleasant festive season.

'I should ruddy well hope so, after the trek down here. Why they don't get rid of this place, God only knows. It's rundown, freezing, and the roof looks as if it leaks. I'd say you needed to spend ten to fifteen thousand on the place before it'd be habitable ... Social ruddy climbers, this place must be breaking the Judge. He'll no doubt touch me for money, as usual.'

Richard snapped that perhaps they kept the Hall because they liked it. Not everyone was as obsessed with money as his father was.

'You ought to know about that, Richard, never having

earned a brass farthing – yet you manage to spend more in one week than a man earns in a year of hard labour! If all Eton taught you was to play goddamned backgammon, then I for one wish I'd never sent you there.'

Throwing up his hands in despair, Richard walked out, leaving BB, his father, to take over his position by the fire, warming his rear end.

'Leave him be, dearest,' Sylvia remonstrated feebly, 'you always criticize him. He's a dear boy, and means no harm ... Did you bring your hunting jacket?'

BB bit the end of his cigar, spat it in the fire and bellowed for Fred to get him a drink to warm him up.

The thundering sound of Buster charging down the hall announced the arrival of Mrs Simpson. She proffered her cheek for Sylvia to kiss, while BB complained bitterly about not being able to take a bath after their journey. Mrs Simpson pursed her lips and murmured that there was a war on. BB snorted, 'Don't tell me they're rationing hot water now, Edna, for Gawd's sake.'

Sylvia could see her sister was furious, so she suggested Edna might tell them when it would be convenient for them to take their baths.

'Well, come along now, dear, and I'll show you your rooms and explain the intricacies of the plumbing system at the same time.'

They left BB still hogging the fire, his trousers sizzling. Sylvia followed her sister upstairs, noting Edna's pathetic attempts at flower arranging. 'My dear, perhaps you would like me to make a few Christmas decorations? I can paint some twigs and put some coloured balls and ribbons on them – they look very festive.'

'We don't really go in for that kind of thing ... The gardeners haul a tree up outside the house and the Judge switches on the fairy lights – that, my dear, should suffice. And we're not sending Christmas cards this year – rather goes against the grain, but there is a war on.'

Sylvia sighed. There was indeed a war raging, but somehow here in the depths of the country it seemed very far away.

Feeling a bit miffed at Sylvia's condescension, Edna ushered her into her bathroom and explained how the hot water supply worked. Noting how many trunks her sister had brought from London, she said, off-handedly, that they had been invited to the Duke and Duchess's house party the following weekend. Of course, she would call and ask if she could take her sister along.

The two women were so different, one five foot eight in her stockinged feet, the other five foot nothing. Their only similarity was in their plummy, aristocratic voices, Edna's hoarse from constant shouting and Sylvia's husky from chain-smoking. Sylvia must at one time have been very pretty in a doll-like way, with her big, liquid eyes, tiny upturned nose and cupid's bow mouth.

Edna looked around the bedroom and folded her arms. She loved to take digs at Sylvia, as if they were still children. She'd always been jealous of her younger sister. It was unfair that Sylvia should have all the looks, but the fact that she herself had married a judge, and now mixed with high society, was reward enough. The family beauty was married to a South African, and a rough diamond at that, and Edna never let an opportunity pass to rub it in. 'I can't say for certain that the Duchess will oblige – they must have so many guests ... It's rather an honour, you know, to be invited, but then the Judge is very well thought of in these parts. The rumour is that he may even become Lord Chief Justice, did I tell you that?'

'Yes, you did, dear, and I'm thrilled for you both.' Sylvia fluttered her eyelashes, which were thickly coated with mascara, and looked so down, so hesitant and nervous that her sister felt quite sorry for her.

'No doubt Richard will be roped in. Young men are always in demand, there are so few about with the war on ... I don't suppose you've got any dresses that would suit Harriet, have you? We really should do something with the gel. She'll be coming out in a year or two, and she's not the slightest bit interested in fashion. Would you see what you can do with her? The wretched child cut off half her hair, you know. Her best feature and she ruins it ... Well, not the back, it's just that the front's gone fuzzy.'

'I'm sure I can find something appropriate for Harriet ... She's out riding, I hear, with – Edward, isn't it?'

Edna snorted and strode to the window. With all the students up at the university Allard could at least have brought home someone less peculiar. 'Chap hardly speaks, you know. Good-looking, I suppose, but I find him rather disturbing. He's sly in a funny sort of way – can't fathom out his background at all. Welsh, or his family were, but then Allard was always one for collecting lame ducks.'

Sylvia carefully placed a silver-framed photograph on the bed-side table. It was of two blond, angelic-looking boys, arm-in-arm and smiling into the camera. She touched the frame fleetingly, a sad, motherly gesture as if she were touching the child itself.

'You shouldn't carry that around with you, Sylvia. A constant reminder like that doesn't do any good, you know, not after all you went through. I'd put it away somewhere.'

Sylvia ignored her, but she continued, 'I don't know why you put up with that husband of yours, I really don't. He's so dread-fully coarse and loud. He may be rich, but that's not everything. Does he still run after the ladies the way he used to?'

Sylvia blinked, her nervous little hands trembling as she began to arrange her pure silk underwear, all neatly packed in layers of tissue paper, in the drawers. But she said nothing.

Edna pressed the point. 'I do care about you, you know. You are my sister, after all.'

Sylvia shut the drawer very carefully and blinked, gave a tight little smile. 'And I care about you, my dear. But I am perfectly well now, and BB takes care of us all, in more ways than one. Don't be cruel about him, he is a good man.'

Silently thanking God that he was also a rich man, Mrs Simpson kissed her sister's powdered cheek and walked out.

Left alone, Sylvia sat on the bed and looked at the photograph. Her tiny hands fluttered above the two beautiful, smiling boys, then dropped like birds to her side. Her eyes filled with huge tears and brimmed over, staining her cheeks with mascara.

BB walked into the room. For a moment his face puckered with pain, then he assumed a neutral expression and breezed over to lay a hand on her curly, blonde head. 'Hold on, there's a good girl, keep yer pecker up – we don't want you having to go away again, now do we?'

She smiled up at him, and he took out his big silk handkerchief and wiped her tears away as though she were a child. She patted his hand and managed a small smile, saying she was perfectly all right, it was just that her sister sometimes got the better of her.

'All I know is I got the best of the sisters. By God, I couldn't survive that creature for long.'

BB watched his wife pull herself together, take her little silk make-up bag and go quietly into the bathroom to patch up her face. He sighed. She was so fragile, he could never tell her everything he felt, everything he was going through. The photograph of the two blond boys caught at the big man's heart. He gritted his teeth and frowned, then took the frame and laid it face down so the two boys would not be looking at him, not forever making him feel guilty . . . He wished he could love his last born as much, but somehow he had closed off a part of him when his two eldest sons had died.

'Be quite a social time here, Sylvia, my lamb. You'll like that, and you know something – you'll be the prettiest woman they've seen in these parts for years. Always said you're the loveliest woman I ever set eyes on.'

She came out, refreshed and repainted, kissed his cheek lovingly. BB turned to leave the room. 'Well, I'll leave you to it, old gel, see you down in the arctic lounge.'

Harriet held her feet up to the fire. In the cracked, stone-flagged floor were little blue-flowered weeds, and she picked them one by one and threaded them through her toes, then held her foot up and laughed. She leaned on her elbow and looked at Edward, who was staring at the wall, a strange, expressionless look on his face.

'What are you thinking? You're miles away.'

He moved to her side and touched her hair, hair like gold, just like gold, just like his mother's, so long that it hung below her waist. He remembered brushing it by the old grate, how Evelyne had loved her hair to be brushed. 'You remind me of someone.'

Harriet smiled and leaned back against his shoulder, a natural and unprovocative move. The fire was low, there was no more wood in the chapel, and Edward noticed the rain had stopped. But he made no move to go. The quietness, the peace, was nice.

'Did you love her, this person I remind you of?'

He smiled down at her and nodded his head. He found himself talking freely, unashamedly, and for the first time without any pain inside him. 'I loved her, loved her very much.'

Harriet touched his face softly, looked into his dark-brown eyes. 'You've got all the girls running after you round here, haven't you? Is this a girl in Cambridge?'

He laughed and whispered to her that it was his mother, she had red hair too, long, long red hair.

Harriet snuggled into his shoulder, said that she was glad it wasn't some woman. Edward coiled a strand of her hair round his finger, rolled it and let it drop into a ringlet on her shoulder . . . She caught his hand, kissed it, and he kissed the top of her head, very, very gently . . . He shook himself back to sanity. 'We should go, Harry – come on, it's stopped raining.' Standing up, he lifted her to her feet. She was too close, his hands involuntarily tightened around her – he knew he should push her away, but he couldn't. She looked up into his face. There was a calmness in her, an adultness that took his breath away. Gently, she pulled his head down to hers and kissed his lips. The sweetness, the innocence of the kiss, her lips so soft –

no tongue searching, thrusting down his throat – it was a childish kiss, no hands swarmed over his body, or clutched at his trousers to feel him. She was simply there, so warm and so pure that it made him gasp. 'We'd better go, come on, get your boots on.'

She began to tie her hair back, and got into a mess so he had to do it for her. As he tied the ribbon, he lifted her thick hair and kissed the nape of her neck, then tapped her tight little bum and told her to get a move on . . . He walked out, hampered by his erection and knowing he had to get away from her before he ripped her skin-tight jodhpurs off.

At seven-thirty, Edward was freezing to death in the bathroom, in a cold bath. The dinner gong, obviously repaired, boomed out, and he hurried to his room to dress. Harriet hurtled into his bedroom in a dreadful pea-green dress. The hooks and eyes were undone at the back, she had only one shoe on and her hair was like a wild hedgerow. 'Will you do me up, Allard's not in his room? I hate this dress, it looks dreadful, doesn't it? Mother says I have to wear one for Uncle and Auntie.'

The dinner gong chimed again. Edward adjusted his immaculate, perfectly tied bow tie and, silently congratulating the late Clarence on his taste and style, hurried down the stairs.

Mrs Simpson was talking loudly to her husband as Edward entered the sitting room.

'A real stallion hound, darling, is frightfully rare nowadays.'

Sitting astride her chair as though it were a horse, Mrs Simpson gave Edward a cursory smile and kept talking. The Judge rose to his feet as his wife went on at great length about what, in her opinion, a good hound should look like. He poured a sherry and handed it to Edward.

'Straight, beautiful neck and shoulders, depth of girth, bone and feet. Must have that essential muscle, refinement of skin, back quarters like a horse. Frightfully important that it's quick of hearing. Get a deaf dawg . . .'

'Thought you were describing me for a minute there, Edna.'

BB and his wife, with their son trailing slightly behind, made a grand entrance, and were introduced to Edward. His wife, tiny and demure, fluttered in a chiffon dress that seemed to trail myriad floating panels like scarves. The room reeked of Chanel No. 5, and her shrill, nervous laugh mingled with the clinking of her many bracelets.

BB accepted a whisky from the Judge. He was a lot older than his wife, and wore an immaculate grey suit and stiff white collar, with a blue foulard tie in an old-fashioned dimple knot and a large diamond pin. His complexion was florid, his white hair, though balding, thick at the sides of his red cheeks, and his small round eyes were like flints. He shook Edward's hand in a grip like iron, and stood nearly as tall as Edward, his wide shoulders tapering to his once-slim waist showing that, although he was too heavy, he had at one time been a very fit, athletic man. He raised his glass high, including everyone in the room in a toast to the family.

His son paled beside him, although he had his father's colouring and was exceptionally handsome, the similarity ended there. Richard Van der Burge was slim and dandyish, and Edward reckoned him to be around the same age as himself, although far more sophisticated.

Richard laughed up at Harriet who loomed over him as he sat on the sofa, and observed that she was growing faster than he was. Then he got to his feet and gave her a kiss. She pushed him away and wiped her cheek, telling him he was a ponce. The butler nervously approached Mrs Simpson and whispered to her, asking if he should announce dinner. Edward took stock of the guests. They were, it was exceedingly obvious, 'money'.

Allard swept in, his cheeks flushed with the evening air and slightly out of breath. He apologized to everyone for his lateness and linked arms with his mother. They all drifted into the dining room.

The table was beautifully laid, and a rotund cook peered through a hatch that led into the kitchen. She was handing the dishes to a young local girl who had come in to help out, and to old Fred. Fred, obviously a 'man of all trades', was acting butler. Edward couldn't help but notice that he was even less adept at this than he was at driving. Edward was placed next to BB with Harriet opposite. While the others at the table discussed family outings and previous dinners together, Edward became fascinated with BB.

'I have not shaved myself in over twenty years. I was in New York, and I realized that it was non-productive and time-consuming. In the time it would take to shave, I could have been reading, say, a company report, and no doubt made a decision that could possibly bring in a million dollars, maybe more. So I detailed a unique tonsorial network between myself, my chauffeur and my barbers. The barbers were briefed to be standing by to attend to me instantly, and they got a good tip for being ready and waiting.' His shaggy eyebrows and piercing blue eyes roamed the table, demanding attention. He spoke in a strange, guttural manner, clipping the ends of his words. The family, obviously having heard most of his stories before, continued their chatter. Richard paid no attention to his father, but Harriet was avidly interested in her uncle and asked questions Edward was too shy to ask.

'Did you make millions, Uncle BB? In America? I thought you were in mining? You've got mines in America too, I suppose.'

BB roared with laughter while he picked at the dreadful dinner on the plate before him. Edward gathered that the Van der Burges were in gold- and diamond-mining in South Africa, and that BB must have made a fortune in the early twenties over there and opened up some kind of banking operation in America. He fascinated Edward as he patiently described the mysteries of the Stock Exchange to Harriet. 'You got different types of markets, Harriet, we give them names. First we got the "bull" market, that's the one in which the majority of share prices have been, and continue to be, rising. Then you got what we call the "split up" – that's when the value of a company's stock goes very high. Market dealings are made easier if the value of the stock is reduced, and the number of shares correspondingly increase as the "split up" happens, understand?' BB continued to talk, holding forth with gestures so expansive that his wife carefully removed his cut-glass wine and water tumblers from his reach. 'A man known as a "bear" is a person who believes prices will fall, and the "bull" is a man who expects them to rise.'

Both her elbows on the table, Harriet's eyes twinkled as she asked BB which of the two he considered himself.

'You tell me, Harriet, eh? Which one do you think I am, Harriet, lovey?'

BB gave the butler a small nod of his head to clear, and by that small movement placed himself as the head of the table — not that the Judge seemed to notice, he was too busy pouring himself another glass of wine. He was arguing with his wife about the vegetables, telling her they should be lightly boiled and not stewed to a pulp. Mrs Simpson haughtily repeated his suggestions through the hatch to the cook. At the same time Harriet spoke even louder to BB, 'Does that mean you are rich then? I mean, diamonds are worth a lot of money, Ma's got a diamond ring and that's worth thousands, isn't it Ma? Not as big as Auntie Sylvia's, though. Did you sell them in America? Is that what you did over there, Uncle?'

Harriet was reprimanded for asking impertinent questions, and it gave Edward the opportunity to talk to BB. Buster appeared at this moment, at least, they could smell him and he had to be removed. He was dragged unceremoniously out of the doors, and the Judge remarked that if the dog was fed the same stewed veg as he was, no wonder he farted.

BB quietly explained to Edward what they meant in the City by 'selling short'. He smiled and murmured that he was, if anything, a bear, and selling short was a favourite device of a bear. This was done if you believed that a stock was going down. A bear would sell, but the stock he sold was not necessarily his own – or not as yet, because he knew he was able to borrow it from a broker for a time, for a fee. 'Then, Edward, I deliver the borrowed shares to my buyer, collect the payment and wait for the price to fall. Once it goes down, I buy the same shares at a lower price – you with me? – and give them to the broker to replace the shares I initially purchased ... my profit is the difference between the price at which I sold the borrowed shares to the buyer and the price I paid to replace them. Now, you can get yourself in a right bad situation if the prices unexpectedly go up instead of down. In 1930, rules governing the short-selling system were imposed, aimed at the likes of me so that there could be no possibility of the system actually causing prices to fall.'

Bored by her uncle's conversation, Harriet concentrated on stuffing herself with trifle. Edward asked BB if the Wall Street Crash had affected him. The big man put his napkin down and turned to Edward, although he threw his voice to the whole table. He thumped the table, making the pudding spoons jump, and said he had got out in time. 'I wish I could say the same for many of my friends – good friends that were bled dry, men who had to face creditors and so gambled on the markets that had already crumbled beneath them.' He swept the dining table with a theatrical gesture, forcing everyone to listen as he described the fate of many of his colleagues in New York. Mrs Simpson raised her eyes heavenward, having heard this story, like everyone else, many times before.

'There were men appealing for time, many became foolish, taking risks they would never have attempted before the crash ... One close associate who shall remain nameless, but a true, dear friend of mine and my dear wife's, tried to recoup his losses, based on the old Roman maxim, *caveat emptor* – buyer beware!'

Richard Van der Burge looked at his mother and yawned, but his father held forth and fixed his son with such an icy stare that the boy pursed his lips and looked down at his plate instead. BB continued, 'In 1933 the Securities Act effectively made it mandatory in all stock dealings for the seller to beware. It was a tough new legislation, and I was lucky to get out without undue losses. Men were up to their necks in lawsuits, all resulting from disputed market dealings and loans. Bankruptcy is a terrible thing, and a friend of mine who fell foul of the hungry vultures wrote on a notepad over and over again, "My life is worthless, worthless, worthless, I am a failure." Then he shot himself in a New York cocktail bar. That man's life had been a veritable victory, rising from nowhere, nothing, to dominate the banking world for ten years.'

BB was finally silenced by Allard waving his spoon in the air and loftily asking if anyone knew what Beau Brummel's last words were?

'As they carried the dying Brummel from his impoverished room in Paris, he was heard to say, "I owe no one."'

When dinner was over, Mrs Simpson stood up, saying she, Sylvia and Harriet would take coffee in the library. Allard and Richard sprang up and both rushed to the doors, giggling. The Judge only lasted until he had drained his brandy glass, then departed to his bedroom, complaining of wind. Edward was thankful they had left him alone with BB, and began to question him in a roundabout, flattering way. BB was a sharp man. He smiled, poured himself a glass of port and held it to the light, murmuring that he hoped it would not be of the same poor quality as the rest of the meal. 'I am a self-made man, Edward lad, and I am proud of it, proud. I began in South Africa, I went over there with one hundred pounds in my pocket, and eight years later I was a multi-millionaire. Ever heard of the great Kimberley mine, son? Look at this, see, this was the first diamond I mined with my own hands, look at the colours, beautiful, isn't it?' He held his tie-pin up to the light, then placed it in Edward's hand. Edward held it and turned it over, then returned it to BB's big, open palm.

'The gold pin was made from my first gold nugget. I struck it rich, my boy; my quarry returned five thousand ounces of gold from thirteen tons of ore, my shares rose from one pound to one hundred and fifty. Those were the days, these hands raking the ground hour after hour, but my God, when you strike, there's no better feeling on this earth – better than sex, lemme tell you. No woman on earth can give you a climax like the one you get when you strike it rich. I've seen a gold nugget the size of that decanter, weighing in at twelve pounds – the Peacock nugget – Jesus God, my friend, I seen men weeping just looking . . . and I was there, right at the beginning. Gold, it can't clothe a man like wool, can't even arm them like iron, warm them like coal, feed them like corn, but – and pay close attention to this, lad – gold can buy all the others, and that's what it's all about.'

It was two hours later when Edward and BB joined the rest of the party, BB having consumed an entire decanter of port. His face was flushed and his small eyes glinted, and he strolled into the lounge with his arm around his new friend's shoulders. The others were playing charades, and BB shattered the relaxed, informal atmosphere as he strode into the centre of the room and declared that he wished his own son had the intellect of his new-found friend. 'There's a job waiting for this lad when he gets out of university, and you're all my witnesses. This lad is going places, I know, I can tell, which is more than I can say for everyone else gathered here. Finance is what rules the world, and I say there would be no war on right now – no bastard Germans herding Jews into the concentration camps – there wouldn't be a war if there had been no Wall Street Crash.'

Embarrassed by his father, as everyone else also appeared to be by now, Richard tried to hand him a cup of coffee, but BB stood in the centre of the room, legs apart. 'You young people don't understand finances. Take the Messerschmidt – now then, when the crash came, where was Willy Messerschmidt, tell me that? I'll tell you – in Germany, waiting to see if the Eastern Aircraft Corporation at Pawtucket, Rhode Island, had crashed, and when he discovered it was in trouble his hopes of building a secret air force to prepare Germany for another war were dashed, but had they? No! The bastard facing financial ruin was kept going by Hitler himself. It was Hitler who knew the man was a genius, and financed him, and, by Christ, look what havoc those planes are creating. There would be no war – no war – if the Wall Street Crash hadn't happened. It caused Germany's growing economic crisis to escalate, just as it improved Hitler's chance of gaining office. The Reich was tied to the American economy more closely and – not many people know this – massive loans from Wall Street helped finance the German reparation payments and the post-war reconstruction projects. That's how that man got into power, the Wall Street Crash should never have been allowed to happen . . .' BB swayed, still standing in the centre of the room.

Harriet, bored, curled up on the sofa with a copy of *Horse and Hound*. Allard kept taking sneaky looks at his watch, and twice he tried to exchange amused glances with Edward, but received no reaction, so he turned back to Richard. Unlike his father, Richard had no South African accent. He had been educated at Eton and was, so Edward had overheard, going into his father's business. They were at present negotiating with two renowned dealers in Hatton Garden.

As they prepared for bed that night, BB commented to his wife, 'Good chap, that young fella, Edward. Liked him – reminded me of myself at that age.'

The next evening Edward again spent most of dinner talking to BB. The man knew everything there was to know about mining, and Edward was so involved that he didn't look at Harriet once throughout the meal. She was hurt by his ignoring her and reverted to childish behaviour, squabbling with Allard and Richard. As usual, the Judge and his wife discussed hunting and the details of preparing the horses.

'How's the chap doing, Harriet? Can't have one of us letting the side down – have to go over and have a word with the master of the hunt as it is. What do you say, Harriet, he make it, you think?'

Edward heard Harriet say that he would be able to hold his

own, he could more than likely outride Richard already. Richard laughed, looked at Edward and said that he had tamed the wildcat, Harry was actually being nice to someone. Allard joined in the teasing, shouting across to Edward that Harriet was love-struck. She blushed, and threw a tantrum, hurling a bread roll so hard it bounced off the table and hit the Judge.

'That's enough, Harriet, now go to bed. Now! We've had enough of your antics. Out – I mean it – out!'

Harriet stormed out, slamming the door. They finished their dinner without further interruption. Later, Edward played draughts with BB, who would not stop until he had won three sets. He sat opposite Edward, chewing on his cigar, slamming his fist down on the board when Edward beat him.

'Right, my friend, one more set, and this time I'll get you on the hop.'

It was after twelve when the evening broke up and everyone drifted off to bed. The plumbing creaked from the extra usage. His teeth chattering, Edward went to his room and dived between the chilly sheets. He could still hear the distant murmur of voices, but eventually all was quiet. He was just dropping off to sleep when the bedroom door creaked open.

Harriet, her face tear-stained and glum, stood there in her thin cotton nightie. 'Why were you so nasty to me at dinner, you totally ignored me. What have I done?'

Edward sat up and told her to go back to her room immediately, she hadn't done anything, far from it.

'What do you mean? You didn't look at me once.' She crept to the bed and sat down, her bare feet blue with cold.

'Harry, you are fourteen years old, and it's not done to come to a fellow's bedroom at this time of night.' In a whisper as loud as most people's normal speaking voice, Harriet asked why?

'You know why, it's not on, what if anyone were to see you here? Now be a good girl and go back to bed.'

Stubbornly, she remained sitting, rubbing her chilled feet against each other.

'Harry, I'll see you in the morning as usual, now go back to bed.'

She slunk off the bed, pouting moodily, padded to the door and glared back at him. Then her eyes filled with tears and she turned to walk out.

'Harry, don't get upset with me, I didn't mean to ignore you, I give you my word, it's just that . . .'

She cocked her head to one side, her long hair tumbling around her shoulders. 'Just what?'

Edward held out his hand and she crept back to hold it tightly.

'Just nothing, I'll see you in the morning, goodnight.'

She flung herself in his arms and hugged him. He could smell Pears soap. Then she bounced off the bed again, happy, gave him a cheeky grin and banged out.

Edward closed his eyes. She was so noisy, he thought, she would wake the whole house. He listened, but all was silent. He knew he would have to tread very carefully with Harry, she was as frisky as a puppy. He pulled the bedclothes around him and could smell the Pears soap, feel her warm, lovely body. Christ almighty, he had a hard-on again, he knew he would have to get himself laid soon, the sooner the better.

One night, after his draughts session with Edward, BB appeared, puffing, on the top landing. 'Look, old fella, been going through my wardrobe. Put on a lot of weight, doubt if I'll make the hunt – gout, you know – but it's a pity to waste all this gear . . . Now then, you're a big chap, what do you think?' He held out an armful of hunting togs, jackets, boots, a polished black topper. Edward knew why he had come up, and he invited BB into the cold bedroom. BB had a look at all the books laid out on the desk, then sat down.

'See you're still hard at it, jolly good, interesting.'

Edward showed BB his work, and they discussed mining. BB rubbed his hands complaining of the cold, and disappeared briefly to return with two glasses and a bottle of brandy.

'I hear you've no family, son. That right?'

Edward told him it was, and that he was having difficulty making ends meet, but he was determined to finish his studies at Cambridge.

'Short of cash are you, lad? Well, we'll see to it that you make ends meet. In return, I want you out on the first seaplane to South Africa when you've finished at university. What do you say? It'll be the chance of a lifetime, and you'll have more than opportunity – you'll have me, and any introduction I can give you. It's wide open there for the likes of you, prepared to work hard for their chance.'

Fortified by the Judge's excellent brandy, BB found himself talking more like a father to Edward than his own son. 'I had two good boys, you know about them? They were like me, you know, eager to go into the business, good, hard-working lads, and I've always maintained that if you want to go into a business you start from the bottom, work your way up, whether you're the boss's son or not. If you don't know what the workers do, you don't understand them ... My father was a penniless immi-grant in the East End. He slaved to get me my stake, never saw me strike it rich, but I owe him a debt ... never forget your debts, son, that's another important lesson.'

Edward was taken aback when the big man suddenly sat on the bed and took out his silk handkerchief. 'They died along with twenty-five kaffirs. When they dug them up, the eldest boy had tried to save two of the workers, his body lying over theirs ... It took them five days to dig out the youngest lad.'

Edward poured another measure of brandy and handed it to the big man.

'I'm not a chap to show my emotions, got to keep up a front for the wife. Marry a strong woman, Eddie, one who'll stand by you through thick and thin, or never get yaself hitched. There's women the world over that'll give you any satisfaction you need below the belt – have that rather than tie yaself down ... not worth the heartache.'

The intimacy of their friendship in that huge, cold bedroom

was never shown to the rest of the family. BB would revert to his usual blustering self with the others, arguing with the Judge on politics, war, anything that took his fancy. The other side of this complex man was reserved for his private drinking sessions with his new pal Edward. But occasionally the big, robust man could not help but give an affectionate pat to Edward's shoulder, the fondness glowing in his flinty eyes. These familiar, almost loving, gestures did not go unnoticed by the rest of the household.

Allard couldn't resist making snide remarks to Richard. 'Watch out, old chap, that's a very ingratiating fella – even got Harriet eating out of his hands like one of her nags . . . Appears he's done the same with your father.'

Richard did take note, and had a quiet talk with his mother. She assured her son that his father was just being friendly. He missed his friends back in South Africa and appeared to have a lot in common with Edward.

'Just so long as it's not Pa's money, that's fine, keeps him out of my hair.'

The morning of the first meet was clear, and the whole household gathered in the hall. Mrs Simpson looked almost attractive in her black habit, black topper, lace veil and immaculate, gleaming boots. Allard, the Judge and Richard, all equally smart, checked their appearance in the hall mirror. They were joined by Edward, who felt uncomfortable in BB's riding kit, and even more by their scrutiny, concerned he might let the side down. Seeing him so well kitted out, however, they accepted him and the Judge even fixed Edward's cravat for him. He gave him so many instructions about what to do and say when he met the Master of the Hounds that Edward's head reeled. He began to understand why the Judge kept quiet about being only a clergyman's son, why they were so delighted with the invitation with the gold crest . . . they really were as much social climbers as himself, and it amused him because they were taking him right along with them. Their obsession with the correct procedures for the hunt arose from the fact that they were not original members of the local social set, and now they were about to move up a notch. As they walked out to the stables, Edward was feeling as buoyant as they so obviously did.

Harriet moved to Edward's side. She looked quite beautiful under the black lace veil, her red hair braided as if to match her horse's tail. 'Remember everything I've told you. Keep well to the back, don't try and be clever, just hold him in and don't let him take the lead. Control him – he'll want to join the leaders. Keep him reined in – he's very powerful, but you'd not be able to keep up with the Master, so let him know who's boss. As soon as you see riders breaking away, you can leave without disgrace ... If you fall, remount, ride on, don't let the hounds worry you.'

His head was teeming with instructions, and it didn't help that BB's hat was a trifle too tight.

Along the way the farm workers stopped in the fields and waved to them, and the Judge, leading the group, touched his crop to his topper. Long before they reached the village they could hear the hounds, and as they turned into the square the noise became ear-splitting. The loose hounds ran back and forth, baying excitedly, and the eight pairs held by the handler on long leads barked hysterically. Edward was surprised to see how many riders there were – on beautifully groomed mounts with braided manes and tails. The horses were frisky, some rearing and trotting sideways, others jerking their heads up and down. Above the noise of the hounds and the restless horses could be heard the high-pitched voices of the riders.

A large silver tray of punch was being offered around, and the public house, The Feathers, was overflowing with farm workers and valets. Six of the mounted men wore hunting pink, and three more stood on the cobbles, horns at the ready. Edward stayed on the edge of the circle, and nearly lost his topper when he leaned down to take a small silver cup of punch.

A palomino, its tail braided with black ribbons, began to sidestep as if dancing. His woman rider bent forward and patted his neck, and he kicked out again. She trotted on, wheeling him round to calm him. She sat side-saddle, wearing a long, black skirt, a black jacket tight at the waist and flared over the hips. Her cravat was white, and her flat topper was veiled with black, a long swirl of black net trailing behind her. 'Walk on, thatta boy, walk on, good boy.'

She was stunning, her arrogant head held high, her black leather-clad hands holding the matching crop, and Edward stared. Suddenly she turned the horse and trotted towards him. As she approached, he realized it was Lady Summercorn. She brought her horse to a stop and gave him a tiny smile. 'We've missed you. You promised to come over and see us. Perhaps later on today, unless you have a prior engagement?'

Edward touched his topper, flashed a smile. 'I would like that, thank you.'

The Master commanded the hunt to 'walk on', and the riders began leading their horses out of the village square. Edward stayed at the back of the pack, as instructed, and Lady Summercorn rode beside him. The pace was easy and slow as they manoeuvred their mounts through the narrow village lanes.

'There's a field off to the right, just before the main gallop. I doubt it will last longer than that. My chauffeur is waiting at The Feathers. Riders generally splinter off about that time, I'm sure no one will miss us.'

She stared directly ahead, and might have been talking to her mount. She heeled the horse forward until Edward was slightly behind her, then turned and gave him a secret smile.

The hunt was on, but Edward had already caught his fox. He didn't give a damn about the four-legged one.

Edward did not return to the Hall until after one o'clock in the morning. He had called the Simpsons and said he had taken a fall, and left his horse with Fred to lead to the stables.

Allard was sitting in his father's armchair, very drunk, and heard Edward arriving home. He staggered out into the hall. 'Well, you slut, Lady Summercorn's gels treat you all right?'

Edward shrugged. 'Rather boring, actually. Came a hell of a cropper. How did it go?'

'Go? Go . . .?' Irritated by his sarcastic tone, Edward turned on his heels, but Allard continued, 'Harry's in hot water, she took that fence by Hendley's brook.'

Edward turned back, concerned. 'Is she all right?'

'She is, the bloody horse isn't, though. All hell to pay – Pop's blown a fuse. Listen, you on for tomorrow? We're invited to the Gaskills', could be a good do.'

'Actually, no, I accepted an invitation to dinner.'

'Well, well, well. Got into the inner sanctum, have we? Lady Summercorn . . . well, well.'

Edward said nothing, gave nothing away. He was as exhausted as Allard, the only difference was that his horse had been of the two-legged variety. Her Ladyship had been very demanding. Edward slipped his hand into his pocket and felt the cigarette case she had given him. He wondered if he would get a lighter to match at dinner the following evening.

Harriet was in the stable, lying in the straw next to her horse. She had been poulticing his injured leg every half-hour since she returned from the hunt. The horse could not put his leg down, and old Fred and Harriet were taking turns to sit up with him through the night.

Edward woke with a start, sat bolt upright, then flopped back when he saw by his bedside clock that it was only four in the morning. He rubbed his head, he was freezing cold and got up to put a jumper on, then heard footsteps below in the court-yard.

Harriet was huddled by the stable wall, her shoulders shaking. Fred was standing a short distance from her. He tried to put a blanket around her shoulders and pointed towards the house, but she refused. Then Edward saw her march towards the kitchen.

Edward dragged on his trousers, threw on his coat and went

down to the kitchen. He made her jump, he entered so quietly. He saw she was loading a shotgun.

'What on earth are you doing?'

She told him curtly to mind his own business and walked out. He followed her across the yard and into the stable, then stopped when he heard Fred's voice. 'Let me do it, miss, I'll do it. You've no need to put yerself through this. Go back to the house now, there's a good lass.'

Her voice was not harsh or childish, it was quiet and firm. 'No, Fred, go on, leave me, make sure you shut the doors behind you – I don't want to wake the whole household ... I mean it, I want to be on my own. He's mine – it was my fault and I have to see it through, that's the way it should be. Please, Fred, I know what I'm doing.'

Edward slipped into the shadows and watched as Fred walked away, glum-faced. He stopped to say he would get the cart ordered for first thing in the morning, she wouldn't have to see him taken away. He'd not let her go through that.

The heavy door was dragged shut behind Fred, and Edward walked towards the stall. He couldn't see her, but he could see the hind quarters of her horse, lying wrapped in a blanket. He was shuddering and making strange panting noises. Harriet was sitting with his head resting in her lap, stroking his nose to comfort him. 'You'll be out of pain, boy, not long now, shhh, not long, no more pain, there's a good boy.'

About to speak, Edward was stunned into silence. He saw her carefully place a blanket over her beloved horse's head to deaden the sound of gunfire, stand up, aim the shotgun right at his head and pull the trigger. The horse jerked, kicked his legs out in a frantic spasm, then lay still.

She lowered the gun and slid down the side of the stall to end up squatting by the horse's head. She didn't remove the blanket, but expertly placed her hand on the pulse points.

'Harry ... you all right, sweetheart?'

She gave a sad, soft sigh, nodded her head, got to her feet and said she hoped the shot hadn't woken anyone. 'He was in agony,

I couldn't stand to see him go through more. We did what we could, but his leg was broken, and it was all my fault. I shouldn't have taken the jump.'

Edward was astonished at her strength, her calmness. He took his coat and wrapped it around her shoulders. They walked slowly back to the house and she told him they would come for the carcass in the morning.

She stared up at the stars and told him she wouldn't go back into the house – she was going for a walk. He watched the straight-backed little figure in his big overcoat striding across the fields. It was hard to believe she was only a child, she constantly threw him off-balance, the child-woman. He didn't follow because he wouldn't have been able to trust himself; at least he had some decent qualities. The further away from her the better. He decided he would pull some strings to join Lady Summercorn's house party as quickly as he could.

Alex Stubbs was transferred to Durham Jail, known for its hardened criminal inmates. He was over eighteen years old now, and eligible for an adult prison. With his record of violence, he was placed in a top security wing, with two men to a cell. Stubbs, Prisoner 49861, wearing his grey uniform and carrying his few belongings, was led along the corridors to a cell at the end of E Block. The wardens opened the door and Alex walked in. The door closed behind him. There were two bunks, one already occupied. He put his things down.

'You a friggin' fairy, Stubbs?'

'No.'

'Get this clear from day one, Stubbs, I don't wanna know anythin' about you, I don't want you yakkin' on about your family, your kids, your fuckin' wife, nothin' . . . I don't wanna know you, I don't want you askin' me any questions about my life. I'm in here for eight years, armed robbery, I got three to go an' I intend gettin' out without any aggro. That clear? You stay on one side of the cell an' I'm on the other. I don't drink, I don't smoke, an' I don't want any fuckin' trouble from the barons. You start anything, anything, an' I'll tie your balls so tight you'll wish you never met me.'

George Windsor glared at Alex. He looked almost scalped, his crew-cut red hair was so short. His thick neck sloped down to massive, muscular shoulders. Windsor was about five foot eight but built like a bull, even his hands were broad and stubby.

Alex turned and looked at him, and for a second Windsor was nonplussed. The lad was younger than he had at first thought, and he was a hell of a size. His blue eyes glared fearlessly, and he moved to Windsor's bunk, rested his hands on the side. 'I don't wanna know you either – know anyfing about you. I'm just gonna serve me sentence, I don't even want to talk to you. I want out as badly as you do. I don't smoke and I don't drink, I work out, an' you screw anyfing up fer me and it'll be your balls wrapped around your neck.'

Windsor shook Alex's hand and lay back on his bunk. He watched out of the corner of his eye as his new cell-mate carefully placed four books on his small corner table. No photographs, no knick-knacks, nothing.

On Windsor's table was a neat stack of comic books and nothing else. Around them could be heard the catcalls and ribaldry of the other prisoners, but the two remained silent. Cell doors clanged, and there was the all-pervasive stench of urine. Alex lay back on his bunk and closed his eyes. The years ahead loomed like a nightmare. He knew he would have been out, a free man, but for his foolishness. He tossed and turned, angry with himself, angry at little Eric. Desperate for sleep to envelop him, he counted the years, and memories of Edward reared up. This was his fault, Edward was to blame for everything. He'd put Alex in prison to begin with, it was all his brother's fault.

Alex tried to picture Edward's face, but that too had become blurred by time. At last he fell into a fitful sleep, calmed by his assurances to himself that when he did get out, he would find Edward and make him pay for what he had done. 'I'll kill him . . . I'll kill him.'

Windsor looked up. The lad was talking in his sleep. That was all he needed – a friggin' nutter in with him. Well, if he was, he'd straighten him out fast enough. He stared at the sleeping figure. The boy's face was a mess, and it looked as though he had a cracked cheek that should have been attended to. There were fading yellow bruises all over his face and shoulders. Windsor lay back, thinking that whoever this kid wanted to kill had better watch out – he, for one, wouldn't like to bump into him on a dark night.

Chapter Eight

Edward left Haverley Hall to spend the rest of his vacation with Lady Summercorn and her guests. The Simpsons felt rebuffed, especially as they encountered him on a number of social occasions. He was very much in demand, for reasons they were totally unaware of. Edward was being passed around as the 'stud' of the season, screwing anyone who would pay him for it. Lady Summercorn was desperate to keep him, so she upped the ante until Edward was 'bought' for her sole use. He loathed and detested the lot of them, with their high-pitched voices and artificial manners. They all wanted the same thing – his body in bed.

Edward had not even said goodbye to Harriet; he just packed his bags and departed in Lady Summercorn's Rolls-Royce. The only person he paid careful attention to was BB. He wanted to take up the offer of work in South Africa, so he made sure the old boy knew exactly what he was up to.

'As you said, sir, work your way up from the bottom . . . all depends which bottom. But right now, I need cash, so I'm on the move.'

BB roared with laughter and pulled Edward towards him. 'You mean she's keeping you? Good for you, lad, that's the ticket. Make 'em pay for it, strapping young fella like you. Here, this is a little something for when you get back to college.' BB tucked a fiver into Edward's pocket. Edward had expected more, but thanked him. He knew BB would be discreet, and he was pleased that he was leaving the Simpsons with his blessing.

'Good lad! If I were younger I'd come with you ... Go on, give her one from me ...'

Only once did Edward feel any remorse. He went to a cocktail party where, to his surprise, he saw Harriet. She was sitting alone, looking awkward and out of place in a dreadful yellow dress, a bored expression on her face. He slipped to her side and stood looking down at her thick mop of hair.

'Mind if I join you?'

Harriet's grim expression quickly changed to a glowing smile when she saw who it was. Then she kicked him in the shins. 'You are a rotter, leaving without a word. I've been going to these awful bashes just in the hope of seeing you, to give you a black eye.'

Edward sat down, laughing, took her hand and kissed the palm.

'Oh, stop that, you're as bad as all these wets. You stink, you know, you missed my birthday. I hate you.'

'No you don't, Harry, not really.' He was teasing, but he saw a hurt expression cross her face. He kept holding her hand. 'Tell me, where in God's name did you get that frock?'

'This "frock", as you so quaintly put it, happens to be a Balmain number my mother insisted I wear and which Auntie Sylvia bought in the year dot ... Makes me look as if I've got jaundice, doesn't it?'

He had to laugh, she was so outrageous, and she elbowed him, leaning closer. 'Are you screwing any of these old bags? Allard said you were. Are you?'

'Where did you learn to speak like that? You should be ashamed of yourself, a nicely brought-up young lady ... What else did Allard tell you?'

Harriet shrugged and muttered that he was probably jealous. She giggled and nudged Edward in the ribs again.

Edward saw Lady Summercorn raise an eyebrow at him. It annoyed him, but he rose to his feet. She might pay for his services, but that didn't give her the right to order him around like a skivvy.

'What's the matter?' asked Harriet.

He looked down at her and shook his head. 'Nothing, it's nothing ... I'd better circulate. Maybe I'll pop over and say goodbye before I go back to college.'

Harriet glanced up at him, then turned away. 'I still ride every morning, go to my chapel. Maybe you could walk over one day – it's not far from ...'

Edward was whisked away to be introduced to a plump woman, a very close friend of Her Ladyship's. When he turned back the sofa was empty, Harriet had gone. It depressed him, just as much as the possessive hand clutching at his arm. The fat, jowled face smirked up at him. 'I've heard so much about you ... I'm having a few friends over for a small dinner next week ...'

The red-painted mouth dropped open as Edward spun on his heel and walked out. He searched half-heartedly for Harriet, then walked out into the snow and sat on a bench in the garden. He took out his gold cigarette case, tapped a cigarette on the lid and lit it with a gold lighter. He turned the lighter over in his hand.

Later that night, Lady Summercorn came into his bedroom. She fiddled with her bracelet, muttering that the catch had broken, then tossed it on to the dressing table. 'My husband's coming home on leave. Perhaps it would be best if you left a few days earlier than we'd arranged. It's been fun, but it's over. Maybe I'll contact you at Cambridge ... Would you mind if a few of my girlfriends make your acquaintance?'

Edward picked up her bracelet and fingered the small gold links. 'I don't think that will be necessary – I have their numbers, in more ways than one. I'll leave tonight.'

*

Edward left Lady Summercorn's estate before the household was awake. He decided to walk to the station and take the train back to London, perhaps pay a visit to Dora before returning to college. The station was closed, and Edward hesitated a moment until a guard wandered down the lane towards him. When Edward asked the time of the next London train, he shrugged and said he hoped there would be one around ten, but there were always delays. He took Edward's bags inside and promised to look after them, and Edward walked off. He knew it was madness to go, but he needed company, needed something clean and honest.

'Hello.'

He rested his arm along the back of the old pew in the chapel and saw her standing in the doorway, her cheeks like rosy apples and her hair wild. She sat beside him.

'You have a nice Christmas?' he asked.

'Yes ... it would have been nicer if you had been with us. The tree went up in flames, the fairy lights short-circuited, or something. The Judge was livid because Allard said he had put the wrong fuse in the socket ... Anyway, made Christmas finish with a bang.'

'Did you get some nice presents?' Edward asked.

'Oh, yeth, I got a dolly ...' she lisped. 'Why are you talking to me as if I were ten years old? If you want to know, I got some new stirrups and a silver-topped riding crop from BB. What did you get? Not that I'm interested, I didn't get anything for you.'

Edward replied, 'Ah, but I've got something for you — it's a belated Christmas-cum-birthday present.' He took out the broken bracelet and held it up. Harriet looked at it as he held it aloft, dangling it in front of her. She held out her wrist and he bent his head to fasten the chain around it, although he knew the clasp was broken. He suddenly felt guilty and caught the bracelet in his hand, put it in his pocket. 'That was a lie, you don't want it, it's cheap and nasty.'

He expected her to delve in his pocket and ask what he

meant, but instead she said softly, 'I would still like to have it, may I?'

Edward hesitated, then handed it to her. She gave him a sweet smile as she tucked it into the pocket of her jodhpurs. 'Thank you.' She held up her new crop. 'Here, take this, I want you to have it.' As he shook his head she said, 'Please take it, I've got another one and this is real silver.'

He stroked her thick, curly hair for a moment, then said, 'If it's real silver, then you keep it.'

She turned her cheek and his hand brushed her soft, fresh skin. She kissed his fingers and he pulled his hand back sharply. He got up and kicked at the pew saying he shouldn't be there, he should be at the station. He wondered what he was doing in the middle of nowhere, in a broken-down chapel with a child.

'Harry, get on your goddamned horse and get out of here. Go on, be a good girl, just get the hell out of here. You drive me crazy, you know that? Oh, Christ, come here, come here, Harry.'

She went into his arms and he held her, held her tight, so tight she felt the breath squeezing out of her lungs and it was the sweetest feeling she had ever known in her life. He spoke into her hair, his face buried in the red-gold curls that still smelled of Sylvia's Chanel No. 5. 'I'm not much good, Harry. There's a lot of reasons and I can't tell you but . . . I have to succeed, I have to make it, and I'll use anything, anyone, to get wherever it is I am trying to go . . . You are no use to me, in fact you're a menace, because you make me feel, you touch some chord right down inside me . . .'

She felt he was smothering her, but she didn't move, she couldn't, he was holding her so tightly, but he didn't frighten her. She looked up at last into his handsome face. 'I belong to you, I do, I know it.'

He held her at arm's length and said in a harsh voice that she belonged to no one but herself, least of all to him. He flicked up the collar of his black cashmere coat and smiled, but his eyes were holding on to her – dark, black eyes. 'Maybe one day, when I've made it, I'll come back for you, just don't lose your-self, Harry, don't grow into a woman.'

She spoke so softly, looking down at her old riding boot, 'Everyone has to grow up, Edward.'

He turned away, faced the wall. 'I have a brother, you know, younger than me ...'

'What about him?'

'Well, I have to succeed for both of us, you see. I owe him ... I owe him.'

She could barely hear him, and moved a little closer. His fists were clenched as he fought his emotion and she saw his face twist with anger. 'Why am I telling you this, why?' Neither spoke for long moments until he whispered, 'I owe him his free-dom.' The word 'freedom' hammered inside his head and he struck out at the wall, his back to her. His voice was hoarse with emotion. 'That was my father's name – Freedom – he was a Romany gypsy, a gyppo ... You see what I mean, you don't know me.'

'I think it's a beautiful name ... Freedom.'

Hearing her say it with such gentleness calmed him, but he still wouldn't turn and face her.

'He always loved my brother best. He bought him a dog once, I remember. I wanted a dog so badly, but I pretended not to like it. One night, one night, Harry, we had this argument ... You wouldn't understand, you couldn't, I'm a liar and a cheat, I'm cheap ... I come from the slums, Harry, real poor, you know? But I won this scholarship and ... and ...'

She remained standing, not moving closer, just standing there. He could feel her behind him. He pressed his head against the brick wall and the tears streamed down his face.

He turned to her, lifting his hands in a helpless gesture. Her huge eyes looked deep into his. She was so different from all the women he had known – it was a direct gaze, innocent, and she wasn't frightened by what he had told her. It was a terrible puzzle to her – his disconnected words showed his anguish and torment. She didn't even lift her arms when he cupped her face in his hands. He kissed her gently, chastely, on her wonderful mouth, so soft and warm. A loving kiss. She loved him and he knew that he loved her. He held her face until his fingers marked her cheeks.

But Harriet was a child.

He turned on his heel and walked out. She stood staring after him. It was the most decent thing he had ever done in his life.

Dora had been in tears all day. Johnny Mask had been picked up for black marketeering. Not only that – when he was arrested they discovered that he had also skipped conscription. He chose to go into the army rather than jail, and so arrived at his taste-less apartment with his head shorn and wearing a corporal's uniform.

He was philosophical about it all, reckoning that the war wouldn't last all that long, and by the time they'd got him trained he would be back at the club. Dora wept buckets, she could see him opening fire on rows of Germans and being shot to pieces.

'Darlin', listen to me, I'll be confined to bleedin' barracks for three months before they can even ship me over. What you howlin' for? I keep on tellin' you I'll be all right, for Chrissake . . . Dora, will you shut it!'

She gulped and mopped her tear-stained face. With Johnny gone, who was going to run the club? Who was going to look after her? She started up again, her face puckering, and he threw his arms up and threatened to slap her around, he had work to do and she was part of it.

'They got me on a load of gin, but I got a warehouse full of stuff scheduled to come in tomorrow night. Now I can't trust any of those sons of bitches I got workin' for me, so I need someone on the inside.'

Dora started to think, her little brain teetered around and she tossed a few names to Johnny, who shook his head.

'Yer not wiv me, are yer, you stupid cow? Look, you know the club racket – you should do, you've been runnin' it wiv me long enough, even get the girls in for me, so . . .'

Dora suddenly felt the tears departing. Sharp as a tack, she picked up on what he was saying. She wasn't going to be ditched, far from it.

'I'll be able to get out on weekend leave, right? All you gotta do is run the place until I'm fancy free again. I can even start a racket going down the barracks so I'll need you even more on the outside, workin' for me.'

Dora gaped, then threw her arms around his neck, kissing him, and he had to shove her away. 'We got no time for that stuff. First I'll take you over the accounts, the orders, who you got to bung a few quid to on the side so we don't get any aggro from the law ... Dora! Siddown and fuckin' pay attention! Gawd almighty ... I must be outta me head.'

Dora sat, attentive, and Johnny opened the safe, taking out papers, and to her stunned amazement, rolls and rolls of banknotes.

'An' another fing, Dora, you handle this right an' I might even make an honest woman of you, when I'm out, like ... Don't start howlin' again!'

She was over the moon, he was going to marry her – she asked if he really meant it? He relented and sat her on his knee, saying she'd never let him down, all the years they'd been together she'd never let him down and he appreciated it. Of course he meant what he said – when he got out of the army he would marry her. 'Here we go! It's not real, it's what they call a zircon, but no one would know it's not the real fing. You like it? I got it off Harry the Jew over in Paddington, does it fit?'

The ring, three sizes too big, sparkled as Dora held out her hand. She was so happy she danced around the bed. 'Johnny, I love it, I just love it, and it's perfect ... Hey, I'm engaged, I'm engaged!'

He tossed his head and grinned. He liked the way she was so tickled, but he was also making sure she would tell everyone she was his 'intended'. There were reasons behind it – he reckoned that if the lads knew this woman who was running the place was not just a tart they might leave her alone.

Dora sat at the reproduction antique desk and began sorting

through the papers – who had to be paid off, who to order the booze from, who to welcome into the club and who to warn off. He had two good men for the door and the bar, and an 'inside man', who would be the one she would signal to if a customer was giving trouble.

'Fing is, Dora, we gotta keep up the nice class of our customers. We can clean up, officers, you know – elbow the likes of me, we don't want the riff-raff in, keep it classy. That goes for the girls too, an' make sure they're clean, any with a dose get 'em out quick.'

He went to great lengths to show Dora the bookkeeping. One set for the government, one set for Mr Mask. She was to bank only the takings from book one, everything else went into the safe. They didn't want to be copped for taxes and busted, they had to keep it legal and straight.

Dora ended up with so many instructions and lists of arrangements that had to be made over the next month that her head reeled.

'Another fing, gel – now we're an official couple you don't lay the customers. It don't look right, you're the boss, an' you gotta act like one, so you get respect, understand me? So you stick to ginger ale. I hear one word you get yourself legless and I'll be out an' you'll be for it.'

They spent the night together, Johnny so eager to get Dora clued up that he was unable to get a hard-on. She giggled and said it didn't matter, they would have lots of time for that when they were married.

'Johnny, we gonna have kids like normal people?'

He flopped back, still desperate for an erection, and gave up.

'Gawd 'elp us, we only got engaged an' you're arranging the bleedin' nursery . . . Go an' get the baby oil, will you, and shut up?'

Johnny left the following morning, handing out instructions as he went. He had to come back as he had forgotten to kiss Dora goodbye. She started getting tearful and he gave her one of his looks that was usually followed by a slap. She forced a brave smile.

'Thatta girl, I'm dependin' on yer, so don't fuck it up, all right, darlin'?'

She had only a few moments of doubt and sadness at Johnny's departure. Returning to the satin-covered bed, the open safe, she suddenly perked up and flopped back on to the bed, laughing.

'It's all mine! Bloody hell, Dora Harris, you're rich.'

The train from Yorkshire ground to a halt yet again, and Edward swore, went to the window and lowered the sash. 'What's the problem? What's the delay?'

A guard, running down the track swinging his lantern, shouted something inaudible and kept on running. All the lights on the train went out, the signals, the station two miles up the track blacked out . . . The train remained stationary for about half an hour and was then shunted into a siding. The passengers heard the drone of planes overhead, but no bombs . . . the planes passed over and were gone. Looking up, they asked each other if they were 'ours' or 'theirs'.

Miles away they saw the sky light up like bright red and yellow fireworks and they knew they were German planes. The train began a slow backward shunt and halted again. Crowds of soldiers began to board and filled the front carriages.

'Got a light, mate?' The soldier looked no older than Edward. He clocked the gold cigarette lighter and lit up a thin, hand-rolled cigarette. 'Thanks . . . thanks, mate.'

The boy and four more soldiers were told by their commanding officer to get back up front. Their vacated seats were taken by officers who sat back, eyes closed. Edward put his glasses on and buried his head deeper in his jacket collar. It was the first time he had felt any form of guilt.

The young officers were all very well-spoken, their upper-crust voices loud. He listened to the conversation as one officer stared out of the window.

'Rocket, I'd say.'

The other officer shook his head, said that the rocket sites were in Holland, too far away.

'That was a rocket, I've seen them before.'

'Wait, we'll soon know if it was a rocket or not, only takes a few seconds . . .'

They were all silent, then suddenly they heard it, a huge explosion. They sat back again in their seats.

'Told you it was a rocket, saw the flash.'

'Our chaps are overrunning them now, don't see many more coming. The Allied Forces are wiping them out, thank God.'

'I knew it was a rocket, I knew it was one of those V2s. One landed near our chaps, centre of the road, smack on a junction . . . It was not long before ten-thirty and one pub had run out of beer so all the customers were moving on to a bar in McKenzie Road. Bloody place was jam-packed when the bloody thing came down. The bar-room floor collapsed, the poor fellahs were dropping through into the cellah, whole building came down around them . . . Foggy night, too, and a bloody one, we had to tunnel under the debris, poor bastards screaming . . . But every time we removed a part of the building the rest just crumbled on to those below. I still hear them, you know, still hear them screaming.'

The train began to move and Edward lurched in his seat, heard the soldiers in the front carriages give a cheer. The officers, all bomb-disposal experts, relaxed in their seats and slept for the rest of the journey. They were exhausted, their mouths open and snoring as the train made its slow, unsteady journey to Paddington Station. In the station buffet they heard a newscast of the latest report.

'The Fourteenth Army is advancing through Burma, the Japanese in full retreat.'

The soldiers in the buffet let rip with a cheer, and stretched over the counter for mugs of tea and stale bread rolls. The newscaster ended his report with a rousing, 'Let's hope the longed-for end to these long years of war will soon be here.'

The soldiers raised their mugs of tea and cheered, and their officers barked orders for them to get themselves to platform three, they were on the move again.

Edward sipped his tea, watching the boys barging out of the doors towards the platforms. The woman behind the counter looked over the glass case. 'Bastards hit the East End again last week, it wiped out my husband's allotment, all his onions gone, not one left. Pulverized the whole onion bed and yer could smell it fer miles around. See, they was cookin' in the fire, I dunno ... Oh Gawd, 'ere they come, the Yanks are back.'

The buffet filled with American soldiers joking loudly with one another, and Edward walked out to wolf whistles and lewd remarks. He picked up a taxi, it was past eleven.

'I can only take yer as far as Hyde Park Corner, guv, they got the road up round Marble Arch, crater in the road size of this station.'

They rattled through the blacked-out streets. The cab driver was an authority on German warfare, Hitler's strategy. 'I'm tellin' ya, mate, he made a mistake. See, he was so close – Jersey, you know – they was that close, yes, fella in the cab yesterday hadda get out. See, if you don't have actual documents sayin' you was born in Jersey then you hadda get off the island, he'd left everything he'd worked for. But they occupied the bastard, an' I'll tell you somethin' else, the Americans, if they hadn't hit Pearl Harbor they wouldn't have backed us up ... Now then, with them behind us we'll wipe those German buggers off the face of the earth ... I've nothin' against 'em, the Yanks, they may be shaftin' all our girls, but my daughter's got herself a lovely fella, he's brought us the best corned beef I've ever tasted in me life, tins of the stuff. Works in the canteen, see ...'

Edward was glad when the cab pulled over. He refused the offer of certain items that could be got for a good price, and of introductions to some good clubs, and by the time he'd paid the cab off he would have liked to throttle the driver.

Dora had spent a lot of Johnny's money on clothes, but she told herself that that was what she should be doing, she had to look the part. She had a new platinum rinse, silvery-blonde, almost white, and her face had been made up in the beauty department at Harrods. Her eyebrows were plucked, and she wore the new, deep-red lipstick. Her hair was scooped into a roll on each side of her face, the back curled into a pageboy. The clustered pearl earrings and matching hair slides made her look very sophisticated in the little black dress with the padded shoulders. It was nipped in at the waist and tight over her little bum. She had put some sticking plaster around Johnny's ring so it didn't swivel around her finger, and she flashed the ring and her long, red nails. She was smoking Lucky Strikes from a gold cigarette case, and couldn't keep her eyes off herself. She kept catching glimpses of herself in mirrors around the club and liked what she saw so much that she constantly tilted her head and touched her hair.

The club was full, and the girls were working hard at entertaining. Edward sat at the far corner table, watching Dora swanning around the club. She hadn't seen him yet, and she disappeared through a small door marked 'Private'.

'You on your ownsome, darling? Would you like company? We can offer some lovely champagne, and there's small snacks if you're feeling peckish. You feeling peckish, lovey?'

He smiled at the pouting young girl and shook his head. He asked for a whisky and soda and said he was waiting for Dora.

'Oh, Miss Harris. She know you're here, does she?' She stepped back, dropping the big come-on act as he looked at her.

'I'll wait for her, thank you.'

'There's a geezer sittin' on his own, Miss Harris, says he's waitin' for you.'

Dora pursed her lips and picked up her small black handbag, took out a compact and flicked it open. 'Phyllis, you do not call customers "geezers". How many more times do I have to tell you that? Who is he and what's his name? You ask what he wants and then you come to me an' you say, "Miss Harris, there's someone who wants to speak to you." That clear, lovey? Now, which table is he at?'

Dora moved aside the small flap covering the peephole in the door and Phyllis peered over her shoulder, said he was the customer sitting at the back table in the alcove. Dora let the cover slip back into place and smiled to herself. 'Bring the gentleman into my office, would you, and bring us a bottle of Dom Perignon, one of the real ones.'

'Well, Eddie, this is a surprise. Sit down – thank you Phyllis, that'll be all for now.' Phyllis left the champagne in its ice-bucket and slipped out.

'You want a drink, Eddie? It's good stuff, none of the muck we serve out there ... You look well, nice suit, how do you think I look?'

He gave her a nod of approval, refused the drink, and noticed she didn't touch it herself. She sipped from a long, thin glass of iced water, and crossed her perfect legs.

'How's your mother?'

Dora waved her hand vaguely, said her mother had snuffed it months ago, couldn't even remember how long. 'Pity, really, I'd like her to see me doing so well. I manage the place, you know? Well, more'n manage it – I run it, see. Johnny got enlisted, terrible shame. They picked him up for black marketeerin' and then found out he was a draft-dodger. I worry about him because he's in the bunkers and he suffers from claus ... er, claus ...'

Edward finished the word off for her, '. . . trophobia'. Dora nodded. 'Yeah, it's some kind of phobia, he don't like enclosed places, ever since he was in the nick one time ... Well, tell me about you.'

When she saw the gold cigarette case, the gold lighter, she gave him a quick once-over. He let the smoke drift out of his nostrils ... He was still the best-looking man she had ever set eyes on. Trouble was, he knew it, he had that manner about him. 'Very sure of yourself, aren't you, Eddie?'

He laughed and suddenly he looked younger, and said he could say the same for her. He stood up, crossed over to her and held out his hand. 'Let's cut the crap and go to bed, I'm tired and I need a place for the night.'

She wanted to say no, wanted to say she wasn't his for the taking, not any more, wanted to say she was engaged to be married, but she simply nodded her head. 'Go out an' get a cab to Johnny's place, it's same as last time – only difference is, it's mine . . . I can't be seen leaving with you, not now I'm runnin' the place. Doesn't look good. I'll be with you in a few minutes, just sort out a few things. Here's the keys, let yourself in.'

He caught the keys and walked out, closing the door behind him. Dora remained sitting for a few moments before she buzzed for Arnie Belling.

At first Arnie had not liked taking his orders from Dora, but Johnny had given him a twofold assignment. He was to act as bouncer inside the club, and he was to look out for her. He was paid extra for the latter. Only after Arnie had seen her spot a barman fiddling the till and observed the way she handled him did he begin to respect her. She had asked him simply to stand close, close enough so the barman would be aware of his presence. Then she had smiled sweetly, sat the man down and offered him a drink. The barman had relaxed, drinking, saying they were doing good business and that Johnny would be proud of her.

'Yeah, he would be proud of me, but he'd have your balls, love. Now then, don't make excuses, don't even try because it would embarrass me, and it would annoy Arnie. See, your fiddle's been copped. It's two in the till for the club and one in the pocket for you . . . Don't interrupt, let me finish. Now then, you're a good man behind the bar, and you got a good line with the customers. We are making a good profit so why don't we say two and a quarter in the till, a quarter in yours, the rest to Arnie? That way the pair of you can watch out for each other.'

Arnie watched the guy hesitate, then realize he was on to a

good thing. So it was a deal and, because he was getting a share of the profits, a straight share, he worked even harder.

'Lock up for me will you, Arnie? I got ever such a headache.'

Arnie helped her on with her mink and said he'd have a taxi outside in a minute. Dora checked her appearance once more in the wall of mirrors, made sure her seams were straight, touched her hair in the familiar gesture and swanned out.

Edward looked around the place, impressed. New wallpaper, new curtains – not exactly elegant, but certainly a vast improvement.

'I'm very impressed, place looks quite nice. You've been busy.' He helped her off with her coat, noted the label, and tossed the mink to one side.

Dora walked straight through to the bedroom and began to take off her stockings, kicking her shoes across the room. 'I got a maid comes in every day to keep the place tidy. I'm obsessed with everything being tidy. I got a place for everythin', probably because all my life I hadda . . . had to share everythin' with me sisters an' brothers, not even me own bedroom. Now this is all mine, at least until the war's over, anyway . . .' She was trying to sound posh, trying very hard not to drop her aitches, and Edward was amused. She reminded him of himself not so long ago. He began to undress.

'What you laughing at?'

He stripped off his shirt and tossed it on to the small, pale pink velvet chair, then pulled off his trousers and, stark-naked, walked over to an ashtray to finish off his cigarette. He blew out the smoke and then ground the cigarette into the pristine cut-glass ashtray.

'I'm doin' well, Eddie, really well. I'm stashing it away and I'm enjoying myself – life's good, really good.'

He flipped back the clean silk sheets and got into bed while she slowly removed her underwear. He watched her as she wriggled sexily out of the black lace brassière, then her panties giving them a small twirl. 'Figure's good, ain't it? Not bad for my age?'

Perfect legs, tight belly and big tits – she was lucky, they were well rounded so didn't sag or droop. He watched her cream her face, sitting naked at the neat dressing table, first the cream, then the dabs of astringent, and each piece of cotton wool she used went into the small pink velvet waste bin. She checked her eyes in the mirror, the little lines, then took the stopper from a perfume bottle and dabbed her neck, elbows, behind the knees . . . admiring herself all the time. Then, ready, she turned with a smile.

Edward lay with his eyes closed, and she stood up, hands on her hips. 'Bloody hell . . .' Flipping off the lights she climbed in beside him, and he grabbed her, laughing. He wasn't asleep – far from it – and he mounted her before she'd even pulled the sheet over her . . .

Dora drew her pink silk dressing gown closer around her and carried the coffee into the bedroom. 'You'll have ter get a move on, she'll be 'ere – here any minute an' I don't want her finding you. You know the way maids talk.'

She stood at the bathroom door, watching him as he rifled through Johnny's shaving gear and lathered his face. 'You know, you really are the best. I'm not just saying it, I really mean it, an artist. You could make it your profession.'

She surveyed his body, sipped the thick black coffee and reminded herself not to use too many beans in the American coffee machine, a gift from one of her customers. 'When will you come again, Eddie? Eddie . . .?'

He splashed cold water on his face, walked past her into the bedroom and began to dress.

'Eddie, you hear me, when are you coming back? You don't really give a tinker's cuss about me, do you? You know, I thought you did, last night? What did you need, a room for the night? Eddie, you deaf? Why don't you answer me?'

Slipping into his fresh shirt he started doing up the small pearl buttons. 'Because I don't like to be called "Eddieeee . . . Eddieee."'

'Oh, all right, then, Stud, is that a better name?' Furious with him, she opened her handbag and took out two folded tenners, chucked them on to the bed. 'You got a posh voice, Eddie, you got all the right gear. You got the lighter an' cigarette case, but that don't make you any different from me. You're goin' through one school, an' I'm goin' through another, but we're the same.'

He was putting his coat on, going to walk out on her. She blazed. Nobody walked out on her, she was somebody now. She certainly wasn't going to take it from a kid from her own back-street slum. She hurled a pot of cream at his head, but she missed and it spattered over her new wallpaper.

Dressed to perfection, his coat on, Edward snapped his overnight case shut. Then he gave her his smile, and she wanted to cry. 'Damn you, Eddie Stubbs, damn you.'

Picking up a handkerchief from the dressing table she blew her nose.

'I earn good money, Eddie, and with Johnny away you could stay here, stay with me. I know how to handle the punters, I could really make it . . . You like me, don't you?'

He looked around her bedroom, picked up his case.

'This isn't for me, sweetheart, and nor are you . . . Thanks anyway.'

She followed him through into the small hallway with the pink rose-patterned carpet. 'Will I see you again, then?'

He opened the door, gave her a wink and said, 'Sure,' then he was gone. When she went back into the bedroom she noticed that he had taken her twenty quid, and then she saw the cream dripping down the new wallpaper. 'Me wallpaper, look at me bloody wallpaper.'

Evelyne Stubbs' solicitors were taken aback when the smart young man presented himself as her son. He apologized, and said he had intended calling to see them months ago, but due to his studies he had never been able to get to London on weekdays.

They reviewed Evelyne's will in detail. Edward had hoped that the land his mother's house had stood on would be of some value. The whole street had been bombed, and they were building prefab houses – in fact they had already rebuilt part of the street and were rehousing the homeless.

'The land, really, is virtually worthless. Of course, that may not be the case after the war, but at present there are vacant plots of land all over London, in some places more land than houses.'

Edward took their advice to retain the plots until they were worth selling. He then asked about Evelyne's money in the Post Office; it was a simple matter of the verification of his signature and the money was his. He stopped at the first Post Office he came to after leaving the solicitors' office, and withdrew the 123 pounds in cash. The assistant asked if he wished to retain the old book, as there was still one pound, fifteen shillings and sixpence of accrued interest.

Edward chuckled, slipping the book into his pocket. 'I think I'll leave that in, for emergencies, thank you.'

After opening a bank account – his first – Edward made his way to the station and sat on the train, waiting for it to leave for Cambridge. He had hoped, of course, that his mother's land would be worth a lot more. He recalled the days of Miss Freda and Ed, the Meadows family, and how hard his mother had saved and fought for them not to be evicted. What had it all been for? To end up as a worthless piece of wasteland. He gave no thought to Alex, beyond being relieved that the solicitors had not mentioned him. It did not occur to him that half the money he had just banked rightly belonged to Alex, or that half the property was also his. All he could think of was that now he could continue his studies, not exactly in the lap of luxury, but with more than enough to see him through.

By the time he let himself into his rooms, Edward was quite cheerful. He had only just taken his overcoat off when there was a knock on the door. He recognized the light, nervous tap, and called for Walter to let himself in.

'I've just been with the board again, it's unbelievable. They're sending me off to the War Office, to decipher bloody codes or something. I mean, how can they do it to me, smack in the middle of term?'

Edward commiserated. Poor, blind-as-a-bat Walter. He even offered to make the poor boy some cocoa, but Walter was so depressed he refused. Walter was nudging ahead of Edward in the tutorials, he was exceptionally clever . . .

'You should take it as a compliment – only picking the chaps with specially high IQs. Never know, Walt, you may yet make a career for yourself in the Foreign Office.'

Walter picked at his spots, squinted and moaned that he was just completing an analysis of specimens down in the lab, he doubted if he'd be allowed to complete even that. Edward offered to take a look, and together they walked over to Downing Laboratory.

His hands stuffed in his pockets, Walter kept complaining until Edward patted him on the shoulder. 'Think of it this way, you've got all the London cinemas – most of the pictures at the locals here are years out of date . . .'

Walter cheered visibly, and began talking about the possibility of working with microfilm. He lost Edward in the technical pros and cons of film-making.

But Edward was anything but lost when he read the results of Walter's research – it was too interesting. They sat in the library, discussing Walter's tests, then together they went over to the chemical laboratories.

Walter had drawn maps and detailed diagrams of many of the famous mines of South Africa. His tiny, meticulous print was difficult for Edward to read.

'What I've done is to take all the famous mines and break them down into scales – where the strikes occurred, how they were discovered. This one, for example, is the De Veer mine, coming in at the west side angle – the west-end shaft was burnt out – check down the layers of basaltic rock, black shale, melaphyre, and at eight hundred feet they hit quartzite. Smack in the middle you've got the different reef levels. Now, I reckon you should be able to tell the quality of the quartzite areas by the texture of the top basaltic rock – see? Look at the difference in quality – all those listed in Chart A, Chart B, have the same consistency. Now then, look at the mines that struck lucky, and look at the chemical formation of the top layer . . .'

They continued their talk until late that night. Walter was enthusiastic, excited. He believed he could, given the time, find some method of testing the top layer of rock and know, without have to spend millions on drills and pumps, just as they were able to test for oil, what areas were more likely to contain the precious minerals.

Edward asked if he could hold on to Walter's precious papers and read them overnight. After hesitating for a moment, Walter agreed, and went off to pack his clothes. He was due to leave the following morning.

By dawn, Edward had copied all the notes. He congratulated Walter, saying he was certainly on to something, and he hoped they wouldn't keep him away from college for too long.

Edward worked hard, taking Walter's theories a step further, and was excited that he would have one hell of a paper for the end-of-term exams.

Chapter Nine

The prisoners were all gathered in the canteen for their dinner. The Governor called for silence. He had a speech prepared, but only got as far as telling the men that the war was officially over, Germany was taken and Hitler was dead, the long nightmare was over. The men cheered and shouted, and the rest of the speech was lost as the prisoners roared their approval.

The fact that the country was at long last at peace really meant very little to those serving sentences, but they celebrated along with the rest of England, the rest of the world. They filed into chapel and offered prayers for the dead, prayers for peace to be long lasting.

All across England the long-awaited peace gave rise to street parties and celebrations. Not everyone celebrated – peace would bring an end to the black-market racketeers, and night clubs folded overnight. Soldiers, sailors and airmen arrived home first to cheers and then disillusion as they tried to readjust to civilian life, to the fact that they had missed their children's growth, their jobs were lost, in many cases their wives were gone, and mass unemployment loomed again.

Men trapped in the insulated world of the prisons were given film shows of the invasions, the signing of the peace treaty. Newsreels were shown, and the prisoners on their rows of hard-backed wooden chairs watched the screen with awe, which turned to horror when they saw footage of the liberation of Hitler's concentration camps. Many hardened criminals wept at the appalling atrocities on the screen.

Alex lay on his bunk, still trapped in the nightmare of those starving millions, the skeletal shapes of men's, women's and children's bodies being tipped into the anonymity of the mass graves. The haunting, pitiful faces were so remote, so unreal, that they hung over his head like a cloud, part of a terrible dream.

'Alex, you think them films were real? I mean, really real? Like, I know some of us inside here have done things in their lives, like meself even, but, but no one could really do what we saw, could they? Starve all those people like animals, I mean, they didn't even look human . . . were they?'

Alex sighed and turned over, looked at the big, bull-necked man who was so disturbed, so disbelieving . . . He was like a child. 'Takes all kinds, George. It wasn't just one man what done it, it's a whole country. They must all be as bad as each other.'

George swung his legs down from his bunk. 'You tellin' me that ordinary people stood by and let it go on wivout doing nuffink? I mean, there was kids operated on wivout anyfing to put 'em out! Jesus, they wouldn't even do that in the nick.'

Alex didn't want to talk, he was as overwhelmed as George by what they had seen. He rolled over to face the wall, but George continued, 'I get my hands on that bastard, on Hitler, I'd bleedin' kill him, I would. I'd give him his own torture, then shove 'im in the gas chambers. I'd round up the Gerry bastards and gas the whole fuckin' lot of them. Not one of them should be allowed to live, gas the bleedin' lot.'

Alex told him quietly that if he did that he would be no better than the Germans.

'I believe in an eye for an eye, a tooth for a tooth, that's in the Bible, that's in the bleedin' Bible.'

Alex was unable to get any peace with George banging around the cell, picking up his comic books and slapping them down again. 'One million Jews die, so they should take one million Germans and wipe 'em off the face of the earth . . . I'd not leave one SS officer alive – not one of those cunts would survive – that's what I'd do. For however many Jews was gassed, pay 'em back. What you say, Alex, never mind this trial. What they doing, anyway, givin' them animals a trial? Fuckin' hell – you and me know what a good lawyer can do, they'll walk away, you watch 'em, walk away and . . .' George Windsor, 'Mister Tough', 'Mister No-Talk', 'Mister Stay-Off-My-Back', broke down in tears, his square, muscular body shaking as he sobbed his heart out.

George was not the only man in the prison unable to face what had gone on outside, beyond their safe world, and it caused a mass outbreak of rioting and destruction. No more films were to be shown until the prisoners had settled back into their daily routines. But the films had another, more positive effect on many of the men. They all volunteered to work in the Red Cross department making blankets, to contribute in some small way. Jew-haters suddenly wanted to help Jewish prisoners.

George soon began to drive Alex nuts. He had to slink off to the library to read, and George even pursued him there.

'You mind if I ask you somefing personal, Alex? It's just that, well, I've been thinkin' over some of the things what you told me, and, like, I got anovver year . . . Well, look, Alex, will yer teach me ter read and write like what you do?'

Alex led him along the rows of books and found a children's story book, took it back to his table. He was now a 'trusty', allowed in the library and able to borrow books at will.

'I'll work wiv yer in the gym, if you like. I was a trainer, see, a boxer, an' there's nothin' I don't know about the 'uman body – injuries, the lot, so it'd be a fair swap, all right, mate?'

So George began learning to read and write. He looked up to Alex as if he were some kind of hero, because of his superior intelligence.

At first Alex ignored George's offer to help in the gym, but eventually he let George begin training him. His already large, six-foot-two-inch frame changed radically. His wide shoulders tapered down to a firm, tight waist, and he built up his legs and arms on the weights.

One day while George was barking out the time like a drill sergeant and Alex did press-ups, he stopped counting. 'Alex, your name's Stubbs, ain't it? You related to a boxer, ex-champ?'

Alex picked up a towel and wiped his forehead. 'Why do you want to know?'

'Well, it's the name, like, he was called Freedom Stubbs. Bit before my time, mind, but me old man, my dad, he was one of his sparrin' partners down at this big country house. Always said he was one of the finest men he'd ever seen box, man was like lightning, with one hell of a reach. He was an enormous geezer, six foot four, used to wear his hair long like, yer know, he was a gyppo.'

Alex tossed his towel aside, for a moment he was tempted to tell George.

'Never heard of him.'

'Yer know in the washrooms – well, last cubicle, 'is name's scratched into the wall. He must've served time 'ere . . . He was British Heavyweight Champion, oh, must've been, now let me think . . . 1925 or '26 . . .'

Alex walked along the cubicles and into the stall at the far end. He found his father's name scrawled beside a date. He leaned against the tiled wall, feeling sick, and tried to remember the dates his father had been away, but it was all so long ago, a blur.

George was released four months later, but he promised to write, and to arrange a place for Alex to live. Alex had the cell to himself for a month. He now had the best bunk, and he waited to see who they would put in with him.

Brian Welland was a pretty boy, and Alex knew at a glance that he was queer. He tossed his book down and stared hard. 'How old are you?'

'Twenty-seven, sir.'

'What you in fer?'

'Fraud.'

Alex came on as the heavy 'con' at first, almost repeating George Windsor's welcome when Alex had first arrived at Durham. Brian was well educated, his speech refined. But it was the row of books that Brian carefully laid out by his bunk that interested Alex. Classical volumes, with a few thicker books on banking and taxation. Brian gave Alex a sheepish smile, expecting a crude remark, but instead Alex picked one of the books up and asked if he could read it.

'I doubt if that one will interest you, it's accountancy.'

'That what you are then? An accountant?'

'Was, I was . . . and I doubt if I'll be allowed to practise when I get out.'

'I'll make a deal wiv you. You could get a lot of aggro – I'll see the blokes leave you alone. In return, I want you to teach me everyfing you know . . .'

This was the last thing Brian expected. He was so relieved he would have promised anything to have Alex on his side – he had been terrified while being held on remand. But he did not anticipate Alex's almost obsessive desire to study – the moment he woke up he reached for a book. Every moment he didn't spend in the gym he spent with Brian, ploughing through everything they could get from the library. Brian was a good teacher, and had worked for the Inland Revenue. As a fledgeling tax inspector, he was able to guide Alex through the complex taxation system.

Brian had become involved with a man who had manipulated him into a banking and taxation fraud. He had been used, but in the course of the scam he had travelled extensively, and organized tax havens for his friend in Jersey and Switzerland.

Alex was fascinated, and questioned him on everything, often until the early hours of the morning . . . and the relationship deepened. Alex, not Brian, made the first move. He had already had a number of homosexual so-called affairs, but Brian was different. Alex actually cared for him, and the feelings were reciprocated and eventually consummated. Alex learnt a great deal more than accountancy from his lover, who now corrected his grammar and picked him up on his dropped 'aitches'. At first Alex had been temperamental about being constantly corrected, but he soon realized it was done out of affection. In the end he worked just as hard on speech defects as on his other studies. Being with Brian gave Alex a new confidence in himself. He was less aggressive, more quietly assertive than he had ever been.

Brian was broken-hearted when Alex left. They promised to write, and Alex gave his word that as soon as he had a place to stay he would send Brian his address. But he had no intention of ever seeing him again, the relationship was over. For Alex, like most prisoners, homosexual practices until Brian had been a pure necessity . . . but there would be no more Brians, he had served his purpose. He would have one label, 'ex-con', and he didn't want another.

Alex set his sights on climbing back to the top of the mountain, to breathe that clean, fresh air once more. He vowed to himself that he would never see the inside of a prison again.

True to his promise, George Windsor was waiting for Alex outside the gates of the prison. He had rented a small flat in Dulwich. The next day they bought a second-hand suit for Alex. Being 'outside' was not easy at first, and he had to hide his shyness at talking to strangers. The next step was to find a job, but with hundreds of soldiers back from the war, work was hard to come by. Alex began a depressing round of job interviews, arranged by his probation officer.

Edward walked out of the examination room, exhausted. His head ached from concentrating and his shoulders were stiff from hunching over the exam papers. He breathed in the lovely, fresh spring air as he walked across the quad. He had done well, he knew it. Not one question had beaten him. It had been his last exam in two weeks of finals, and now all that was left were the results and freedom. He felt almost light-headed as he walked along the river bank.

The May Ball signified the end of term, and everyone was excitedly looking forward to it. But Edward decided he would give it a miss and await his results in London.

Edward's bedmaker was just finishing his room, and told him a letter had just arrived — it was on his desk. 'You do well, you think, sir? In the exams, sir? I hope so, you've certainly worked for it if I may say so. Very dedicated student if I may say so, pleasure to bedmake for you, sir.'

Edward smiled, he knew the man had hardly given him a moment's thought, but it was now coming up to the time for tipping, and he wanted to ingratiate himself.

'Well, I'll be off, sir, all shipshape, thank you very much, sir.'

Edward didn't even turn his head to thank the man. The door closed and shut out the sound of his muttering. He opened the letter. It was from Harriet, and the energetic loops and coils of her handwriting reminded him of her. It was misspelt and full of underlinings and double underlinings for emphasis:

> I am coming to the May Ball as Allard's partner. Will you be there, will I see you?, can I see you. It is imperatife . . .
>   Love, Harry.

> PS You have not written once. I have been incarserated at boarding school, then diabolickly removed from boarding school, and threatened with being sent to Switzerland to finishing school.
> PPS Please reply to this, I am esconced at London address.
> PPPS you forgot my birthday AGAIN.

Edward thought about replying to Harriet's letter. He had not spoken to Allard for months; they passed each other without any acknowledgement. As he had made up his mind to take up BB's offer of work, Edward booked a passage on the seaplane to South Africa. This made a considerable dent in his mother's legacy, but he still had the gold cigarette case and lighter.

The pieces of furniture and the paintings from Charlie's attic that Edward wanted to keep were crated to be put into storage. He packed his personal belongings into his trunk, discarding a few articles that were very worn.

All around him the students were hell-bent on preparing for the ball. Hotels were booked, girlfriends and fiancées began to arrive by the train load to be ready for the big night. Edward kept himself busy completing his packing. He would be in Southampton the night of the ball and, even if he had contemplated staying for it, forking out the one pound and ten shillings for the tickets was, he felt, a waste of his cash.

'You leaving before the big bash, sir? Well, that is a rum thing.'

The gatekeeper inspected Edward's list of instructions for the things that were to be picked up. His trunk he would take with him.

'Going somewhere nice, sir?'

Edward smiled, and said airily that he was going to see friends in South Africa.

He walked one last time along the river. He had to see Emmott and a few other tutors before he left, but basically it was over, and he wanted one long, last walk.

'Edwaaaaard! Edwaaaaaard!' It was Harriet, wobbling alarmingly on a bicycle. He knew it was her not just by the bellowing, but the long red hair that streamed out behind her. She was wearing a printed summer dress, and had tucked the skirt into the leg of her knickers so it wouldn't catch in the spokes. Her skin was lightly tanned, her long legs bare, and she was wearing brown leather sandals. She careered up to him and he caught the handlebars to stop her.

'Gateman said you were walking this way so I borrowed this, no idea whose it is, but he must be a very tall chap, I can hardly reach the seat.' She had grown taller herself, and must have been at least five foot eight in her flat sandals. But it was as if there had been no time since their last meeting, she was as familiar with him as if they had parted only yesterday.

'Said you were about to leave, thank you very much, not even a word to me ... My, you are even taller than I remembered.'

He tucked her hand under his arm, he could say the same for her, she was almost as tall as her brother.

'What's gone on between you two? I mentioned your name and I thought he would throw up ... Oh, look, a mallard!'

She dropped to her knees on the river bank and stared at the duck. 'You two have a falling-out, did you?'

'No, not a falling-out, more just sort of going our separate ways.'

'Well, he is a bit odd ... Ahhh, look, more ducks – I love ducks, I once had a nanny, and she used to take me to Regent's Park to feed the ducks, lovely woman, with terrible BO, but she knew all the ducks by name, well, the ones she'd given them to.'

They walked on, arm in arm. Harriet chattered to begin with, then she went quiet and they walked together in silence until they came across a floating, empty punt.

'Shall we capture it? Go for a punt?'

Edward reached out with a stick and pulled the punt towards them, looked around for a pole, but there wasn't one.

'We'll just float along, let it take us where it wants, come on, get in ... Where are you going, anyway? Why are you leaving before the ball?'

Edward said he was going travelling. Harriet lay back and hitched her skirt up so the sun could get to her legs. 'Ma says I shouldn't sunbathe because my freckles'll all join up into one dark red–brown blob, but I love the sun ... Where are you travelling to then?'

'I don't know yet.'

'I haven't cut my hair, you will note, it's now much longer and the front is growing again. You know Pa has been made Chief Justice Simpson now? He swans around, very puffed up, he's so proud of himself.'

Edward kept his distance from her at the far end of the punt, watching as she trailed her hand in the water. She filled him in on all the family news. 'The Van der Burges have gone on a world cruise, then they come back and go home, thank the Lord. They really were becoming part of the fixtures and fittings . . . BB consumed most of Pa's stock of brandy and never replenished it, which infuriated him.'

The sun was getting hotter and hotter, and Edward closed his eyes, the cool, slight breeze off the river was delicious.

Harriet pointed to an ice-cream seller on the bank. 'Oh, have you any money on you? Come on, paddle over, I'd love a cornet.'

They paddled with their hands and Edward handed her sixpence. She waded into the water, and with wet dress and sandals she marched up on to the bank, coming back carrying two dripping cornets. She climbed back into the punt and Edward pushed off from the bank.

They fell into silence again as they drifted on down the river. A few punters passed them, shouting as they poled on.

'I am being made to go to Switzerland, did I write and tell you that? Finish me off, and then I return to be paraded around town for my "coming-out" . . . Crikey, I loathe them all, I really do.'

Edward sat up and tossed the cornet end to the ducks. He leaned on his elbow, smiling at her. 'What do you want to do, Harry? Really do with your life?'

She finished her cornet, not giving a crumb to the ducks. She had ice cream all round her mouth, which she wiped off with the back of her hand, and licked the trace from her lips. 'You wouldn't like it if I told you.'

He tapped her foot and told her to go on, he wanted to know. She bent forward and took one sandal off, laid it on the seat beside her then did the same with the other one. He leaned forward and tapped her bare foot, asked her again to tell him what she was going to do with herself, what she wanted out of her life.

'Okay, I would like . . . One, for you to take me into a big, white, soft bed, really thick and squashy, one that you sink into ... I would like then to have four sons, all of them as tall as you, all of them a criss-cross of our looks, two with reddish hair, two with your black, black hair, but all with your dark eyes ... Then I would like to live with you and our sons on a big farm, like abroad somewhere, maybe South America, somewhere where there is hot sun, wild animals roaming, a few horses, my own stables, a cook, because I hate cooking ...'

She was lying stretched out, legs bare, eyes closed and her hand trailing along in the water, causing miniature whirlpools to form and disappear. 'What about you, Edward, any of that take your fancy at all?'

He shaded his eyes and looked at the river bank because he couldn't think of anything to say. He had a lump in his throat, and he swallowed hard. The punt banged into the bank, and Harriet reached up to a hanging branch of a willow tree to hold the boat beneath it. He could see the glint of the sun on the thin gold bangle she wore.

'Course, you don't have to reply, make any decision immediately ...' She tossed her head back and laughed, her hair flying around her, and fell back into the punt, legs in the air. She continued to laugh as he moved along the punt on all fours, leaned over her and looked down into her freckled face. 'You, Harry, are as mad as a hatter.'

She wrapped her arms around him and looked up into his face.

'You will never have anyone love you as I do, they will all be older, experienced and boring, but you can have me untouched by any other human hand ...'

He kissed her nose, but remained hovering just above her, looking down into her upturned face. 'What if I don't want you? What if I have other plans for my life that do not involve a lunatic?'

The big, blue eyes filled with tears, brimming over, and she whispered, very low, 'You will break my heart.'

Edward moved back and sat on the seat. He rubbed his head. 'Harry, I have to go away to find some work. I have no money, nothing to offer you, and added to that you are still a kid with romantic notions you've got out of some magazine.'

She threw water at him and drenched his shirt. 'Bollocks, I am not a kid, as you put it, I am sixteen years old, you are just making excuses. I'll wait, I'll wait for two years, but I won't wait any longer ... Ma will have a fit, Pa will have a heart attack, especially if he's laying out all the cash for my coming-out, but ...' She looked at him, she wasn't joking, she said it softly, so earnestly, it was touching. 'I'll wait for you, Edward.'

She toyed with the branch, and the willow shuddered above her head. Then she let it go and sat up, looking at him very seriously, very straight-faced. 'Only, you'll have to give me something, something so that I know you'll come for me, I don't want letters, just your word ...'

Edward pushed at the bank to make the punt move, but it remained stuck by the willow. 'I can't give it to you, push from your end, come on, Harry, push it away.'

He leaned out and pushed, the punt turned and he fell towards her, landing with his head in her lap, between her legs. He lifted his hands and held her tightly, pressing his face against her, and she folded her arms around him and bent to kiss the back of his head, then wriggled until her body was beneath his, and he let her. Knowing he was mad, knowing he must be out of his mind, he remained lying on top of her.

The punt drifted off down the river, and they lay wrapped in each other's arms. Content to hold him close, Harriet lay quiet, made no move. Slowly, gently, he pushed her skirt back until he could feel the edge of her knickers, grasped them and began to ease them down. She kissed his head, his hair, with soft, sweet kisses. 'What should I do? Tell me.'

His voice was husky, she could feel his breath on her face as he said, 'Nothing, nothing ...' and she rested her head against his, so happy she wanted to cry. She had dreamed of this moment, dreamed it so many times she felt she needed to pinch herself to prove that this time it was really happening ...

She knew he had undone his trousers, she could feel him

now ... he pressed her legs apart, and as if he were afraid to look
at her, he turned his head away as he gently eased himself into
her ... At last he kissed her lips, and found them as rounded and
soft as her thighs, her breasts, and his kiss hardened as he moved
inside her, gripped her tightly, thrusting himself into her until
the boat rocked in the water ... She moaned, and he looked at
her face, in anguish that he had hurt her ... but she smiled, her
face so filled with love he felt himself wanting to weep.

He was so caring, pulling up her knickers, straightening her
skirt, and she did up each fly button on his trousers. They lay
close and he promised that he would come back for her, gave his
solemn oath that he would be back and give her four sons.

'I don't want a girl, Edward, not a girl, they are such pests.'

He laughed and cuddled her, said she was the only girl he
wanted, and she was right, four sons would be perfect.

They bumped into an empty, drifting punt and retrieved the
pole. Edward poled the boat back towards the bridge, towards
the town. 'Harry, you must never tell anyone what we've done
today, your father would come after me with a shotgun.'

She wagged her finger at him and said he had better keep his
promise then. He helped her jump on to the bank, and as he
was tying up the punt, he heard a sports car careering across the
bridge.

'Oh, damn it, here comes Allard.'

Edward looked towards the bridge as the bright red car
screeched around the corner. 'Go to him, go on Harry – no
goodbyes, no nothing, just go ...'

She turned back only once, then she ran towards the red car,
waving her sandals above her head. 'Allard, whooo hoooo,
Allard!'

Edward heard Allard shouting, asking where the hell she had
been, they had all been looking for her. Then Edward heard the
car turn and drive back over the bridge. She sat at the back, he
saw her turn, give a small wave ... and with her red hair flying
out behind her she was gone in the little red sports car.

*

George thundered up the worn, lino-covered staircase and rushed into the bedsit. 'Now then, Alex, I got some good news for you. This bloke I work for, right, I've told him all about you, said you was good at bookkeeping, an' he wants to meet wiv yer. It's a real job, with wages.'

Alex asked George if he was sure the man was straight, as he had to report to his probation officer every week.

'I got it all worked out. He knows you done time and he still wants to meet you. He's honest, Alex, a real nice bloke – you can at least try it.'

Suddenly George stopped and looked around the small flat. 'Oi, what you been doin', you moved everyfink.'

'It was untidy, I just cleaned it up and put what we don't need away. I hate mess.'

George sniffed and checked his things, discovering that Alex had allocated space for each of them in the drawers, places for shoes, shirts and jumpers.

'Hey, just don't make it too tidy, don't wanna be reminded of the cells, like. But it's nice.'

'I'm going to get some paint, see if I can clean the walls – it's that wallpaper, makes me go nuts.'

George rather liked the heavy, maroon flock wallpaper, and it was quite new, but he said nothing. When he went to the tiny cupboard they used as a kitchen, he gasped. Every pan was polished, every cup washed and neatly stacked. Alex had even rinsed out the dishcloth and hung it on the sink to dry.

'Oh, yes, you done a real fine job, yer could eat yer dinner orf this floor, Alex. You'll make me a good wife.'

George whipped round as Alex sprang towards him, his fists clenched.

'Hey, hey, it was just a joke, all right?'

'I just like a clean place, that's all, George. There's nothing nancy about that.'

George sighed. Sometimes Alex could be so touchy. Grinning, he said there was no harm meant, then he put the kettle on. He even wiped the drips of water off the small draining board. He noticed Alex had his nose stuck in a book again. Not that they were real books to George, no stories, just rows of calculations. He began to hope that Alex would get a job soon, because he doubted if things would work out between them.

Harry Driver was very sceptical about the new chap Stubbs. He had always run his business single-handed, but lately he had been branching out. He had a small drinks place, but his main income was from five back-street tailoring and dressmaking sweatshops. He put Alex to work on his club books first so that, having complete knowledge of his accounts himself, he could test the lad out.

With his paunch and his ever-present stubby cigar Harry was a real character. He was from a Russian immigrant family that he complained were forever bleeding him dry. Harry did take care of a vast family, having six kids of his own plus various aunts and uncles. And in the sweatshops he was always discovering yet another impoverished relative who had come looking for work. He was a penny-pinching man, but a decent one, and he had got very fond of George Windsor, so if George said the chap was a good'un, he was inclined to believe it. He put Alex on trial for three months at half the salary he would have dared offer any man with credentials. 'Understand me, Alex, I am taking a risk on you, so I can't shell out the money before I know I can trust you. All you gotta do is prove yourself, you'll not hear a bad word about Harry Driver, but you gotta prove your worth first.'

Alex pored over Harry's books, and made careful, detailed notes alongside his figures. He checked the bar takings, the warehouse, the staff, leaving nothing out, and by the end of the week he made Harry nearly swallow his cigar.

'I think, Mr Driver, you are losing between one and two hundred a week, it varies at different times of the month. I've made a list of the takings from the club for each week over the past six months, and I think you'll find my assessment interesting.' He went over each detail with Harry, who hummed and hawed and shook his jowls until his head spun. 'Added to that, Mr Driver, you are paying certain taxes that need not necessarily be paid if you purchase articles within a certain time limit. If you are outside that limit, then you are paying more tax. They work by the fiscal years, you see, sir.'

Harry chomped and spat and relit his dog-eared cigar. He told Alex to leave the work with him, he would have a look at it.

'Wally, listen to me, I've got a lad here I think you should have look over your books, he's a whiz-kid, I've not seen anything like it. I'll let you have him on loan, mind, he works for me, but I want to see what you think of him.'

Alex was put on a salary of seven pounds a week by Harry Driver, and he was tickled pink. He knew, of course, that he was earning it, and he knew he was worth twice the amount, but he had to start somewhere.

George and Alex went shopping in Petticoat Lane for suits, shoes and ties. Some were second-hand, some new, and Harry gave them both special prices on his sweatshop goods. Alex displayed his new wide-collared, single-breasted suit. It was brown with a thin blue stripe, and he had bought a brown-and-pink striped tie and polished brown shoes to go with it.

'Gawd help us, Alex, wiv the briefcase, my son, you could be a City gent.'

Alex marvelled at his friend's stunning bad taste. George loved the wide, hand-painted ties, the huge square jackets with the padded shoulders and two-toned shoes reminiscent of the old movie gangsters.

Alex was now also on loan from Harry Driver to a number of East End Jewish tailors and stall-holders. They joked between themselves that for a goy, a non-Jew, he was the meanest man they'd ever come across.

'This boy, Solly, he knows the tax system better than I know

the wife, no word of a lie. You know how much he just saved
me? Fifty quid – I got it from the government – and know
what else this boy can do? Save on your taxes – save! If you
knew the loopholes that are legal . . . On my word, this boy is
gold dust.'

Alex was passed from manufacturer to tailor, to sweatshop, to
clubs, and Harry Driver reaped the benefits and raised Alex's
salary to twelve pounds a week. Alex was no fool, he was getting to know everyone with the best cash flows in the East End.
At the same time he was still learning.

Once a week Alex had to report to his parole officer, who
would shake his hand and congratulate him, saying that they
were proud of how well he had adapted to his new, straight life.
While he was on parole they could, at any time, walk into his
flat or his place of business to see if he was doing what he said
he was.

Alex bided his time, waiting for the day when he would be
free of the probation officers. He was determined not to put a
foot out of line until he was not only free from prison but completely free of prying eyes. He wanted to find his brother, to
confront him, but he was careful never to mention his name. It
became an obsession with him and this, along with his shyness,
added to the strange, solitary air about him.

George popped into Harry Driver's sweatshop on his way to
work to see Alex, but was told he always had that particular
afternoon off. This puzzled George, as Alex had never mentioned it. Harry insisted George stay for a cup of coffee,
anyway. 'Look, I'll come right out with it, George. This guy
you sent me seems too good to be true. I mean, he works
like a friggin' beaver, and don't talk to nobody. Now don't
get me wrong, I can't fault his work, he doesn't even stop for
a bite to eat. So, what is it with him? I mean, what makes
him tick?'

George was guarded, not liking to be questioned about his
mate. 'Like you said, Mr Driver, he works his butt off for yer, so

why don't you just accept it? Just don't cross him, leave him alone. You an' me both know you're gettin' 'im cheap.'

George went off to his job as a bouncer, but Driver's remark nagged at him. He wondered why Alex had never told him about his afternoons off.

Alex wished he'd worn something old, he was getting filthy digging around the grave. It was in a terrible state, the weeds choking his mother's cross. He dug and snipped with his scissors and filled the tin can with water from the tap to put the flowers in. He told himself he'd get a nice stone urn or something for next time. The grave was looking nice now, the grass cropped around, all neat and tidy, and he placed the flowers on it and stood back.

'Doing all right now, Ma, I'm doing all right, you'll see, I'll make it, gonna be somebody, you got my word on it . . . Amen.'

He was washing his hands at the tap when he saw her, her blonde hair rolled into a tight bun at the nape of her neck. She looked one hell of a lady, with her black mink draped over her shoulders and her ears glinting with what looked like diamonds. She was wandering up and down between the gravestones, peering at each one, a ten-shilling bouquet of flowers in her arms. Alex straightened his tie, smoothed down his jacket and followed the searching figure.

'Dora . . . Dora!'

She turned, bewildered, and stared at him.

'It's me, Alex Stubbs . . . it's Alex.'

She almost dropped her flowers, then she smiled and shook her head. 'Well, I hardly recognized you, good heavens, it's been years, hasn't it? How are you?'

He felt embarrassed as he put out his hand to shake, but she just waved her gloved hand. 'I'm lookin' fer Mother's grave, but it's been so long I can't remember where she is, isn't that awful, I know she's 'ere somewhere.'

Alex followed her as she teetered around on her high heels,

peering shortsightedly at one gravestone after another. Eventually she stopped by some old grave and dropped the flowers. 'I can't ruin my shoes any more. Give me your hand, Alex, it's ever so muddy.'

He guided her back through the narrow lanes and they reached the gates.

'You need a lift anywhere?'

He marvelled at the way she looked, the way she spoke, it was hard for him to believe it was the Dora he'd known.

'I haven't a car, I come by bus.'

She walked over to a white sports car and told him to get in, she'd give him a lift.

They drove along the familiar streets and she pulled up outside his flat.

'So you're back in this neck of the woods, are you? I must say I couldn't stand to live here. Besides, I couldn't leave my motor outside, the kids would wreck it. What do you do with yourself now then?'

He told her about his job with Harry Driver, and she nodded, said she knew of him, he'd got a small drinks place. 'You married are you, Alex?'

He shook his head, looked at her hand but couldn't see whether she was wearing a ring or not because of her gloves.

'I was, remember Johnny Mask? We got married but it didn't work out. I ran a club, well, bit more than that, actually, you must come down sometime, Mayfair – Masks. Just mention my name at the door. How's that brother of yours? I've not seen him down the club for ages, what's he up to?'

Alex stared at her, then gripped the side of the car window. 'You know where he is? You got an address?'

Dora laughed and switched on the engine. 'You must be joking, he's quite the toff now. He used to come down the club a few times. Look, I got to go, nice seeing you, Alex.' In her mirror, Dora could see him standing like a big oaf, watching the car. She shuddered, he reminded her of her own past. She hoped he wouldn't show up at the club, not in those dreadful cheap clothes he was wearing, anyway. Robert Mitchum had a lot to answer for, all the East End villains tried to copy his look.

While Dora was changing, Johnny walked in, yelling that she had left all the lights on again. What did she think he was, the London bloody Electricity Company?

She came out of the bathroom, her mouth set. He reeked of booze, and his eyes were red–rimmed.

'Been playing poker, have you? I dunno, I work all the hours God gives me for you to squander it at the first opportunity. Who you been playing with this afternoon then?'

Johnny flopped down on the bed and said he'd been over the East End. He lit a cigarette.

'Don't toss the match on the carpet, Johnny, honestly, how many times do I have to tell you? They leave burn marks.'

Johnny snorted and got up to pour himself a drink. She clocked it but said nothing.

'I been playing wiv Harry Driver and a few of his mates, lost a bundle an' all, he's very flush all of a sudden. You hear about him? He's opening up more businesses than I've 'ad hot dinners.'

Dora began to cream her face. The lines were worrying her now – fine lines around her eyes and mouth, and she couldn't hide them. 'Funny, I met an old friend – remember the Stubbs boys? It was one of them – Alex ... He's doing Harry's accounts for him.'

Johnny scratched his head. 'Alex? Christ, I remember 'im – skinny boy, blond. They picked 'im up outside one of the dosshouses, didn't they? He was a good kid, what you say he's doing?'

'You never bleedin' listen to me, do you? I said he was doing Driver's accounts.'

'Yeah, I remember – Christ, he was good even then, and he was straight. He used to bring all the cash down, every penny accounted for. Well, well, working for Driver, eh? I owe him, you know, that kid. He kept mum about me, not like that little shit–head – what was his name? Talked like a canary, he did, that's why they picked up Alex.'

Dora watched as he poured yet another drink. 'Oh Johnny, don't get pissed tonight. There's a big crowd comin' down and you make such a fool of yourself. It's not good for business.'

'You see the lad, tell 'im to come an' see me.'

'Lad? He's more like a gorilla nowadays. I tell you, I wouldn't have recognized him. Mind you, he would make a good bouncer . . . Ah Johnny, please don't drink.'

Johnny slapped her so hard she slid off her stool. She blazed at him. 'That is the last time, Johnny, the very last time. Sod you, I've had you up to here.'

He hung his head in shame, mumbled that he was sorry, he was sorry. 'I dunno why I do it, I don't, Dora, but yer git me so mad sometimes. An' usin' that phoney posh voice of yours gets on my nerves.'

Dora started unloading underwear and clothes from the wardrobe.

'What yer doin', Dora, what yer doin'?'

She snapped that she had warned him that if he ever hit her again it would be the last time. Well, now it was, she was through and she was walking out on him. 'An' I'm walkin' out of the club, too. I can get a job in any place around town, don't think I can't. I'm sick of covering up for you and taking your violence. You've done it, Johnny, I quit.'

He knew that without her the club would fall apart, and he begged her, then got on his knees and clutched the hem of her dressing gown, crying and begging.

'I'll stay on one condition – that is, stay here, in your bed and in the club – if you make it out on paper that I own half – half, Johnny, it's only fair.' She had him by the balls and she knew it. She got him another drink, a real stiff one, and cajoled him into signing half the club over to her. Then she undressed him and put him to bed. He lay snoring, mouth wide open, and she looked at him with distaste.

She called her lawyers to make sure the contract was legal,

then left for work. All the way to Mayfair she was thinking that now she'd got one half she'd keep Johnny boozed up until she'd got the other half for herself.

Dora was squinting at the accounts when Arnie knocked on the door to tell her there was a gent waiting to see her, name of Stubbs, looked a bit of a punk.

'Show him in, will you, Arnie? It's all right, he works for Harry Driver. Apparently he's a whiz-kid with the accounts. Maybe we should try him out, that bastard we've got costs us an arm and a leg.'

When Alex entered she could see that he'd made a great effort. His hair was slicked down, his suit pressed and his shoes polished until you could see your face in them. Dora felt sorry for him, the trouble he'd taken.

'Well, you found the place, then. Can I get you a drink? Champagne? You name it and I'll get it sent in.'

Alex said champagne would be just fine, and sat there like a dummy. He was all fingers and thumbs, and spilt the champagne as he poured it. He had to lick it off his hands. 'Er, when I saw yer, you said somefink about Eddie. I come round to see if you got his address.'

Alex could hear his old cell-mate correcting him, 'No, no – it's not somefink, something, it's a soft G.' He caught Dora staring at him and looked away. She was checking him over and he knew it.

'Like I told you, I've not seen him for a long time ... They say you know all about taxes and accounting, Alex. How come? If you don't mind me saying so, you don't look like the pin-striped City type.'

Alex shuffled his feet, blushing. 'Let's just say I had a long time to study.'

Suddenly he looked up and gave her a shy smile. She smiled back and poured him some more champagne. 'You certainly made a mess of your face ... You know, accountants cost. Maybe I could let you have a look over our books. I'd be glad of a few tips and I'd pay you for your time.'

There was another knock at the door and Arnie appeared. Dora looked up, annoyed at the interruption, but he whispered something to her and she got up to look through the spyhole in the door.

Johnny, obviously very drunk, was leering around the bar. She flipped the cover back in place. 'Arnie, get Cathy over to him and get him out fast as you can. There's a big party due about eleven-thirty and they're real money, I don't want him around. If he won't go quietly, bloody well haul him out.'

She clinked ice into a tall, thin glass and poured herself a glass of water.

'Crazy, isn't it? My dear husband, partner in a business that's worth God knows how many thousands, and he's out there boozing it up and carrying on with the girls.' Dora lit a cigarette and put it in a holder, blew out the smoke and crossed her still perfect legs. 'You be interested in doing the accounts, Alex? No need to mention it to Driver if you don't want to.'

Alex murmured that he could always do with some extra, and if she handed over the books he'd contact her as soon as he'd been through them.

Dora got up and went to a wall safe, twirled the combination and turned, smiling and licking her lips. 'Goes without saying there are two sets, but I'm sure you would know all about that. I can trust you, can't I, Alex? I mean, these are private.'

Alex could feel her looking at him and flushed, put down his glass and told her she didn't have to worry. She took out all the books and put them into a shopping bag. He was fascinated by her perfectly manicured long red nails.

'I'm sure I can trust you, Alex, we go back a long way together, you and me. Here you are, dear, and I'll wait to hear from you.'

Alex worked all night on Dora's ledgers, and when he had finished he chucked down his chewed pencil. 'Shit, that little tart's worth a bleedin' fortune . . .'

The club was a gold mine, but it was losing more than it needed to through mismanagement. Alex knew he could get back a lot of the tax the club was paying. She could be claiming for God knows how many more employees than she was. Alex quickly began to calculate the savings. He paced the small bedsit, constantly drawn back to the books. Dora was earning a living wage, but right in front of him he saw a way to make a lot more. When George arrived home at four in the morning, he was amazed to find Alex still working.

'Whatcha up to, son? You been out? 'Bout time yer got yer leg over . . .'

Alex quickly covered the books while George was hanging his coat in the small wardrobe they shared.

'I'm movin' out, George. Need a bigger place. Maybe you can get that bird you see to move in an' keep the place tidy . . .'

George's face fell, and Alex went to sit next to him on the bed. 'I been offered a job. It's straight, but . . . there's another reason. You see, I need to find somebody, and I just got a lead on him. So, in a way, I'm killin' two birds . . .'

George watched Alex undress, revealing his big body, and the powerful way he moved. He hung everything neatly on a hanger in the small wardrobe.

'You want to tell me about it? I mean, who is he? Who you got this lead on then?'

'It's a relative, that's all.'

'Well, you make sure you don't do nuffink that'll put yer back inside.'

Alex turned to him. Sometimes he frightened George. His blue eyes were filled with hatred, and yet he had a soft smile. 'I'll never be put behind bars again – I'm going to make sure of that.'

During the flight to South Africa, Edward settled back in his seat. It would be a long journey with many stopovers for refuelling. He recalled BB telling him he had arrived in South Africa with only one hundred pounds and made millions – well, Edward had, after paying his fare, exactly eighty-five pounds to his name. He was, nevertheless, determined that he too would make his fortune.

Ahead of Edward lay his future, and he was itching to begin. He knew he was taking a chance, knew it, but he was ready for it – longed for it – and he would let nothing stand in his way, nothing and no one.

Edna Simpson waited at the airport for her daughter. The plane was delayed, and she paced up and down. The family had said all they could say on the subject, and they had made their decision. As soon as she got off the plane she would be taken to the Harley Street clinic where she was booked. The minor operation had been easily arranged. No one would find out, no one would know. Harriet was still a child, and the more Mrs Simpson thought about it the worse she felt. Her daughter had been a problem since the day she was born, when Mrs Simpson had almost died giving birth to her. It had been one heartache after another ever since.

'God, why couldn't she have been a boy?' The season would soon be upon them, and Harriet's 'coming-out' dance would go ahead as arranged. Mrs Simpson was so immersed in her own thoughts that she jumped.

'Hello, Ma, dreadful bumpy ride, pilot was terrific.'

Mrs Simpson pursed her lips and kissed her daughter frostily on the cheek, then took her suitcase. They walked to the car, which was waiting outside the terminal.

'We are going straight to Harley Street, everything's arranged.'

Harriet beamed, said there was absolutely no need, she felt wonderful.

'That is not quite the point, dear. You will only have to stay overnight, I'll collect you in the morning and no one will be any the wiser. Now get in the car and don't talk about it, I don't want the chauffeur to know – talk about anything but you-know-what.'

Harriet stopped short and folded her arms. 'What you talking about, Ma?'

Mrs Simpson pursed her lips even tighter. 'You know perfectly well, an abortion.' She hissed the word, and Harriet's mouth fell open. 'Daddy and I have sent off all the invitations, get into the car, dear. So far we have got a jolly good set of replies.'

They got into the car and Mrs Simpson watched the chauffeur putting Harriet's case into the boot.

'Oh, God! You're not serious, Ma, you haven't arranged a dance, have you?'

Her mother gave a nod for the chauffeur to drive on, and settled back. 'Well, of course we have, it's your coming-out ball, you know perfectly well. We had to book our dates at the Dorchester ballroom weeks ago.'

Harriet giggled and leaned back in the seat. 'Well, I'll certainly be coming out in more ways than one, Ma.'

'No you won't, I won't hear one word more. It is all arranged. Now then, do you want to see your guest lists?'

Harriet gazed out of the window, sighed and took her mother's hand. 'I'm truly sorry, Ma, about the dance, but I am not going to any clinic, I refuse ... You see, I want him, want the baby more than anything else in the world, and I don't think I have ever felt so happy in my whole life.'

Mrs Simpson thought she would faint, she had to wind down the window. 'Please keep your voice down, please.'

Harriet looked at her mother, and then at the stiff-backed chauffeur. She leaned forward and dug him in the back. 'I am going to have a baby, Henson, isn't that wonderful?'

The car veered towards the centre of the road. Henson flicked a quick look into his mirror and then concentrated on driving.

'Didn't you hear me? I am going to have a baby.'

Mrs Simpson slapped her, said she was most certainly not and she was to stop this silliness at once.

'It's not silly, Ma, it's the truth.'

'I know it is, haven't you been sent home in disgrace? Do you know how your father feels? Have you any consideration for your father, for Allard? Let alone myself, don't you care what we think?'

Harriet tried to take her mother's hand again, but she withdrew it. 'Oh, Ma, don't you care what *I* think, what I feel?'

Mrs Simpson took out her handkerchief, blew her nose, and said it was quite immaterial what Harriet felt. They had decided and it was final.

'It's my baby, mine, and I want him, and what's more I am going to have him and I don't care what any of you think or feel, he is my baby.'

The chauffeur swallowed and took another quick look in the driving mirror. The conversation going on behind him was riveting.

'Who is the father, we want to know who did this – and my God, if I get my hands on him, if your father got his hands on him, he would tear him to pieces . . . How could you, dear, you are only sixteen.'

They argued for the rest of the journey, and the poor chauffeur kept being told to go to Harley Street, then Harriet would scream that he had to take them home, he didn't know which way to turn.

'Your father will settle this – Kensington, Henson! And you haven't heard a word of our conversation, is that clear?'

Allard strode into the hall as they arrived, looked at his sister then at his mother. 'I say, is it a joke, you been playing a joke on us, Harry?'

Mrs Simpson said that she most certainly had not, then looked with a glimmer of hope in her eyes. 'It isn't a joke, is it, Harriet?'

Harriet looked at the two of them and laughed, then asked if they wanted her to waddle for them or stick a cushion up her school tunic. 'I am preggers, and I am delighted and happy, so stick that up your nose.'

'Harriet, come down this instant, you hear me, I want you in my study now.'

She marched in and sat down in the big, black leather wing chair and swung her legs. He had his speech all prepared just as if he were in court, but suddenly the words disappeared and he got up and pulled her into his arms. 'Oh, Harry, Harry, you silly, silly gel, what a mess you've got yourself into! But not to worry, we'll get it all sorted out.'

She hugged her father, this show of emotion was so unlike him and she felt sorry, sorry for all the upset, but she was resolved, and would not be persuaded. 'Pa, I want him so much, I want this baby, and I am going to have him. Please, please, don't make me lose him, don't let them take him away . . .'

The Judge tried everything, and in the end he had to admire his daughter. He asked her time and time again for the name of the father, did she love him?

'I do, I love him with all my heart.'

The Judge sighed with relief. Well at least that was one thing in their favour. 'Well, then, you'll have to marry the chap, who is it?'

Harriet bowed her head and looked at her shoes.

'Come on, gel, out with it, I'll go round and see his family, is he foreign? You meet him in Switzerland?'

The Judge gulped down his Scotch and sat down next to his wife, took her hand. 'Gel's got a will of iron. She won't have it aborted, and she won't say who the father is, only that she loves the chap and she wants his brat. I don't know what we are going to do, be a bloody rum do her coming out six months' pregnant, be the laughing stock . . . Some birthday party, what?'

Mrs Simpson felt the tears rising again, and sniffed. 'Now, now, don't break the taps, old thing, we'll sort something out. We can pack her off to the country – that cousin of yours, farm down in Dorset. Nobody'll see her there, know her . . . she can have the thing and . . .'

The more they discussed it the more it became a vicious circle of problems. If she was allowed to have it and then returned to London everyone would know.

'Don't suppose we could farm it out, no, she wouldn't

accept that. We could say we've adopted it, lot of it going on
nowadays.'

Harriet came in, downcast but unashamed, and repeated how
sorry she was, and how sad to make the whole family so
unhappy. 'I'll marry the father one day, I promise you. It's just
he has things to do. I don't mind staying down on Auntie's farm,
I can even take my horse.'

Mrs Simpson told her that she was even more stupid than she
had imagined. 'You can't ride in your condition, you silly gel.
Who is the fellow, why won't you tell us? I mean, if he needs
money perhaps Daddy can help out.'

'Bloody take a shotgun to him, more like it . . . whoever he
is needs a ruddy thrashing. You're only sixteen, for Gawd's sake.'

Harriet got up and put her arms around both parents' shoulders and kissed them. 'Just know that I love him, I really do, and
I want his son.'

At that moment she seemed so grown up, so much older than
her parents even, and they looked at each other and gave in.

The Simpsons prepared a press release to the effect that Harriet
Simpson's forthcoming dance would be cancelled due to illness.
Then they crossed it out – the Judge said it sounded better if
they said, 'due to a family bereavement' . . . In truth it felt like
one, they had suddenly lost their little girl.

Harriet adored the country. Her Auntie Mae was a distant relative, and one they usually kept out of the way. She was a big,
rotund woman with two grown-up sons married and living
close by, and she welcomed Harriet with open arms. Her husband was reluctant at first, but the Judge gave them a handsome
allowance to keep her until the child was born.

She roamed the fields in her old print frocks, she didn't
bother with maternity wear. She simply left the zippers or hooks
and eyes open. She wore an old pair of sandals that looked as
though she had worn them to go paddling.

As the months passed, her belly grew, and she loved the feel of her baby inside her. She wrote long stories in her diary, they were love stories, but she never mentioned the name, the person she wrote them for.

The local doctor and district nurse checked her over, she was fit, healthy, and her child never seemed to cause her a moment's problem. She yelled the first time he kicked, and made everyone feel her huge belly.

'How come you're so sure he's a boy?'

She wrinkled her tanned face, her freckles all joined into one, and roared with laughter. 'Because I know, and what's more I am going to have three more, and they'll all be enormous!'

Harriet ate like a horse and grew plump and round, her long legs tanned. She would pinch her fat, swearing like the farm labourers. 'Bloody hell-fire, I'll have to go on a diet, when he's home and dry, I'll be as big as a house.' She waddled like a duck to make the lads laugh, and they adored her. There was nothing they would not do for their madcap Cousin Harry.

Aunt Mae sat sewing by the open kitchen door. 'She looks so beautiful, like a wild thing. She's so happy, so full of life, it breaks my heart.'

Aunt Mae had tried once to ask Harriet about the father of her son, but she had wagged her finger and sworn she would not be tricked by anyone into telling.

'It's just that he's missing so much, to see you as you are now. To touch your belly, feel his unborn child, is something important to a man, Harry, and he's missing it.'

She wished she hadn't brought it up when she heard Harriet up in her little room, sobbing as if her heart would break.

The next day Harriet was all sunshine again, but her aunt detected a sadness that wasn't there before. 'I dare say he'll be with you for the next lot you want to have, so it makes no difference, really, does it?'

Harriet gave her aunt one of her sweet smiles and that funny little wrinkle of her nose. They both knew in their hearts that the first-born was very special.

'You got a name for him, lovey? What you going to call this chap?'

Stretching her arms above her head, Harriet said that it was a secret, and when she lowered her arms she felt the first pains. She clapped her hands . . .

'Oh, Auntie, he's coming, he's coming, he's on his way.'

Chapter Ten

Edward received no reply from his many letters to BB. He was not unduly worried as Harriet had told him they had only just left for South Africa. He bided his time working in bars in and around Southampton, saving for his passage. The months passed and still no word came, and so he sent a cable saying he was on his way, hoping that by the time he arrived BB would be expecting him with the job offered to Edward waiting for him. He eventually made it to South Africa after a nightmare journey, by seaplane, tram boat and a two-seater mail plane. He was sweating in the intense heat, for even though the taxi had every window open, the air was still and arid. He began to worry about the length of the drive, conserving his hard-earned money as always. 'Is it much further to Rosebank?'

The driver coughed and spat out of the window. 'Not far, boss, it's another ten, fifteen miles along the highway. You can't miss it when you see it, where the rich live.'

Half an hour later the scenery changed and the houses became very grand, almost baronial in style – some low to the ground like sprawling bungalows, others tall and pillared like the houses of America's deep south. The taxi swept up a wide gravel drive, the palm trees clustered along its edge giving shade from the boiling sun. The house was three-storeyed with a verandah running the whole length of the ground floor. Painted awnings hung over the windows with shutters to match, and Edward got out and stared in admiration. He paid off the taxi and walked up to the front door.

The bell resounded through the house with a strange echoing effect. Edward rang again, waited, stepped back and looked up at the house. 'Hello . . .? Hello . . .?'

A black maid opened the door and peered out.

'Edward Stubbs, I cabled that I was coming over, is Mr Van der Burge at home?'

She opened the door and turned back into the house without a word . . . to him. She shouted, 'Meester B . . . Meesteeeer B! There is someone here for you!' The woman waddled across a long, polished floor. She banged on a door, shouted again and then turned. 'He's in here, but he's sleeping. He expecting ya?'

BB yanked open the door. His suit was rumpled, his collar stained, and his face was so flushed that Edward hardly recognized him.

'Vat you screamin' fer, woman?'

'Mr Van der Burge, it's me, Edward, Edward Stubbs. I cabled you . . . Edward Stubbs, sir, we met at the Simpsons'.'

BB swayed, stared hard, and then his eyes lit up and he opened his arms. 'My friend, my friend, come in, come in . . . Zelda, get us something in here fast, come on in . . .'

Edward left his case and followed BB into the room. It was cool, the shutters drawn so that it was in semi-darkness. The floor was of pine with rugs scattered over it, the furniture was wicker and a Hoover fan twirled overhead. There were also, Edward couldn't help but notice, a lot of whisky bottles, many of them empty.

BB poured himself a brandy, stumbled against the side of a large, polished table. 'Coffee . . . damned black bitch . . . Coffeeee Zeldaaaa.'

He staggered to an armchair and fell down into it. 'Sit down, lad, sit down, how long are you here for then?'

Edward began to think he was going out of his mind, he sat

and looked at the room then mentioned the job BB had offered him.

'What job, my friend, what job?'

Zelda thudded into the room with a tray of coffee and a few stale biscuits, and banged it down on the table. 'You should not drink, Meester B, it's no good for ya.'

BB glared at her and Edward rose. He followed Zelda out, closing the door behind him. BB seemed not to notice his departure.

'How long has he been like this? He's dead drunk.'

Zelda shrugged her fat shoulders, tried hard to remember exactly how long BB had been drunk, but she rolled her eyes and gave up.

'Is Mrs Van der Burge at home, Zelda?'

She shook her head, then made a circular motion with her finger near her head, rolling her eyes. 'She's in the home again, and this time she don't look as if she ever come out – crazy.'

Edward leaned against the polished banister. 'Oh Christ, I don't believe this. Where's his bedroom? I'll get him up there – he looks like he needs a wash.'

Together they hauled the big man slowly up the stairs. When they reached the landing he fought them off, swayed, and was about to topple backwards, but Edward caught him.

'Bastards, sons of black bitches, all of them bastards.'

They had a struggle to get his clothes off. Zelda informed Edward he had not changed his clothes for weeks, and they smelt like it. When the big man was clean they rolled him into his double bed. He seemed for a moment to focus, held out his hand as though to shake Edward's, then it flopped on to the bed and he snored, falling into a deep sleep.

Edward walked around the house. It was filthy, every room filled with dust and dirty dishes. Eventually he opened a door on the same landing as BB's bedroom. It had been converted into an office, and there were papers in every corner, stacked almost to the ceiling. The desk was a mess of open drawers, and more papers were strewn across it and the floor.

Edward remained in the room for most of the night, and by morning his back ached and his eyes itched from reading. BB was broke. How he had been living in London God alone knew – probably on credit. Edward struck the desk with his fist – BB, the great financier, had lost everything in the Wall Street Crash. He had only useless mines and overdrafts – Edward took his fury out on the papers, hurling them across the room. Judging by the mess, that was more than likely what BB had done himself. He went to BB's room and looked at the big, beached whale as he snored and right there and then he wanted to kill him. But he closed the door, went to his room and sat hopelessly on his bed, beside his unopened suitcase. He lay across the musty-smelling bed, and then was gripped by a sudden, terrible wrenching pain. He doubled up, clutched his belly. He was terrified, what in God's name was the matter with him?

The pains swept over him in engulfing waves. They would subside only to come back, wrenching and shaking his body . . . Sweat dripped off him and he felt them coming again and again . . . He rolled on the bed, his legs thrashing, in agony . . .

Slowly, as the sun came up, the pain diminished. He lay exhausted, gasping for breath. An overwhelming sense of grief and loss engulfed him. He touched his face, half surprised to find he was crying, the tears streaming down his face. He got up and stared at himself, stared at the weeping man in the mirror.

He ran down the stairs, leaping the last ten to the landing below, kicked open BB's door and grabbed the startled man. BB was sober but confused, and Edward was like a madman.

'Call London, call London, you have to call London . . . listen to me, you have to call London . . .'

Somehow he got through to BB, who unearthed the telephone number. Edward snatched up the receiver and waited for what seemed an interminable age of misdialling, operators' voices and strange noises, until finally he heard a distant ringing tone.

BB fought to get his befuddled brain into order so he could speak. Edward gripped his arm so tightly it was like a vice. 'Speak to them, ask them if everything is all right, now, speak to them now.'

BB took the phone, breathed in and licked his lips. 'Hello ... hello, can you hear me? It's BB! What? It's a terrible line, hello? Allard, it's BB, just making the yearly how–de–do call. Everything all right there, old chap? Can you speak up, it's difficult to hear ...'

Edward released his hold on BB's arm, his eyes searching the man's face. He wanted to grab the phone from the pudgy hand, but he contained himself. He was sure the Simpsons wouldn't approve of him even trying to speak to Harriet. He wished he'd just asked for Allard, made some excuse to speak to him.

BB listened, his face red, the sweat trickling down his chin. He mopped his brow with a dirty, stained handkerchief. 'I can't hear? What ...? Oh, Sylvia? Well, she's not too good. Is everything all right there?'

BB battled with the bad connection, his voice rising. 'What? She is? No ... no reason, just rang to say hello ... what?' He looked at the phone and shook it. Edward could hear the buzz of the dialling tone ... He seized the phone.

'It's no good, been cut off. Lines are always bad, terrible connections.'

Edward's eyes frightened him, deep, black eyes.

'Harriet? Did they say anything about Harry?'

BB scratched his head. His eyes filled up and he looked at Edward, helplessly. He was hardly able to recall what had just been said to him. 'Think they said something about her being a bit under the weather, not "coming out" this season ... What is it, lad? What's wrong, what have I done?'

Edward felt his whole body relaxing, the pain in his stomach eased and he slumped into a chair. 'Nothing, nothing ... Sorry if I yelled at you, I just ... I just had a gut feeling ... an odd feeling.'

The pains had subsided completely, the awful wrenching at his belly was over. BB stuck his hands in his pockets. Tufts of white hair stood up on end around his bald head. Edward stared through him, and then his eyes focused on the old man. His voice was quiet now. 'I need you, BB – need you to make my fortune. What a joke, what a fucking joke. You don't even know who I am, do you? Do you . . .?'

BB's face puckered as he sat in the chair, his feet planted wide apart, a shell of the man he once was.

It was all coming back to him now, he remembered who Edward was. He slumped before the younger man, head bowed in shame. He could find no words to express his feelings. He was a drunkard, a bankrupt, and a liar. Edward clenched his fists in anger as he saw the light dawning on the old man. BB's voice was hoarse, whisky-soaked. 'Allard's friend . . . yes, Eddie. Oh God, my mind's so fuddled.'

Edward gripped him tightly. 'Then you're going to have to get straightened out, you're all I've got. We're partners, you and me, and we'll do it on a handshake. I'll get you back on your feet, I don't know how the hell, but, by Christ, I've not come all this way for nothing. Shake . . . shake, BB.'

The old man looked Edward in the eyes and shook hands. He gave a wobbly smile. 'We used to play draughts . . . yes, yes, I remember . . . You played a good game of draughts. I've not played for a long time now, a long, long time.'

'We'll play anything you want, BB . . . after I've made my fortune.'

BB thought he was joking, but Edward's face was like a mask, with no trace of humour. There wasn't even a glimmer of a smile.

The birth had been easy for Harriet. Even so, she had screamed the place down. The midwife had blushed at her language, and the doctor had laughed as Harriet kept up a steady flow of verbal abuse. She had swung her fists in the air, writhing around on the old-fashioned bed. 'You bloody amateurs, what in Christ's name are you doing? Get that stupid bitch out of here, I want a vet! A vet knows better than you two! Ohhhh, Jesusssss . . .'

But when the baby was born, and laid on her breast, Harriet softened. She glowed like every other mother the doctor had seen. She held her son in her arms, not wanting to part with him even to be washed. He weighed eight and a half pounds and was perfect, with a mop of jet-black hair. His eyelashes were so long they brushed his cheeks. His tawny skin was neither reddened nor wrinkled ... he was like a doll, sleeping contentedly.

'Oh, look at his fingers, Auntie Mae, have you ever seen such perfect hands – and his toes, each one is simply perfect.'

They were beautiful together, she with her rosy-red cheeks and her auburn hair tumbling around her shoulders. The baby was strong, his tiny fists clenching and unclenching. He had such a pair of lungs the whole farm knew his arrival had been accomplished successfully. The lads all gathered outside Harriet's window, and she held up her son with pride.

'See, what did I tell you? It's a boy! Look at him, isn't he just wonderful?'

Harriet was so strong and healthy she was up and about the following morning, singing at the top of her voice. Auntie Mae was preparing her breakfast when she burst into the kitchen.

'I want eggs, bacon, porridge and tea, and – oh, yes, toast, with lots of marmalade – your home-made stuff. Oh, don't bother with a tray, I'll eat down here – he's had his breakfast. Guess what his name is – go on, guess.'

Auntie Mae shook her head in wonder. Most women spent at least a week in hospital when they had babies, and here was Harriet charging around the kitchen. She was stuffing food into her mouth like a naughty schoolgirl. In all truth she really was just that, her aunt thought to herself. She ruffled Harriet's hair and Harriet gave her a bear-hug, then nuzzled her neck. 'I think I am happier than I have ever been in my whole life, my son is ... Oh, Auntie Mae, he looks just like his father.'

She began to tickle her aunt, who tried unsuccessfully to

guess not only the father's name but the secret name Harriet had chosen for her son.

No one would have expected it, or even dreamed it could happen. Two weeks later, while Auntie Mae was preparing Harriet's bumper breakfast, one of the farm boys popped in with a bunch of wild flowers. He stood at the kitchen door, grinning and asking if anyone had guessed the baby's name. Harriet had promised a ten-pound note to the first person to get it right, so the farm hands were always dropping in with hopeful suggestions. Mae took the flowers and put water in a vase for them. She laughed and told the boys she was sure their Harry wouldn't call the boy Ned, that was the old carthorse's name.

'Well, I tried all the others I can think of, and it'd be just like her to call him something different. So my money's on Ned.'

When Mae had sent the boy back to work, she realized how quiet it was – too quiet. She had not heard either the baby or Harriet, and it was after seven.

'Harry? You all right, my love? Only I got breakfast near done. That was the boy from Barrow's Lane, you've got 'em all guessing – he says you'll be calling him after the old carthorse ... Harry?'

Mae listened at Harriet's door. The silence worried her. She lifted the latch and peeked in.

Harriet was standing in the centre of the room, wearing a long, white nightdress. The buttons were undone, her breast bared ready for feeding. The baby was cradled in her arms.

'Oh, why didn't you answer me? You gave me such a fright.'

Slowly, Harriet turned her stricken face to her aunt. She tried to speak, but couldn't.

'What is it, lovey? Harry? Dear God, child, what is it?'

Aunt Mae moved closer, peered at the baby. His eyes were closed, as if he were sleeping. She reached out to touch him, but Harriet stepped back.

'Now, love, just let me take a look at him ... Harry?'

She stepped forward again, and this time Harriet allowed her to touch the baby. He was cold, his tiny hand was ice cold.

'Will you let me hold him a while? There's a good girl.'

Mae took the baby from her, and knew he was dead. She wrapped a shawl around him.

Harriet's voice was barely audible. 'He was cold when I went to give him his feed in the night. I've had him close by me, I've kept him warm, but he won't wake up.'

Aunt Mae took the baby downstairs and called for one of the farm boys to get the doctor, fast, although she knew it was too late, nothing could be done for the child. She covered his face and hurried back to Harriet.

She was still standing in exactly the same position, her arms half lifted as though she still held her son.

The doctor came immediately. He could find no reason for the baby's death. He said, sadly, it was a tragedy. No one was to blame, no one could ever have predicted it. He spent a long time sitting with Harriet, trying to make her understand that it was not her fault. He was very perturbed that Harriet did not cry, and more worried when he realized she did not accept that the child was gone. He gave her sedatives to make her sleep, and Mae sat with her for two days and nights while she lay, dry-eyed, staring at the ceiling. Deep, shuddering sighs shook her body, and she clasped her aunt's hand tightly, but no tears ever came.

The baby was buried in the Simpsons' family chapel, a cloak of secrecy over the proceedings. Harriet had not given the child his name, and he had never been christened. She played no part in the funeral arrangements, and refused to name the father on the birth certificate.

Mrs Simpson sighed with relief. The baby's death saddened her, but at the same time it did save the family any embarrassment. She expected Harriet to pick up her life as if it had never happened, unaware of how deeply the loss had affected her daughter.

*

Mae took Harriet back to London, and her heart broke when they said goodbye. She even offered to stay in town to take care of her, but Mrs Simpson dismissed the offer, insisting that all Harriet needed was time. Mae left a changed girl behind her in the Kensington house.

It was accepted that Harriet would not 'be herself' for a while, and the Simpsons were not unduly worried by her quietness. She withdrew from the family, preferring to eat alone in her room. Mrs Simpson put up with Harriet's moody idleness for as long as she thought she should mourn. But when she remained locked in her room months after the funeral, she began to wonder if Harriet should see a doctor. Her room was untidy, dirty, with plates of rotting food pushed under the bed. She refused to wash or dress, but lay on her bed, staring into space. She had a habit of picking at bread, making it into small hard balls, and odd piles of her endeavours littered the room. She began raving against her mother, accusing her of spying, and would put a chair under her door handle in addition to turning the key in the lock. She grew very thin and refused food, until Mrs Simpson was at her wits' end.

The Judge tried to talk to his daughter and was spat at. He was astounded at her filthy language. She became abusive if any of them tried to make her eat. Allard tried, but was told he was a nasty old poofter. He beat a hasty retreat in case the Judge should hear her.

The family doctor gave Harriet another supply of sedatives. He discussed her symptoms with her parents, and put it down to severe depression after the loss of her baby. He did, however, say that if her 'illness' persisted she should see a psychiatrist.

Harriet's condition not only persisted, it grew steadily worse. The climax came when the Judge found her in the kitchen. She was setting two places at the table, and talking in a hideous, high-pitched voice to someone she accused of trying to kill her. The Judge was mortified.

'Harry, old gel, there's no one else here but me. It's four in the morning, why don't you let Daddy take you back to bed?'

She lunged at her father with the kitchen knife, narrowly missing him. He shouted for his wife, and together they managed to get Harriet back to her room. For what remained of the night they could hear her, crying and shouting jumbled words. She was obviously putting herself through hell.

The next morning she was laughing, cooking eggs and bacon. On the surface it appeared she was suddenly all right again. She ate ravenously, and chattered non-stop about things she wanted to do and places she would like to go to. When Allard came downstairs she teased him and laughed so much the tears rolled down her cheeks. They watched her dancing around, then she thudded back up the stairs to get dressed for a 'mammoth shopping spree'.

An hour later they found her lying on her bed, staring listlessly at the ceiling. Judge Simpson arranged an appointment for her in Harley Street with Mr Montague Flynn, a kindly psychiatrist, who diagnosed schizophrenia. He had a long discussion with the Judge, who refused to believe there was anything of that nature wrong with his daughter, insisting it was just depression. Mr Flynn assured him, quietly but firmly, that Harriet's condition was a little more than that.

'You see, sir, schizophrenia symptoms are fluid. It's a changing process, rather than static. Your daughter may demonstrate different signs of her illness from day to day, even hour to hour. She may show different symptoms in different situations. Often diagnosis is difficult, but she has all the classic signs of disordered perceptions – she hears voices that blame her for the death of her child. Her logic is overborne by the strength of her delusions. She has changed radically in the past few months from a happy, outgoing girl to a recluse. She is very self-critical, and exceptionally anxious. Your daughter, sir, needs help, she is crying out for it in the only way she can ...'

*

The Judge blamed everything on his wife and her sister. 'I have never had any of this kind of trouble in my family, but your sister went off her head when her boys were killed. Runs in the family – your family.'

Mrs Simpson sipped her gin and tonic, her foot twitching. 'I blame whoever got her pregnant, that's whose fault it is, and if I ever find out who he was, I'll wring his neck.'

The Judge picked up the *Evening Standard*, muttering that if he ever found out who it was, he'd take a shotgun to him. He retired behind his paper, the print blurring before his eyes as they filled with tears. Seeing his daughter that way had hurt him more than he would ever be able to tell.

His wife continued, 'Well, she won't be coming out this season, that's for sure.'

The Judge turned the page. 'I don't want to talk about it, subject's closed.'

Mrs Simpson sighed, wondering if there could be any truth in the suggestion of a connection between Harriet and her sister. She dismissed the thought immediately, blamed the entire illness on the father of Harriet's baby. She banged her glass down. 'I hope he rots in hell.'

The following day Harriet left to stay at a clinic. She went quietly, without argument. She looked older – strangely old – wearing a hat pulled down to hide her face. When Mrs Simpson went into her daughter's room she found an auburn heap on the untidy dressing table. Harriet had cut her hair.

Chapter Eleven

Alex sat with Dora in the office. He had taken a while to come back to her with his analysis of the club's accounts. She was slightly afraid of him – he spoke so quietly, and was obviously nervous himself. He made it brief – the gambling part of the club was badly run. They had just a few poker games, private sessions, which could be opened up into a much more ambitious operation, a much bigger money earner. First, she should put in a roulette wheel.

'Well, I know that, darlin', but if you've got a partner that plays your own tables, forget it. I did have one for a while, but I had to close it right down.'

Alex waited for her to calm down. 'Johnny's boozing and gambling away all the profits, right? Well, you're his partner, and I'm telling you the accounts indicate you could double the earnings on this place. But you've got to off-load your husband first.'

Dora threw up her hands and said she was working on it, but there was only so much she could do.

'What's his share worth, Dora, twenty-five grand? That's being generous. You could buy him out. This place is leased, you don't even own the building – all you got is the licence, the lease and the fixtures and fittings.'

He had her full attention now. She listened, sipping at her

water. 'I've not got that kind of money, Alex. You should know, you've got the books, for Chrissake.'

Alex stared at her and his eyes frightened her, they were so expressionless. 'First you have to have a legal document stating what the partnership is worth, how much cash. That I can do for you.'

Alex was making notes on a small slip of paper, and he said that rather than go for the highest estimate she had to go for the lowest. 'Forty thousand, you want the place insured for that, all legal, just so should anyone ask you know exactly how much you want if someone offers to buy you out . . .'

Alex continued, she had to make Johnny sign another document making her a legal partner, the papers she had at the moment would not really stand up to scrutiny.

'I'll sack that bloody lawyer of mine, he's useless. He was supposed to do it.'

Again Alex waited patiently for her to calm down, then in his steady, low voice he went on. 'The papers must be verified by a good company, a known company. There must be someone who works for some big law firm among your customers – use him, use his company. Legal, it has to be legal.'

Dora hesitated. She knew everything Alex had said was true, but there had to be a catch. 'Okay, come on, out with it. Why are you doing all this?'

'I took a fall for Johnny, years ago, but what did he do for me? A few words here and there with some prison barons, but he never came to see me, never asked how I was. I don't owe Johnny anything – so listen carefully. I've found out Johnny owes money all over town, even at Harry Driver's. He plays for high stakes, likes poker sessions . . . he's also hooked on the booze. You an' me, Dora, we'll pull a sting, one that'll leave you owning the club outright.'

Dora's jaw dropped. There he sat, like a big oaf, and yet he talked as if he knew exactly what he was doing.

Taking his time, Alex outlined the plan, and Dora didn't interrupt once. When he had finished she sat chewing her lips for a moment. 'What do you get out of it?'

Alex smiled, lifted his hands in a casual gesture. 'I'll run the place for a nice wage. Better than sittin' on me backside in Harry Driver's sweatshops.'

Alex was already packing his briefcase. Dora sighed. 'All right, let's do it.'

Alex gave her one of his strange smiles. 'That's a clever girl.'

Edward knew exactly the scam he and BB would pull to make them rich. It was far-fetched, requiring a lot of time and hard labour. It would take at least four years. This was summer 1947, and Edward had been in South Africa almost a year. Under Edward's instructions, BB had purchased four 'dead' mines. He already owned five non-productive mines, all lying dormant. He questioned Edward as to why he was to buy still more, but as always there was no reply. BB had grown accustomed to the mask-like expression Edward used when he didn't wish to discuss something. He could be jovial, even laughing, but as soon as BB pushed for information his eyes went blank. It was chilling, this ability to switch moods so rapidly. At times BB felt afraid of him, but his usual good humour and friendship touched the old man, and he eventually stopped probing.

However, things began to change after BB received a letter from his son Richard, who was living in England. He went to Edward's room and found him sitting at the microscope on his makeshift desk, as usual, surrounded by hundreds of test tubes and stacks of notes and files. BB coughed and waited for Edward to give him a nod that it was all right to speak.

'Just got a letter from Richard. He's doing quite well, working for De Veer's in Hatton Garden. He says he'll be coming over quite soon ... Edward? I said I got a letter. You met Richard at the Simpsons', didn't you?'

Edward dropped his pencil, moved the microscope aside and rubbed his eyes. He held out his hand for the letter, and read it while BB wandered around the room looking at the hundreds of sample phials filled with sand and rock, all neatly tagged.

Edward shook his head in disgust, the contents of the letter infuriated him. 'He's asking for more money! What does he want another house for?'

BB stared at one of the ampoules, taking it out of its wooden rack.

'Don't touch anything, BB.'

Poor BB jumped nervously and immediately replaced the thin glass tube. Edward continued, 'You should let him earn his own money if he's got such a good job. What's he coming to you with his hand out for?'

BB straightened his tie, stood with legs apart. 'He's my son, that's why. Look, I think I'll take a little trip into town, all right with you? Anything you want? Zelda's got *bobotie* for your dinner.'

Edward was already back at work, squinting intently through the microscope, and he didn't answer. After shuffling his feet for a moment BB departed. Edward worked on, and when Zelda brought him a supper tray he looked at his watch and was startled at how late it was. 'BB not back yet, Zelda? He called at all?'

She shook her head, then went to the window and lifted the blind. The old Bentley could be heard churning up the gravel outside. She let the blind drop. 'I made you a nice *melktert* for your pudding ... Eh, eh, he's home, boss, and he drunk. He cut right across the flowerbeds again.'

She rolled her way out and padded along the landing as the front door crashed shut, making all Edward's glass tubes shiver. Edward pushed his supper tray aside and marched out on to the landing. He looked over the banister and yelled, 'Where in God's name have you been?' He started down the stairs. 'Most important, did you tell anyone I was here? Look at you, you're a mess, you wonder why I don't tell you anything? This is the reason! You're pissed out of your mind, for Chrissake, you could ruin everything.'

Swaying and blinking, BB puffed out his cheeks. 'I've just had a couple at the Pretoria Club, and why not? You sit here all day, all night. I don't know what the hell is going on in my own house. All you get me to do is buy up useless mines ... So I went to a soccer match. Good game, Cape Coloureds played well. You know, man, those Bantu fellas kick the ball around like the devil. Mind you ...'

Edward interrupted him. 'You tell anyone about my presence here? Did you? Well, did you?' BB burped and gave Edward a shifty look. Edward reached out and pulled BB to him. BB was wearing his best suit, and Edward picked up his silk tie. BB eased it away from him and tried to straighten it, but he stumbled and fell into a chair. 'No one knows, I have told no one, man, but I had a little business to do. I'm not a damned prisoner, for Chrissakes, man!'

Edward snapped that he was until he was told differently. 'This is part of the plan, BB, and if you foul it up now how can I trust you later on?'

The old man looked crestfallen and Edward pulled up a chair. He gave a little wink to show he wasn't angry any more. BB rubbed his head until what little hair he had left stood on end.

'Okay,' said Edward, 'this is what you do. Might work well ... You cable Richard, tell him to get a flight over. When we get the dates I'll tell you more, but get him out here.'

Edward walked out, and BB padded after him, pleading like a child. 'Tell me, tell me what you've got up your sleeve. You make me feel so useless. I want to help you, man, you said you needed me?'

Edward turned, put his arm around BB's shoulders and led him into the study. He decided that perhaps it was time to let BB in on part of the plan. 'Okay, sit down, look around. See these samples ... I'm going to need a hundred times this amount. Maybe Richard's coming will be more than useful, I've got to get into one of the major companies.'

Edward tried to explain to BB in simple terms what he had been working on at Cambridge – Walter's initial hopes of a breakthrough in assimilating tests for minerals taken from the surface of the land. He made no mention, of course, that the experiment was instigated by Walter. 'My theory was that, by testing the minerals, I could say without doubt whether or not the ground had the right amount of mineral deposits – that it would produce diamonds, gold, semi-precious stones even. This would bypass the vast expense of drilling equipment and initial layout of . . .'

Edward couldn't finish as BB roared with laughter, shaking his head. 'Well, man, that's a tall order, and pretty nigh impossible. For one, the diamonds can be found on the surface of a productive mine, or close to water, you don't have to dig, boy. The land is littered with diamonds, opals; washing plants are what you have to set up, wash for 'em. It's the building of the water plants that takes the initial cash, and then it's wash, gallons . . . you find a glimmer of a fissure all hell breaks loose, and when it's dried up your luck is out, like mine, finished. Left with thousands of worthless acres.'

Edward was whistling, impatient for BB to wind down. But BB continued, 'You've got to have blasting licences, the machinery alone would set you back half a million, you can't move in mining on a few hundred thousand, unless you get a strike . . . an' I know of men who have kicked, kicked the ground and turned over jars the size of eggs, diamonds big as my fists in the old days, but you'll never find those again. Land that can be had cheap is drying up.'

Edward banged on the side of his chair and BB glared.

'You haven't listened to me. Do you think I would be going to all this trouble if I was trying for a goddamn strike? I know what sort of cash we have – you have – and I know how much we would need to even attempt a mining venture. That is not my concern. I am going to prove that dead, known mines can be productive.'

Again BB guffawed with laughter. 'You'll need more than a theory, son, and I'm telling you straight, you'll never be able to prove it for years, years.'

Finally losing his patience, Edward jumped up and paced the room. He snapped, 'I never said my theory was proved, but what if I could prove it? What if I could, for example, guarantee that your dead mines were actually alive?' He sat down on the edge of his chair. BB pursed his lips. He could see Edward's excitement.

'Take it one step further – what if, after I had stated that I could guarantee your mines would produce again, this statement were leaked to the press? Not by any old sod, but by a scientist actually working in, for example, the De Veer labs, thereby giving credence to the experiment? What if, after that statement, your mine did produce again? Any mine, come to think of it, that had been a dead zone for years. What do you think would happen then?'

'You'd have a bloody stampede, man, for your services! You know, lad, if there was even so much as a suspicion that there's diamonds in this area ... We have to be bloody careful, any findings of valuable minerals ... Jesus, I start to open up my places, my mines, that costs in itself. You're looking at machinery that'll cost at least ten thousand, you have to show we are actually working, that work is in progress ... No mine in production is without washing plants, and everyone knows it is the only way diamonds are generally discovered. The workers cost nothing but a few rand and a good meal a day so that's not much outlay, and they are so thick they wouldn't know what the hell we were up to. But everything, everything we set up, needs money. See, you rarely find diamonds just by turning gravel over, so we need diggers, then we got to make an elaborate show of security – no productive mine is without security, wouldn't look right.'

BB strutted across the room, chomping on his cigar, his face shining.

Edward smiled. 'It'd be an elaborate charade, but it would mean that your dead mines would become valuable assets overnight, wouldn't you agree? Even more of a proposition if you were forced by bankruptcy to sell in auction all the mines that had recently been discovered to be productive again. You with me?'

BB dragged on his cigar. Slowly, it was dawning on him why Edward had made him acquire more defunct mines.

'The banks have already loaned out enough to open the mines. Now we start borrowing more and more, until they call in the loans and you are forced to sell – forced just when it is made public that they are rich! Rich, BB!'

'Jesus Christ, man, you'll never get away with it! The De Veer company would never allow it, that's if you can ever get a job in one of their labs in the first place. There's no certainty, and even if you did, and say it was De Veer's, they'd be over your shoulder like hawks.'

Edward pulled his chair closer, so his knees were touching the old man's. 'I can do it, I know it! I can make the scam work, but it will take time, years. Each sample will have to be doctored by me, and when I'm through they will have thousands and thousands of samples. Now, when I begin to leak my work to the press – not from Pretoria, from right across Africa – the theory will have to be refuted. That will take time because I will have made up so many thousands of samples, and they will have to check them all before they can say my experiments are a load of crap . . . But by that time, we will already have sold, understand me? We coincide the leaks about your mines precisely with the banks foreclosing on their loans. You have no alternative but to sell, but by Christ you'll kick up a storm, desperate not to sell . . .'

BB couldn't quite follow. 'You fix each ampoule? That's what you're doing? What're you using, chippings? Real stones?'

Edward waved his hand around at the already tagged samples. He gave a wink, tapped his nose. 'It will take me years to "gather" this lot, but I will gradually take them into the lab, the lab of a well-thought-of company with a big name. They will receive them carton by carton, so it will look like I'm working on each one, one at a time. They will have no idea I've doctored them, right? With me? I'll need to be taking trips out to mines every day, and I need gold, diamonds and gems to grind and roughen. It will cost every penny you can borrow or beg.

You will have to borrow more from the banks, do you understand?'

BB's brain began to tick. It was a wild, far-fetched scheme,
but Edward's enthusiasm was contagious. 'You've got to get
inside one of the major companies, the only way to pull it off,
need them behind you.'

Edward knew the old boy was hooked, and he grinned.
'Richard will get me in, I know it. If he's already working for
De Veer's he may be able to get me an introduction, added to
which I have a first-class honours degree from Cambridge, plus
my professor is sending me glowing reports – reports, BB, on
my work at Cambridge, which is . . . the theory I've just told
you. But I have to gain authenticity from one of the big companies. So, I want to get Richard out here, and fast.'

'Consider it done – partner.'

Chapter Twelve

Johnny was shaving when Dora took in his coffee, put it down and asked him if he remembered one of those rich fellas from the other night, the one with the Greeks?

'I dunno! What other night? What the hell are you talking about?'

She sat on the edge of the bath and said that the reason she was asking was she had been asked to set up a game in the club – a real private one for high stakes, on a Sunday when the place was closed.

Johnny was immediately alert, she could see just by the way he continued shaving and said nothing.

'Only that Sunday I gotta go to Brighton, it's Hylda's birthday party. You know Hylda, girl with the long blonde hair and the lisp ... Well, she's having her twenty-first, I can't get out of it.'

Johnny rinsed his face, patted it dry with the towel. 'What you want me to do?'

She told him the most important thing was that he didn't even think about playing. These were big money boys with a lot of cash to throw around. 'What you say, Johnny, you around Sunday?'

He was so annoying she could have hit him. He combed his hair and said he might be, he wasn't sure.

'All right then, I'll get Arnie in to see to it. I dunno, I don't ask you to do much, but I would have thought you could at least show some interest. By the way, is it true you took cash out of the till again last night . . . Johnny, I'm talking to you.'

He sprayed her cologne over himself and admired his new suit in the mirror.

'Johnny, will you answer me?'

He tossed her comb on to the bed and went out into the hall. 'I hear yer! I hear yer, what else yer want from me? Any more bits of fucking paper yer want me ter sign? You can go stuff yourself! You got that ape Arnie counting out all the money I take out. So I owe yer a few quid, so fucking what, it's my club. Anyone calls for me, tell 'em I've gone away, fend 'em off, will yer. And Sunday I'll be there, I'll be there.'

She stopped him at the door and made him promise not to play, and then he slammed out. She dived for the phone. 'Alex? Alex, he's hooked, I know it. Can you set the game up, you sure? This Sunday, yeah, I'll have it for you, I will, no problem.'

Dora dressed quickly, went straight to the bank and made an arrangement to withdraw twenty-five thousand pounds, saying she would be in to collect it on Friday. Alex was waiting for her, and she stood on tiptoe and kissed him, then drove off in her little white sports car.

The three Greeks looked smart, and each carried a briefcase. Alex met them outside the club and gave Arnie the signal to open up and let them in.

Arnie switched all the lights on as they passed through. The smell of stale booze and cigarettes clung to the flock walls and, empty, the place seemed seedy. It surprised Alex as he had only ever seen it in full swing, with flowers on all the tables and a bevy of pretty girls. Now in the cold light of a Sunday afternoon it disgusted him.

No sooner had they entered when George Windsor arrived. He gave Alex a look, and behind him came two girls dressed in evening clothes to serve the drinks. There was no sign of Johnny Mask.

'Where the hell is he?'

Johnny waltzed in and apologized for being late but he had been busy. Alex could see he had already been drinking. Johnny stared hard at Alex and moved to his table, put an arm round him. 'Hey, Alex, you son of a bitch, how ya doin'? Jesus, truck run over yer face or what? Never would've known ya.' Then he pulled Alex to one side and whispered, 'You playin' with these wops?'

Alex assured him he was, then smiled and nudged Johnny and said after all he was an accountant now, and had made a few bob. Johnny seemed satisfied, and Alex caught the gleam in his eye as the Greeks dug deep in their pockets and laid thick wads of notes on the table. Alex joined them, and the girls moved around the table with drinks.

New packs of cards were ready on the table. Alex took his seat and, like the Greeks, took out a wad of money. Johnny perched on a bar stool, poured himself a Scotch, and watched the seal on a pack of cards being broken and the game begin.

Alex was up by two thousand, the men hardly speaking except to bid, and Johnny's fingers began to itch. The phone rang and Arnie answered, then looked across to the table. 'Call for you, Alex, important, sorry.'

As he passed Johnny, Alex spoke to him out of the side of his mouth. 'I thought these guys were supposed to be sharp, I'm creamin' them.'

The game went quiet, the men covered their cards. Alex swore into the phone, looked back at the table, then slammed the phone down.

'I got problems, I got to walk – I'm sorry about this.'

The Greeks argued among themselves, and Johnny moved to the table.

'No need to break the game, I'll take his place if you agree. Alex, what you say?'

Alex put it to the men and they refused, saying they would need to see the colour of Johnny Mask's cash. They knew about him, about the markers, and they were not interested. They wanted his money on the table.

Johnny swore and went to the till, sprang it open. It was cleaned out. As planned, Alex took Johnny aside and told him to get the papers from the safe in the office. He could put his share of the club up as a stake, and Alex would lend him cash in return. 'It's just between you an' me, Johnny, up to you. It's your choice, only I got to go.'

Johnny signed his half share of the club to Alex, and was handed twenty thousand pounds.

Alex walked out of the club as the game proceeded. He gave Arnie a look, and George walked with Alex to the exit. 'Gawd almighty, he fell for it, he's off his rocker.'

One hour later, Johnny was five thousand up, flushed and drinking steadily. He was playing well, and he was beginning to raise the bidding higher and higher. The Greeks won, lost, won, lost, making sure that Johnny believed he was on a winning streak. They had been playing for over two hours when the game began to move into really high stakes. The stakes were being pushed up by Johnny himself. He started the bidding on one hand at five thousand . . . Slowly the tables turned on him. The Greeks were good, and although Arnie watched closely he couldn't see how they were doing it. He would never play a game in one of their joints, that was for sure. They were wiping Johnny out, hand by hand. As Johnny began to panic, he doubled up his betting to try to recoup his losses.

At midnight Alex returned. Johnny looked exhausted, his collar undone, sweating, and stubble darkened his sweating cheeks. He seemed hardly to notice Alex's arrival, he was dealing, and his cash, once stacked so high in front of him, was down to about two or three thousand at most.

'He's lost every hand for the past hour, couple more big pots and he's finished.'

'Okay, I'll go five and another two on top to see you.'

'Fucking hell, shit . . . Shit!'

Johnny swiped at the table and the cards tumbled on to the floor. Arnie went immediately and gathered them up, replaced them with a new deck.

Three o'clock and Johnny was cleaned out. He walked away from the table, running his hands through his hair. 'Give us one for the road, Arnie old son.'

Arnie placed a double Scotch in front of him and he knocked it back, then gave a short, harsh laugh. 'You know, my Dad, he was a gyppo. He thought he had the luck, he gambled all his life. He died in a Salvation Army hostel ... Any of you lot know where I can find the nearest one?'

You had to admire the way Johnny straightened his tie and turned with a flashing smile to Alex. 'Tell Dora, will ya? Tell her I finally did it.'

Alex paid off the Greeks and gave them the two whores as a present. Then he paid Arnie and leaned on the bar, looking around. 'You know the first thing I'm gonna do? Get some new tablecloths, this place looks like a dive.'

They both turned as Dora entered, her mink coat slung over her shoulder. Alex gave Arnie a look which told him to disappear and he murmured, 'Okay, boss.'

Dora heard him, and cocked her head to one side. Alex tossed the papers to her and she caught them, laughing. 'So you did it? How much do I owe you?'

Alex walked over to the table, which was still stacked with the cards and the cash. 'Twenty-five grand ...'

She thought he was joking, but he wasn't. 'You're not serious ... What the hell do you take me for?'

Alex handed over the papers Johnny had signed. 'Look at the papers, darlin', I am serious. Johnny signed the club over to me – all legal, just as we agreed.'

'You bastard ... you dirty bastard! You thievin' git!'

Alex sighed and told her she could choose – either give him the money or accept him as her new partner.

'I need that money, you know I do. I got wages to pay on Friday, all the girls, the barmen, the booze . . .'

Alex handed her the briefcase. 'Well then, it's simple, isn't it – partner?'

Dora knew he had beaten her, but then she looked on the bright side. Maybe it would be a good thing to have a man around. And, if Alex were true to his word, she wouldn't be the loser, far from it. She began to look at Alex in a different light.

'Will you do one thing for me, then, Alex? For God's sake get yourself a decent suit.'

Alex drew back his head and laughed. It took her by surprise – it was an infectious, bubbling laugh.

'You know, I thought your brother was a bastard, but I reckon you're one step ahead of him.'

The smile disappeared, and Alex's face froze. 'If ever, ever, he walks into this place, no matter what hour of the day or night, you call me . . .'

He frightened her. 'He owe you, like Johnny did?'

Alex snapped the briefcase shut and wouldn't meet her eyes. 'Yeah, he owes me.'

At Johannesburg Airport, Edward slipped in among the throngs of travellers as they left the terminal, ending up at Richard's side. 'Richard . . .? You on flight 054?'

Richard turned, puzzled for a moment, then recognized Edward. 'Good God, it's Stubbs, isn't it? Well, hello there! How are you doing?' They walked into the brilliant sunshine outside the terminal.

'I'm hoping for a job at De Veer's mining laboratories.'

As he looked round for his father, Richard said he might be able to help out as he was employed in their valuation department at Hatton Garden. He spotted his father's old Bentley as BB tooted and waved. Edward had polished the car himself, and it gleamed.

'Pop, this is Edward Stubbs, remember him?'

BB gave Edward a non-committal look and shook his hand.

He had to hand it to BB, he carried it off brilliantly, even seemed to get a kick out of it. Richard threw his case into the back of the Bentley. 'I say, can we give you a lift, Edward?'

'Actually, I have to book into a hotel, not got things arranged as yet.'

With a look to his son, BB waved his cigar and said surely they could put the young chap up for a few days. Edward saw Richard hesitate, but then he smiled and gestured for Edward to climb aboard.

Richard was very much 'on top' and wanted to flaunt his affluence to Edward, insisting they dine out together that evening at one of the best hotels. Edward murmured that he was a little short of cash, and Richard waved this aside. BB gave Edward a covert look as they entered the house.

While they were dining at the Fairmount Hotel, Richard rose from the table as two grey-haired men in dark suits approached them. They shook hands as Richard introduced his father, then as an afterthought he introduced Edward. The two men were in top executive positions at De Veer's, and Richard almost grovelled at their feet to persuade them to join their table. BB surpassed himself. 'You shouldn't miss this opportunity. This young friend of my son's has just stepped off the plane from London. He was at Cambridge – firsts in every subject and honours in Geology and Petrology . . . looking for work. If I had my day again I wouldn't let this chap go . . .'

Mr Johnson took stock of the handsome young man, and leaned forward. 'How long have you been in South Africa?'

Edward flushed and looked down, acting the shy student. 'I just arrived, I was on the same plane as Richard, actually.'

Johnson nodded, then turned to Richard. 'Bring this young chap along with you on Thursday, be interested to hear what he has to say for himself. Nice to meet you, Mr Stubbs, BB . . . until Thursday then, Richard. Thanks for the drink.'

Richard waited until the two men had threaded their way through the restaurant before he looked angrily at his father. 'I only just got my own foot in the door, Pop, I don't want to push my luck. Maybe another time, Edward, all right?'

BB rose from the table as Richard, obviously still angry, held Edward's arm. 'I don't want to sound hard, Edward, but the old man does go on a bit. It's taken me a lot of hard work to get this far in the company, and Pop's not exactly got a snow-white reputation.'

BB turned to his son, his face flushed. 'I heard that, and you'll take young Edward here with you. Always give a chap a leg-up, Dickie, you never know when you might pass them on the way down – and I should know. Right, let's get me to bed.'

'Mr Johnson, there's a gentleman here to see you, says his name's Stubbs.'

Edward took the phone from the receptionist. 'Edward Stubbs, sir, met you with Richard Van der Burge at the Fairmount Hotel the other night . . . Yes, yes, well I'm here in reception right now.'

Mr Johnson was waiting at the lift as Edward stepped out. 'I have to go over to the labs this morning, you busy later?'

Edward grinned and said he was more than free, and they walked into the office.

Richard made no attempt to mention Edward. He had had long talks with the marketing board, and they discussed the new sales brochures they were about to print, spending considerable time looking over the new designs. The diamonds had been given more commercial-sounding names: 'Brilliant', 'Marquise', 'Pear'. Richard was beginning to get a headache, but he tried to appear interested in the conversation. They went on to the problems they had been having with the Central Selling Organization getting their shipments on time.

Fascinated, Edward listened as Johnson explained the Central Selling Organization, or CSO. With such an attentive audience he held forth in great detail. 'Our principles are very straightforward. As we, the CSO, handle the major proportion of world sales, we can best maintain an adequate supply of diamonds to the cutting centres at stable prices . . . If you look at this map, Edward, it'll give you some idea just how many mines are producing quality merchandise.'

Johnson pointed to a wall map and picked up a pen, gesturing to each country as he spoke. 'The Belgian Congo, Tanganyika, Bechuanaland, Basutoland, Namibia, Sierra Leone, Ghana . . . all from Africa, we here in South Africa are among the many. Co-operative marketing depends not only on the ability of the CSO to sell diamonds, as with your young friend Richard, but also on its financial strength to cover stocks. Whenever production of particular sizes exceeds demand, then these categories can be carried in reserve until the market needs them, therefore keeping some kind of equality . . . excuse me.'

Edward jumped as Johnson barked on his intercom, then switched it off and checked his watch. 'Look, you want to have lunch? Show you not only the laboratories but some of the cutting experts of the world are in town today, would you like to meet them . . .?'

Richard was amazed to see Edward being guided through the canteen by one of the Great White Chiefs, and ushered into one of the private dining rooms. Edward gave Richard a slight smile and followed Johnson.

The food was good, and served by waitresses wearing pretty pink caps. Johnson introduced Edward to the others, and they discussed in detail a programme they were setting up. A white-haired gentleman seated himself opposite Edward, next to Johnson.

'You the young chap with the glowing degrees from Cambridge? Who was your professor, not Emmott by any chance?'

Edward was 'in', and he smiled. They talked for a long time, at the end of which the man shook Edward's hand and said, 'Call me Ernest.' His love of diamonds was obvious, and he kept

Edward fascinated with his descriptions of the two main methods used for mining diamonds, 'pipe' and 'alluvial'.

Time and time again Edward tried to interrupt Ernest but,
like Johnson, once he got started on his precious diamonds he
was unstoppable. Just as he was about to launch into the alluvial
mining process, Edward managed to interrupt.

'It's quite extraordinary, sir, I was making vast progress in the
testing of above-ground materials to avoid the time it takes to
pinpoint the exact location of the central mine. Stones, I know,
can be carried miles on river beds, and the miners work backwards to trace the source . . . But what if, by using chemicals on
the layers of earth at surface level, one could detect, and be
almost one hundred per cent sure, that there would be diamonds
or gold seven or eight hundred feet below . . . ?'

Johnson did not like to break in on the conversation, as the
chairman was obviously enthralled by the young student. Sir
Ernest Lieberson tweaked his moustache as he listened to
Edward's theories, which he found interesting, to say the least –
especially when Edward took Emmott's notes and copies of his
final papers from his briefcase.

Sir Ernest had been credited with great ingenuity. He was known
to be a resourceful man, and was the one BB had pinpointed for
Edward to reach, telling him that it was Lieberson who had
steered the diamond industry out of the depression in the thirties. Edward had struck gold on his first introduction to the De
Veer company. He had made such an impression on the chairman
that he was not only shown all the laboratories but was asked to
have lunch with Sir Ernest, whose son was at Oxford, the following day. He wished to discuss Edward's theories further.

Edward returned home to find a furious row raging between BB
and Richard. BB had taken to using a silver-topped cane to help
him walk about, and as Edward came into the room he was
using it to prod his son in the back. 'Only way you'll get those
mines is over my dead body. Your brothers were killed in the

Fordesburg, and I have personal attachments to the others. Try anything and I'll cut you off without a bloody rand.'

Furious, Richard turned on his father. 'From what I can gather from your cronies at the Pretoria Club, you don't have a rand to your name anyway.'

Purple with rage, BB shouted that if it was true then his bankruptcy was due to his, Richard's, spendthrift ways. Richard was taken aback. 'You're not serious, Pa . . . Edward, would you mind leaving us alone, this is a private matter?'

Edward gave BB a meaningful look as he left the room, and heard the old man's puff of breath as he flopped into a chair. 'You can sell off your mother's jewels, what's left of them.'

Afraid that BB might divulge something to Richard, Edward hovered outside the door. The crackling laugh made him smile.

'Ah, see, that's brought you to your senses. Those sons of bitches at the club biting against me as usual, are they? And what the hell have you been doing there? Playing the tables again? Haven't you learnt anything from London?'

At dinner, Richard was quiet, picking at his food. Bad-tempered, he asked when Edward was thinking of leaving.

'Perhaps tomorrow, depends on my luncheon. I think I will be offered a job at the laboratories.'

Richard had served his purpose in getting Edward into De Veer's, now Edward wanted him out of the way. 'When are you due back in London, Richard?'

Shrugging, Richard said they were waiting for a new consignment of roughs to be delivered, he was to carry them back to London.

BB looked at his son and sighed. 'Come to that, eh? Got you carrying the stones? Well, they must be testing you, so be sure you take care.'

Richard snapped back at his father. 'I have no intention of continuing as their errand boy. I have been assured of a position within the company as an executive.'

*

Shortly after dinner Richard left for town. Edward patted BB's hand and the old man gripped it tight. 'How am I doing? Not let you down yet, have I? Keeping my old brain ticking you are, makes me feel good.'

'No, BB, you haven't let me down. I know I'm going to get into the labs and then we're home and dry. I've arranged for you to buy two more mines.'

Laughing, BB put his arm around Edward. 'That's what I like to hear, think big and your dreams will grow, think small and you'll fall behind . . . think big, son, think big.'

But Edward was thinking far bigger than BB ever dreamed.

Chapter Thirteen

The following day Edward charmed his way into Sir Ernest Lieberson's office. As he had hoped, he was offered a job in the laboratories, pursuing the theories he had first begun at Cambridge.

Richard returned to London and Edward moved into a cheap hotel. It was imperative that he had no traceable association with BB. But, as promised, he kept in touch. He knew it was necessary, even though at times he could have done without the nightly calls. He worked all day, moving from mine to mine, making careful studies and collecting samples, filling his specimen bottles with soil and rock gradings. He travelled extensively, and his preparations were diligent in the extreme. It was vital now for Edward to have rough diamonds and gold. He needed samples of both in quite large quantities.

BB's part in the plan began. He employed a group of kaffirs to rewire the fences on all his mines. Every mine they had was to look as if work were in progress. They would work on a turn-around system, in split groups, one day leaving only one boy on a site but with a piece of heavy machinery to make it look as though a lot was going on. It appeared that eight dormant mines were now being worked, which naturally stirred up interest in the local communities. The mines were many miles apart, and the news was left to spread slowly by itself.

Edward's work was inspected, but the four scientists were doubtful of any beneficial outcome. However, Edward requested a month off to begin taking samples from as far afield as the Belgian Congo, Ghana, and the Ivory Coast. He wanted samples from as many 'live' mines as possible to counter-test with the dormant ones.

Edward was granted two months' sabbatical, paid for by De Veer's. He did not, as they presumed, begin work immediately, but searched around Pretoria for the haunts of local journalists. He became a regular visitor, sitting chatting and drinking with reporters in pubs and clubs, making it his job to get well acquainted. He was amused that all the bars he went into had 'Men Only' signs up, and no women were to be seen drinking.

The barman at the Night Light Club, Nkosi, proved an invaluable asset. Edward was looking for a very specific kind of journalist, and had begun to despair of finding one when Nkosi whispered to him that he should, if he had nothing better to do, come and meet a friend of his called Skye Duval.

Edward was waiting for Nkosi when the tiny bar closed, and they drove out of town on to a dirt track. They veered off, and Edward stared around him, trying to get his bearings. He began to feel uneasy, not knowing where he was, but eventually they stopped at a small shanty with lights streaming from every window, the threadbare curtains unable to prevent it. Loud music blared from the shack.

Nkosi tapped on the door and entered. It was closed behind them by a beautiful black girl who beckoned them into the shanty's living room. Edward was surprised to see white men sitting with their arms around black girls. It was, of course, illegal to fraternize, and everyone stared at the door as Edward entered. Seeing Nkosi leading him in, they relaxed again, and the room was soon filled with the hubbub of their chatter.

Nkosi talked quietly with a fat-bellied man who sat with his arm around a very young black girl. The man had some information for sale and the pair of them slipped outside.

Skye Duval was the most handsome man Edward had ever set eyes on. He entered the room to a few ribald comments from the men, and he smiled. He was very tall – not as tall as Edward, but lanky so that he appeared taller. His hair was black and worn long, but it was well cut. His almond-shaped eyes were dark amber, his nose almost hooked, the wide cheeks and small mouth made the face strangely pretty yet arrogant. Skye had a dimple in his right cheek and a lopsided smile. He was stoned out of his mind, and he walked as if on air, a cigarette stuck in the corner of his sweet, girl's mouth. Edward watched him closely as he kissed two of the girls, obviously a familiar customer of the house.

Skye caught the can of beer someone threw him and moved with hazy eyes through the lounge. He opened the beer, which sprayed all over his cream-coloured suit, but didn't bother to wipe it away. He drank from the can while he surveyed the room. Edward met the eyes, glinting amber, tiger-like, which flicked over him, and Skye raised one finely arched eyebrow. He may appear drunk, thought Edward, but the man's taking everything in, and no one enters or leaves the room without those strange eyes recording it.

Skye made his way over to Edward. 'Well, you're a strange face ... Skye Duval ... no, don't get up, I'll join you.'

Skye's method of joining Edward was simply a slow, languid collapse on to the sofa next to him. His voice was very upper-class English, drawling, and Edward noticed a heavy signet ring on the small finger on his left hand.

'So which are you here for, the news items or the broads?'

Edward estimated Duval could not be much older than himself, yet he seemed very worldly and confident.

'I'm just passing through.'

'Aren't we all, but you were brought by the infamous Nkosi or whatever they call him. He usually drags in the most dreadful types, sometimes it's hard to call the place home ...'

'Is this your house?'

Still lolling on the sofa, Duval turned his head. 'You joking? ... Christ, my shoes are crippling me, it's the heat, makes the feet swell.'

Skye stared at his scuffed shoes, then caught a beer can tossed to him by one of the black girls. It hissed as he pulled the ring off and guzzled the beer, spilling it over his clothes again. He wiped his mouth with the back of his hand. 'I am a reporter, Johannesburg *Sunday Express*, don't suppose you've got a scoop for me? If I don't send them something soon, I'll be out of a job. You're English, aren't you? Where are you from?'

Edward gave him Allard Simpson's address, and Skye laid his slim arm along the back of the sofa. 'Kensington? Know it well, my family lives in Cadogan Place. What are you then, a student?'

'I was, at Cambridge. Now I'm just travelling.'

'Travelling, are we? Oh God, I'm buggered. I've got to get out of this dump, it's driving me nuts ... You drive, Cambridge fella?'

Edward put his beer can down and Skye promptly picked it up and drained it. He burped, then flung an arm round Edward's shoulder. 'We English should stick together – you got any money? Show you a nice time, or you can show me ... Ha, ha, ha ...'

Skye got into the driving seat once they were outside the bungalow, and drove so recklessly that Edward hung on for dear life. They went on a club crawl that made Skye so foul-tempered he got himself thrown out of the last one.

'Well, that's that for the night, another day passed, another day gone that I won't see again.'

He drove around the town, then headed out for his own place. He didn't seem interested in where Edward lived, or even if Edward wanted to go with him. He simply accepted that he was there.

Inside Skye's house Edward tried to talk sense to him, but he was blasted out by Purcell, played so loudly it nearly shattered his eardrums. Skye passed out on the sofa and Edward looked around the place. He moved quietly into the bedroom, saw the unmade bed, the clothes strewn around. At the side of the bed was a photograph of a very beautiful girl, a blonde, standing on a beach and shading her eyes to look at the camera.

Skye appeared behind Edward. He had taken off his shoes and Edward hadn't even heard him walk in. 'Trouble is, I'm sick of this fucking country, they want you to act as spy, every fucker is spying on everyone else ...' He flopped down on the bed, rolled over. 'You know, I did this article on travelling across the Sahara on camels, with my friend ... He was my friend, understand, really close friend. When we got back, they all loved the story ... but it wasn't enough ... editors want blood, prefer shit like "Suspect I observed yesterday has a pen friend in Moscow and he collects Russian stamps. I think he could be a Communist." You believe that kind of crap? An' I'll tell you something else. Every one of those guys you saw tonight screwing the knickers off the little black whores – even the most liberal Afrikaner – if approached by the security branch and asked to spy would. Bastards leak rumours if you don't spy, and that fucks you over, and the police will destroy you anyway even if you do spy. There's no chance in this shit-hole of not being a goddamn sodding spy.'

Edward, trying hard to decipher what on earth Skye was talking about, asked him if he was a spy. Skye turned on him in a fury. 'Course I'm a fucking spy you arsehole, what in Christ's name do you think I've been talking about – I fucked him over, didn't I?'

He swayed drunkenly in front of Edward and shouted, 'I'm talking about my mate, the one that came on the caravan with me, I'm talking about him.' He slumped into a chair, and his lower lip trembled ... 'Like a bear he was, Cambridge blue, rugger forward, maybe a prop, I dunno.'

He gulped at his drink and lay back closing his eyes.

'They put pressure on him, secret police, he told them to sod off, so they leaked a rumour that the poor son of a bitch was a spy. They framed him, and to increase the rumour they put a lot of pressure on his black friends; so the poor sucker was running to black and white trying to make them believe he was straight. You know what he did? He walked into the fucking lab, man, into the photographer's darkroom, and gulped down a mugful of chemical fixer. They said it was suicide ... some bloody suicide.' His face streamed with tears ... and he finished his drink, throwing the glass at the wall.

Edward made sympathetic noises and watched as Skye stripped off his clothes. He was down to baggy white underwear when he turned to Edward. 'Well, what are you waiting for? Into bed, prick.'

Edward backed off fast and said, very embarrassed, that he was straight.

'Why on earth have you stuck like glue to my side all night long if you're not queer? Isn't it obvious? Aren't I obvious?'

Edward sat in a chair by the chaotic dressing table while Skye propped himself up in his bed. He lit a cigarette and lay back on the pillows. 'Ahhhh, deary me, my sob stories usually get the boys into bed with me. Don't you just love their tight black bums? I just die for them ... did very well tonight, see, real tears. Maybe one day I'll be able to tell the truth, there again maybe I won't ... Eh? You want some coffee, you able to cope with that percolator thing in the kitchen? If so, I'd adore a cup.'

As Edward got up to go into the kitchen, he again caught sight of the photograph of the beautiful blonde. 'Who's the girl? She's lovely.'

Skye picked up the picture and snuggled down under the bedclothes. When Edward came back with only half the percolator, the other half, sadly, missing, Skye was fast asleep with the photograph held tightly in his arms. For a moment Edward thought he resembled an innocent child. As he crept back to the door, it creaked open, and he winced, hoping the sound had not woken Skye ... it hadn't, his body remained still deep in a drunken sleep.

Edward wandered around the messy house. He searched all

the rooms thoroughly. There were books piled in heaps and on every available surface. The bookcases were crammed full. Many were on politics and there were plays from every period. Several shelves were devoted to film-making and there were stacks of movie magazines. Mr Duval was a complex character ... Edward also reckoned he was a dangerous one. Why did he tell him the long elaborate story about his friend's suicide? To get him into bed, or to alleviate his own guilt? Edward was more than sure Skye Duval must have assisted if not organized the frame-up that caused his friend's death. He began to read a folder of press cuttings relating to Skye's articles. They made fascinating reading and were well if rather flamboyantly written. He replaced the folder and searched the drawers, finding a lot of clothes with good labels that were badly in need of washing. The wardrobe contained many suits in similar condition, and to Edward's surprise a set of women's expensive clothes. Everything was muddled, haphazard. In a desk drawer Edward found so many bills that he gasped. Skye owed money everywhere. His bank statements were old and torn, his entire overdraft facility having been exhausted months ago.

The record collection was mostly classical, a few big jazz bands, Swing along with Sammy Kaye, Horace Heights and his Musical Nights, Louis 'Satchmo' Armstrong and Billie Holiday plus a few blues singers, some German records and a couple of recordings of black pop groups. They were dusty, many without covers or in the wrong ones. Edward was about to stroll out to the verandah when he found another bunch of folders. These contained photographs of Skye in flowing robes and the story of the trek across the Sahara in manuscript form. Looking through the photographs Edward again got the impression that Skye was one of the handsomest men he had ever seen.

A car drew up outside and Edward walked out to the dark verandah. The small Volkswagen, which a young black boy was driving, parked and he saw a very attractive white girl sitting in the back seat. The boy got out and it looked as though he was carrying something for the woman, falling into step behind her as they entered the house. They walked in silence, and then Edward heard her laughter, the lower tones of the boy. At first he had presumed him to be the girl's servant, but there was familiarity in that laughter. They did not enter the lounge, but went straight to the spare bedroom and closed the door.

Edward was unsure if he should make some noise to let them know he was in the house. He knew they would be arrested if discovered. Any romance across the colour line was illegal in South Africa, the land of so-called racial purity. If they had ever shown in public that they were on equal terms they would have been arrested immediately. Skye would also be charged if it were discovered that he allowed his home to be used by them.

Edward waited for a while and then lay on the sofa, eventually dozing off.

Around dawn, Edward was woken by the sound of the lounge door opening. Skye entered the room. 'Christ, are you still here? I thought you'd have gone. Do you want some wine? It's chilled in the kitchen.'

When he returned with the wine, Skye said abruptly, 'Well, what do you want? You've certainly waited long enough.'

Edward noticed the change immediately – Skye's lisp had disappeared, and he seemed tired. Edward detailed his plan, but the only indication that Skye was listening was the constant twitching of his foot. When Edward finished, Skye set his wine glass down carefully and lit a cigarette from a half-smoked butt. He gave Edward a lopsided grin, and his lisp returned. 'My, my, you have been busy. And, well, what can I say? It's certainly interesting.' He leaned back in his chair, his foot still twitching and getting on Edward's nerves. Again he grinned, but this time it was more like a smirk. 'How old are you, my Cambridge friend?'

Edward added a few years and said he was twenty-six. Skye raised his eyebrows. 'Same as myself . . . you look younger, but there again, perhaps not. Be a good fellow and bring the bottle, will you?'

Skye's eyes were shrewd and watchful. He picked up the telephone and dialled, and Edward came back in time to hear him speaking. His heart lurched – Skye's voice was sly and his lisp was obvious. He was rocking back and forth in his chair. 'I may have something for you, but, you bitch, I want my passport . . . Yeth, yeth, yeth, fair exchange.'

He removed the bottle from Edward's hand and poured for himself. He did not look at Edward as he spoke. 'About this offer – you're on, it will also help me out of a rather nasty situation – not merely financial. Well, I think you overheard – my passport is being, shall we say, "held", against my will. It's rather debilitating to say the least.'

Skye drank most of the bottle of wine as he told Edward that ever since he had arrived in South Africa he had loathed and detested apartheid. He had broken every rule in the book, hating how the rich whites lived. He had stayed mostly in black townships, knowing he was breaking the law, for to enter a black area a white must first obtain a special permit and he had never bothered. He had, therefore, been under the watchful eyes of the South Africa security police, and was listed as an 'undesirable alien'.

'I was ordered to leave South Africa within seven days, that was three days ago. I have had to do certain things to be able to remain here, like retrieve my passport from the police.'

Edward asked why he wanted to stay so badly if he hated the country so much. Skye laughed, but it was a humourless, bitter laugh. 'Because, old chap, I was born here. My mother took me to England on a false passport when I was a baby, helped by a certain group of people, and unwittingly I returned here, I wanted to become a reporter so I ingratiated myself with the inner sanctum of the Pretoria secret police. It was easy enough – as I told you, I just betrayed my friends . . . Rather good at that – in fact, fucking marvellous.'

Edward had noticed the Volkswagen from the previous night had already departed. He began to feel uneasy. He looked at Skye, puzzled, and asked why he didn't go to the British Consul if he was a British subject. Skye stared at him. 'Someone – a woman named Julia – also has my birth certificate, so I can't go. I'm trapped here until I get it back.'

Edward told him he could send away to Somerset House, they would forward a copy of his birth certificate. Skye shook his head at Edward's stupidity and spoke coldly, quietly. 'I'm black, you stupid bastard. My father was black, a political embarrassment, he was one of the highest members of the banned African National Congress . . .'

Edward realized that Skye was an even more fortunate find than he had believed possible.

'My mother was very young, her family dripping with fucking coalmines, and she got herself knocked up by a bloody black houseboy. Needless to say, I was kept very much in the dark, haw haw haw, but I was well educated and although I was shipped about somewhat, things weren't too bad. Anyway, she got herself married, and, naturally, the husband doesn't have the slightest knowledge of moi.' He fell silent for a moment, sipping his wine.

Edward noticed the foot-twitching had stopped, and Skye appeared very still. He had a haunted look, and he was distant, but he continued. 'So, buddy boy, that's Skye Duval for you. Now you know – I have entrusted you with my life.'

Edward didn't reply, but Skye appeared to read his thoughts. 'It's imperative, you know, if two people are doing a con trick, that they trust each other, have something on each other. You even attempt your little scam without me and I'll know. Understand me, man?'

At his hotel later in the morning, Edward looked through the newspaper. He glanced only fleetingly at the front page, then flipped back to it. There was a photograph and he recognized the girl's face. The article was by no means prominent, just a small bulletin, but the girl had been arrested with her black lover. There was no name to the article, but Edward knew it had to have something to do with Skye. He was also very aware of the importance of the information he had just gained. If he were to tip off the blacks about Skye Duval's secrets, the man would be a walking target. This made Edward think hard. Why had Duval opened up to him? Was it simply, as he had said, trust? Or had he in actual fact bitten much harder on Edward's offer than he had thought? Edward concluded that Skye was indeed a manipulator, and even though he joked about it, he would be in the scam whether Edward wanted him or not.

Edward knew he had Skye when they met that evening. The girl in the newspaper had hanged herself. Yet another death lay at Skye's feet and he was in a nasty, belligerent mood. 'Get me out of this shit-hole country, man, before I put my head in a noose like everyone else. A voice keeps whispering louder and louder, "You're black, Skye Duval, you're a fucking black." And you know what? I wanna be black. The whites here are made of vomit, one day they will all spew their guts out and we will rise up and swamp them.'

Edward knew he had to get Skye on to a different subject, so he asked about the woman called Julia.

'This woman, the one holding your birth certificate, is there any way we can get to her? If we have that you'll be off the hook.'

Skye shrugged, and said she kept it locked in her safe.

'At her home? Couldn't we get it somehow?'

Skye had been sceptical about Edward, but now he looked at him with interest. Even more so when Edward suggested that the two of them together could surely break into the woman's safe. Skye went to telephone Julia and then returned to the table. 'She'll see me tonight . . . we can at least try.'

Julia Keevy was overweight, and wore her dyed blonde hair in a tight, lacquered set. She wore rings on every finger, and a kaftan to hide the rolls of fat drooping from her body. Her small eyes were like speckled duck's eggs, and her skin had been exposed to the sun for so many years that it was as wrinkled as a walnut. She was grotesque, welcoming Skye with a glossy, thickly lipsticked smile. She had dismissed her servants for the night, and had the champagne on ice.

Edward waited outside. Skye had described the exact layout of the low, sprawling bungalow. Skye would open the back door, and had warned Edward to be careful of the screen door squeaking.

He moved stealthily into the kitchen, banged his shin on the fridge and held his breath. Had she heard? He could hear a deep, throaty, gin-sodden laugh from the bedroom. He slipped into the dining area, took stock of the rooms, and eventually found the lounge.

The safe was like a vault, with a heavy combination lock. He scratched his head – no way could he open it – and jumped as Skye appeared silently beside him.

'We'll never open the bloody thing, look at it.'

Skye gritted his teeth and swore, squinted at the numbers.

'Baby, what you doing? Skye, honey, what you doing?'

Skye muttered to Edward to keep still, they had come this far and he was not going to give up. He walked to the bedroom, smiling sweetly as he carried the bottle towards the beached whale on the bed. 'Sorry, the first one I took out wasn't chilled enough, just let me open it ...'

When Skye popped the cork out of the bottle with a loud bang, Edward nearly had a heart attack in the next room. Suddenly Skye went crazy. He leapt on top of her, ramming the neck of the champagne bottle into her mouth so hard that she gurgled and flayed the air with her hands. He sat on top of her and pushed the bottle to the back of her throat.

'What's the combination of the safe, you fat bitch? The combination – now!'

She tried to fight him off but she was choking, the bottle being forced further and further to the back of her throat. The champagne frothed and bubbled down her chins and her eyes bulged, then she flopped. Her body went limp, and a horrid gurgling began in her throat. Skye removed the bottle and slapped her face from side to side.

Edward was searching the desk when Skye appeared with a gun in his hand. He walked to the safe and blasted at the lock, bullet after bullet.

'Jesus, you crazy? For Chrissake . . .'

Letting the gun fall to his side, Skye stared as the safe door swung open. He began to hurl the contents out. Bundles of bank notes fell around his feet as he scrabbled and searched. He checked inside envelopes and folders. 'Where is it? Where the fuck is it? The bitch, the bitch!'

Edward stood frozen at the window – what if someone had heard the gunshots? There was silence, ominous, but it gave Edward confidence that no one had heard. He went into the bedroom, leaving Skye searching like a madman. The scene that met his eyes made him want to vomit – the grotesque sight of Julia on the bed, mouth wide open, eyes popping out of her head. The sheets and body dripping with champagne. He shouted to Skye, 'Get in there and clean the bottle and glasses, your prints'll be all over the bloody room. I'll look for it, go on, move, those shots could bring the law any minute.'

Edward filled a carrier bag with jewels and cash, then dragged Skye out. They left by the back way, wiped the door, then ran across the gardens and down two streets to the car. This time Edward drove, slowly and carefully, so as not to attract attention.

They returned to Skye's bungalow and Edward tipped the contents of the carrier bag on the bed. There was at least fifteen thousand in cash, but the jewels and the gold bangles were worth, he knew, at least twenty to thirty thousand more. He examined Skye's birth certificate and slipped it into his pocket.

*

The newspaper reported that Julia's houseboy had been arrested and charged with her murder. The motive for the killing was obviously robbery.

Neither Edward nor Skye waited around to hear the outcome of the murder trial. The houseboy was jailed for life.

Book Three

Chapter Fourteen

The last eight years had been good, no one could deny that, Dora least of all. She and Alex had moved into the lucrative years of the flourishing London clubland. She had changed her looks – now she went in for the Diana Dors style, with pencil-slim skirts, shoulder-length hair and pale lipsticks. She always wore thick, false eyelashes, with midnight-blue mascara, and she had made sure she kept her figure. She squeezed herself into the skirts, wore uplift bras to help her sagging tits, and still looked younger than her age, but only at a distance. The small lines had deepened and the more she tried to cover them the more aware of them she became.

The club just about ran itself, but they had to deal with a lot of aggravation from villains demanding protection money. Alex always paid without a murmur, as he had seen what happened when other club owners didn't. The places were 'fired', or fights broke out among the guests, uninvited guests who drank a skinful and then picked rows and broke mirrors and noses. Dora had been all for fighting the thugs, calling in the police, but she had as usual given way to Alex.

After the first few months Alex had realized he was not a good front man. His scarred face didn't actually add to the ambience, and so he left it to Dora. He was always working behind the scenes, though, always there when needed, and the club ran

like clockwork. He had fingers in many other small businesses –
he had bought out Harry Driver years ago, and ran his sweatshops and betting shops as well as his small drinking clubs. As he
did at Masks, Alex paid protection money to keep things quiet,
but there was a growing undercurrent of violence as gang warfare raged between rival East End gangs for territory. Alex played
no part in the violence, and became known as a 'steady', a man
anyone could rely on, a man who always kept his word. He was
an honourable man and it paid off. He was left to run his clubs
and his offshoot businesses without much trouble.

After resisting at first, Dora gave way as she watched many
clubs being taken over by the gangs. She also complied for her
own safety. She had branched out, no longer living in Johnny
Mask's old place, and had bought herself a three-storey house in
Notting Hill Gate. Johnny's flat was known as the 'dossing pad',
where the hostesses from the club took back their tricks – all
part of the club's 'social benefits'.

Dora kept her own special stable of girls clean and on a quick
turnaround, but like Alex she also had a second string to her
bow. The Notting Hill Gate house became known as a 'party'
place, with girls even more beautiful than those at Masks. They
were from all kinds of backgrounds, but classy, and all in it for
the fast money. The films and 'private cabarets' were expensive,
and only for those with a lot of money or connections. Dora
was a 'madame', and a tough one. She tolerated no nonsense
and her house was tasteful and, above all, well run. Even more
important, it was safe. The law was paid off; politicians, magis-
trates and the aristocracy were welcomed along with the odd
chief of police and foreign diplomat. The Notting Hill Gate
house was a very lucrative business on its own.

Trusted and well liked, Dora was paid handsomely for her
small parties. She was also earning a fortune. Alex, of course,
knew about her little 'perks', said that as long as she didn't
involve him it was fine, but he refused to take part in any of the
activities although he kept an eye on her books.

Dora also ran a team of girls known as the 'cash and carry', who were planted in the casinos with ready money supplied by Dora. The big, high-rolling gamblers, the female ones with only a certain amount of money to spend each week, would sell off their jewels to continue gambling when their cash ran out. The women were mostly foreign, Arabs, Lebanese, and whenever they removed a bracelet or a ring Dora's girls would move in and buy it for cash at a quarter of its value.

Wrapped in her white mink coat, Dora sat in the back of her Rolls. She was nervous, wondering what Alex would say. She knew how much he depended on her, and she chain-smoked, stubbing out the cigarette after one puff and lighting another immediately. The Rolls stopped at a traffic light, just a short distance from her home, on the corner of Ladbroke Grove. She leaned forward and pressed the button, the glass slid back. 'Pull over, just for a minute.'

The Rolls glided to the side of the road and stopped, engine ticking over. Dora thought it was fate – it had to be – all these years and not a word, and tonight of all nights she saw him, knew it was him just from one look.

Johnny Mask, wearing a filthy raincoat and with a hat pulled down over his straggly, greasy hair, was picking through a waste-bin at the side of the road near the traffic lights.

'I want you to do something . . . You see the guy, the dosser on the side of the road by the wastebin? Take your hat off, put your collar up.'

Dora lowered the window and watched the chauffeur walk behind Johnny Mask and drop two twenty-pound notes on to the wet pavement. Johnny had stopped rummaging, was staring at something he had taken out of the bin. The chauffeur tapped Johnny on the shoulder, pointed to the ground.

'You drop something, mate?'

The chauffeur walked on, crossed the road and returned to the Rolls.

Johnny Mask looked down at the folded bills, gave the chauffeur a look and then a smile, his old smile, patting his pockets.

He bent down and picked up the wet notes, gave a shifty look round and beetled off down Ladbroke Grove.

Down and out, Johnny was still the same. Dora pressed the button and the window glided up. She knew he would be drunk out of his already addled mind within the hour. So much for the past, she was now sure where her future lay.

Dora entered the club. It was early, so there were few punters about. Those that knew her smiled, and Arnie gave her his usual welcome.

'Hello, Lana, how's things?'

Arnie had a fixation on Lana Turner, and as Dora looked like her he had always called her Lana. She smiled and patted his arm, knew she would miss old Arnie. She weaved her way through the tables, stopped to fix a flower arrangement, looked over at two of her girls and gave a small wave. Then she opened the door to the inner sanctum.

Alex was at his desk as she knew he would be. She tossed her mink over the easy chair and poured herself the usual iced water, and leaned on the small corner bar.

Alex barely looked up from the accounts. He had not changed much – he wore his hair slicked back, oiled with Brylcreem, but he didn't seem to have changed. His thick-set shoulders and heavily muscled arms were still courtesy of George Windsor, as they still worked out together regularly. Because he frequently had considerable amounts of cash to bank, he carried a gun in an underarm holster, and his suits were cut by a skilled East End tailor to disguise it. He did not bother applying for a licence; with his record he was sure to be turned down.

Always immaculately dressed, Alex looked more like a City gent than a club owner in his pale blue shirts with detachable white collars, and dark, pinstriped suit. Dora often wondered if he only had the one suit, as he never wore any other colour or style. Only his face distorted the image.

Dora had never been to Alex's flat in the East End. At one time she had wondered what it would be like, but when she dropped hints for an invitation they were ignored. Eventually she put Alex down as a skinflint because he showed no outward signs of his new-found affluence. He did not smoke or drink, and seemed to have no friends apart from George Windsor. However, he did buy a Jaguar every year, and listed it as a company car for tax purposes, although no one else was ever allowed to drive it. Alex paid Arnie a tenner a week to make sure it was waxed regularly and remained in pristine condition.

Dora sipped her iced water, thinking what an oddball he was. 'Alex, do you mind if I ask you something personal?'

He didn't even look up from the books, just lifted his pen towards her and carried on writing.

'You got a girl hidden at your place?'

Alex laughed and said there were enough around the club without having one at home. She knew he occasionally took girls up to the old flat, but never twice, or if he had she didn't know about it. Sometimes the girls talked to her, asked about him.

'That your personal question, is it?'

She clinked the ice in her glass and perched her bum on the edge of the desk. 'Nope ... You're not gay, are you? I mean, really gay, sort of a closet queen?'

He jabbed the pen into her side then dropped it on the desk. 'No, I am not a closet poofter, what's all this leading to? What d'you really want, Dora, come on, out wiv it.'

Dora saw him grimace. He tried so hard to speak correctly, but still he used words like 'wiv' and 'somefink' when he wasn't concentrating. She found the way he tried to copy the toffs' accent endearing. She herself had taken elocution lessons for years, and had suggested Alex do the same. Her voice now had little or no trace of her own East End origins.

Alex tapped the books and asked again what she wanted. She sighed, chewed her lips. 'Is this all you want out of life, Alex? This place, your little sidelines – don't you want a family, kids – you know, the things most people want?'

He picked up her hand, her left hand, and looked at the ring. He laughed, but didn't let go. 'What's this? Don't tell me that Texan wants to make an honest woman of you? That what all this is leading up to? Well, don't ask me to walk down the bleedin' aisle.'

Dora snatched her hand back. 'Do me a favour! You think I'd get married here, with all these apes looking on? Oh, he knows all about me, don't get me wrong, but we'd get a quickie licence in Nevada, or some place like that. What you think of him, Alex?'

Alex shrugged and picked up his pen. 'I'm not marryin' him, you are. Seems an all right enough bloke.'

Dora paced up and down for a moment, then sat on the edge of the desk again. 'It's my chance, Alex. I can make a new life for myself, no worry about running into some "john" I had God knows how many years ago ... He lives in Houston, don't think I ever laid anybody from there.'

Alex stared at her, knew she was serious, and he rubbed his nose. 'So how much do you want? I'll buy you out.'

Just like that, no arguments, no recriminations, no sarcastic remarks. She wanted to cry.

'What's the matter, I said the wrong fing?'

'No, no, you great big idiot, you said just the right thing and I love you for it, I really love you, Alex.' She hugged him, but he gently pulled his arms away and opened up the safe.

'I saw Johnny Mask tonight – he looked like a dosser, thieving out of a wastebin. It must have been fate, sort of helped me make up my mind.'

'You'd never end up like that. Here you go, let's sort through the contracts.'

Watching him laying out the documents on the desk, taking out the chequebooks and cashbox, Dora thought to herself that he wasn't wasting a minute. 'You think I'll make a good wife?'

'No, lousy. Yer can't cook, can't do nothing ordinary – but then, you never could ... Yeah, I'd say you'll make 'im a great wife. Now put yer name on the dotted line.'

'Alex, if you asked me, I'd stay. But you don't need me here any more, do you? Place runs itself, more or less.'

Alex twisted the pen, then suddenly held out his hand to her. He fingered her tiny white hands with the long, blood-red nails. She knew he was the best friend she would ever have, and began to get tearful. She really cared for him. 'You know, Alex, you should take a break. Everybody has to at some time. He won't come down here now. I know why you're always here. But Eddie's not coming back, not here.'

His hand tightened on hers and his grip began to hurt her. His voice was quiet and cold. 'One day he'll come back – if not for you, he'll be looking for me. An' I'll be ready, waiting. I'll surprise him. Now sign these contracts if that's what you want.'

In his clean, neat flat Alex sat with his arms folded behind his head. He owned Masks outright, plus Dora's Notting Hill Gate property, and he began to calculate just how much he was worth. He grinned to himself, he was doing all right – more than all right, he was making it and he was going to go even further. He had to admit the buy-out had almost cleaned him out of ready cash, but he would soon be flush again. He began to think about buying the year's new model Jaguar XK120, the sports model, he'd have it custom made.

Going to the bathroom, he picked up his toothbrush and squeezed some paste on to it. He stared at his muscular body in the mirror, then began to brush his teeth. He was always very self-conscious about an ill-fitting plate he had to use after losing two front teeth at the hands of his prison guards. He kept it by his bed at night in a small cup. He splashed cold water over his face and patted it dry.

He would have liked to celebrate his success, but there was no one he particularly wanted to see. He pulled on his freshly laundered pyjamas and turned back the bed. From habit, he always made it as he had been forced to in prison. The small flat was bare, only his precious, worn books were on display. The cleanliness and neatness of the two white-walled rooms verged on the obsessive. A kitchen table and two chairs were the only other pieces of furniture. He had painted them white, and often a vase of fresh flowers stood on the table. His writing paper, pens and sharp pencils stood in groups in a small holder. Every garment had its hanger, socks and shirts had their space. Each drawer was lined with paper.

At night Alex would spend his time reading, always aware of the limits of his education. He liked routine, and every night when he returned from the club he would put in two hours' work. He was taking several university courses by post. He never intended to take any of the exams, it was purely for his own enjoyment, and these hours were precious to him.

He sat at the table, his exercise books in front of him, but he couldn't concentrate, so he lay down on his bed instead. There was someone he would dearly have liked to show off his success to, and that person was Edward. He whispered to the white walls, 'I can wait, Eddie, I can wait, and I'm going to get rich waiting.'

Chapter Fifteen

While Alex climbed to success in England, Edward's preparations for the 'big scam' in South Africa were moving towards their conclusion. Skye Duval worked at the press releases for the reopening of the mines, all due to the assurance of a young scientist carrying out experiments on their owners' land. The mines were mostly fictitious and so far afield the reports would take some time to verify.

BB was deliberately getting himself deeper and deeper into debt with the banks. Mortgaging the house was the last move. All his defunct mines were now open, and to all intents and purposes active.

Rumours began to spread like a small bush fire, continually fuelled. The De Veer Corporation placed a notice in the newspapers disassociating themselves from the 'new chemical method of assessing mining areas'. Edward was unobtainable, supposedly travelling across Africa. A group of technicians were put into Edward's laboratory to take over his experiments. Hundreds of thousands of phials took time to assimilate, none could be taken at face value. They had to begin taking their own samples from the same areas, but they had Edward's notes and positive samples, all linked directly to the reopening of the mines.

*

Edward had a secret meeting with Skye. They had to have a headline, and fast. They needed bulk findings quickly, and they needed names and photographs. They were running out of money, running out of the jewels Edward was using for the samples, and running out of gold. They were so close and yet, without substantive evidence to back up the claims fed to the papers by Skye Duval, the whole scam could fall apart like a pack of cards.

Luck was on their side, in the form of Sylvia Van der Burge's death. Richard arrived in South Africa for the funeral, and his visit coincided with a consignment of stones being sent to England.

BB was not expecting his son. He had not had time to mourn his wife's death, or even take it in properly, and he looked sadly at his only surviving son. 'I'm sorry ... so sorry the poor old gel's gone.'

Richard was irate, and stormed at his father. 'Sorry? I like that! I've had to drop everything to fly out here. On top of that, you haven't paid the nursing home bills, and then there's the cost of the funeral.'

BB wanted to block out his son's carping, vicious voice. His face flushed bright red. 'Inconvenient, is it? Your mother's death is inconvenient?'

Richard gritted his teeth. 'Yes, yes, inconvenient. And that's being truthful. The news hasn't exactly bowled you over, has it? She was your wife.'

'Yes, God bless her, she was my wife, and – God help me – your mother.'

Richard clenched his hands and swallowed. 'The nursing home has to be paid, the funeral costs ... I don't have any cash, you'll have to put a notice in the papers.'

BB shuddered – how Sylvia had doted on this boy. He took out his big handkerchief and blew his nose. 'You know, Dickie, she was a sweet soul, but when my boys died they took part of her with them, left nothing for me. She gave you all the love she had left, along with every penny.'

BB sobbed, his handkerchief over his face, blubbering like a child. Richard was about to put his arms around his father, hold him, but he heard BB moan the names of his dead brothers. Even now he wasn't weeping for his wife, but for his beloved first-born sons. Richard felt the old familiar jealousy sweep over him. His brothers' deaths had not only destroyed his mother, taken a part of her with him – they had taken all of his father's love, leaving nothing for him.

Richard helped himself to a drink and they discussed the arrangements. 'Perhaps you should also know that the bank will be calling in your loan any day now, I suggest you put those worthless pieces of crap on the market while I'm here. It'll just about cover my expenses, and the bank will more than likely take the house from under your feet.'

BB knew exactly when the bank loans would be called in. He was worried that someone might put two and two together; it was, after all, Richard who had introduced Edward to De Veer's, and someone might remember. They were so close now that Edward too was worried, and he went to meet BB.

'Old girl kicked the bucket, that's why Richard's here.'

'Sorry, I'm so sorry . . . You holding up all right, are you?'

Richard would have been blind with fury if he had seen the way his father's eyes glowed for Edward. 'Aye, I'm better now I've seen you, son. I need a bit of human contact. We'll see it through, though, eh? We'll get the buggers, won't we?'

Edward nodded. Any day now the banks would call in BB's markers and he still had one move to make.

'I have the explosives boy standing by – Thin Willy, good chap, trust him. But without the goods we can't do a damned thing . . . You know, in the old days I kept an old jamjar full of rough cuts, all the old-timers used to keep one stone per haul as a good luck stake, now . . . well, there aren't many of us left, not the old-timers.'

Edward couldn't sleep, the millions and millions of rough stones pouring out of the De Veer mines daily were, like his scam, so close and yet so far. The security was tough, no one could get near them. Edward sat up. No one? What about Richard Van der Burge himself? He not only got close but he carried bloody bags full back and forth to England.

Edward approached Richard almost immediately after his mother's funeral. He talked about mundane things – did Richard still see Allard? Then, nonchalantly, he asked if Richard was still carrying for De Veer's.

'Yep, still the blessed errand boy, what about you? Oh, you work for them, of course.'

It was obvious that Richard had only half his mind on Edward, the other half on some matter of his own.

'You all right? Seem a bit down?'

Richard shrugged and said that was putting it mildly. 'Truth is, old man, I am in what one could only describe as a tight corner, so tight I'm choking to death, and I can't see a way out.'

Edward played him deftly, not pushing for explanations, not too eager, but still interested.

'Might as well tell you, I suppose. Got myself into more of the old trouble, lost a lot of money on the tables.'

Edward hinted that his own fortunes were about to change. He became cagey, but let out the information inch by inch until he could tell Richard had taken the bait. When Edward let slip that it was a little bit of a scam that'd bring in about a quarter of a million, Richard grabbed his arm. 'Can you tell me about it?'

'Can't really tell you too much. It's a bit dodgy, and I'm not the only one involved . . . You might even know one of the chaps, so I can't really.'

'Oh, come on, tell me. You know I won't say a word, really I won't . . . Must be crooked, the way you're so wary. Come on, tell me.'

Richard had swallowed the bait, and slowly Edward gave him enough details, not that he would be able to trace any of it for himself.

Richard laughed. 'So when this reporter chappie gives a big

splash about the mine reaping you'll sell ... Well, wish you luck – sounds easy, bit too easy ... Where you getting the roughs to throw about?'

Edward shook his head, then grabbed Richard's arm. 'Listen, we could cut this guy out, the one we've got lined up. You would be perfect, my God ... Look, aren't you carrying back a load this weekend? You'd pay off all your debts, no one would be any the wiser – plus you'd have money in your pocket. Look, I may be able to let you in on it, just a possibility, I'm not sure ...'

Richard fell for it hook, line and sinker. 'It would be easy enough for me to do. You see, we keep the stones in a safety vault, but I take them with me on the plane. I'll change my flight to the next day and I'll still be able to get the stones delivered on time because it's the weekend.'

Edward left Richard hanging on tenterhooks to see if he would be able to bring him into the scam.

Without mentioning who he was using to place the gems, Edward called BB and gave him the news it was 'on'. He then called Skye, instructing him to get cracking. He had the stones, they could do it, but Skye had to move fast to set up the mine.

The girl was hired, a prostitute brought from Johannesburg and installed in a hotel. She was to be paid five thousand for her part in the scam, and she would return home the same day so she would not be able to answer any questions.

Skye met with Thin Willy to prepare the explosives, and all the men hired by BB were gathered together, waiting. Five more journalists had been tipped off, and had their cameras ready.

Skye photographed the prostitute posing as the granddaughter of the mine owner, holding in her hands the rough diamonds like blackened, muddy stones. The mine was cordoned off as the press interviewed the girl, and the men patrolled the new fences with guns at the ready.

'Miss Smith', with Skye taking photographs all the time, was driven to the diamond weighing and verification office. The press gathered around them, flashbulbs popping. She was photographed outside the office doors, smiling and waving a bottle of champagne.

In her hotel room, Edward waited to collect the stones. She was slightly drunk from the champagne, and seemed not to care about her body search. Edward replaced the stones in their little white bags, then into the case, after which Skye took 'Miss Smith' to the airport and saw her safely on her way.

The next day Skye had sold his story to every paper, with different pictures to go with the stories. The photos of the visit to the diamond merchant's office to verify the stones were of excellent quality, and the ones at the minehead showed Miss Smith displaying the stones as the boys grouped around. There were also shots taken by flash down the newly blasted mine.

All the newspaper reports stated that Miss Smith had been prepared to sell until a young scientist from the De Veer Corporation had assured her that her old grandfather's mine was indeed alive and kicking not more than another hundred feet down. Skye's article also mentioned that the experiment had been verified and that Japan was fighting to get a share of what would be the biggest breakthrough in the history of mining. The news caused an uproar, and an even greater ripple passed through the laboratories of De Veer's. When they checked the exact location of the mine, they found that Edward Stubbs had already earmarked it as being live. Again De Veer's declined to make a statement as to the authenticity of Edward's experiments, saying they were not prepared to disclose their findings before further examination.

With trembling hands, Richard retrieved his case and Edward gave his word that he would be paid in full by banker's draft in any currency he desired within the month. All the stones were intact, and Richard returned to England.

BB now played his final hand at the Pretoria Club. He weaved his way in and declared that he was buying drinks for everyone in the house. The news items littered every table. 'That lad's a genius, he's proved it once, now it's my turn.'

Edward made the call to the club and BB's voice boomed at him down the line. For a moment he thought BB was having a heart attack, then he started to laugh as the old boy gave the performance of his life.

He would have laughed even harder if he had seen BB stagger to his chair in the club, gripping his arm. 'The bank, those bastards are foreclosing on me.'

He began to think he had overdone it, because he could actually feel a burning pain down his left arm.

They all watched as the old boy, his face flushed bright red, gritted his teeth and marched, leaning on his stick, to the car, and drove himself home. Edward was waiting, ran to him, clapping his hands. 'My God, BB, we're going to do it, look – the bank's publicized their foreclosure on your loans, when that auction starts we'll clean up.'

BB felt terrible, his chest hurt and his arm was stiff. He nodded and asked Edward to bring him a brandy.

Concerned, Edward stepped back, looked the old boy over, and hurried to the drinks cabinet. He carried the bottle back and poured a stiff measure, helped BB's shaking hands lift the glass to his lips.

'I'll be fine, just fine ... Now then, son, you know where everything is kept, don't you, never know, old ticker's playing me up.'

Edward held the old man close, gripped him tight. 'Now listen to me, you old bastard, I do know where everything is, and in no way are you opting out of the last stage. You not got the guts for it? Backing out at the last minute?'

The old boy swiped the air with his cane. 'Am I hell, I'll be at the bloody auction, I'll be there.' He let the cane slide to the floor and held his big hand out. Edward knelt down beside him.

'God bless the day I met you, you've made an old man happy.'

Edward kissed him on the top of his bristling white hair and said he would be waiting. 'Think big and your dreams will grow, think small and you'll fall behind.'

The next day BB drove himself to the auction of all his worldly possessions in his gleaming old Bentley. As he entered the room, a hush fell over the crowd. He pointed his stick at two bankers and told them they were vultures. He sat up at the front as the auctioneer took his place. The house went under the hammer for a ludicrously low price. From the front came the boom of BB's voice, 'Bastards . . . bastard bankers.'

Next on the agenda were the mines, to be sold as a job lot. BB waved his stick, screaming that the bankers were taking his very life.

The bidding started, and BB had to hold on to his stick with both hands. He wished Edward, his adopted son, could be there . . . he closed his eyes and the bidding sounded like sweet music . . .

'I am bid five . . . and six million . . . and one and two, eight . . . I have nine . . . and one, ten million . . . twelve . . .'

The Van der Burge mines went under the hammer for sixteen million. Cheap at the price – if they had been as good as the reports they should have fetched twenty times that amount. BB didn't feel he had cheated in any way. The vultures deserved it.

BB could see Edward waiting as he stepped out of the car and he beamed, held up four fingers four times . . . Edward slid down the wall of the house, rolled on the ground and screamed with delight. 'We did it, we did it!'

That afternoon BB signed over all the deeds to his dead mines. He kissed the cheque lovingly, and banked it the same day. Edward placed his mines on the market and made five million each. Like his partner, he deposited the cheque the same day. They were moving as fast as possible, knowing that at any moment the ludicrous 'gold rush' they had instigated would be proved a con. BB had already signed the drafts of the major sums over to Edward as agreed. The rest he retained, leaving very little for himself. Overnight Edward earned himself fifteen million. The dam would burst at any time, and preparations for him to leave South Africa began to move ahead.

Skye Duval threw himself at Edward's feet and kissed his ankles. 'We did it! We fucking did it!'

Edward turned on him. He was so tense he was like a coiled spring. 'I've got to get out. I'm the one who started this rolling, so they'll be coming for me. I'm leaving for London on the next plane.'

Skye crawled across the floor and hauled himself up into a chair. He had been drinking steadily, and was so flushed with the success of their scheme he couldn't stop laughing.

Edward left Skye opening a bottle of champagne and went upstairs to BB's study. Hearing Edward coming, BB knew he had done the right thing. Edward would receive his share too if anything happened . . . He had made Edward his heir.

Edward went to the old man and held him tight. 'I've got two tickets, one for you as well. You packed? We'll move out this afternoon. The vultures won't take long, BB.'

BB's eyes went moist, and his voice was gruff with the effort of trying not to show how deeply touched he was. 'No, lad, you go and make more, much more. Put all you have to good use, make yourself powerful and untouchable. I did it once and, by Christ, with your help I almost did it again. But Edward, son, I've no more mountains to climb, I'm satisfied now and I'm in debt to you.' He stuck his will in Edward's top pocket, and Edward opened it. He gripped the old man's knees. 'You can't do this, BB, what about Richard?'

'He'll hate me, but that won't be anything new. He deserves no more than he gets. Now, lad, bugger off. Any day the news'll break what you got yourself up to. You'll not only have them after you, but the police as well. Go on, go on, and don't look back. Just walk out, and remember, Eddie, think big and all your dreams will grow, think small and you will fall behind. Think that you will . . .'

Edward walked out and didn't look back, he couldn't. Skye

was waiting for him outside the room. He was staggering drunk and flung his arm around Edward's shoulder. 'Let's you an' me go on a long jaunt together, eh? Take the place apart, just you an' me, brother.'

Edward scared Skye as he shook his arm away violently and picked up his suitcase. 'You're not my brother, and you're drunk out of your skull. You go your way, Skye – I'm going back to London.'

Skye couldn't believe what he was hearing. He trailed after Edward as he rang for a taxi. 'Eddie, what's the matter? Has something gone on between you and the ol' boy?'

Edward turned to Skye, his face like a mask. 'There's some land we should think about buying. I made a few discoveries when I was doing the collections – perlite's there, make a bundle with it in the building trade. I think you should stay around here. No one can touch you about the press releases – you were just doing your job. Blame the whole scam on me. I think you should stay.'

Speechless, Skye backed away from Edward.

'I'm going alone, Skye. Here's the details of the land and some things for you to look into. I'll be in touch as soon as I'm set- tled in London.'

Skye felt as though he had been punched in the stomach. He shook his head. 'Oh, man, I don't believe this. You're just walk- ing out on me, leaving me here? Well, fuck you, buddy boy – I'll be on that plane with you . . .'

Edward sighed. He could see the taxi drawing up outside the gates. He signalled to it and the cab turned into the drive. 'I don't think you quite understand. You're staying put, I might need you here. You've got nothing to leave for, and you've got enough cash to buy as many black boys and as much booze as you want.'

Skye gripped Edward's arm. 'You know I did all this for you, for us both . . . for you an' me, buddy, an' if you're getting out of this fucking country, so am I.'

Edward stared at him, then reached through the open taxi

window and touched Skye's face. 'You stay here, I need you here. We're not through with this place, buddy boy. Now you've got the smell of money, think about doubling all those dollars . . . I'll call you . . .'

Skye watched the yellow taxi drive away. He leaned against the villa walls, crying . . . then suddenly he was running to his car. He drove like a crazy man back to his bungalow, ransacked the drawers, knowing all the time it wouldn't be there. He tipped out the last drawer and, sure enough, his passport and birth certificate were gone. He was so stunned at the implications, at how Edward had used him, that he collapsed on the bed. He had walked straight into Edward's carefully prepared trap.

'You bastard . . . Oh, you bastard . . .'

With a wondrous gleam in his eyes, BB surveyed the havoc he and Edward had wrought, revelling in it. Greed had made men he had thought were his friends grab at dried, dusty, empty earth – men who were too greedy to wait for the scientists to approve Edward's theory.

He drove to the black area of town and pulled up outside a small shanty. Children gathered around the old black Bentley in the dusty road. BB banged on the broken-down door and called for Thin Willy.

A gnarled, thick-set man with muscles as strong as iron standing out on his arms, greeted BB warmly. They had a genuine affection for each other.

'Time, Willy, it's time.'

Willy nodded his thickly curled greying head and walked back into the house. He came out carrying two sticks of dynamite. BB put the keys to the Bentley into the black man's hands, and they both climbed in. 'Yours now, so you drive.'

Willy beamed his cracked-tooth smile and shook his head, laughing. Then he drove carefully, hunched over the wheel, to the Fordesburg mine, the only one BB had retained as it was in his wife's name.

Willy parked the Bentley and took a torch to help the old man across the fields and the overgrown, unused tracks. With an iron rod he heaved away the massive stone that had been placed in front of the old shaft. At last it rolled back far enough for them both to squeeze through. Thin Willy guided BB, holding on to his arm, until they reached the first shaft, the gates rusted, the ropes rotting. Pulling hard, Willy looked with some trepidation at BB. 'May not take your weight – twenty-five years a long time, boss.'

BB waved him aside and climbed into the old-fashioned cradle. Willy handed him the explosives, they shook hands, and then Willy began to turn the cradle's wheel.

Far below Willy heard the clank of the bucket as it halted, and the echo of BB's voice, then he felt his way out of the mine. He rolled the rock back into place. Two names were carved into the rock; John Van der Burge and Michael Van der Burge. Willy patted the rock and sighed. There was no record of the names of the other boys who had died with the two white boys, but then they had only been kaffirs.

Willy walked back to the Bentley. The promise he had made to BB more than twenty-five years ago was now fulfilled. He waited, the keys in the ignition, until he heard the low rumble and boom from deep below the ground. BB was laid to rest with the ghosts of his sons. He had gone the way he had chosen, with pride. Willy knew BB would make headlines one last time, as by morning the papers would have received his letter.

The letter did make headlines, and the photo of BB was centre page. He had taken total credit for the outrageous con trick, and by doing so also took all the blame. Edward Stubbs was cleared as being nothing but an innocent young student with a hopeful but foolish idea that he could find out with chemicals what the mighty bowels of the earth contained.

The rocks that fell around the old man, burying him, had the last laugh. They shed over the dead man a mound of small, pebble-like objects. Diamonds.

*

Edward was excited as the pilot requested the passengers to fasten their seat belts, they would be landing at Heathrow in ten minutes.

Eight long years had passed since Edward's arrival in South Africa. He had always known it would take a considerable time, but had not anticipated just how long he would be away from England. It was 1954, and he stared down through the clouds at the City of London far below. The Thames was like a snake curving through the city. He leaned back against the headrest as the plane dipped and took up its position in the stack. He was moving into a new phase of his life; he was a multimillionaire and still not thirty years old. He felt as if he had the world in his hands, and laughed aloud. Edward Stubbs had done it, he had made it, and now he was back and determined to climb even higher. Money he had, now he wanted power.

Chapter Sixteen

Edward settled back into living in England. He had made a couple of half-hearted attempts to trace his brother, but there had always been some urgent matter that took precedence. A year after his return he drove in his new Silver Cloud Rolls-Royce back to the East End, back to his roots.

The Roller cruised along, past his old home, or rather the debris of where a prefab had once stood. He got out and walked along the entire road; he owned plot twelve, Evelyne's house, he owned the corner site, the Meadows' old house, plus the plot at the far end, Freda and Ed's.

The council developers could not move with the land at each end and dead centre being privately owned, and they sold the whole stretch of land to Edward at a ridiculously low sum. The next time Edward drove along the old street he owned it, every brick and every piece of debris, the whole street, with the canal running along the back and direct views over the Thames.

Edward had formed a building company, bought it off the peg. It was already called the Barkley Company, and he liked it, liked the sound of it, repeated it in his mind a few times. Offices with a yard were purchased for the building company, and Edward stood up to watch the sign, 'Barkley Company Ltd', being painted. Four men were employed to erect corrugated iron fencing the whole way around the street site.

'What you going to build, Mr Barkley, sir? Offices? Warehouses?'

He smiled and said nothing, just instructed the men to complete the fences, he hadn't decided yet.

Edward noticed a property for sale in Greenwich and studied the brochure. The place was ridiculously cheap, described as 'a small, stately manor house, giving direct access to the river'. He took a boat trip along the Thames, standing breathing in the cold river air and the sights. He had missed England and was glad to be back. The river, the barges and the bridges gave him a sense of freedom.

The house was so run down that the roof had sunk in, the gardens were overgrown and the access to the river was blocked by driftwood and leftover debris of bombed-out wharves. The estate agent bowed and scraped to Mr Barkley as he opened the front door, and their voices echoed through the dark marble hall. The dusty cobwebs hung in swathes, and everywhere was filled with rubble. One room had been used by tramps – they had left their empty wine and meths bottles, and the stench of their urine pervaded the air.

The master suite overlooked the river, directly across from his old home. He could stand at the window and see where he had been raised. 'Tell your company, I will give them ten thousand below the asking price, in cash. Contact me at my office tomorrow morning.'

The agent almost fainted as he calculated his commission, and his luck in being the one to be given the keys to show Mr Edward Barkley of the Barkley Company around the old manor. As he locked and bolted the thick oak front door, he noticed, for the first time, the strange carved gargoyles looming from the eaves of the dilapidated roof. He made a mental note to contact his 'knocker boy' friends. The old place would be demolished, and there could be a bit of cash made from 'devils' heads' up the King's Road.

Within one week the deeds belonged to Edward, and within a month of the completion twenty-four builders started work. They were not going to demolish the manor as everyone thought, far from it. Mr Barkley was going to be in residence, and he wanted the best, nothing but the best.

Driving away from the manor house Edward was very happy. The work was going along fine. He turned on the car radio and suddenly decided he would visit his mother's grave. He veered off the bridge and headed for the East End cemetery.

He stared down at the neatly cut grass, the marble urn filled with fresh flowers. The caretaker told him someone came most Sunday afternoons to tend the grave. Edward tipped him well, very well, and the old man took off his cloth cap. 'You want me to look out for him, sir? Tell 'im you was askin' after 'im?'

Edward hesitated. It would look strange if he didn't say something. 'No, no need, thank you all the same.'

'It'd be no trouble, guv, you jest gimme yer name an' I'll pass it on ...' the caretaker trailed after Edward and looked at the Rolls parked along by the railings. 'Didn't catch the name, sir?'

Edward stopped and turned, irritated by the man's persistence. 'Barkley, the name's Barkley.'

The old man pushed his cap back, scratched his head. 'Barkley ... you any connection to the Barkleys, that big tombstone up by the grass verge? Only the geezer don't do dat one, he does the small one up by the taps.'

Edward shrugged the man off and opened the car door, then as the old boy shambled back into the gatehouse he walked across to the Barkley tomb. It was massive, and an archangel stood on top as if on guard. The Barkley family were titled until 1864, then the title dropped, and the last names added made Edward bend down to brush off the creeping moss.

'Edgar, Andrew, the dearly beloved sons of Edith and John Barkley ... Rest Forever In Peace.' The whole family had been wiped out in the Blitz, not that Edward felt any pity, it was the dates that interested him. Edgar and Andrew had been born in the same years as Edward and Alex Stubbs.

Edward spent a long time at Somerset House trying to check on the Stubbs family; Freedom and Evelyne had never married – both he and Alex were illegitimate. Freedom's name was on both birth certificates as the father, but there was no marriage certificate.

Turning to the Barkley family, he made copious notes and detailed the family history. He was informed by the clerk that many records had been destroyed in the fires of the Blitz ... There was no record of the deaths of the two boys, Edgar and Andrew, at Somerset House. Armed with a copy of the birth certificate of the dead Edgar, Edward applied for a new passport ...

Shortly before two o'clock two Sundays later, Edward arrived at the cemetery. By four o'clock he was ready to give up when he saw the silver Jaguar draw up. He didn't know for sure, but he had a gut feeling it would be his brother.

Almost able to touch him, Edward stood right behind Alex. 'Hello, Alex.'

Alex straightened, clenched his fists, and froze.

'Been waiting for you, came last Sunday too.'

Alex's stomach turned over. He couldn't move, and his mouth went dry. He felt the hand on his shoulder like a massive weight, and still he couldn't turn. The hand rubbed his shoulder, then moved to his neck, skin contact. Slowly, Alex turned to look into his brother's face. He had to lift his eyes just a fraction, but then Eddie had always been slightly taller. The brothers remained silent as they looked at one another – into each other's souls. Edward's hand dropped, but their eyes were locked, each trying to see into the other's mind.

Edward reached out and traced his brother's face, the scars, the broken nose, the crushed cheek and the ear, the one bent like an old boxer's ear. His hands were manicured and soft, his touch gentle. Alex could only see his father, Freedom, standing before him, the thick black hair and black eyes, the straight nose and high cheekbones. Edward was a mirror image of Freedom.

Gently, Edward wrapped his arms around his brother. Alex went stiff, his body rigid, his hands clenched at his sides, ungiving, unwilling to bend to the embrace. He could smell sweet perfume in his brother's hair, on his soft, shaved skin. He was helpless, so many emotions exploding inside him . . . He gritted his teeth, waiting until the arms fell away, until Edward stepped back.

This was the moment Alex had been waiting for all these years. His heart was pounding, and he swallowed. He tried to make his voice sound natural. 'Hello, Eddie – will you have a drink with me?'

Edward smiled, and they both turned and walked away from the grave towards their separate cars. Hands shaking, Edward brought the Rolls behind the Jag. He lit a cigarette and his whole body shook. Jagged pictures flashed before his eyes. He began to sweat. As if replayed again and again, he saw his father coming towards him, his arms open wide . . . coming towards him, towards the knife . . .

Alex blasted his car horn, looking back at the Rolls, then waved his hand for Edward to follow. Alex was calm now, icy calm. He had been thrown by Edward's resemblance to Freedom, it had unnerved him, but now he was back in control. They drove off one behind the other.

Alex stopped to pick up a bottle of rum. He didn't know why he chose rum, he didn't care. The Rolls drew in behind the Jag and parked, Edward locked it. He looked around the run-down street, not two miles from where they used to live. He followed Alex up the stone steps to the third landing and neither spoke a word.

The room was spartan, and Edward looked around as he took off his coat and flung it over a plastic-covered chair. The table was laid with one plate, one knife and fork, and one cup turned upside down on its saucer, the teaspoon not in the saucer but lying beside it. Every item in the small two-roomed flat was meticulously placed, even the salt and pepper, the folded paper napkin.

Opening what looked like a cupboard, Alex revealed a small sink and drainer and a two-ring gas cooker. The only glasses were two thin, polished tumblers. He put them carefully on the table and unscrewed the cap of the bottle, poured two measures and replaced the cap.

'Rum.'

Edward picked up a glass and held it. Alex offered no toast, just gulped at the rum. It burnt the back of his throat and he coughed. 'I don't drink.'

'Nor do I.' Edward tossed his down and it burned. They both coughed, put the empty glasses down on the clean table. There was a gaping void between them. Alex topped up the glasses and they drank again.

'We've got to talk, Alex.'

Alex was aware of his brother's deep aristocratic tones. He chose to speak badly, as if separating himself from his brother. 'Oh, yeah? I've got nuffink ter say ter you.'

They drank again, emptying their glasses and putting them back on the table. Edward could feel the booze beginning to take effect. He reached for the bottle and poured for them both.

The suit, the posh voice, the style, brought Alex's anger rushing up, like vomit. Edward knew his brother was working up to something, and did not try to stop it. They finished the bottle and Alex put it away carefully. The rum was having the desired effect, and he eased up.

'What do you want?'

Edward thought about it, licked his lips. 'I owe you, and I'm here to ... to ... settle.'

Alex gripped the edge of the table. He was trying to stand up straight but the floor moved.

'I'm a rich man.'

'So what, so am I.'

'But I'll make you richer.'

'You got nuffink I want.'

Edward gripped the other side of the table, half rose, and the floor moved under him, too ... 'Your floor's uneven.'

'Nuffink wrong wiv my fucking floor.'

Edward stood and swayed on his feet and Alex stood opposite him and swayed. 'We're drunk.'

'I'm not.'

'Yesh you are.'

'I bet you any money I can walk dat edge of de carpet.'

Edward turned his back and walked to the carpet edge. Alex slid open the kitchen drawer and took out a knife. He had found it in a drawer at the club. It had belonged to Johnny Mask, and was razor sharp, an old stiletto, a gyppo's cut-throat razor.

Alex watched as Edward moved very carefully to the edge of the carpet and balanced on the fringe, his arms out like a trapeze artist.

'One million I can make it from here to there ... you on?'

Alex swayed, nodded his head ... he glared as Edward began his balancing act ... midway along he wobbled, one foot edged off the fringe of the carpet.

'Well, thassit, I owe you, one million ...'

He slapped his chequebook on the table, fumbled for his pen, scrawled out the cheque ...

'Very funny.'

'Not a joke, Alex, cash it, you'll see.'

Alex moved like lightning and held the knife at Edward's throat. This was it, the moment he had dreamed of, lain awake planning. Now it was here – he could kill Edward. But the face that stared back at him wasn't Edward's, it was his father's, with the same dark eyes. Alex froze, unable to use the knife, then in a fury he hurled it across the room. Edward let out a hiss of breath, put his hand to his throat as the knife hit the cupboard door and sliced into the wood. 'Jesus Christ.'

Edward tried to rise to his feet but Alex, having missed his long-awaited chance of revenge, felt his rage unleashed, like water bursting from a dam. He grabbed Edward by the hair and yanked his head back so hard he heard a crack. 'You take yer fucking cheque, you cunt, and stuff it up yer arse, eat it, eat it!'

Alex began to stuff the cheque into Edward's mouth, and Edward kicked him in the groin. Alex buckled up and backed away – then he straightened and began to roll up his sleeves. Edward slipped his tie off, broke the gold cufflinks as he too began to roll up his cuffs. Alex gestured with his hands, snarling. 'Come on, come on then . . . come on, pay me, pay me for the years, Eddie, pay me.'

The two brothers fought like boxers to begin with, throwing punches at each other, punches that found their mark and hurt. They were one and the same, they were out in the back yard but this time there was no Freedom to yell instructions, no mother standing at the back door shouting for them to stop. They boxed, sparring, jabbing at each other until Alex smashed his fist into Edward's face and his nose began to bleed . . . Alex then fought dirty, kicking, lunging, throwing any article of furniture close to hand. The chair crashed down on Edward's head, and Edward hurled his body at Alex and they fell on the table, smashing it in two beneath their weight . . . They rolled on the floor, biting, slapping, kicking, shouting and screaming abuse at each other. They made so much noise that the old woman from the flat above began banging on the ceiling with her cane for them to shut their racket, but it went on and on . . . A chair was hurled through the window, smashing on to the street. Edward ran at Alex and caught his arm on the jagged glass, blood sprayed over the wall, and like a mad bull Alex charged, head down, butting Edward against the door . . . It splintered, and Edward hammered blows into Alex's stomach . . . Alex brought his two hands, clasped together, up under Edward's jaw and sent him reeling, sprawling backwards.

Alex threw himself on top of him, holding him up by the hair with his left hand, his right fist crashing again and again into Edward's face. Edward's head jerked from side to side as he caught blow after blow, and neither of them even heard the police siren, the screaming neighbours shouting that someone was being murdered.

The banging on the door as the police pounded against it, tried to force it, brought Alex to his senses, and he hauled his brother to his feet. Edward's face was covered in blood, his shirt drenched with it, his eyes puffy and already swelling. The door burst open and the police officer gaped at the two bloody men. 'Iss all right . . . is all right, officer . . . we're brothers.'

Alex had to hold Edward up on his feet, hands beneath his armpits. The police officer looked around at the wrecked room, the broken windows, gave them a lecture about disturbing the peace and told them to clear up the mess in the road.

Left alone, Alex let Edward slither to the floor, ran water in the sink and splashed his face. The blood streamed from his nose and mouth and he was heaving for breath as he leaned against the wall. Edward staggered to his feet and fell down again. Alex took him a wet cloth. ''Ere, wipe yer face.'

Edward held the cool cloth to his bleeding face.

'Get out, Eddie, we're quits.'

'I'm going nowhere without you.'

'It's too late, Eddie, you're too late, go away.'

'I'm rich, don't you understand? I'm rich!'

Alex dunked his head in the water and stood up, shaking the drops around him. 'So am I . . . I don't need you, I don't need yer money, I don't need nuffink, nobody.'

'You married?'

'Noooo! Fuck off!'

Edward picked up the remaining chair, set it down carefully and sat on it, folding his arms. 'Will you just hear me out before you throw me out?'

Alex sighed, and at that moment the chair collapsed beneath Edward and he landed in a heap at Alex's feet. Alex swore and hauled him to his feet yet again, and they caught sight of themselves in the mirror and started to laugh. Alex left his arm around his brother's shoulders and they laughed, laughed at each other ... and their roaring laughs turned into sobbing tears. They clung to each other like lovers, holding each other, afraid to let go. With tears streaming down his face, Edward held his brother's broken and bloody face between his hands, kissed him, and Alex buried his head in his big brother's neck.

'We're brothers, Alex, remember, and we're going to be them again, I promise you, I swear to you.'

Chapter Seventeen

The brothers' reunion did not unite them immediately. Alex was not that easily won over; he could not rid himself of the bitterness he felt towards Edward. All that he had been so proud of acquiring appeared small and shabby when reviewed by Edward. He felt self-conscious under his brother's scrutiny; Edward's ever-present sophistication threatened him. Alex balked at changing his name; in fact, he turned against everything Edward suggested. He had been his own boss and, in his own way, happy with his accomplishments. To have them derided, almost sneered at, made him react violently.

Edward knew he had to take his time, yet he was impatient for Alex to match him, to be able to stand alongside him. As things were, he was an embarrassment. Edward made sure they were never seen together in public, and he always made the approach when he wanted to see Alex.

He had been waiting for Alex for over two hours, sitting in his car parked outside Alex's squalid flat. He watched the Jaguar draw up, watched his brother carefully wipe the fingermarks off the bonnet. Alex looked like a crook, like a cheap con man, and Edward decided it was now or never.

Alex looked up as he approached, then turned back to inspect his motor.

'Can I come up? Got a minute?'

Alex nodded, and walked into the building. As he waited for Edward to catch him up he could smell his cologne.

'You smell like a whore's bedroom.'

'Fifty quid a bottle makes her high class, you got that kinda bird working for you? Business must be looking up.'

Alex tossed his coat over a chair and snapped, 'Yeah, go on, Eddie, any chance you can to get a dig in. What d'you want? Get off me back, will yer?'

Edward looked around the bare room then down at his polished, manicured nails. He noticed that the chair they had broken in the fight had already been replaced.

'I'm going to give it one last try, Alex, then, if that's the way you want it, I'll walk.'

'You do that! What's wiv this Barkley crap, eh? Who d'yer think yer kiddin', poncin' about? You should watch out fer yer motor, kids round 'ere don't know yer, you'll 'ave no wing mirrors . . .'

'Oh yeah? They leave the crooks' cars alone, do they?'

'I'm no fuckin' crook, but I'm known around here, all right?'

Edward began to unbutton his coat, shaking his head. They always had to go through this banter, it was beginning to get on his nerves.

'Okay, Alex, I'll give it to you straight. I'll buy you out for any price you want, and I'll put one million aside for you on top.'

'Look, I heard you the first time, I'm not interested.'

Edward stared at him, his face set, then he sprang forward and gripped his brother by the neck, pushing him towards the mirror.

'Take a good look at yourself, Alex, a real good look. The cheap suits, the face . . . what do you see? How far do you think you can go, Stubbs? You've got a record, and it's stamped right across your forehead – ex-con!'

Alex swung round, shrugging his brother away. 'I am what you made me, Eddie.'

'Do you think I don't know that? You think I come here

grovelling out of anything but guilt? I'm rich, I want to help you. I want to put things right, and you won't let me. So tell me, what will you let me do?'

'Nothin' . . . I don't want nothin' from you. Stew in yer guilt, Eddie-boy, fuckin' stew in it.'

'Okay, so you won't do it for me – how about doing it for Ma, for her? You know all she ever wanted was . . .'

Alex could feel the tears welling up inside him. He jabbed the air with his hand. 'You got no right to even mention her name, you bastard! You got no right to come into my life an' make everythin' like a piece of shit. I worked for everythin' I got, an' I'm proud of what I done. I don't need yer, I don't want you around. You keep pushin' me an' I swear I'll fuckin' kill you. This time I won't chuck the knife away, you'll get it just like you gave it to Dad, hear me? You hear me?'

Alex was spoiling for another fight, as if it was the only way he could communicate with Edward. There had been too many years lost between them. Edward chose his words carefully, knowing he was on dangerous ground, clinically talking his brother down, determined to win him round. He began with flattery, telling Alex just how impressed he was with his business, saying that if he had given the impression he was not, he wanted to rectify it.

'You think if I wasn't impressed by you I'd be here now? I thought I was sharp, but you, Alex . . . Come on, I'm not putting you down in any way. All I can see is how much further you could go, and I want to give you a hand up.'

'I need you, huh? That's what you're sayin'? You're full of bullshit, you always was.'

'I need you, it's me that needs you. I want to be big, Alex, but I can't do it on my own, and all I'm offering you is a partnership. But we've got to be clever, you know? People know who you are. What if they didn't know you, eh? Didn't know anything about you? Look in the mirror, your face, Alex . . . what do you see? Broken nose, cheek smashed in, and your ears look as if you've been in the ring for years.'

'Yeah? So what? It's my face, I can live wiv it.'

'You don't have to. You were a hell of a good-looking kid. Get the nose straightened, cheek fixed . . .'

Alex stared at his reflection, then at the handsome features of his brother. He could feel Edward's hands on him, and he turned away. Edward held him gently, made him look at himself again.

'You want to go through the rest of your life like this? Don't give me your answer now, think about it. Here are some brochures of clinics in Switzerland . . . We'll take it stage by stage, see it through together.'

Alex took the brochures and flicked through them. He chewed his lips, looked at Edward and back at the glossy pamphlets. 'What about me business? You leave it more 'n a few weeks an' all hell breaks loose. I can't just piss off, I run the show.'

'I'll take care of it, all of it, and I'll give you the best price. You want it back after, then you'll have it. I reckon we can really go places together, just so long as it's together.'

Alex felt at a loss, pulled so many ways, wanting everything that Edward dangled before him but at the same time distrusting him. Edward was relentless, swinging the carrot, knowing he was at long last winning Alex over.

'Plus a million on top – You've got to let me give you my guilt money, I won't take no for an answer. It'll be in a Geneva account in both our names. I'll keep the club running, what's-his-name will show me the ropes. You can't lose, Alex.'

'Arnie, 'is name's Arnie. He's a good pal ter me.'

'Yeah, I'll take care of him, no problem. What do you say you sleep on it? It's a new start for both of us, I need you with me, I want you with me. You're my brother, we're brothers.'

Alex sat on his single, neatly made bed. His expression was so childishly confused that Edward put his arms around him, kissing the top of his head.

'I love you, Alex. Let me do this for you. Then it's you and me going right to the top. I've got contacts; I'm already branching out, trying for big building projects. That's where the money is, property, and I've got the finances to buy now while the time's right.'

Alex remained sitting, staring blank-eyed at the clinic brochures. He knew Edward had won him round, just as he had always done when he was a kid. He turned slowly to stare at his reflection ... the mirror blurred ...

The nurses whispered together, checking his pulse, his drip. 'How are you feeling, Mr Barkley? Your brother's waiting to see you. Feel like a visitor? Yes?'

Alex was in such pain he could do nothing. His bandaged head throbbed, and he felt as though a truck had run over his face. He could smell the familiar cologne, the heavy, sweet, musky smell, and knew his brother was in the room.

'Hey, you still using that whore's perfume spray?'

Edward laughed and held Alex's hand. 'That's my brother talking! How are you feeling?'

'Terrible, bleedin' terrible. Me 'ead feels like someone kicked it in.'

Edward remained at the bedside until Alex slept. He came every day, and even spent two weeks with Alex at a rest home in the Alps. It had really only just begun, there would be more plastic surgery, involving a series of operations.

Alex's nose was remodelled, his cheeks built up with bone taken from his hips. His ears were reshaped, his jaw rebuilt, and his teeth capped and straightened so he no longer had to wear a false plate. His face was black and swollen for many months, and he grew depressed and irritable, as if he would never be free of the bandages or the pain.

Edward discussed his brother's progress with the doctors, and worried about his fits of depression. Alex had been away from London, from the world he knew, for almost a year, and had grown so dependent on Edward he no longer even asked about his club. The surgery had given him a complex; he didn't want to go out, aware of the tell-tale scars, and said he felt everyone was looking at him. Instead of giving him confidence in himself, the operations had done the reverse. He had never lived in such luxury or been so well taken care of, and he was at a loss how to accept it and deal with it. He was not ready to go home, yet Edward knew he must start preparing him for his eventual return. He planned a short holiday, driving through the south of France.

Alex sat sullenly at his side, wearing dark glasses, hunched in his seat.

'I got you some records, for speech therapy ... you listening, Alex?'

'Yeah, you gonna make me a friggin' film-star next, are yer? Feel a right git, all these bleedin' operations and fer what? I look like a bleedin' patchwork quilt.'

'They'll heal. You should stay in France, learn the lingo.'

'Yeah, I hear you. Who've I got to bleedin' talk to, meself?'

The trip was a disaster. They argued and bickered their way through village after village until eventually Edward's patience snapped. He was almost ready to throw in the towel when he discovered Alex in his hotel room, staring at his new face in the dressing-table mirror. The swelling and bruising had indeed gone, and there was the ghost of the old Alex, the handsome face nearly healed.

Alex turned to Edward and smiled. 'Hey, not bad fer an ex-con, what you think?'

Edward knew then that Alex was on the mend. The following morning he had arranged a special trip, refusing to tell Alex where they were going, saying it was to be a surprise. They tried out their schoolboy French as they headed towards Cannes.

Later that afternoon Edward showed off his surprise – the Château La Fontaine, his gift to Alex. A twofold gift, because he was more than aware that Alex needed even more time to adjust to his new image. Edward wanted him to start losing his East End accent, wanting him to adapt at his own pace to his new-found wealth. He calculated, not in weeks or months, but in years, so he set up a project, yet another carrot that would also keep Alex occupied, and would free Edward from his nursemaid duties. He knew he had made the right decision as they drove through the château gates.

'Imagine, Alex,' Edward told him, 'imagine what you could do with this place! You have carte blanche, as much cash as you need. Go ahead, take it back to basics and build yourself a palace.'

The Château La Fontaine, buried in the hills only an hour from Cannes, was originally built in 1769. During the occupation, the Germans had taken over the property and let it run to ruin. The once-splendid gardens and orchards were overgrown and tangled, but somehow the château, even though crumbling at its very core, retained a magnificent power.

Alex began to work on it with trepidation, then slowly the excitement of the massive undertaking took hold. He set the wheels in motion to completely reconstruct and refurbish the château.

One of the estimates he obtained for the interior, from Michelle Marchalle of Marchalle Fabrics, came in under budget. The company sent a representative to meet Alex and discuss the project in detail. So Alex met Miss Imura Takeda and within half an hour he had offered her the job.

Miss Takeda, who wished to be known simply as 'Ming', was a diminutive Japanese woman. She had arrived at their first meeting in her small Citroën, and he had been taken aback by her composure and businesslike manner. She was wearing a Chanel suit and was perfectly groomed, her glossy black hair cut in a heavy fringe reaching almost to her perfect almond eyes, and cropped short into her delicate white neck.

Ming offered to cook Alex dinner at her home. He found her workshop and apartment in a small, run-down cobbled street in Cannes. She gave him a calm, small bow as he entered her showroom. There were only two pieces of furniture on display, a small table and a single chair set against a cream silk wall and standing on a highly polished wooden floor. A tiny white vase contained an arrangement with a single flower.

Ming led Alex through to her workshop, where again the furnishing was sparse, with four girls working on designs at two trestle tables. The walls were plain with only two prints hanging, and there were stacks of fabric samples in fine wooden frames. Alex was shown designs, materials, and careful copies of original wall-hangings that Ming had drawn.

'I am most grateful, Meester Barkley, that you have chosen my company. We are very small but I give you my word that the work will be done to a very high standard.'

She made tea, her movements quick yet unhurried, and placed before him perfect cups of the finest bone china he had ever seen. She watched him touch the table, bowed her head.

'It is very beautiful, yes?'

Alex, sitting on a low cushion, nodded and sipped his tea.

'The table is seventeenth-century Chinese. Many people think only of porcelain for that period but, you see, many pieces of Ming furniture were also made.' Ming giggled as she said the word 'Ming', then whispered that it was not her real name, but one she had chosen for her work. 'Many people in the trade simply call this period of furniture "Ming".'

They continued their conversation while Alex watched her tiny hands prepare the most delicious supper of raw fish and vegetables. Ming gave him a book on seventeenth-century Chinese furniture, which as soon as he arrived home, he spent the rest of the night reading.

Alex grew increasingly enamoured of Ming. They travelled across France together in her little Citroën, attending auctions and antique fairs. They flew to Paris for the major 'in house' auctions, and he was guided by her taste and flawless eye for detail in everything. She would make him walk mile after mile through every fabric section of every store, never satisfied, until she found exactly the right texture, the right shade. Her own company set about hand-dyeing silks, and she employed six Japanese women to begin making up the drapes.

Alex was aware of the change in himself. Ming introduced

him to the high priests of Paris couture, and under her influence, a hint here, a word there, he set about buying his own wardrobe. Hesitantly, he asked for her approval, and gratefully accepted her advice.

They were together every day, but at about ten o'clock in the evening she would always excuse herself and return to her own apartment if they were in Cannes, or to her hotel room if they were on the road. Alex was like a teenager, not knowing exactly how to take the first step towards changing their working relationship into a more personal one. The completion of the château drew closer day by day, and Alex was unable to sleep at night for thinking of ways he could keep Ming near him, close to him. The château was obviously her pride and joy, and she took such delight in finding each special piece of furniture, never making too much of the decor, allowing the majestic rooms to speak for themselves. He ached to kiss her, to hold her, but he was tongue-tied in her presence, flustered. If she was aware of his infatuation, she gave him no hint.

Ming and Alex stood together in the entrance hall of the château, surrounded by the smell of fresh paint, of polish, while the bright sunlight streamed through the stained glass windows.

'Well, Alex, I think we have finished. Are you happy? Are you pleased?'

He adored the lilting sound of her voice, her accent when she spoke French. He made up his mind, it was now or never. 'Ming, I have to talk with you, not about the house, something personal . . .'

He towered above her, and she raised her almond-shaped eyes to his, then lowered them. She bit her lip until it hurt. She had been unable to make him out; at first she had thought him clumsy, because of his desperate shyness, but then slowly she had realized that it was due to his schoolboy French. Then she had wondered if he was homosexual – they had stayed in hotels together, been in each other's company day in, day out, and not once had he made a pass at her. She could not take the initiative herself to turn the relationship round. Her business depended on him, she couldn't risk it. He was more than a meal ticket to her, he had taken her out of the red and into heavy black figures, and when they started to show the château in the glossy magazines as she intended, she knew her name would be made. She had done more than a magnificent job, she had surpassed herself.

Alex caught her tiny hand and she saw him flush. This was it, he was going to make a play for her at last. She gave him a demure smile.

'I was wondering if we could have dinner together tonight? I have made a reservation in town.'

Ming had to stand on tiptoe to reach his lips. Her kiss was soft and swift, and he gasped.

'I would like that so much. I shall miss the château, I shall miss you.'

Ming had never seen a man so pleased by a few simple words.

'You will? Do you mean that?'

Ming laughed, and fell into step beside him along the marble hall. He was so childlike, and she knew he was unaware of the admiring glances he received from the many women they had met, it was as though he simply didn't notice them. Ming paused, the hell with it . . . she held his arm and whispered.

'Take me upstairs now, take me up there in your arms.'

For a moment Alex stood, nonplussed, then he swept her up into his arms. She rested her head on his shoulder, felt his pulses thudding. He carried her up the stairs and into the master bedroom suite with its drapes and the vast bed they had bought from an Austrian castle. As he laid her gently down, she reached up and took his face between her tiny hands, pulled him towards her. But before their lips met, they heard the sound of a car on the gravel drive below.

Edward was impressed, more than impressed; he was astonished. He gazed at the château through the window of the Rolls. 'Mind you,' he thought to himself, 'by the rate of knots the cash has been flowing out of the account, I should be impressed.' Now he could see where it had all gone.

He parked the hired Rolls and walked up the steps to the entrance, which was flanked by urns containing a profusion of budding flowers. He turned to survey the gardens. The orchards, the hedgerows, were all a riot of colour and richness, a wonder to the eye. It was hard to believe that it had been a wilderness less than eight months ago.

He was equally astonished at the interior. He strode from room to room, taking it all in. Nothing jarred – the furnishings, the fabrics, the colours, all blended so perfectly that he felt something akin to awe.

Alex was surprised to see his brother, but not as taken aback as Edward was by him. For a moment he did not recognize Alex, having seen him only fleetingly since the last plastic surgery he had undergone. There had been numerous operations until his face had been completely reshaped, and now Edward could see the full extent of the change. There were no scars or puffiness – he looked like a different man. Edward held him at arm's length. 'Jesus Christ, you look good, you look good.' He inspected Alex's face closely, shook his head. 'My God, what a job they did on you ... what a face! Now you're my brother again ... I love the gear, nice jacket.'

Edward touched his brother's face, his cheek, then wrapped him in his arms. Alex seemed not quite at ease with his brother, a little withdrawn, and Edward picked it up immediately.

'What's the matter, something wrong?'

'No, no, nothing wrong ... well, tell me, what do you think of the place?'

He watched Edward as he wandered around, picking up objects, looking at the fabrics. He was pale, not tanned like Alex, but there was that strength to him, that confidence. He picked up an ornate vase, a very expensive one. 'This a copy or the real thing?'

Alex smiled, amazed he wasn't able to tell. 'It's real, Ming Dynasty. It has an unusual fault in the glaze that makes it special.'

'You don't say? Well, I believe you, thousands wouldn't. What did that set us back?'

'Twenty-five thousand.'

Edward nearly dropped the vase in shock. 'Fucking hell, twenty-five grand and it's got a bleedin' fault . . . You're sure you know what the hell you're doing?'

'Yes – it's already increased in value.'

Alex began to feel annoyed as Edward continued his inspection. He noted that Edward's cashmere coat had a small rip in the pocket and a stain down the front. Edward somehow looked old-fashioned, scruffy, his suede shoes in need of a brush.

It had been almost five years since they had been reunited. For the first three years Alex had undergone extensive plastic surgery. He had recuperated in Cannes, and grown accustomed to living in style, a style he had adapted to with ease. He now spoke fluent French, and had taken a year of elocution classes to, as his brother put it it, 'Get rid of that bleedin' East End tag.'

Edward and Alex had struck a deal, one that Alex could not really refuse. He had agreed to leave England, undergo surgery, and hand over the reins of the club and his other business interests to Edward. Alex had drawn up the contracts, selling out for one million. Edward had then placed a further two million in a Swiss bank account for Alex's use. The château had been Edward's idea on one of his infrequent visits. He had suggested that they buy it and renovate it, even teasing Alex that although he was having a well-earned holiday, there was always money to be made in property, and it would give Alex a goal. But Edward had not bargained for Alex's enthusiasm, his dedication, or the vast expense of the refurbishment. He kept a watchful eye on the Geneva account, and had cabled even more money to Alex when asked. The more money he paid the less guilt he felt. But he was careful to make notes of every withdrawal, every transaction.

Ming could hear their voices as they strolled from room to room. She waited for what she deemed a respectable time before making an appearance. Then she entered the drawing room silently, standing just inside the ornate, arched doors. Alex watched his brother when he turned towards her. At times Edward's resemblance to Freedom was truly unnerving – the eyes so dark, hair so black that it had a blue sheen to it.

'Edward, this is Ming. Ming and I have been working closely on the whole project – in fact I couldn't have done up the place without her.'

Edward smiled at her, but his eyes were expressionless. His French was not as good as Alex's, and he spoke to her in English. 'Done a great job, I'm very impressed . . . what about a small tour?'

He picked up the looks between the two of them as they led him around the château. They were very much a couple, pointing out one piece of furniture or another, explaining where it came from and exactly which period. Ming talked about the colour schemes, the wonderful carpets they had shipped in, and Edward said not a word. She could feel his eyes, taking stock of everything, taking special note of her. So this was the big brother she had heard Alex speak of. She could see how different they were, in manner as well as appearance, and she could feel the energy flowing from Edward, could sense his danger.

Alex grew quiet as they neared the end of their tour. He noticed the way Edward stood close to Ming, rested his hand on her shoulder when he asked about a painting, stepped back and laughed with her when she described the auction where they bought it.

At last the inspection was over, and Edward walked slowly down the great stairway. Halfway down, he stopped. 'Well, we shall have to throw a party before we leave. I shall call London, start making arrangements . . . what about staff, have you anyone moving in yet?'

Alex hesitated. He had not hired anyone as yet, he had been taking care of himself. But Edward paid little heed to his reply, he was congratulating Ming again, but at the same time dismissing her. 'Do you have transport?'

Ming smiled and said yes she did. Edward looked over at Alex.

'Well, no doubt we will meet again ... Alex and I have a lot to discuss, I am only here for a few days, then we return to London.'

Alex ushered Ming to her car. She knew he was angry, his face was set, but he smiled, said he would collect her for dinner later in the evening. He stood and watched her drive away before turning back to the château.

Edward was lounging on a silk sofa, his feet resting on frilled silk cushions. 'We'll have a good dinner, then we'll go over all the papers you have to sign. I'll be here for a couple of days, but I want to send them back by courier tomorrow, then I can relax. May take a dip later, I must say the pool looks very inviting.' He paused, looked searchingly at Alex. 'You look fit and well, Alex, really tanned, it suits you ... She's a cute little thing, isn't she? Very talented, too ...'

Alex clenched and unclenched his fist.

'You'll have the office next to mine, but I've not furnished it ... after seeing your taste, well, I think you'd rather do it yourself. *Très* impressed, old boy.'

'Good, I'm glad you like it. I ... well, I love the place, and it must be obvious to you that I'm very happy here – not just in the château, but in France. I like it, I like the people, and I've been thinking.'

'Obviously. Well – go on.'

'Well, I can't just continue spending, this place will cost a fortune to run. But I'm sure I could open up the vineyards. And perhaps I could start buying some of the farm land surrounding the orchards, make it a productive business. We've already started – we'll have a good crop, and the season's not even begun.'

'You don't know anything about farming! Besides, I've made arrangements.'

Edward cursed himself silently for not coming to France more often. He should have guessed something like this would happen. He lit a Havana cigar, puffing slowly, taking his time and choosing his words carefully. 'Trouble is, you've no option really.'

'Whaddya mean by that?'

'Watch it, Alex, the accent slipped there.'

'Screw my fucking accent! What do you mean I've got no option? If I don't want to come back to London, then I won't . . . And would you use the bloody ashtray?'

Edward turned on him, his voice controlled, but spitting out the words. 'Maybe I need you, maybe you've overspent out here – do you think I'm running the Bank of England? While you've been lazing about over here in the sun, I've been working my butt off for you – yeah, for you . . . Here – passport, birth certificate – Alex Stubbs is dead, Alex Barkley's coming back to London with me.'

Alex didn't even pick up the envelope. He stuffed his hands into his pockets. 'You owe me, Eddie, you gave me that cash, what is this? You want it back? Not a lot to pay for near ten years.'

Edward went to his brother, put his arms round him. 'You've got it all wrong. I'm needled now because . . . because, Alex, I want you with me. I want you to take a look at what I've been doing, that's what I've been knocking myself out for since you've been in France. Between us, together, we can go places, you know? You haven't even seen what I'm working with in London, and you're going to step right in, right in next to me . . . You opt out of it, then it'll all be worthless. Don't run out on it just because of some Jap bitch.'

Alex pushed him away, had to get away from his arms. 'Maybe I need her.'

Edward sighed, rubbed his fingers in his hair. He tried another tack. 'You look closely at her, Alex my old son. She's no twenty-two-year-old, she's forty if she's a day. Not quite the sort you want to settle down with and have a family.'

Alex was getting angrier, his fist itching to throw a punch.

Edward opened his briefcase. 'Take a look at how deep I'm

prepared to go for you, how far I'm prepared to go to get you out of that cheap shit-hole of a club you ran. You are free, no one can trace you ... Alex Stubbs, the ex-con with the off-the-peg suits, is gone. Read it, bottom of second page.'

Alex opened the English newspaper, searched the columns, unsure even what he was looking for ... The article was only a few lines long, but it was a nightmare: 'GANGLAND KILLING SUSPECTED ... Alex Stubbs, a Mayfair club owner, was found burnt to death in his Jaguar early this morning. Police suspect ...' The print blurred, and Alex couldn't read any more. He swallowed, stammered, 'What the hell is this, for Chrissake?'

'Like I said, Alex Stubbs is dead. You've a new passport, new birth certificate – you come back as Alex Barkley. I'm already making waves – we've got a property business, investment company, plus that old club you ran ... I didn't sell it, you only had a short lease, so I bought the whole building. We'll open a club, it'll be the best in London – gambling, dining, cabaret ... I've already sunk over two and a half hundred grand in it, going too fast for you, am I? Whichever way you want to look at it, the jam is spreading very thick and fast. Going to make you rich, brother, richer than you ever dreamed.'

Alex's mouth was dry, his mind reeled. Edward leaned back on the sofa and laughed. 'I've been over all your old accounts, and you are good. As I said, I need you.' He sprang to his feet, bursting with excitement, and strode around the room. 'I want this place in every magazine, every glossy from *Paris Match* to *Vogue*, *Elle*, you name it, and then we'll throw a coming-out party, for you, for me. We'll get the Rainiers, the Windsors, big names, have them all here kissing our hands, and then, brother, we are in, all you need is the social acceptance ... Alex? Heyyy, buddy ...'

Alex sighed and rested his hand on the Louis XIV marble-topped table. 'It's maybe what you want, but ...'

Edward snapped, his face flushed with anger, 'Can't you see what I'm offering? Remember Ma, her dreams? Not just for me, but for you. We're going to be everything she ever wanted, and more. If you need time to think about it, fine. But I won't wait long, and don't think this came cheap.' He held out the newspaper, shoved it under his brother's nose. His voice dropped almost to a whisper, 'You had a pretty poor funeral, old son – two bouncers and a wreath of friggin' yellow roses from a tart ... that what you want? You make your mind up.'

Edward slammed out of the château, and Alex heard the Rolls churning up the gravel. He walked from room to room, and as he passed through the bedroom he caught his reflection in the long mirrors. He stopped, stared, then walked closer and looked at himself. He did look different, his hair bleached almost white by the sun, his tan, his new face. He put out his hand and touched his image in the mirror. It was true, Alex Stubbs was dead.

Ming knew it would be Edward, she just knew it. He walked straight in, straight through to her sparse, white sitting room.

'Okay, I'll give it to you straight – I think you are good, and I intend making the château famous. I will get every major glossy magazine to cover it, that means you will benefit. I will promote you, make you, but I want a cut ...'

Ming sat demurely in the high-backed, polished wood chair. Edward lit a cigarette, carefully placed it into the gold holder. 'I have companies in England, office blocks, properties. I also want to branch out in the States, more offices ... I want you to do the interior design for them all ... have to change your name, but I'll back you to the hilt.'

Her hands folded, she waited for him to finish. Edward flicked ash off his cigarette, leaned forward and continued, 'I'll make you a rich woman, and a famous one ... I detected traces of an American accent, you educated in America? What happened? Had to run for it when your lot hit Pearl Harbor?'

Ming caught her breath – she detested him, he was even sharper than she had given him credit for. He was silent, watching, waiting for her to answer. 'I was educated in America, my family sent me over to finish my studies there ... Pearl Harbor really has very little to do with either myself or my work ... I am residing in France because I wish to.'

Edward stood up and laughed, stubbed out his cigarette in a crystal bowl. Before she could say anything he was walking up the narrow staircase to her workshop. He lounged in the doorway. 'You know how much the château cost to refurbish, sweetheart? Did you think for one moment I didn't have your credentials checked out? I know all there is to know about you, and I also know you were in debt up to your little Japanese neck in the States. You were left high and dry with no cash to finish your so-called studies. You were brought over to Cannes by a French pimp, dumped by him, then you worked in a couple of massage parlours. You have a stream of relatives coming in illegally to work for you, cheap labour ... Don't mess around, don't think I am as dumb a bastard as my brother – do you want to be rich or not, that's all you have to think about.'

Ming gasped. She was shaking with rage and humiliation. Her family was impoverished, but her father was a samurai. They had no knowledge of her troubles, and to hear Edward speak in such a manner made her want to kill him. But she showed not a flicker of her thoughts or emotions on her face, which remained set and impassive.

'I will retain the name "Ming", I think it is very simple and very easy to remember. The Americans like that, plus I can use the Ming Dynasty logo.'

Edward threw back his head and laughed. He pinched her chin between his fingers, looked down into her face. 'You're hungry for it, aren't you? Takes one to know one ... There is just one other thing. I want you to stay away from Alex – I'll give you a few thousand now, pack up and leave France for a short holiday until I get him back to London. Then I'll start all the arrangements for you to move to New York. I'll have my lawyer send over the contracts.'

Edward was congratulating himself on how he had manipulated Ming. He knew instinctively that 'Little Lotus Flower' would be a good investment. He almost forgot to drive on the right-hand side of the road, and only just swerved back in time as an Aston Martin roared past with its horn blaring. The white Aston was being driven far too fast, and he could hear the screeching of rubber as it disappeared from view round a bend.

Harriet swore as she spun the wheel – some stupid old dodderer hogging the road. She slowed down considerably as the road narrowed and made a sharp turn on to a farm track.

Pierre Rochal turned on the outside lights of the barn as Harriet drew up. He was wearing an old tee-shirt and shorts, and was deeply tanned. He was in the process of converting the barn into a summer residence. The farm was a further two miles up the track.

Harriet sang out, '*Bonjour, amigo!*' She hopped out and ran along a plank to fling her arms around him. He kissed her lightly, then they began to unload the boot of the car. Harriet filled her arms with the groceries while Pierre lifted out the paint. He looked at the label. 'Yellow? Yellow?'

'Oh, don't you like it? I thought it would be lovely ... like daffodils. Can you imagine turning into the lane and seeing our barn, like one enormous daffodil?'

Pierre smiled. If she had bought bright pink he wouldn't have cared. To see her so happy and relaxed was enough, and the fact that she said 'our' barn made up for the terrible choice of paint. He watched her searching for the corkscrew, and leaned against the stained pine kitchen door. 'Second drawer down, we celebrating?'

'Yep. It's only plonk, and look – candles! We can eat on the planks outside. I am going to cook – now don't pull a face, I have to practise. A doctor's wife needs to be able to run a smooth ship.'

Pierre wrapped his arms around her, kissed her neck. 'Am I to take it that the answer, at long last, is "yes"?'

Harriet blushed and nodded. Then she delved into her grocery bag and held up a record. 'Plus, *mon cher*, I shall be able to speak your lingo ...'

Pierre laughed. The fact that he didn't even have a record player in the barn had obviously escaped Harriet's attention. She insisted he sit outside until she had prepared dinner, and he carried the candles with him. He arranged some orange boxes to sit on, while she sang at the top of her voice.

He had first met Harriet on the ski slopes in Switzerland. Met her? He chuckled as he remembered how they had collided head on, Harriet falling at his feet in a tangle of skis. At that time he had no idea she was one of the patients in his father's clinic. They had spent the day together, and by the evening he was besotted.

There had been bitter opposition from his father, of course. Harriet's emotional stability was erratic, and over the years she had spent a considerable time in various clinics. However, Pierre's father could not help but see the good effect the relationship was having on his patient. His son's happiness was eventually what persuaded him to accept the situation, but he made sure that Pierre knew Harriet's problems in detail, giving him access to her records. Although Pierre was a doctor, not a psychiatrist, he was fully aware of Harriet's condition. His obvious love and care was touching to see, and under his influence she had been on an even keel for a considerable time.

Harriet had only once discussed her illness with him – using it as an excuse to refuse Pierre's offer of marriage for almost a year. She had wanted him to be very sure, to 'know what he was taking on', as she put it. Pierre did know, and it seemed, if possible, to make his love for her even stronger. He was so engrossed in his thoughts that she made him jump as she appeared at the door.

'Would the affluent Parisian *docteur* mind if his steak was rather charred?'

Pierre held out his hand and she went to him. She smelt of frying, and her hair was standing up on end.

He asked, 'Have I told you today how much I love you?'

She laughed and sat on his knee. He wound a piece of silver

paper around her engagement finger, and she held up her hand to admire it.

'Tomorrow we'll drive into town and choose a ring.'

'No – this is just perfect ... this place is perfect, you are perfect.'

Pierre smelt the steaks burning, and rushed into the kitchen.

Caught in candlelight, the silver paper glittered. A small voice in Harriet's head whispered, 'Look, Auntie Mae, look at his hands, and his feet – each toe is just perfect.'

Harriet watched Pierre through the open window. He was tossing the salad expertly, and she sighed. She did love him, she cared for him so much, and he was so understanding. Unconsciously she unwound the silver paper from her fingers and rolled it into a tiny ball.

Alex heard Edward's car, and walked down the stairs as the front door banged open. Alex winced as the delicate stained glass shuddered.

'You've had a few calls from London – I've left a note of them on your bed. You're in the west wing – I won't be late, but don't wait up.'

'My, my, you look very smart – like the suit. What's the material?'

'Linen – it's made locally. See you in the morning.'

Edward watched Alex drive away. He knew he was on his way to Miss Takeda, and he chuckled. He doubted if Alex would ever know about his 'Lotus Flower'. He had not told Ming just how far he had delved into her affairs, or that he knew how much money she had creamed off the refurbishing of the château into her own pocket. She was as devious as Edward, and it amused him, but he reckoned that Alex would be better out of the grasp of her tiny, white hands.

When Alex arrived he found Ming wrapped in a floating white kimono. She held the door open a fraction, then bowed slightly as he stepped in. He had bought a bunch of roses from a flower seller in the town, and Ming held them close to her chest as she led him into her sitting room. She fetched a white vase and filled it with water, began to arrange each bloom with care.

'Well, you met my brother, what do you think of him?'

'He is very charming.'

'I wouldn't describe him as that.'

Alex wanted her to look at him, wanted her to say something, but still she attended to the flowers with studied concentration. Alex stood close to her. Suddenly he felt so shy, so uncomfortable. Gently, he placed his hand on her shoulder. She touched his hand, brushed her cheek against it. He lifted her into his arms and held her tightly.

'Be my wife? Will you? Will you marry me?'

He could feel her shaking, and he tilted her chin up to look into her face. She moved away from him, gesturing for him to sit down – not close, a little apart from her.

She told Alex the truth about herself. She left out nothing, even the time she had spent in the 'massage parlours'. When she had finished, she sat with her head bowed, tears streaming down her face.

Alex hesitated for a moment, then he said, 'I had better tell you about me.' And piece by piece he told his story, for the first time in all the years. It came out without violence, without hatred. He told it simply, his voice low, and Ming was silent throughout. Alex's voice only faltered when he described the death of his father, Freedom.

'I loved him, I loved him so . . . but, then, Edward . . .'

Ming could feel his pain, knew instinctively not to speak. Alex told her of his years in prison, and as he talked the hatred of all those years eased from him, little by little. At one point he smiled at her – at long last someone else knew, knew what he had been through, what he had done. He even told her about the surgery on his face, he left nothing out, as if once he had begun he was unable to stop. At the end he was drained, empty, and he sighed. It was over.

They both sat as if stripped naked, the void between them a

vast distance neither of them knew how to span. Suddenly Ming put out her tiny white hand, and there was no void, no more emptiness between them, they were in each other's arms. While they held each other tightly, Ming told Alex of Edward's visit. She saw the flash of rage in his eyes, and she held him, calmed him. 'Listen to me, I want to be your wife, but I want everything he offered me, too. I want what he offered, do you understand?'

Alex did understand, because he too wanted, or at least needed, to try to achieve everything Edward had dangled before him.

'We can do whatever we want, there's no need for us to be separated . . .'

Ming laughed softly, hugged him close. She knew Edward would stand between them.

'In a way I think he's scared of me, he wants you all to himself. Well, let him think he has you. We can wait until the time is right. Perhaps it will be better if he thinks he has succeeded in separating us.'

'You think so?'

'I know so . . . You see, I love you, I love you, Alex.'

Alex blushed beneath his tan. He tried to say what he felt, but he wanted to leave, it was crazy. More than he wanted to stay, he wanted to leave. Uppermost in his mind was the fact that he had beaten Edward at his own game.

Ming was disturbed that Alex didn't make love to her. She watched him from her workshop window as he hurried away, and remained standing there long after the car had gone. Slowly, the armour Ming had carefully constructed around herself cracked. She had let the only man she had ever cared for walk out of her life. She looked around her workroom, the bales of material, the stacks of fabric samples. Why hadn't she taken him to her bed, why? Almost unaware of what she was doing, she began to draw on a large sheet of paper. She drew the Ming logo, then pressed the pen over and over the drawing until the paper began to tear ... Ming ... Ming ... Ming ... It would not be long before that simple logo, and her name, was known worldwide.

Edward heard Alex's arrival home, heard him moving around below, and was surprised when he walked into the bedroom. He was carrying a bottle of Krug champagne and two glasses, and Edward again marvelled at the change in him. As Alex uncorked the bottle with a single practised movement, he looked so handsome, so sophisticated. He sat on Edward's bed. 'Ming has disappeared. I was upset at first ... now, well ... I've been thinking over everything you said, and I am ready to return to England, so we had better begin arranging this "coming-out" party ... Cheers.'

Edward toasted his brother in the champagne, which was chilled to exactly the right temperature. He patted the pillow beside him. 'I've already started, take a look at the "A" list.'

Alex lay next to Edward on the vast double bed, their heads resting on frilled white Victorian pillowslips. They laughed as they went over the names, made references to childhood events long forgotten, until they both drifted off to sleep, side by side. In his sleep Edward turned, and his arm rested across Alex's body as if they were lovers.

Book Four

Chapter Eighteen

Edward returned to London and went directly to the new club to inspect its progress. The building had begun to take shape – dining rooms, tearooms, kitchens and rest rooms. Three floors were totally dedicated to gambling – roulette, chemmy, baccarat tables, and private card rooms. The place was filled with designers and decorators, and no expense was spared. The papers had begun to speculate on the owner of the new, elegant club, which would be membership only, exclusive.

Edward had been taken aback at his brother's obvious adeptness at accountancy, and now he rubbed his hands in satisfaction. Alex was going to be more than useful. Edward had disposed of all Alex's small business interests, and had taken over only what he saw as reasonably profit-making establishments. Growing slowly now on the site of what had been their old home, number twelve, was a fifteen-storey tower block. When the building was finished he would have a sign erected the size of the roof saying simply, 'Barkley Ltd'.

He worked like a man possessed – he was everywhere, like a whirlwind. He seemed to have inexhaustible wealth, and soon the City was taking notice of Edward Barkley. The property company had expanded, and he was buying up land at such a rate that he swung the property boom even higher, and in doing so doubled his profits. The small building yard had now grown into a vast concern with over two hundred employees. Edward bought, rebuilt fast and sold. He used bombed-out areas as car parks, and with only one man required to sit in a small hut and take the money, it was an easy, lucrative business – one speculators began to watch out for. Edward Barkley had fingers in every pie, and yet no one seemed to know where he had come from.

Edward needed little sleep, often working right through the night in his office. He went through the stacks of files he had taken from the old Masks Club. Dora's notes made more than interesting reading. Her lists of clients were what attracted him – not the ordinary customers but her own private business. Edward thumbed through the pages and what he found made him laugh aloud. 'Dora, Dora Harris, you little slut ... You lovely little muckraker!' The lists contained not only the names, but also their references. From judges to politicians, film stars to the landed gentry and, under 'R' – the royals. With the lists were carefully documented films, tapes, photographs. Edward knew he had a small goldmine, and he was going to tap it to exhaustion.

The following morning Edward met with his PR company. There were now some extra names he wished to add to his guest list for the party at the château, ones he knew would not be able to refuse, thanks to Dora. However, they would be dependent on very high society names accepting the Barkleys' invitation in order to swing them into the upper echelons on both sides of the Atlantic. If the Windsors agreed to be present, the floodgates would open.

The Duke and Duchess of Windsor now resided in the south of France with a hard core of both English and French society surrounding them like an army. It was known that the royals were not above being paid to make an appearance, and Edward suggested a possible approach on those lines. He was told, however, that Mr Barkley did not even warrant that.

Edward refused to take no for an answer, knowing that with

the Duke and Duchess making a social appearance his and Alex's names would be placed on society lists throughout the world. He persisted, never actually negotiating appearance fees, but offering vast amounts to charities the royal couple were known to lend their names to, and eventually he received a short cryptic note of acceptance. It was now ensured that the party would be one of the biggest and most aristocratic of the season. With the royal couple as bait, acceptances would be assured.

The preparations reached fever pitch. Teams of waiters and caterers flocked over the lawns, blooms were shipped in from all over the world for the ornate floral displays. The society columns had a field day, quoting the names of the guests, and soon there was a scramble for invitations to the opening of the château.

One hundred waiters and eighteen chefs had been inspected, and everything was ready. Edward admired himself in his dressing-table mirror, then went to see Alex.

'Oh, you're wearing a white tux, well . . .'

Alex looked far more sophisticated in the new, fashionable white tuxedo. Edward fingered the collar, stepped back to get a better look. 'Excellent fit, who's your tailor?'

Alex laughed, and told him that was rather a dated expression, his designer was a young Frenchman. Edward immediately took another look at himself. 'Do I look all right, then?'

Alex nodded. He was more worried about his greetings to the royals, going over his carefully rehearsed instructions yet again.

'Right, this is it, Alex. Let's get it over with – we walk down together, okay, side by side.'

The two brothers moved to the head of the staircase and began to walk down to greet their guests.

Alex wondered how on earth he had arrived at this point in his life. He felt strange, ill at ease, and part of him knew that this was a turning point in his life. He didn't want to let Edward down in front of their three hundred guests, but he felt like an actor about to open in his first play, shaking with first-night nerves. He wished he had someone he could at least feel close to, someone he could associate with, but there was no one. Did he want this charade? He didn't know, couldn't fathom how he felt, and suddenly it was too late for doubts.

He stood at his brother's side, shaking hands and welcoming everyone, knowing no one. Time and time again Edward gestured for Alex to join him in a throng of people, and he smiled shyly, shaking hands, his face stiff from smiling and bowing and thanking everyone for their congratulations. He felt exhausted.

The party was going without a hitch, but there was tension as the guests waited for the Windsors to make their appearance. They murmured to each other, constantly watching the brothers, but were polite and cordial at the same time as they consumed vast quantities of champagne and the delicious food.

The Duke and Duchess of Windsor arrived two hours later, and set the château buzzing as everyone took sneaky looks at the couple standing talking to Edward Barkley. Alex was brought over to meet them, and was so desperately shy he could say nothing. The Duchess asked to be given a tour of the château, and Edward, about to lead them into the lounge, froze. 'Please excuse me, Your Grace . . . Alex, please . . .'

Alex gestured for the couple to walk ahead of him, glancing at Edward for a moment, afraid to be left alone with them. 'Edward, you all right?'

'I'm fine, I'll join you. Go on, don't keep them waiting.'

Edward's heart was pounding. He was sure, sure he had seen Harriet. He threaded his way among the guests, shaking hands automatically and smiling his thanks at their compliments. He reached the far end of the marquee, stared around. He told himself he must be mistaken, why would she be here? But he couldn't stop searching every face. Memories flooded through him, swept over him. He had once read her name in a society magazine, and had even thought about trying to contact her, but decided against it. He straightened his bow tie, and was about to hurry back to Alex when he heard her laugh.

Harriet was standing with her back to Edward, wearing a simple white cotton dress. Edward could see the freckles on her back, even though she was tanned to a wonderful golden colour. She had a glass of champagne in one hand and a small white clutch bag in the other. Pierre Rochal was at her side and he, too, was laughing. One of their party turned and saw Edward.

'Oh, you must let me introduce you ... this is Edward Barkley, our esteemed host – Edward, come and meet some dear friends of mine.'

Harriet turned. As she was introduced, she tossed her champagne glass over her shoulder. It was an unconscious gesture as she held her hand out. Everyone thought it was very amusing, except for an elderly gentleman who looked on in stunned amazement.

'We are gatecrashers, you don't mind, do you?' said Harriet brazenly. 'Only, we couldn't resist Jasper when he said we could tag along. Do you know Dr Pierre Rochal? And this is Daisy Millingford ... and, oh, I'm so sorry, I've forgotten your name?'

A blonde woman introduced herself, nudging Harriet in irritation as they had been at school together. The moment of forgetfulness was the only indication Harriet gave that she was shocked at seeing Edward again. She showed no interest in him, and soon made her way to the buffet. Edward excused himself and followed. He stood behind her as she surveyed the vast spread of food and one of the staff stood poised to serve her. Harriet picked up a chicken leg and bit into it.

Edward's voice was husky with emotion. 'You've cut your hair.'

'You've changed your name.'

'Can I see you?'

'What on earth is this slimy stuff all over the chicken, it's awful.'

'Where are you staying?'

Pierre joined them at that moment, and smiled apologetically at Edward's discomfort.

'Pierre, don't touch the chicken, it's dreadful ... Did you meet my fiancé, er ... Edward? Do you mind, Mr Barkley, if I call you Edward?'

Pierre smiled again at Edward, then told Harriet they were leaving. He appeared rather embarrassed by her rudeness, and thanked Edward for his hospitality. As they turned to go, Edward caught her by the hand. 'Where can I find you?'

She withdrew her hand, and her brilliant, sparkling eyes glittered. She tossed her head and walked away without a backward glance.

Alex sat with the Duke of Windsor, Her Grace having departed to talk with other guests. They were discussing seventeenth-century furniture, and the Duke was fascinated. Alex leafed through his book and showed a Chinese painting table, Huang-Hua-Li wood with a carved bamboo motif.

'So what price would a piece like that fetch?'

Alex told His Grace it would be in the region of seventy-five thousand dollars. Together they inspected the few pieces Alex had already purchased, the small lute table in hardwood, and they walked into the master bedroom to stand side by side looking at a Chinese rectangular side table, again made of Huang-Hua-Li, but sixteenth century.

'They are very good investments, sir. You see, there are nineteenth-century copies that are fetching extremely high prices. These will always rise in value because of their rarity ... the most rare piece would be a seventeenth-century bed, no one has ever found one.'

They got down on their hands and knees to feel the highly polished wood and examine the joints. The Duke was absolutely intrigued ...

Sitting at a small garden table in deep discussion with Edward was Count Frédérique Rothschild, who offered to purchase the château, with all its contents, outright. He wanted to spread his vineyards right across the valley, and the château was perfectly placed for the champagne-growing region. They shook hands and agreed to meet within the next day or so to arrange the price.

Edward was beginning to get irritated. The party was clearly a hit, but his brother was nowhere to be seen. Guests were leaving without Alex there to bid them farewell.

He looked around for his prize guests to get them to pose for photographers and wondered if they had left after only a few moments, as was their wont.

Moving from table to table, his computer-like brain stored names and faces for future reference, and still there was no sign of Alex. A butler moved unobtrusively to his side and whispered that the Duke and Duchess of Windsor's car was being brought round to the main entrance. Edward posed with some of the other guests for the photographers, then weaved his way towards the main entrance where a chauffeur waited with the white Rolls-Royce, engine ticking over. Edward hurried back into the hall and through the group of people who stood there chatting, and was just about to go in search of Alex when he stopped, open-mouthed.

Down the staircase came the Duke, his arm resting loosely on Alex's, their heads close, in deep conversation. Edward watched in amazement as the Duke reached the bottom of the stairs and a waiter appeared, carrying a small wooden box.

'Oh, this is really most kind of you, most kind, I shall treasure this, and I assure you I will take an avid interest from now on. This is really an exceptional gift.'

The Duchess joined her husband and he displayed his precious gift, the small seventeenth-century box. Rather casually, she waved her hand for the waiter to take it to the car. The Duke jumped to attention at her side, while Edward stood at the door to see the most important guests to their car. They barely looked at him, but gave Alex a firm handshake before they drove away.

*

It was late evening when the last hangers-on departed, and the debris of the day was cleared away. At last Alex was able to take a long, soapy, relaxing bath. He felt exhausted. He didn't even know if the event had gone well or not, he was too tired.

'Well, well, old chap, you surpassed yourself, and what was that thing you handed over to your new pal? Couldn't believe my eyes! What on earth did you give the Duke?'

Alex explained that the Duke had been taken with the small Chinese box, and Edward laughed. Perhaps they should get a collection of them to hand out if they were so popular. Alex soaped his hair, too tired to go into details.

'Got some news – place is sold, lock, stock and barrel, doing the deal first thing in the morning . . . We did very well, buddy boy.'

'Why sell, in God's name, why? After the months I've put into it, and just like that you're selling, it's madness.'

Edward toasted his brother, and said that four and a half million did not sound like madness to him. 'Alex, you can buy yourself another place, do it up, but the chap wants it, with all the contents.'

Alex climbed out of the bath, saying there were a few things he would like to keep.

'Take 'em, ship 'em back, no problem.'

Alex wanted his Chinese furniture. He knew and loved each piece, so he gave in without a murmur. Edward raised his glass.

'To London, to your return . . . Mr Barkley.'

Alex couldn't sleep. He was returning to London. It had been a long time, and his nerves were on edge. It was after three in the morning, and he was surprised to find a light still on in the kitchen.

Edward was sitting, staring into space, a bottle of Scotch at his elbow. He turned bleary eyes to Alex – he was drunk. His words were slurred, 'Ehhhhh, I wake you up? Did I wake you?'

'No, couldn't sleep. Do you think it went well?'

'Yeah, yeah, went well . . . want a drink?'

Alex got a glass and sat down. Edward poured most of the whisky over the table. 'I'm thinking of getting married.'

Alex fetched a cloth to wipe the table. He laughed. 'You joking? Getting married – who to, in God's name?'

'Girl I know.'

'Well, I didn't think it'd be a bloke! Who is it?'

'I want a son, four . . . four boys . . . yes, cheers.'

Edward lurched to his feet and raised his glass in a grand toast, knocking his chair over. In the end Alex had to help him to bed. He tried to undress him, but Edward was so drunk it was virtually impossible.

'I'm getting married.'

'Yes, you said . . .'

Edward passed out. Alex stared at him for a moment, then went out and closed the door quietly. He wondered if Edward would still be getting married when he sobered up.

In the press the following day there were many pictures of Edward, and a few of Alex, always in the background. But the most important thing was that they were on the inside track – at least, it was important to Edward. Alex looked at his brother – hung-over, propped up in bed with all the newspapers littered around him, reading all the relevant articles aloud to Alex. He made no reference to his forthcoming marriage. As he read, he was downing 'the hair of the dog' from a tumbler. His shirt was stained, and he had tossed his trousers on the floor. He was brash, loud, and Alex was thinking how uncouth he was. With a big Havana cigar clamped between his teeth, he was struggling to translate the French papers. Suddenly, Alex started to laugh.

'What's so funny?'

Alex didn't say, he couldn't explain, but he had made good use of his years in France. If anything he was more of the gent than his brother. The one who had looked like, and been, a thug had overtaken the other and he knew it. Alex found it exceedingly humorous.

'So when's the date? Last night you were getting married – still on, is it?'

'Yep – just got to straighten a few things out – like her fiancé for starters.'

'So you've not actually asked her, and she's engaged to someone else? Well, I wish you luck. Who is she?'

'You know that twerp, Jasper thingy, has the big boat in the harbour? Get him over for lunch ... No, fuck the lunch, ask him for a drink this morning, would you?'

Alex checked his watch and reached for the telephone. 'No sooner said than done. You don't mind if I give it a miss, do you? There are a few things I'd like to get organized before we leave for London, and I should like to get a detailed inventory of the château ...'

Edward threw back the bedclothes and rubbed his head. He was still badly hung-over, and wearing his socks. Alex noticed one of them had a large hole in the heel. 'I'll get you some socks while I'm in town ...'

Waiting for the operator to connect him with the boat, Alex looked around the bedroom. It was unbelievably messy and reminded him of when he and Edward had shared a bedroom as boys. Jasper Hamilton's lazy drawling voice gave Alex no chance to dwell on the past. Jasper was a strange effeminate man, known to be biding his time until he inherited a family fortune, a fortune made from a special brand of mustard. He had also seemed on familiar terms with both Harriet and Rochal at the party. Jasper was known to have considerable debts as he chose to live in great style and without the means to pay for it, his 'hot mustard money' still clenched in the hands of his ancient mother.

Edward didn't beat about the bush. Within minutes of Jasper's arrival he was offered money for information regarding Pierre Rochal. Jasper's eyes lit up, and he sat back to feed Edward any scrap of gossip he could think of. This included the restaurant the couple used regularly on the harbour front.

*

Edward obtained a prominent table for lunch at the restaurant, and had just started his meal when Pierre and Harriet sauntered in. He asked them to join him, but Harriet politely refused, saying they were expecting friends. They sat in a booth and Edward finished his meal alone. No one joined them.

Pierre could see Harriet was on edge, and asked her if it was anything to do with Edward. Deftly filleting her trout, she laid the bone on the edge of the plate, refusing to answer the question.

On the beach later that afternoon, Pierre checked his watch to see if he had time for one last swim before going back to work on the barn. Shading his eyes, he could see Harriet mono-skiing way out in the bay. He waved his towel, and started to pack their beach bag. He looked up a moment later to see Edward Barkley sitting on the sea wall. He wore dark glasses and a seasonal, open-necked shirt, but with a dark suit over it. Edward gave Pierre a nonchalant wave and gazed out to sea.

Harriet was an extremely good water-skier, and was now executing a jump. The water sprayed out behind her ... the boat made a wide curve and headed inland. She released the rope and glided into the shallows.

When she and Pierre walked up the beach, she gave Edward a polite nod. They climbed into the Aston Martin and roared along the quayside, but Harriet did not even turn her head in Edward's direction.

Alex was furious – Edward had raided his wardrobe. The doors stood open, his suits were thrown across the bed, shirts had dropped off their hangers.

'Edward? Edward! If you want to borrow my clothes have the decency to ask! You've chucked everything all over the room.'

'Well, you're shorter than me, but what d'you think, look all right?'

He was wearing a pale blue cotton suit with a white tee-shirt underneath it. His face was tanned, and his teeth shone whiter than white.

'Where are you going?' asked Alex. 'Do you know what time it is? It's after ten.'

'Yeah, well, the discos don't hot up until late, I've been told the groovy people don't arrive until after ten, so ... You don't have a comb? Can't find mine.'

Alex handed him a comb and watched as Edward stepped back from the mirror to admire himself. 'She can't resist me tonight, eh, buddy boy?'

'I've released the staff as from tomorrow, that all right? And I've arranged a meeting with Rothschild ... Eddie? Edward!'

'Fine, you handle it – whatever you say. See you in the morning.'

Pierre was beginning to get irritated. It was quite obvious that Edward Barkley was trailing around after them. First at lunch, then the beach, even the intimate little restaurant they used for dinner. He was always alone, always asking if they would care to join him, when it was he who obviously wanted to join them. Harriet gave him not so much as the time of day. His appearance at the disco made her burst into laughter, but she still refused to talk to him. The latest thing to annoy Pierre was Edward walking up to them on the dance floor and asking if he could cut in. Harriet put her hands on her hips and cocked her head on one side. 'Cut in? Oh my God, I haven't heard that expression since I went to dances in the church hall.'

Edward still stood in the centre of the small, square dance floor. The music was so loud it was almost impossible to hold a conversation, so Harriet bellowed, 'Do you mind, Pierre? Perhaps if I give him one dance he'll leave us alone.'

Pierre shrugged and went moodily back to their table. Their friends asked him about Edward – the papers had been full of his château and the party he had thrown. They all watched the couple on the dance floor with interest.

Harriet danced around while he made pitiful efforts to mimic the strange movements of the other dancers. In the end he pulled her close to him.

Close to him, feeling him against her, she couldn't play any more games. He bent his head to talk to her, shouting above the music. 'I want two minutes with you alone, two minutes.'

Pierre watched them thread their way among the tables. He had seen the intimate way Edward had drawn Harriet into his arms, the way she leaned close. Whether she liked it or not, he would have it out with her that night. It was obvious she knew the intrepid Mr Barkley very well.

Harriet and Edward walked along the sea front. He didn't attempt to touch her – they kept about a foot apart. When they stopped, he laid his hands on the rail, and she did likewise. She was even taller than he remembered, and her body was taut, lithe ... He could see the strength in her hands as they gripped the rail. Her curly red hair was cropped like a boy's, and gave her an urchin quality, a tomboy look. He had her to himself, and he was dumbstruck. Not knowing how to begin, he inched his hand closer and closer to hers on the rail, until they touched. The contact helped him, but when he spoke, his voice sounded alien. 'I love you, Harry, and I want to marry you. I love you.'

He wanted desperately to hold her close, but she moved her hand away, and he could see her knuckles whiten as they tightened on the rail. She gazed at the sea as she spoke. 'You know how many times I have dreamed of this moment, dreamed of you saying exactly that ... I waited, you know, I waited for you ...'

He touched her cheek gently, a soft, stroking gesture. He felt her stiffen, turn her head away from him. He couldn't speak, didn't know what to say to her. Pierre was at the entrance to the club, holding her wrap. He called out. 'Harry ... Harry ... Harry!'

'You are too late, Edward, leave me alone, please, go away from me.' Her voice was no more than a whisper, but so cold, so unemotional he turned and walked away. He couldn't help but look back, and Pierre was wrapping her shawl around her shoulders. She remained staring out to sea.

Edward ran along the dark beach, ran until he flopped exhausted on to the wet sand.

Pierre had to prise Harriet's hands away from the rail. He guided her to the car and drove her home in silence. When they pulled up outside the barn, she turned to him. In the dim light the tears sparkled on her cheeks.

'I can't marry you, I'm sorry, I'm so sorry.'

'We'll talk about it tomorrow. You're freezing – come on, I will make you a hot drink.'

'No . . . I'll stay with Daisy – it's better that way. I'm sorry, please don't ask me to explain.'

'I think I deserve some explanation, for God's sake. It's him, isn't it? Edward Barkley?'

He thumped the steering wheel with his fist. She gave him a wobbly smile. 'At least I saved you forking out the price of a ring.'

'This is no time to joke, Harry. At least come inside and talk about it.' But Pierre could not persuade her to leave the car. Eventually he slammed the door and walked into the barn.

It was quite a while before he heard the engine revving, then the car roared off. He downed a large brandy in one gulp and hurled the glass at the wall. The next second he heard the screech of brakes outside. He ran to the door. 'Harry? Harry?'

Edward Barkley stood in the pitch dark, his Rolls-Royce parked precariously near to the edge of the open well.

'I want to talk to her, let me talk to her.'

'She's not here . . .'

'Don't bloody lie to me . . .'

Pierre shouted, but Edward charged him like a mad bull . . . disappearing down the well with a howl. Pierre peered down the deep hole. 'I tried to warn you – I've a good mind to let you stay down there.'

'Fucking hell, I think I've broken my nose.'

Pierre examined Edward's face. His nose was intact, but he would have a very black eye. His temple was already turning a dark, angry purple. Pierre handed him a damp cloth. 'You'll live. You want a drink?'

'Christ, I feel such a bloody fool.'

'I guarantee you'll look even more like one tomorrow, you'll have a real shiner. Here – it's brandy, but more than likely not the vintage you're used to.'

'Where is she? I have to talk to her.'

'When you've finished your drink I'll put the storm lights on. You'll have to back down the track . . . she's staying with friends.'

'Where?'

'Why don't you just get the hell out of here before I throw you out?'

Edward downed his brandy and stood up. He towered over Pierre. For one second he even thought about throwing a punch, but instead he walked to the door. Turning, he held out his hand. His suit was sodden, his face bruised, and there was a helpless air to the big man.

'I love her . . . I'm sorry to come here like this. If I'd been in your shoes I'd have let me rot in the well . . . Harry and me, we go back a long time. You take care of her . . . I won't bother you again.'

Pierre had never seen such raw and desperate emotion in a man before. It made him feel inadequate. Edward obviously loved her and, given the choice between the two, Pierre was sure he would be the loser. In truth he already knew he was.

Pierre told Edward where he could find Harriet. He even held a torch so Edward could reverse safely down the track. Then he walked back to the barn. Half-painted in bright daffodil yellow, it called out her name . . . She was everywhere he looked, and he made up his mind to leave for Paris, cut short his holiday.

It wasn't until Pierre had packed that he felt a strange sensation of relief – a confusing and unexpected emotion. He tried to analyse his feelings, and eventually they were clarified by a moth-eaten teddy bear. The small, worn bear sported a hand-knitted vest with the letter 'E' embroidered very badly on the front. The bear travelled everywhere with her, and he knew she would be frantic without him. But this was no longer Pierre's responsibility – it was Edward Barkley's.

Edward rang the bell beside the electric gates. There was not a light to be seen. He kept his finger on the button, rattled the gates, but still there was no answer. After prowling around the walls, he got into the Rolls and drove it close to the wall – so close he scraped the wing on the driver's side. He then climbed out of the passenger door, on to the roof, and scaled the wall.

Once inside the grounds he made his way to the main entrance. As he stepped on to the porch all hell broke loose – two Dobermann pinschers galloped across the lawn, teeth bared. Edward almost pulled the door knocker off its hinges while he shouted at the dogs. Suddenly, lights blazed in the hallway, he heard voices shouting and the frightened face of Daisy Millingford's father appeared through the frost glass door panel.

Edward just made it into the hall before he lost his trousers to the dogs. A gardener in a dressing gown dragged them back, snarling, to their kennels. Daisy rushed down the stairs, pulling her hair rollers out while trying to explain to her father who Edward was.

In the midst of the confusion, Harriet appeared at the top of the stairs. Edward, in his filthy, mud-splattered suit, sporting a black eye, ran up the stairs two and three at a time. The family looked on aghast, while Daisy shouted that he was Edward Barkley, the Edward Barkley from the château.

'I love you, Harry, I love you . . .'

Edward showed not the slightest embarrassment at his extraordinary behaviour. Harriet sat on the stairs, her legs shaking. She was wearing a ridiculous, frothy pink nightdress of Daisy's.

Daisy ushered her family and the housekeeper into the kitchen, leaving the lovers alone, but before she closed the door she took a quiet look . . .

They were sitting side by side, their arms about each other.

If Harriet turned him down now, Daisy would be up those stairs like a hare . . . She closed the door, and tried to explain to her family what was going on.

Alex woke with a start when his bedroom lights came on. Edward beamed at him from the doorway.

'Alex, I want you to meet my future wife . . . Harry, this is my brother, Alex.'

Alex stared from one to the other. Harriet was still wearing the frothy pink creation, with the addition of a blanket around her shoulders. Edward had ruined Alex's suit, and to cap it all he looked as though he'd been in one hell of a fight. Alex was speechless, but Edward was already on his way out.

'I'll leave you two to get to know each other . . . this calls for a celebration.'

Alex ran his fingers through his hair, then gestured for Harriet to sit on the bed. She curled up like a cat at the far end and scrutinized him. He flushed, and tried to think of something to say.

'I told him not to wake you, but he insisted. This isn't my nightie, it's Daisy's.'

'Ahhh, I see – that makes all the difference.'

She giggled, and he looked up shyly. Suddenly she crawled up the bed to sit closer to him. She took his hand, kissed his cheek. 'You look so uncomfortable – you're not at all what I expected.'

'I could say the same for you.'

Again she giggled infectiously, and Alex began to relax. She had certainly taken him by surprise – she was not at all the type he would have expected Edward to be interested in, let alone want to marry. She slipped her arm through his as if she had known him for years, and started to tell him how she had first met Edward. Alex had never met anyone like her; as with everyone else who came in contact with Harriet, he fell instantly under her spell.

Alex went shopping with Harry to help her choose her wedding dress. She cavorted around the designer shops, tripping out of the changing rooms in creations worth thousands, the dreadful veils perched on her bouncing curls. She never seemed to tire, and Alex found her exhausting, and often infuriating. Eventually they chose a simple white silk dress in the new, short length. It was even shorter on Harriet, as she was so tall. She didn't want a veil, choosing instead to wear a small crown of daisies.

Alex also helped Edward buy a suit, and discovered how well matched the couple really were – both were tremendously impatient, and neither had any real interest in style.

None of Harriet's family was invited to the wedding. Harriet went to great lengths to find a chimney sweep to act as witness. Alex worried about him turning up in his filthy overalls, but Harriet roared with laughter and said she had promised to pay him extra if he did just that, and carried his brush; it was supposed to bring good luck.

On the morning of the wedding Edward was panic-stricken, and made Alex go and check that Harriet was getting ready. Between the two of them Alex was exhausted. It was not enough for Harriet for the pair of them to spend their pre-nuptial nights in separate bedrooms – they had to be in separate wings of the château. She would not sleep anywhere near the groom until she had a signed, valid contract to do so.

The two of them were boisterous, like noisy children, and very obviously in love. Edward showered gifts on his bride-to-be – little boxes of jewellery were delivered, unpacked, inspected, and laid out on Harriet's dressing table. Alex never saw her wear a single piece. She was forever dressed in a pair of old shorts and a tee-shirt, and barefoot.

Harriet screamed for Alex – her new satin shoes were too tight. He was kept running from one wing of the château to the other as bride and groom yelled for cufflinks, knickers, socks . . . He managed to get Edward ready, and planted him in the hall to wait for Harriet. He was about to collect her when she called down the stairs, 'Both of you close your eyes and hum the "Wedding March", I'm coming down . . .'

The brothers stood side by side, humming in unison, then both opened their eyes and stopped at the same time. Harriet was moving slowly down the stairs, the white dress setting off her golden tan, the daisy garland framing her face. She was like a child, looking so innocent it was hard to believe she was nearly twenty-nine. Alex had grown to understand why Edward had been obsessed with her, wanted her — now he saw something else about her he had never noticed before. Harriet resembled their mother, in the colour of her hair, her tallness, and her smile.

Edward whispered, 'I love her, Alex, my God, I do love her.'

It was not until they were sitting in the registrar's office that Alex realized Harriet was barefoot. She gave him a sweet, secretive smile, and turned to Edward with such adoration that Alex found himself close to tears.

In a way, Alex was happy to be going back to London now. It was a long time since he had tended his beloved mother's grave. She could be proud now, happy — her sons, the brothers, were together again. Alex did not yet know just how wealthy Edward was, but he was soon to find out.

Chapter Nineteen

Alex, with Mr and Mrs Edward Barkley, returned to London. Alex moved in to Edward's manor house at Greenwich. The heavy, flocked wallpaper, the windows draped in velvet, the motley collection of furniture from Tudor to Victorian, appalled Alex's new-found taste. Squashed in alongside antiques were modern leather sofas, anything that had ever taken Edward's fancy was purchased without a thought of its matching or suiting the manor. There was a sense of decadence, of weight, to the house which Alex found overpowering. Among Edward's purchases were many old oil paintings, a selection of which hung down the wide, sweeping staircase. Edward surveyed his home with pride, and indicated the portraits. 'This is your new family, aunts, uncles, parents – take your pick. I got us a good cross-section of ancestors – army fellas and a few sea captains.'

Alex unpacked his bags and gazed out of the bedroom window, across the river. There was the office block, the Barkley Company Ltd sign facing the manor. He was ill at ease – he had only been away five years and yet he felt as if it had been a lifetime. Edward pounded up the stairs, shouting for Alex to get a move on as he wanted to take him to the office.

Harriet rushed from room to room, shouting down the

curved staircase. She stuck her head over the banister. 'What time do we expect you back?'

Edward was already walking out to the drive. He waved and said they would be late, then gestured for Alex to get a move on. It was Alex who blew Harriet a kiss and said, 'I'll get him to call you – see you later.'

Alex had met many of Edward's employees, and his head spun. They all shook his hand, addressing him as 'Mr Barkley'. Edward showed him off as though he were a prize racehorse, laughing and joking, telling stories about how he managed to persuade his brother to leave their estate in France. Edward carried bundles of magazines featuring the château. No one questioned his story about Alex, or Alex's position as his partner. It was unnerving, as if they had somehow been expecting him.

At long last Alex made it to the inner sanctum, the top floor. Edward flung open the door to an empty office and bowed. 'I'm right next door. You employ as many secretaries as you need, Miss Henderson here will show you the ropes.'

Miss Henderson, a plain nervous woman in her late thirties, gave Alex a small nervous smile and bade him welcome.

'I'll need a desk, a chair, anything will do for now, a telephone and a good calculator.'

Miss Henderson made fast shorthand notes as Edward roared for her to hurry to his office. She excused herself, and left Alex alone in the empty room. It was not empty for long as everything he had requested came to him with remarkable speed. He set to work, and at lunchtime Miss Henderson brought in coffee and sandwiches. Two secretaries followed behind her with arms full of files. Alex already had two stacks either side of his makeshift desk. He looked enquiringly at Miss Henderson.

'Mr Edward has instructed me to bring all the company files to you. He said he will be back in two to three weeks, something unexpectedly turned up. The car keys and house keys are in reception.'

Although stunned, Alex said nothing. For Edward to up and

leave on the first day, without a word, amazed him. But he had little time to be fazed by his brother's disappearance as the office began to fill up with files, brought in by four typists.

It was after eight when Alex received a telephone call from Harriet. He had completely forgotten to ring her as he had promised. She went very quiet when told that Edward had been called away on business, so Alex made the excuse that it had been very urgent. Harriet hung up.

Over the next few days Alex hardly saw Harriet, as he left very early each morning and returned late. He had made up his mind to move as soon as he could find a suitable house.

One evening when he arrived home, exhausted, he discovered Harriet, covered in paint, decorating one of the bedrooms. The paint was a very bright yellow, and he raised his eyebrows. 'This the nursery?'

He was surprised at her sharp reaction to his innocent question.

'No, no ... it's going to be my studio – there won't be any nursery. Now, if you'll excuse me, I have to get on, I want this finished as a surprise.'

Alex put the brittleness of her manner down to his imagination, his tiredness. Later, alone in his room, he put a call through to Ming. Her soft voice soothed him, and she agreed to come to London as soon as he had found a suitable house. She mentioned that her company was doing very well, and she would have lots of ideas and fabrics to help furnish his new home.

Alex began the mammoth task of reviewing the company files. They continued to be brought into the office all week, and he worked on them throughout each day. The only reason he took time off from the office was to view houses. Eventually he found one to his liking in Mayfair.

There was no word from Edward, where he was or what he was doing, and Alex simply worked on. No one interrupted him except Miss Henderson, who kept up a constant stream of fresh, black coffee.

*

Exhausted, his eyes red-rimmed, Alex walked beside the river. He had worked day and night for a month, and now he was drained. He was due to move into his own house, but he waited for Edward to return, waited in trepidation and anger, combined with disbelief. The first two days of sifting through his brother's files had been an eye-opener, but then it went beyond that. Edward Barkley had amassed a vast network of companies, many offshore, with so many people, so many illegal transactions, that Alex was stunned that his brother had got away with it. The frauds were like a spider's web, weaving and interlocking. There were fake firms as fronts, covering insurance policies in Panama, Brazil ... classic cases of ships losing cargoes, the losses obviously fictitious. In one case Edward had sold a cargo of olive oil to a small company at a very low price. The ship had put to sea and blown up, but as well as the insurance payment Edward had been paid for the cargo. Two more ships had supposedly gone down with their cargoes, only this time the ships didn't even sink – oil streaks were left on the ocean, but the ships sailed into a port, were repainted, renamed and sold ... and that was just one of Mr Edward Barkley's scams. The list was endless, from small-time fiddles to big-time fraud. The details of the pay-offs read like a telephone directory: government officials, Lloyd's underwriters, Stock Exchange runners. Edward had so many illegal businesses that Alex could hardly keep count.

The building firm employed two hundred men, and it paid wages for two hundred, but Edward actually had over five hundred men working for him on the construction side alone. He found it as beneficial to save two pounds as he did two million.

The Barkley Company actually owned only the fifteenth floor of the tower block, the rest belonged to different companies – but all those companies were, in fact, owned by Edward. Alex had seen turnaround businesses before, but this was on a different scale, in a different league ... and the money was being constantly shifted, like dogs on a racetrack. The property developments were vast, the net spread right across London. Blocks of apartments were bought, given a lick of paint and sold again within days. Edward seemed to have a monopoly on blocks of flats coming up for sale – leaseholders were bought out, and the buildings were sold at three times the purchase price with vacant possession. Edward was pushing the property boom forward, but he held on to large areas of prime building land. To enable him to do this he had to have a very fast turnover on the properties.

Car parks appeared on bomb sites, bringing in an incredible amount of cash. Some of the takings were declared, the rest was diverted into housing developments. How could tax officers know how much money a car park took each day?

Alex went through lists of numbered companies in detail. They were on separate sheets, and were obviously smaller than the others Alex had examined. They had no names as such, simply code numbers, and it was obviously all some kind of fraud. The business ranged from toiletries to household and fancy goods for the wholesale trade. Under the heading of 'Outlets' were the same businesses again, plus over fifty warehouses dotted all over South London. Then there were scrapyards, transport companies, delivery companies ... Alex calculated that the number of staff required to operate all these must run into hundreds. There were no names, no payroll details, no accounts. The scrapyards collected anything from household waste to industrial and government assignments. He began checking each one to try to make sense of it, and details of more fraudulent transactions began to emerge.

Many of the proceeds Edward had ploughed into housing estates, but no accounts were attached. Alex kept on matching tax numbers, and realized that Edward had been using false numbers and channelling goods in quick buy-and-sell transactions that, taken together, were so immense Alex could only surmise that he had been handling cash flows of between one and two million, and recorded none of it.

Miss Henderson buzzed through to Alex's office. 'Mr Edward has just returned, sir. You asked to be informed immediately.'

'Thank you, Miss Henderson.'

Alex checked his watch, looked around his office. The whole room had been redesigned, with hi–tech equipment: telex machines, calculators, direct lines to the Stock Exchange, all modern and economical, streamlined and efficient. Alex pressed his fingertips together, drew a deep breath. He was going to have a showdown, and he wouldn't back off.

Edward's office door was ajar, the keys dangling in the lock. As Alex entered, he turned and waved for him to sit down. He was on the telephone, so Alex sat in a heavy leather wing chair and surveyed the room. He had not been in the office before, the door was kept locked. There were the same heavily built panelled walls, a carved stone mantel with a false coal fire, and a plum–red carpet. The desk was massive, with huge claw feet. A couple of wing chairs were the only other furniture in the room. The desktop was empty apart from a row of telephones. Alex smiled to himself at his brother's obvious taste for the old-fashioned, old–world style of living; the room could have been lifted straight from the manor. Somehow it matched Edward – he was so tall, his frame running slightly to fat, but his shoulders were like an athlete's. The ever-present cigar was sticking out of his mouth. 'Fine, tell them we're not interested . . . Yes, tell them that. They refused the first offer, tell them it goes down every week they delay, it's up to them . . . Maybe, but I also happen to know the company's going bankrupt, so we'll see how they react . . . fine, call me.'

Edward replaced the phone and went to the fireplace, twisted a carved lion's head on the mantel. 'I had this made, you like it? It's my safe.'

The safe was concealed behind a portrait in oils, and Alex thought the subject was the Duke of Wellington.

Edward removed some files from the safe. 'Right, this is it, more or less. It'll take time for you to sift through them all, but you'll have to. The accountants are listed along with the documents – different man for each section, but you'll take responsibility for them overall.'

He went back and forth to the safe, stacking ever more files on the desk. Lights flickered on the phones, but Edward paid them no attention. 'Got something for you, one for you, one for me . . . had 'em made specially.'

He opened a drawer in his desk, took out a small leather case. 'We've changed our names, but we must never forget where we came from. Whenever things go bad – God, hope they never do, but if they ever should, this'll help. One look at it'll make things all right, because we can never go back – we never want to, but I'm not ashamed, it's necessary.'

Alex couldn't think what he was working up to and was surprised when, for a brief second, Edward looked vulnerable. He went to stand by his brother's side.

Edward continued, 'Remember Dad saying about how they buried the Romanies' precious things with them? Well, I buried her necklace in the grave.' He opened the small leather box, and unwrapped some tissue paper. 'I went back, about a month ago, dug it up – I made it all neat again, so don't worry. I had these made up from the gold, one for you, one for me.' He held out a small gold medallion on a fine gold chain. Alex turned it over – it was only the size of a sixpence, and engraved on it was the single word, 'Stubbs'. Edward slipped his own on and tucked it down inside his shirt collar. 'Put it on, after all the trouble I went to get it. Go ahead, put it on.'

Without a word, Alex slipped the chain around his neck.

Abruptly, Edward sat down in his leather chair, swung around and tapped the files on the desk. 'South Africa's wide open, doing a few deals, should have some good results by next week . . . They still live in fucking mud huts. We start a housing project over there . . . Alex my old son?' Receiving no reply, he looked searchingly at Alex. 'Something wrong? What's up?'

'How does twelve years for fraud sound?'

Edward's face changed, suddenly sharp, vicious.

'You got something niggling you, why don't you say it?'

Alex threw his arms up in fury. 'Niggling? Niggling me? Jesus Christ, Edward, you're a fucking crook. I've never seen accounts like them, and what's more, I don't see how you've been getting away with it.'

'Because, old chap, on the surface I am a very respectable citizen . . . I also employ a team of men whose sole job it is to make sure I don't get copped, and now it's your job. You think any of my little businesses are too risky, fine – I'll get rid of 'em, because I can't afford at this stage to have even a murmur go round. I admit there's a few petty fiddles . . .'

'Petty? Eddie, you are fiddling on every side of every business! It'd take just one, just one nosey little tax inspector, and you'd fall like a pack of cards. You're moving money from bank to bank, next month shifting it to another – you keep on buying more and more businesses and you'll be wiped out.'

Edward shrugged and said fine, Alex should get rid of any he felt were not viable assets, that's what he was in the business for.

'It's not just that. The whole structure of the company stinks. You've got more offshore companies than you know what to do with, half of 'em you've shelled out money for just for the names, you haven't even used them . . . Unless what I read in the files is a lot of bullshit and you're keeping stuff from me, and if so we can't work together. You've got to come clean with me, Eddie.'

'Don't call me that!'

Alex raised his hand in a gesture of submission. 'Okay, okay – Edward, that all right? I can sort through these companies and get rid of them, fast. You cannot be associated with these frauds. All the pinball machines, the fruit machines, we can hang on to, but the scrapyards and the warehouses stocked with hot goods have to be cleaned out, and we start afresh. No documents here either, nothing must link you to them if there's ever an investigation.'

Edward sighed, bored. 'The law's paid off, I've paid them enough to stop any investigations.'

Alex was round the desk before Edward knew it, grabbed him by his lapels. 'Paid off, is it? Listen, I know every tax dodge there is, I can clean up the mess for you. But, by Christ, you don't take me down again, not this time . . . I want any bribes, any shit, cleaned up, because I'll never go back to jail, hear me . . .? You got it?'

Edward pushed him away, straightened his suit. 'Okay, okay, I hear you, no need to get uptight.'

Alex reached for the folder on South Africa and Edward snatched it away. 'You got your work cut out for you – go on, sell off anything you don't like the look of. This is just a mining project I'm interested in.'

Alex concentrated on his polished nails. His voice was quiet, controlled. 'Ten years inside and the smell, the stench, never leaves you, it's in your clothes, your hair. You go on this way and by Christ that's where you'll end up . . . You've got to be sharper, not so greedy, take it stage by stage. You recognize a good deal, but you can't stop your left hand grabbing.'

For a moment Edward seemed to hesitate, then he thumped Alex on the back. 'You make a donation to charity, a big one, big gesture – get the Duke of Edinburgh's youth clubs or whatever, bung it to them. We'll clean the slate of the dodgy companies, then it'll be right by the book, all right my son? All right, Alex?'

Alex was still uneasy, he didn't altogether trust his brother. But he shook the outstretched hand, then said he was about to move into his new house. Edward smiled, but his eyes were cold. 'You've been very busy while I've been away. Who's done it up? You get the Jap woman over?'

Alex turned his back on Edward, walked to the door. 'No, she was too busy on one of your projects, I managed on my own . . . Have you thought about contacting Harry yet? You just upped and left, you know, you might have had the decency to call her. I'll be in my office, should you need me.'

Edward drummed his fingers on the desk. He would have to tread a little more carefully with Alex breathing down his neck. He decided there and then that Alex would be informed only so far, certain deals he would keep to himself.

*

Edward burst through the front door, his arms full of gifts and an enormous bunch of red roses. He called Harriet's name and she appeared, wearing an enormous pair of men's overalls. She waved a paintbrush at the roses. 'You'll get those wrapped around your neck, Edward Barkley ... What the hell do you mean by pissing off without a word?'

'I'm sorry, sweetheart, really urgent business cropped up, and I had to drop everything and run ... You want to see what I've brought you?'

'No.'

Edward threw everything up in the air and smiled at her. 'Okay ... how about getting those overalls off?'

'Not bloody likely. I'm working, very urgent business cropped up, darling. I'm sorry, now do excuse me ...'

Edward chased her up the stairs. Laughing, she flicked her paintbrush at him, then pulled him by the hand into her new studio. He blinked, and rested his elbow on her head. 'Now, I'm not a very critical sort of chap, Harry, but don't you think it's rather bright ...'

'It's supposed to be ... Don't you like it?'

'Oh, yeah, I love it ... and I like the spotted pattern on the floorboards – how did you do that?'

'They're drips, you bastard ... See, I did the ceiling – have you any idea how I've slaved over this room?'

Edward pulled her close and kissed her neck. She smelt of turpentine and paint. He asked about dinner.

The kitchen was in a shambolic state – dishes piled almost to the ceiling, empty soup tins stacked in a corner ... 'I think I'm going to demand a refund on you, Harry – look at the state of the place.'

'Well, Alex left, and I can't cook ... We can go and get a takeaway ... Indian – shall we have Indian? Or there's Chinese ...? Fish and chips? What do you feel like?'

Edward tossed her the car keys and said she could decide, he was going to take a bath. A short while later he heard her call up the stairs that dinner was served, and went down to the dining hall in his dressing gown. Several small cartons of Chinese food lay on the table, and a note, attached by a drawing pin, which said, 'Enjoy your dinner.'

Alex was surprised to receive a call at his office so early in the morning. Harriet said he was not to worry, she had been called away on very urgent business, then she hung up. Alex had no idea what she meant.

Alex was working on diligently, gradually putting things in order. Back taxes were being settled, the hundreds of workers legally employed, with insurance cards and tax codes. No fool, Alex was accounting for every penny – profits, valuations, securities, leases, pensions, overseas subsidiaries, losses ... he wanted no loose ends, everything carefully documented.

Just as Alex was leaving the office, Edward strode in, unshaven and obviously very worried. 'I can't find bloody Harriet, have you any idea where she is?'

Alex slapped himself on the head and apologized for forgetting to mention her call.

'What urgent business, for Chrissake? Did she tell you where she'd gone?'

Alex shook his head, picked up his briefcase. Edward sighed, then suggested Alex take him back to see the new house. He was in need of a decent meal. But Alex covered fast, saying he would prefer to leave it to another time, he wanted to have the place finished before anyone saw it. Edward didn't seem to mind, and sat down in Alex's swivel chair.

'She's doing this on purpose, you know, and the place is a tip. Kitchen looks like a bomb hit it.'

'Well, you didn't marry her for her culinary expertise, why not get a housekeeper?'

Edward fiddled with Alex's neat row of pens and began to doodle on the immaculate blotter.

Alex asked, 'Nothing wrong between you, is there?'

Shaking his head, Edward tossed the pen down. 'Maybe you're right, I'll get a housekeeper – maybe she can make an appointment for me to come over to your place.'

Alex took the sarcasm without comment, and waited for Edward to pass by him before he locked his office door.

Alex breathed a sigh of relief as he let himself into his new house in Mayfair. He walked into the lounge and fixed himself a cocktail, then sat down and surveyed his creation; the semi-gloss, Peking-yellow walls, the ceiling painted in three subtle tones of beige, the cornices and high, trompe-l'oeil skirting boards simulating Siena marble. The curtains were in two shades of golden-yellow pleated taffeta with heavy beige fringing, hanging from pale wooden rods. The sofas and armchairs were covered in a wonderful deep citrus-yellow shantung with scattered marigold-yellow cushions. Several of the chairs were covered with a special chintz copied from an early nineteenth-century design. Alex's use of colour was so tasteful, and he sat admiring it. The house made him feel content.

The front door opened again, and Alex turned. Ming entered, went straight to him and kissed him. He fixed her a drink. 'Edward is back, you'll have to leave.'

Ming shrugged and began to flick through one of the magazines from the orderly pile on the glass-topped coffee table. 'That's okay, I have a meeting in New York, I've got to do decor for the new shop ... Oh my God, have you seen this, it's in the *Tatler*, look ... "London's most eligible bachelor, Alex Barkley".'

Alex handed Ming her drink and leaned over her shoulder to read the article. 'He was right, that donation did the trick – we've been handing out thousands to every charity you can think of. I've been in "Jennifer's Diary" three times ...'

As Ming skimmed through the magazine, her own fabrics featured prominently. There were also spreads in three new interior design magazines. She picked up her drink and sat down, crossing her perfect legs. 'I met a possible client today, Barbara Hunter Hardyman – Texan woman, she came into a fortune. She's bought a penthouse in New York ... I'd like to get into Texas, good property there ... Oh yes, can you get a few days off? Just that her father's ranch is being auctioned off, and I may

be wrong, but he was a collector of seventeenth-century furniture ... Maybe we could kill two birds with one stone, I get a
new client and you add to your collection.'

Alex kissed her and said he would do what he could, but
there was a lot of business to sort out.

'But this would be business! I may be wrong, but it looks as
if there might be part of a bed ...'

Alex was hooked. No bed of that period had ever been discovered, it was every collector's dream.

'I'll see if I can arrange a couple of weeks off. I certainly
deserve it. I'll wait a few days, see if Harriet reappears.'

Ming raised an eyebrow. 'You mean she's left him?'

Alex sipped his iced Manhattan, picked up the cherry and
popped it in his mouth. Ming asked again after Harriet.

'No one knows where she is. She'll turn up, I think she's
done it on purpose.'

'You like her, don't you?'

'Yes, I do, as a matter of fact. I think ... oh, I don't know, I
just have a feeling that Edward will have to watch out for her,
treat her gently. He thinks she's doing this disappearing act to
teach him a lesson. In a way I agree, but I doubt if it'll work.'

Ming murmured sarcastically that Edward couldn't treat
anyone gently, it wasn't in his nature, then went to the kitchen
to prepare dinner. Alex sighed. He knew she was right, but he
felt saddened – he wouldn't like to see Harry hurt. His mood
changed as he looked at the beautifully set dining table. Ming
had brought out her own line of tableware, and he was very
impressed.

As Pierre Rochal was closing his surgery, the receptionist buzzed
through to tell him he had a visitor. He was slightly irritated as
he had arranged a small dinner party for his fiancée.

'*Bonjour, amigo.*'

'Harry? Why didn't you call, let me know you were coming?'

'Oh, I just popped in on the off chance. If it's not convenient,
I can come back.'

Pierre opened his arms and she came to him, hugged him close. He knew instantly that she was troubled, there were all the tell-tale signs. She looked drawn, with deep circles beneath her eyes, and spoke rapidly, as if her thoughts were racing ahead of her. She was trying desperately to be her usual, ebullient self, but her body was rigid with tension, and she was threading her fingers round and round the strap of her holdall.

'Are you in trouble?' he asked. She nodded her head, her face twisting as she fought back her tears. He excused himself and made a quick call to Michelle, his fiancée, to say he was running a little late.

Harriet was not very fluent in French, but she had been with him long enough to understand every word he said. 'Who's Michelle?'

He told her, 'She was my nurse. In three days she'll be my wife. You'll meet her later – now, why don't you just tell me what's wrong?'

Harriet wandered around his surgery. She had been to see her mother, she told him, to ask about her Aunt Sylvia, basically wanting to know more about her own illness. Her mother had been less than helpful, and more worried about the Judge going into hospital for a prostate operation. Pierre watched her, picking up books and replacing them, chewing her nails. Eventually she blurted, 'Is schizophrenia hereditary? That's what Aunt Sylvia had, I'm sure, and when I was first ill . . .'

Pierre kept his voice low, soothing, 'Now you know, Harry, the first diagnosis wasn't correct. You have a depressive problem, one you can control, you know that.'

'But what if I am schizoid, and your father was wrong? He could be wrong . . . I feel it coming on.'

'Well, that proves you're not, because if you were really schizophrenic, you wouldn't be aware of the change. I'll prescribe something for you, a new drug, lithium – it'll help when you begin to feel tense and nervous.'

'I don't feel like that, I feel as if someone's tied a bloody big weight around my neck, and I just can't get it off me. He just walked out of the house, never even said goodbye, and he didn't come home for three weeks. How could he do that?'

Suddenly her eyes blazed, her hands clenched at her sides and she began shouting and swearing. Pierre was thankful his receptionist would by now have left. He listened to Harriet's tirade against Edward, until she slumped in a chair in floods of tears. Pierre insisted she stay with him, and drove her back to his apartment.

Michelle prepared the spare room for Harriet, who was subdued and drowsy, although feeling guilty about her intrusion. Pierre was grateful for Michelle's understanding – she showed no jealousy, required no explanation. He had told her all about his relationship with Harriet.

Before their guests began to arrive, Pierre checked that Harriet was sleeping, then went to his desk to retrieve her small teddy bear. He slipped it between her arms – he had been right, he had known one day she would come back to him, and now more than ever he was relieved that he had not married her. Michelle, the elegant, immensely rich Michelle, was everything he ever wanted.

Harriet took to Michelle instantly, and was invited to stay for the wedding. She began to recover slowly, although she was unusually quiet, childlike and listless at first. With the drug Pierre prescribed, her depression began to lift, and her old spark returned with a vengeance when Michelle took her on a shopping spree in Paris. Michelle could not help but notice that money was no object with Harriet, and she had only to say she liked something for Harriet to insist on buying it for her. At the House of Dior Harriet's naturally sunny nature revived. She wanted a new image, and under Michelle's guidance she chose well. She bought so many outfits and hats that they needed a separate taxi to carry everything back to the apartment.

For the wedding, Harriet wore an Ungaro coat with matching dress. She had chosen a small beret to top the outfit, and her hair, since she had met Edward again, had grown long enough for the latest pageboy cut. She looked stunning and, her confidence renewed, she decided to return to London.

The Barkley Company was now in a secure position, and Edward was well pleased. He congratulated his brother, and handed him a thick white envelope with a flourish. 'A little bonus, brother.'

The bonus was all very well, but it was time for them to sit down and discuss their personal finances. Edward was as evasive as ever, but Alex knew exactly what the business was worth – or thought he did. Edward still kept some bank accounts secret. But, as promised, he paid Alex his share of the proceeds from the château, minus the extras he had put in, of course.

Alex was not happy with the arrangements – suddenly Edward was treating him as an employee. 'I'm your partner, Edward. I thought that was what we agreed, everything split down the middle.'

But Edward itemized the cash he had given Alex, the cost of the cosmetic surgery, the château, the Mayfair house, the million for the club, the small businesses . . . it all added up. Alex began to get impatient – he knew exactly how much Edward had laid out; he had, after all, done the accounts. 'So what are you saying, Edward? That I'm not your partner? What am I, then, an employee? Your accountant? That what I am?'

Edward laughed and said of course not, it was just that he wasn't all that flush with cash at the moment.

'Edward, who do you think you're kidding? I know exactly how much you've got. Remember, this is Alex you're talking to, me, Edward . . . Now, am I your partner or not? Just tell me right now.'

Edward turned on Alex in a fury, saying he had been more than fair. His voice rose as he told Alex to take a good look at himself, take a look at what his brother had made of him. 'And there's a few more costs not exactly accounted for, costs I couldn't put down in any ledger – like your death. You want me to write down how much that cost? It set me back thousands.'

Alex faced Edward and snapped that he knew how much a funeral cost, he could hand Edward the cash right now from his wallet if that was what he wanted. Edward calmed him down and gave him a twisted smile. 'It wasn't the funeral that carried the heavy price-tag, it was a bit more involved than that.'

Refusing to let the matter drop, Alex matched Edward's calmness and took out his wallet. 'I'll settle now – how much?'

'All right, but don't say I didn't warn you. It wasn't as simple as it sounded, you can't just dump a body in a car and set light to it. Gotta have someone the right size, got to have someone to identify the corpse . . . that costs a lot, I brought someone over from Brazil . . .'

Alex leaned against the desk, licked his lips. He knew there was more. Part of him had heard enough, but he had gone too far to drop it. 'You brought someone over from Brazil to do what?'

Edward hissed at him. 'Christ, you want me to spell it out? I had a guy bumped off – right size and weight – then I paid off a geezer to give false dental records . . . Look, it's over, finished with, forget it.'

Alex began to sweat. He felt chilled, but he wouldn't leave it alone. 'Where'd you find this . . . you just pick some poor bastard off the street?'

'Look, forget it! He was a bouncer, a bum . . . no family and nobody missed him. Besides, he started asking questions about you, wanted to know where you were, who I was, so he needed to be got rid of anyway.'

Alex didn't have to ask the name. He knew it was Arnie, Arnie from the old Masks, who had stood by him, who had given him so much loyalty and friendship when he had taken over from Johnny Mask. 'I don't want any part of your stinking money. From now on I'll earn every penny, earn it, and by Christ don't you ever try anything on with me, because I'll wipe you out.'

Edward seemed not in the least bit worried – in fact, he seemed relieved that he didn't have to part with his hoards. However, he did make it clear that on the subject of Alex's death they were bound to each other to keep silent.

'I don't have any alternative, do I?'

'No, I guess you don't . . . Well, I'd better get on, got a lot to do.' He strolled out of the office as though they had just had a simple business meeting. Alex sat at his pristine, marble-topped desk, shaken and profoundly aware that he was bound to his brother in more ways than one.

Alex put in a call to Ming. He felt better at the sound of her voice, and began to relax, telling her he would be flying out to New York at the end of the month. Ming's voice was slightly distorted, the line fuzzy, and she wanted to know exactly which plane, what time, as she had so many business commitments.

'Alex? Can you hear me? That auction I told you about, shall I arrange for you to fly to Dallas? Alex . . .'

He paused a moment before he replied. 'Yes, fine, you arrange it.'

He replaced the receiver, realized the time and hurried home. He had employed a cook and a cleaner, but was still interviewing butlers and valets. Like his accounts, he wanted his home run like clockwork, kept in meticulous order, and today there were three men to interview, all with good references and experience.

Alex chose the last man, James Scargill. His references were not in quite the same category as those of the other two applicants; as an ex-prisoner he had to report regularly to a probation officer. He was a dapper, stiff man, an ex-army batman, and he blushed with shame when Alex questioned him about his record.

'That is all behind me now, sir, I was a very young man, sir, and went into the army as soon as I was released.'

'The job is yours, Scargill. I shall require you to double as my valet, butler and chauffeur . . . is that acceptable?'

Scargill could hardly believe his luck, he had been turned

down by so many people. 'Yes, sir, and I give you my word, sir, you will never regret it. You are, if I may say so, a gentleman.'

Alex gave his new valet a smile, and shook his hand.

Miss Henderson smelt the strong perfume and looked up as Harriet strolled into reception. She had bought Aunt Sylvia's favourite scent, Chanel No. 5. She wore a black straw hat and a fawn and gold braided two-piece Chanel suit from the latest collection, a black mink draped around her shoulders. Her high heels made her even taller, and Miss Henderson gasped.

'Would you tell Mr Edward Barkley I'm here?'

Flustered, Miss Henderson looked at Edward's appointment book, but could see nothing further listed for the day. 'I'm so sorry, do you have an appointment, Miss . . .?'

'Just tell him it's Mrs Barkley, would you, Mrs Harriet Barkley?'

Miss Henderson blushed and apologized profusely. She had never met Harriet. As she buzzed through on the intercom, Harriet picked up a glossy magazine.

Edward flicked off the intercom, relieved and angry at the same time. He opened his office door and stood back as Miss Henderson ushered Harriet in. He was speechless.

With a small smile of thanks to the nervous Miss Henderson, Harriet sauntered into the room. Her heels made her almost as tall as Edward, at least six feet. He watched her drape her fur over the back of a chair, then parade slowly up and down the room, finishing with a flourish. 'Well, how do you like the new image?'

'Where in God's name have you been? I've been worried stiff, why couldn't you have had the fucking decency to call me?'

'Ahhh, you like the outfit, do you? Good, because it cost you a lot of money.'

'The outfit is fine – where have you been?'

'Oh, it was just something that cropped up, and I had to rush off – you know, just like you had to . . . Cigarette?'

Edward raised his hands in exasperation. She flipped open a

gold cigarette case and extracted a Gitane. 'Do you have a light?'

'What in Christ's name are you playing at? Don't you know how worried I've been? I was going to contact the police.'

'Oh, I called Alex, didn't he tell you? Well, aren't you going to offer me a drink?'

Edward lit her cigarette and snapped the lighter closed. 'I'd like to tan your hide, my girl, and stop playing silly buggers . . . You've been in France? Is that where you've been?'

He became more infuriated as Harriet calmly sat at his desk. He couldn't help but be struck by just how beautiful she looked, but he was seething with jealousy. 'Pierre? You've been with him?'

Harriet stubbed out her cigarette, rested her chin on her hands. 'I'll make a deal with you, Mr Barkley. From now on, you treat me with respect. If you are called away on business, then you let me know, and I shall let you know where I go.'

'Ahhh, so that's what it's all about, is it?'

'You were worried where I was – what do you think I felt when you upped and left without a word? Is it a deal?'

Suddenly Edward began to laugh, moving round the desk to her. Taking her hand, he pulled her to his feet. 'It's a deal, Mrs Barkley . . . and before I forget, you look beautiful. From now on, you'll know my every move . . .'

'Promise?'

'I promise.'

Miss Henderson tapped on the door to say she was leaving. She bobbed out again quickly when she found Mr and Mrs Barkley wrapped in each other's arms. The following morning she informed the typing pool that Mr Edward's wife was a Paris model with the longest legs she had ever seen in her life.

Chapter Twenty

The long-awaited opening of Edward's club was constantly delayed. It was already May 1961 and nothing had been officially approved. The place was standing ready and waiting, with only a brass plaque beside the door to give any sign that there was a club in the street, but it could not function without a licence. Edward had hoped he would be able to pull strings, but then Alex received a frantic telephone call from him. He was beside himself, they had been refused permission once again. Alex made a few enquiries, and then went round to the club.

Commercial gaming tables, casinos, were illegal. The Royal Commission in 1951 prohibited commercial gaming of any significance, stating that:

Anyone who plays, elsewhere than in a private house, any game in which there is an element of chance for money or money's worth runs a grave risk of committing a penal offence. There are certain games such as roulette which it is even illegal to play in a private house ...

The Betting and Gaming Act went even further than the Commission's recommendations in allowing a fixed charge to be made in advance to members (of twenty-four hours' standing) of a club. The Act did not stipulate, as the commissioners had recommended, that the charge should be limited to an amount that would cover the cost of providing the facilities.

Edward listened intently as Alex outlined the gaming laws. They could not move without a licence for their club. If they opened without one they would be shut down and fined heavily. Edward was furious, knowing that illegal clubs were coining it all over London.

It appeared to Edward that Alex was doing everything to dissuade him from continuing the club project. Alex, however, had learned fast and his initial desire to be one hundred per cent legitimate was beginning to bend. He knew more than anyone the potential earnings from clubs, he had after all run one himself.

Edward swung backwards and forwards in his chair, giving Alex sidelong glances. 'Your nose twitching, is it, brother? I thought you were sidestepping my deal. What d'you want?'

The curse laid to rest with Freedom's talisman now moved like a shadow into the room. They carried it close to their hearts in the shape of the small gold medallions. The brothers, unaware of its existence, felt nothing untoward happening, but Alex, who had until now refused to participate in any underhand dealing, was changing. Edward felt it, but put it down to simple greed. 'Well, what d'you want? Part of the club?'

Alex shook his head, leaned forward smiling. 'I get a percentage of whatever comes through the company, just taking care of my interest ... now, will you pay attention and listen. The law has no right of entry into any club to do checks, therefore any criminal proceedings would be slow. That could give us a chance to switch the games. We could stay one jump ahead of the law quite easily, but we will have to think about cabaret, dancing, making the restaurant larger ... We can also get around it by bringing in customers. Advertising here is cut to a minimum – in other words we aren't even allowed to advertise as a club – but there is nothing to stop us bringing in customers from abroad. We hire special flights, give them special deals, overnight memberships ...'

Excited, Edward clapped his hands, thumped Alex on the back. He was making phone calls before Alex had finished.

The brass plate outside the club said simply, 'Banks'. The closed membership had given rise to many people fighting to join. The gaming rooms contained American roulette (with double zero giving advantage to the house), blackjack, punto banco, French roulette, craps, and baccarat, and there were two rooms for private high-stakes poker games.

On the ground floor was an exclusive restaurant, with a larger room leading off containing a small dance floor and a cabaret stage. The interior, so elegant and ornate, drew people like magnets. High-class American acts were hired, and a six-piece band. The staff wore uniform, the hostesses dressed in fashionable evening gowns. All the girls had been hand-picked for looks by Edward himself.

It was made clear to the girls from the word go that he wanted no tricks being turned, no girls earning extras on the side. They were there only for decoration and to be pleasant to the customers, without behaving like hookers.

Six young chorus girls were hired. Their costumes were showy, glitzy and sexy, their routines provocative. They were to open the two sessions of the cabaret, at nine o'clock and midnight. There was just enough room for their routine on the small floor.

Tirelessly, Edward supervised every item in the club, double-checking with Alex, vetting the first night's guest list for class, contacts and, above all, wallets. 'No good getting in a crowd that don't have a cent to their names, so make sure we mix and match.'

Alex was kept on the go, organizing the cashiers, checking croupiers, barmen, doormen. They had to have exemplary credentials, otherwise they were dismissed without wasting a second. The brothers had to watch their backs, knowing how much could be siphoned off.

At last everything was set, and Edward called all the male staff into the restaurant – the chefs, waiters, doormen, croupiers and cashiers. As always, Alex remained in the background, watching from the office door as Edward called them to order. The whole room hushed as Edward waved his hand for silence, standing taller than any of them, wearing a white dinner jacket, a cigar clamped between his teeth. His speech was short and to the point, telling them simply that they had been hand-picked, they were special. He stressed to them that if the club did well they could all expect a bonus. 'There will also be a large bonus for any member of staff discovering any in-house fiddling, back-handers, from the roulette tables down to the ladies' powder-room tips. If any member of staff even suspects something is going on, they must come to me in confidence, and they will be rewarded for their loyalty ... I don't have to tell you what will happen to anyone caught with their fingers in the till. The reason I have called you all here, from the head waiter to the washers-up, is that this is a family, one big family, and anyone stepping outside the family circle must be dealt with. The success of the club depends on you all, and I assure you, the more successful we are the higher will be your financial rewards ... Thank you.'

Alex watched them file out. They were cocky, self-assured, proud. Edward had such a manner that even the lowliest of the kitchen staff behaved as if they had a share in the club.

Alex and Edward sat together in the private office and Edward, expansive as ever, opened a bottle of champagne. 'Christ, what a night it's going to be, this place'll be a gold mine, bloody gold mine! I'll have punters fighting for membership – that's the trick, don't let 'em in easy and they come knocking at your door ... here's to us, to Banks.'

Alex raised his glass and toasted the club. The intercom on the desk buzzed, and he flicked it on, then picked up the phone, covered the mouthpiece. 'Just give everything the once-over for me, would you?'

Dismissed, Alex gave a mock bow. 'Anything you say.'

As soon as the door closed behind Alex, Edward spoke into

the phone. 'Send her in ...' He picked up Alex's untouched glass and held it out to Jodie as she entered.

Chosen for her background and experience in three other clubs, Jodie was the head girl. Tall, with elegant shoulders, she wore a long, skin-tight, sequinned dress that flared from the knee into layers of net. Her hair was dressed in a neat coil at the back, swept up to show off her perfect neck and high cheek-bones. She closed the door and leaned against it, smiled and arched one of her carefully pencilled eyebrows. 'I've contacted everyone, they know the score. And I put the list in the top drawer of the safe.'

She took the glass of champagne Edward offered her, her long red nails brushing his hand. 'Cheers ... Let's hope it goes off well.'

'There's no hoping, sweetheart – it's imperative, and I've left nothing to chance – nothing.'

More than anyone else Jodie knew just how careful Edward had been, and why he had chosen her above all the other girls. She was on a big salary, double that of most of the others, and she had a dual job. She was to oversee the girls employed in the club, but she was also to make sure that certain clients were taken care of. Using Dora's stash of films and list of clients, Jodie's job was to make them aware that their little foibles could be well taken care of. Not at the club, but Jodie would be their contact. Edward had kept Dora's information to himself – Alex had not the slightest idea it existed.

Jodie sipped the champagne and smiled over the rim of the glass. 'Club's name's good, Banks ... "in" joke, is it? Barkley's Bank?'

Edward laughed, then got down to business, following Dora's initiative. He had bought a large house in Notting Hill Gate, in a very exclusive area. From the outside it looked eminently respectable, but all its bedrooms had been carefully decorated to suit certain clients' 'tastes'. Jodie's hand-picked girls would be under her direct supervision. It was another, very exclusive, part of Banks.

'Just make sure, Jodie, that my name is never, never mentioned. There must be no connection whatever between me and the house. One word leaks out and you'll be out of a job along with the girls, so make sure they don't even know my name.'

She hitched up her dress, adjusted her stocking seam and told him it was all taken care of. She gave Edward a small salute and swanned out.

Watching her leave, Edward thought, 'what a waste'. She was a very beautiful woman, but then so was her girlfriend. The reason Jodie was in control was because she hated men, and Edward had gone to great pains to find her. He laughed – that old slag Dora had certainly known her business.

Harriet wore a stunning pearl-encrusted white gown. Her hair was coiled into a thick long braid of false hair, threaded with pearls. Edward introduced her to everyone, and they all were impressed with the very glamorous Mrs Barkley. Harriet appeared to know already a lot of the society people, and took Alex by surprise. She gave no outward show of nervousness. Her familiarity with the upper echelons of the English aristocracy was obvious. Her class reared its head, and she made many introductions, never putting a foot wrong. She was very calm and serene; the tomboy quality had been replaced by a new sophistication.

Alex stood to one side, he remembered Dora, the small Masks club. He smiled to himself thinking how she would have loved to swan around tonight. It was all going very well, in fact better than he had dared to hope and he turned to search the room for his brother. Edward was always easy to find, head and shoulders above everyone else. Like Harriet, he had the same ability to appear attentive, always giving the other person the impression that whatever he or she was saying was of the utmost importance, but somehow Edward had perfected the act and could actually note everything else that was going on around him while he was listening. He didn't miss a trick. They make a good pair thought Alex as he turned from Harriet back to

Edward. Alex saw the flash of pride in his brother's face as he edged further into the shadows, unnoticed, and able to watch as his brother passed behind her. He saw him rest his hand on her neck. The caress was somehow showing her off as his property and that touch made her stop in mid-sentence and rub her cheek against Edward's hand. She turned to follow his progress through the milling guests. Alex was fascinated, her eyes were bright, like a child's, and then her smile froze and he could almost feel her panic. Alex had to crane his neck to see who Edward had joined.

He was speaking to Jodie, his head close, and he was whispering something. Jodie then stood on tiptoe and cupped her hand over her mouth to hide what she was saying. They appeared intimate, close, and Alex's heart sank. If he had seen it and felt something was going on, then he knew Harriet must be aware of it too. He moved quickly to her side. 'Everything all right?' he asked.

'Everything is fine,' she retorted, 'who's that blonde woman with Edward?'

Alex shrugged, said she was just one of the girls. They both saw the secretive pair enter the door marked 'Private'. Alex reached for Harriet's hand, and gave it a squeeze. He looked at her eyes closely, her pupils were enlarged. 'What are you staring at?'

'Nothing . . . nothing, I was just thinking what a lucky man my brother is.' She had obviously seen Edward's interaction with Jodie. Her whole body was tense with jealousy. Before Alex could calm her down he heard someone screech. 'Harryyyy.'

Moving towards them with a lot of waving and floating panels of chiffon came a heavily pregnant Daisy Millingford. She was flushed, and dragging a chinless, equally sweating husband. 'Gosh Harry, I was hoping I'd see you, this is Charlie, you remember Charlie?'

Harriet turned with any icy expression. 'No, and you are?'

Daisy was taken aback. 'Oh Harry, don't be so beastly, it's Daisy. I'm married. I sent you an invitation, don't you remember? Charlie Lambert, this is Harriet Simpson, or I should say Barkley.'

Poor Daisy was met with such a disdainful look she turned nervously to her Charlie. 'Oh sweetheart, I'm in dire need of a fizzy drink, would you mind?' He jumped to attention hurrying after a waiter. Daisy tried to cover the embarrassing moment holding out her hand to Alex. Harriet made no effort to introduce him. 'Hello, I actually met you at your wonderful château in France, but I'm sure you won't remember me.'

Alex murmured that he was delighted to renew their acquaintance. He insisted they move to a table. When they were seated, Alex leaned close to Harriet, who stared with a fixed glower towards the still closed office door. He whispered that he would bring Edward to meet Daisy.

The two girls sat opposite each other. Daisy began talking non-stop. 'I'm preggers, due in two months . . . we've bought a sweet little mews house in Maida Vale. It was in a dreadful state, but then Charlie isn't qualified yet, he's a law student.'

Harriet was staring into space and quite obviously not listening. Daisy battled on, her high-pitched voice getting slightly hysterical. 'I say, have you seen anything of that Froggy chap you were engaged to? What was his name? You know that barn is still there. Oh, someone bought it and did it up, resold it for a fortune . . . do you live in town?'

Still Daisy got no response from Harriet. She couldn't believe Harriet could be so rude. She gave a nervous laugh, patting her hair into place. 'I'll just go to the powder room. If Charlie comes, tell him I won't be a moment.'

Daisy had to ease herself up, and pull down her dreadful dress. Suddenly, she turned angrily to Harriet. 'I don't know what I have ever done to you, Harry, but I was your friend, I've thought of you so often, even wished I could see you. You've changed, and if you don't mind me saying, I think you are fucking rude . . .' Daisy pushed her way to the ladies' cloakroom.

Charlie brought Daisy's drink to the table, hesitantly brushing his hair back with the palm of his hand. 'Sorry I took so long but it's freshly squeezed orange. She's all right, isn't she? Er . . . is it all right if I sit down? . . .' He sat, and almost pulled the cloth off the table as he inched himself round on the velvet booth's seat. 'Whoops sorry ...'

'Are you happy, Charlie?' Harriet asked him.

He appeared a trifle thrown by her question, then nodded his head. Harriet ordered a bottle of champagne and said she would go and look for Daisy.

She found her sitting in floods of tears on one of the small stools in the ladies' powder room. 'Oh, Daisy, Daisy, I am sorry, so sorry.' Harriet sat next to her friend and hugged her close.

Daisy sniffed, and gulped back tears. 'I'm being stupid, it's just you look so beautiful, and I feel such a fat, dumpy idiot.'

Harriet wiped Daisy's face with a paper tissue. 'Daisy, you look lovely, you know a pregnant woman always looks radiant, didn't you know that? You are lovely, with your little round tum ...'

Daisy looked into her friend's face. She knew instinctively something was very wrong. 'What is it, Harry? Have you had that old trouble again? Have you been ill again?'

Harriet bit her lip, and her eyes filled with tears, she swallowed, and then pulled a tissue from the box and blew her nose. Daisy remained quiet, simply sitting close. Harriet reached for her friend's hand and held it tight. She was like a schoolgirl again, and once she'd started she couldn't stop. 'Oh Daisy, sometimes I just don't know what to do. I love him so much, and I try so hard to be what he wants. You know, I have spent hours at the beauty parlour today, the hairdresser, this bloody false hair, even my nails are false ... I'm on these pills to keep me calm, and it's like I'm wrapped in a cocoon, but I'm scared to stop taking them in case I have one of my turns ... you see I'm not what he wants, not really ...'

'Oh rubbish, what do you mean not what he wants, even Charlie's eyes were out on stalks when he saw you ...'

'You don't understand.'

'Well, why don't you try me?'

Harriet began to pace up and down. She turned and stared at herself. 'I never was one for all this kind of thing you know. I

mean, I try, of course I do ... but, right now he's in his office
and he's with another woman, and I don't know what to do
about it ... Daisy, tell me what to do.'

Daisy snapped her little gold evening bag closed. She wagged
her finger. 'Well for a start, Harriet Simpson, you've got to stop
thinking like this ... you just remember how that man hounded
after you in France. He didn't marry one of those bleached
blondes out there with dangling earrings, he married you ...
now just you get back to being Harry. If he's bonking some
bloody woman ...'

'What? ... bonking?'

'Yes, it's the latest slang for getting the old leg over ... if he's
having a bit on the side, give him a wallop and get off those
bloody pills, do you have to take them?'

Harry gripped Daisy's hand tightly, desperately. 'Oh God, you
won't tell him, will you? He doesn't know about me.'

'Oh don't be stupid, I don't even see you any more ... you
want my advice? You go out there and make sure that dish you
hooked toes the line. If he won't, give him that left upper cut
you've got ...'

Daisy was now well into the role of maternal know-all.
Harriet laughed, and hugged her friend with such force she
almost toppled off the stool. Daisy grabbed the dressing table.
'And I thought you'd changed, you're still as clumsy as ever, you
know the only time I've ever seen you co-ordinated was when
you were sitting on a horse. You remember that time you rode
on to Daddy's lawn and he chased you round with the hose? ...'

Harriet shrieked, her hand over her mouth remembering the
occasion. Daisy began pulling more tissues from the box to wipe
away tears of laughter, recalling how her father had soaked
everyone with the garden hose, he had been in such a rage ...
Harriet went quiet, her lips trembled as if she were going to cry.
Instead, she gently touched Daisy's big swollen stomach. 'I don't
ride ... not any more. Take care of your baby, take care of
him ...'

Daisy cupped Harriet's chin in her hands. Her puffy face was serious with concern. 'You know sometimes, Harry, it's best to turn a blind eye; not all the time, but you know what I mean . . . your old man will have a lot of temptations with this place, but you're his wife . . . he chose you. You love him, don't you?'

Daisy felt as if she were talking to a child. There was a help-lessness about her friend, a vulnerability that made her so touching . . . even more so when a single tear trickled down her face as she whispered, 'I love him so, Daisy, I hurt inside, hurt so much sometimes I wish he'd never come back into my life. Do you feel that way about Charlie?'

Daisy laughed, 'Good God, no . . . I just grabbed what I could get, and you should get out there before someone grabs what you've got . . .'

In five seconds Harriet was a different person. She wiped her face with the back of her hand, sniffed, and then did a comic Groucho Marx walk to the door. Daisy asked if she could have the name of her hairdresser as she rather fancied a similar false braid down her back. The next moment Harriet pulled off the hair switch and threw it across the room. Harriet winked, gave a small salute, and was gone.

Daisy picked up the hairpiece. The colour reminded her of Harriet's chestnut mare, she wondered why Harry didn't ride any more. The baby inside her kicked, and Daisy dropped the hairpiece into the bin, it was the wrong colour for her anyway.

Alex collided with Harriet as he came out of the office. Her hair was standing up on end, and he thought she was drunk. She gave him a dazzling smile. 'Is he bonking that blonde in there?' Without waiting for an answer, she entered the office. 'Just what have you been up to, Mr Barkley?' she said, her hands on her hips like Calamity Jane.

Edward walked round from his desk, and cocked his head to one side. 'Well, Mrs Barkley, I could ask the same of you, you look as if you've been dragged through a hedge backwards . . . come here, menace, right here and close your eyes.'

'What have you done with the blonde?'

'Ah, she's in the filing cabinet. Now are you going to come here, or do I have to drag you?'

Edward pulled her to stand directly in front of him. He instructed her to close her eyes. She shut her eyes, and waited. She felt the warmth of his hands at her neck, and then something icy cold being draped around her. 'This is an anniversary present, and it comes with my love ... I love you, Harry ... I love you.'

He held up a mirror in front of her so she could see the spectacular diamond necklace. His face was concerned, wanting her approval ... The outrageous necklace was tasteless and meant nothing to her. The words 'I love you, Harry' made her feel as if he had given her the world. She lifted her hand and with the tips of her fingers traced his mouth. An electric shock ran through his body, he wanted to draw her close, but he couldn't. He was held by the expression in her eyes. There was such pain, such fragility ... so much love. Her soft, barely audible 'thank you' made him want to break the moment, as he could see her as she had been all those years before standing in the broken chapel with the tiny gold bracelet. He pulled her roughly into his arms, too shy, too afraid she would see such vulnerability in him. 'Oh, my Harry, I'm so bloody proud of you, you are the best-looking woman out there, do you know that?' He sniffed, not allowing himself to cry, and he joked. 'Well, you were, what the hell have you done to your hair?'

'I gave it to Daisy Millingford.'

He laughed, and he was back in control of his emotions again. He stood back to admire his necklace. He bowed to the door. 'Your public awaits you, princess.'

Alex watched them enter the main club room, their arms entwined around each other. Jodie's voice made him start. She stood quietly at his side. 'Eighty-five thousand pounds around her neck, each stone is perfect, he picked each one himself ... he's opened the box so many times it's already worn ... I think it's rather old-fashioned ... what do you think, Mr Barkley?'

Alex said nothing. He had already said enough when Edward

had shown him the necklace. It was similar to the one treasured by their mother only, instead of pearls, Edward had chosen diamonds. Alex touched the gold chain round his neck, and his mouth tightened. Edward had shown off the necklace with such pride, but Alex had been furious without really knowing why. He had even asked what had happened to the pearls; he knew where the gold was, round their necks, but the pearls? He had been stunned when Edward had told him they were buried with her, buried with their mother, and if he didn't believe him, he suggested Alex should dig up the grave.

Harriet became the centre of attention. Everyone admired the necklace, just as Edward confided to everyone exactly how much he had paid for it.

Harriet danced over to Alex, with a glass of champagne. She made a camp, theatrical gesture with her hand indicating the necklace, then she giggled.

'Rather makes me look like some ancient grand duchess, don't you think?' She hooked her arm through his, and snuggled close. 'You know, I remember a poem I read once. It said something about painting a picture of the world, a big, big picture, and everything was painted on this picture, you know, everything that was beautiful, and then . . . then it was rolled up into a big ball . . .'

Alex listened with only half an ear. He was tired, he wanted to leave. It was after twelve. Suddenly, she lifted her arms and spoke loudly, making everyone around them stop and stare. 'I painted a picture of the world for you, and I rolled it into a ball, and let it roll to your feet. You picked it up in your arms, and threw it back.'

Edward gave her a small frown of disapproval and she whispered to Alex. 'He must have thought I was playing.'

Alex excused himself. He asked Harriet to tell Edward he was leaving. She gave him a kiss, and made him promise to call her the following morning.

Alex had always been aware of her strange energy, from the moment they had first met. Now he found it disturbing. When she was excited, she drew people around her, he could see it even now. The delighted faces of people listening to her, telling them stories, making them laugh. But it was all for Edward, her energy was fuelled by him; it was as if he, and he alone, could control it . . . just as she had said, if she could give him the world, wrap it up for him, hand it to him he would kick it back, thinking it was a game. She knows, he thought to himself, that crazy little lady knows. 'Oh be warned, Alex,' he told himself. 'Never get to be the one in the middle; best stay well clear, get off their roller coaster or she could take you down with her.'

Alex returned to the office to get his coat. He picked up the empty diamond case . . . the lid snapped shut. It was like an omen, and from that moment Alex made the decision to distance himself from Harriet.

Harriet did call Alex a number of times to invite him for supper, even to meet him in town for lunch as she wanted his opinion on two trouser suits. Alex had refused, very politely. She detected the coldness immediately. She never called him again, never even mentioned it to Edward. She was saddened that he, Alex, could not have talked it over with her, but she understood. She had looked upon Alex as a friend, and was intelligent enough to be aware that perhaps it was not the wisest relationship. She missed him, she had liked him and she had very few friends. She made no attempt to contact Daisy whose forthcoming baby would remind her too much of her own dead son. She made a conscious effort not to allow old emotions to creep back. She was loved, and she was happy, she was safe in Edward's love, and she stopped taking her pills.

'Banks' became established overnight, and the brothers watched the money roll in. Aware that the major part rolled straight into his brother's pocket, Alex had mixed feelings, but he also watched it roll straight out again as they poured more and more money into legitimate businesses.

The Panamanian company, sitting unused and unwanted, was

turned into an insurance company. Edward flew out to install a manager, and when he returned, the company had one desk, one chair and one employee. The Barkley Company had yet another string to its bow, offering high-risk policies to all the major insurance companies. Edward was about to contact certain 'friends' employed by the massive Lloyd's of London when Alex appeared, and he put the phone down. He didn't want Alex to overhear his conversation.

'Something up?'

Alex asked if it would be all right to take a week off.

'What for?'

Alex told him about the American collector of seventeenth-century furniture who had died, and the auction was to be in Texas. He mentioned the possibility that something he was interested in would come on to the market.

'Can't you send someone over there for you?'

'Not really – you see, if the rumours are correct, there will be a lot of dealers after it. I'd like to get in first, before them, and ... Well, I don't know who I could trust to authenticate it.'

'What the hell is it?'

'Well, it might be a bed – there's never been a record of one on the market. It would be an investment. On the other hand ...'

'Bed? What the hell are you talking about? For Chrissake, send someone over from Christie's or Sotheby's; you don't have to go yourself, do you?'

About to reply, Alex was interrupted by Edward's telephone. 'Who? Oh, yeah, yeah ... put him through in two seconds.' Covering the phone with his hand, Edward said irritably that if Alex really felt he had to go, then go he should. Alex was dismissed, and Edward swivelled round in his chair, flicking the intercom switch. Alex had wanted to discuss other matters, but, faced with the back of the leather chair, he gave up and walked out. He paused briefly at the door, however, and overheard a little of Edward's conversation.

'Walter ... Well, a voice from the past. Better not talk on the phone, why don't we meet?' Edward swivelled round again to make sure Alex had gone, then satisfied that he was alone he leaned his elbows on the table. 'Best if we were to discuss it in private, Walter ... No, no, it's personal ... are you free this evening? No? Well, you name the day.'

When he replaced the phone, he gave it a little pat of pleasure. Walter was now in a very high position in the Government, a position that would be useful to Edward, and the more he thought about it the better it seemed that Alex would be out of the country. He was going to ask his old friend Walter a small favour, one he knew he wouldn't be able to refuse. He was sure a man in Walter's position would not like a whisper getting out about a certain boating accident in Cambridge.

Alex arrived in New York and went straight to Ming's apartment. She did not return until evening, and even then she had to make four or five business calls before she could sit and relax over dinner. Unable to divert her mind from work, she consistently questioned him about the business, about the club. Had they had good press coverage on the decor, had he brought any of the press cuttings with him? Alex took her hand, pulled her to him. 'I've come here to get away from the club, away from business.'

Ming smiled, kissed him. 'I'm sorry, but I have been with my accountants all day – it just gets to me sometimes, all the money I have to carve up and hand over to Edward – and for what? He doesn't do a damned thing.'

Alex didn't want to get into an argument with her, but he still made his own feelings quite plain. 'Not quite that, Ming. He did front your business, and without him you might still be in the south of France.'

'You know that is not true. I would have made it. Maybe not quite so fast, but I would, on my own – without Edward. You can tell him that, and you can also tell him I am about ready to buy him out of his share in the company as he agreed I could, if the time came.'

Alex released her hand and ran his mind back over Ming's accounts. She must have been making a lot more money than she accounted for, because Alex knew precisely how much she was declaring.

Ming sensed his withdrawal, and she slipped on to his lap, kissing his neck. 'You know, you should be my partner – is there any way you could get Edward to give you his contract, make it over to you? Don't tell him it would be me buying him out, you do it, and then . . .'

Alex buried his face in her neck, kissing her softly, but his mind was racing. Could Edward have been right about her, was she out for all she could get? Did she really care for him? 'Have you given any thought to getting married? We will have to tell Edward sooner or later . . . and then, well, I would like a son . . .'

He felt her tense in his arms, although she still held him, still stroked his cheek. 'We're just fine as we are, and, well, I don't think I am really the maternal type . . . Did I tell you I have arranged for us to fly to Dallas? I've already made some drawings for Mrs Hunter Hardyman, and Alex . . . all I need is one good contact, she is like royalty out there, and rich.'

She slid off his knee, glowing as she told Alex that every time Barbara Hunter Hardyman drew breath she made a million. 'I just need one intro, just one, then I can take it from there . . .'

Suddenly Alex felt tired, his head throbbed. He excused himself, saying he would just lie down for a while, it must be jet lag. Ming was very attentive, bringing him iced water and aspirin. She laid a cool cloth on his head, and he closed his eyes. She sat next to him, looking down into his handsome face as she spoke. Her voice was soft, distant. 'Alex, I can't have children, I'm sorry, I should have told you.'

He lay still with his eyes closed and said nothing. Eventually he felt her move from the bed and leave the room. He got up, opened his briefcase, took out his calculator and began to go over Ming's accounts. If there were discrepancies, she had covered them, but still he felt uneasy, in some way betrayed. Edward's voice echoed in his brain: 'She's old, she'll never give

you a family ... she's out for all she can get. You're her meal-
ticket, only you're too dumb to realize it ...'

Unconsciously Alex began to twist the gold medallion; it had
become a habit when he was disturbed. He also thought that
perhaps Ed had been right, just as he was right about so many
things, almost as if he had second sight.

At breakfast the following morning Ming was as sweet as ever,
teasing him that he had been in such a deep sleep that she had
not liked to disturb him. She was dressed in a neat black suit over
a white blouse with an Eton collar. She was ready to travel.
Together they caught the flight to Dallas.

Ming had brought all the brochures for the auction, and she
showed Alex the details of what they hoped was a bed. It was
described as, 'Various Kang table legs, made from Huang-Hua-
Li wood, apron carved with dragon design'. There were also a
number of other pieces from the same period, as the old billionaire had been a renowned collector. Alex was fascinated, and
at last he began to relax, asking Ming what she knew of the
Hunter Hardyman family. She told him they were oil barons,
and what she had gleaned from the society columns. Then, as
businesslike as ever, went on to say she had cabled the ranch,
they were expecting him, and she had booked them into a hotel,
in adjoining rooms. She laughed. 'We may be in luck, we are
three weeks ahead of the auction and the valuation officers are
still there. They have been sent from both Sotheby's and
Christie's, but I am sure if you offer the right price you will get
the pieces, everything, everyone, has a price ...'

Alex looked at her, then turned to stare out of the plane
window. He wondered if Ming, too, had her price.

On their arrival in Dallas, they booked into the exclusive Del-
a-Mare Hotel, then hired a helicopter to take them on to the
Hunter Hardyman ranch. Ming handed Alex a local newspaper
with an article marked for him to read.

Already there had been some press coverage of Alex's visit,

and he knew Ming must have organized it as the article said that Alex Barkley, the previous owner of one of the most magnificent châteaux in France, was in New York to discuss further projects with Ming, the successful and most sought-after designer, and to talk about possible residence in Texas. He had to hand it to Ming, she wasted no time, and already the hotel desk clerk was passing him numerous invitations from Texan high society, requesting his presence at charity balls.

'Well, you have been a busy girl . . .' He couldn't help feeling irritated, and his mood worsened when she took the invitations and sifted through them.

'Good, this is good. I will make sure my secretary sends them my own brochures, there is a property boom over here, perhaps you should think about buying some land.'

Again Alex had that niggling feeling at the pit of his stomach, but he said nothing.

They had been travelling for over three-quarters of an hour when Alex asked the pilot, Jeff, how far it was to the Hunter Hardyman ranch. He shouted back over his shoulder. 'We've been over their land for the past ten minutes. Far as the eye can see, everything from now on belonged to the old man . . . He was one helluva guy, take a look below and you'll see what I mean.'

Alex was stunned. There were hundreds of square miles of land from which rose oil wells and refineries, buildings with bright-red letters twenty or thirty feet high saying, 'Hunter Hardyman'. They flew over what looked like silver-topped warehouses, but were actually aeroplane hangars. Alex shouted to the pilot, 'Those hangars filled with private planes, Jeff?'

'Hell, no, they're filled to the rafters with stuffed animals. The old guy was the last of the great white hunters, crammed the place with all his trophies. There are more stuffed tigers in there than they got left in the goddamn jungles . . . They say he was after the white buffalo, an' shot everything in sight hopin' it'd be the poor bastard . . . Okay, now you're hittin' their cattle land, look, far as the eye can see, and it's still Hardyman land. And off to the right, that's the biggest tile factory in the United States, ships them all over the world ... More cattle coming up on your left ... An' up ahead you see the herd of horses, thoroughbreds all of 'em – you ever seen a herd like it?'

As they flew on and on, the overpowering wealth of Hunter Hardyman began to dawn on Alex. He had thought himself rich – now he was seeing wealth beyond his wildest dreams.

'You can see the oil wells, the fields stretch for two hundred miles east, see the pylons?'

Coming into view in the distance, rising out of the heat haze, was a sprawling ranch house, four storeys high with eight white pillars before an arched entrance. Miles of velvety lawns were sprayed constantly with water to keep them lush and green. A vast swimming pool at the side of the house was surrounded by changing rooms, a barbecue and a tiled patio. Sunbeds with brightly coloured canopies littered the poolside. Alex's stomach lurched as the 'copter began its descent. Now he could make out the guards patrolling the white perimeter fence.

'Are those guards armed, Jeff?'

'Yep, sure thing, sir. They got a hundred of 'em, the old boy was paranoid about kidnapping ... Okay, here we go, buckle up and sit tight.'

Way below them by the Olympic-size swimming pool, two figures lay sunbathing. Ming stared down at them through a pair of binoculars, then turned to Alex. 'I think they must be her daughters, she has two. She's divorced now ... she must be older than I thought, they look quite old. Here, do you want to see?' She offered him the binoculars, but he refused, and she began to survey the ranch.

'Oh, by the way, she's called Mrs Taverner, Barbara Taverner.'

The entrance hall was so vast it could have been a ballroom, with a tiled floor and marble in such profusion it dazzled the eye. Alex found the hall cool, almost cold, the chill of the marble adding to the effect of the air conditioning. No servant appeared to greet them. She looked at Alex and shrugged. The crystal chandelier, out of place in the ranch house, tinkled in the cool air.

Three men wearing light suits and open-necked shirts, with their ties pulled loose, appeared through double doors from a room off the hall. Alex introduced himself, but the men seemed none too interested. Alex was not prepared to turn round and go back after coming all this way. The men were about to move on. Firmly, Ming took charge. 'Mr Barkley cabled from New York that we would be here, surely there must be a secretary, someone we could speak to?'

One of the men hesitated, and Alex cornered him. 'Would it be possible for me to look at the pieces I am interested in?'

The man pointed towards the room he had just left, and said that Alex should talk to their head man, Mr Dean.

They were taken aback by the appalling taste of the vast lounge. Although the place was cluttered with boxes, and various pieces of furniture had been dragged to the centre of the room, the awful decor was obvious. The room was dominated by a painting of a man with white hair, wearing a linen suit that even in the painting looked crumpled.

'That's the old man himself, impressive, isn't he?'

Alex made a point of charming Mr Dean, and was given a brief rundown on the family. Mr Dean was the head man from Sotheby's – pleasant, open-faced and balding, sweating even with the air conditioning and constantly wiping his head.

'The old boy seems to have had various families, no one can quite work out the intricacies of the family feuds. But after he died there were three women and three families grabbing . . . he lost his sons in a plane crash, perhaps you read about it? The fortune's been divided up and this place left to a granddaughter. Have you met Mrs Taverner? Well, she wants this place sold as fast as possible – hates it, and hated him from what I've heard. But it means we are working night and day to get everything catalogued and ready for the auction.'

Alex chose his words carefully. First, he asked about Hunter Hardyman's china collection, and Dean told him they had not even started assessing that yet. The porcelain experts were flying in next day, and in the meantime the men were just listing the articles. The pricing would be done by the experts. Alex mentioned the lists he had already seen.

'Yes, but they're incomplete – there's fifty times more than that. We had no idea the job would take so long. You know the ranch itself is up for sale? Are you interested?'

Alex was not interested, and there was nothing worth looking at in this room. Somehow he had to steer the conversation around to the seventeenth-century furniture. 'I'm wanting to have a look at a couple of pieces – not of immense value, but I'm just starting my collection . . . You think I could take a look at items 500 and 600?'

Dean was no fool. He smiled at Alex. 'They're in the dining hall, but I have to tell you, they've not even been valued yet.'

Alex said he would still like just a quick look at them, and eventually Dean led him from the room.

Alex followed him through the double doors at the far end of the room and down a long corridor. When they reached the far end, Mr Dean looked over his shoulder, then unlocked the door. 'I would have liked to have been at his funeral, rumour has it a couple of the old boy's ex-wives turned up, and all hell broke loose.' He lowered his voice to a confidential tone, 'He was a real money-grubbing old buzzard – made his fortune from scrap, bought land, and the rest is history, but I've never met anyone who has a good word to say for him. And he was paranoid, believed everyone was trying to kidnap him. That's why the place is wired up like a fortress. There are more bells and wires around this place than Fort Knox . . . Freezing in here.'

The room was dark, shuttered, and there was the icy blast of air conditioning. 'Old man kept the place ice cold, at least he knew that much. The pieces in here are in excellent condition, and some of it he never even used. There's a Queen Anne desk over there – in all my life I have never seen one in such condition. Look, would you mind if I leave you, come back in a few minutes? I still have a lot to do.'

The door closed behind him, and Alex stared around the cold, draped room. Just one look told him that Dean was right. Even to Alex's untrained eye some of the furniture was indeed special. He searched around for the seventeenth-century pieces, lifting cover after cover away from highly polished Queen Anne, Tudor, Victorian chairs, desks and card tables, but he could not find the treasures he had travelled so far to see. Frustrated, he was about to give up when he saw a chair in a corner, piled high with old newspapers. Removing the papers, he stood back.

The yoke-back armchair, Huang-Hua-Li hardwood with a perfect matted seat, was in superb condition. Alex got down on his knees to touch the smooth wood. Then he spotted the legs of a bench seat, horseshoe-shaped, and he knew it was the same period. Excitedly, he uncovered three more pieces, and began to think he might be right, somewhere here there might just be the most sought-after article for any collector, a bed.

The door opened behind him, and a cold voice, almost as chilly as the room, said, 'Mr Dean, the servants have laid out lunch in the breakfast room. I would be most obliged if you would ask permission to use the swimming pool – one of your men is in there right now, and I must ask you to have them refrain in future.'

Taken aback, Alex stood up and straightened his tie. She was very tall, wearing a simple white dress, but a dress that would set any woman back a few thousand dollars. Her skin was a pale golden colour, and her blonde hair was swept up in a Grace Kelly chignon. She wore a gold necklace and many bangles on her slender arms.

Alex moved towards her. 'I really must apologize for my presence here. We haven't been introduced – my name is Alex Barkley, I cabled from New York. Are you Mrs Taverner?' He looked into steely, penetrating eyes the colour of turquoises. There was not a scrap of make-up on the flawless skin.

'I am Mrs Taverner – I'm sorry, I didn't catch your name?'

'Alex Barkley.'

She did not take his outstretched hand for a moment, and he

was about to withdraw it when she suddenly slipped her cool fingers into his grasp. It was a fleeting gesture, and he felt foolish. Mrs Taverner turned back to the door, paused a moment. 'Barkley, you said? And English, from your voice?'

Feeling exceedingly uncomfortable, Alex nodded. He felt she was scrutinizing him from head to toe. 'I think I should tell you that I am a private collector, I am not connected with the auctioneers.'

She twisted the diamond ring on her wedding finger, held her head slightly to one side. 'You spoke to my secretary? Well, I'm sure if you have permission then it's all right. Don't let me detain you.'

He could smell her perfume in the cold air, a fresh, clean smell. He remained standing as the click, click, click of her heels receded down the corridor. Then there was silence. He returned to examining the furniture, putting Barbara Taverner out of his mind.

But Alex was in Mrs Taverner's mind. She walked into her study where Miss Fry, her secretary, was typing at a large desk. 'Miss Fry, who is Alex Barkley? And why is he here?'

Miss Fry blushed and gestured to Mrs Taverner that she had someone waiting. Ming rose to meet her, hand outstretched, smiling. 'Mrs Taverner, I am delighted to meet you, I am Imura Takeda.'

Ignoring Ming's hand, Mrs Taverner turned to her secretary. 'Miss Takeda is the designer you were interested in for your New York apartment.'

Ming smiled again, although tempted to walk out, she was given such a thorough once-over.

'Is Mr Barkley your client?'

Ming unzipped her portfolio and began to lay out the large colour photographs of Alex's château, together with the press cuttings of the other houses she had done, and Mrs Taverner glanced through them, showing perfunctory interest. 'Well, this is interesting, really fine ... does Mr Barkley live in New York?'

Ming gave Mrs Taverner details of Alex's background, embroidering everything, while she displayed more photographs and brochures. She did it so cleverly no one would have guessed it was a 'hard sell'. Throughout Ming's presentation Mrs Taverner's long, blood-red fingernails tapped on the edge of her desk, then she held out a languid hand for the press cuttings and sat down. 'Miss Fry, why don't you see to some coffee . . . I'm sorry, what did you say your name was?'

Ming repeated her name, and received a dazzling smile.

Mrs Taverner turned on the charm while Ming sipped her coffee. 'Your client, Mr Barkley – perhaps he is interested in buying the ranch?'

Ming informed her that Alex had come to look at some seventeenth-century furniture.

'Oh, yes, you said . . . Well, I am impressed, this château is splendid . . . Would you like to look over the plans for my apartment in New York? You'll be able to get some idea of the size of the place . . . Miss Fry, would you see about a little lunch for Miss Takeda . . .'

She followed Miss Fry out of the room, closing the door behind her, and sent her off to invite Alex to a private luncheon, one Ming was not invited to.

Half an hour later, Barbara Taverner knew virtually every corner of the château, Ming giving her a highly professional sales pitch. She now knew that the Duke and Duchess of Windsor were personal friends of Alex's, and she surmised that Alex was one hell of a catch, rich enough himself not to be after her fortune. Not that his money amounted to anything approaching Barbara's inheritance, only another oil baron could match her vast income.

Alex was led into a small lounge on the first floor. Bright, deep-seated sofas in yellows and greens with orange scatter cushions offended Alex's sense of colour, but the glass-topped table on the verandah, set with chilled champagne, looked inviting.

'Mrs Taverner will join you shortly, Mr Barkley.'

A Spanish maid attended him, offering him champagne, then stood quietly in the shadows.

Barbara Taverner was used to making entrances. She had changed, and was now wearing another simple, wildly expensive dress. Alex rose from the sofa, and she waved her hand for him to join her at the table. She spoke in fluent Spanish to the maid, who served them cold poached salmon and salad.

'This is really most kind of you, Mrs Taverner.'

'Please call me Barbara ... Alex, isn't it? I just adore your designer, and I desperately want her to begin work on my New York penthouse. She's looking over the drawings right now ... more champagne?' She rang a small gold bell beside her plate, and the maid refilled Alex's glass. Barbara made polite conversation, charming him, and he could smell her lovely fresh perfume. He also noticed that she hardly touched her food, waiting politely for him to finish, then placing her knife and fork together and ringing the tiny bell. Alex made a point of being very attentive, smiling at her remarks, but if asked, he could not really have recalled one thing she said to him. She fascinated him with her coolness, her precise gestures, her softly drawling voice and husky laugh. For her part, Barbara noticed everything about the Englishman. His perfectly tailored suit, his gold cufflinks, his shoes, his tie – his well-manicured hands and broad shoulders. She was making a list in her head and he was getting tick after tick ... She could tell his body was firm beneath the starched shirt. 'Are you staying locally, Alex?'

He told her which hotel he was booked into, and that he would be leaving within the week.

'Oh no – I see I will have to persuade you to stay a little longer. You have to see Dallas, meet everyone, I insist you at least promise to have dinner with me. Have you met my daughters? I married very young, and I'm divorced now, but that is too long a story to go into at our first meeting. Would you like me to show you over the ranch, the rooms they won't be pawing over?'

Stealing a quick glance at his watch, Alex smiled and gave a formal little bow. She took his arm and they toured the house. Alex was charm itself, giving all the right responses, but wondering all the time how long it would take to get to the point – how much Barbara Taverner would accept for the pieces. And he had still not unearthed the prized bed.

As she led him from room to room, she divulged little bits of her background, her relationship to Hunter Hardyman. 'He was my mother's father, and I think she loathed him almost as much as I did . . . He was a dreadful man, domineering, and the most ruthless man I ever met in my life. I was left this, and all I want is to get rid of everything he ever touched. He destroyed my mother's life – and even mine. My marriage was over before it really began. I was sixteen, and HH arranged it, as he arranged the life of every member of his family. I don't know if you have heard the gossip, but Grandpa had numerous families, and none of us really get along.'

She was open and at ease with Alex, and he began to enjoy her company. Of course, Barbara was making sure he knew she was divorced, unattached. Finally Alex looked at his Rolex and said he really had to watch the time as he intended to return to his hotel before nightfall. Barbara wasn't about to let this catch out of her hands – she smiled sweetly and told him it would be madness to return to the hotel. He must stay to dinner.

'That really is most kind, but I'm afraid I really do have to go back to London as soon as possible. Perhaps if you would be willing to come to some arrangements regarding the pieces of furniture I'm interested in, I am willing to settle a price for them now, if it's agreeable. I will match any other offers, and then have them shipped over to England.'

Ming appeared with her portfolio, talking intently to Miss Fry about schedules and estimates. Barbara excused herself and went off with Miss Fry, leaving Alex and Ming together.

'Well, I not only have the commission for the New York apartment, but she wants me to find a suitable one for her daughters.'

Alex congratulated her, then looked at his watch, he said they should thinking be about leaving. Ming stood close to him and whispered, 'I will have to leave straightaway, she wants these estimates by the end of the week – but you stay. I think she's enamoured, maybe you'll get the furniture at a good price . . .'

Barbara made an entrance. She was smiling. 'Mr Barkley, I have arranged for the pieces you want to be shipped out to you at the first opportunity. I am told it won't take too long.'

Alex looked nonplussed, and she laughed. 'Please accept them as a gift, on condition that you stay for dinner, and give me just two days of your time to show you the sights.'

Alex murmured his thanks and said that he really could not accept her invitation as he had to return to New York with Ming.

'Oh, I simply won't take no for an answer – I have my own plane, why don't you let Miss Takeda go and I'll arrange for your luggage to be brought back here? You simply can't refuse.'

Alex looked at Ming for help, but she insisted on returning alone. Alex walked her to the helicopter, and she laughed at his confusion. 'Oh, for heaven's sake, Alex, stay. You'll enjoy yourself and you said you needed a holiday. Besides, with all this extra work I won't have much time to spare. I'll see you when you return to New York.'

Alex gave way, and watched the helicopter as it took off. Ming waved once, then turned to talk to the pilot.

Alex was like putty in Barbara Taverner's hands, and she swept him along in her wake. He was flattered by her attentions, and she never ceased to amaze him. Flying her own plane she managed, in the two days, to take Alex to cocktail parties, lunches, teas, and a charity ball.

There were envious looks from the Texan society ladies as Barbara led the elegant and charming Englishman around on her arm like a champion. To Alex's blushing embarrassment she never failed to bring up the fact that he knew the Duke and Duchess of Windsor intimately . . . However, Alex began to enjoy his 'star status', the flattery and the fawning, and Barbara was a stunning-looking woman. Alex was falling in love, and it took little persuasion for him to agree to stay another week.

Edward arrived home from the office even later than usual. He was greeted by his rather frazzled cook-housekeeper, who told him that there was a Mr Dewint waiting to see him, he had been waiting for two hours.

'Who? Dewint? Never heard of him . . . and Agnes, would you get something fancy for tomorrow evening, dinner for six – but it could be eight. De what, did you say?'

Agnes disappeared into the hall and returned to say that Dewint had been sent by the Kensington Staff Agency. She passed Edward a small, strange, handwritten card. ' "Norman Dewint, butler" . . . ingenious chap, it appears! Show him in. Oh, Agnes, is my wife about?'

'Well, she was, sir, but then she said something about going to her pottery classes. She's left a shocking mess in the upstairs bathroom, sir.'

'Thank you, Agnes . . . show De what's-his-name in, will you?'

'Sit down, Norman, help yourself to a drink.'

Dewint sat at the far end of the eighteen-foot refectory table and thanked Mr Barkley, but he did not partake of alcoholic beverages.

'Right then, Norman, tell me about yourself.'

Dewint coughed, straightened the razor-sharp creases in his black and grey striped butler's trousers, and in his rather high-pitched voice, paying close attention to his aitches, began to detail his past employments. 'I 'ave, sah, worked in the Queen Mother's establishment at Balmoral. Hi think you will find, sah, that they was, if I may say so, pleased with my services. I have detailed hall the 'ouses I have subsequently had the honour to be in service with, and I am a qualified valet stroke butler.'

His plummy, high-pitched voice with its strange aitches and his small pale face made Edward laugh. Dewint was like a pixie –

pointed nose, pointed chin – and he had large, pointed ears. His flat, Brylcreemed hair shone, as highly polished as his shoes.

Edward sent the neatly stapled references spinning back down the table. 'Thing is, Dewint, I am not a man of, shall we say, habit, or consistent movements. My wife is not domesticated, quite the reverse, but we do entertain a lot. When I am away, I like the house to be kept running in some sort of order – won't be easy, not with my wife and her hobbies . . .'

Dewint launched into an involved history of the time he worked for Churchill, but Edward cut him short. 'Can you start first thing in the morning?'

Dewint beamed, his pixie ears twitched. 'Hi can, sah, and may I say it will be a pleasure, sah. I've read about you in the society columns, I like to keep abreast of things.'

Dewint gave a hop and a skip as he departed down the drive. He had been desperate, and he knew he would be able to get along with Mr Barkley. He had seen the house could do with a thorough clean, and he would be ready, with his green pinny on, first thing tomorrow. He checked out of the hostel and was back at the manor by seven-thirty the next morning.

He woke Edward with an elaborate breakfast tray. Harriet's tousled head peered over the blankets. 'Oh, scrummy, I'm starving.'

'I shall bring more toast immediately, sah . . . modom, may I say how very pleased I ham to meet you.'

Harriet was already tucking in to her breakfast. She waved her fork and Dewint bowed out. She spoke with her mouth full, 'He's just divine, how on earth did you find him? He looks like Noddy – you know, Noddy and Big Ears . . . Pass the tomato sauce . . . ta.'

Edward ate as hungrily as his wife, and said that someone had to get the house organized. Harriet hopped out of bed with marmalade all over her cheek, and opened the bathroom door. 'An artist of my calibre cannot be bothered with the mundane, boring, day-to-day running of this tip . . . Look, I made this in class.' She held up a strange-looking pot with a very thick rim.

'What's that?'

'Well, it's supposed to be a sugar bowl, but I didn't quite get the wheel going right – what do you think?'

Edward didn't even look, but opened the *Financial Times*, then laughed, 'Bloody hell, he's ironed it! Look!'

The bathroom door slammed shut.

Down in the kitchens Agnes and Dewint were at loggerheads. He was giving his critical assessment of the very tarnished silver. Agnes slapped her dishcloth down on the table. 'Listen, by the time you've cleaned up after that Mrs Barkley, you'll have no time for cleaning ruddy silver. She had a pigeon in here yesterday, ruddy pigeon she'd found in the garden.'

'I'd be grateful if you did not speak of my hemployers in derogatory terms. If you'll excuse me, I'll take the 'ot toast up, and in future, wrap it in a napkin, hit keeps it warm.'

Edward came out of the bathroom and found that Dewint had already stripped the bed. Over a chair hung a clean shirt and trousers.

'I 'ave not has yet 'ad time to familiarize myself with your wardrobe, sah. But given time I will know exactly what your preference is . . . I believe you are going to the office this morning, so I have laid out what I think is suitable, sah.'

Edward smiled and thanked Dewint, who walked out with a bundle of sheets. By the time Edward was dressed and ready to leave, Dewint was on his hands and knees on the stairs with a dustpan and brush. Edward gave him a small pat on the head as he passed, and went on down the stairs.

'Might I 'ave a quick word, sah? The wine cellar is rather depleted, and I wondered if you would like me to order for you . . . St James' is a good company, and very reliable.'

Edward looked up, leaning against the banisters. 'I'll leave it to you. If need be, open an account with them. And check the larder. In fact, check everything and make some kind of an inventory. Looks like you and I are going to get along fine.'

Dewint had just reached the bottom stair when Harriet called out – or rather, shrieked – from the studio, 'Deeeewint!'

He blinked slightly at the brilliant yellow walls. Harriet was covered in wet clay, her pottery wheel spinning wildly out of control. A strange, malformed blob sprayed the daffodil-yellow walls with specks of brown.

'Yes, modom?'

'Could you switch the thing off? It's that plug on the wall, the pedal's stuck or something.'

Dewint caught a speck of clay in his eye, wiped it and pulled out the plug. Harriet puffed with relief, then apologized profusely for the mess. Dewint wiped his face, gave a polite cough, and suggested that if modom was in agreement, he'd stock up the larder.

'Yes, modom is – and you can call me Harry ... and don't worry about me interfering, you will be a godsend. Come here.' Dewint moved closer, and she whispered to him, 'Do you think we can give Agnes the heave-ho? I can't stand her.'

Dewint's eyes twinkled. 'I must hadmit, mod ... Harry, I'm not exactly enamoured myself. Would you prefer hit if I settled the matter?'

'Oh, yes. Now then, tell me, what do you think of this pot? I know the rim's a trifle thick, but do you like it?'

'Oh, yes, it's a splendid piece.'

'It's yours ... Right, off you go, I'm going to try and fix my wheel.'

Carrying his strange gift, Dewint returned to the kitchen. Agnes snorted, 'Gawd almighty, night classes, workin' all hours up there an' that's what she's finished up with ... What the hell is it? The lift don't stop at the top floor with that one, I know it, I can tell.'

'It's a large-lipped pot, and, oh, by the way, you are fired.'

Dewint opened accounts with the wine merchants, grocers and butchers, and simply handed the bills over at the end of each month. Edward came to entrust him with more and more of the basic running of the house, and his salary rose along with Edward's trust. He seemed to know instinctively when to remain with Edward for a nightcap and when to leave, and he turned a blind eye to any 'goings-on'. He adored the outrageous dinners, never knowing who would be there. He recognized many of the faces from the television.

Dewint had become a part of their lives, and he felt it particularly keenly one evening when he was laying out Edward's evening clothes. He felt Edward's hand on his shoulder.

'Has Alex, my brother, called at all while I've been out?'

'I have not heard from Mr Alex, sah . . .'

Edward appeared disappointed. 'It's my birthday – the years start moving faster once you pass thirty, don't they?'

'Oh, yes, sah, they do, and may I wish you a very happy birthday.'

Edward checked his appearance in the wardrobe mirror, and Dewint bowed himself out. Edward picked up his white silk scarf and headed downstairs. As he passed the doors to the dining hall, Harriet flung them open, revealing a big birthday cake with candles. On the cake, in bright pink icing, was written, 'Happy Birthday, Edward – 35 Today.' Harriet was dressed in one of her Paris creations, singing, 'Happy Birthday to you . . . Happy Birthday to you – ' at the top of her voice. It took him completely by surprise – he couldn't recall ever telling her when his birthday was – and she dragged him into the room to blow out all the candles. There were gifts, neatly wrapped and tied with bows, and Dewint stood by to open the champagne. Edward looked at his watch, and Harriet picked up the tiny gesture immediately, trying to hide her disappointment. 'Do you have to go wherever it is? Can't you put it off? I thought we'd go out for dinner.'

'Sweetheart, I can't – but I promise not to be late. We can save the presents until I get home, okay?'

She kissed him, and she and Dewint drank his health. It was Dewint's turn to feel sorry for her, she looked so deflated. She had been working for days on the surprise, hiding the gifts, ordering the cake. 'So much for the surprise ... Ah well, cheers ... cheers ...'

Dewint watched her walk slowly upstairs. He knew it wasn't his place, but he couldn't stop himself. 'As you won't be dining out, I've prepared a small chicken, perhaps you would like ...'

She didn't let him finish his invitation, didn't even turn to face him. 'No thanks, I'm not very hungry ...'

Edward had finally made contact with Walter, and they had arranged to meet at Banks. Walter had been very dubious about the meeting, and had cancelled twice, but in the end he went along.

He was very impressed by the club. Edward had reminded him that he was no longer called Stubbs, and not to mention that name. So Barkley was the name Walter asked for at the door, and it certainly made everyone jump.

Walter had changed a lot since university days. He was balding, and his spots had left pockmarks on his face. He still had to wear thick glasses. He nibbled nuts from the dish on the table, checked his watch. Edward was late. A waiter asked him if he had changed his mind, if he would care for a drink, but he refused and asked where the telephone was. The waiter promptly brought one to his table, and he called his wife.

As Edward entered the club and looked over at his table, he had an opportunity to view Walter without his knowing. Edward's usual bottle of Dom Perignon was brought over as he greeted Walter, towering above him.

'Well, well, it's been a long time ... No, don't get up, Walter.'

Having come straight from the office, Walter was still in his dark navy pin-stripe, and he blushed. Edward looked elegant, his suit beautifully tailored, and he was even more handsome than Walter remembered. 'Strange thing, you know, saw some photographs of you once, and I remember thinking how like you this Barkley fellow was. Must congratulate you, place is very chic.' He pronounced it 'chick'.

Edward noticed immediately that the northern accent had

gone, along with the spots and the National Health spectacles.
Walter now sported a pair of fashionable rimless glasses, which
magnified his eyes as his old pair had done, but also made him
look affluent. Walter was no longer nervy, he seemed confident
and his manner was relaxed.

'I should congratulate you, Foreign Office, eh? You're up for
the Minister's replacement, I hear? Aren't you going to join me?'

Again Walter refused a drink, and said he didn't, only mineral water. A glass of iced water was brought, and Edward asked
if his table for dinner was ready, they would eat. Walter murmured that he had really only a few moments as his wife was
expecting him home for dinner.

'Nonsense, you'll eat with me – use the phone, call her, say
you're with an old friend from Cambridge.'

So Walter called his wife again and told her to cancel dinner,
while Edward looked over the evening's menu.

The table in the restaurant was also always reserved for
Edward. Walter was impressed again, this time by the standard
of the cuisine. He was no fool, and kept asking himself why,
after all these years, Edward had suddenly made himself known
again. He found out soon enough, and flushed.

'I want the building contracts for all the areas I've mentioned,
and I know that with a word and a helpful nod from you I can
bypass any other companies, and it goes without saying that you
would benefit from the deal.'

Walter couldn't eat another mouthful. He pushed his plate
away and said Edward must understand that at this stage in his
career he could not afford any scandal to be so much as whispered. 'If I get you in on any other level than a totally
viable . . .'

'Bullshit, Walter, that is exactly why we're having this little
tête-à-tête, because that is precisely what I want and I know you
can do it . . . Now then, you look as if you really need a drink.'

Gulping down the brandy, Walter began to sweat. He knew
what would come next.

'At this stage in your career you can't afford any rumours

about a young woman student who drowned in a boating accident on the Cam.'

Walter wiped his mouth with his napkin, sweating even more. 'You wouldn't bring that up?' But he knew Edward would, and his heart sank. All the years of hard work, and he could see everything suddenly slipping out of his grasp. 'I'm sorry, it's out of the question.'

Edward rose abruptly from the table, tossed his napkin down. He towered over Walter like a giant. 'Fine, so we know where we are. Thank you for coming. I'll put in my bids for the contracts and simply keep my fingers crossed. Goodnight, Walter.'

Walter hurried after him on the pavement. Edward's Rolls had already been brought round, and he was opening the door.

'Can we talk about this, please?'

Edward opened the passenger door, Walter got in, and the car sped off.

They drove straight to the house in Notting Hill Gate, and Walter found himself out of his depth. The women, the flowing champagne ... He made two more calls to his wife in Clapham. By the end of the evening he was thoroughly drunk, and the two blondes looked so like Marilyn Monroe that he was ecstatic.

'Make sure he really enjoys himself, that clear? And this one's on the house, anything he wants, just mark it down.'

Edward let himself into the manor. It was in darkness. He walked quietly into the dining hall where his cake and gifts had been left for him. He looked at his watch – it was after three. Without bothering to open the gifts, he took off his coat and crept up the stairs.

She was awake, he knew, and he slipped his arms around her. 'Sorry.'

'It's always "sorry", isn't it? You ever think how little I see you? And tonight of all nights couldn't you have given me just one evening, just one?'

'I'm sorry, but how was I supposed to know you'd arranged anything?'

'It was supposed to be a surprise, that's why. There's no point in even talking to you – besides, you stink of stale cigars and booze. Have a nice time, did you? Go to your fucking club, did you?'

'Don't swear, I hate you swearing.'

'Oh, well, fuck you and the horse you rode in on. What do you take me for? What am I supposed to do? Sit here and wait? Wait for when you have a spare half-hour you can give me . . .'

'You can do anything you like. I don't ask you to sit waiting, I never have. It's your choice.'

'Oh, fine, fine. Isn't that what a wife's supposed to do?'

'Since when have you played that part?'

She turned over and thumped her pillow. He looked up at the ceiling, the drapes of the canopied bed. He sighed with tiredness, becoming irritated with her. 'I love you, Harry, it's just right now I'm in the middle of negotiations with South Africa. It's a very big deal, and tonight I had a meeting with a man who can open doors there for me.'

Harriet hunched over, further away from him. He rolled over and curled himself around her back, pulling her close. It was a simple gesture, but one she had grown to love, the way he pressed his body against hers.

'You're not going to get round me, I hate you.'

'No, you don't.'

'I fucking do, I'm going to run off with Dewint.'

Edward laughed and kissed her back, massaged her neck. Eventually she rolled over and looked into his face. He kissed her lightly on the nose, and then traced her cheek with his finger. 'You know, maybe we should think about starting a family. You're always talking about me breaking promises, but as I recall a certain young lady gave me a promise in a punt. Four sons – well, don't you think we should start? Neither of us is getting any younger, so I'd settle for two.'

Her body arched, stiffened, and he was shocked when he saw her face change. He was so close, he could see the darkness in her eyes. 'What is it? Harry?'

She was out of bed, pulling a robe around her naked body. 'What do you think this is, a stud farm? Well, screw you, I'll sleep in the spare room.'

Dewint heard the doors banging below. He thought to himself that they were at it again – but they always made it up. He woke, hours later, to the sound of muffled sobbing. He crept to his door – the sobbing was coming from her studio. Obviously they hadn't made it up yet.

Edward breakfasted alone, and didn't even go up to the studio. Dewint knocked and placed a tray outside the door, but it was still there at lunchtime.

Edward spent all morning in his office, mulling over his offer to Walter. It had all been too easy, and Edward waited for some kind of retaliation, but none came. He started on the arrangements for the workforce he would need in South Africa.

Two weeks later, knowing that Walter had returned to the Notting Hill Gate house five times, Edward received a call. Walter said simply that Edward's company had won the contracts for South Africa.

A case of champagne, two dozen red roses and a cheque for two thousand pounds arrived on Walter's doorstep. Edward knew that if the cheque was returned, his plans could go wrong, but he had done his homework. Walter's three children were all at boarding school, he had a mortgage and an overdraft. The cheque was cashed. Edward received no thanks, but he knew he had Walter in his pocket. He donated a lot of money to Walter's political campaign, and for that he did receive a note of thanks.

Edward was in good spirits when he arrived home. Harriet had been sleeping in the spare room, and he was making a special effort tonight to make it up to her. It had not occurred to him to try before, he had been too busy, and as usual the time he chose was the most convenient for himself. He had bought her a bouquet of red roses, bottles of perfume, and theatre tickets. He knew she loved the theatre, and he had tried to cover everything. He whistled as he took his coat off, and Dewint appeared from the kitchen, looking rather sheepish.

'Excuse me, sah, but . . . would you mind if I talk to you very personally? I'm sorry if I am out of line, but I think something must be said.'

Edward beckoned him into the lounge, where a fire blazed in the grate. His whisky and soda stood in readiness.

'Christ, you're not thinking of leaving, are you? I mean, we can't do without you.'

Dewint closed the doors. 'It's Mrs Barkley, sah. She's really not very well, and she's hardly touched a morsel for days. She won't come out of the studio – I think, sah, she should see someone, she needs to see a doctor.'

Edward leapt up the stairs, four at a time, panic written all over his face. He pushed at the locked door, then knocked. He received no reply.

'Harry? Harry, open the door . . . Harry, it's Edward, come on, sweetheart, open the door . . . How long has she been in here?'

'Quite a while, sah. I have the spare key.'

Edward unlocked the door. Dewint stood directly behind him, but he slammed the door in the concerned pixie face. Edward knew instantly something was terribly wrong. Harriet was hunched in a corner, plucking at the skin of her hands. Her eyes were vacant, and her face so pale it frightened him. 'Harry? Harry, what's all this about? Aren't you well? Darling? Harry . . .?'

Her chest heaved in a long, drawn-out sigh. The yellow walls were covered with drawings, like a child's scribble. Her pottery wheel was smashed, and all her misshapen pots were broken. Edward tried to take her hand but she recoiled and covered her head with her arms, pressing herself further and further into the corner. She spat at him, 'Leave me alone, leave me alone.'

'No . . . come on, give me your hand, I'll get you cleaned up.'

'Don't touch me – don't touch me.'

She sprang at him, lashing out at him, screeching at the top of her voice. He pinned her arms to her sides and shook her. 'Harry, for Chrissake what's the matter . . .? Harry?'

Dewint stood in the hall while Edward called for an ambulance.

She would not let Edward near her, but she seemed to accept the gentle cajoling voice of one of the ambulance crew as they helped her down the stairs. Edward shook his head, almost pleading with the ambulance men, 'Oh, Jesus Christ, what's the matter with her? Do you know? What's wrong with her?'

Harriet would not let Edward travel in the ambulance. He watched it drive away, and turned to Dewint for an explanation. He mentioned the pills Mrs Barkley kept in her bedside cabinet, and Edward found them. Pierre Rochal's name was on the label, but when he phoned Paris, he discovered that Pierre was away on holiday.

When Edward arrived at the hospital, he was told that without Harriet's medical records they could not say exactly what was wrong with her at this stage. She was very dehydrated, and in an extremely tense condition. She was under sedation, and until they had obtained her medical history there was nothing anyone could do. They would contact him.

Edward couldn't believe it was happening, just as things were going so well, the company riding high. But only Edward could turn such a sad circumstance to his benefit, however unintentionally. It came about because he contacted Allard Simpson, Harry's brother. Allard lived in a shabby but still genteel area of Kensington. He had hardly changed since the days at Cambridge, apart from looking seedier and being obviously low on funds. It had been twenty years, but might have been a matter of months.

The same old mocking Allard looked Edward up and down. 'My, my, the elusive Mr Barkley, my brother-in-law, no less. Well, to what do I owe this unexpected pleasure? Barkley? Good

God, couldn't you have thought up something with a little more savvy? Do sit down, I'm sure I can find something to wet the whistle.'

Edward's glance took in the threadbare carpet, the dirty ash-trays. Allard lit the gas fire and rummaged through a cupboard, bringing out a bottle of brandy and two misty-looking glasses. 'How's sis? She keeps well out of the family's way, can't say I blame her ... Well, cheers.'

'It's Harriet I've come about.'

'Well, I didn't think you, Mr Celebrity, would be here without a reason. What's she up to?'

Edward hedged, looking for the best way to broach the subject, then thought, 'To hell with it,' and blurted, 'What's the matter with Harriet?'

'Good God, how should I know? I've not seen her since she rushed off to France with that Frog doctor ...' He looked at Edward speculatively, 'Unless ...'

'Unless what?'

'Well, there was a bit of drama, so long ago I can hardly remember it. But, well, she was very dodgy for a time.'

'Dodgy? What do you mean, dodgy?'

'You know she cracked up, the Aunt Sylvia syndrome ... Christ, look, why don't you ask her yourself, or Ma – she knows more about it than I do.'

'Right now she's in no condition to be asked anything. Sylvia? BB's wife? Why did you mention her?'

Allard snorted and wagged a finger at Edward. 'Come on, old chap, don't pull the leg – you know very well, or you should. After all, you cleaned poor Dickie Van der Burge out of his fortune. You know the poor sod's bankrupt? Can't keep him away from the tables, gambling every night. I'm surprised he's not turned up at your posh club with a sledgehammer, he loathes you ... So would I – how much did you get from the old boy? Heard through the grapevine that you made megabucks, that true?'

Edward's mind was in turmoil ... Sylvia? Sylvia syndrome?

He gulped at the brandy as Allard leered at him, swinging one foot with its down-at-heel, scuffed shoe. He laughed, twirling his finger by his temple. 'Sis gone a bit nutty again, has she?'

'Allard, talk straight, or so help me God I'll smash this glass straight into that smirking face of yours.'

Allard backed down fast, poured himself another brandy. 'All I know is, Aunt Sylvia was a bit dotty. Everyone put it down to her losing her two sons. Harriet went the same way after . . . Look, this is her business, you'd better ask her yourself.'

'Why don't you tell me . . .'

Allard did actually have the decency to become serious. He even showed a flicker of emotion when he told Edward about Harriet's baby, about the cot death. Edward felt as if he had been punched in the heart. Allard continued telling him how Harriet had been diagnosed schizophrenic . . . Edward sat back and closed his eyes. 'Jesus Christ . . . was the father the French guy . . . was it . . .?' He swallowed, his mouth dried out, he couldn't even bring himself to say Rochal's name. He was so shocked he didn't ask dates, times, all he could think of was that she had had a child, and the sense of betrayal consumed him, sickened him. Allard continued unaware of the emotional impact of his revelations . . .

'I don't know all the facts, and she would never say who the father was, maybe it was Rochal, doesn't really matter . . . all I know is she went off to some psychiatrist in Switzerland, and he said it was manic depression. That's all I know. I presumed she'd got it all under control – she's in a bad way, is she? She's always been a bit odd, you know up one minute and down the next. Drink? Another drink? Are you all right?'

Edward sat with his head in his hands. He pressed his fingers against his temples, forcing himself, pushing himself towards controlling the explosion burning inside him. 'Yeah, yeah, I'm okay. No more, thanks . . . so tell me, what about you? You follow the Judge? Did you take up law?' Edward was sweating, and relieved as Allard casually discussed his own career. Having failed his exams he was now working for a well-known insurance broker. Edward listened intently, commiserated when Allard bemoaned the fact he had not gone into the theatre as he had always wanted. He heard himself offering Allard a table at the club any night he chose. He was totally back in control. Sharp enough to ask Allard not to mention to anyone his change of name, just in case it worried Harriet. He detected the vicious glimmer in Allard's sly eyes, and reckoned he would delight in stirring things up whether it affected his sister or not. So he talked fast.

'I have a couple of high-risk insurance companies, like to do a little "I'll help you if you help me" racket . . . You must be in a position at your company to know when they are coming in with big profits at the end of the year. I want you to start shoving out high-risk claims on a couple of things – you know, safe, sure ones. There'll be a lot of money in it for you . . . What do you say?'

Allard snorted and said he wasn't in a high enough position to do anything even a trifle dodgy.

'Nothing dodgy in it, old chap. All you've got to do is take a gander at the profits for the forthcoming year, farm out a few high-risk policies in my direction, make yourself a couple of hundred thousand for starters . . . Get yourself a better flat, want to think about it?'

Allard opened the brandy, finished the dregs of it and smiled. 'Christ, I always knew you were a crook . . . Fuck off, I'm not interested, old bean.'

'How's Henry? Hmmmm, old bean?'

Allard laughed, told Edward he could not blackmail him with that – it was common knowledge. 'Even Pa knows my preferences, Eddie, so that angle won't work.'

Edward picked up his coat. Allard surprised him, and he was not, after all, going to be easy to sway. 'Maybe you should have a chat with your old boyfriend.'

Allard sneered. 'You don't seriously think he even talks to me now, do you? Far too important . . .'

Edward put on his coat, then increased the pressure. 'I think he will if you whisper in his ear that I would . . . I would talk to him and a number of other people. It would ruin him, so don't beat about the bush, Allard. Earn yourself a few bob and get a decent pair of shoes. You can't attract much looking the way you do, male or female.'

Allard hated Edward, his Savile Row suit, his still strikingly handsome face. 'You got a card or something so I can contact you?'

Shaking his head, Edward said that he would contact Allard. 'I'll give you five days to think about it.'

Edward had a long talk with the doctors. They were very helpful, assuring Edward that it was nothing more than a temporary relapse. Given time, his wife would be back home and perfectly able to cope with life. She was not an invalid, but he must keep her condition in mind. They put her on tranquillizers, and she was to go into a rest home for a few weeks. They warned him that she would appear drowsy and slightly disorientated. Edward puffed on his cigar, paced the room and eventually blurted out what it was he wanted to know. 'Is this hereditary? She had an aunt who was institutionalized ... It's just that should ... I mean, if she were to have a baby ...'

'Your wife, Mr Barkley, is not schizophrenic. We have all her records here from three different clinics. She has a history of manic depression. It can be inherited, but it is not a foregone conclusion. Her condition can be triggered off by emotional upheavals ... In this case it's very clear that it was caused by the loss of her baby.'

'What was wrong with it?'

'The doctor who delivered the child, a boy, said he was in perfect health. We still have little or no knowledge of why these cot deaths happen, but they are quite common. To your wife it was such an emotional loss that she had a complete nervous breakdown. You will have to be gentle with her, take great care until she feels confident, feels herself again. You must also learn to watch out for the symptoms, never forget that your wife does have this illness.'

'You mean, if I detect anything unusual, this can be avoided?'

'Well, it can most certainly help to prevent her getting to the advanced stage she is in at present.'

'So, what are the symptoms?' The doctor felt as though he were on trial. Edward had such an angry, blunt way of questioning him. 'Well, what do I watch out for?'

'Elation, almost euphoria, with sudden switches to irritability, anger, is the most obvious. If she should appear more active than usual, talking more ... an inflated sense of self-esteem, grandiose ideas ... In some cases ...'

'I don't want to hear about other cases, Doctor, just my wife's.'

'She may very well appear deluded about her identity, need less sleep, be very easily distracted, and over-react to trivial or irrelevant stimuli ... I am, you understand, Mr Barkley, covering all possible symptoms of depression, manic depression.'

'I hear you, Doctor, and I am trying to assimilate it. Is there anything, could there be anything else?'

The doctor smiled. Now he could see the chinks in Mr Barkley's armour – he no longer behaved in such a brusque manner, he actually seemed helpless. 'It's not so bad as it sounds, but tell-tale signs can include sudden shopping sprees, even sexual indiscretions.'

Edward ran his fingers through his hair. He was quieter now, and gave the doctor a half-smile. 'She always was a bit of a handful ... What will be the next move?'

'As soon as she is physically tip-top, I want to put her through a course of psychotherapy. She's had a number of therapists before, but I am not sure at this stage which type of therapy would be most beneficial. Perhaps a group would be best, as she has had a considerable amount of cognitive and behavioural therapy through the years.'

Edward said that there were no financial problems and he wanted the best there was. The doctor rose from his seat and shook Edward's hand. He realized now that the bravado had been a strong cover-up, and Edward was obviously very disturbed and shocked.

'You know, Mr Barkley, a good marriage, a strong marriage in which there is total openness and understanding, is likely to discourage Harriet's depressive states from becoming regular occurrences. External events can trigger a depression, and when this happens, outside help is always advised ... You obviously care; you love your wife a great deal. Perhaps together you can beat it.' He noted the fleeting look of anger cross Edward's face before he gave a charming smile and said it was time to visit Harriet. As he reached the door, still with his back to the doctor, he said, 'I love my wife, guess I'm not the easiest person to live with. But from now on I'll give it a damned good try. Thank you for your time.'

Edward spent a long time sitting outside Harriet's room. He digested everything the doctor had said, and the future seemed daunting to say the least. He couldn't bring himself to face her, to cope with her.

A nurse came out of Harriet's room, carrying a tray. When she saw Edward, she paused and put her head back round the door. 'Oh, your husband's here, Mrs Barkley ... It's all right, Mr Barkley, there was no need to wait. Can I bring you a cup of tea?'

'No ... no thanks.'

He picked up the big bunch of Harriet's favourite flowers, tapped on the door and walked in. She was sitting propped up on pillows, surrounded by so many bouquets of flowers the room was heavy with perfume. She smiled brightly. 'You've overdone the flowers, place looks like a funeral parlour! There's a sweet little Indian girl down the corridor, and I've sent quite a lot of them to her ...'

Edward laid down the flowers almost afraid to look at her. She had that flushed look, her cheeks rosy, hair shining. It had now grown to her shoulders, and she had tied a ribbon around it.

'I didn't notice before how long your hair's grown, looks nice. Dewint's in a terrible state without you to clear up after. He's started polishing everything in sight.' He pulled up a chair and she offered him grapes, oranges – he caught her hand and held it tight. 'It's okay, sweetheart, it's all right . . .'

Her eyes brimmed with tears and she chewed her lip. 'I'm sorry, I'm so sorry . . . have they told you all about me?'

'Yes, no stone unturned. You're going off to a nice place for a rest, then they say you'll be back home as good as new. And, I've got instructions from Dr Wilson on how to be a good husband. I've not tried hard enough, I know it, but I'll make it up to you. We'll go on a holiday together, wherever you like.'

'You know I might get a bit wobbly again, I mean, I'll try not to, but did they tell you?'

'Yes, they did. Dewint and I will keep our beady eyes on you, make sure you're stocked up with pills, all you have to do is get yourself fit and come home fast.'

'You still want me, then?'

'I'm your husband, what the hell do you expect? You've got me under contract, haven't you?'

She smiled, then her eyes drooped, and he held her hand until she fell asleep. She was comforted that he had taken no phone calls while he sat with her, and had not looked at his watch once . . . He leaned forward and kissed her brow, then crept out and closed the door silently behind him. He felt so depressed himself he wanted to weep.

Edward had always made a point of never associating with Jodie's girls. They were for his punters, but tonight he needed someone. He got very drunk, and went up to the rooms with the prettiest and youngest of the girls. Jodie gave strict instructions, this was no ordinary customer . . .

It became a nightly arrangement. He never asked for any particular girl, taking anyone available. But Jodie always made sure he got the very best. He treated the girls with great courtesy, and although he owned the place he tipped them well and sent frequent gifts. They all liked him. He was still a very handsome man, and his prowess in the bedroom made their work a pleasure.

Edward changed his drinking habits. He had never been one to overindulge, but now he started drinking heavily. Many nights Dewint found him passed out in the drawing room, and in the mornings he would be hung-over, often asking for a drink as soon as he awoke. He never brought any of the women home, which was a blessing, but it was Dewint who sent the flowers and gifts on his master's behalf.

Allard took longer than the five days, but he did eventually agree to work for Edward, for cash in hand. As an added incentive, Edward gave him carte blanche membership at Banks, and a special introduction to the house in Notting Hill Gate. He then secured four high-risk policies, and farmed them out to his own insurance companies, two in Panama and one in Brazil. He had still had no word from Alex, and with money pouring in he prepared for a long-overdue visit to South Africa.

The records of his 'hits' remained in a separate file, one that was not to be seen by Alex.

Harriet came out of hospital and moved into a rest home. Edward was a regular visitor, although he never stayed long. He was always attentive, and brought flowers and gifts. There was a growing void between them, and she felt helpless, unable to reach out to him, and blamed herself. Often after these visits she regressed, and her therapist soon connected part of her trouble with her husband. Edward refused when it was suggested that he join Harriet in therapy, feeling that as he was paying vast sums of money they should be able to get his wife straightened out without his assistance. The therapist therefore concentrated on Harriet's relationship with Edward in their sessions. Piece by piece, Harriet imparted snippets of valuable information concerning her emotional ties to her husband, and it became clear that she placed him above everything else in her life.

She showed no marked improvement until she began drama classes. Suddenly she found a release, and a vocation. A month went by, and Dewint visited instead of Edward. Hesitantly, he explained that Edward had gone to South Africa, but would be in touch as soon as he returned. In fact, Edward had not yet left, he was sitting at home by the telephone. He placed a call to Skye Duval and waited. The line was buzzing, there were echoes of different operators. At last he heard Skye's familiar voice. 'Duval speaking, who is it?'

'Hello, buddy boy, I need a meeting with you, we're on, want to start things rolling fast.'

'Okay . . . I'll meet you at the airport, just say when.'

'Don't bother, I'll come to you . . . two days' time.'

Skye replaced the phone and reached for the vodka. Edward had walked back into his life once before. The first time Skye had tried to tell him to go to hell, but he was broke, boozed up and easy for Edward to manipulate, just as easy as it had been all those years ago. He smiled as he recalled the days of Edward's first big scam, and wondered what he would have in mind this time. He knew intuitively that it would be crooked.

Alex began to get edgy. He had been away from London far too long, and was worried that his telexes to Edward had gone unanswered. But he had been enjoying himself so much that he put off his return even longer. The auction of the Hunter Hardyman estate was now imminent.

Barbara showed not the slightest interest in the auction; all she wanted was to be rid of the place, with its reminders of her hated grandfather. Alex was fascinated by the old man's massive wealth. There were, however, many branches of the Hunter Hardyman family, a few of whom he had met and found loud and uncouth in comparison with Barbara.

'I owe that to my mama. She hated him too, and I was educated in the very best school we have to offer, and so were my daughters. But I'm afraid they've inherited some of the worst of the family traits. They both need to go to France or Switzerland to complete their education, what do you think?'

At times she was so innocent, turning to Alex for guidance, but it was often quite obviously calculated. She didn't really need anyone; she had a mind like steel, and yet she could smile so like a child that it touched him. 'You know I was married at sixteen, I really never had any time for myself, with two young daughters and an alcoholic for a husband. Now I want to live, Alex, really live.'

She had tried to steer Alex towards the bedroom, but had never pushed it. She was much too calculating and, although he was attentive, he had never so much as kissed her.

When he told her he had to leave for England in two days, and suggested she and her daughters might like to visit him some time, Barbara bit her lip. It was an invitation, but a very open-ended one. He mentioned no dates. She decided she would have to work even harder on him, she had held off the seduction for too long.

A bottle of champagne, on ice, was waiting for them when they entered his hotel suite. Barbara slipped off her chiffon wrap, trailed it along the floor and murmured that it was dreadfully hot. He opened the balcony windows and turned up the air conditioning, but that was not what she had in mind. She insisted on taking a bath to cool off. She turned on the taps of the vast double bath, trailed her hand in the water and sipped champagne. Alex could see her through the open door, and she knew he was watching. Slowly she took off her diamond necklace and earrings, then even more slowly she untied the chiffon sash at the front of her dress.

Aroused, Alex moved to the bathroom door, watching intently. The dress seemed to slip away from her of its own accord, and she sat naked on the side of the bath. 'Take your clothes off, slowly, Alex, do it really slowly.'

He loosened his tie, pulled it off slowly and dropped it to the floor, then began to unbutton his shirt. She sat, sipping champagne and watching. His initial nervousness dropped away as his shirt did. He unzipped his flies and still she watched, sipping and smiling up at him.

Barbara had found him an intensely attractive man, but now as he stripped in front of her it took all her willpower not to rip his trousers down and go down on him there and then. Her first husband had been a drunk, but a very experienced man, and a kinky one. He had trained his blushing bride well – too well – and his alcoholism had resulted in his sweet, not-so-innocent young wife moving on to fresher fields, taking his carefully taught sexual prowess with her. She had had many lovers, and when she realized she had outgrown her husband, she divorced him on the grounds of his drinking. Now she put all her experience into this one night – she was going to seduce this quiet, handsome Englishman, and what's more he was never going to forget it. It was a gamble, but Barbara never gambled without being very sure she would win.

Alex would have taken her as soon as he was naked, and moved to hold her, but she slipped away from him, the bath forgotten, and walked into the bedroom. In her hands she held a bottle of sun-tan oil from the bathroom ... She smiled and held out her hand to take him to the bed.

'Lie down, lie down ... come on, baby, lie down.'

Alex moaned, hardly able to contain himself, and he lay face down on the bed, clutching the satin cover. Barbara sat astride him and began to oil his shoulders, and he gasped, gritting his teeth ... He was back in jail with Brian, in their cell ... She smoothed the oil over his back, over his shoulders, and was kissing his neck and his ears, all the time her expert hands moving up and down his body. Twice he tried to turn, but she pushed him back, oiled him and smoothed him until her hands reached his buttocks ... She licked at him, she was driving him crazy, and eventually he turned over and pulled her beneath him ... Still she fought him off, kissing his chest and murmuring all the time, soft, lewd words ... 'Beg for me, Alex, beg for me, come on baby, beg for me. Tell me how much you want to fuck me ... Come on, baby, tell me ...'

He wanted to scream, she was sucking him, biting him between his thighs, and he was helpless, her hands were everywhere, smoothing, pulling, oiling ... and then he grabbed at her head, pulled at her hair until she cried out, pushing her face against his thighs, pushed so hard that her teeth cut into his leg . . . and then she put her perfect mouth around his prick . . .

Alex came with a shudder that shook the bed. He put his hands over his face, he didn't want her to see the extent of the pleasure she had given him, but she pulled his arm away . . .

'Now it's your turn . . .'

Alex did not leave the bedroom the next day. They remained together, food was sent in, eaten, and then they were back to screwing again. Alex had never known such pleasure, he made up for all the lost years . . . until even Barbara was exhausted. He never stopped, this Englishman was more than she had ever bargained for . . .

'You're really going to leave me, go back without me? You can't leave your baby, can you? Alex? You can't leave me now, can you?'

He moaned and held her tight, her body slithering in his arms like an eel, and he kissed her. 'I'll take you with me.'

Barbara was determined she would somehow trap Alex into marrying her. Marriage to Barbara had, naturally, crossed Alex's mind, along with the massive fortune that went with it. He certainly found her the most sexually attractive woman he had ever encountered, but then he had not had all that much experience with women.

He lay on the bed and thought about Ming, then his mind wandered back over all the years to Dora. He closed his eyes, let the memories flood through him, and he had a sudden impulse to see Dora again. He reached for the telephone wondering if the operator would be able to trace Dora's husband with just the name Kinnerton. He couldn't remember the man's first name . . . On second thoughts he decided against it. He rolled off the bed and walked into the bathroom, where Barbara was lying in the bubble-filled tub. She flicked water at him, and sat up so he could see her beautiful breasts, the soapsuds around her like a cloud.

'Tell me about your husband, what was he like?'

Barbara blew bubbles at him from her hand, but her eyes narrowed. Why did Alex want to know about her husband?

He sat on the side of the bath and gently soaped her shoulders. She caught his hand and kissed it, kissed each finger, sucking at them, and he bent down to kiss the top of her head. The damp, steamy atmosphere in the bathroom had made small curls form by her ears, and he twisted one around his finger.

'I hated him, Alex.'

'Not at first, surely?'

'Oh no, I was sixteen, and he was very glamorous. He used to ride up to see Daddy, and he was always bringing me little gifts ... But he was thirty-eight, married four times already.'

'So, go on ... you agreed to marry him?'

'Daddy married us – wanted him to oversee some of his oil-fields, and then they had this new pipeline running through Alaska or something, I don't know. But it was more of a business deal. Contracts were exchanged.'

Alex looked at his nails. 'And? Go on.'

Barbara was desperately calculating how much she should tell Alex about this part of her life. She remained silent, flicking at the soap bubbles with a fingernail. She had trailed after her first husband, panting after him like a chubby puppy. She had been as overweight as her daughter Selina, and so besotted with this handsome, debonair man that she had persuaded her father to somehow arrange that he marry her. At first her father had refused, but at the thought of how much business he could acquire by joining the two together he changed his mind and pressured Joe Taverner to marry his plump, spoiled brat of a daughter. Taverner had accepted the deal, and Barbara.

He had never let her live it down. In the first year of their marriage he tormented her, forcing her to beg to be taken into his bed. He found his young bride only too eager to act out his fantasies. She became a slave girl, a mute, a willing partner in every sexual game he could devise. For the first three years she lived with him, tied to his bed in chains, whipped in the stables, dressed in kinky leather costumes made to his own designs. He turned away from his many mistresses – his wife had supplanted them. She balked at nothing, and took him to such a sexual peak that his obsession inverted itself. He became the slave, the mute, and her fertile young brain devised many more perverted games – he became the one bound to the bed, tied up in the cellar, now he was the one to crawl and beg for her favours.

Taverner had always been a hard drinker, and with a wife whose energy was directed into nothing but sexual gratification, he spent more and more time at their ranch, drinking. Two daughters were born, and immediately handed over to nannies and nursemaids. The games began again as soon after the births as possible. Then Taverner made the mistake of introducing third parties. At first it was other women, but when Barbara had tired of that, he brought home men of all shapes, colours and sizes – paying them to screw his wife.

By the time she was twenty-one, Barbara had had more lovers than most women would have in three lifetimes. She tormented her husband with them and drove him to distraction. Her puppy fat had disappeared and, as though emerging from a chrysalis, she had been transformed into a stunningly beautiful woman, insatiable and obsessive in her desires.

Taverner lost control of his drinking and wrecked his business. Rumours of his wife's behaviour were spreading – she was becoming notorious, not only for her sexual perversions but for her outrageous spending sprees. Having always had plenty of money, she had never known a moment when she could not have whatever she wanted when she wanted it. She threw parties, bought speedboats, yachts, racehorses, even a plane, and grew bored with them almost before the ink had dried on the cheques. Taverner, sodden with drink and broke, was cast aside. Barbara's father threatened to cut her off unless she behaved herself, so she controlled her urges and limited herself to one man at a time in the privacy of her own home.

And this was what was lying in Alex Barkley's bathtub, this beautiful sophisticated woman was more of a whore than any of

Dora's girls – even Dora herself. Barbara Taverner was a slut in thousand–dollar dresses with a billionaire's daughter tag around her neck. The veiled looks that Alex had detected from Dallas society and presumed were envy, really meant 'sucker'. They knew all about her, and they pitied him.

'My husband, Alex, wasn't a very nice man. He would subject me to horrible things, tie me up and beat me . . . It was terrible because I was so young, I had no one to turn to, no one. My father wouldn't listen, and then when Joe got so drunk, so drunk he couldn't screw me himself . . . Oh I can't, I can't tell you . . . I am so ashamed . . .' Tears rolled down her perfect cheeks . . . 'I hated him so much, and I could do nothing . . . Now you know, I am so ashamed, oh God, he beat me, and . . . Alex . . .' She turned her tear-stained face to him, held out her arms. 'Sometimes he even made me enjoy it. Help me, oh, don't leave me, I need you, Alex, I would die if you left me . . . You're every-thing he wasn't. I trust you, I trust you so much, and you have made me respect myself again, when I never thought I could.'

He knelt and took her in his arms. She seemed so childlike, so desperately lonely. He kissed her forehead, her cheeks, her lips. Barbara knew it was now or never, and she clung to him, held him tight. She became girlish and coy, nuzzling his neck, giggling. 'I would be such a good wife to you, Alex, entertain-ing – and something I've always wanted is to be part of English society, you know, mix with the titles and meet everyone. I'd be such a good wife, I would – do you mind me being so rich? Is that what troubles you? But it mustn't – think, darling, oh think what we can do together, what we can accomplish . . .'

She climbed out of the bath and danced around the room, putting on a plummy English accent, bowing and curtseying, then knelt at his feet and looked up into his handsome face. 'I love you, Alex, I love you so much. Whatever you want I want, I love you.'

Alex hugged her tight and said over and over again that he loved her too. He had never spoken those words to anyone in his life before, and it was as if she had opened a floodgate inside him. Taking her by the hand he dragged her into the bedroom, opened a bottle of champagne and poured them each a glass. 'Will you be my wife?'

She wept, flinging her arms around him, shouting over and over, 'Yes! Yes! Yessss ...'

Skye Duval discovered just what Edward wanted him to do. Even if he wanted to, he couldn't back out.

'See, old chap, I need someone here I can trust, someone who will keep their mouth shut and run the business this side. You'll have a lot of money passing through your hands, and as I said, I need someone I can trust.'

Skye shrugged. 'I don't have much choice, do I? Hey, listen, I'm not arguing, I need the bread ... but there's got to be something more in it for me than cash, I want my papers back.'

Edward gave his word, he would return them, even if Skye didn't agree to do the business. Skye laughed, he had to hand it to his old buddy boy, he could still lie better than anyone he had ever known. Skye knew he was caught in Edward's web, Edward could eat him alive if he wanted to. 'Okay, you're on ... make me a rich man again, eh?'

Edward held Skye's shoulders. 'Yes, but keep off the booze. You foul it up and I'll kill you.'

Skye laughed again and told Edward he would have a hard time – he had been dead for years. Edward then took him completely off guard, held him in his arms, like a caress. 'I need you, buddy boy, don't let me down.'

Skye's voice was barely audible as he gazed up into the strange, dark eyes. 'You know I won't, you're all I've got, even though you're an incorrigible bastard.'

Edward began to tell Skye of his plans for buying up vast areas of land for mining perlite.

When Edward returned to London, he was angry that Alex had still not returned. He responded to Alex's many telexes by telling him to 'get his arse back to London'.

Dewint noticed how unkempt Edward looked, and he was drinking more heavily than ever. He did not ask after Harriet, and made no effort to visit her. He prowled moodily around the manor, eventually giving Dewint instructions to have the studio repainted. Looking at the bright-yellow walls, he said, 'It's enough to drive anyone nuts. Get it cleaned up.'

'Yes, sir . . . do you have any particular colour in mind, or will you be asking Mrs Barkley when you see her?'

Without replying, Edward walked out. Dewint watched him drive off far too fast, clipping the gatepost. He decided to paint the studio a pale lemon, he was sure Harriet would like that.

Edward tried hard not to think about Harriet's eventual return. He felt guilty about the thoughts that kept creeping into his mind. He wanted an heir, a son, and it was obvious to him now that Harriet would never have a child. Harriet's love had always made him feel good – her almost innocent attitude to sex meant that it was always he who made the first move. It was this innocence that had always attracted him to her. Having had a surfeit of sexual experience in his youth, he had not given it a great deal of importance in later years. But now, the girls in the Notting Hill Gate house had whetted his appetite, brought desire to the surface again. Now he made up for lost time. Harriet seemed like a ghost from the past, and one he was seriously considering consigning to the past. He was not sure how he should go about it given her precarious mental state.

The last person in the world Edward wanted to see was Richard Van der Burge. One of the staff informed him that Richard was trying to get into the club, and had mentioned Edward's name. Edward excused himself from his table, leaving the attractive Brigitte Bardot look-alike pouting. He strolled out to meet Richard.

Richard looked terrible, down-at-heel and as scruffy as Skye. He was shaking, and his fingers were badly stained with nicotine.

'So, Richard, how's life?'

Richard shrugged and smiled nervously, and lit yet another cigarette.

'You still work for De Veer's?'

After inhaling deeply on his cigarette, Richard replied, 'No, no I don't . . . Not working at present. Had a bit of trouble, you know, chaps kept getting promoted over my head. Got difficult, so I walked.'

'You all right for cash? You know, if you need tiding over while you're out of work?'

Richard asked for ten thousand and, without batting an eyelid, Edward wrote out a cheque. Then he offered Richard a job in the insurance office. He suggested quite a high salary, more than he had intended. 'It'll be old pals' time – you see, you'll be working with Allard Simpson.'

'Oh, that's fantastic . . .'

'Yes, that's the good part . . . the bad part is that you'll be in South Africa.'

Richard agreed, and with a hesitant look in the direction of the gaming rooms he left to pack his bags. He didn't thank Edward for the cheque, believing that he was owed more than a meagre ten thousand, much more – and he intended to get it.

Edward drank heavily for the rest of the evening, embarrassing his beautiful escort so much she left the club in floods of tears. Too drunk to drive himself home, he took a taxi.

Dewint wondered what Harriet was up to. He had been surprised to see her home, and knew Edward was not expecting her. He gave a silent prayer he would not return with a woman. His initial nervousness was dispelled within moments of her arrival. She kept him in such a state of laughter as she mimicked the doctors and patients, he was exhausted. She firmly instructed him to retire to his pigeon loft and she would wait up for Edward.

As the hours ticked away and Edward did not return she

grew more nervous. She rehearsed what she would say to him, holding his photograph in front of her and altering her script as often as she changed her clothes. She eventually got into bed, curling up in her thick nightdress. He wasn't going to come home and she couldn't really blame him.

Edward managed to open the door. The hall was in darkness and he bellowed for Dewint. She peered at him through the banisters. 'It's his night off, will I do?'

Edward stumbled to the stairs, then patted the wall searching for the light switch. He muttered drunkenly about his intentions to visit her. He couldn't look her in the face, but tried to apologize for his lateness.

'It's all right, I understand – business ... you want a hand?'

Even though he leaned against her as she helped him up the stairs, he could not look into her face. He fell across the bed face down.

'Right, I'll start with the shoes and work upwards ...' She tossed each shoe into a corner of the room, happy to have something to do for him. He rolled over and leaned on his elbow. His face was flushed. Their eyes met and he looked away embarrassed not knowing what to say to her. There was an awful silence, a helplessness to them both. He loosened his tie. 'You look good, is that a suntan? Where've you been then?'

'I've been using a sun lamp, and I've put on weight, lean forward and I'll get your shirt off.'

She began to undo the buttons, slowly moving closer, touching him. Her hands were shaking. He wrapped his arms around her waist burying his head against her. His voice was muffled, 'You all right?'

She stroked his head. 'Yes, I'm all right, my love.'

His grip tightened around her. 'I've missed you, missed this bloody flannelette nightgown ... Oh God, Harry, Harry, I've missed you, this place is a morgue without you.' Slowly he lifted his head, and looked into her eyes. He was drunk enough to be honest, to be open about the way he felt and his vulnerability touched her. 'Christ I'll take care of you, you're never going away again . . .'

She rocked him in her arms . . . 'I'm home now, I'm home now.'

There was no void, no shyness between them.

Later, when she lay next to him, he reached out in his sleep and pulled her close, the way he always had. She closed her eyes. She could feel his powerful body and pressed her backbone against him, surrounded by him, curled against him. Now she was home.

Feeling buoyant, Edward whistled as he entered his office. Miss Henderson handed him a cable, and he started to laugh as he read it. He ordered her to get his wife on the telephone. It was only nine o'clock but he poured himself a brandy.

The intercom buzzed and he picked up the phone. 'Harry, hey guess what? Alex, the sly son of a bitch, has got himself married . . . married! Alex! Just sent me a telegram. Doesn't say who the hell to, how about that? You want to go to the theatre tonight? Okay, pop into the office . . . See you later.'

Replacing the phone, Harriet gave it a loving little pat. It was a start – Edward had begun asking her to meet him at the office and taking her out to lunch. She called to Dewint that Alex had got married. He had never met Alex, so he wouldn't know him if he fell over him, but he said all the right things.

Dewint was delighted to have Harriet back, looking so well and obviously happy. She had adored the pale lemon of her studio, and had set about reorganizing all the furniture.

'You know, Norman, when I was away, one of the things we used to do was act out dramas. I just loved it, and I am going to start taking drama classes, what do you think?'

At one stage in his life, Norman Dewint had been a 'hoofer' – not that he would ever have mentioned the fact unless asked, and it was something he left off his curriculum vitae. Now he did a quickstep down the stairs, ending with a flourish.

'Mrs Barkley, I can think of no one who'd be better on stage.'

'Why, Norman, you're very light on your feet – how did you do that step?'

Dewint flushed with pleasure. 'I used to be able to tap dance, it's all to do with relaxation. It's a very simple, old-time step used by Fred Astaire – one, two, three, side-step, side-step, bend and twist . . .'

Harriet applauded, then persuaded Dewint to teach her more in the dining hall. They pushed back the table and rolled the rugs aside, leaving the wooden boards bare.

'Right, you be Fred and I'll be Ginger . . . Oh, music, we must have music . . .' She burst into song, 'I could have danced all night, I could have danced all night, and still have begged for more . . .'

Dewint watched her dancing up the stairs. The whole house had come alive again. Everything was back to normal.

Alex, with his new wife, met her battery of lawyers and legal advisers. Only then did he realize the magnitude of the fortune that came attached to his wife. Barbara was as uninterested in her financial powers as only an incredibly rich, spoiled woman could be. She daydreamed of being introduced to society and of becoming a famous socialite.

Alex flew to New York, leaving Barbara to make the arrangements for herself and her two daughters to travel to England. He knew he should have contacted Ming, explained to her, but it had all happened so fast, and he was unsure how she would take it.

Ming was not in her Manhattan apartment or her office. He was told she would be 'on site' at, of all places, his wife's new penthouse. Alex bought a ridiculously ornate bouquet of roses and arrived at what was to be his own apartment.

Ming was standing at the window, holding up pages of a large pattern book. She looked up at Alex and smiled. 'Good heavens, you look wonderful! I have called London so many times to speak to you – where on earth have you been?'

Alex handed her the roses and she gathered them in her arms, buried her face deep in the flowers. 'Oh, they smell delicious . . . now, come and see what I've done to this place, it will be magnificent.'

Alex didn't know how to tell her. She was so excited, leading him from room to room, and as always he was impressed with her taste and her innovative designs. She led him into the master bedroom. 'See, I have made everything in different, just slightly different, shades of pink . . . I don't think it looks too bad, more than likely she will hate it, her type always do. She'll want gilt mirrors and hideous gold angels . . . Alex? Is something wrong?'

Alex sat on the oyster-pink satin bedspread. He ran his hand along the cover, then gestured for Ming to come to him. She slipped into his arms as she always did, curled up on his lap.

'I got married, in Nevada last week, I married Barbara.'

As quickly as she had moved to him, Ming slid away, turning her back to him. She was rigid, but her hands fluttered slightly, like birds' wings. 'Well, she is very rich . . . I am making over a million dollars from this commission alone . . . Then I will have more, because of her daughters' apartments.'

'She won't be living here, I am taking her and her daughters back to live with me in England.'

Still Ming remained with her back to him. 'I see . . . does that mean you and I . . . What about us?'

Alex moved closer to her, wanting to hold her in his arms.

'I love her, there will be no more of you and me. I still want to be friends with you, of course I do . . . I still want to see you.'

She turned on him, her eyes like a Siamese cat's, narrowed into slits. 'Oh, that will be nice! Well, thank you for telling me, now if you will excuse me . . .'

'Ming, please . . .'

'You know, if you had said "I have married her because of her millions" I could understand, really, I would understand that, but love . . . You love her? She's tasteless, she's cheap, she's coarse, the only thing that smells sweet about her is her money . . .'

Alex bowed his head. He didn't argue, he didn't want to, he

knew he had hurt her and he felt guilty. 'I'm sorry, Ming, but ...
I love her.'

She laughed and walked to the door. When she reached it,
she turned to face him. 'You don't know the meaning of the
word, but you have what you deserve. I am sorry for you, she's
notorious, did you know that? You see, I have a number of
other clients now, courtesy of your new wife, and none of them
could wait to tell me ... You've married a whore.'

Alex's temper snapped. 'I don't think you have any right to
bring that up, you of all people.'

Ming's voice was icy. 'I slept with men because I needed to
eat, I was poor. She pays for her men, she buys them! Look at
you – how much is she paying for you, Alex? And does she
know about you? Does she know what you are?'

Alex hit her, hard, so hard that she slammed into the edge of
the door. She rubbed her shoulder. 'Get out ... please, leave me
alone, I never want to see you again.'

Alex left the apartment. He felt sick at the way he had struck
out at her, guilty, hating himself. He stepped out of the lift fifteen floors below and Ming watched him from the penthouse
window as he hailed a taxi. She would make him pay, she hated
him now as much as she did Edward. She knew their secret, and
if they didn't let her buy her shares back, buy them both out of
the business, she would make damned sure they would be
sorry ... Alex and Edward Stubbs, socialites – she wondered
how popular they would both be with the English aristocracy if
it were known that Edward had murdered their father, that they
came from East End slums. She laughed softly – she would plan
carefully, let them climb the ladder just that little bit higher ...
The higher they were the further they would fall, and she would
make them fall so hard that neither of them would get up again.

Ming straightened the bedspread. The roses lay on the floor
where they had fallen. She bent and picked them up, trying so
hard not to cry, but her mouth quivered, and she sobbed. She
had pushed Alex into Barbara Taverner's arms, and her anger at
her own foolishness dried her tears. She tore each rose from its

stem and hurled it across the room. She had come cheap – what a pay-off, a damned bunch of roses, pink roses.

With his new family, Alex returned to England a week before Kennedy was assassinated. Their arrival went unnoticed except for a small paragraph in one of the gossip columns stating that Alex Barkley and Texan billionairess Barbara Taverner of the Hunter Hardyman fortune had married.

Book Five

Chapter Twenty-One

Alex breezed into the office, was congratulated on his marriage by all the staff, and walked straight into Edward's office. The door was closed, and Alex tried to open it, infuriated that it was always kept locked. Miss Henderson appeared.

'My brother not in today?'

'I'm sorry sir, he left two days ago.'

'Do you know where he's gone?'

'I'm sorry, sir . . . shall I bring the mail into your office now?'

Alex's initial good spirits deflated, and he gave her a brief nod. He had expected Edward to have left at least a note, perhaps even shown some interest in his marriage, his wife, but there was nothing. He sat down and began to sift through the backlog of work that had piled up in his absence. Everything seemed in reasonable order. He began to flick through the night-club accounts, then sat back and let out a long, hissing breath. As Edward had predicted, it was a gold mine, money was pouring in, and Alex knew he would have his work cut out moving it around. He would have to work fast before they were crippled by taxes.

Edward had indeed cut and run, after an emergency call from Skye Duval. Richard Van der Burge was causing trouble and needed to be removed from South Africa. He was bad-mouthing

Edward, and the last thing Skye wanted was the slightest whisper getting out about the nasty situation he and Edward had been involved in with Julia. Edward had literally dropped everything and caught the next flight out. Miss Henderson rang Harriet and told her not to expect Edward home for a few days.

Harriet had given Dewint the night off, as she and Edward had planned to go to the theatre. She had been to the hairdressers and the beauty parlour, and her new evening gown had cost a fortune. She was about to take the dress off again, thinking of the waste of the two tickets, when she remembered Dewint. She climbed the stairs to the attic where he had his room and opened the door.

Dewint was sitting at his small dressing table in full make-up, looking rather like Joan Crawford. He was wearing a dark-red satin dress, high heels and long sleeves. He froze, clenched his gloved hands, and his body shook with nerves at being caught out. Harriet took in the bizarre situation in a moment. She tilted her head to one side, saying, 'Sorry, I should have knocked.'

Dewint stuttered apologies. His terrible shame was pitiful, he was close to tears. 'I only ever do this in my time off, really . . . I cannot say how sorry I am . . . Oh, God.' The pixie face crumpled, and he wept into his gloved hands.

Harriet stood close behind him and patted his powdered shoulder. 'This is your domain, Norman, you can do what the hell you like.'

She was gone before Dewint could say another word. Picking up a large pot of Pond's Cold Cream, he began to smother his face, then he realized he'd not taken off his gloves and burst into tears.

Harriet decided to watch TV. She sat in full evening dress and tuned in to *Dr Kildare*. The show had her groping for a tissue as it was all about a poor crippled girl who wanted a famous movie star's autograph. The young girl was dying, but the movie star refused point-blank even to see her, being too involved in her own drama ... Harriet gasped, it was Joan Crawford ... she ran to the stairs and shouted at the top of her voice for Dewint.

'Oh, quick, quick, she's on TV. Joan, your idol ... hurry or you'll miss it.' Dewint scurried down the stairs. As he entered the lounge, the programme had been interrupted by the announcement that President Kennedy had been assassinated. They stood side by side in stunned silence. They spent the evening together waiting for the news flashes ... eventually the 'National Anthem' played and she turned off the television with a sigh. Dewint blew his nose for the umpteenth time. 'Oh Mrs Barkley, what a shockin' thing, what a shockin' thing to have happened. A man like that cut down in his prime ...'

She continued to stare at the blank TV screen. Her face was concentrating, frowning. After a moment, she said to him, 'You and I have just witnessed a modern-day tragedy ... but it's strange, when you turn that little square box off, it sucks it all back in. As if it weren't real. Tragedy is personal, it clings, holds on to you, stays inside you and you can't turn it off ... it won't go away. I wish I had a small switch at the side of my head. I think I'll take myself off to bed now, goodnight Norman.'

Dewint locked up the house. As he passed the master bedroom, he heard her crying ... the sound was eerie, and he hoped Edward would come home soon.

Edward found Richard Van der Burge in his bungalow. He was sitting staring at the wall. His suit was sweat-stained and his shirt grimy. The room stank of his body odour, dirty socks and discarded clothes. Edward closed the door quietly and chucked the key on the dressing table. 'I thought Skye Duval was a bum, but you – look at you! What are you trying to prove, that you can drink this place dry?'

'Ahhhh, so fucking what? Way I hear it, you've been trying hard enough ... Well, join the AA, Eddie, that's the "All-time Arseholes". Trouble is, we're not too anonymous, haw, haw,

haw. Christ, what did you make me come back to this place for, man? That bloody fairy you've got working for you is a fucking nutcase, plays ruddy music all day, all night. He tell you I flew out to Pretoria? Yesss, bastard spat at me. That's what you did, Eddie, you did that!'

'Here's five grand – take it and get the hell out of here.'

'Fuck your five grand, Stubbs . . . You brought me out here, an' now you'd better cough up if you want me swept under the carpet. Maybe you'd like to blow me up in one of Dad's defunct mines . . . You're not just a thief, oh no – I've been checking up on you and that poofter.'

Edward knew they had to get rid of Richard fast. He walked out to the waiting car and sat with Skye.

As he drove, Skye kept an eye on Edward. His hair had grown longer and he was fatter, but he was still the most handsome man Skye had ever known.

Edward was miles away. He remembered now, the mine where BB's sons had died . . . He also recalled Sylvia and BB sitting puffing on a Havana, telling Edward to be sure and marry a strong woman. God, what a joke! The Sylvia syndrome had come full circle.

Skye was still talking. 'Dickie's been ostracized, they won't allow him into any of the clubs. Memories out here are long. He's pretty objectionable anyway, a real prat.'

Edward leaned back and closed his eyes. 'We've got to get him off our backs, Skye. He said he'd been doing some checking up, don't want him to get wind of that little incident with Julia, could be very nasty.' He sucked in his breath.

Skye leaned casually across Edward and opened the glove compartment as they sped along. He was still a showman, and made no attempt to remove the .38. He knew Edward could see it. He snapped the compartment closed.

'No, Skye, it's got to be more subtle, and we mustn't be involved. Can't you set him up? Right now I don't want anything to interfere in our business stakes, things are just coming together. Perhaps . . . if it were known he had some cash on him,

known to a few of your friends, they might do the job for us –
you with me?'

'Loud and clear, brother – loud and clear.'

Alex led Barbara up the steps of the manor house and rang the
bell, shading his eyes to look through the glass panels of the
door. Barbara was dressed in a white Courrèges outfit with
matching white boots. She was still tanned, and her blonde hair
fell in a straight, silky sheet to her shoulders. Alex stepped back
and looked up at the windows.

'There's lights on – can you see anyone?'

Dewint inched the door open.

'Is Mrs Barkley at home? Would you tell her it's Mr and
Mrs . . . Harry? Harry, that you?'

Harriet yelped, ran straight into Alex's arms and hugged him
close. He introduced Barbara, but Harriet gave her only a cursory glance and led them into the sitting room, sending Dewint
scuttling down the dark passage towards the kitchen. Papers littered the room, piles of books were strewn on the floor.

Harriet took hold of Alex's hand excitedly. 'I've started drama
classes, and I'm trying to get an audition prepared. Dewint is
absolutely marvellous, he goes over all my lines.' She bit her lip
and pulled Alex close, whispering, 'Can I talk to you, it's important . . . Would you mind, Barbara, I just want to show Alex
something?'

Alex gave Barbara a small smile and followed Harriet out into
the hall. Left alone, Barbara surveyed the mess – this was not
what she'd expected. She picked her way across the room to
look at the photographs on the mantelpiece among the many
invitations. One small photo caught her eye, of Alex, Harriet
and Edward together. She recognized the château, but she was
more interested in Edward, thinking what a handsome man he
was. She wondered why he had married such a strange-looking
creature. There was a slight cough behind her, and she turned
as Dewint carried in champagne and chilled glasses on a tray.

Harriet was huddled with Alex in a corner of the hall. She

asked him over and over where Edward was and how long he would be away. Alex couldn't give her any information on where his brother was. Eventually he insisted they return to Barbara. As he turned to walk away, Harriet caught his hand again.

'Have you been told about me? Has anyone said anything about me?'

'No, I've only recently got back to England. To be quite honest, I did think perhaps you might have called to invite us over, to meet Barbara and her daughters . . . Has he not been in touch?'

'No, he just upped and left as usual . . . Is there someone else? You would know, is there someone else, Alex?'

'Harry, I don't know anything, really I don't. Come in and sit with us, come along, we're being very rude.'

Harriet moved past Alex and threw open the sitting-room door. She smiled, charm itself, and offered champagne, suggested they stay to dinner. Barbara had never met anyone quite like her, and was not sure how she should deal with the situation. Harriet's main topic of conversation was the plays she had been to see, and the performances of actors Barbara had never heard of. At one point she flushed with embarrassment, and Harriet guffawed. 'What? John Gielgud? You've never heard of him? But he's a knight, he's one of the most famous actors in England! Laurence Olivier, now you must know him, don't they have theatres in Texas? Where did you find her, Alex? What about Paul Scofield?'

Harriet launched into a detailed, scene-by-scene account of a production of *Romeo and Juliet* she had seen at the Old Vic. Alex received a frigid look from Barbara to get her out fast. He made excuses while Harriet continued to describe the costumes and the direction all the way to the front door. As they walked down the steps they heard her shouting to Dewint, 'She's never heard of Sir John Gielgud, can you imagine it?'

Barbara was furious. She sat, tight-lipped, in the back of the car, refusing to sit in the front with Alex.

'She was just so damned rude, whatever excuses you want to make for her. I won't be going back there, that's for sure. No wonder your brother's done a disappearing act, with that at home, who wouldn't?'

Harriet licked her lips and began the balcony scene for the third time, Dewint reading Romeo's lines. When the phone rang halfway through, she snatched it up, hoping it would be Edward. 'Hello . . . oh it's you.' She pulled a face to Dewint, 'It's Allard.' She sat on the edge of the sofa swinging her legs. 'Well, what do you want, you old shirt-lifter? What . . .? Oh, but that's terrible.'

As she continued the call Dewint gestured to see if she wished him to leave the room. She shook her head and placed her hand over the mouthpiece. 'It's about Dickie, my cousin, he's dead.' Yet she didn't seem particularly disturbed by the news, in fact quite the reverse. She replaced the receiver. 'Well that's the end of the line for the Van der Burges, killed in a hit and run accident. Surprised he was standing up long enough to be knocked over by anything, dreadful boozer . . . but it gives me a jolly good excuse, so start packing, Romeo, and I'll call the dreaded Miss Henderson to arrange my flight . . . I'll give Edward the shock of his life. Oh, pack something black for the funeral.'

Dewint gathered up the pages of their script as she danced into the hall, singing at the top of her voice. Dewint called up to her, 'Will your black woollen coat and matching dress suffice, Mrs Barkley?'

She grinned back to him. 'Good heavens, no. Something cotton, I'm going to South Africa.'

Dewint almost dropped the papers. 'South Africa? But don't you think you should contact someone first? What if you arrive and the funeral's over?'

She winked, 'I'm not really going for that, it's just a marvellous excuse to surprise Edward. Let's get cracking, it's going to be a hard job finding my passport.'

*

Dewint tapped on the bedroom door, a suitcase already wiped down and ready to pack. She was standing with her back to him, staring out of the window. She had been crying, but waved for him to come in and wiped her face with the back of her hand. 'Just thinking about poor Dickie, I really should have tried to see him, but I never got around to it. We used to have such fun when we were kids, up at the old Hall. I loved that place, keep meaning to go there, but I never do . . . I don't even call Ma and Pa, I suppose I should let them know about Dickie, not that they cared a hoot for him, but he was family after all.'

Dewint began selecting clothes, holding them up for her approval, as she searched the desk drawer for the telephone code for Yorkshire. 'Ahhh, we need look no further, my passport's here.' She tossed it to Dewint and as it fell open he could see her photograph. 'It's a real shocker, isn't it, I couldn't keep my face straight, that's why I look so fierce.' Dewint carefully placed the passport to one side and continued packing.

Harriet dialled, swore under her breath and dialled again. She cupped the mouthpiece under her chin carrying the base to the wardrobe to inspect her clothes. She peered in, pointing to a black hat as her call was put through. 'Ma? It's me, Harry . . . Harry.' She rolled her eyes, and slumped on to the bed, as her mother obviously gave her a lecture about how she never contacted them. She held the mouthpiece up for Dewint to hear, and then interrupted Mrs Simpson. 'Ma, I don't have much time, I'm going to South Africa . . . South Africa, it's Dickie, he's dead . . . All right, I'll start again, Richard van der Burge, your nephew, BB's son, has been killed, in a hit and run accident . . . I don't know any facts, just what I've told you, and what Allard . . . Allard, have you gone deaf?'

The call continued for another ten minutes, and then she lay back and let the phone drop from her hand on to the bed. 'I feel terrible, she's as deaf as a post, and Pa's still got something wrong with his prostate. He's sold all the horses . . . poor Pa, how he loved hunting . . . we all did.' She carried the phone back to the bedside table and walked out of the room.

Dewint saw her standing in the garden. She had her arms wrapped around an oak tree, her face pressed against it. He made a pot of tea, constantly looking into the garden from the back door and still she remained holding the tree. It was getting dark. She had made no arrangements for her ticket. He knew Miss Henderson would have left the office and he was relieved. Dewint didn't think it a good idea to surprise Edward. If he behaved away from home as he had done when his wife was in the clinic it would be Harriet, not Edward, who would be in for the surprise.

Harriet eventually came to the kitchen door. Her face was pale, and she shivered with the cold. 'It's funny, isn't it, how episodes of your life suddenly come back to you?' She poured herself a mug of tea and heaped in three teaspoonfuls of sugar. 'We'd all been hunting, Pa was furious with me, I took a fence badly, spent all night in the stable, but I knew it was hopeless, just as I knew it had been entirely my fault. Just as I know, deep down, I know it was my fault he died.'

Dewint presumed she was referring to her horse, he had no idea she was talking about her baby. She gulped at the hot tea, and her hands shook. 'I kept riding, you see, I loved to ride so much. Early morning, when the grass is wet, everything's clean and fresh, and they come out of the stables, snorting, pawing the ground and they want to run free. Up you get, and you have to hold them in, hold them tight, then you let go, and you feel that surge of power as they are released, the sound ... ba-ba-ba-boom-ba-ba-boom.' The tea spilt as she punched the air with the mug. Dewint could not take his eyes from her. She was so alive, her cheeks flooded with colour and her eyes sparkled. She slapped the draining board, making the sound of running hooves ... 'All that energy, Norman, all that life and ...' She spun round holding her arm out straight, her fingers shaped to form a gun. 'I killed him ... BANG.'

Dewint's hands flew to his cheeks, gasping like an old woman. 'Oh Mrs Barkley you didn't ... you didn't, God help me if I ever break my leg.'

Just as that energy had flooded through her, he saw it drain away. Her whole body sagged, and she said she would lie down for a while. He followed her into the hall, watched her move slowly, heavily up the stairs. 'What shall I do about South Africa, Mrs Barkley?'

She paused, seemed confused. 'South Africa . . .? Oh yes, well I suppose you'd better arrange my ticket, you sort everything out that's necessary, don't want to talk now, can't talk now.' Dewint hovered at the foot of the stairs.

'Are you sure you still want to go?'

He saw her hands clench and she snapped, 'I need to see my husband, I want to see Edward. Now leave me alone.'

Edward lay beside the swimming pool, his body oiled and relaxed. He was tanned to a deep, dark brown, and his hair had grown even longer. He was smiling because the joint Skye Duval had presented to him was taking effect. Skye had harvested his own illegal crop from seeds brought in by one of his men. The grass was very strong, and Edward felt as if his head were opening up, his body drifting on a cloud.

Swimming length after length of the pool was Skye Duval. Eventually he swam to the side and hauled himself out. He was naked, and a young houseboy threw him a towel. Skye flopped down on to the sunbed next to Edward and took the joint. He drew heavily on it, letting the smoke drift from his nostrils, moaning softly. He rolled on to his stomach. 'This is the life, eh? Sometimes this place isn't so bad.'

Edward picked up the newspaper, the English *Times*, and tossed it to Skye. He stretched, yawning. 'I put an obituary in for Dickie, felt I owed it to BB.'

'That was very decent of you. I'm sure the old boy wouldn't have given a bugger.'

Edward laughed, took the joint back for a last drag before stubbing it out. 'He couldn't have timed it better. What beats me is what he was doing in that section of town, he must have been out of his mind.'

'Aren't we all! Shall I roll another?'

Edward closed his eyes without replying. Skye gave him a hooded, hesitant look before rolling the joint. He used straight grass, no tobacco, and his joints were strong. He leaned over and switched on the transistor radio – and The Doors blared out across the pool, 'I'm Your Back Door Man'. Jim Morrison's heavy voice was joined by Skye Duval's gusty laugh, he found the link between the lyrics and his own preferences hysterically funny. Stoned, he jumped up, danced around, puffing on the cigar-sized joint.

Edward turned over, began to rub more oil on his shoulders. He put on a pair of Skye's mirrored shades, and continued to watch him dancing. He held up his hand as Skye proffered the joint. Edward gripped Skye's wrist tightly. 'What was Richard doing in the wogs' area, Skye? Do you know?'

Skye released his wrist, backing off. 'Sure! He liked black ass, always made his way there after a drinking session. He must have played around with someone's wife, or daughter, his sister or mother – who gives a fuck. Whoever zapped him did us all a favour.'

'Who was he having this booze-up with, Skye, do you know?'

Skye's doorbell rang, and the houseboy moved as if to answer it. Skye waved him back to mixing drinks at the poolside bar and wrapped a towel round his waist. He ambled off, still dancing, to answer the door. Edward dragged on the joint, inhaling the grass deeply into his lungs. He had a bloody good idea exactly who Richard Van der Burge had been with that night. Skye Duval.

Edward had his eyes closed. Skye bent close, whispered in his ear, 'You've got a visitor, and a very attractive one. I don't know where you get the energy from, man, and this one's far out.'

Edward half rose, then blinked in the strong sunlight. He reached for the shades again, and his hand froze. He tried to stand, but was so stoned he flopped back. Harriet stood on the verandah. She was wearing a black dress, a wide-brimmed, black straw hat. 'Jesus Christ.'

Skye made a sweeping gesture for Harriet to come to the poolside. Out of the side of his mouth he said, 'This one even I wouldn't mind shafting.' He called out, 'You want a drink sweetheart . . . what did you say your name was?'

Harriet remained on the verandah, half in the shadows, half in the sunlight. Casually, she took her hat off and shook out her hair. Skye clapped his hands . . . 'Oh yes . . . get 'em off, she's lovely . . . Eddie, I gotta hand it to you, you know how to pick 'em.'

Edward pushed him aside. 'Shut it, it's my wife.' Skye curled up with laughter, thinking Edward was joking. He yelled . . . 'Man here says you're his wife, that true?'

Edward glowered as he made his way to the verandah, and Skye shut the music off. Now he shaded his eyes watching with interest, more than interest. Wife? Edward had never mentioned to him that he was married.

Harriet's heart was thudding, Edward moved up the steps into the shadows. 'Hi. I was just passing on the way to the shops and thought I'd drop in, have I interrupted a business meeting? I mean I can always come back.' He didn't make it easy for her, he didn't take her in his arms, even seem too surprised. Instead, he leaned against the wooden railing.

'How in Christ's name did you find me?'

'Allard called me about Dickie, so I came for the funeral, ashes to ashes, you know, that kind of thing.'

'He was buried a week ago.'

'Oh well, in that case I'll go home.'

Edward stared at her, his mind racing. He had always covered his tracks so well and if Harriet could find him, God knows who else would. 'You tell Alex you were coming?'

'No, but Allard knew where I could contact you, I didn't know he worked for you?'

'He doesn't . . . come on down to the pool, I'll introduce you, Skye, this is Harriet . . . Harriet, Skye Duval.'

Still he did not touch her, did not show any sign he was pleased to see her, in fact the reverse. Skye on the other hand held her at arm's length, raved about her hair, her eyes, and promptly ordered a bottle of champagne to be opened in her honour. All the while Edward made no attempt to move near her, he picked up his towel, and casually said he would take a shower. He walked to the side of the pool and stepped under the ice-cold water. Distanced from her he could look at her, watch her sitting in her neat black dress, shading the sun with her hand as Skye chattered away. He saw Skye pick up her straw hat and stick it on his head. He sat close to her lounge chair, talking non-stop, asking about her flight, her hotel.

Edward dressed and combed his hair before joining them at the poolside. She was more relaxed, yet Skye had seen her nervousness, her eyes straying to Edward every few moments. What fascinated Skye was the change in Edward. If his wife was nervous, his dear friend was all over the place. First he had put his shirt on inside out, and his shoes on the wrong feet. Buddy boy was stoned out of his tree, and trying to be straight. Skye started to snigger, this could be fun. Just as the thought crossed his mind, the smile was wiped off his face. It was as if he, Skye, didn't exist, wasn't there. Edward's shadow loomed over Harriet, and she took her hand away from her face, no longer needing to shade her eyes. She looked up. 'Christ she's beautiful,' thought Skye. Edward spoke so softly Skye could only just hear.

'Hello, Harry.'

'Hello.'

Gently Edward cupped her face in his hands and kissed her lips. Skye had seen him with more women than he could count, but he had never seen this protective, gentle side. She glowed with love, it shone in her eyes, in her every gesture. He watched her touch Edward's hair, say softly how long it had grown, and that she liked it.

Skye did a dive into the pool, swam a length almost entirely beneath the surface. His lungs felt as if they would burst. He wanted to explode with jealousy. He loved Edward, was in love with him, always had been. They had been getting on so well, nothing sexual, but for Skye just to have him close was enough and now he saw what closeness really was, and he hated her. Even more so as they walked to the verandah, Edward giving a casual wave to Skye, the only indication they were leaving. She, however, smiled, thanked him for the champagne. The champagne she had not even touched. She also called out that he could keep her hat, said it suited him better. Skye heard the car drawing away and, towelling himself dry, trod on the straw hat, crushing it with his foot. So much for Mrs fucking Barkley.

Edward carried her cases into the hotel. He had switched her room demanding the best they had, and it was the bridal suite. He gave the bellhop a big tip, too big, to get rid of him, before he scooped her up in his arms. She clung to his neck and they both fell on to the enormous bed together. 'So tell me, how in God's name did you find me?'

He began to take off her dress as she repeated what Allard had told her. He again asked if Alex knew, and she flopped back on to the pillow. 'No, no one knows I'm here, except Norman – why? Is this place a secret or something?'

Edward told her that he was in the middle of a complex deal, and didn't want even a sniff of it to get back to London until he was ready. She began to undo the buttons on his shirt, kissing his chest. 'Well, you can leave me with that dreadful lizard-type gent at the pool, I won't get in your way, I promise, just needed to see you.'

Edward pulled off his shirt and got up from the bed to take off his trousers. 'The lizard, my love, is Skye Duval. He does the odd bit of work for me.'

He moved back to the bed, and took her shoes off. She rested her head against his shoulder, rubbing his back with her hand. 'You know, sometimes I forget just how you look, I think I know but I don't. I love you, Edward, I do love you.'

He held her, rocking her slightly. He didn't tell her the effect she had on him, seeing her there, standing in the shadows of the verandah. His initial anger, his instinct for self-preservation and concern that no one knew his whereabouts had made him angry at her intrusion. Now he could think of nothing he wanted more . . . 'Tell you what, I'll get through all the business, then we'll go some place, what do you say to that?'

She mimicked Barbara, Alex's wife, using a soft Texan drawl, 'Why honey, that sounds divine . . .' She laughed, describing Barbara to him as he had never met her. She insisted on entering the room from the wardrobe, giving him Barbara's performance in their manor and he lay back on the bed with his hands behind his head. She could always make him laugh, and she was so unselfconscious that her whole performance had been done stark-naked.

He held out his arm for her to lie next to him. Her skin was so pale against his dark tan, and he found himself instructing her to take great care if she went out in the sun. They lay side by side, completely relaxed with each other, and he pulled her even closer. His arm slipped around her, resting on her belly and drawing her body into his own curve. It was a simple gesture, but one she always associated with him, with security. He kissed the nape of her neck . . . his hand stroked her body, and he felt the tiny stretch marks at her back. He knew what they were, maybe she was even unaware of them herself . . . they were the marks from her child, the child he believed had been Pierre Rochal's. Even thinking about it, about a part of her life he had never known, made him jealous. He held her closer. 'I want you to have our son . . . no, no, now don't turn away from me . . . I want your belly growing fat with my boy, our son . . . Why not? You've been well, and you're fit and strong . . . what do you say?' She looked into his face and they kissed . . . he took it to be an answer and, aroused, he began to make love to her.

The black cloud inched fragment by fragment across her mind, weighing her down, engulfing her. 'Don't think about it, don't think about it.' She repeated it to herself over and over . . . She moaned for him, her legs opening to him, but her mind began closing, the voices screamed inside her head, 'Push . . . push . . . he's coming, push Harry . . .' and the pain engulfed her, making her gasp as if she couldn't breathe. The black cloud burst with the fragmented picture of their dead baby's face. Unaware of what she was doing, she was pushing Edward away from her, her body rigid . . . but he came into her, climaxing into her until he shook.

'I'm sorry,' she whispered . . .

He moved from the bed and walked into the bathroom, closing the door. Suddenly he kicked it open. 'What in Christ's name is wrong with you? . . . If you tell me what I do wrong, then we can work it out. Jesus Christ, you drive me crazy, do you know that? You think I don't feel it? You think I don't feel you freeze up on me? What am I doing wrong, do I hurt you? Harry? . . . Harry?'

'I'm just tired from the plane, I said I was sorry.'

He stood for a long time looking at her. Then he sighed. 'I'll take a shower.' She pressed her face into the pillow, not wanting him to hear her crying.

When he came out, he sat on the bed. 'I'll book a table, invite Skye, is that all right . . .? Harry?' She held her arms out, wanting his forgiveness . . . wanting to tell him why, what happened to her, in her mind . . . how could she tell him that the son he wanted died in her arms. The fear of her own madness linked to the loss of the child, the baby she blamed herself for losing. Her guilt was more powerful than her body, her desires, and yet she loved him completely.

As she bathed, Edward lit a cigar. He had already booked the table, and was dressed and ready to leave. Skye had invited them for drinks first . . . sex with Harriet had never been the mainstay of their relationship . . . he reconciled himself to the knowledge that it never would be. Sex he could get wherever he wanted . . . he would just have to make do with loving her. He paced the room, even thought about going elsewhere, for another woman to father him a son . . . he stubbed out the cigar, grinding it into the ashtray. Trouble was he wanted the mother of his child to be Harriet . . . he didn't want just any woman's brat.

Edward didn't remark on how beautiful she looked when she came out of the bathroom. She had made a great effort, even making up her face. He just said, 'Let's go.' But as always, when she looked at him in that tentative nervous way, his whole body wanted to hold her, say it was all right . . . but tonight, like so many other nights, she had pushed him away . . . He knew he would be won round soon enough, but he wasn't going to make it easy for her.

They drove to Skye's in silence. She was biting her nails, looking at him, needing him to be kind, but he purposely remained silent. It was not until he parked the car outside Skye's bungalow that he made a conscious effort to be nice to her. 'You look lovely . . . and don't worry, we'll work it out, okay?' She nodded her head, then flung herself into his arms. 'I love you, I do love you.'

'I know, I know . . . and by the way, don't take one of his joints, they're lethal.'

Skye did not get the slightest hint that all was not well, far from it. Edward bounded in, hand in hand with Harriet. The champagne corks popped, and this time Mrs Barkley drank. They also had more champagne at dinner. Harriet and Skye began to interact fast, she picked up his camp humour and then had not only Skye weeping with laughter, but Edward too. She repeated the story about discovering Dewint dressed as Joan Crawford, but she made Edward promise never to mention that she had told him. His mood eased, and he started to enjoy himself for real. He could see the way Skye was being captivated by her and he liked it.

She had ordered snails, and then held up one of the shells, and with a serious face looked at Skye. 'Did you know that the shell is the most delicious part of the escargot? You really must try it . . .'

Skye bit into the shell and almost lost his front tooth before he realized she was joking.

Edward didn't find it quite as hysterically funny as they both did, but concentrated on ordering a good wine to go with their main course. They had all ordered different dishes.

When the meal was served, Harriet was very disgruntled by what she called 'her shrivelled chicken'. Skye, getting well drunk, admired with relish his Dover sole. He made a great show of offering his plate to her, then withdrawing it, saying she could only have it if she gave him a forfeit. Edward sliced into his steak, warning Harriet against the 'deal', and Skye splashed more red wine into his already full glass . . . 'Don't be so bloody boring, come on, Harry, yes or no? Yes? Okay . . .'

Skye thought about it, and then pointed to the pianist sitting playing a very soft rendering of show tunes. 'Okay, Mrs Barkley, I want you to go across the room, and ask him to play something . . . and you have to sing, in front of everyone . . . if you do, you'll get my Dover, if you don't, you are stuck with that very sickly chicken.'

Edward wiped his mouth with his napkin and suggested she simply call the waiter and order something else. 'No, that's not the point, it's not the point, is it, Skye?' Edward was slightly embarrassed, they were already louder than any of the other diners. Skye was obviously encouraging her, and at the same time giving sly little nudges to Edward. Harriet was having a ball, she banged the table. 'I'll do it on the condition you do one as well.'

Edward had almost finished his steak, he put his knife down. 'This is getting stupid, just order something else, or I'll order it for you.'

She clapped her hands not listening to him. 'You, Mister Duval, have to go across to that table and act as a waiter.'

Skye turned to the group of people already raising their eyebrows and giving disapproving stares.

Edward threw down his napkin. 'That's enough Harry, just call the waiter and stop this.'

'But I am the waiter, dear heart, I am.' Skye was lisping, and being overtly camp.

Before Edward could stop her, Harriet was at the piano. The pianist, who had very rarely had a request and could play his medley of show tunes with his eyes closed, became quite animated. There was no microphone, and Harriet sat next to him on the piano stool. He flipped through his books and she helped him to find the music.

Edward finished his steak. Skye leaned close to him. 'She's wonderful, just wonderful, I adore her ... how in the hell did you find her. My God, she's going to do it ...' Skye drew the entire restaurant's attention as he applauded loudly. He knew Edward was getting more uptight, and he revelled in it, pouring even more wine. 'Ease up, Eddie, I reckon she knows what she's doing.'

'Do you, she's never sung before in her life, and when I want more wine, I'll bloody ask for it.'

Harriet began singing, softly at first. 'Blue Moon, you saw me standing alone, without a dream in my heart, without a love of my own ...'

Skye never took his eyes from her, and slowly Edward, too, turned towards the piano. There she was, eyes closed, swaying against the pianist and her voice was as sweet as a bird's. He felt a helplessness sweep over him, she captivated him as she did the entire room. He applauded along with everyone else.

Skye was up and removing a tray from a passing waiter. He slipped his napkin over his arm and tangoed between the tables. Even the elderly foursome managed a half-smile of amusement as he insisted on serving them, and cleaning their breadcrumbs from the table.

He then ordered a very good bottle of port as a peace offering. With the tray held aloft he turned to Harriet who was still standing by the piano. He fell to his knees. 'I love you, I am in love with you.' He led her proudly back to their table, bowing low and kissing her hand. 'Mrs Barkley, you are exquisite ... I don't suppose you have a sister do you?'

Edward lit up a cigar, his voice was quiet, nasty. 'She doesn't have a sister, Skye, but I think you might prefer her brother. He's an iron hoof too.'

Harriet saw Skye flinch, the slight flush in his face and she frowned at Edward. She then cupped her hand to Skye's ear and whispered. 'Pa calls him a shirt-lifter, isn't that funny?'

He bent down and gave her a swift kiss on her lips, catching her completely by surprise. His eyes were serious, painful . . . 'You don't believe me, do you? But I meant what I said . . . I am in love with you.'

Edward pushed his chair back, clicking his fingers for the waiter. The cigar clenched in his teeth. 'Oh she likes compliments, she likes to tease, but doesn't come up with the goods.' He gripped her arm. 'Let's go.'

Just as she had seen the hurt in Skye, Skye saw Edward's remark hit home, but he didn't bargain for her reaction. She jerked her arm free. 'Want to see my next trick, Mr Barkley . . . LADIES AND GENTLEMEN I SHALL REMOVE THIS TABLECLOTH, LEAVING ALL THE CROCKERY ON THE TABLE . . . AHHH ONE, AHHH TWO . . .' Edward walked out as the crockery smashed to the floor. The bottles of wine, the glasses . . .

He sat in cold fury in the car waiting. They came out arm in arm, and the manager bowing and scraping. It reminded Edward of Cambridge, of Charlie, and his fury grew. She was one of them, the bread-throwing English upper classes. As they reached the car, Edward got out and pulled her round to the passenger seat. He pushed her roughly inside.

'Oh my God, there is no need to be so butch, dear, I can get in all by myself.'

Skye had his hand on the door, as Edward shoved him aside. 'Get yourself home, you've done enough for one night, show time's over.'

Skye watched the car career out of the parking lot. He shouted, waving his fists.

'I love you, I love you Mrs Barkley.'

Harriet folded her arms. 'That was unnecessary, and very silly.'

Edward drove fast, too fast. 'Silly? . . . the two of you behaved like schoolkids and you call me silly, Jesus Christ.'

She glared out of the window. 'Only having a bit of fun, you didn't have to say that about me, or what you said about him, and stop the car . . . I want you to go back for him.' He didn't stop. 'Did you hear me?'

The car screeched to a halt and she slid forwards banging her head. 'You think you know him, do you? You think you really know him! Well, believe me, you don't. There's more to Mr Duval than you could ever imagine, take it from me.'

'Ah! Does that mean you know everything about him?'

'Yes, yes I do. Now let's forget it.'

Harriet was already sitting on the balcony eating breakfast when Edward, very hung-over, stumbled out from their suite. She peered over her bright pink-rimmed sunglasses. 'I hope we are in a better mood than we were last night. Coffee?'

'What's the time, I've got a meeting at nine.'

'Well you've just missed it, and I suppose you'll say that's my fault. Here, sit down and have your coffee and I'll order some eggs and bacon.'

'Christ, no! I couldn't face eggs and bacon, just coffee. I must have had more to drink than I thought.'

'Is that an apology?'

'No.'

'Well it should be, you know you left Skye in the car park?'

'Well somebody had to behave like an adult. You two are not safe to be let out together. I am supposed to be here on the quiet, doing subtle business deals, and what happens? The wife gets up with that ancient pianist and sings, then pulls the whole fucking tablecloth off ... very subtle, can I borrow your sunglasses?'

Harriet continued to read the paper eating her toast. Edward sat in moody silence. She looked up and then back to her paper, hiding a smile. He was feeling dreadful, she knew it, and he was now wearing her bright-pink sunglasses.

'I've got to go to Pretoria, do you want to come?'

'No, thank you, I just want to sit and relax by the pool.'

He took his coffee inside. She could hear him on the telephone, then he came back out again. 'Right, I'm going then, you sure you don't want to come with me?' She flicked through the paper, pursing her lips.

'I don't understand you. Why don't you want to come with me?'

She flicked the paper again. 'Because you are foul. To discuss your wife's sexual problems in public is to my mind the ultimate in bad taste ... would you mind standing to one side or the other, you are blocking the sun.'

He sighed, shaking his head. 'You are something else, you know that. You come all the way out here, and now you're having a go at me ... I don't even remember what I said ...'

She looked at him over the paper, then carefully folded it. He reached over and took her hand. 'All right, I do, and I'm sorry, I'd had too much to drink ... and he was all over you, I never got the chance to tell you something.'

She left her hand in his, and he lifted it to his lips. 'I liked your song, but before I could say anything he was in like Flynn ...'

She beamed. 'Do you mean it? You liked it? Honestly?'

He kissed her hand ... then caught the time on her wrist-watch. 'Shit, I'm going to miss my next appointment ... come on, your coat's on the bed.'

He grinned at her, and she punched him. 'You bastard, you always win me round so easily ...'

He ducked the next punch, still smiling. 'Was it that I liked your song or the hand kissing?'

She got him a good left, and he picked her up and threw her over his shoulder. 'You can sing to me in the car, it's a long drive ... and tonight we'll go dancing, but without Skye Duval, is it a deal?'

Edward was cramming his white panama hat on to Harriet's head as the Rolls Corniche screeched out of the parking lot. She was driving. Skye rolled down his window but he knew they hadn't seen him. He had a bunch of wild flowers for her, and he tossed them away. He sat in the boiling hot car, brooding ... he hadn't been able to get her out of his mind.

She belonged to Edward, maybe that was why he wanted her

so much ... he lit a cigarette, wondered what Eddie boy had meant when he had said she liked to tease, was that what she had been doing to him? ... the cigarette followed the flowers as he started the engine, crashing the gears. 'Bitch ... they're all the same, bitch ...'

He drove as fast as Harriet out of the hotel. He turned the music up loud. 'I'm Your Back Door Man' ... he was Eddie's back door man all right, he was that schmuck, well, he'd taken enough. By the time he arrived back at his bungalow, he was seething with impotent jealous rage. He rolled up a joint, inspecting his hidden stash, warning himself to go easy, his crop was almost through. He looked at the joint and laughed. If he could get Mrs Barkley to take one of these, he'd show her what teasing was all about.

Skye did not see Edward or Harriet for two days. He was in constant contact with Edward, but he never said a word about their last meeting, or his wife. Edward was no fool, he kept them well apart, knowing that Skye was a bad influence. He was, however, very busy and constantly in meetings, and after two days trailing around with him she grew restless. Unable to sit in the sun for long she went on shopping sprees buying a strange assortment of African carvings. She arrived back at the hotel as the phone rang. It was Skye. He asked what she had been doing, and if she ever had a free afternoon, he would love to show her the sights. She accepted, but said she would have to be back by six as she was expecting Edward then.

'Eh, no problem, get a cab over to my place and we'll take it from here.' He let the phone drop back on to the hook ... She was at the door before he had finished drying his hair. She handed him a small packet.

'It's something I saw, it reminded me of you.'

It was a small carved wooden tiger, and he held it in the palm of his hand.

'Reminded you of me? Don't know how to take that, Mrs Barkley.'

She smiled a little self-consciously. 'It's your eyes, it was a toss-up between that and a green lizard, but I wouldn't be offended, I bought Edward a chimp.'

She strolled out on to the verandah and asked where his houseboy was. Skye said it was his day off. It wasn't. He was banished to his room.

'I wouldn't mind a swim, do you mind? Only I never really like swimming in hotel pools, because you never know how many people have pissed in them.' He smiled, waved for her to help herself. He pointed to the shower area, and said there were swimming costumes if she wanted one.

He sat rolling a very big joint as she changed. She came out, and posed in a terrible flowered one-piece suit. 'Dear God, what kind of women do you have here, this is thirties, isn't it?'

He licked the paper, and she screwed her eyes up. 'Do that again.' He did. 'I should have bought you the lizard.'

She then executed a perfect dive into the pool. She was a strong swimmer and he began to lose count of the lengths. Eventually she swung herself up the steps, her hair dragged back from her face. 'Ohhhhh that was good, so good.'

She flopped down beside him and he lit the joint. He drew heavily on it, feeling it fill his lungs, and then held it out. 'You want to try it? It's home grown, pretty good.'

She curled her tongue over her lips, and then nodded. He instructed her to draw in the smoke, to suck it in on a breath so she would 'feel the benefits'. She held on to the thick joint, and gulped, coughed and wafted her hand ... then she tried again.

'You feeling the benefits?'

She cocked her head to one side. 'Not sure what they are, but it tastes foul.'

He encouraged her to continue smoking, then took the joint back.

'Holy shit, my head's exploding, is that the benefit? It's like being drunk ... Whooo, lemme have some more, it's great.'

Skye passed the J back to her and lay back, he was feeling nicely stoned ...

'You want some music . . .? Harry? Shall I put some music on?'

She didn't answer so he got up and walked into the house. He chose one of his favourites, Berlioz. She saw the way his strange eyes closed as he listened to the music. His face with his eyes shut had no brilliance, was ravaged, gaunt. His flowing caftan gave him a sexuality that was both male and female. He hadn't heard her enter, and his eyes opened. She listened to the music for a moment.

'Ahhh, the *Symphonie Fantastique.*'

'You like classical music?'

'Mmmmm.'

She was wrapped in a white bath towel, and he thought she was the most perfect creature he had ever seen. Her thick red hair still damp from her swim clung to her head forming tiny curls. She sat cross-legged in the centre of the room. 'You know I think I am feeling the benefits, sort of woozy . . . but nice, Edward will be furious.'

'Don't talk about him.'

'Why ever not?'

'I just don't want you to talk about him, I want you to talk about yourself . . .' He lay on the sofa staring at her, leaning his head on his elbow. 'I've waited for you, did you know that? . . . I wanted to get you stoned, then I wanted to take you to bed.'

He saw her blush, her cheeks went rosy red, and she plucked at the carpet. He stretched out his body, at the same time rubbing his hand down his thigh, his fingers tracing himself, and she could see his erection.

'Don't you like him?'

'Who?'

'You know who, Edward.'

'Ahhhhh, Eddie, sure I like him. If you want the truth I more than like him, we go back a long time. I met him in a whore-house, a black whorehouse. You want a drink?'

'Does he still go there?'

'Sure, he takes whatever I deliver, he's a great stud, a stallion, but you know that ... you do know that, don't you, Mrs Barkley?'

He moved past her, so close his gown touched her. He slowly unscrewed the bottle of vodka and drank it neat. He swayed around her like a cat, a cat playing with his catch. He couldn't see her face, couldn't tell what she was thinking. Her hair hid her eyes, and he crouched down offering the bottle. Suddenly, she tossed her head back, and stared at him, then she reached over and touched his face.

'Oh, Mr Duval, you are a dangerous man, with a beautiful face, and a very disarming manner, but you're just an alley cat, a seedy alley cat with vicious sharp claws.'

He pulled her to him and kissed her, forcing her mouth open, his tongue searching her mouth. An open, wet, frantic kiss, as he pulled the towel away from her and pushed her backward until he lay on top of her, his hands grasping her wrists. She made no effort to fight him off. She showed no fear of him. He was at a loss ... the hunter had netted himself. She pushed him away from her and he flopped back on the carpet.

'Let's go.'

'Christ,' he thought, 'not the bedroom now,' he couldn't get it up if she were Ben Hur.

'To the whorehouse. I want to see what goes on when I'm not around.'

Edward was exhausted, it had been a long, hard day. The mining rights for three of his perlite investments were causing problems. Added to that two hospital complexes were behind schedule and a high-rise apartment block built in shifting ground. This meant his men had bought land cutting corners on the surveys, but they had charged him the full rate. The men had to be sifted out and dealt with.

He walked into the hotel and took the elevator up to their suite. He wanted a hot bath and food, his shirt was sticking to his back. He dropped his briefcase on to the bed, pulled his shirt off and threw it aside. 'Harry? You on the balcony?' Getting no answer he looked at his watch, it was after eight. He crossed to the phone to ring down to the main dining room and saw her note. He angrily placed a call through to Skye. No reply. He ordered room service, and then took a shower.

He rang Skye three more times during the evening. His anger turned to genuine worry when at eleven o'clock she still had not returned ... at twelve o'clock he was driving around the streets looking for Skye Duval's car. He stopped at a phone booth and called Skye yet again, and still could get no reply. He called the hotel, and Mrs Barkley had not returned ... he sat in icy fury in the car and banged the steering wheel. Where would that bastard take her at this hour?

Skye was exhausted, he sat slumped on a bar stool. Harriet was sitting between four blacks and a hooker known as Tricks, because she never missed one. Harriet was holding forth about black rights, and Skye couldn't believe it. One drive through the black shanty towns and she was an authority on what had to be done. They all listened avidly, because she also ordered drinks every two minutes for anyone who cared to join her group.

Skye had tried to take her out, but one of her new friends had pushed him aside ... pushed him a little too roughly. They were in the black area, and not wanting trouble he went back to the bar.

Skye became more and more wary as the evening went on. He knew he would have Edward to deal with, never mind getting his wife out. He didn't know who he would be more scared of – Edward or the blacks that surrounded him ... or were surrounding Harriet.

Encouraged by her friendliness, they were openly touching her, accepting her free drinks. White women didn't come in their area. Shifty looks passed between dark eyes, her gold necklace, her diamond ring, even better was the thick wad of notes they saw in her wallet ... any moment now they would make their move and take her outside – and Skye knew he could do nothing to stop them.

Edward Barkley entered the dark, seedy bar. Everybody fell silent as the tension built. Harriet waved across to him and then turned to the men. 'It's all right, he's my husband . . . Edward, I want you to meet some friends of mine.'

He walked straight through the lot of them and took her elbow. 'Time we went home, you got your bag?'

He turned to Skye, his face was a mask; he gave Skye a small nod of recognition. The men formed a circle, surrounding Harriet and Edward . . . a tight silent group. Still holding her with one hand, he took from his inside jacket pocket a wad of notes, he tossed them to the bar . . . he looked to each man. They moved aside, and the couple walked out of the club. Edward opened the car door and slammed it shut so hard the car rocked. Before starting the engine he leaned over, flipped the glove compartment open and replaced the gun.

She didn't know what she was more afraid of, the change in her so-called friends, or the violent cold anger from her husband. His hands clenched the wheel as he drove back to their hotel. She could see a muscle twitching in the side of his face . . .

'I'm sorry, I should have let you know where I was.'

He gave her a look that frightened her.

They went up in the elevator in silence. He unlocked their hotel room, jerked his head for her to go in before him and she moved quickly to the bed. He didn't switch the light on, but stood in the dark. His voice was unrecognizable, 'You have a good time, white trash?' She had never seen him so angry. 'Well? You going to answer me?'

'Yes, and I am sorry, I should have called you . . .'

'You should have called me . . .?'

She moved towards him. 'Don't come any nearer, I've never hit you but, by Christ, you're close . . . what the fuck do you think you were doing? Did that prick get you stoned? Well . . .?

You better answer me, Harry.' She didn't have to, he knew by her silence.

'So then what? Don't tell me he fucked you? That would be too much of a joke . . . well, I'm waiting?'

'Go screw yourself . . .'

He was across the room like lightning, he got her by the hair and threw her down across the bed, his hand came up, and she was as fast as he was, rolling away from him. 'This is how you treat your black tarts, is it . . .? Beat them up? That is where you pick them up from, isn't it? Which one do you go for? Tricks? You go with her?'

He had wanted to hit her before, now he could have killed her. Instead he chose his words, knowing he would get to her, hurt her. 'I go with any woman who won't freeze up on me, that likes me inside her, wants me inside her, unlike the frigid bitch I'm married to, all right?'

Her dress hit him first, then her right shoe, she stood in front of him and swished her hips. 'You want to rip my pants off, or shall I suck you off?'

He tore her pants off, and picked her up. 'You asked for it and you are going to get it.'

She was spreadeagled on the bed, his hands gripping her wrists. Skye had tried to rape her in exactly the same way . . . but now she fought, struggling and kicking with all her strength, but she couldn't move. Slowly he lowered his head and kissed her, releasing her hands, and pressing her legs open. She tried to move from beneath him and he grabbed a fistful of hair and yanked her head back. She screamed, biting at his hand, but he kept on, his hand roughly pushing her legs further and further apart. Slowly she began to move with him, not against him. Her whole body opened to him, and just as she reached out for him, he moved away.

He laughed, standing at the end of the bed. He began to peel off his clothes. He then reached over for the lights.

'Don't turn it on, please don't . . . don't turn the light on.'

He lay down on her, and with his right hand flicked the

switch, light flooded the room. She tried to hide her face, but he turned her roughly to look at him. 'You are going to know who's fucking you . . . now look at me . . .'

There were no fragmented dreams. No nightmares . . . they made love over and over again. She came to him, openly, with no fear, and her mind cleared, lifted. She was free.

Skye Duval was, to put it politely, shitting himself. He had half a bottle of vodka beside him to give him the nerve to walk into the hotel. When told to go straight up to Mr Barkley's suite, he had another large vodka in the bar. He tapped on their door sweating. Edward called that it was open and for him to walk right in. He hesitated, licked his lips, thought that if he was going to take a beating he might as well get it over with.

Edward was sitting up in bed, just the white sheet draped over him. Skye hovered by the door, and Edward smiled, his teeth gleaming in his tanned face, and his hair loose, as if he had just showered. He lit a cigar and tossed the match aside.

'Siddown . . . drinks on the table, help yourself.' Skye was even more at a loss, he looked to the balcony. 'She's in the tub, okay? I've got all these papers for you to sort out; the cables I want sent today and the rest you can do when I've gone. I want monies transferred to the five accounts I've listed . . .' As the bathroom door opened, Skye was so nervous he swallowed an ice cube. She was fully dressed and smiled at him. As she crossed to the bed, she knelt close to Edward and kissed him. 'I'll get them to collect the cases – you want anything from reception?' Edward shook his head and she walked out. Pausing at the door, she cocked her head to Skye. 'Bye Mr Alley Cat.'

Skye flushed, looked nervously at Edward, his foot began twitching . . . still he got no adverse reaction.

'Okay, that's about it, there's four folders, this stack of letters and the rest are cables. We're leaving, but I'll contact you in a few days, okay?'

Skye nodded, his foot still twitching . . . she was right . . .

compared to Edward he was nothing ... just a seedy alley cat, because there before him was the king – the cigar clamped in his teeth, the broad powerful shoulders. As he got up from the bed tucking the sheet around him he seemed like a giant. 'What you waiting for? You want something?'

'No.'

He towered above Skye as he whispered, 'You're getting off light this time my friend and you know it, now get out.'

Skye gathered up the papers, and moved as fast as he could to the bar for another booster. He was shaking, not really believing he had got away with it. She hadn't told him ... he just couldn't understand it ... all he knew was, whatever the game, Edward always beat him, was always one step ahead of him. He could never be free of him, the power he held over Skye was unbreakable, unless he killed himself, and Skye was too much of a coward to do that.

On their return Dewint was given so many African statues his 'pigeon loft' looked like a market stall. He had never seen them both looking so well and happy.

It was even more unpleasant therefore for him to give Harriet the news that her father was dying. She left for Yorkshire the same day.

The following morning Dewint carried in Edward's breakfast tray. Although he said not a word, he couldn't help but notice Edward's appearance – the long hair, the tan so dark he could have been a Red Indian, or one of those hippies from America.

'I'll run a bath immediately, sah.' He behaved as though Edward had been gone only a few hours, and asked no questions.

'Dewint, contact Miss Henderson at the office, tell her to bring everything that's been dealt with while I've been away. She's to say nothing, I don't want anyone to know I'm home yet. I also want back numbers of the newspapers – get copies from the library or whatever . . . And Dewint, the house looks good, just fine.'

In contrast to Dewint's reaction, Miss Henderson nearly dropped all the files, and her mouth gaped open.

'Something wrong, Henny old girl?'

She flushed to the roots of her mousy hair and bit her lip, trying to hide her shock by turning away to put the files down. Dewint closed the door as he went out, and Miss Henderson swallowed hard and took another look at Edward.

He looked just like a wild gypsy. He smiled at her, reached out and gripped her chin. 'What's going on in that little head, eh?'

'I'm sorry, but . . . well, excuse me for saying this, but you look like a gypsy, Mr Edward. I don't mean to be rude, but you do, you really do.'

He tilted his head to one side and smiled again, his teeth whiter than white against his dark skin. 'I do, do I? Well, well, I look like a gypsy, what a thing to say.'

She looked so nervous that he patted her shoulder. 'Just joking, I don't mind – and you never know, Henny, I might just have a drop of the Romany in me . . . Right now, to work. Tell me everything, all the gossip, and don't miss out a single thing. Let's start with Alex.'

He listened, wandering around the room in his dressing gown, barefoot. His long hair had been washed and combed back from his face.

Miss Henderson talked for at least two hours, and was tired at the end of her lengthy monologue. Edward didn't interrupt her once, gave no hint of what he was feeling. Finally, he said, 'That it? How's your mother, any better?'

Miss Henderson shook her head, said she was worse, and now it was becoming very difficult to cope.

'You need a break, Henny. Find a good nursing home, and don't worry about the cost, that'll be taken care of. Just go out and have a shopping spree, buy yourself a few things.'

She was going to cry, but he picked up a file and started talking business.

In the early evening Miss Henderson departed, trying to thank him, but he waved her thanks aside, then cupped her face in his enormous hands. 'I don't want to lose you – you go on doing too much and I will. So get that old lady of yours sorted out. I'll be in the office first thing in the morning.'

He kissed her frazzled brow and she hurried out. By the time she reached the gates she was crying openly. She had never met anyone like Edward – she knew a lot of people didn't like him, but as far as she was concerned he was a god, and she worshipped him.

Edward reached for the phone. He didn't bother to check the time, he just dialled Alex's number and waited. After a moment Alex answered.

'Well, well, buddy boy, while the cat's away, huh . . . I'm home, see you in the office tomorrow.'

He didn't wait for Alex to reply, just put the phone down and lay back on the sofa. He wondered what this Barbara woman would be like, and if he would approve of her. He got up and carefully opened a small, mirrored box, carrying it to the table. He had changed from smoking joints, he had found something far more stimulating. He opened a small square of tin foil, picked up a razor-blade and cut two long lines of cocaine. He rolled up a crisp new pound note and snorted both lines. He whistled, sniffing, then licked his finger and removed all traces of the powder from the mirror, rubbing it along his gums. This was something else Skye had introduced him to, and he liked it, liked the way his head cleared, the energy that flooded through him.

Padding across to the record player he selected an album, dusted the record off, and put it on the turntable. Jimi Hendrix – 'All Along The Watch Tower'. Edward swung his hips and danced, singing along at the top of his voice.

Way up at the top of the house, Dewint cocked an ear to the music and Edward's loud singing. He closed his eyes. 'Dear God,' he thought, 'not again. Why can't he play something soft and gentle?' If it wasn't this record it was Bob Dylan and his ruddy 'Tambourine Man'. It appeared that Mr Barkley was swinging along through the sixties with a vengeance.

Chapter Twenty-Two

Everyone said 'good morning' to Alex: the receptionist, the doorman, and the lift man. The lift doors opened as Miss Henderson was walking by with a thick pile of letters.

'Mr Barkley's waiting in his office, sir, I'll bring coffee.'

Alex pursed his lips and let himself into his own office. Putting his briefcase down he took off his raincoat, hung it carefully on a bronze coat stand, checked his hair and tie and then walked along the corridor to his brother's office.

Edward was on the phone when Alex entered, and waved him in, paying no other attention to him. 'Well, if it's a popular street we'll make it even more so, run a string of boutiques along the whole length of it, stocking all the newfangled gear the kids want ... Yeah, okay, I'll be in touch.' Replacing the receiver, he clapped his hands. 'We're going into the fashion business, Alex. I've been reading all these mags, the Carnaby Street boutiques are doing a roaring trade – fancy the mini-skirts myself ... How you doing, old fella, long time no see?'

Alex couldn't speak, he simply stared. The cowboy boots, the denims, they were not the reason ... Edward, with his long hair, looked like a ghost.

'What the hell's the matter? The gear? Don't worry about it, I'll get organized soon ... Alex?'

His face white, Alex dropped into the chair opposite his

brother's. He swallowed, Edward carried on talking, heaving files on to his desk and slapping the top one. 'We got trouble, eh? They want to close the club down, right? Fucking bastards . . . I'll find a way round it, Jesus, what the hell is the matter with you?'

Alex snapped at him that perhaps he should take a look in the mirror. If it was some kind of joke, it was sick. 'We build this whole thing up and for what, you want the world to know, is that it? You changed your tune, look at you – Freedom, want me to start calling you Freedom?'

Edward ran his hands through his long hair, then he leaned back in his chair and roared with laughter. The gold chain was visible round his neck; with his tan he looked fit.

'Oh, Jesus, Alex, it never occurred to me, I just never bothered to cut it . . . hey, easy, take it easy, man, I'll get it cut . . . we gotta talk business now, and fast.'

Barbara was furious. She had changed her dress eighteen times, had her hair done, and was about to set out for the Ritz when Alex called to say the lunch was cancelled. He gave no reason, irritated at her questions.

'When do I get to meet him, then?'

Covering the phone with his hand, Alex asked Edward if he would be available for dinner that evening. Edward, caught up in the mound of files, shrugged. 'Come over to my place, we'll eat there, meet her there, right now we've got more important things to discuss . . .'

He swung back and forth in his chair, and then stuck a match between his lips and cocked his head to one side. 'So you want to buy in, eh? Fine by me, but I want the money placed in a bank in Geneva, this wife of yours arrange that? And the other condition is, as partners, we go hand in glove, no cheque, no letter, not one document leaves this building without a double signature. You agree to that, then let's get the lawyers in and away we go.'

Alex agreed readily, and they spent the rest of the morning

discussing their massive network of business activities. One by one. They were only a quarter of the way through when Edward threw in the towel, yawned and said he had had enough. 'We have to start selling, Edward. Lot of these small businesses take up too much time, and with the club going bust on us we'll need more funds to lay out on certain projects we've not yet discussed. But the more of the smaller businesses we release the more finances we'll have to buy bigger concerns. I think we should put in a bid for Buchanan House, they have a tremendous turnover and they are on the market right now.'

Edward sniffed, then concentrated on the heel of his cowboy boot. 'Why, if Buchanan House has such a big turnover, do they want to sell; it doesn't quite add up?'

With pride, Alex handed him a neat file. 'They don't, not yet, but I have inside information that there's one hell of a family feud going on. We can buy a major stake, they have guaranteed three other members of the family will follow suit – it's all here, Edward, read for yourself.'

Edward yawned, picked up the file and scratched his head. 'I'll take a look at it at home, see you around.'

'Edward, we'll be over about eight-thirty, is that all right?'

Edward shrugged his shoulders and walked out.

As Alex returned to his office he overheard Edward at the reception desk, asking about the new security system he had ordered to be installed.

'They had begun work, sir, but we were unsure about certain specifications you had made, and they have to wait for some parts to come from Japan . . .' Edward swore, and then the doors banged closed.

'What was that about the security system?'

The receptionist explained that Mr Barkley had requested monitor cameras to be wired into all the offices, and then the night watchmen would be able to watch on screens in the basement.

*

It was already after eight when Edward returned home. He had been discussing the security system with the company, and was armed with a vast number of leaflets. He bellowed for Dewint. 'I'll have something to eat in the bedroom, I'm ... shit! Look, can you knock up some kind of meal, my brother's coming over, anything'll do ...'

Edward could hear Alex's Rolls coming up the drive, and he swore, tossing the leaflets aside. He hadn't bathed, changed, nothing ... 'Dewint, they're here, get them drinks and I'll be down.'

Barbara was wearing a sequinned, full-length white evening gown, off the shoulder on one side, a single sleeve on the other side reaching to a point on the back of her hand. The skirt fluted out from the knee, and she carried a matching sequinned hand-bag and a silver-fox wrap. Alex was dressed in a white evening suit and black tie, more to suit Barbara than for Edward. He had told Barbara little, just that Edward was as difficult as ever but had agreed to the buy-in, and was considering the Buchanan House deal.

Dewint served chilled champagne and murmured that Mr Edward would be down shortly. Then he shot up the stairs to warn Edward to dress, and found him still soaking in the bath.

'Are you expecting any other guests, sah? They are wearing formal attire.'

Edward swore, heaved himself out of the bath and grabbed the proffered towel. Then he fetched his address book. 'Call a few regulars, some from a show, and tell them to come on later – make it about eight to ten of them, okay?'

'Would that be for dinner, sah?'

Pulling out clothes from the closet, Edward told Dewint just to get a few faces along after they had dined.

'Stars, Dewint, look under "S" for stars, they'll be here.'

Dewint hovered, squinting at Edward's scrawling writing and shook his head as Edward held up a grey suit.

'I don't think so, sah, they are, as I said, dressed.'

*

Alex and Barbara sat in silence. The clock ticked and they could hear the constant pinging of the telephone.

'Where has he been, did he tell you?'

Alex said he had asked, but Edward had been as evasive as usual. She began to tap her foot in irritation. 'I presume he is aware that we are here? How long does he intend to keep us waiting?'

Alex stared out of the window across the river, where the Barkley Company Ltd sign loomed high in the sky. He sipped the champagne, then lit a Havana cigar, carefully clipping the end.

'I must say the place is frightful! Who on earth did the interior for him? A lot of it looks almost threadbare ... and all those terrible paintings, Alex, in the hall.'

Puffing his cigar alight, Alex went to stand at the fireplace. 'Oh, they're family.'

Harriet sounded very distressed on the telephone. The Judge was nearing the end and she found Haverley Hall very cold and her family in a similar state. Edward asked if she was all right, and not getting too upset, and she retorted that of course she was upset, anyone would be under the circumstances.

'Look, sweetheart, I've got to go. Alex is downstairs, I'm to meet the new wife. I'll call you tomorrow, okay?' He replaced the receiver.

Alex and Barbara both looked at the phone as it pinged again, and Barbara stood up, smoothing her dress over her tight, firm figure. 'Perhaps you should go and bring him down. He's obviously on the phone – it's ridiculous keeping us waiting like this.'

The double doors opened with a bang as she finished, and Edward beamed, open-armed. He wore a white silk suit and a pale blue shirt, open at the neck, a thick, heavy gold bracelet, and his long hair was tied in a thong at the nape of his neck. Barbara's jaw dropped, but she recovered rapidly as Edward strode towards her.

'Well, you must be Barbara ... I have to apologize for keeping you waiting. There'll be just the three of us dining, and then some more guests will be joining us.'

Edward bent his head over her outstretched hand and kissed it. She could smell a heavy, musky perfume, and found herself blushing. 'Alex, you are a sly old dog. You never said you'd married a raving beauty ... Sit down, sit down and let me look at you – champagne, let me toast the pair of you.' He raised his glass and drank, then sat opposite Barbara, smiling, and continued to flatter and tease her. When she told him about her daughters he laughed, tossing his head back, saying she had to be lying, no woman who looked like she did could have two grown daughters.

Barbara warmed to Edward, laughing and joking with him. She did not mention her anger at being kept waiting, or make any reference to her previous visit. He asked her all about Texas, and when Dewint entered to say that dinner was served he leapt to her side, guiding her into the dining hall.

Rows of candles shed their light on the long table, which was set out with heavy silver, polished and dazzling, as for a banquet. There were big silver goblets, bowls of fresh fruit, large chunks of bread in silver bowls, and Edward was the perfect host. If Barbara spoke, he gave her his full attention, his eyes never leaving her face as if everything she said was of vital importance. She was flattered, and the flow of conversation continued throughout the meal.

Alex toyed with the thick, home-made chicken soup, and hardly touched the roast beef, which was overdone and too thickly carved for his taste. The wine flowed, good wine, and Edward kept their glasses filled as Dewint moved around silently, clearing and setting, as unobtrusive as ever.

Barbara regaled Edward with stories of her old devil of a grandfather, and even though they were not particularly amusing he threw back his head and laughed as if she were the wittiest woman he had ever met. Alex watched his wife blooming under Edward's encouraging attention. Occasionally Edward would reach over and pat his arm. 'You lucky man, you lucky man ... Barbara, another toast to you both. My brother's a lucky man, but I warn him, he should keep you tied to the home ...'

Alex felt very emotional. Again and again he saw the ghost of his father in Edward. Sitting in the throne, with his huge shoulders and thick black hair, the only difference was that Edward was a year older than Freedom had been when he died. It was as if Freedom had come back to say, 'Look at me, this is what I would have been if everything had gone well, if my life had been different ...'

'You're very quiet, Alex? Have some more wine, I've lots of people arriving to meet your wife, so I don't want you crawling off with one of your headaches ...' Alex's lips tightened – Edward made him sound like an old woman. But he smiled, and accepted the wine as Dewint passed round a mediocre selection of cheeses.

The doorbell rang a couple of times, but Edward gave not the slightest indication that he had heard it. They could hear voices, people arriving, laughter, but still Edward concentrated on Barbara. It was not until Dewint murmured that coffee was served in the lounge that Edward jumped to his feet and withdrew Barbara's chair. But as the three made their way past the long refectory table towards the lounge, Edward stifled a yawn.

Barbara recognized several of Edward's film-star guests. She listened as they discussed a columnist who had written a scandalous piece about a drug addict, but she had no idea to whom they were referring. The doors constantly opened to allow more guests to enter. Two of the men were obviously gay, wearing extraordinary thick platform boots and flared trousers with torn tee-shirts. The next couple were both in seedy evening dress, but they all greeted Edward with familiarity, shrieking with laughter when they saw him.

'Eddie, the hair! Dahling, I mean, it's Buffalo Bill!'

Edward grinned and laughed with them all, completely relaxed. He kept the stereo playing all the time, with Bob Dylan, Joan

Baez, and then a band so loud that Barbara could no longer hear the film stars' gossip. 'I'm a back door man, Yes ... Yes I am ...' Barbara noticed that a joint was being passed round – not that it came in her direction, it bypassed Alex and herself discreetly.

Alex sat quietly on a sofa, tired, wanting to leave. A group of actors was holding a heated discussion about a production of *Hamlet*, and on the other side of the room the pros and cons of mini-skirts held sway, the comments light and flippant. Alex flicked a look at his watch, it was past midnight and he wanted to go. Barbara was enthralled with two actors, accepting free tickets for an opening night. The music grew louder, another Bob Dylan record.

'Barbara, I think we should leave, I have an early appointment in the morning.'

Barbara would have loved to stay. She had spent most of her time in London with quite a different set of people and she loved this noisy, flamboyant group. However, she bowed to Alex, and waited for Dewint to bring her fur. Everyone kissed and waved goodbye, and went back to talking even louder as Edward ushered Alex and Barbara to the door.

Sitting at her dressing table Barbara creamed her face while Alex sat on the bed and asked her what she thought of Edward.

'He's divine, and such a character. The girls will adore him.' Alex kissed her neck and she moved her head away, saying she was tired, and continued cleaning her face.

'I'll see you in the morning, goodnight.'

Barbara watched him through the mirror as he stood for a moment at her bedroom door, then gave her a small smile and walked out. She sighed, tossed the cotton wool into the waste bin and followed him, slipped into his bed and held him, performed well for him, dutifully.

It was strange, Alex was just as handsome, but Edward? She traced Alex's face softly with her finger, bent and kissed it. He murmured and turned over.

When Barbara returned to her own room, she couldn't sleep.

She went over the whole evening in her mind – Edward's smiling face, his perfume, his roaring laugh … She had known instantly, almost the moment she saw him, that he was different – there was something intensely exciting about him. That was what really set the brothers apart – Edward was dangerous. When she finally slept, her body turned and she reached for the pillow, pulling it to her – pulling Edward into her arms.

Installed in Alex's elegant house, Barbara caused an uproar with the servants as she moved furniture around, and hired two more maids. She couldn't wait to begin her career as a socialite. She found Alex as sweet as ever, but lacking in the one thing she had married him for – social contacts. She began to get bored, itchy, with everything set up in the house to entertain and no one to lavish invitations on.

Alex closeted himself in his office with calculators and files, trying to determine the flow of finances and redirect them into various projects of his own. The property development side alone was now an incredible size, and with the profits from the night club Edward had been buying buildings with cash. According to what Alex had fathomed out he now owned almost a two-mile stretch of warehouses and Thames waterfront. The discrepancies between the accounts and the cash were enormous, and night after night Alex worked on the terrifying jumble of scraps of paper, leases and deeds, until he threw his hands up in despair. The company could be prosecuted at any time, the Inland Revenue would have a field day.

Edward's return did not make his appearances in the office any more frequent. Alex could never contact him, he was either out supervising his new boutiques in Carnaby Street or he was at the night club. Alex left him messages, memos, but never received a word in reply. Also, a couple of Alex's own business ventures were not going as well as he had hoped. Yet again he was warned that, with the new gaming laws being introduced, their club, and hence a valuable asset for laundering money, was near to closure.

Bundles of documents would be left on Alex's desk – more new companies, more lists of salaries to be paid out, instructions for large sums of money to be withdrawn, all with hastily scrawled messages telling him to lose the transactions in the books.

Alex worked late every night, not helped by a constant stream of workmen installing Edward's new toy, the security system. Loose wires hung in every corner of every office.

Nor was there any respite for Alex when he went home to Mayfair. Barbara would be sitting waiting for him, wanting to go here or there, wanting to be introduced to everyone she could think of, and Alex was so tired he simply wanted to eat his supper and collapse into bed.

'Alex, I'm bored out of my mind, for Chrissake, I sit here all day, I sit here all night! What in God's name do you expect me to do? I can't just sit, I wanna do things, I gotta do something . . . is there nothing I can do in the business?'

Her Texas twang grated on his nerves, and he snapped that perhaps she should take some elocution lessons.

'Fine, I'll start tomorrow . . . You want eloquence, fine, you mind telling me who's gonna even hear my goddamn voice? We don't see anyone, we don't meet anyone, I am bored! Jesus Christ, I come all this way and the only people I meet are goddamn Americans over here for the season – I bought a horse for the girls, stabled it in Hyde Park, that should keep them quiet. Alex, are you even listening to me?'

She snatched the newspaper from him and threw it across the room. 'Alex, will you just listen for a minute, all you have to do is to tell me what to do and I'll do it, but I don't know where to begin.'

Alex got up, kissed her, and apologized. 'Okay, my love, start donating to charities. Make sure they are the big ones and directly connected to royalty. Donate, then offer your time to help out at functions. You want to meet people that's the way to do it . . . Then . . .' He picked up the newspaper and opened it, and Barbara was about to shout at him again when he passed it to her and pointed out an article. 'That bank's in trouble. It's a private bank run by a family. See if you can't get to them, they're well connected, but rumours in the City have it that they're on their way out. See what you can find out, open an account there or whatever, send the lawyers in first and say you want to make a large deposit . . .'

Barbara moaned that that wasn't really what she had had in mind, but Alex kissed her neck and unbuttoned her blouse. 'I think we should maybe take the bank over, the family's got the connections but they're broke – that's your task, sweetheart, so get cracking.' Suddenly he sounded, even to his own ears, like his brother.

Barbara donated massive sums to charities, and soon got caught up in so many charity functions she hardly had the time for her elocution classes. She was invited to lunches, balls, dances, teas, and for the first time since she came to England she started to enjoy herself.

The St James' Bank was overawed by Mrs Barkley. Her lawyers had paved the way and there was quite a reception waiting for her. She made an impressive entrance – the Rolls, the chauffeur, the furs, but most important was the amount of money she wanted to transfer from her Texas accounts. She was evasive, play-ing them along and suggesting that perhaps they should take time to think about the arrangements. Next, Barbara invited the bankers to a small dinner party, knowing they would come, and set about making sure her guest list was full of society names.

Alex was impressed, Barbara was doing far better than he had ever bargained for, although he could do without the frequent dinner parties. He found her circle of 'friends' growing in number, and they were useful to him. The dinner parties became bigger and better, and at long last she began to feature in the society columns. Soon she had every gossip columnist eating out of her hand, and paid for it highly. She became close to the American Ambassador and his wife, and began to dom-inate many charity functions. She was a natural hostess, and learned faster than Alex would have given her credit for. He began to admire her, and to love her even more.

Barbara was in her element, she had made it, and she was now even more choosy about who she talked with, who she invited to her dinners. Now she was looking for openings to move yet another step upward.

Barbara's daughters had both been shipped off to finishing school in Switzerland. On their return to London, the elder girl, Selina, had found it difficult to adjust to her new life and a whole circle of new people, and became very quiet and withdrawn. However, Annabelle, the younger, took to it all with an energy and vigour inherited from her mother. She made many friends, ensuring that they were all from titled families, and moved effortlessly into the young jet set.

Barbara put all her efforts into making good marriages for her daughters, and she discussed a possible suitor with Alex. It would not only mean a good step forward into society, but a strong business move. The St James' Bank heir, Conrad St James, was hand-picked for Selina, financial arrangements with the family having been concluded satisfactorily. Alex Barkley took over the bank, giving Conrad a job for life, and in return Conrad married Selina. She had very little say in the matter, led like a lamb to the slaughter.

The wedding was an elaborate occasion, the cathedral packed with four hundred guests, followed by the reception at the Grosvenor House Hotel in Park Lane. It made every society column, and took up the whole of the gossip diary in *Queen* magazine.

When the newly weds departed for Rome on their honeymoon, Barbara heaved a sigh of relief. Next, she wanted to get Annabelle married. Annabelle had grown taller, and she had her mother's perfect figure. Lord Henry Blackwell, who was as shy as Selina, had been earmarked for her. Unlike her sister, however, she did not bow down to her mother, and they fought like cat and dog. She had a mind of her own and a strong one; she knew exactly what she wanted, what clothes she wanted to wear, and she was as adept at social climbing as her mother. With her friends from school, many of them titled, she could always get around her mother by saying, 'But Lady Somerton's daughter was with me.'

Alex let Barbara do exactly as she wanted, content that she was out of his way, for he was in the midst of the takeover of Buchanan House. He had sold off numerous small businesses and was amassing the cash in readiness. He and Edward argued over virtually every sale, every clause, and their terrible rows echoed round the office. Alex was infuriated by his brother, who would appear and disappear at will, always on some deal or other that he had in mind. These were never of interest to Alex, he wanted more and more to move into the City, but Edward kicked against it. 'Stocks and shares, buddy boy, why get into that, we do all right this way . . . Someone's got to do the dirty little deals, and we're way ahead of everyone else. You start playing the stock market and you'll get your fingers burnt . . .'

Alex was insistent, just as his wife was climbing socially so he wanted to have the City's respect. The Barkley Company had a bad name for under-dealing. Alex wanted to move up and out.

'Edward, why break your balls on this club, close it, let it go.'

Edward hit the roof, screaming at his brother that if he would just go through the accounts he would see why not. They could launder money through it, cream it, just like the old days.

Trying to keep Edward on the straight and narrow was virtually a full-time job, and a desperate one for Alex. 'Why? Why, for Chrissake, take these risks? We are legitimate, and yet you always want to branch out into back-alley deals.'

Edward lost patience, snapping at his brother that he had made the Barkley Company, not Alex. He had made it on the backs of his deals, and if Alex didn't like what he was doing he could go fuck himself and see how well he would do without Edward. The rows between them became a daily occurrence, secretaries and typists would cringe as the bellowing rang through the office. Edward terrified them all, rampaging along the corridors arguing at the top of his voice.

Alex had to spend days trying to fathom out what new moves his brother had made. The Carnaby Street boutiques, which Alex had been against from the first, were going from strength to strength.

'I got the nose, buddy boy, I got the nose ... listen to me, and you'll be where you want, believe me.'

The office was still in turmoil, with workmen carrying wires and monitor screens in and out of Edward's office installing his elaborate security system. Every room was fitted with cameras. Edward's new toys whirred and bleeped, and he was forever rushing down to the basement to check how they worked.

'How long are these men going to be here, Edward? I've got two board meetings this morning, and I don't want ladders everywhere and white overalls dodging in and out.'

Edward beamed and told Alex it was all completed, dragged him down to the basement. 'Okay, now take a look – see, we get anyone breaking in and all the guys down here have to do is flick switches ... see ... There's now a camera in every room, right? They can check out the place with a couple of switches ... bingo!'

Alex looked around the room and sighed. He was beginning to think Edward was paranoid. At times he acted so crazily. His hair was longer than ever, and he wore his denim jeans and cowboy boots every day. While Alex was striving for respectability, Edward was joining in with the 'Swinging Sixties'. The rock music from Edward's office was so loud at times that Alex couldn't hear himself think.

'Edward, maybe you need some kind of rest, you know?'

Edward swore at him, said he was simply moving with the times.

'Bit old, aren't you, to be wandering around like a hippy?'

Edward roared with laughter. 'Brother ... maybe I'm making up for all the lost years of hard labour I put in, so what?'

Alex quietly reminded him that he himself was more than familiar with hard labour. Edward flung his arms around him in one of his crazy gestures. 'Hey, trust me, you got to trust me, Alex old son. I know what I'm doing – you do your thing, man, and I'll do mine, okay?'

Alex hesitated, then asked point-blank, 'She's bad again, isn't she? Harry?'

Edward was suddenly deflated, and made a strange, half-hearted gesture. 'Always comes out at strange times, you know. I was on tenterhooks when the Judge died, but she coped, right as rain. But she's acting up now . . . I dunno what to do, Alex, I just don't. She joined some fringe theatre, all I hear about is this bloody play, she's obsessed with it . . . I don't know if it's in her mind or what, she's wearing black from head to foot all the time now, and she's started shutting herself up in her studio again.'

Alex suggested she should see a doctor.

'Not as easy as all that, she's so paranoid.'

'Well, that makes two of you. With all this equipment you've been installing I'd say you were one and the same . . . if you like, I'll invite her over, or call and see her.'

'Sure you can fit her in? With your busy social schedule I'm amazed you have time to get into the office. But thanks and no thanks. How's your takeover doing?'

Alex was immediately on guard, murmuring that it was going along fine. But Edward was already striding down the corridor, not even interested.

Barbara was not too pleased to be told at the last moment she had two extra guests, Edward and Harriet. She rearranged the table, moved her place cards in a desperate bid to seat Harriet where she would be the least trouble.

Dinner was set for nine o'clock, by eight forty-five there was still no sign of them. Alex called the manor only to be told they had just left. They did not make an appearance until after nine and Barbara was furious. Her guests sat very formally sipping cocktails as Edward, wearing a white tuxedo but no tie, strolled into the sitting room. Harriet remained in the hall wearing what could only be described as an assortment of scarves pulled together to form a dress . . . she also had one wrapped around her head, but worse than her appearance was the fact that she was holding a pigeon she had found in the drive. She appeared at the door as everyone turned to stare. 'Edward, what should I do with it? It's got a clubbed foot! The poor thing's starving.'

'Give it to the butler.'

Barbara's butler, Scargill, turned from handing round the drinks tray. Barbara gave him a look, waved her hand, and knew by now the chef would be throwing a fit in the kitchen. In the end it was Alex who removed the pigeon and took it outside. He simply threw it out of the back door and then assured Harriet it was being fed and cared for.

Dinner was announced and Edward, deep in conversation with a New York banker, sat down in the wrong place. This put all the seating arrangements out, and so it was musical chairs until at last everyone was seated.

The consommé was being served by two white-gloved waiters. Harriet was seated next to a judge, and she fell into a deep conversation about her father and his prostate operation. Everyone had finished their soup and the waiters hovered as Harriet hadn't touched hers. Edward leaned on his elbow and enquired if she had finished, everyone was waiting. 'Oh sorry, you can take it away . . . sorry, Barbara, but we were talking about my father.'

Barbara enquired how Judge Simpson was and Harriet looked astonished. 'Oh he's dead, didn't you know?' Everyone murmured their condolences, and Alex quickly changed the conversation.

Harriet grew very quiet as she knew nothing about banking, and had no interest in political matters. She couldn't help but notice how at ease Edward was and felt more than inadequate. She also noted what a very good hostess Barbara was . . .

*

As they drove home, Edward yawned. Harriet was biting her nails. He slipped his arm around her shoulders. 'You went very quiet.'

'Well I felt a bit out of my depth, the white-gloved treatment is a bit over the top.'

He drove up the manor house drive. 'Maybe, but sometimes it's good for business.'

Harriet lay awake most of the night. She made elaborate plans to begin working with Dewint. To redecorate the manor, and get lots of white gloves ... suddenly she could hear the Judge, his booming voice bellowing through the old Hall ... 'For God's sake, Edna, that fella looks as if he's in a black and white minstrel show, the Duke's comin' for a bite to eat, not a ruddy cabaret.' She slipped out of the bed and crept to the window. She loved to look out of this particular window, down to the big oak tree.

His approaching death had frightened her father, his bluster had gone, and when she had sat with him, he had cried ... held on to her hand. 'How's my country gel then, eh? Good of you ta come up and see us, place always quiet without you ... this is where you belong, not in that filthy city.'

The Judge's request to be buried with his favourite hunter was dismissed as senile ramblings. After his funeral Harriet found the old horse's grave. The horse her pa had refused point-blank to send to the glue factory. He had dug the grave himself. She laid a bunch of wild flowers and a small card ... 'From Your Country Girl'.

As the train arrived back in London, her heart had already begun to ache for the fields, for the fresh clean air, but Edward wasn't there, and where he was, she had to be.

Alex was preparing for the takeover of Buchanan House, a twenty-three-million-pound deal. The news hit the City, and Mr Alex Barkley's face began to appear in the *Financial Times* columns. He was referred to as a new breed of tycoon. He began to relax. Maybe his brother was right, he should let Edward get on with his side of the business. He negotiated the renaming of Buchanan House, listing all the subsidiary companies they could combine. He thought about going public, so he had many meetings with brokers and financiers, closeted in his office or in the boardroom for hours on end. The poised, whirring cameras were soon forgotten, became part of the walls. But Alex was unaware of just what a tight security system his 'dear' brother had had installed. Although Edward's office appeared as it always had, the mammoth desk had been modified, as had the walls. Behind five oak panels were monitor screens, and his desk was computerized, the sides opening up to reveal the controls. Without moving out of his office, Edward Barkley could tape and record every meeting that took place in the building. Every single negotiation, every single phone call that went in or out of the Barkley Company, he recorded. By this method, Edward felt free to roam, leave London whenever he wanted, assured that his office was ticking away all by itself.

Edward had decided that a meeting with Ming was called for. It was not particularly urgent, he just wanted to get away from London, from Harriet – she was heading for one of her depressive bouts. He knew it was wrong, that he should tell her what he was doing, but he did his usual disappearing act anyway.

Dewint had the unfortunate task of telling her, one that often landed on his frail shoulders. Her play was about to open, and Dewint knew how important it was for her to have Edward there on her first night – she needed his approval. She had worked so hard, and at long last she had her Equity card. But she took it very well, shrugging her shoulders and saying it was only to be expected. Dewint tried to make up for Edward's absence, telling her that by the time he returned from New York the play would have had a chance to 'run in', and her performance would no doubt be better for the experience.

This was her first professional engagement, one she had

worked hard to get. She had joined the Bush Theatre at Shepherd's Bush as an assistant to the stage manager. She was an obvious choice for the part of Christina in their production of *The Soul of a Whore*, and so far the rehearsals had gone without a single hitch. As the opening night approached, Harriet's nerves were in shreds. This was no passing whim, as Edward had believed at first, but a serious stab at making a career for herself. She had made considerable donations towards the running of the theatre, and although no one liked to admit it, this had swayed the company into not only staging the production but also offering her the role. They were touched when she insisted she auditioned like anyone else, even though she was the 'angel'. She didn't want to destroy the play's chances of success. Harriet had won the role fair and square, and her position in the company was confirmed.

She rarely, if ever, mentioned her husband, and used the stage name of Harriet Simpson. It had become very important to her that she prove herself, without any influence from Edward.

Dewint watched over her, fussing around, almost as nervous as she was. Alex had been asked to attend, but he had declined due to a prior engagement. Allard, however, was bringing a crowd of his friends to support her.

The small theatre at the top of the pub was crammed. The young author sat biting his nails as the critics squeezed into the rows of benches.

Dewint's nervousness evaporated within the first ten minutes. Harriet's performance was astonishing – she seemed perfectly at home on the stage, and her performance had depth and great humour. She had a rare quality that riveted the audience. She walked a dangerous edge, switching a laugh line into a violent tirade against the men she picked up in her character of a whore. She dominated the stage, and at the end the small theatre gave her a standing ovation.

Dewint waited outside the pub's 'stage door' until Harriet appeared with Allard and his crowd of friends, who were absolutely overwhelmed by her talent. They went off to celebrate, and Dewint caught the bus home. He sat up until four in the morning, when she arrived, exhausted but jubilant. She had done it – she didn't need anyone to tell her, she had felt it from the stage. She handed Dewint a newspaper with the only review so far.

'I'm a star, Norman . . . twinkle, twinkle.'

'Oh, Mrs Barkley, you are, and I'll be there every night.'

'I'd like that, Norman, I'd like that . . . Don't wake me until late. Goodnight . . .'

The following morning as Dewint cleared Harriet's breakfast tray from her bedroom, he noticed all the bread had been rolled into tiny pellets. He checked the pill bottle in her bedside table and found it open.

Ming was reading the morning papers, including the English ones, from cover to cover. There was yet another article about the Barkley empire in the financial section, plus an announcement in the social columns – Alex's second stepdaughter, Annabelle, was to marry Lord Henry Blackwell. But there was little or nothing about Edward Barkley.

It was chilling that, at that precise moment, her houseboy informed her that she had a visitor . . . a Mr Edward Barkley.

Ming kept Edward waiting until she had changed, made up her face, and felt ready to meet him. He was waiting in the lounge, spreadeagled across the sofa reading one of her magazines. She had a moment to take in his dishevelled appearance, his long hair, the denims.

'Well, I see we are very much into the swinging style, would you care for coffee?'

Edward beamed at her and swung his cowboy boots down from the sofa. 'You look good . . . in fact, you've not changed at all.'

Primly she sat down, as far away from him as possible.

'You know, Ming, when I heard that Alex was married, I

thought it was you – I knew the pair of you were carrying on your little affair – but I was wrong.'

'Yes, you were. Well what do you want?'

He laughed, ran his hands through his long hair, and she noticed he wore a gold bracelet. He seemed at ease with her, as if they had seen each other only a few days previously. 'I've got some more projects for you to take over, in Mexico, couple of hotels . . . and I may have a deal for you. What do you think of shipping your fabrics back to Japan? Be a lot of money in it, and they are very interested . . . You free for lunch?'

Ming was impressed, Edward's ability for making contacts never ceased to amaze her. The Japanese project was, as he had said, worth a fortune.

Having made the introductions at lunch, Edward left Ming with the four Japanese buyers to negotiate the contracts. On his way out he let his hand rest just a moment too long on the nape of her neck. 'Why not drop into my hotel later, spot of dinner . . . 'bout nine?'

Ming inclined her head slightly to show her acceptance, then gave her full attention to her countrymen. The deal was an excellent one. They were very interested in Ming's company, interested enough to want to buy into it as part of the deal. They questioned her closely on Edward Barkley's association with her business, hinting that if he agreed to sell them his shares, they could guarantee that shops for her fabrics would open in Japan. As their discussions continued, it became increasingly clear that the deal would only go through if there were no third party involved.

Ming knew that her long wait was to come to an end, now, tonight. During dinner with Edward Barkley tonight she would make her move, and be free of him for good.

Edward had not even changed. He was sprawled on his bed watching cartoons on television when Ming entered. He smiled and patted the bed for her to sit beside him. She hesitated, then sat in a chair.

'I thought we could have room service, or would you prefer to eat out? How did it go? Did you finalize the deal?'

Ming smiled, then cocked her head to one side. 'I'm not hungry, Mr Stubbs. I've come here to discuss business, nothing more.'

She noted the slight twitch, but he gave her no other sign that her use of the name 'Stubbs' had affected him. He switched off the television, and Ming opened her briefcase, tossed him the morning newspaper. 'Alex is really doing well, his stepdaughter, too, marrying a baronet . . . they entertain royalty, according to that article.'

Edward picked up the paper and began to laugh. The world was so small – Lord Henry Blackwell, Allard's boyfriend, no less. Ming was taken off guard when he chuckled. Then his manner changed and he tossed the paper aside. He stared at her, his face hard, his eyes expressionless. 'What's with the "Stubbs"? What's going on in that conniving little head, Miss Takeda?'

Ming folded her hands, licked her lips, and spoke very quietly, but clearly. 'I know all about you, Edward, just as I know all about Alex. I am prepared to forget what I know in return for your twenty-five per cent share of my company.'

She waited, watching him as he stared at her, but he remained silent. She continued, 'I know, Edward, and I am sure Alex would not want it divulged to the English press, that he was convicted of murder. He served a sentence, didn't he? But he served it for you . . . I think it would make fascinating reading, and I could make a considerable amount of money selling the story to one of your more dubious newspapers . . .'

Taking out a cigarette, Edward tapped it on the bedside table, then searched his jeans for his gold lighter. 'So they want me out, do they? Only to be expected, they're a devious bunch, the Japs . . . Well, I suggest you go ahead – and shut the door when you leave, sweetheart.'

Ming sat for a moment longer, then rose to her feet, straightened her skirt, and walked to the door. 'Very well, but don't say I didn't warn you.'

'I hear you ... You don't have time for a quick massage before you go, do you? I like the girls naked, sitting astride, you know? But I'm sure I don't have to teach you the business, do I? I'll pay you extra if you toss me off.'

Ming's hand tightened on the door knob. She knew she had lost this round, he had beaten her at her own game. She looked back at him; if she hated him before, now she wanted him dead. 'Goodnight, Mr Barkley.'

'Oh, Ming, don't try to undercut me, it's a waste of time, you ungrateful little bitch. Try anything and I warn you, I'll take you down with me ... Now go back to the Japs and say I want in, or there's no deal.'

Ming closed the door silently. She knew she could not win with Edward, perhaps she could stand a better chance with Alex. In the meantime she would play the Japanese company along, saying the Barkley shares were being bought out.

Alex Barkley had made it, and he revelled in it. He was happier than he had been in his whole life, with his beautiful wife at his side, two well-connected sons-in-law, and a three-quarter share in a private bank. His own income was staggering, and combined with that of his wife he deserved the title of 'tycoon' the newspapers had given him. He was proud of his achievements, his home and his business. Princess Margaret was a regular guest. Mr and Mrs Barkley had become an 'A list' couple. There were still some slight hitches with the Buchanan takeover, but nothing that alarmed Alex, only Edward could do that.

Edward's increasingly erratic behaviour was not confined to the office. The manor became an open house to dropouts, welcomed by Harriet, who always surrounded herself with groups of actors and musicians. Edward took little interest, his main occupation of late was his night club. He still managed to hold the reins of Banks, being the ninety per cent shareholder, and he was adamant that he would not lose one of his lucrative assets. They were beneficial to him, not just financially.

Edward tried every 'hit' he had used in the past, but to no avail. Clubs were being closed down all over London, and the exclusive Banks became a government priority when it was noted that Edward had returned to London with the notorious George Raft. Mr Raft, it appeared, had Mafia connections. Edward flaunted Raft at the club – flash-bulbs popped as he sat, cigar clenched in his teeth, with his arm around his new friend's shoulders. Next day, the photograph accompanied the headline 'Tycoon's brother involved with Mafia.'

Alex drove to Edward's house. He was trying to control his anger. Dewint was pushed out of the way as Alex passed him. 'Edward! Edwaaaard!'

Edward appeared at the top of the stairs, grinning from ear to ear. 'Hi, man, something up?'

'Don't you play silly buggers with me, Edward. What the hell do you think you're doing? You seen the papers?'

'No – in them, am I? Well, that makes a change – I mean, you're the Barkley Company, according to the press. Tycoon's brother, what?'

Dewint heard them quarrelling at the tops of their voices. He turned away a car-load of guests, and still the brothers argued.

'The Home Office is going to bar George Raft from re-entering the country, why in God's name didn't you tell me he had a share in the club, why? And why, for Chrissake, are you getting mixed up with these guys? You don't need them, you don't even need the club. Just as we are doing so well, the last thing I want is the company name besmirched with this kind of press . . .'

Edward looked at Alex, his face a mask, and when he spoke his voice was so calm that it sent chills through Alex. 'How about headlines like "Barkley tycoon uncovered – ex-con Alex Stubbs"? You stupid bastard, you know Ming threatened to sell our story? You with all your fucking press agents, your social-climbing wife – well let me tell you, your bloody high-powered friends would drop you like dog shit . . .'

Alex paled, so shaken he had to sit down.

'It's all right, it's all right, I doubt if she wants her "true life" history plastered across the papers either. But why didn't you listen to me, I warned you about her . . .'

Alex closed his eyes. 'Oh, Christ . . .' He helped himself to a drink and sat down again.

Edward put an arm around his shoulder. 'Look, don't panic about the club, it'll blow over, but I was made an offer I couldn't refuse – three-quarters of a million for a thirty per cent share in Banks. In return I get a share of a casino in Nevada – it would have been madness to turn it down. When are you going to learn, your big brother has the Midas touch? Listen to me, don't try to do me in, ride with me. You're my brother, I'd never do anything to harm you, you know that . . . Look at me . . . you ever dream you could be where you are now? Well, did you? But never forget where we came from and keep your mouth shut tight . . . and if you ever feel like gabbing, take a look at your medallion, that way you'll always remember.'

Alex asked if Edward still wanted to keep the club open, knowing it was being investigated by the Home Office.

'They won't find anything wrong, Alex. And besides, I have my own contacts in the Home Office, so why don't you just back off, you aren't involved.'

Without touching his drink, Alex walked out. Apparently unconcerned, Edward sat with his feet up on the sofa, whistling. He would find himself a new partner, one person, someone high up in the City, and they would run the club, he would show Alex. He cut and snorted more cocaine, he was doing a line on the hour almost every hour now.

Later, he put it down to the cocaine, and the fact that he was still jet lagged. He always had to have a reason, but however he fooled himself, there could be no excuse for his flagrant disregard of everything the doctors had said about Harriet.

The argument began over dinner. She was dressed in a strange forties' dress with padded shoulders. He looked her up and down. 'Do you go out of your way to make yourself unattractive? Where in God's name did you get that dress?'

'My mother, if you must know.'

'Well I'd give it back.'

'That would be rather difficult ... don't you want to know why?'

'I'm sure you will have some amusing elaborate story ... so tell me!'

'She died three weeks ago ...'

'I'm sorry, you should have told me.'

'How? I never know where the hell you are ... what made it worse, I couldn't even get to her funeral. The play ... remember the play I was in, just another thing in my life you missed.'

'I've said I'm sorry – what more do you want me to say? Well?'

'Nothing ...'

'Are you going into any more of these theatrical ventures?'

'That's my business.'

'Not quite, I do happen to be paying for them, and if you want my opinion I think they're conning you. I had a look at your accounts ... and like I said you've shelled out a lot of cash.'

'Shelled? ... Christ you sometimes sound so vulgar ... where did you pick that one up from, little slit eyes? Dingley ding Ming?'

He bit the end of his cigar and spat it out. She drummed her fingers on the table spoiling for a fight.

'I was just trying to fathom out how much longer this fad of yours was going to last ... that's all, no need to get uptight.'

'Fad? ... the theatre is not a fad. I happen to like it, more than that I love it, the warmth and the friendship I get from the people associated with it ...'

He interrupted her, 'How long do you think this so-called warmth would last if your cash dried up? You should put it to the test ... couple of months you'd be left high and dry, sweetheart.'

She jumped up shouting, 'You are the one that's high; you

should look at yourself – you're stoned out of your mind most of the time, and don't call me sweetheart ... save it for your tarts.'

Dewint was about to enter the dining room with a large trifle, but stepped aside as she rushed out of the room. She was quickly followed by Edward, and by the look on his face there was more than a storm brewing. He took himself and his trifle back into the safety of the kitchen. They had had rows, and he was used to them, but this one he had felt coming for quite a while.

Edward cornered her at the top of the stairs. 'You think this is any place for a man to come home to? All those queens poncing around, you got up like something from the ark? Well do you? When will you try learning the part of a wife for a change?'

She kicked out at him. 'When you play the part of a husband, you egotistical bastard, that's when ...'

'You saying I'm not? That what you're saying? Well you tell me who picks up the pieces? I got the leftovers, didn't I? Well didn't I? And you know who I'm talking about.'

'No, I don't ... you're so stoned it's difficult to follow your train of thought, now let me past ... get out of my way.'

He leaned both hands over her so she was trapped beneath him. 'I'm referring to the French man, Pierre Rochal ... go on, run to your hiding hole, go on ...'

She edged past him, and he sneered. 'He didn't put up much of a fight, did he? Know why? Because he knew all about you, guy couldn't wait to get shot of you ...'

Harriet was almost at the top of the stairs, she looked back at him. 'You were the one that ran after me, and if you've got to rake up that far back, then you really are pitiful.'

'Yeah, you said it ... but if I'd known about the baby, maybe I wouldn't have come after you. I was the one who wanted sons remember? Me!'

He began to move up the stairs. 'It was his baby you lost, not mine, but I've had the shit thrown at me. Surprised?

You didn't think I knew about it, did you? Don't you tell me about being a good husband, you got the better side of the bargain.'

He waited for her to come back at him, ready to continue the fight. Like a boxer coming in for the kill, knowing the punch had found its mark, he waited . . . his opponent, his wife reached down to the ache inside her. The pain that had haunted her, that she had denied him, was released. Her face crimson with anguished rage she screamed . . . 'It was your son, you bastard.'

The fight turned tables, a boxer when hurt can be more dangerous . . . more vicious because he knows it's the last chance . . . Harriet took it, took it and gave punch after punch to his heart. 'He was perfect, Edward, perfect. Imagine what it felt like to hold his cold body in my arms – whisper his name, beg for his lungs to move . . . what was his name, can you think what I would have called your son, can that putrid, festering mind think . . . tell me his name?'

His mind reeled, he pressed his back against the wall. She came closer, closer, now she moved to stand in front of him, her arms stretching either side of him as she looked into his face. She whispered the name he already knew . . .

'Freedom . . . I called him Freedom.'

Slowly he moved his arms around her as her body caved in. He cried for what he had done, he cried for his son . . . and at long last they wept together for their loss. Later they slept in each other's arms, afraid to let go . . . drained . . . bound to each other as they had always been. Edward woke and felt for her body, but she was gone. He prayed he would be wrong, but he found her in the studio. This time, though, she allowed him to drive her to the doctor.

> For who steals the charm of the dukkerin's son
> Will walk in his shadow, bleed with his blood
> Cry loud with his anguish and suffer his pain
> His unquiet spirit will rise again.

It was almost ten o'clock when Edward returned. Dewint made him fresh coffee and took it into the lounge. Edward stood staring into the fire, he turned a sheepish, sad face.

'How is she, sir?'

'Not too good, may be away for some time . . . I'll be at the club if anyone wants me.'

Edward began his drinking again, staying out until the early hours of the morning. Dewint didn't serve his breakfast often until noon. He always tapped nervously . . . afraid to wake him because he could have such terrible moods. This morning he was awake, and Dewint carried in his tray.

'Mrs Barkley's downstairs, sah . . . Mrs Barbara Barkley.'

Edward smiled, began to eat. 'Show her up, and bring a bottle of champagne.' Barbara walked in and tossed her mink on the bed. She noticed he was wearing only his pyjama bottoms, and the gold medallion around his neck.

'Well, you proud of yourself? Alex says he's tried to reason with you, now it's my turn. He says you've been offered a lot of money for a percentage of the club. Well, I'll match it if you back off, get rid of it.'

Dewint entered with the champagne and popped the cork, while Edward lay back, arms behind his head. Barbara waited until Dewint had gone then she sat down a good distance away. 'Annabelle's just married, everything is good right now, and Alex can't afford to lose out on this thing he's got going. Why do you do it, Edward? Why?'

Edward sipped his champagne and patted the bed for her to come and sit close. 'Maybe I'm bored, maybe I've been through Alex's trip and out the other side. I don't care any more, I don't give a fuck what the right people think of me, it doesn't matter. You know, the only thing that does is money – need I say more? Look where it got you.'

Barbara threw the glass of champagne straight at his head. It splashed down the pillow and Edward laughed. 'Do you really care what those stuffed shirts think? Who gives a shit? You got one life, Barbara, and I've spent most of mine licking other men's fucking boots . . . Why don't you get your clothes off and get into bed with me.'

Barbara slapped him and he caught her wrist. 'Temper, temper . . . only teasing. But you can rest easy, I'll be a good boy, no more headlines, all right? I was just bored, that's all, don't you ever get bored?'

He watched her sigh and pour herself another drink.

'Now you've met the so-called English aristocrats, you telling me you really get on with those wankers?'

Barbara, walking to the window, asked him to refrain from speaking to her like a tart.

'Ohhh, I'm sorry, I'll mind my p's and q's, won't use any naughty words in front of Her Ladyship. Why don't you be honest, honey child, you're as pissed off as I am . . .'

Barbara picked up her mink coat, slipped it round her shoulders. 'I happen to like my life. Just because you have nothing worthwhile in yours, don't think everyone feels the same way.'

She couldn't have said anything worse. Edward threw back the bedclothes and stood, barring her exit. She tried to push past him, but he grabbed her and she tried to force him away. He held on, and she fought, kicked at him and scratched him, grabbed his hair. The leather thing holding it snapped, and his hair fell loose, down to his shoulders. Barbara resisted by letting her body go limp. 'Please don't, let me go, Edward. Don't do this to me, please.'

He opened his arms, released her, and then cupped her face in his hands, gently. 'Sorry, sorry, sorry . . . go home to him, go home like a good girl.'

He moved back to the bed and sprang up on it, then flopped down like a child. The door closed and he glanced up; she was leaning against it. She began to unbutton her blouse, kicked off her shoes, and Edward, propped on one elbow, watched her. 'You are a rare beauty, Barbara, you know that? Untie your hair.'

She sat on the edge of the bed and allowed him to toss her

hairpins aside one by one . . . He eased her blouse away and with one finger unhooked her bra, kissing her shoulders, her back, and she leaned against him . . . He pulled her back until she lay across the bed, and he ran his hands through her hair. He began to ease her skirt off, and she made no move to either stop him or help him.

They lay side by side, one so fair, so blonde, and the other so dark . . .

'You know, you look like him sometimes, and you both wear those medallions. What have you got on yours?'

Edward looked down at her and smiled. 'Exactly what Alex has on his.'

He touched her breast, slowly tracing the nipple, then he whispered that perhaps she should just close her eyes and make believe he was Alex, and then she would be able to make regular visits . . .

'Would you want me to?'

Edward kissed each of her breasts and said he would, he would like her here with him all the time. She held him, wrapped her arms around him and kissed his neck.

'I want that too, you know I want that too.'

Edward hadn't expected her to be quite so easy, but he did fancy her; she was a beauty. He made love to her gently, lovingly. She was slow to be aroused, she behaved straight, not seeming to want anything 'unusual' . . . and it was not until he had come into her that she started. He wouldn't have minded a quick snooze, but she rolled on top of him. 'You go to sleep, Mr Barkley, and I'll suffocate you.'

She put the pillow over his face, told him to keep still and not move, then she got off the bed, went to the champagne bucket and brought back a handful of ice cubes, dumped them on the bedside table. She took one and ran it gently along the side of his thigh. He squirmed.

'No, no, don't move, you'll like it . . . wait, you'll like it.'

Edward grasped the pillow and pulled it over his face as the ice slithered over his body, between his thighs, his balls, until he was jumping, writhing ... but she kept pushing him down, started to kiss and rub his chest. He tossed the pillow aside. 'Where else have you got an ice cube, madam?'

Barbara leaned back, laughing, and eased him into her.

'My God, where did you learn all this – Alex?'

She moved on top of him and smiled, Alex had not had this treatment, he preferred something else ... 'I'll try out Alex's treatment on you after, he always likes it a certain way ... now why don't you shut up talking about him and enjoy it.'

Edward pulled her down to him. 'You think I'm not enjoying it? Well, I'll teach you a few things.'

Lying awake in his room, Alex heard Barbara arrive home, and waited to see if she would come into his room. She tapped on his door and opened it.

'Edward wouldn't listen to me. I even offered to buy him out, but he was so beastly I went over to see Margaret and had a late dinner ... I'll see you in the morning, darling ... night–night.'

Barbara was so exhausted she almost had to crawl the last few yards to her bed, and fell asleep instantly.

Edward hated Barbara to ring him at the office, and what had started out as a fling was now very heavy going. She would arrive at any hour she chose, never calling first, expecting him to be ready like a stud. Otherwise she would demand to meet him in hotels or secret restaurants.

Edward paid weekly visits to Harriet, but this time her recovery was slow. She had become a vegetarian, preparing for her release to eat her way back to health. She had endeared herself to so many nurses and patients it was difficult to have a private conversation with her. She knew everyone's name, and her sunny nature made the doctors joke that no one ever wanted to leave. They also informed Edward in all seriousness that it was taking time because she was still afraid to leave the security of the nursing home. Edward was relieved, life was becoming a little tricky, with Barbara appearing whenever she chose. She had no regard for Harriet, and rarely asked about her.

He couldn't help but smile, they certainly were poles apart . . . he stood by the greenhouse door and watched Harry with a small trowel digging at a tomato plant . . . Barbara would never have been seen dead in a pair of wellington boots, but there was Harry elbows in soil – her face filthy. She gave him a wink, and then wrapped her arms around a very plump girl who appeared to be in tears. She joined him outside and jerked her thumb back to the greenhouse . . . 'She's very upset, her pet's died.' She slipped her arm through his.

'I didn't know you could have pets here?' he said.

'Oh, you can't, not really, it was a toad, called Herbie, but she was very fond of him, she's known him since he was a tadpole.'

'Ah well, in that case they'd have a strong rapport.'

She laughed, and he pulled her close . . . then he sniffed.

'God, what's that smell?'

'Manure . . . it's the new perfume by Dior, very popular.'

As always she had him laughing, and he kissed her soil-stained face. 'Want you home soon, Dewint is walking around like Dracula's mother . . .'

He felt her tense up, then she was serious. 'I'll come home when I'm strong, won't be too long, okay?' She waved him goodbye from behind the gates, placing the trowel to her lips and giving him a Hitler salute. She returned to her tomato plants and he to a young, skinny model he had begun an affair with. He was in a very good mood, perhaps it was because he knew Harry would be home soon.

Dewint looked disdainfully at the young girl. Edward took him aside and gave him strict instructions that if Mrs Barkley, Mrs Barbara Barkley, was to call he was not available – ever. He knew he could get rid of the model easily enough, but Barbara was too close, too dangerous when Harry came home, he didn't want anything to upset her.

*

Dewint tapped on the bedroom door. Even though he had told Mrs Barkley that Edward was not at home, she was refusing to leave. She swept past him, straight into the bedroom, and closed the door in his face.

'What the hell are you playing at, giving that idiot orders to say to me, to me, that you are not in when I know damned well you are?'

The poor, nervous 'beanpole' hovered in the bathroom, a towel wrapped around her skinny body. Barbara shouted that it was the third time she had tried to see Edward, and that he had not returned any of her calls, but she was stunned into silence when the bathroom door opened and the girl, pink with embarrassment stood there, shaking.

'Get this thing out of here, Edward, and fast – I mean it.'

Edward kissed his little girlfriend and handed her her clothes, saying he was sorry but there was obviously some kind of family crisis . . . It was nothing, 'she' was just his sister-in-law.

Dewint was given the nod to get the girl out, and Edward wrapped his dressing gown around himself and went to join Barbara in the lounge.

'You bastard, you bastard, why haven't you answered my calls? Because that, whatever you call it, was in your bed? Why don't you grow up, you're a bit old for her, aren't you? What is she, sixteen, seventeen?'

Edward lit a cigar and lay on the sofa. 'She's actually twenty-two, but she looks younger . . . was there something you wanted?'

Barbara walked around to the other side of the sofa so she could face him. 'I'm pregnant.'

Edward beamed and congratulated her, said Alex would be thrilled.

'It isn't Alex's, it's yours, it's yours. If you recall, when I first came here I didn't happen to have my cap in my handbag . . .'

'So what do you want to do about it?'

She sighed, asked him what *he* wanted to do about it. He walked to the window, pushed it open. 'Will you tell Alex? I know a good doctor . . .'

Barbara stepped away from him as though she'd been slapped. 'What did you say . . .?'

'I said I know a good doctor who will see you, be over with, if that's what you want . . .'

'What do you want, you bastard?'

Edward sighed, rubbing his head. 'Does Alex have any idea about us?'

Barbara opened her handbag and took out her compact, began dabbing her eyes with a handkerchief. 'No . . . no he doesn't, and he won't. He'll think it's his, I'll make sure of it.'

She blew her nose and refreshed her lipstick, but her eyes filled with tears. 'You know, I thought you really cared about me. But you don't care about anyone, do you? I must have been out of my mind. Well, I'm going to make it up to him, so stay away from me and if you so much as even hint at what has gone on between us I'll . . . I'll . . .'

'Give me some credit, for Chrissake, he is my brother . . . He'll not hear it from me, you have my word on it.'

He heard the snap of her compact, then she sniffed. 'Well, do something for him. Get rid of that club, sell it, do whatever you have to, but don't be involved in it any more.'

'Okay, if that's what you want.'

'Even more than that, I want you to stay out of our lives, stay away from us, and leave him alone. He's decent . . . I wish to God I'd never met you.'

When she had gone, Edward poured himself a brandy. What a bloody mess. Part of him, the part that had always wanted an heir, was saddened by the fact that, of all the women in the world, the one who carried the child he'd always wanted should be his brother's wife.

Dewint came in to say that if Edward was going to visit Harriet, he should set out soon to avoid the traffic.

'Ahhh, yes, we must avoid the traffic at all cost. Right, let's get on the road then. Did you get some flowers and the things she likes from the vegetarian shop?'

'Yes, sah, everything's here. You'll give her my love, won't you?'

Edward took the carrier bag and nodded, saying quietly, 'Yes, old fella, I'll give her your love.'

Harriet was waiting for him in the sunny lounge. She sprang up and hurried towards him. She looked wonderful, and it never ceased to amaze him how quickly she changed. The terrible, drawn, haggard look had been replaced by a youthful bloom.

'I have some news. I've been bursting to tell you, but I wanted to see your face when I told you — guess what?'

'Why don't you try telling me, and here — all the stuff you wanted from that weird shop.'

'Oh, I'm coming home! Still, we can take it back with us ...' Her laugh bubbled up and eventually he was caught by her good spirits.

'So, what is it, eh? What do you want to tell me?'

'You are going to be a father.'

He stared, open-mouthed, then swallowed. He looked around the room, then back to her in disbelief. For a moment he was so confused he was speechless.

'I — am — going — to — have — a — baby ...'

Book Six

Chapter Twenty-Three

After the initial shock, Edward set about preparing for father-hood like a military campaign. He dragged Harriet to every possible doctor and discussed any foreseeable problems with the pregnancy. Harriet was tested, pummelled and prodded by the best gynaecologists in Harley Street. They discussed at length whether or not she should keep on with her medication. It was decided that she should stop, unless it became necessary again, as she wanted to breastfeed the baby. Edward read every book he could find about expectant mothers, babies, and depression. He was worried because Harriet's age put her in a high-risk cate-gory.

He had even discussed this with Alex as Barbara was even older. Alex suggested that Edward talk the matter over with Barbara, but felt that as she had already had two children, she was not unduly worried. Barbara was the last person Edward could talk to, instead he took himself off to yet another specialist. He wanted to know the risks of mongolism, and whether the child could inherit its mother's manic depression. He also brought up the matter of Harriet's age. Edward had always lacked a great deal as a husband, but now, his care and attention to every detail was touching. His misgivings were discussed thoroughly by the specialist, and relieved by his confidence that after all the examinations Mrs Barkley should have a perfectly normal birth and most important, a healthy child. Edward even held the instruction book for Harriet while she learned the exercises. He attended sessions with a nurse brought in to instruct them both, and didn't appear to mind panting and puffing alongside Harriet. A lot of the time she got into such fits of giggles that he was the only one left panting, the nurse standing over him telling him how to push. But under his loving care, she blossomed.

Harriet began to feel she had finally turned a corner in her life. She paid careful attention to her health, and took great pains to obey her doctors' orders to the letter. Her vegetarian meals were carefully chosen and cooked to give her a balanced diet. She was blissfully happy, and what made her happiest of all was Edward's adoration.

Work and the office could not be further from Edward's mind. But when he received an urgent call from Skye Duval, Harriet persuaded him to go. He was reluctant to leave her, but she insisted.

Barbara heard about Harriet's pregnancy from Alex. Edward had been loath to tell anyone about the forthcoming event because he wanted to be one hundred per cent sure nothing could go wrong. It was bizarre that both brothers should be expectant fathers, but even more ironic that both wives should be carrying Edward's children. Alex had not the slightest notion that Barbara's baby was not his, and was as excited and overwhelmed with the prospect of having a child as Edward. But Alex was left to run the company virtually single-handed, as Edward had done his usual disappearing act.

Alex had discovered the deeds for Banks on his desk the day Barbara told him she was expecting his child. He felt it was a lucky sign, that Edward had agreed to sell. He had no idea of the part his wife had played in persuading Edward to agree to the sale.

At first Alex presumed that the club was an embarrassment because of the bad press it had received, but when it was put on the market the interest didn't come from the seedy club world he had once known. It was eventually sold to two financiers, both with excellent reputations in the City.

Aware of the club's Mafia connections during Edward's ownership, Alex had always disassociated himself with Banks. Now, with the club going legitimate, he made sure that he kept a share, seeing his opportunity to act as a silent third partner. The new owners closed the club for six months while it was refurbished, and when it reopened it was an exclusive gambling club for members only. It was fronted with such good names and links to the City that it seemed above reproach, and, as Edward had always known it would, the club became a gold mine.

Alex quietly paved his own way in the City, enjoying his forays into high finance more and more. He took a particular interest in arbitrage, a very complicated form of dealing which made money by seizing on anomalies in world currencies and interest rates. He opened up his own office and employed three slick young brokers, whose job it was to watch the money markets for opportunities. For example, if the dollar was 1.29 in Frankfurt, but in New York was fetching 255 Japanese yen, they would find a broker in Milan willing to sell Dutch guilders for 70 yen apiece. Meanwhile, the pound might be changing hands in London at 4.3 guilders. So if they pushed a million pounds through the sequence while the rates held good, from Frankfurt to New York, to Milan, to London ... they could end up with a vast profit for very little time and effort. This was what attracted Alex to the City, it was like a chess game, and he was making a fortune.

The three young men spent their days scanning Reuters' screens and 'running' on the Stock Exchange, enabling Alex to amass great sums of money with one hand while attending to the Barkley Company with the other. Also, since he had taken over the St James' Bank, he was able to delve deeper into the property business unhindered by the necessity for loans from City banks. He worked best alone, without interference from

Edward, and was more than pleased that his brother was out of the way. All company cheques required double signatures, but Edward trusted his brother's business acumen and left signed cheques for him to use. Alex was going from strength to strength, ploughing Barbara's fortune into the Barkley holdings and beginning to structure the massive takeover of Buchanan House, a vast corporation which owned restaurants, shops, and four department stores, nationwide. As he grew more confident of his prowess as a tycoon, Barbara became his ally, always at his side. She considered their social calendar, entertaining lavishly, and their connections enabled them to push their business upwards, step by step. Alex was happy – he was to be a father, and at last he felt fulfilled and contented.

Barbara never mentioned Edward's name, and she rediscovered her love for Alex. In truth, she couldn't help but notice that when Edward was absent, Alex was far more at ease. He appeared to be very much the head of the Barkley Company, and the business was run according to his instructions. Everything was legal, he was becoming a public figure, and the baby's birth was imminent.

Edward didn't stop to take his coat off. He hurtled up the stairs, dropping baby clothes and toys as he ran. 'Harry, Harry, I'm home . . .'

Harriet waddled out to the landing. She was wearing a white maternity dress, and her hair was so long she had plaited it down her back. Wild curls framed her forehead, and escaped in small wisps at her neck. Edward thought her more beautiful than ever. He clasped her to him, crushing the flowers he had brought her and dropping more toys. He was deliriously happy. 'God, I've missed you, have I missed you!'

'Well you've not been off the phone – for a man who never used to bother to call you're certainly making up for lost time. Now, wait until you see the nursery. It is, though I say it myself, a triumph . . . The cot was Dewint's find, it's got more frills than

I personally would have chosen, but ... Look, what do you think?'

The room was decorated in eggshell blue. All along one wall were toys, trains and boats and aeroplanes. 'I've had such fun picking out everything.'

'You've not been doing too much? You know you have to look out for yourself, remember what the doctor said ...'

She gave him a slap, and told him Dewint even carried her handbag for her. She giggled and said she thought he quite liked it.

They sat before the blazing fire, discussing names. Neither of them mentioned the name Freedom, that was the past, this was the future ... Suddenly, as she leaned forward to poke the fire, Harriet gasped, and put her hands to her swollen belly. The colour drained from her face and she winced with pain, clung to Edward ... 'Oh, God, something is wrong, get an ambulance ... Oh my God, Edward, I'm losing him, for God's sake help me ...'

The ambulance took Harriet to the local hospital as there was no time to drive across London to the clinic they had booked. Harriet's doctor was there within the hour, and she was rushed into the delivery room. Edward, who had studied all the procedures, had to remain outside, frantic with worry. Nurses came and went. He paced the corridor, lighting cigar after cigar, until at long last the surgeon came out and removed his mask. 'Well, she's all right – we've saved her.'

'What about the baby?'

'It's the baby who's all right, she's a tiny little soul, but a fighter. You can see her as soon as she's cleaned up. Harriet's still out, she'll be coming round in fifteen, twenty minutes.'

'A girl? It's a girl? Does Harry know?' He shook his head. 'Of course not ... Is she all right? Is my wife all right?'

The surgeon led Edward to a chair before he could fall down, then sat next to him. 'She's a little cracker, but be prepared – she's very tiny, weighed in at two pounds. But she's got everything in the right place. She's in the incubator, but you can hold her soon enough, okay? Want to come through? Then you can see your wife ...'

He led Edward to the Special Care Baby Unit, past rows of bawling babies, to a side ward. There, in something that looked to Edward like a huge cake stand with a clear dome over it, lay his tiny daughter. A nurse, her eyes smiling over her face mask, beckoned him.

'She's a sweetheart, come on, take a look. You know, we had a fight on our hands, and she fought along with us.'

Edward's heart was thudding in his chest, his lips were dry. He swallowed hard, leaned over and looked down into the incubator that was keeping his daughter alive. He gasped and smelt the disinfectant on his own mask. The little girl was like a miniature doll, and all he could think of to say was, 'Look at her hands, look at her hands.'

The child was wriggling, and her miniature fingers were splayed out, pushing at the tubes in her nostrils. The nurse let him stay for ten minutes, and then they told him he could see his wife, she was coming round.

'Has anyone told her yet? Has anyone told her the baby's all right?'

The nurse shook her head. Harriet was not fully conscious, and he would be the one, he could tell her himself.

Edward took Harriet's hand and she moaned, turned her head and realized he was there. As soon as her eyes opened he bent close, kissing her, whispering, 'Baby's fine, it's all right, you did your stuff. We got the wrong sex, but who cares? She's beautiful, and she's all right.'

'It's a girl ...? It's a girl?' She gave a deep, shuddering sigh. 'Oh, it's a girl, a girl ...'

'Hey, now listen, maybe it's fate, and I don't want any nonsense. We just thank God we have her, and I won't leave here until you smile ... Come on, give me one of your smiles.'

He stroked her forehead gently, and she smiled wanly. 'Poor Norman will have to redecorate the nursery, we got the wrong colour.' Her face puckered and she wept.

Edward kissed her tears. 'My God, she's the image of you, spitting image . . . Now you get some rest, I have to go and get some of your things, you left in a bit of a hurry.'

Alex arrived at the small, private clinic shortly before the child was born. Barbara was ready to go into the delivery room, but the nurse left them alone for a few moments. Alex sat close, wearing a green gown and mask and holding Barbara's hand as she went into labour, never leaving her side throughout the birth. When at last he heard the baby's cry his heart thudded, and he found himself weeping.

'You have a son, Mr Barkley, and what a boy, he's so strong.'

Alex was beside himself with joy as he held his son. He turned his tearful eyes to his wife. 'Barbara, look at him, he's perfect, he's the most perfect baby I have ever seen . . . nine and a half pounds, nine and a half pounds . . .'

The baby was laid gently on Barbara's stomach, and they both looked into the tiny face with the long, black eyelashes. Already he had curly black hair, and at less than one hour old he was the image of his father, Edward Barkley. Barbara could see only Edward's face, the baby was so much his child that Barbara hated him. She turned away, unable to bear it.

Alex picked up his son and showed him off, proudly, to anyone he could find.

'This is my son, my little boy . . . isn't he the most perfect baby you have ever seen in your life?'

Left alone, Barbara prayed that Alex would never find out, never know the truth. She had spoken only a few words to Edward since hearing about the birth of his daughter. Harriet was still in the hospital, and rumour was rife about Harriet's condition, her mental state – no one imagined there could be anything physically wrong with her. Barbara had said simply that if Edward ever gave so much as a hint of the true facts about her child she would make sure his darling wife tripped over the edge she was always teetering on. Edward was disgusted, and even signed a paper Barbara's lawyer had drawn up.

Barbara had no fear that Edward would ever try to see his child, and she knew she would never be welcome at the manor. She had hoped for another girl, they were so much easier than boys. She wondered how Edward would feel about the situation now, she knew he had been as desperate as Alex for a son. She pursed her lips, thinking it served him right.

After a great deal of argument, Alex had put his foot down and chose the baby's name. He had called Edward to tell him – he would be known as Evelyn. Barbara hoped he would change his mind and agree that Evelyn was not a boy's name, but when she tackled him yet again he suggested she take a look at Evelyn Waugh's novels. Barbara retorted that she'd never heard of her, either. Alex laughed and said he simply wanted to call his son after his beloved mother, and in the end Barbara had acquiesced.

Later that night, when the nurse came in, the baby was crying.
    'Don't you want to hold him, Mrs Barkley?'
    'No, I'm too tired, you give him the bottle, I'm too tired.'

Harriet came home from hospital. She had recovered from the Caesarean operation, and showed no signs of the post-natal depression that everyone had been expecting. Edward sighed with relief, but it was just like Harry to break all the rules. The doctor did say to Edward that until the baby was well enough to leave the hospital he should keep a careful watch on his wife.
    Harriet accepted her daughter, and called her Juliana. Joking with Edward one night she said that the baby was jinxed as all her nursery toys were for boys, and they referred to her as 'Jinks'. The nickname stuck, and Juliana was known as Jinks from then on.
    With Dewint, Harriet visited the baby daily for two months. The doctors believed that not bringing her home straightaway had worked to Harriet's advantage. They felt that Harriet's attitude to Jinks was slightly standoffish, she didn't seem to want to pick the baby up or hold her. Part of the problem was that

Harriet was afraid to – the baby was so tiny, so vulnerable. But the time she spent at the hospital with the nurses, learning to care for her, to feed her, gradually enabled Harriet to grow accustomed to handling the baby. Edward went along as often as possible, and it was with relief that he noticed Harriet's increasing eagerness to visit her.

When at last Jinks was brought home, they hired a nurse to help out, at the doctor's suggestion. They had chosen a pleasant Scottish girl who, being a vegetarian, had something in common with Harriet. The two got along very well. Mavis McCormick was sensitive and intelligent, and fully aware of Harriet's problems. She knew when she should interfere and when to stand aside.

Edward had waited until his daughter was safely home before he broke the news that he would have to go away for a few weeks. There were problems in South Africa just as all the hard work of the last few years was coming to fruition. There were serious hitches and financial discrepancies that would have to be sorted out fast. Skye Duval was not answering Edward's telexes, and his office phone had been left off the hook.

Edward left details with Mavis of how to contact him, day or night, if it should prove necessary. He was very reluctant to leave, but really had no option. Harriet was philosophical about it. She carried Jinks in her arms to see him off, waving the little girl's hand as Edward got into the car. Then he got out again to give them both another kiss.

'Okay, now you take care of your mother,' he told Jinks seriously, 'and when I come home I'll bring you something special.'

Harriet, smiling, said if he brought anything more home for the baby, they would never be able to get into the nursery.

Edward had never been so relaxed and happy in his life, and he hated leaving. The thought of his family fed his anger on the flight to South Africa.

Skye had never seen Edward so angry. In all the years they had known each other Edward had never shown this icy fury, and he was terrified. Skye sweated it out as Edward went from site to site, checking and double-checking the company's building projects. To all intents and purposes Skye had been running the company as Edward instructed, but there were big payouts, five thousand here, ten there, which were not accounted for.

Skye stuttered. 'That MP you got, he's in and out of the place all the time. Every time he comes here he wants more, he gives us a project and his hand is out ... Take a look, he's got an account here, one in Switzerland, and he's even got me setting up schemes for his wife, his kids ... I've been warning you about him, I sent you telex after telex ...'

Edward swore. Walter was going over the top, feathering his nest at Edward's expense, and yet they could do nothing. They needed him – his name had already got them into Mexico.

'You think we could get these deals without him, Skye? Do you?'

Skye said they could, the company was now very prestigious, but he doubted if they could lose Walter. He would want to milk them on everything they built.

'We'll see about that ... Mexico, how's that going?'

Pulling out the drawings and the files, Skye showed Edward that Walter had once again taken a ten thousand pound bribe for his connections in Mexico. 'He wants a share of everything, Edward. The guy is so greedy, he wants to be a rich man and he's doing it on your back. But I don't see how we can stop him. If word of his share in all these projects leaks out, it'll finish his political career and at the same time wipe us out. The government would step in right away.'

They dined together at a very elegant restaurant. Edward chose a table at the back of the room, in a small alcove. He poured Skye a glass of Dom Perignon and toasted him.

'Got some business to add to your already expanding duties. That land I own over at Ghost Mountains, I'm ready to begin work on it. I want all the tractors and digging machines driven over there at the beginning of next month. I have all the licences for blowing the place apart.'

Skye whistled. He had been waiting to see why Edward had been steadily buying up vast areas of land to add to the millions of acres he already owned.

'It's not for diamonds, it's perlite ... I've done a deal with some Americans to start mining for perlite.'

'What do I get out of it, apart from more work?'

'You'll be handsomely paid, old bean, as always.'

'The official will want a cut, plus the government, you know that?'

Edward ordered for them both, and Skye tossed the menu aside. He downed his champagne, ordered another bottle.

Edward mused, twirling his glass around. 'Been thinking of floating the company on the London Johannesburg stock exchange, raise more money from Joe Public – make you a tycoon, Skye. I've made an appointment for you to see the solicitors tomorrow, Main Street, they'll be waiting. I'm not interested in the stones, it's the perlite I want. You'll have the best man to help you, an expert on sedimentary rock, he'll do all the assessments. I want to corner the whole market, become the sole owner of every perlite mine in South Africa, so I don't want any leakage. I don't want anyone to suspect there might be valuable stones there as well ...'

Skye lit a cigarette and blew out the smoke, which formed circles above his head. 'You'll have to be fucking careful, man, that place could be more productive – surrounded by fucking oyster beds, you know, near the fucking coast. Could be showered with pearls, never mind fucking diamonds.'

Edward didn't speak while the waiter served their meal, then he jabbed at the steak with his fork. 'I'm arranging a method for getting the stones out and over to England ... We are mining for perlite, sweetheart, anything else keep quiet about. I'll get it out of South Africa, no problem.'

Skye toyed with his food, pushing it around his plate, his cigarette still burning between his fingers. 'You're the boss, man, but you want to get on the side of the blokes running the so-called "Illegal Diamond Division". I'll give you their names. They'll turn a blind eye as long as you pay them enough.'

Edward nodded, chewing his steak, then spoke with his mouth full. 'I don't want a single mining house to get wind of this project. Next week I want you to go over to Sbwana Bay, and take your fucking quinine with you, it's bush and more bush. You don't go near the map companies, I've got some worked out. This is mouth shut time.'

'Okay by me – fancy a trip, bored out of my mind on the building sites. You know how much the machines will set you back? Around fifty thousand – pounds, not dollars, sweetie.'

Edward pushed his plate away and wiped his mouth with his napkin. 'I don't like to push you, but I have a lot of money tied up in this deal, and I'm trusting you with it. Fuck me over, Skye, and you're dead.'

Skye sighed, his voice quiet and pitiful.

'I know, I know . . . I'll see it through for you as I do everything else. Goodnight.'

Edward mentioned neither Harriet nor the child to Skye, and Skye didn't dare to broach the subject. There was no friendship between them now and he knew it, had known it ever since he made that stupid pass at Harriet.

Edward, after a delay of over a month, eventually returned to London and went straight home. Even though it was after midnight, he went to the nursery to deliver the promised gifts. His daughter lay sleeping, her blankets kicked off, her fists curled tightly in sleep. He felt such a strong surge of emotion he wanted to pick her up and hug her, but he gently covered her and crept into the bedroom.

Harriet was sitting up in bed, a pair of glasses perched on the end of her nose. She gave him a wink and tapped her book. 'Just checking up on the pros and cons of motherhood. She is extraordinary, I'm sure she's advanced for her age. Do you know, I'm sure she almost said something . . . Did you see how long her hair's grown? And she has a front tooth coming . . . You've missed so much, she's nearly walking, and she holds on so hard. And when she laughs she tosses her tiny head back and gurgles ...'

Exhausted, Edward undressed and climbed into bed. Harriet switched off the light and he pulled her close. 'I love you, I love you both ... I'm sorry to have been away so long, you get my letters?'

'You know something, I asked that snooty bitch Barbara if she would like to have a double birthday party, and she refused. So I told her to bugger off. They'll no doubt have the Savoy Grill, but ... Edward?'

Edward was sound asleep.

The next morning, Edward went to see Jinks before leaving for the office. She was standing up in her cot waving a rubber hammer, and he picked her up, loving the smell of her. She nuzzled his neck and then whacked him over the head with the hammer. He laughed, and the little girl looked afraid, unsure, so he put her down and pulled a funny face. She responded with a smile that made his heart lurch.

He gave Dewint instructions to throw out his jeans and cowboy boots, then went straight to the barber's to have his hair cut. He was buzzing, filled with energy and ready for anything.

Arriving unannounced at the office, Edward took the place by storm. He was like a whirlwind, and everyone jumped as he rampaged through the offices. 'Where's Alex, Miss Henderson, where's Alex?'

Miss Henderson told him Alex would be at the Stock Exchange. Edward walked straight into his brother's office and began sorting through all the business the company had done during his absence.

He picked up a vast ledger on Alex's proposed takeover of Buchanan House. The major deal had fallen apart. Alex had been investing on the Stock Exchange and, by the look of it, had taken some bad setbacks, costing him a lot of money, added to which the property boom was beginning to slide. They were left with millions of pounds' worth of properties they could not offload.

Edward paced the office as he discovered more and more of Alex's disastrous ventures. He had taken over the St James' Bank, and that was now being investigated for astronomical losses, and they stood to lose millions. Edward threw up his hands in despair. The property boom was fast becoming a landslide, and Alex had allowed loans to companies, taking their properties as collateral. Now many of those companies were sinking so fast that the bank looked as if it was on the brink of closure. On the good side, however, the Carnaby Street shops were making huge dividends, the money rolling in in waves. But Alex was moving it out again, and without Edward's signature.

Edward checked over the Banks sale to Jasper Golding and Sir Francis Coleman, and discovered that it was yet again a flourishing, successful business. Renamed, the private gaming house was making a vast profit. From the documents he found in Alex's desk he reckoned that the men's stakes of one million each had already trebled ... he also discovered the shares Alex had hung on to. He was furious, Alex was cheating him, going behind his back. Edward's trust in his brother suddenly disintegrated – he was just like everyone else, like Walter, lining his own pockets.

Edward turned to the company's financial records. It was more and more obvious that Alex had been steadily losing money, the company's money. Edward sighed, so much for honest, straightforward dealing. To date, he alone had been responsible for the lucrative side of the Barkley Company.

He returned to his own office and began to outline a plan to salvage the failing St James' Bank, to try to recoup the losses incurred during his absence. He was so engrossed in working his way through the files that he didn't even look up when the door opened.

'Well, well, this is your Uncle Edward, go on, say hello.'

Alex carried his son in his arms. Although the same age as Jinks, he was twice her size, and had thick, black, curly hair. His eyes were dark, his skin tawny, and his lungs were in good working order. He bellowed, wriggling to get down.

'This is Evelyn – what do you think of him?'

He put the little boy down and he clung unsteadily to the desk, then fell over. Edward bent down and picked him up. He could feel how much heavier Evelyn was than Jinks.

'He looks like him, doesn't he Edward, like Dad?'

Edward looked down into the upturned face. Papers tumbled to the floor as the little hands grabbed.

'You've got your hands full here, Alex, eh? What a big fella. So this is what's been keeping you away from the office?'

Alex picked up the insult fast, and immediately led Evelyn by the hand to the office door. 'Go to Nanny, there's a good boy ... bye-bye.'

Turning unsteadily on his fat little legs, Evelyn waved to Edward. Beyond the door a nanny in uniform waited for him. As soon as the door closed, there was a scream which continued into the distance as the nanny carried the wailing child away.

Alex looked at the closed door, then at the desk. 'I see you've been over the files. I admit we've taken a few setbacks, but we lost the takeover of Buchanan House because you weren't here and the board wouldn't accept the deal without you ... And you have the nerve to make digs about me not being in the office ... where in God's name have you been?'

A cigar clamped between his teeth, soberly dressed and with his hair cut short, Edward was back to his old self.

'Well, it's a bloody good job I showed up when I did, you're certainly making a right balls-up of it. Christ, whatever made you buy stock in that fucking heap?'

Alex tried hard to control his temper. 'I made a list of the properties we can let go, cover our losses.'

Edward tossed Alex his own list of companies they could sell off fast. Alex looked at them quickly, noting that they were mostly his own deals, and threw the paper back.

Miss Henderson heard the argument escalating into a

full-scale row. Before long everyone could hear the brothers screaming at each other.

'There's not a memo or a note on Ming's contract with the Japs that I set up. Do I have to do everything, for Chrissake? If she's gone into business without us then we get over there ... Plus we get shot of this prat of a son-in-law, what's his name, Conrad St James. Guy couldn't run a bowling alley, never mind a fucking bank! I want a meeting set up with all the board members of the bank and I want it fast ... Think you can handle that, buddy? Think you can do one simple thing and not cock it up?'

All through dinner Alex was quiet, and Barbara knew something was wrong.

'Edward's back, things have not been going all that well, especially at the bank ...'

'Why didn't you tell me, Alex? What things?'

Alex didn't usually discuss business with her, but slowly he began to tell her about the problems. Conrad St James was proving incapable of running the bank, and Alex had delayed confronting him because he was married to Alex's stepdaughter, Selina. 'Edward wants to take a look at the accounts. I've had to fund a lot of the bank with Barkley monies ... He has every right, I'll go over and have a talk with them this evening.'

Barbara sighed. She had had very little to do with her daughter since she had been married off. With either of her daughters, come to think of it – her new life left little room for them. She was a grandmother now, and didn't like that, either.

'I won't be able to join you, darling, I have a charity meeting for the Spastic Association, do you mind going alone?'

Alex held her hand and kissed it. 'Just a few things to remember ... Keep quiet about my stake in the club should Edward start sniffing around. Now he's back, he'll be poking his nose into every transaction I've done since he left.'

'Did he ask after Evelyn at all?'

Alex smiled. 'I took him to the zoo this morning and then

Edward met him at the office. You know, he was jealous, I could see it in his face.'

'You spoil that child, you know. Maybe you've been spending too much time with him.'

Alex gave Barbara a strange, veiled look, and spoke quietly. 'Well, one of us has to.'

Barbara pursed her lips. She didn't want to discuss it, they invariably argued about Evelyn.

Suddenly the little boy ran into the room. 'Daddy ... Daddy ...' He threw himself into Alex's arms, and chortled with laughter as his father twirled him around, tossed him up in the air and caught him.

'Who's Daddy's boy, then, eh? Who's Daddy's boy?'

Watching them, Barbara was terrified that Alex would notice Evelyn's likeness to Edward, it was so obvious to her. 'I don't want Edward seeing him, Alex, he's such a foul-mouthed man. I don't want Evelyn near him.'

Alex held his son close and buried his face in the thick curls. 'We'll keep him away from the big, bad wolf ... Now, Daddy's got to go out, but ... tomorrow, what are we doing tomorrow?'

'Zoo ... zoo ...'

Alex carried Evelyn to the nursery and the nanny smiled. He so obviously adored his son, in a way he made up for the lack of motherly affection. Evelyn began crying because he didn't want Alex to leave, but he got a tap on the nose and was told Daddy had important work to do.

When Alex arrived at Selina and Conrad's house, he found his stepdaughter alone. She was a strange, quiet girl, and although he was fond of her he found her trying, she was so shy and introverted.

'How are your boys?'

Selina murmured that they were all well, then lapsed into silence.

'I really need to talk to Conrad urgently, you expecting him soon? If so, I'll wait.'

Selina shrugged, her mouth turned down. 'He comes and goes as he chooses, perhaps you should try at the office in the morning.'

Alex tilted his head to one side. 'Nothing wrong between you, is there?'

Selina laughed, humourlessly. 'There's nothing between us, but I'll pass your message on if I see him.'

'I'd appreciate that, tell him we're in trouble, Edward's back, and kicking.'

Alex felt sorry for her, and made a mental note to have a word with Barbara, perhaps she should talk to the girl. He sighed, irritated by Selina's lack of energy. She had everything money could buy, a handsome husband, two lovely boys, and yet she was never enthusiastic about anything.

Edward was sitting up in bed with stacks of files on each side of him. Dewint brought a dinner tray, and Edward lay back. 'I dunno, I leave for a few months and he gets us into such deep water, you know what's the matter with him, he's a big softie; can't do business on favours, keep it in the family, doesn't work . . .'

Harriet shrieked for Edward. He leapt out of bed, overturning the tray, and ran from the bedroom. He threw open the nursery door. 'What, for Chrissake? What is it?'

'She's cross-eyed – look for yourself, she's cross-eyed. Mavis agrees with me – can you see, hold your finger up . . . See, it's her left eye . . . Oh my God, she's cross-eyed.'

Edward picked up his daughter and stared into her face, while she tried to ram her fingers in his mouth. She had round, rosy cheeks and auburn hair, darker than her mother's, and strange black eyebrows. No one could actually describe her as beautiful, but to Edward there was nothing wrong that he could see. 'She's not, she's just got strange-coloured eyes! You're not cross-eyed, are you sweetie?'

'She is! Give her to me and I'll show you. It's bad enough to have hair like a burnt orange, now she's cross-eyed. There! See – the left eye swings in towards the corner . . .'

Mavis was hovering at the door, and Edward brought her into the debate. 'What do you think, Mavis?'

'Well, I'd no say it was crossed, maybe a wee bit lazy.'

'Oh, bloody hell, you know what's going to happen – she's going to be one of those children with glasses and a patch over one eye. She certainly suits her name, she's jinxed all right.'

Edward carried Jinks on his shoulder for a third opinion, and Dewint peered up into her face. 'Well, I couldn't say for sure, sah, but they can do wonders nowadays, you know. They can straighten it out.'

Proved correct, Harriet gave Edward a smug look. 'Right, Mavis, we're taking her to Harley Street. The last thing I want is a cross-eyed daughter.'

Edward shut himself in his study for the rest of the day. Late in the afternoon, Harriet returned with Jinks and stood, hands on hips, at his door.

'Well, I was right, she's cross-eyed, and it's got to come from your family because none of mine squint – mentally a wee bit unstable, as Mavis would say, but no cross-eyes.'

Edward laughed, and she sat on his knee. It was the first time she had ever referred to her own condition with humour. She became serious, and told him they could operate, but not for a few years, then she burst into tears. 'Oh, God, Edward, she's going to have to wear glasses, and when she goes to school they'll call her four-eyes, or three, because one side of the glasses will have to be blanked out. I knew it, I told you.'

Edward rubbed his head. His mind was still on the work littering his desk. He suggested they should get opinions from two or three specialists before they took any drastic steps.

'I've been to the very best man at Great Ormond Street, and they said they will give her glasses and operate when it's time. Well, you're obviously busy and I'm obviously interrupting you, so I'll let you get on with it.'

She waltzed out, and Edward shut the door. But after a moment, unable to concentrate, he went up to the nursery. He sat with Mavis – he found her a pleasant girl, and she adored Jinks.

'Mavis, you know about Mrs Barkley? Well, she seems just a little frantic over this eye business. How do you think she is?'

'Och, she's lovely, and she's such a sweet nature. She's the easiest child I've ever taken care of.'

'I meant Mrs Barkley, Mavis . . . Do me a favour and watch over her, just as much as Jinks. If she starts . . . well, acting a little bit strange, even the tiniest bit, let me know.'

'Oh, yes, Mr Barkley, I will . . . And I'd like to say . . . well, I'd just like to say how much I like working here and how much I like your wife – she's a verra special person.'

'She is, Mavis, she is . . .'

Alex had to admire the way his brother had grasped the complexities of the banking system, and the formula they would use to put the bank back on its feet. All loans would be foreclosed on immediately, and those unable to meet the deadline would have to offer their companies to the bank. The Barkley Company was ready to 'take a spin in the City', and Edward had earmarked certain companies they would be able to 'pump up' and use inflated share prices. Conrad was staggered, said they could not even attempt to hoodwink the City in that manner, it would have a catastrophic effect on any later dealings.

'The City has its own laws, we would be blacklisted.'

Edward snapped that they would only be blacklisted if they were caught. From what he had gathered, the City was as crooked as any other business. 'All bloody used car dealers, Conrad son, and we will go in right at the top, offering companies that have good turnovers. The attitude to take is, if they can't come up with the repayments then it's their loss, the bank will not take the fall. They will all have the opportunity, and the Barkley Company will stand behind the bank, taking forty-five per cent of the shares of those with a high turnover . . . My company, however, will not make a penny from the issue, just the shares after the float.'

Conrad gasped as Edward continued to earmark one company after another, and he interrupted Edward. 'Does your company have the financial backing for these negotiations? You are talking about millions?'

Alex looked at his brother and waited.

'We have the finances. Second in line for this morning's meeting is the takeover of Buchanan House. Alex lost to an Arabian company, and I believe they have over-extended themselves, judging by their unaudited mid-term accounts for '74. Their interest payment is five million, but the Buchanan's board of directors show a profit of thirty-eight million. Therefore it's inevitable that interest payments on Buchanan's own borrowings are a substantial hole, the company had to borrow extensively to get Buchanan House ... So, Alex, let's move in fast, this is not for public knowledge.'

Before Alex and Conrad had a chance to digest all of Edward's schemes he had gone, hurrying to his next meeting.

'He'll never pull it off, Alex, it's madness. We'll all go down, not just the bank.'

Alex was already on the phone, arranging to meet the brokers for Buchanan House. He put his hand over the mouthpiece. 'Do exactly as he says. I mean it – don't trust him, ever, but believe me, he has the Midas touch.'

Edward had never lost money, not on any of the insurance companies, his properties, his sidelines. Everything he touched turned to gold. As much as Alex hated his brother, he would never question his decisions again. He would do what he was instructed to do, and do it to the letter.

Edward continued to work at the pace he had set himself, day in, day out. He was at the office from seven in the morning until after nine at night. He was aware of Alex's change of attitude – he listened attentively, never argued, and carried out Edward's commands with precision.

Edward's own businesses, his private deals and the bribes were for his eyes only, no one else ever knew what he was doing.

Walter was still proving troublesome, and even though he had made his fortune from Edward's backhanders he wanted more. His political career was taking off. He was in the public eye, and he lived well, spending many evenings at the house in Notting Hill Gate.

Once again Edward would use his 'hit list', his old blackmail tricks. Allard was easy to keep silenced and in line. He was still employed by Lloyd's, but now in a higher position, he would never want it known about his payoffs. Edward worked behind the scenes, and Henry Blackwell was taken aback to discover exactly which family he had unwittingly married into. When he had met Annabelle Barkley he had been totally unaware of her connection with Edward Stubbs, the student he had known at Cambridge. He had kept his secret, and was now even more desperate to keep his past relationship with Allard quiet, not only for the sake of his rich young wife, but there was also his political career to consider. He was treading the same dangerous ground as Walter, accepting money from Edward in the same way. In return, he leaked crucial information on companies just before they went public, enabling Edward to buy in at just the right time. Edward's move into the City was rapid, and caused a storm; within months he became a force to be reckoned with. Once again the Barkley Company was rearing its head as a formidable power.

Alex was unaware of how Edward was able to secure so many intros into the City in such a short time. He settled down, obeying his brother's instructions. Edward only allowed Alex access to certain accounts, and just as long as he kept in line, behaved himself, Edward would carry him along. Their nets spread, the brothers moved upwards yet again, becoming accepted in every social circle. They were pillars of society, and the more respect they gained, the more financially secure they grew.

Once the company was ticking over smoothly again the Barkley Company was stronger than ever, and Alex didn't question Edward's decisions because it was Alex who enjoyed the fame, received the glory. In the society columns they always tagged the word 'tycoon' to his name. It was as if he had won himself a title, and confirmed that he had arrived.

To the outside world he might be 'Mr Tycoon', but in the office he was still under Edward's thumb.

Edward buzzed to ask Alex to go in, and tossed him a first-class air ticket. 'I want you on the first plane to New York – I want this Ming affair settled once and for all. If you can't handle it, telex me – but try, Alex. All you've got to do is read through all these notes I've prepared for you and that's it, all right?'

Alex nodded and picked up the papers. He walked out, shutting the door quietly behind him. The higher they rose, the more delight Edward took in treating him like a clerk. If Alex protested he was told that he got the publicity, he was the Barkley tycoon, and if he wanted to keep it that way there had better be no arguments.

Alex and Ming were like strangers. She was very cool and restrained. They had not met since his marriage to Barbara, and Alex knew he would have to broach the subject sooner or later. He ordered dinner in his room, feeling it would be easier to talk there, in privacy, than in a restaurant. He tried to relax, but he was tense, ill at ease. She looked stunningly beautiful, and gave him her familiar bow rather than shake his hand or kiss his cheek.

Her obvious refusal to acknowledge their previous relationship made it somehow easier to raise his reason for the meeting. 'I'll come straight to the point – Edward wants to issue a writ on your company for a complete audit of your accounts. If it should go through you'll be hit hard for tax evasion – he knows you've been "creaming" – but as long as he gets the lion's share he'll be happy. He also wants a progress report on the deal with Japan.'

Ming sat demurely, waiting for Alex to finish, then she smiled. 'You know, you begin to sound like him.'

A waiter tapped on the door and wheeled a trolley in. Ming

fell silent while he set the table. She was very much aware of the change in Alex – he looked far more handsome, with a slight greyness at the temples. He was immaculately dressed and exuded sophistication, a man of the world, with a confidence he had previously lacked. She was impressed.

Alex indicated a seat for her, dismissed the waiter and served the dinner himself. Ming watched his deft, quick movements, the way he tossed the salad. He was so different from Edward, and yet she detected a similar quality she had been unaware of when they had first met. The brothers were growing more alike.

'I asked Edward if he would allow me to buy him out, I have completed all the contracts in South Africa, plus two more in Mexico, I am sure you know all about them . . . But I no longer wish to work for you, and again I offer to buy out your percentage in my company. I will double my first offer.'

Alex tried to cover his confusion, but Ming had found that tiny chink in his armour and set to work, laughing softly. 'Well, it appears Edward is still up to his old tricks . . . I thought you were partners.' She began listing building companies, businesses he had no knowledge of.

Alex couldn't eat, he felt sick. Just as he had begun to trust his brother, just as things were going smoothly, the water rippled and then giant waves swept over him . . .

'I want Edward out of my company. I have not, as he suspected, been given the contract for Japan, they do not want a third party involved . . . Alex, is there any way we can work this together, exclude Edward?'

Jinks was operated on. Edward and Harriet brought her home with her little glasses on, one lens covered with sticking-plaster. She was so good, she hardly cried, but Harriet had made up for that as they waited outside the operating theatre. She had sobbed and sobbed, and although Edward tried hard to comfort her it was obvious that he was as upset as she was. Seeing their little daughter unconscious on the theatre trolley had touched them both.

They bought special gifts for Jinks, including a musical box. She was very careful with all her toys, keeping them neatly laid out in the cupboard, and she took a long time unwrapping each one, holding her head at an awkward angle so she could see clearly.

Jinks' hair was very thick, and she wore it in pigtails – one always higher than the other as Harriet usually plaited it for her. It gave her a strange, lopsided effect which was not improved by her new glasses. She had a gruff voice which always made them laugh as she sounded like an elderly gin-sodden lady.

Edward was forever watchful over Harriet, worried that the stress of Jinks' operation might take her near the edge. He persuaded himself that that was why he was feeling so pent up: he felt bound to the house, to his wife. His old wanderlust returned and, bored, he began venting his frustration at work, taking on more and more deals, buying and selling, anything to occupy his mind. So much attention was paid to Harriet's condition that Edward's feelings were often swept aside. Only Dewint, whose loving care had been the mainstay of the household for so many years, could feel the undercurrent and waited with trepidation. Dewint knew Edward was drinking heavily, and he suggested that perhaps Harriet and Jinks should go to the country, to Haverley Hall, for a short holiday.

If Harriet was aware of Edward's drinking she said nothing, she was so wrapped up in her new role of motherhood. She agreed that Jinks would benefit from some fresh air, and proceeded to pack. Edward drove them both to the station, and as he watched the train pulling out of the station, his daughter's face pressed against the window as she waved goodbye, his depression deepened. He couldn't really understand himself why his moods changed so radically and why, whenever he felt content, felt that life was good, something inside him, like a sickness, made him try to destroy that happiness. He caused mayhem when he returned to the office that morning; he was already drunk, his behaviour erratic. He screamed instructions to Miss Henderson and made her wish for Alex to return to regain some semblance of order.

Alex did not return for a week as he had been in Mexico trying to decipher the companies that Edward had, without a word to him – his so-called partner – been running for years. Miss Henderson was more than relieved to see him. She was close to tears and she showed him the bedlam created by Edward: his manic instructions, his new shares and business transactions were a confused mess of papers. Alex listened, his fury mounting at the destructive and foolish deals his brother had begun and left half finished.

'You'd better give me the keys to his office, Miss Henderson. God knows what else he has got us involved in.'

'I'm sorry, sir, I don't have a spare set, no one does . . .'

'Well, if that's the case, I'd better go and find him. Is he at home?'

'I don't know. I can call the manor, if you wish.'

'Don't bother, I'll go personally. Make a list of all these new transactions and leave them on my desk.'

Dewint opened the front door, and looked aghast as Alex stepped in. 'I'm afraid, sah, Mr Edward . . . he has company, sah.' He told Alex that Harriet and Jinks had gone off to spend a few weeks in Yorkshire. But Alex would not be put off.

'Tell him I am here, would you, Dewint, and I have no intention of leaving.'

Alex looked into the lounge; the room was a mess. Bottles were strewn everywhere, dirty glasses. From somewhere in the house he could hear music. Then he heard Edward's voice, shouting, telling Dewint he didn't want to see anyone. Alex strolled back to the hall door and saw two scruffy tarts being hustled out by Dewint. He sighed, about to turn away, then froze.

Edward appeared, unshaven, his eyes red-rimmed. Alex could smell him a mile off, and he was reeling drunk. He started shouting, incoherently, then slumped on to the sofa. Alex calmed him down and tried to talk to him, begging him to rest. He was sure Edward was an alcoholic, but he just could not fathom out what had caused the change. He seemed hell-bent on destroying everything they had built up.

'Why, Edward, in God's name, what is the matter with you? Just as everything is going so well . . . Are you ill? Is that what all this is about?'

Edward stared at him without replying, then began to pick up empty bottles.

'You need a doctor? You carry on this way you will destroy everything we've built up together.'

'Together? Don't be so fucking crass, you an' me aren't together, you line your own pockets like every other bastard I come into contact with . . . fuck off, leave me alone!'

Alex sat down, tried to keep his voice calm. He played for time, his mind reeling, wondering what Edward had discovered. 'Maybe that's your fault . . . you see, every time I think I can trust you, I find out something that makes me more wary of you than ever . . . what the hell have you got going in South Africa?'

Edward sneered at him, poured himself another drink. 'Whatever I've got going keeps you out of the shit, so why worry . . . I'll go to prison, not you, haw haw haw.'

Alex wanted to shake him, hit him, but he gritted his teeth and tried once more to discover what Edward was working on in South Africa. 'Is it legal, just tell me . . .?'

Edward laughed, a boozed, humourless laugh. Then he switched on the stereo so loud that it was pointless to continue.

He watched Edward as he moved around the room, trying to dance to the music. It was pitiful. Alex closed the door and switched off the stereo as the music ended, determined to talk things through. Edward smiled at him, fumbled in his pocket. 'Look, I've been making out my will. You get the lion's share, on condition you take care of Harry and Jinks. Christ, look, I'll come clean – I am bored, understand? I am so bored, and . . . and I packed them off to Yorkshire. I'm thinking of upping and leaving, you know . . . Oh, you won't understand,

I get these feelings inside of me and . . . I feel trapped here, I'm trapped.'

Alex read the will. Sure enough, Edward had left him every-thing apart from some legacies to Harriet and Jinks. He looked up as Edward poured himself another drink. 'Here, take it back. And if you want some advice, grow up. You've been a selfish bastard all your life – just for a change, think about Harry, about Jinks, and what they'd do without you.'

'Think about them? Jesus Christ, I spend my whole life wor-rying about her and the kid . . . Well, I can't take it, it's like living with a bloody time-bomb – I never know when she's going to blow. Have you any idea what it's like . . .'

'Getting yourself drunk won't help matters. Maybe you should take a holiday, you've pushed yourself to breaking point. You can't be an easy man to live with, Edward, and, well, you've got your daughter to think of . . .'

Edward drained his glass. 'Yeah, little Four-eyes. She's so damned well behaved, so quiet, she's like a fucking mouse. Even the nanny creeps about like a fucking nervous cow.'

Edward leaned back on the sofa, turned his bleary eyes to his brother and, out of the blue, asked about Evelyn. Alex shrugged and said he hadn't seen much of him lately as he had only just returned from New York.

'He a good little chap, is he?'

Sighing, Alex replied that he was a bit of a handful, and they were unable to keep a nanny for more than a few months. Edward stared sullenly into the fire and hurled his glass, shat-tering it on the tiles. 'I'm going out, fancy a night out?'

'No, I'm on my way home, and if I were you I'd get to bed, sleep it off.'

Edward began to swear to himself, and he didn't even notice when Alex walked out.

On the back seat of Alex's car lay the tell-tale newspapers, and he picked one up. It showed a picture of the 'tycoon's brother', drunk and being thrown out of Tramps nightclub. Alex swore and waved his hand for the chauffeur to drive away.

'Go on, drink yourself to death, you bastard, and the sooner the better.'

Edward continued drinking, and by daybreak his initial mood of despondency had switched to belligerence. He decided to wipe out all the men he knew were waiting with their hands out for the payoffs, for his bribes. He wanted to destroy them, they were making him sick, making him drink, the vultures ... Well, he would get rid of them all, start with a clean slate ... And last, but not least, on his list was his brother. He had plans for Alex – he would take Evelyn from him. The boy was his, Evelyn was Edward's son.

He weaved out of the room, clutching the banisters to help him climb the stairs. Dewint, coming out of the kitchen, looked up in horror, Edward's face was unshaven, his eyes unfocused. There was a helplessness about him that was heart-breaking. Dewint hurried up the stairs ...

'You'd best lie down, sah. Here, let me give you a hand.'

Dewint buckled at the knees as Edward put his arm around his shoulder, and leaned heavily against him. Together they swerved like dancers to the master bedroom.

'You are a good chap, Dewint, good chap. You think you could get me cleaned up a bit? Old hands shaking and I don't want to cut my throat, though there are many who would love it if I did.'

Dewint swished the shaving brush round the bowl, and gently soaped Edward's face. He was propped up in bed, his eyes vacant, staring ahead.

'What if I were to run you a nice bath, sah?'

'Thank you. You're a good chap, Dewint.'

He busied himself running the water in the big porcelain tub, laying out the fresh sheet-sized bath towels. When he returned to the bedside Edward had not moved. He was weeping soundlessly, tears streaming down his face. As Dewint made quietly to leave the room, Edward reached for him.

'Just sit with me for a while, old fella, I'm in a bit of a mess ...

need a bit of company, need ...' Edward wept, holding tightly to Dewint's hand ... twice he tried to stop the tears, giving Dewint a sad half smile and a little shrug of his shoulders. But the tears continued. The bath water grew cold as they sat, Dewint not knowing what to do to comfort Edward. Suddenly Edward lifted Dewint's hand to his lips and kissed it ... whispering so softly that it was hardly audible ...

'Thank you. I'm all right now ... I'm all right now.'

And it was over. Abruptly Edward reached for the telephone. He dialled a number and waited. He turned to Dewint ...

'Top up the bath and lay some clean clothes out. Then you'd better fix me something to eat – omelette, one of your specials, okay? Hello? It's me!'

Dewint sprang into action as Edward was stripping off his shirt, talking to Miss Henderson at the office. Gone was any sign of emotional turmoil, instead he was sharp and abrupt.

'Alex was round asking about South Africa; fend him off, Henny. I don't want anything to do with my business out there getting into Alex's hands. Tell him anything, but make sure he sees nothing ... that includes telexes, cables and any reference to Skye Duval. I'll leave it to you then and, Henny, this is important to me, understand? Good girl. I'm fine. Yes, I'm fine.'

After his bath Edward sat eating hungrily as Dewint kept up a steady refill of piping hot coffee. Edward ploughed his way through a stack of old newspapers, flicking over the articles that referred to himself. There was no hint of the man who had sat weeping, but Dewint knew, more than anyone else, that Edward was cursed with a consuming despair. A despair that he seemed to try to reach out to, as if he craved to be punished, for what Dewint couldn't even contemplate. What impressed him was the way Edward fought back ... He loved this man, admired him, and yet was always, would always, be a little frightened of him. Edward caught Dewint watching him as he checked over his appearance in the hall mirror. He gave his extraordinary wolfish and yet boyish smile as he said softly, 'He's mine, and I am going to get him. Clear the place up will you? I shouldn't be too long ...'

Edward drove straight to Mayfair. Checking his watch, it was four o'clock. His son would be home from school. He had decided he would walk in and take him. It was as simple as that. Evelyn was his son. He parked opposite the gates of Alex's house, and was just about to get out of the car when he saw Evelyn pedalling round and round the garden on a small tricycle. He fell off twice, but picked himself up and sped around the garden again. His thick black hair had been cut short, and he wore strange, burgundy-coloured knickerbockers and long, wrinkled socks, part of the uniform of the small, private Hill House School. Edward shook his head and muttered to himself – what a terrible get-up for his son to be wearing. Again he was about to cross to him, when he saw Alex coming out of the house ... the little boy turned, leaped from the bike and hurtled towards Alex, flinging himself into his arms. Alex twirled him round, to the boy's delight ...

'Do it again, Daddy. Do it again.'

Edward watched as Alex threw Evelyn up into the air and caught him, putting him up on to his shoulders. They went back into the house. Edward sat for another ten minutes before he drove to Hill House School and enrolled his daughter for the next term. It made him feel better. The time had not been right, but with the two children at the same school he would be able to keep an eye on Evelyn, get to know him ... then he would take what he had always wanted, a son, his son. Edward lit a cigar. He flicked a look into the driving mirror and ran his hand through his black hair, hair identical to his son's.

Edward breezed into the office, gave Miss Henderson a bunch of roses, kissed her frazzled head and waltzed along to his office. He unlocked the door, whistling as Alex came to his own office door. He was always taken aback at the way his brother could switch from mood to mood, but he had been sure his recovery this time would have taken considerably longer.

'Well, you recovered fast. Binge over, is it, or was it something I said?'

Edward gave him a strange smile. 'Maybe something you've got is worth sobering up for, brother, be with you in a minute.'

Half an hour later Edward again took Alex by surprise by laying on his desk the contracts for his companies in Mexico, not only details of the projects but also very well kept accounts.

'I hear you went on a trip to see for yourself? What do you think of the project?'

'Now that I actually know it exists, it'll take time to assimilate, just as this load of extra deals you've made will take time to assimilate . . .'

'But on the surface, brother, things don't look quite as bad as you thought, and there's your name, sweetheart, in black and white. You're not cut out of anything . . . Right? Am I right? So I'll leave this with you. I'm going to collect Harry and Jinks, won't be more than a few days . . .'

Edward was already on his way out when Alex rose from his chair.

'Hang on, I'm going to need your signature on some documents.'

'Can't they wait? I'll only be a couple of days. How was Ming?'

Alex caught the nasty sideways look, and pursed his lips. 'The Japs won't consider a third party involvement, there's no deal unless we sell our shares.'

'Well, that's that then, no deal . . . I can wait. They'll come round eventually, it's too good a proposition, unless you have other ideas. You got any other ideas, Alex?'

Alex flushed slightly and shook his head. Right now his share of the Mexican companies was too big a prospect for him to jeopardize because of Ming. 'No, but I would like to know what is going on in South Africa.'

It was Edward's turn to flush, and he swung the door backwards and forwards. 'Okay, I'll come clean, I'm looking at some possible land, mining land, but as yet there's nothing concrete . . . haw, haw . . . that's a joke. There are possible perlite mining facilities, but I'll keep you informed if and when it looks like I can pull it off.'

'Who've you got over there? Anyone I know?'

'No one, it's just me. Don't push me, Alex, start adding up the figures of what I've just handed to you from Mexico. I'll never rip you off, you should know that by now. You can trust me, Alex, just like I trust you ... Pity we sold out on the club, looks like a gold mine. I would still like to have a hand in it but, well, that was down to you ... Right, I'm off. Take care, give my love to Barbara.'

Alex could say nothing. He knew that Edward had discovered he still owned shares in the club.

'Yes, say hello to Harry and Jinks for me.'

'Okay, and you say a big hello to your son, to Evelyn.'

Alex looked up, but the door had already closed behind Edward. Almost in an involuntary move he ran his finger round his collar and pulled at the gold chain, as if it was cutting into his neck. He reached for the files on Mexico. His hand rested a moment on the covers, then he rang through to Miss Henderson.

'Get me anything you can find on perlite mining, would you, in South Africa.'

He flipped off the intercom button. Opening the files he tried to concentrate, but could not get rid of the strange feeling, as if Edward remained in the room. He looked to the closed door.

'What are you up to now, Eddie? What?'

Harriet had not read any of the newspaper reports about Edward. She was enjoying life at Haverley Hall, relaxing and growing vegetables in the garden. At seven and a half, Jinks was an unusually quiet child, and still wore her glasses. She was getting taller, but was painfully thin and nervous. Mavis was still with them, but Harriet knew it would soon be time for her to leave – Jinks was already at primary school. Harriet had kept Mavis on as she had become a good friend, but she had a boyfriend now and her own life to lead.

Jinks seemed unconsciously aware of how to deal with her

mother, often behaving as if she were the child. Harriet continued to have her schemes, her hobbies, but had settled down much more as she approached middle age. She looked a little eccentric, with her hair in a messy bun at the nape of her neck. She wore loose, flowing garments to disguise the fact that she had put on considerable weight, due partly to lack of exercise and partly to her medication.

Harriet was weeding the garden, unaware that Edward had been standing watching her for nearly fifteen minutes. He had always been aware that she looked like his mother, but now the resemblance was uncanny. When she looked up and flashed him that wonderful smile he couldn't help but feel good. It was always the same – away from her he could forget her, but as soon as he set eyes on her again he felt that rush of emotion. He opened his arms for her as she ran to him, and swung her around. 'My God, you've put on weight, nearly put my back out.'

Calling for Jinks, Harriet led Edward around her vegetable patch, pointing out the lettuces and showing off her tomato plants with pride. Jinks came shyly to the door. She was a timid child, and had always been slightly afraid of her father.

'Look who's here! Surprise, surprise, it's Daddy.'

Edward held out his arms and she went to him, gave him a small peck on the cheek and promptly stood back, looking down at her feet. Edward lifted her chin to look into her eyes, and she blushed.

'Your mother's given you a complex, you've got wonderful eyes. Come here and let me see – they're green, well, well, Jinks has got green eyes.'

'It's because Ma makes me eat so much of her lettuce.'

Edward laughed at her attempt to make a joke, then they all went inside for tea. Jinks still would not meet her father's eyes, but hung her head at the table until he grew angry with her. He started to argue with Harriet, and Jinks left the table.

The next morning they drove back to London. Jinks hated the dark rooms of the manor, and always had nightmares. She was also highly nervous about starting her new school, and even when told she would at least know someone, as her cousin would be there, she pursed her lips in identical fashion to Harriet. 'I've never met him.'

'Oh, you will, darling, you two are going to be friends. You can invite him back for tea and things like that.'

Harriet snorted, 'Oh God, if he's anything like his mother she won't. And speaking of Barbara, this arrived this morning, it must have slipped by her. I've been invited to this luncheon ... She's chairman of Save the Animals, Save the Whale, and God knows what else – look, it came yesterday. Shall I go? It'll be a laugh, don't you think?'

Examining the embossed invitation, Edward agreed she should go. He thought no more of it until he walked into his office one morning a few weeks later.

Alex buttonholed him. 'Barbara is absolutely furious with Harry – you know she turned up at a Save the Wild Animals lunch with a fox fur wrapped round her neck?'

Edward gave him no more than a cursory shrug of the shoulders. Nothing ever surprised him where his wife was concerned.

In an abrupt change of subject, Alex commanded all Edward's attention. 'I want to ask your advice.' Alex never asked for advice, he usually offered it. 'It's Evelyn, he's becoming a hell of a handful for Barbara. And, well, I put him down for Eton and Harrow. You don't know anyone who has any influence with one of them, do you?'

'You're asking me? Me? Listen, your dear wife wouldn't even let him come over to our place for Jinks' birthday party last year, how come I can suddenly play a part in his education?'

'Well, I've got enough contacts of course, but ... Well, he isn't what I'd call academic. Give him a rugger ball and he's happy as a lark, but he won't study, he's way behind.'

'So, what can I do?' Edward couldn't help smiling. All these years he had wanted some contact with his son, and now it looked as though he was going to get it.

'Well, I just thought, with all your Cambridge friends, you might be able to pull a few strings.'

'Can't Barbara?'

'She's trying, but I'd like a second opinion. He's only nine and she wants him boarding, it would be for the spring term, after Christmas. I doubt if he's as bright as we were, remember the scholarships we both won? Anyway, if you'd ask around I'd be grateful . . . she can't get rid of him soon enough.'

Edward agreed to do what he could, and to Alex's amazement he seemed quite pleased to be helping out. But when Alex told Barbara she hit the roof, demanding to know, of all people, why did he have to choose Edward?

Of late they had not been getting along at all well. Barbara attended so many functions he saw her rarely, and her lack of participation in Evelyn's upbringing drove him to distraction. She had no time for the child, and had even missed his sports day at Hill House. Evelyn had won four races and was so popular and outgoing that Alex had been as proud as Punch.

He had sat with Harriet, who moaned to him that Edward was off on one of his trips. She even said, laughingly nudging Alex, 'And we all know what he'll get up to. You know, it used to destroy me, but . . . Well, now I must close my eyes, ignore it. If it makes him happy then so be it, and he has settled down. He's stopped drinking, did you know?'

Alex knew about Edward's liaisons, his so-called business trips, and he gave Harriet a small smile. Through all the upheavals in their lives they had remained friends, even if they did see each other rarely.

Harriet watched as Jinks came in second to last in the egg and spoon race, and grimaced. 'Well, at least she's brainy although not very well co-ordinated, is she? But then, it's her eyes, she squints, did you notice it at all, Alex?'

'Not really. Does she have to wear those terrible glasses? Why don't you get her a better pair?'

'Oh, I can't be bothered, really, and of course she won't have to wear them all her life, you know. It's just to straighten out her eye, it's the left one, goes right into the side – terrible affliction.'

Meanwhile, Evelyn was getting into a fight on the other side of the field. Alex sighed. 'God, he's a handful. You know he tied Barbara's bathroom door closed and she was trapped for hours? It was the servants' day off, all hell broke loose, as I'm sure you can imagine. Anyway, I gave him a good talking to, but it just drips off him like water.'

'My father always used his old military belt. He made us run up the stairs like soldiers, with our socks down, and he whopped us with it. We got big red welts on our legs. You know something funny, I've never thought of it before – but you don't think that's why Allard's such a big poofter, do you? Have you ever met him? He worked for you on and off, with Dickie Van der Burge in South Africa. You hear anything of Skye Duval at all? I often wonder about him . . . Ah well, years go by.'

Alex had been listening with only half an ear until South Africa was mentioned.

'Who is Skye Duval?'

'He works for Edward. Right, that's it, tea time.'

Alex remained sitting on the bench, deep in thought, while Harriet marched across the field to collect Jinks. He had come to the conclusion that Skye Duval was some sort of alias Edward used from time to time, but now it was quite clear he actually did exist.

Harriet waved to Evelyn, and he turned and grinned back. She was already busy collecting her daughter's plimsolls and gymslip.

'Well, darling, you did very well, at least you weren't last.'

Jinks was gazing across the field at her handsome cousin. He had hardly ever said two words to her, and unlike her he was extremely popular. She had once tried to make friends, but he had stuck out his tongue then crossed his eyes, mimicking her, so she had never tried again. She trailed after Harriet, who appeared to know everybody, and kept stopping to chat. She was laughing with Jinks' teacher, as outgoing as ever. She patted her daughter's odd pigtails.

'Well, she can't be top in everything. It's her glasses, you see, I'm sure without them she would run like the wind, wouldn't you, darling?'

'Honestly, Mother, it's got nothing to do with my glasses, I just can't run very fast.'

'Well I know that, darling, but you might at least have won the egg and spoon race. When I was at school we used to stick ours to the spoon, but everyone's so honest these days.'

Alex tried to discuss Evelyn's prowess in the sports events with Barbara. Uninterested, she continued writing her diary, reminding him that they were dining out that evening.

'I said he won . . .'

'Yes, I heard you, but perhaps you should encourage him to do his homework. It's all very well winning prizes for running, but that won't get him into Eton or Harrow, which is your fault, you should have put his name down. There's a waiting list, I couldn't believe my ears . . . waiting list for a school, sometimes this country is ridiculous, it really is. Now I'd better start dressing, I'll tell Scargill to run your bath, was there something else?'

Alex shook his head, but she had already walked out without waiting for his reply.

When Alex went upstairs to change, he passed his son's open door. He was lying across his bed, still wearing his sports kit, and his face was filthy.

'You eaten? Evelyn? Have you eaten?'

'No, I'll get Scargill to fix me something when you two have gone out.'

'You have any homework?'

'No, Father – in case you hadn't noticed, we broke up, it's the Christmas hols . . . Ma said she'd give me a tenner.'

Alex put his hand in his pocket and handed over ten pounds. His son grinned and pocketed it fast. Alex gave him another, saying it was to go towards Christmas presents.

'Can I go out on my bike?'

'No, Lyn, it's dark, and you've no lights. Ride it in the morning.'

'Okay.'

When his father had gone, Evelyn got out his A – Z of London, and began to plot his route. He had no intention of staying at home and not riding his bike.

Alex had changed for dinner, and he found Barbara in her room painting her nails.

'I suppose we should get a tree, for Lyn, but I just hate the needles dropping everywhere ... He's going to spend the actual holiday with the Hope-Swindowns, so perhaps I won't bother this year. I think it's rather a good idea as Charlie Hope-Swindown is that bit older and very clever. His mother's on the board for the Mentally Handicapped, she's related to ...'

Alex interrupted, 'Christ, it's Christmas, you know I like him around then. And what's a few pine needles? You don't have to clean the place.'

'Well, I won't be here! Oh, Alex, we've discussed this how many times? You know I have an arrangement, I've told you all about it. It's just a small operation, and well, Christmas seemed an ideal time to have it done. Then I'll go to a health farm for a few days, are you listening?'

'Fine, fine, I'll go to New York.'

Barbara's eyes narrowed, but she said nothing. She screwed the top of the nail varnish on carefully, gave herself the once-over in the mirror and admired her firm jawline, courtesy of the best plastic surgeons in the country. She was going to have her breasts lifted, and to avoid anyone finding out, she had said she was going abroad for Christmas. She licked her perfectly glossed lips and stood up. She caught Alex looking at her.

'You look beautiful.'

'Thank you, darling ... It's so rare nowadays you even notice me.'

Alex sighed as she swanned past him. He followed her

downstairs, passing Evelyn's room. The lights were still on, the comics littered the floor, but there was no sign of him.

Evelyn pedalled over Westminster Bridge in pouring rain, his A – Z stuck in the handlebars of his bike and getting soggier by the minute. He had the twenty pounds he had conned out of his father in his pocket, and he was off on a well-planned adventure. He was going to spend Christmas with his Uncle Edward, the man Mother always referred to as the 'Big Bad Wolf'.

Standing at the top of the ladder, Dewint was having such a good time, lavishly decorating the tree with coloured balls and glitter. Harriet stood beside the tree, bellowing instructions and waiting to hand him the bedraggled fairy she had brought from her old home. The tree reached almost to the ceiling, and around its base were piles of gifts wrapped in brilliantly coloured paper. Harriet had spent hours making paper chains, linking them all together until the whole house was festooned. The fire blazed in the lounge grate, candles glowed, and twinkling fairy lights had been added for effect.

Edward had been out shopping, with the aid of Dewint, and had hidden himself away to wrap his gifts. They had chosen an enormous doll for Jinks, and gardening equipment for Harriet as she was now eagerly nurturing a vegetable patch behind the manor.

Dewint, rather bent with age now, almost toppled off the ladder when the doorbell rang. Harriet shrieked that she would answer it, it was probably carol singers.

Standing on the doorstep, tears streaming down his cheeks, was Evelyn. A policeman stood beside him, his helmet under his arm, holding Evelyn's bicycle. The boy was sopping wet, his teeth chattering with cold.

'Well, well, it's Evelyn, and with an escort! Do come in . . . Edward! There's nothing wrong, is there?'

'We found him up by Greenwich Docks, riding down a dual carriageway with no lights.'

Edward came down the stairs, overhearing the policeman's last few words. He opened the door wide, put his hand on Evelyn's shoulder, and took the wind out of the pompous policeman. 'How very kind and thoughtful of you to bring him safely home, officer. Now I think we'd better get you a hot toddy ... Dewint! A large drink for Constable ...? I presume you are off duty?'

Edward gave an unhappy, saddle-sore little boy a secret wink. The policeman was rather chuffed at his reception, and asked for a brandy. Dewint proffered a glass, but Edward insisted they gave the constable the bottle, he felt sure the lads back at the station would also like a share of the Christmas spirit. Laughing now at the boy's antics, the policeman thanked them heartily and left.

Edward closed the door and smiled at his son. 'Well, we sorted out Constable Plod, so now, my lad, what's all this?'

Hot soup and warm towels were brought and Evelyn was led to the fireside. He explained that he had come for Christmas, and Harriet hugged and kissed him. She brought Jinks down to make him welcome. She was overcome with shyness, hanging her head and unable to say a word. Harriet told her to go back to bed, she would freeze without any slippers on. She went off with Dewint to make up a bed for Evelyn.

'The General runs the house, and we all obey her or she throws terrible moods, isn't that right, Jinks?'

Jinks tripped as she was leaving the room. She bit her lip and replied, 'Yes, Daddy,' but it went unheard. Edward sat on the arm of Evelyn's chair, fascinated by the boy.

'First thing tomorrow we'd better get you some lights for your bike.'

'First thing, Edward, is to get this boy to bed,' said Harriet as she entered the room with a hot-water bottle. 'Look at him, he can hardly keep his eyes open. I've put him in the room next to Jinks, so if he gets lonely in the night she will be next door.'

Evelyn, exhausted, stumbled as he stood up, but Edward caught him before he fell. 'I think I'd better carry the chap up, General, don't want any accidents, not before Christmas Day ...'

Harriet stoked the fire while Edward carried Evelyn upstairs and laid him down in the newly made bed. He was already asleep. Edward tucked him in and stroked his thick, black curls, then leaned forward and kissed his forehead.

Evelyn stirred, and he slipped his arms around his father. 'Thank you for having me to stay, Uncle Edward.'

When the boy had fallen asleep again, Edward left him, making sure the door was half open and the landing light left on in case he should wake in the night. As he passed his daughter's room, he called out, 'Goodnight, Jinks.'

Her whispered reply went unheard. In the darkness her glasses glinted as she looked around her orderly bedroom, some of the toys still in their boxes. She snuggled down and removed her glasses, rubbing the bridge of her nose where they left a permanent indentation.

In the next two days Evelyn learnt what was missing in his own home. The laughter, the excitement, all building up towards Christmas Day. Delivery vans brought supplies, including one from Harrods with all the Christmas luxuries, and Edward took him shopping in Petticoat Lane. They were in their element.

Harriet had a sneaking suspicion that they should have called Alex to check everything was all right. But Evelyn insisted his parents knew he was staying with them for the whole Christmas holiday. Having Evelyn around had a good effect not only on Edward, but also on Jinks, which pleased Harriet. The little girl had a habit of covering her mouth, like a hamster, when she laughed, as if afraid to hear herself. But with the rowdy boy banging around the house she found herself becoming almost as loud.

Harriet was a child's dream of an aunt. She was the first to suggest a game, and not boring cardboard-box games but clever charades, which she usually won. She was as noisy and boisterous as the children, and even Edward joined in. With a sheet over his head, he mimed the exceptionally difficult charade Harriet had dreamed up for him, 'A Sheik in a Pickle'.

'Would you be Valentino, sah?'

'Close, very close.'

'Oi! No speaking, that's cheating you lose a point,' bellowed Harriet, jumping up and down. To Evelyn's delight, when his aunt and uncle argued it was nothing like the bitter, controlled, back-stabbing 'disagreements' that went on in his own house. When Aunt Harriet shouted at Uncle Edward, he yelled back that he wouldn't lose a point as he didn't give anything away. Anyway, he was damned sure there was no such film. Harriet insisted, all the time nudging and winking at her partner, Evelyn. And Jinks, usually so timid, especially when she heard her parents arguing, now had tears streaming down her face, fogging up her glasses as she rolled on the floor, laughing.

'You see, look at your partner, she's collapsed! Out! Time's up! We won that round, Evelyn, that gives us a four-point lead.'

Jinks turned on her mother, wagging her finger. 'Mummy, you are cheating.'

'That's right, Jinks, you tell her ... Cheat!'

They were all bickering and laughing so much that they didn't hear the doorbell, or Alex's strained voice as he asked if they had heard from his son. When he strode in, the room went silent, and everyone turned to look at him as he stood in the doorway, red-faced with fury.

'I think you've both acted very irresponsibly – do you realize I've had the police out looking for him? I have been absolutely frantic, couldn't you at least have had the decency to call me and tell me he was with you?'

'I came by myself on my bike,' piped up Evelyn, and got such a glare from Alex he dodged to hide behind Harriet. Edward tried to explain, but Alex asked that the children leave the room.

The two of them listened outside the door, and Evelyn pulled a face. Nothing Harriet or Edward said could calm the irate Alex. He insisted on Evelyn getting his coat and his bloody bike and leaving with him immediately.

Harriet left the two men arguing, giving the children a glum look. She whispered that it looked like Evelyn wouldn't be staying for Christmas after all, and cheered them up by saying that if they were very quick they could open one of their gifts there and then. She hurried them to the tree and, of course, they went for the biggest boxes and began to rip off the paper. Harriet hurried upstairs and got Evelyn's coat, and the few things he had brought in his saddlebag. As she came back down the stairs, she saw the children, sitting in a mound of wrapping paper, gleefully opening more presents.

'Oi, just one more each, then Evelyn can take the rest home with him. I'll bring a big brown bag.'

Jinks looked at her huge doll, almost life-size, and then put it back in its box. Evelyn couldn't believe his eyes – a police car with flashing lights and a siren that screamed.

Edward had apologized, but now he was getting angry at Alex's attitude. He snapped that perhaps Barbara should have made sure she knew where her son was staying for Christmas.

'He lied to her, he lied to us both. He told us he was staying with a schoolfriend, we had no idea he wasn't with them until we called . . . So, there's blame on both sides. Now if you don't mind, I'll take him home.'

When they went out into the hall, there was no sign of the children. Alex called, and Harriet came downstairs with a suitcase for Evelyn's presents. She suggested they look in the dining room, they often hid in there. Edward approached the closed doors.

'I'll get him . . . Evelyn? Evelyn . . .?'

Jinks followed her mother downstairs, very subdued. Her doll was already lying in the cot she had been given for her birthday. She looked tearfully at her mother, and Harriet gave a little shrug.

'He'll come and see us again . . . Alex? He can come again, can't he?'

Alex was standing at the dining-room doors, and Harriet went to his side. From where they stood they could both see clearly into the dimly lit room. Evelyn was sitting at the table with his head in his hands, crying. Edward was leaning over him, stroking his hair. They couldn't hear what he was saying, but what they saw stopped them both dead. Alex felt as though he had been punched, and his face drained of colour. In the candlelight, Edward and Evelyn were the image of Freedom Stubbs – but they were also the image of each other. Alex and Harriet both knew in a moment that they were looking at father and son.

It was so clear to them now, the eyes, the thick black hair, the dark complexion. Harriet turned abruptly and went up the stairs, saying to Jinks it was bath time but, like Alex, her face was as white as a sheet.

Edward was sitting by the fire, reading. It was after nine, and he wondered where Harriet had got to. The big oak door inched open and Jinks stood there in her nightdress.

'Daddy's a bit tired for a story tonight, ask your mother . . . Where is she, upstairs?'

Jinks was shaking, and her face crumpled as she sobbed out, 'Mummy . . . Mummy's strange, she looks funny . . .'

Edward picked his daughter up and carried her upstairs, calling for Dewint as he went. He came bustling out of the kitchen, wiping his hands. 'Dinner will be a fraction late, sah, this new-fangled Aga has me all over the place . . .'

'Harry? Harry . . .? Is she in her studio, Jinks? Where's Mummy?'

Jinks clung tight to her father's neck, her eyes wide. She seemed terrified, and as they approached her bedroom she screamed and struggled to be put down. Dewint, right behind them, took the child, reassuring her that everything was all right. But it was in the air, it was almost tangible – something was wrong, terribly wrong. Edward reached the doorway and looked in, then whispered, 'Oh, Jesus Christ . . . take her downstairs, and get the doctor, fast.'

Harriet was sitting on her daughter's bed, her blouse open, the beautiful new doll cradled at her breast. She was rigid, her eyes crazy. Edward closed the door, but she appeared not to notice he was in the room, not until he was close. Then she looked at him. Her voice was quite calm – that was what made it so chilling, her calmness, her apparent normality. 'I can't wake him, his hands are cold, he won't take his feed.'

Edward and Dewint both tried unsuccessfully to take the doll away. She became abusive, and screamed at them both.

The ambulance and the doctor arrived within moments of each other. It took two attendants and the doctor to get her out of the room – they cajoled her, and not until she was sedated did she relinquish the doll. She had begun repeating, over and over, 'He's your son, he's your son . . .'

Edward walked into his bedroom. His daughter lay, swamped in the huge bed, clinging to her teddy bear. Her whole body was trembling, and she turned frightened eyes to him. He undressed slowly. It had been a long and terrible night, and one he knew he could never repeat, never risk being part of again. On the way back from the hospital he had made up his mind – this was the end. He couldn't take any more, and with Jinks to think about he decided the risk was too great. He would divorce Harriet.

Jinks watched her father walk into the bathroom. Her teeth chattered and she was cold and fearful. He switched the light off as he came out. She was scared of the dark, she always had been, but she was even more frightened to say anything. The big bed dipped as he got in beside her.

'You awake, little one?'

His big arm swept her to his side, and he held her tight. 'Oh, you're cold . . . Daddy'll give you a hot potato, turn around, that's a girl.'

Jinks lay in the curve of his big body as he breathed on her back, warming her. After a while he stopped, and she turned to face him. In the darkness she could see that he was crying.

'Do you want a tissue, Daddy?'

'No, no . . . sometimes it's best to cry . . . and you and me have a lot to cry about. Mummy's gone away, and – well, I doubt if she'll be coming back. Not because she doesn't want to, but because Mummy is sick. I'll try to explain it so that you'll understand. She doesn't have an illness, like a cold or a pain in her tummy, it's in her head . . .'

Jinks listened in the dark to his soft voice, and began to wriggle away from him, fraction by fraction. He was talking about a stranger, not her mother. His voice, always low, was little more than a whisper.

'I don't want to hear any more. Goodnight, Daddy.'

He looked down at her funny, crinkly hair, the red mark on her nose from the glasses, her eyes firmly shut. 'Goodnight.'

When she opened her eyes, the room was full of strange shadows. She didn't cry, she just moved further away from her father, wanting the coolness of the sheet against her. His body, his warmth, suffocated her.

Evelyn had fallen asleep in the car, and Alex carried him indoors and put him to bed. He turned in his sleep, and Alex could see his long eyelashes, so thick and dark, as dark as his silky black hair – just like Edward's.

Barbara didn't arrive home until after midnight. She was dressed in a long, floating chiffon gown, and she lounged against his study door. 'Darling, you really should try to come to more of these do's. Your grandchildren are growing up, they look so sweet in their little suits . . . Annabelle's girls are getting to be quite pretty. Selina looked frightful, but then she always does – on the other hand, Annabelle is blossoming. You know she's opened her own boutique in Beauchamp Place? She loves being Lady Blackwell. Mind you, that's about all he has to give her, he really is such a weak man. Oh, I need some money for his campaign, you know he is up for the by-election, and . . . darling? Are you listening to me?'

Alex poured his wife a brandy and held it out, letting her chatter on about her grandchildren, her daughters, until she flopped down in a chair and kicked off her gold sandals. 'The

Duke and Duchess of Kent were there. Oh, and Princess Grace, she's so beautiful ... You know, her son is almost Lyn's age – we had lots to talk about ... I'm exhausted, I've danced my feet off, I don't suppose you've heard anything about the Honours List, have you? I mean, I keep plugging away, hinting to everyone I know. Rumour has it, and I'm sure it's true, that ...'

'I heard a rumour tonight.'

Barbara smiled. 'Really? Well, tell me, are you on the New Year's List?'

'I was at Edward's, went to bring Evelyn home ...'

Barbara sipped her brandy and yawned ... then gasped as the glass was knocked out of her hand. Alex leaned over her, his hands resting on each arm of her chair. 'I want the truth, Barbara, no lies ... just the truth ... Evelyn is Edward's, isn't he ...? Isn't he?'

He was too calm, too cool, and Barbara was scared of him. 'Don't be silly, darling, you're frightening me.'

'Then tell me the truth ... whose child is he? He's his, you only have to see them side by side to know it ... Well? Tell me! He's Edward's, isn't he?'

Barbara was trapped in her chair. He loomed over her, wouldn't let her squirm her way out of it. She began to cry, and he finally moved away. She didn't have to say it.

'Jesus God, it's true ... it's true.'

Barbara couldn't stop crying, although she still did not admit it, but the more she cried the more he knew it was true. He stood with his back to her. 'Why? Just tell me why?'

Barbara's mind was racing, trying desperately to think of something, anything, to say to him. She rose from her chair and went to touch him, but he moved away so fast that she froze.

'Why, tell me why? Jesus, you could have had it aborted, any-thing ... Why?' At last he turned to her, and she started to cry again. This time he hit her so hard across the face that she fell against the desk. Alex picked her up by her hair and threw her back into the chair. 'How long have you two been together? Is it still going on?'

Barbara touched her lip, tasted blood in her mouth. 'No . . . it was over before he was born. I . . . I went to him, went to him for you, I didn't want anything to go wrong, you tried, you tried to make him sell the club, get rid of it . . . well, I tried.'

Alex looked at her with loathing. 'So you went to bed with him? Who the hell do you think you're kidding? You say you went to bed with my brother because of me? You did it for me? You've never done anything that wasn't for yourself.'

Barbara faced him, her fists clenched. 'I am telling you the truth, may God help me . . . I did it for you. I didn't love him, I didn't even want him! All I wanted was for you to be rid of that bloody club. You tried, don't you remember how you tried . . .? Alex? Alex . . .?'

He stared at her coldly, and she cried again. He walked to the door. 'You sicken me, you've made loveless marriages for both your daughters – you've done that for me, too, I suppose?'

Barbara snapped back at him through her tears, 'Yes . . . yes . . . and you benefit, so don't kid yourself you don't. Just as you use my money as though it were your own, maybe you don't do anything except for yourself, either, Alex . . .'

He shuddered, repelled. 'He's not to know, understand me? He's never to know, and he's not to be allowed near Edward again . . . I'll move into the spare room.' He shut the door quietly behind him.

Barbara ran after him, yanked it open. 'Is that it? Is that all you have to say? You're moving into the spare room? You might as well have been there for years, you think this is a marriage? I never see you, and when I do you're just going out to some business meeting. I see more of the goddamn butler than I do of you!'

'Fine, maybe you should have an affair with him.'

Barbara went for him, tried to hit him, but he caught her wrist and pushed her away. This time she fell against the stairs.

'Stay away from me, you disgust me.'

'I disgust you? I disgust you? Well, fuck you . . .'

'That's it, Barbara, come on, let's hear what you really are, let's hear it. Bet all those society friends of yours would love to see you now, crawling up the stairs.'

Hauling herself to her feet, Barbara was in such a rage that she screamed. Alex laughed at her, turned away and walked up the stairs, with Barbara screaming after him.

'You'll never get me crawling to you, the only person you can crawl to is Edward . . . When he says jump, you jump . . . when he's drunk you run round there and clean him up like he was your big baby . . . You are married to him, only you don't even know it . . .'

Alex froze, unable to move. He was fighting for control, because he wanted to kill her. All he had to do was turn round and hit her and she would fall backwards down the stairs . . .

She kept coming close, shouting at him. 'It's always been Edward, hasn't it, you keep on about how much you hate him, you don't hate him, you love him . . . he means more to you than I ever did, than ever your son did . . . Yes, he's his!'

Alex turned; the sight of his face, like a mask, made her shut her mouth. She pressed herself against the wall, terrified. 'Don't touch me, Alex, or I'll scream, Scargill will see you . . . Don't touch me.'

Alex smiled and looked down at her. His quiet voice was icy. 'Don't worry, Barbara, I'll never touch you again.'

He left her sobbing on the stairs. He packed a case, then went into Evelyn's room and packed his. Then he gently shook him awake. 'Come on, Daddy's got a surprise, we're going to New York for Christmas . . . come on, darling, wakey, wakey.'

Barbara was still crying when she saw Alex carry his son, Edward's child, out to the Rolls-Royce and drive away.

As the plane took off, Evelyn slipped his hand into Alex's. He was always a little afraid of flying. Alex gave him a fatherly pat, then helped him unbuckle his safety belt as the indicators went off. The air hostess placed a glass of champagne on Alex's table.

'Oh, can I have one too, please?'

The air hostess looked at Alex and he gave a small nod, so

Evelyn sipped his glass of champagne. 'Why don't you like Uncle Edward, Daddy, did he do something wrong?'

Slipping his arm around Evelyn, Alex told him he asked too many questions, then kissed the top of his head.

'I wish I had a brother, he is your brother, isn't he?'

Alex leaned back and closed his eyes. 'Yes, he is my brother, we just don't get along, that's all. Now, I don't want to hear any more, just let me rest.'

Kicking his feet against the seat, Evelyn sipped his champagne in silence. He turned to look at his father, whose head was resting on the pillow, his eyes still closed. He studied Alex's profile sternly, and then decided that Uncle Edward was better-looking, and he was also ... He couldn't quite put his finger on it, but there was something different about the Big Bad Wolf.

Alex was not asleep, he was irritated by the knocking of Evelyn's heels against the bottom of the seat. The dark head was resting against his arm, and he could smell the boy's hair. 'I used to love him so, Evelyn, we used to be like one person.'

Evelyn didn't hear, he was fast asleep. Alex eased the empty glass from his hand and covered him with a red airline blanket.

Edward could not bear to see Harriet, but the doctors confirmed his suspicions that this time her recovery would be very slow, if at all. Arrangements were made for her to be moved to a mental institution and, as always, Edward provided the best medical care money could buy. Jinks was placed in a boarding school. The clothes of the bewildered child were packed by a heartbroken Dewint. Edward spent days shut in his office. Eventually he handed Miss Henderson a thick dossier of instructions, plus a chequebook with his signature already written for Alex's use. Miss Henderson had never seen Edward so subdued, as if mourning a loved one. In a way he was; the Harriet he knew had gone for ever, and he had no one to blame but himself. In one night he had lost his family; he had also lost his hope of forming a relationship with his son. He knew that by now Alex would be suspicious, not like Harriet, but intuitively aware that the boy was his. It was Evelyn that Edward wanted more than anything else in his life. His sense of loss was all–consuming, as if a shadow lay across his heart, weighing him down. Just as he knew Alex would be more than able to cope without him, and more than likely pleased to be rid of him, he knew his brother would never give him his son. He owed Alex for his years spent in jail. At times he even thought the debt was repaid. Edward's mind reeled. Not concerned with the fact that he had destroyed his own and Alex's family, he attempted to push the shadow from him, to search for something that would make Alex give up his son. What if he made Alex an offer of such magnitude he could not turn it down?

Miss Henderson heard Edward locking his office. As he passed her desk he dropped a sealed envelope into her lap. 'Make sure my brother gets that, would you, Henny?'

'Will you be away long, Mr Barkley?'

'I don't know. I don't know where I'm going and I don't know when I'll be back. I'm trying for the deal of a lifetime, Henny. Take care of yourself.'

She watched him walk out to the corridor, press for the lift. As it arrived he turned back to her and gave her a strange dejected look, and was gone.

Ming was waiting at Kennedy Airport, waving to them both as they came through the barrier. Alex kissed the Japanese woman on both cheeks, and Evelyn shook the delicate hand.

'Well, Alex, you never mentioned what a handsome boy your son is.'

Evelyn might not have been very old, but he didn't miss a trick. His father had never mentioned this pretty lady, and he seemed very friendly with her.

'Do you have a big Christmas tree?'

Evelyn got no reply to his question. Alex and Ming were already discussing business, and he was ignored.

Throughout the journey across New York, Evelyn stared

open-mouthed from the limo. He had never seen such tall buildings, and he asked many questions, repeating the phrase 'skyscrapers' with a chuckle. All the cars drove on the wrong side of the road, and the taxis were bright yellow ... Eventually Alex patted his head and told him not to keep chattering, as he was very tired. So Evelyn kept his nose pressed to the window, and didn't say anything when thick snow began to fall. He wondered what Uncle Edward would be doing, New York was much colder, and he hoped the lady would have big log fires like they had at the manor house.

Evelyn thought Ming's apartment was very nice, if a bit too tidy. Everything looked sparse, and there was a place for every precious ornament. The Christmas tree was just some weird-looking, white-painted twigs with a few gold balls.

The tiny boxroom to which Evelyn was shown contained only a white-painted bed, a single white chair and a polished, lacquered chest with a single white cushion on it. The floor was of polished pine. He was afraid to sit down or move in case he left fingermarks.

Ming had not asked why Alex called her in the middle of the night, why he had wanted to spend Christmas with her, why he had trailed his small son along. She was too clever, waiting until they sat alone by the gas 'log' fire. Alex took his time, eventually slipping his arm around her. 'I need you, I need you, thank you for letting us stay.'

Ming smiled and closed her eyes. Once, she had wanted to hear him say that, once, but it was a long time ago. She wondered what had sparked off this unscheduled visit, knew there was something else.

'I don't want to talk business tonight, but in the morning, we have a lot to discuss ...'

Ming smiled again, but said nothing, she simply held out her hand and guided Alex into her white bedroom.

*

Evelyn woke in the night, and the white shapes in the room scared him, so he slipped along the corridor, barefooted, to his father's room. Alex lay beside Ming, both fast asleep, and Evelyn stared, dumbfounded.

Christmas came and went, and Evelyn spent the majority of his time either alone in his room or being driven around New York by a Japanese chauffeur who could hardly speak a word of English. He visited the zoo, the cartoon cinemas, and behaved impeccably. Ming was civil, always smiling, but there was no warmth, no affection. She gave Evelyn a strange game with silver balls rolling around as a Christmas gift.

The bell chimed for dinner, and Evelyn washed his face and scrubbed his hands, then hurried towards the dining room. He could hear Ming's voice.

'I am thinking of going public, selling off the shares in the boutiques and shops. This will give me the cash flow to move into opening a construction company. It makes sense, as I do most of the designs for the major companies, so why not offer construction facilities as well?'

Evelyn reached the half-open door.

'My company could help you there, we have facilities both here and in . . .'

Ming interrupted. Evelyn heard the chill in her high-pitched, snapping voice, and paused in the doorway.

'You don't have to tell me what you have, and isn't it really more what Edward has? From what you have told me there is very little "we" in your company, you can't even sign a cheque without Edward.'

Ming sounded the chimes again for Evelyn to come, and at the same time she pulled out a chair to sit down at the table. Evelyn entered and sat down, apologizing for being two minutes late. Ming flicked him a cold look of irritation.

The food, which Evelyn found dreadful, consisted of raw vegetables and rubber-tasting fish, and made him feel sick. Throughout the meal, Alex and Ming discussed business, but they were both cool and controlled, choosing their words carefully. Ming's tiny hands folded her starched, white napkin into the shape of a flower.

'Daddy . . . Daddy, can we go to see a movie?'

'Not now, Evelyn, I'm busy. Ask the chauffeur . . . go along, I'll see you later.'

Evelyn wandered back to his room and sat on the white bed. He felt lonely, and even as young as he was he could detect a change in his father's attitude. He curled up and wept, trying to think what he had done to turn his father against him.

Ming leaned back against her white sofa, her delicate fingers cupping her brandy glass. Alex stood by the window, looking down on the busy avenue below.

'Did Barbara admit it? She actually admitted it?'

'It's hard not to, you only have to look at him to see the resemblance. I have been such a fool, such a bloody fool . . .'

Ming said nothing, carefully placing her glass down on the polished coffee table. This was not the time to discuss her own business, to repeat her persistent request for the brothers to sell their shares in her company. Instead she commiserated, her voice soft and soothing. Alex joined her on the sofa and gripped her hand tightly . . .

'He beats me at every turn. You were right, some partner he is! I had no idea what was going on in Mexico, but I accepted it without a murmur when he dropped the contracts on to my desk, accepted it because he'd included me. I'm a dumb piece of meat that he has squeezed every drop of blood from . . .'

'I'm glad you came to me, because I have always been there for you. You know that, don't you, Alex?'

He smiled, his grip relaxing, and she slipped her arm through his. 'So what are you going to do? Divorce?'

He sighed and closed his eyes. 'Barbara has millions tied up in the company. It won't be that easy. It's Edward I have to deal with first. Barbara is simple in comparison. You know, I think, truthfully, that Edward is insane. I'm not just saying it, but if you could have seen him when I went back the last time he was drunk and incoherent . . .'

Ming massaged Alex's shoulders, her eyes more cat-like than ever.

'Had anyone else ever mentioned that he could be unstable?'

'You just have to read the papers – drunk, thrown out of night clubs, his driving licence has been taken away so many times, he's crashed his car. Wish to God he'd smash himself up in it, then we would be rid of him.'

'Well, that could be arranged, but surely it would be simpler to prove to the board members that he is incapable of running the Barkley Company, even if he is who he is, and then you could take the reins legally . . .'

Alex turned to her and smiled, cupping her face in his hands. 'I knew I was right to come here.'

'You must tread carefully, Alex. Don't let him get round you the way he always does, not this time . . . You can get control of the company, I know it.'

He threw back his head and laughed. 'Yes, I know it too, and the first thing you'll want me to do is sell back your shares. Am I right, you little minx? Well, sweetheart, I promise you that will be the first thing I'll do.'

'And the second, Alex, is divorce Barbara. Promise me that, too, Alex.'

He looked at her and knew his brother had been right. She was as dangerous as Edward had always said, but he had not bargained for her genuinely loving him. Alex kissed her, swept her up in his arms and carried her to her bedroom. 'First, my darling, I am going to take you to bed.'

Evelyn peeked from his bedroom to see his father with Ming in his arms. He quietly closed the door, afraid to be caught, confused and lonely. He wished he was still at the manor house, wished he was still with his uncle. He took out the gift he had taken from beneath the big Christmas tree, the shiny police car with the bells and the lights, his face twisted as he tried not to cry.

Later that night Alex lay wide awake, unable to sleep, thinking how he should go about taking over the company. Beside him Ming slept, as composed in sleep as she was awake. He studied her face, wondered what their life together would have been like if Edward had never interfered; but then they would never have met if it had not been for Edward. The realization of the immense power his brother had always had over him made Alex even more determined to beat him. He began to twist his gold chain round his fingers, unaware that Edward had in a way already beaten him. There would be no satisfaction in removing Edward because he had quite simply removed himself.

Chapter Twenty-Four

The following day Alex and Evelyn returned to England. Dewint rushed to change out of the taffeta frock he had bought from the Blue Cross charity shop. He scurried downstairs as the doorbell rang again, wiping the cream from his face, still trying to get his make-up off. 'I'm afraid Mr Barkley is not at home, sah.'

Alex pushed past him and ran up to Edward's bedroom, began to search through his desk, through his drawers.

Dewint hovered at the door. 'I really don't think you should, sah.'

Alex straightened up. He was sweating, red in the face. 'Where does he go? Do you know? All these months away from London, where does he go?'

Flustered by Alex's anger, Dewint stuttered, 'W-Well, sah, I-I really don't know, he has f-friends in California, and, er, he goes to Africa, but I really d-don't know where he is at this p-precise moment in time, sah.'

Looking around, Evelyn saw the drooping, bald Christmas tree, the dead fire in the grate. The place seemed cold and lifeless. Dirty dishes were left on a tray, and the warmth, the Christmas atmosphere, were gone. He shivered — the house frightened him. 'Daddy, who are all these people in the paintings?'

Alex pushed past him into the lounge, and snapped to Dewint that he should clean the place up.

'When will my brother be back, do you know?'

'I'm s-sorry, sah, but he never tells me when he is departing or returning, I just ... I suppose you heard about Mrs Barkley? She was taken very bad again just before Christmas, and Jinks has been sent to boarding school. I'm here alone, you see ...'

Evelyn was more confused than ever. The manor house was different – cold and ugly. It was as if he had only imagined the warmth and happiness of the Christmas festivities. He was looking forward to seeing his mother.

Barbara was resting. The stitches were still there but the swelling and initial tenderness of her breasts had subsided. She would soon be back in circulation, and she was already planning functions and parties.

Evelyn rushed to his mother to give her a hug, and she screamed, pushing him away. 'Don't touch me! My God you're so rough.'

Evelyn walked out, pausing in the doorway to give his mother a cold look. Then he slammed the door behind him.

Alex, unaware of Barbara's many cosmetic operations, or the present condition of her breasts, saw only his son's hurt face. 'He only wanted to kiss you, for Chrissake.'

Barbara got up, flustered. She hadn't expected them to return from New York for at least another week. 'Did you have a pleasant Christmas? How is Ming, well?'

Alex smiled. Barbara could never resist getting her small digs in. He ignored the question. 'I don't suppose you've heard from Edward at all, have you?'

Barbara inspected her face in the mirror, gave him a veiled look. 'I'm not likely to, am I?'

Alex looked at her reflection and was struck by her flawless skin, her still-beautiful face. She caught him staring at her, and made a move towards him. 'Alex ... Alex, I've missed you, can't we at least talk?'

Just like his son he walked away from her, annoyed that he had even given her the opportunity to see the effect she still had on him. Unlike Evelyn he did not slam the door but closed it quietly and firmly behind him.

Alex was handed all the documents Edward had left for him. He asked Miss Henderson what had happened, if she knew where his brother could be contacted. All she could tell him was what had taken place the last time she had seen him, and then she handed him the sealed envelope.

'Mrs Barkley is very sick, did you know?'

Alex was confused, for a moment thinking she was referring to Barbara, but then realized she was talking about Harriet.

'She's in a mental institution. She had a nervous breakdown just before Christmas. I have the address, and also Juliana is now in a boarding school.'

'And you don't know where Edward is? Didn't he leave a contact number?'

'No, Mr Barkley. The last thing he said to me was to make sure you received that envelope.'

Alex closed his office door, put down the thick file of all the listed documents left by Edward, saw the stack of signed cheques, and then opened the envelope. There was no letter, just a copy of Edward Barkley's will, naming as sole heir his brother Alex Barkley. He read the small print carefully, but there seemed to be no hitch, no catch ... Edward had disappeared simply handing Alex the reins. He wouldn't know for how long, but he was going to make damned sure he would grab hold of them, maybe hold so tight that Edward would have a tough time getting them away from him when and if he returned.

Chapter Twenty-Five

Evelyn was sent to Harrow as a boarder. In this, his fourth year, along with two other pupils, he went down to Oxford Street and stole two records from a store. The three boys then got very drunk on the journey back to school. Two of the boys returned to their dormitory, but Evelyn passed out on the tennis courts. The housemaster discovered him the next morning as he went to play his regular eight o'clock game.

The boys had stolen the records while wearing their uniforms, and the school had already been informed about the theft. Evelyn was discovered holding the two albums in his arms – one by Jimi Hendrix, and the Beatles' *Sergeant Pepper's Lonely Hearts Club Band*. He was expelled.

Barbara was having her hair blow-dried when he sauntered into her bedroom. 'Good God, what are you doing at home?'

'I thought you knew,' he replied, cockily, 'I've been given the old heave-ho ... Where's Dad?'

'At the office of course, what have you done? Lyn? Evelyn! Will you come back here, I'm talking to you!'

Evelyn reappeared and leaned against the door, picking his nose. 'What do you want?'

'I want to know what you did this time? Have you any idea

how difficult it was for your father to get a place for you at Harrow? It was bad enough in your junior school.'

'No, I don't know how difficult it was, but I'm sure you will tell me, Mother.'

'I'm going to call him, right now. You are the most infuriating person I have ever met – and for God's sake use a hankerchief.'

Evelyn walked out. He was fifteen years old and arrogantly self-assured. His voice had a resonant, plummy tone learned at Harrow. He had gained little, as far as Barbara and Alex could see, from his vastly expensive education apart from his nonchalant way of speaking. Academically he was either close to or bottom of the class. Only in sports did he excel. However, even his sports reports had begun to include the word 'lazy', and 'unsporting conduct' had been mentioned in two memos from his housemaster. Alex had hoped he could get to Cambridge on his prowess in the game of rugby, but of late even that had fallen below par.

He had grown very tall for his age. Although facially more like Edward than Barbara or Alex ever cared to mention, he had inherited his mother's slenderness and would never be as tall or as big-boned as his father.

Alex was not at his office – he was at Harrow, desperately trying to salvage his son's education, hoping to get the expulsion reduced to suspension. Evelyn had made no attempt to cover for his two friends, and they had been expelled along with him. Alex did not expect such sweeping and immediate action for what he deemed a small misdemeanour. All boys got a little drunk, didn't they?

Evelyn's housemaster was well aware of the donations Mr Barkley had made to the school, and it was his unfortunate task to tell him about his son. 'I'm afraid it is a little more than simply getting drunk. Of course boys will be boys, but, Mr Barkley, I think perhaps for Evelyn's benefit you should know the whole truth – and the truth is never pleasant.'

Alex accepted a cup of milky tea and waited.

'We have, as you know, had a little trouble with Evelyn virtually from the word "go". He does not conform, perhaps "will not" would be a better choice of words. To be frank, your son flatly refused to become an integral part of the school. Perhaps we could cope with that in time, many of our pupils come round to our ways of their own accord in the end. However, as I have said, Evelyn has been difficult. You must be aware of his indiscretions, the problems we have had with him. I am afraid, Mr Barkley, your son is a known cheat, verging on the pathological. He seems incapable of telling the truth. Again, we have to deal with all sorts of boys with problems caused by being removed from their own environment – but your son, Mr Barkley, is also a thief . . .'

Alex listened to the list of Evelyn's offences, and the canings that had had no effect. He also heard about numerous letters sent to him by the school that had gone unanswered. The housemaster ate biscuits throughout the entire meeting, finally wiping his mouth with a greyish handkerchief. Alex suggested rather haughtily that perhaps he should not be talking to Evelyn's housemaster but should take the matter to the head himself.

'I am sorry, and I'm speaking on behalf of the Board of Governors when I say this, it is totally unacceptable for Evelyn to return even to finish this term . . .'

Alex found his wayward son at the office, pestering Miss Henderson. With a cold stare, he pointed in the direction of his own room. Evelyn wandered in and sat on Alex's swivel chair.

'Get out, that's my chair . . . Get out, you stupid bastard.'

Evelyn sprang up fast. Alex slammed the door and threw his briefcase down, his face red with rage. He spat out his words, his eyes like knives. 'You're a thief, a liar, a cheat . . . and that's just for starters. You get drunk, vomit all over the tennis courts and are foolish enough to pass out there so the housemaster can't help but find you . . . If I were you, I'd wipe that fucking smile off your stupid, smug face. I paid good money, big money, to swing a place for you at Harrow . . . You had the opportunity of a lifetime, not just the education but for contacts later in life, when you left . . . and what did you do? You chucked it away for a lousy Rolling Stones' record. Well? You got anything to say? You got something to say about it?'

'Well it was actually a Jimi Hendrix album, his first . . .'

Alex backhanded him so hard he fell against the desk. Evelyn picked himself up, rubbing his cheek, which was already swelling. He smiled . . . 'Did you know when you sent me there, Pater, that if a woman is caught in a chap's room one is expelled immediately, but if it's another bloke you just get suspended for two weeks?'

Evelyn took Alex's breath away. Nothing anyone ever said or did to him had the slightest effect. He found himself almost smiling at Evelyn's audacity, his barbed humour. He slumped into his chair, shaking his head. When he looked up Evelyn was smiling, a smile that mirrored Edward's. Alex stared hard at his son until the smile was wiped away. The eyes that met his were identical to Edward's, dark and unfathomable. It was Alex who looked away.

He tried to ease up. 'I'm sorry . . . okay, I shouldn't have hit you, but things are getting on top of me here. I have no idea where your uncle is, and I have more than enough to cope with. I don't need you causing problems, and you are one, you know that?'

'Yes sir, I'm aware of being a bit of a pest. I can get a job if you like, sweeping the office.'

'Add to it cocky, lazy but above all dumb . . . You are dumb, and I don't mean academically . . . You've just blown your chances of getting a place in any other school . . . Wherever you go, you'll be branded a thief, liar, cheat – like it? There is a possibility that I can get you a place in France, it would get you out of my hair . . . Will you look at me when I'm talking to you! Would you try it? Any other school will turn you down after one look at your history. Sometimes money can't buy you what you want . . .'

'Does Mother know that? Seems to me she does very well for a woman who thought Gertrude Stein was a singing nun.'

'Okay, go on, keep it up, you think it's witty?'

'I'd like to go to France, and I'm ready whenever you say.'

Alex's intercom buzzed and Miss Henderson said that he was already late for his meeting. Evelyn was half out of the door, but stopped as Alex called to him, 'Hang on ... don't go, I'm not completely through. Thank you Miss Henderson, I'll be right there.'

Alex walked across to Evelyn and put an arm around his shoulder. 'You know, all this bravado is one thing, but I want your word on something and I want you to promise me you'll keep it.'

'Sure, whatever you say.'

'I'm serious ... They mentioned you'd been smoking this marijuana stuff, well I want you to give me your word you won't mess around with it. Do I make myself clear? You will be in a foreign country, they have their own laws ... You get copped with drugs on you and you're on your own ... Do I have your word on it?'

Alex gave his son's shoulder a squeeze, murmured that he would try to make it home before nine, then walked down the corridor into the boardroom.

Evelyn stood for a while, his shoes half buried in the thick carpet. Along the corridor he could see his uncle's office door, closed firmly. As Miss Henderson came back to her desk he asked if anyone had any news of his Uncle Edward.

'No Evelyn, we've not heard for quite a while. I'm told that Jinks is doing very well, did you know? Heading for Cambridge like her father. Are you all right, dear?'

Miss Henderson watched him as he gave a slight smile, the way he inclined his head reminded her of Edward.

'Er ... Is there a gents' I can use on this floor?'

'Oh well, there's your father's private one, or there's another cloakroom just at the end, first left.'

'Thank you. If you see my uncle, say I asked after him, would you? Nice to see you again.' He smiled, then turned and shambled off.

Miss Henderson set about clearing her desk. She had heard most of what went on in Alex's office, and she wondered what trouble Evelyn had got himself into this week. He was nothing but trouble that one, it was written all over him. She sealed the envelopes for all the cheques Edward had instructed her to send. One to the nursing home where Harriet was, then their daughter's school fees – she even sent off the birthday cards now. She began to think she knew Jinks Barkley better than her own father did. Her school reports came directly to the office, and it was Miss Henderson who read them with pleasure, and sent Jinks her regular allowance. The girl always wrote neat 'thank you' letters back. She was going to be no problem, it was obvious Jinks had a very bright future.

Evelyn locked the toilet door, put the seat down and sat on it. He then opened a small silver box, took out a packet of skins and rolled a joint. He sat smoking it, sitting in the Barkley Empire's john . . . It amused him, only he didn't laugh. He felt ashamed. Not for smoking the joint, but for the shame he had seen in his father's face . . . 'Liar, cheat, thief . . .'

Evelyn drew heavily on the joint and let the smoke drift out slowly. He felt his bruised cheek where his father had slapped him . . . He stood up, tossed the end of the roach into the bowl and pulled the chain. Maybe he would like France . . .

Alex had seen Ming only a few times since their last meeting that Christmas. Now that he had access to the accounts, in particular those in Mexico, Alex had discovered just why Edward had been against selling back her shares to Ming. The company had channelled thousands of dollars through her outlets and it had proved a good method of laundering money. Ming had taken a percentage of the vast sums. As Edward had done, Alex picked up on the discrepancies in her accounts. Ming might love him, but she had certainly made sure she had lined her own pockets. Alex felt betrayed but realized once more how Edward had covered for him, and just how shrewd he was at business. He had begun to think of Edward more of late, wondering where he was ... and what he was doing. His silence, at first welcome, had become rather ominous.

Alex had been so immersed in the old accounts he had forgotten the time. He knew they were entertaining, yet again, and hurried to the bedroom door, mumbling that he had been held up and was he supposed to dress. 'Barbara, is it black tie tonight or not?'

Barbara raised her eyebrows to her hairdresser and sighed. 'Daaarling, I phoned the office ... It's very casual, but smart casual. It's Walter, his wife and Lord Harmsworth, then the ...'

Alex had already departed to his own rooms.

'I've changed my mind, part it down the middle, Timmy.'

Alex made polite conversation throughout the meal. He was tired, and he stifled yawn after yawn. Barbara's charity affairs were always like this, the people all looked the same, they just switched clothes. As they withdrew into the lounge for coffee, Walter, who had been to the far end of the table, asked for a private word with Alex. The two men waited while Scargill poured them brandy, and Alex clipped his cigar.

'I need to talk to Edward, I've called numerous times and I am told he's abroad or not available.'

Alex lit the cigar and puffed slowly, trying to size Walter up. They had met on a number of occasions similar to this evening, but they had never had an in-depth conversation.

'It's rather a delicate situation, but it is imperative I speak to him within the week. Do you know where he is?'

Alex could see the man was sweating. His pockmarked face glistened, and his eyes behind the thick glasses were shifty, drifting away from Alex's gaze.

'Anything I can do to help? You see, I actually don't have the slightest idea where he is – and believe me, I need to contact him too.'

Walter stubbed out his cigarette, immediately lit another, and pulled his chair closer. 'Have you discussed my business with him at all?'

Alex had no knowledge of any business transactions between Walter and Edward, but Walter made the mistake of taking Alex's silence for confirmation that he did know. 'I've tried to contact Duval in Africa for three months, the PM's somehow got wind of the hospital complex, I cannot afford at this stage . . . You know I regained my seat this election?'

Alex was trying to fathom what the hell Walter was talking about, but he couldn't make head nor tail of it. All he could say for sure was that the man was exceptionally nervous.

'Yes, yes, but that was a foregone conclusion.'

Walter paced the room, hands stuffed in his pockets. 'Part of my campaign was that I would begin building a whole new leisure centre. Costs have jumped – escalated – to a ridiculous level, and I need Edward. He agreed to finance the project, but I have not seen a penny as yet. Now it's up before a committee for review and if it seems like I'm going to break my word, it won't look good . . . You have the hospital, everything's gone through, but he's let me down. I need to speak with him, and within the week.' He lit yet another cigarette and began a hacking, chesty cough.

'How much? I'll see if I can release funds to you immediately.'

Walter eased up, sat down and sighed with relief. 'Jesus, if you could it would save my skin, the election was by no means the foregone conclusion everyone thought . . . Well, Edward must have told you . . . Thirty-five thousand, as agreed.'

Alex nearly choked on his cigar, but covered by saying they should both give up smoking for their health.

Walter stubbed out his half-smoked cigarette and gave Alex a strange, sly look. 'With you two bastards I'm amazed I've kept my sanity this long . . . I'll call the office first thing in the morning, all right?' He straightened his tie, wiped his sweating face and gave a small bow. 'Perhaps we should join the party?'

*

First thing in the morning, Alex called Miss Henderson and asked her if he had all the documents on the building works. She replied that he had all she had ever been given to file. Alex sent a memo down to personnel to check out Skye Duval.

Evelyn was being driven to Heathrow, by Scargill. No one had even said goodbye to him, but he was used to that. He had his precious record collection and his guitar, he cared about little else. He wondered what France would hold for him. The place sounded gruesome, if not monastic. The school was run by friars, and it was apparent even to Evelyn that his father had really scraped the bottom of the barrel.

Scargill did not take Evelyn's cases into the terminal. He pulled up outside and waited until he saw Evelyn give the thumbs up sign at his ticket collection desk then he returned to London. The school was St Martin at Pontoise, about thirty-two kilometres north-west of Paris. Evelyn had drunk his fill of free champagne in first-class during the flight. Now the taxi made his head ache, and he felt sick. As they turned a corner, he saw stretching before him what looked like a fortress. He leaned forward. 'Holy shit, this can't be it, it's like a fucking prison.'

Chapter Twenty-Six

Alex had called a security company hire-car as Barbara was using the Rolls-Royce. The navy blue Mercedes was waiting for him outside the Barkley Company. The uniformed security guards locked up after him. The Mercedes' door was held open by the chauffeur, who greeted him with, 'Good evening, Mr Barkley.' He replaced his peaked cap and hurried round to the driving seat. Alex gave the man a cursory glance, snapped open his briefcase, and began to look over contracts, unaware of the driver's scrutiny as he began making notes with a gold pen in the margin. On every housing development contract he had come across, the same government stamp had been signed by Walter . . .

Looking in the driver's mirror George Windsor was sure now, one hundred per cent sure, that the man in the back of his hire-car was without question Alex Stubbs. They drew up outside Alex's house.

'How much?'

George turned. 'Have this one on me, Alex, for old times' sake.'

Puzzled, Alex looked at him, frowning in annoyance at the driver's familiarity . . . Then he felt as if he had been punched in the gut. Somehow he found the control to take out his wallet, extract a ten-pound note. 'Keep the change.'

George gripped his wrist. 'You can't fool me, Alex, this is George, remember? You share a cell wiv someone else as long as what I did, yer get to remember.' He released Alex's wrist and there was a long silence. Alex stared out of the window at his house. Barbara was entertaining yet again, he could see all the lights on, the cars in the drive. After a long pause, thirty years of pause, Alex spoke again. 'How much do you want?'

'Ahhh, don't make me 'it yer! You think I'd try that one? I was your friend, remember me, George? We shared a cell, a flat, an' yer say that to me ... What yer take me for, some kind of fuckin' bum?'

'I'm sorry.'

'I fuckin' buried yer, mate, stood over yer friggin' grave, mate. Sorry!' George turned back to gaze through the windscreen, gripped the wheel tight.

Alex sighed a deep sigh that made his body shudder. This was the nightmare, the moment he had dreaded, when a ghost would rear its head and bring back the past.

'You know, Alex, I loved yer, the best friend I ever had. I loved yer, and I looked up to yer, and I thought you cared about me. I must have been crazy. Why d'yer do that to me, why?'

Alex asked him to drive around, keep on driving. The car moved off slowly, and it began to rain, heavy drops at first. They sounded loud, like Alex's heart.

'Too much happened, George, to even begin to tell you, but believe me, it was not in my control.' The words sounded hollow. 'Look, I had a chance to get out and I took it, grabbed it with both hands. My brother engineered everything and I went along with it until it was too late, too complicated to get out of.'

Windsor looked at Alex in the mirror. 'Don't have ter make excuses to me, Alex. You done all right, more than all right, just hurt that yer couldn't tell me. But then maybe if I'd hadda chance, I'd have done the same.'

Alex laughed, a soft, mirthless laugh; he would never, could never even begin to tell George part of it. He rested his arm along the back of the driving seat. 'George, I've never had such a good friend, not ever. In fact, I don't have a single one now.'

The two of them drove around for over an hour, and at last the car pulled up at Alex's house again.

'I need a friend, George, someone I can trust, trust with my secrets, my life . . .'

Windsor said he was not after a bribe, not even after money, but he would be just as good a friend, any time Alex needed him.

'Then work for me, be my driver.' Windsor said he would report for duty the following morning. He promised never to say a word about Alex. As Alex began to climb out of the car, he stopped and held Windsor's shoulder for a moment in a tight grip, and Windsor touched his hand.

The cab stood at the kerb until the front door closed, then moved slowly off. Windsor whistled, he had played that very well. He would be all right now. Things would be all right from now on.

Alex couldn't face the roomful of talking, laughing people so he gave Scargill the wink and went upstairs to his rooms. As he undressed, he wondered just how far he could really trust George. He soaped his body, he would have to tie George to him strongly, make sure he was well paid but knew his place.

He began to towel himself dry, and caught his reflection in the steamed-up bathroom mirror. He stared, then wiped it clear, looked at himself. His eyes were red-rimmed, he was exhausted. How many more ghosts from the past could rear up and threaten him? No sooner did he make some headway than something or someone dragged him back. Holding the reins of the vast company was a mammoth task in itself, to be working day and night on trying to piece together Edward's transactions was impossible, he covered his tracks so well . . . He still had no idea where his brother was.

'Where the hell are you, Eddie; where?' He was shocked at the desperation in his voice. He wanted to smash the mirror with his fist. He pressed his head against the cold glass, calming himself, but it seemed that every way he turned there was a wall, closing in on him, pushing him under, as if he were drowning. He breathed deeply, he had not felt this violent, so physically angry, since he had been in prison. As it was then, his fury was directed at his brother, at Edward, but it was impotent fury, because he could not discover where Edward had run to ... unless ... South Africa.

George Windsor was half asleep. It was six o'clock in the morning, and the last person he expected to call him was Alex Barkley.

'George? It's Alex. Sorry to get you up so early, but ... I want to work out, the way we used to ... get yourself over to the RAC Club in St James's ...'

George was overawed by the 'gentlemen's club' with the marble swimming pool. But he had little time to take it all in as Alex was already dressed in a tracksuit waiting impatiently. 'Right, put me through it, just the way you used to. I need to be fit, George ... so let's get cracking. We do this every morning, same time, okay?'

George set Alex a tough programme. The good life had put a lot of extra pounds on Alex, but he never said a word, pushing himself until it was George who had to tell him to take it easy or he'd give himself a heart attack. Alex laughed, he felt good, and George began to give him a massage just the way he used to, pummelling his body, his big strong hands oiling, rubbing him down. George looked into Alex's face – it was an eerie feeling, so many years had passed. It was as though Alex knew what George was thinking. He opened his eyes, and his voice was soft. 'I need a friend, George, don't let me down.'

George turned him over and began to massage his shoulders. 'Whenever you need me, I'll be there, you can depend on me, son.'

Alex smiled, and the two old friends shook hands; then Alex pulled George close and held him for a moment.

Fifteen minutes later, Alex emerged from the changing room in an immaculate pin-striped suit, carrying his briefcase. He looked at his gold Rolex, and his voice was sharp. 'Right, bring the car round, I can make a couple of calls here while I'm waiting.'

George watched Alex stride to the reception desk. He seemed a different person, but it took only a moment for George to size up the situation. Alone, they were friends, but in public George was no more than an employee ... So be it, if that was what Alex wanted, that was the way George would play it, just as long as he was paid enough.

Harriet stood in the hall of the manor, her suitcase packed. Dewint gave her a small gift and she accepted it graciously.

'Where will you go, Mrs Barkley?'

'Oh, my brother Allard's got to sell up the old Hall, so I shall be there for a while, you know, sorting through family things. Then perhaps I'll buy a cottage up there. You must come and stay.'

'Oh, I would like that immensely.'

'Where is he? Do you know?'

Dewint couldn't meet her eyes. 'I'm afraid I don't, I got a card from Mexico, and India, he travels ... you know the way he is.'

She patted his arm. 'Yes, yes I know ... Well this is goodbye. Thank you for being here, for all the times you were so very kind to me. Oh, how are my lettuces?'

Dewint walked with her to the door, said it was the wrong time of year for lettuce but her garden was coming along fine. The cab driver took her case, and she gave a small, sad wave of her hand as Dewint shut the door. 'Now don't you cry, you silly old man, we'll see each other again, go back in, you'll catch cold.'

The cab went off down the overgrown driveway, and he stood on the stone steps until there was no possibility of catching another glimpse. She had not stayed long, and not taken very much, only a few clothes and a couple of ornaments she had made. Most of her time she had spent in the main bedroom, and he had not interrupted her. There had been no divorce – the papers were left unsigned, but it was very obvious there was no chance of a reconciliation. Edward had not been to see her once during her recovery – he had sent flowers, but they really came from Miss Henderson, and Harriet knew it.

Dewint made himself a cup of tea, and then took out his clean, well-pressed handkerchief and cried. The house was dying, neglected, unloved and silent. It broke his heart.

Harriet sat well back in the taxi, resting her head against the leather upholstery. She was fifty-four years old, her hair completely grey, and she had taken the scissors to it herself. She had gained more weight and was now almost rotund. But her eyes were bright as a child's, sparkling when she passed familiar areas. She bought a ham and tomato sandwich at the railway station, munching as she wandered along to her compartment, looking for all the world like an ageing hippy.

Allard met her at the station, very disgruntled as the house sale was taking a very long time to arrange. He was as grey-haired as his sister, and wore a flamboyant bright silk scarf with a rose in his buttonhole. The rest of his garb was as crumpled and disarranged as usual.

Harriet looked him up and down. 'You know, for a poof, you are quite the worst dresser I've ever come across . . . Aren't you supposed to be dapper?'

'Good God, look who's talking! You're not exactly straight off the cover of *Vogue* yourself, are you? And what on earth have you got all those rows of beads round your neck for?'

'I made them, that's why. We did it in therapy, and I might go into business, you know, a cottage industry sort of thing. See, each one is painted, hand painted.'

'I think they're ghastly. Oh Christ this fucking hill, the car's only just going to make it.'

They chugged up the hill in Allard's rotting MG and eventually made it to Haverley Hall. The place was as draughty and as cold as ever, and even more dusty than the manor house. Harriet looked up at the crumbling pile and sighed. 'Ah well – home, sweet home.'

'Not for long, the sooner we get shot of this place the better. Have you got any idea how much stuff we have got to sort through and sell? Where are you going? Aren't you going to make us tea? Harry?'

'I'll just go to my room and unpack first . . .'

Book Seven

Chapter Twenty-Seven

Harriet put her suitcase on the small familiar bed. Even though it was cold, she opened her window and stared out towards the old stables, then across the fields to the woods.

'I'm going for a walk.'

Allard stood at the bottom of the stairs hands on his hips. 'But you've only just got here. I've not stopped for a minute, I've not had time to go for a walk.'

'Oh shut up, you look like a demented lurcher.'

'What?'

She marched to the front door. 'It's a cross between a grey-hound and a wolfhound, very skinny, usually rather bald and with a very snipey nose.'

'I know what a lurcher is, and it's a damned sight preferable to a baby elephant.'

She went out wagging her finger. 'I won't forget that, Allard.'

She walked for miles along small winding lanes, the sounds of the crows screeching above her head. Three young girls on their ponies trotted by with their smart jodhpurs and black riding hats ... memories of her childhood swept over her. The riders entered a field and began to canter; she closed her eyes to the sound of their hooves. Babba boom ... babboom ... she belonged here, her father had been right. As she made her way back to the Hall swishing a stick against the hedgerows, she wondered what her life would have been like if she had never met Edward, if he had never taken her away.

Allard was sitting in the kitchen by the fire. He held up an old family photograph album. 'There's some hysterical snaps of us. Remember that old Brownie camera Pa had . . .? There's not one with an entire body in it. Great one of Buster, just his arse, rather fitting as his raspberries were about all he was good for . . .'

Allard continued snorting with laughter as he turned the pages. She put the kettle on and took one of the scones Allard had bought from the local bakery. She lathered butter over it, and with her mouth full leaned on his shoulders to look at the photographs.

'Who's that?'

Allard touched the faded black-and-white snapshot. 'Fella called Charlie, your husband took over his rooms at Cambridge, he was killed at Dunkirk . . . Christ, here's one of me in the Footlights' revue. Well well, fancy the old man keeping that, I would have thought he'd have tossed it.'

'Why?'

'Well, I'm in drag and you know what he was like . . .'

He snapped the book closed, his initial good humour gone. 'Christ, he was a bastard even then.'

Before she could stop him he had thrown the book on to the fire.

'Allard, you shouldn't have done that . . . I would have liked to look through it. No matter what Pa said or did he never kept you short . . .'

Allard gave her a pinched, vicious look. 'I was actually refer-ring to Edward. He took more than Charlie's rooms I can tell you . . .'

'Why did you bring him home that Christmas?'

'You know, I haven't the foggiest. Maybe to use him as a cover for my flirtation with Henry . . . who knows, who cares, all in the past now ... anyway you look at it he certainly trod through our lives. Family is littered with his wreckage ...'

Allard went into the hall changing the subject, intent on sorting out all the furniture for the forthcoming auction.

Harriet gazed into the fire as the photographs charred into tiny black flecks.

Allard was pulling off the dust sheets from the dining-room chairs. He heard her going up the stairs and threw the sheets aside. 'Harriet ... are you going to help me or not? You haven't done a thing, not a single thing since you arrived ... Harry?'

She looked down to him, almost at the top of the stairs. 'I am not wreckage, Allard. If I had the choice, I would choose him again ... whatever place, whatever time, there could never be anyone else.'

Allard applauded. 'When you get through playing *Gone With The Wind*, do you think you could come down here and give me a hand packing up?'

The gong from the first landing was thrown over the banisters. 'How's that for starters?'

Allard and Harriet had never got on all that well, even as children. Now they bickered over what they should do with tables, chairs and pictures. Allard kept one room filled with the things he wanted, and it was crammed to the rafters.

Harriet launched into a tirade. 'How on earth are you going to fit all this junk into a cottage? You keep on grabbing everything from the "for sale" pile.'

'I do not, I simply do not, I am preparing for my old age, and I intend to live it out in comfort, so mind your own bloody business. Some of this old stuff is worth a packet and we won't get a good price from those local idiots.'

Jinks pushed open the front door. She could hear their voices arguing away but could not see them over the jumble of furniture piled almost to the ceiling. She called, 'Mother? ... Mother?'

'We're up here, darling – at last, someone who can act as referee. Helloooo, my lovely girl, how are you?'

'Hello Mother, Uncle Allard – I'm wonderfully well, how are you two?'

Allard was covered in dust, his face grimy. 'Bloody awful if you must know. Your mother is doing nothing but causing havoc here. I was doing perfectly well without her. I wish she'd never come.'

Harriet swiped at him with a duster. 'Half of this is mine and I want to make sure my daughter gets her fair share. If you would excuse us, Allard, we are going into my room, for a private conversation.'

Allard muttered that he didn't give a toss what they said about him and he watched Jinks pick her way up the stairs to reach her mother.

Jinks was no longer surprised by her mother's appearance. She had not really changed, despite her grey hair sticking up on end and the beads clinking around her neck as she bustled along the landing. Jinks couldn't help but smile as she slipped her arm around her mother's shoulders. 'How are you?'

'Well, it's very difficult, you know. Allard's really a little bit odd, he really is. And so finicky about what he eats. Come on, let's have a good natter. I've been waiting for you to arrive for weeks.'

Harriet closed her bedroom door and moved to the bed, patting it for her daughter to sit beside her. Jinks felt a sudden surge of emotion, so strong she hugged Harriet tight, kissing the top of her head. 'I love you Ma, I love you so.'

'Oh, this isn't like you, what are you being so soppy for? Now then, wait until you see what I've got and he – him downstairs – he knows nothing about. It's our secret . . .'

Harriet opened a bag, tied up with string, and began to take out jewel cases, so many that in the end the bed was covered with them. Jinks reached over to open one and promptly had her hand slapped. 'No . . . don't you dare open one. There's a story to each, and I want to sort them out so you can see them in order.'

Jinks watched her mother as she placed the boxes in line along the bed. This took considerable time as she peeked inside each one before she put it down, then switched them around until she was satisfied. She was totally preoccupied with what she was doing, so her daughter could sit back and watch. After a while Jinks inched around the mess of boxes to stand at the window. She looked down into the garden. 'How's your vegetarian gardener's book coming along?'

'Oh heavens, I've not had time to finish it, what with Allard and everything. Now then, I'm almost ready.'

'It looks as if you'll need me to do some weeding, how are your lettuces?'

'It's not the right time of year for them, now don't interrupt.'

Jinks leaned against the windowsill and studied her nails. 'Have you heard from you-know-who?'

'Well I got all the divorce papers, and sent them back, but I've heard nothing. He won't get around to it. Even Dewint doesn't know where he is . . . There you see? I'm muddled now.'

'I've got a place at Cambridge if I want, and Oxford . . . I had my interviews last month . . .'

'Oh that's nice, dear. I'm nearly ready.'

'I got my usual birthday card. Miss Henderson's even started signing it now she knows that I know, so the charade is rather a waste of time. Does he send you money?'

'Good heavens yes, of course, more than I know what to do with. Not that I tell him downstairs, he's such a tight-wad. Oh brill, I'm ready . . . now sit down, I'm going to tell you a story.'

Jinks sat on the edge of the bed, and Harriet, sitting cross-legged on the floor, picked up a red jewel case. For a moment she stared at the box in her hands, hands worn rough from all the gardening. She smiled, hunching her shoulders like a girl, a gleeful gesture. 'Now then . . . take your glasses off, close your eyes, and I shall begin.'

Jinks did as she was instructed and instinctively rubbed the bridge of her nose. She had tied her long, dark auburn hair back from her face. She kept it long hoping in some way it would make her look shorter. Her height meant she even had to hunch her legs to sit down on the bed. She was, embarrassingly, almost six foot in her stockinged feet. The tweed skirt and twin set she wore were given to her by Harriet. The colour didn't really suit her but she had no interest in clothes. She sighed, her thoughts drifting, and suddenly she realized her mother was silent, very silent ... she was holding up a small gold bracelet. The cold winter sunlight caught it, it glittered magically, rainbow colours.

'This was the first present he gave me, I was just fourteen. He was here with Allard for the vacation, from Cambridge. We travelled down from London by train, and by the time we reached the station I knew I loved him ... Oh Jinks, he had such a look to him, such a wildness, like no boy I had ever met ...'

Jinks listened in totally enraptured silence as Harriet told of her first meeting with Edward, the hunting, the dances, the chapel ...

Four hours later the bed was covered with jewellery: diamond necklaces, pearls, bracelets, rings, earrings ... and with each piece, each box, came a story. The date Jinks' father had given it to her mother. Unfolding like a dream sequence in a film was a love story that their daughter had never known, nor under-stood anything of until that moment. At last Harriet finished, and swept all the jewellery into Jinks' arms. 'It's all for you, my darling, all the memories, all the love, is for you ... No, don't say anything, because I know. I know I haven't always been the best of mothers and you have had to put up with dreadful things. But here, here's the proof of my love, and your father's ...'

Jinks couldn't stop the tears, she shook her head. 'Oh Mama, I can't take it, it's yours ...'

'Now it's yours ...'

Allard's irate voice screamed up the stairs. 'When are we going to eat? Harry?'

Harriet flung open the door and shouted, 'Do you think you could refrain from shouting? I am not deaf, I am not in an open field ... and we are going to eat now.' She slammed the door and leaned against it, her face shining. And just as the tiny gold bracelet had been caught in the sun so her face was bathed in golden light. As if suspended in time, Jinks saw the face of a child, and once again had the desire to throw her arms around her mother.

This time she wasn't pushed away, wasn't told she was being soppy. She was hugged tight, and her mother's voice whispered, 'There was never, never anyone like him. I was his from the moment we met . . . Everything went wrong only because my baby boy died. I had promised him, you see, I made a promise – four boys, four wild sons. Freedom, I named him Freedom . . .'

Jinks wiped away the tear that ran down her mother's cheek, cupped that sweet, innocent face in her slender hands.

Harriet's lips trembled as she continued, fighting back the tears, 'You couldn't make up for him, you see, my little boy . . . You were not enough – but he does love you, and I love you . . . And now you have all my past, you can hold me in your hands whenever you want . . .'

Jinks couldn't sleep, tossing and turning in her cold attic room. If she closed her eyes, she could see her father's face, hear her mother's voice telling her the story. Harriet had never said a single bad word about him, and yet he had left her, pregnant with his child, made no contact with her for years. She felt the anger rising inside her body as she repeated over and over to herself, 'You couldn't make up for him, you see, you were not enough.' She threw her blankets aside and sat up. It wasn't her fault she'd been born a girl – and what a girl.

She looked at herself in the mirror – so tall and skinny she had to bend at the knee to see herself. She said aloud to her reflection, 'Why wasn't I born small and beautiful so he would at least love me . . . ? Why wasn't I born a man . . . ?'

She lay on her bed and wept, holding the pillow over her face so no one would hear. She would have changed places with any dumb pretty woman, given the opportunity. She hated herself, hated her body – she even hated her own intelligence.

*

Still red-eyed from weeping, Jinks went down to breakfast. Allard was banging the water pipes with a hammer because they had frozen during the night.

'Where's your mother? It's her job to stoke up the fire at night,' he complained. 'There's no hot water and we have someone coming to view the place this morning. They'll be frozen before they reach the first bloody landing, it's colder in than out, ridiculous. One of the first things about selling a place is to make sure it's boiling hot, potential buyers are always interested in the central heating.'

He continued around the house, hammering, more than likely causing more damage than repair by his total ignorance of the archaic heating system. Harriet still did not appear, so Jinks laid a breakfast tray and took it up to her room. She found the bed made, so she carried it down again to the kitchen.

'Allard, where's Mother?'

'Well, don't ruddy well ask me, we've got a leak on the top floor. Do I have to do everything? They're the first people we've had even remotely interested in the place. Isn't she in her room?'

'No, and her bed is made. What about the garden?'

'Well, she won't be doing any gardening, it's a skating rink out there because of the broken drainpipe.'

'Is the car in the garage?'

'For goodness' sake, why don't you go and look? I can't be expected to look after Harry and run the place – ever since she arrived that's what I've been doing, and it's not fair, it really isn't.'

The MG was still in the garage with blankets over its engine. Harriet had still not appeared by twelve o'clock, and Jinks began to feel really worried. She had to shout over the racket Allard was making. 'Has she done this before? Only, she knows I have to be back in London on the afternoon train . . . Allard! Do you think she's gone into the village?'

In a dire mood, Allard drove her into the village. They waited until the bus appeared, and asked the driver if he had seen her. They stopped everyone they knew, but to no avail – she had disappeared. When they returned to the Hall, Jinks telephoned Miss Henderson and asked her to relay a message to her friends that she had been delayed. Harriet had not been in touch with the office. Miss Henderson offered to put Jinks on to her father – he had returned the week before and Jinks sounded so distressed. Without bothering to reply, Jinks hung up.

Putting on a heavy coat, Jinks walked across the fields, call-ing for her mother. She returned, unsuccessful, and found Allard in a fury. He was swearing about the estate agent, who had brought round a couple he wouldn't dream of selling to. 'They were Jewish. Really, I don't know what the world is coming to.'

Jinks snapped that he should be ashamed of himself, and should help her search for Harriet instead of worrying about the Hall. He retorted angrily that of course he was worried, but his sister was not the easiest person to care about.

'She has thrown out, thrown out, a jug I particularly liked, Art Deco, and it was on the manure heap ... All right, all right, I'll help you, no need to look at me like that. You look just like your grandmother – the Judge always said she had the ability to freeze the pond over with one of her looks – it's your nose, very snipey, dear ...'

By five o'clock Allard was as worried as his niece, and he called in the local police.

Jinks sat on the stairs, still wrapped in her coat, listening to the hushed conversation with Sergeant Titherington.

'You see, my sister has a history of mental disorder, nothing violent, nothing like that ... but, well ...'

'Has she done this kind of thing before?'

Allard looked into the hall. He whispered, 'Has she ever done this before? You know, just walked off without a word?'

Jinks shook her head.

Eventually, the sergeant came out, putting his notebook into his top pocket. 'We'll put her on the missing persons' list if there's no sign of her by morning.'

'And in the meantime, Sergeant, what do you suggest we do?'

'Contact any of her friends, anyone she may have visited and we'll do what we can . . .'

'Do you want a photograph?'

'Oh, we all know Miss Harry, no need for that. Have you been down to the Feathers at all?'

Jinks snapped, her nerves in shreds. 'My mother is not in the pub, Sergeant . . .'

Allard ushered the policeman to the door giving Jinks a frown. 'My niece is obviously a little upset . . . thank you for coming.'

Before the door had closed, Jinks said in a fury, 'Too damned right I am more than a "little upset". Now think, think of anyone she could have gone to see . . . Allard, I'm talking to you.'

'I'm just going to make us a cup of tea. Really. This is typical of her, absolutely typical, you have no idea how dreadful she was when she was little.'

Jinks was close to tears as she followed him into the kitchen. She pulled out a chair and there was her mother's handbag. 'Allard, is this Mother's?'

He filled the kettle. 'Well, it's not mine, so that proves she can't have gone far. When she comes back in, I am going to have it out with her. Total wanton disregard for our feelings.'

Jinks had a strange foreboding, she felt icy cold. 'Allard, will you see if any of her coats are missing . . . ?'

Allard inspected the row of old coats on the hooks by the kitchen door. Mud-stained wellington boots were all jumbled, left where they had been kicked off. Suddenly he snapped his fingers. 'The chapel, she was always skiving off there. We can give it a shot, but we'll have to walk, no through road – and it's quite a way. Perhaps we should wait until morning, what do you think?'

'No, we go right now . . . better get a torch.'

They were out of breath by the time they reached the woods. Allard was cursing the cold, the mud, and the branches that scratched at his face as he pushed through the dead bracken.

Their breath steamed in front of them, whirling in the torch-light, and Jinks grew quieter and quieter. Her mother would have been here all night, and it was freezing. More than twenty-four hours had gone by. Allard kept stopping to get his bearings, still swearing. He shouted to Jinks to keep up, she'd get lost.

At last they arrived at the derelict chapel in the overgrown clearing. Ivy crawled over the roof and walls, and weeds burst through the stones. It had a ghostly air in the feeble beam of the torch.

Putting his shoulder against the door, Allard heaved. The door creaked open on its rotten hinges. Jinks held the torch, stepping into the chapel first. She knew they would find her mother.

Caught in the beam of light, Jinks saw her. She dropped the torch, sobbing. 'Oh, Allard, she's there ... she's there ...'

Harriet was huddled in a corner, a bunch of dried flowers in her rigid hands. Beside her was a tiny grave, obviously newer than the others, on which she had scratched the name 'Freedom' with the penknife that lay at her feet.

Chapter Twenty-Eight

Dwint heard the door open. He looked out from his top-floor window as a black taxi came down the drive. He wrapped his dressing gown round him and pulled on his slippers. The lights had been turned on in the hall, the drawing room and the study. Dewint leaned over the banisters. 'Miss Jinks, is that you?' Edward's voice boomed out. 'No, it's me, you old faggot.' Dewint gasped as Edward strode out of the drawing room.

'How are you doing, old fella?'

'Oh, I'm doing fine, sah. Welcome home.'

They stared at each other. Dewint had not changed at all, but Edward had put on a lot of weight, although he was still a handsome, awesome man. He had no luggage apart from an old worn leather case. Tossing his coat to Dewint, he rubbed his hands, saying he was hungry. Then, as if he had been gone no more than a few days, he marched into the kitchen.

Dewint bustled after him and began frying up bacon and eggs as Edward sat at the scrubbed kitchen table. He never mentioned where he had been or what he had been doing, and he didn't even ask after Jinks. He seemed preoccupied with scratching at one of the cracks in the table with his knife . . . Suddenly, just as Dewint was about to crack an egg into the pan, Edward got up, opened the kitchen door and walked into the garden. The light from the kitchen enabled Dewint to see him touching the big old oak tree, and then he watched as Edward slowly placed his arms around the tree and pressed his face into the bark. As he put the bacon and eggs on the table, he saw that Edward had scratched the letter 'H' ... The loud ring of the telephone almost made him drop the plate. The phone call was from Allard, enquiring if Dewint had any idea where Edward was. When Dewint replied that he had just come home, there was a pause, and then Allard said that Harriet was dead. Dewint continued to hold on to the phone long after Allard had rung off. Eventually Edward came in and took the receiver from him and replaced it.

'Oh, sah, it's bad news, it's bad news.'

Edward patted his shoulder, and walked slowly up the stairs.

'It's all right, old fella, I know. You don't have to say anything.'

Edward caught the first train, and Allard met him at the station. He gave a brief nod and bent almost double to squeeze himself into the car. There were dark circles under his eyes from lack of sleep, and the inevitable cigar was clamped between his teeth. Allard muttered obscenities as they crept up the steep hill towards the Hall, convinced they were not going to make it. The only time Edward spoke was to remind him that he had a first gear ... The car jolted and, with smoke streaming from the exhaust, they eventually made it over the top. Crossing the small humpbacked bridge, they coasted through the village of Helmsley and on to the Hall.

Jinks was waiting, sitting among stacks of furniture.

'Hello, sweetheart,' was the only greeting Edward gave her as he followed Allard into the kitchen. 'Kitchen always was the warmest place in the house.'

Jinks followed them and leaned against the door.

'Congratulations,' Edward said to her. 'It's something to be offered places at both Oxford and Cambridge. Have you made up your mind yet?'

'I don't think this is either the time or the place to discuss that,' she replied. 'Did Allard tell you about the arrangements? She's to be cremated. We couldn't really have a coffin here with the state the place was in so Mr Postlethwaite – he runs the funeral parlour – he's got her . . . she's at his farm. He has some sort of morgue, where he keeps . . . Oh God, it sounds awful . . . Is Uncle Alex coming?'

Edward appeared completely unaffected by his wife's death. He blew on his hands for warmth. 'No, they're busy, wouldn't you know. They'll probably send an ornate wreath.' He found it difficult to meet his daughter's eyes. It had been a long time since he had seen her. She looked older than her seventeen years, with her thick glasses and her thin, pointed nose pink from the cold. Edward tried to make conversation, huddled by the fire in his great fur coat.

'Right, what's to be done? Have you arranged everything?' Somehow he just knew she would have, he could tell.

Jinks found it hard even to talk to him, he dominated the kitchen and her. She didn't mean it, but her voice sounded brittle, unforgiving. 'We all go to Mr Postlethwaite's and follow the hearse to the church. The vicar's arranged the ceremony, two o'clock, and afterwards we drive to the crematorium. It's quite a way, almost to York.'

Edward looked at his watch and suggested they get a bite to eat before they left. Jinks declined and said she would wait for the car. He still could not look at her. 'Fine, I'll see you later. I'll walk to the Feathers, be there if you need me.'

As he opened the kitchen door, Jinks blurted out, 'It was an accident, she never meant to kill herself.'

'Yes, you said on the phone . . . Be back at a quarter to two.'

He strode out into Harriet's vegetable garden. The line of tomato sticks looked like a miniature army lined up for inspection, and he walked slowly past them. He stopped – attached to one of the rods was a piece of paper, flapping in the wind. He trudged across the frozen soil and looked at it. 'Edward' – his name was printed clearly in Harriet's thick, bold writing. He glanced at the house to see if anyone was watching him, then unhooked the note. There was only one line, in the familiar hand: 'You were never unkind, just the wrong time of year for lettuce – Harry.'

Pocketing the note, he stood for a long time in the bitterly cold garden. He knew it was no accident – she had just walked out across the fields to die. He lifted his eyes to the horizon, remembering the hunched figure so many years ago, striding off into the night – the night she had taken a shotgun to her horse.

'He's still there, he's still standing there.'

Puzzled, Allard looked at Jinks and she got up, walked across to the window. Her father stood with his back to the house, like a giant, his fur coat flapping in the winter wind. She rubbed her cold arms and asked Allard, 'What do you think he's doing, he must be frozen?'

His usually crisp, camp voice was soft. 'I think he's saying goodbye to her in his own way.'

Jinks wanted to go to her father then, wanted to feel his arms around her, but instead she stared at him through the dusty window.

The car pulled up outside Mr Postlethwaite's barn, which also served as a morgue. The elderly bearers, in their black morning coats and toppers, carried the coffin to the equally elderly hearse. As they pushed the coffin in, their feet slid on the icy ground. Mr Postlethwaite murmured to the men that they were going to have a hell of a job getting up the hill, it was hard enough just to stand up straight.

Allard was squashed in between Jinks and Edward in the back of the hired Rolls. Nodding wisely, he said to Edward, 'It'll never make it up that hill, any money on it?'

The procession moved off, following the hearse, which seemed bowed beneath the weight of Alex and Barbara Barkley's 'floral tribute', an enormous display of white lilies. Edward and Allard couldn't help but smile. The hearse's gears began to grind . . .

'What did I tell you, it's in trouble,' Allard crowed. Jinks gave him a cold stare to shut him up.

Halfway up the hill, the hearse came to a halt and slowly slid backwards until it bumped into the Rolls. Edward started to laugh, and Allard, his hands over his face, tried desperately not to join in. Their chauffeur reversed frantically, then grabbed the handbrake, but the Rolls rolled on and struck the following car, containing the vicar and three of his parishioners, whose faces looked terrified as they slithered downhill ... The parishioners screamed in unison, like three little balding birds ...

Three times the hearse attempted the hill, only to slide back. Coats were removed and laid under the back wheels, much to the chagrin of Mr Postlethwaite, whose best tails would bear the tyre imprints forever after. But the hearse steadfastly refused to climb the hill. Allard was now laughing openly, and Edward was wiping away tears of mirth.

Jinks, who had tried so hard not to find humour in the situation, biting her lip until it bled, finally caved in. Edward smiled through his tears, 'That's it, sweetheart, you know Harry's engineered this whole thing – she's up there roaring with laughter. Can't you hear her?'

Indeed, Harriet would have split her sides if she had seen her last journey, the coffin tied eventually to the roof-rack of Mr Postlethwaite's new Morris Minor. The hilarity of the journey was echoed halfway through the delayed funeral service when a wedding party arrived. The vicar took their advent as a cue to speed up the service. The poor organist, his frozen fingers struggling with the keyboard, pumped the bellows desperately for the rendering of 'The Lord is My Shepherd'. He was mortified when his precious organ began to emit what could only be described as a deep, resonant fart.

The bride and groom stood aghast as the coffin was carried from the church, followed by mourners in a state verging on hysteria. Allard, beside himself, had to lean on the door to get his breath, declaring loudly that it was better than any revue he had ever seen.

By this time the hearse had made it to the top of the hill, and Harriet was driven more sedately on the last leg of her journey to the crematorium. In the confusion between wedding and funeral, someone had tied a silver horseshoe to the coffin. It trailed behind, but no one laughed. They were all very quiet, subdued, and the bouncing horseshoe somehow reminded them that they would never hear Harriet's wonderful laugh again.

That night they drank more brandy than they should have, sitting in the freezing Hall. They all needed sustenance, and the vicar had to be helped home as he had already overindulged at the wedding reception. Jinks took the opportunity to excuse herself when he departed, and went up to her room. She had only just closed the door when her father knocked.

He was wearing his wolfskin coat, and carried the ashes in a small urn. He had tied the horseshoe to it.

'I wondered if you would like to say goodbye to her? I'm going to the chapel, and I'd like it if you came – would you?'

They walked apart to begin with, Edward carrying the ashes under his arm. Twice Jinks stumbled, and in the end he tucked her arm in his. He knew the way, never stopping once, and he guided her to ensure the branches didn't slap her face.

'Okay, we're here . . . You all right?'

She nodded, and he pushed the door open. Jinks hung back slightly as he moved further into the dark, broken-down chapel. He bent down and brushed the dead leaves from the small stone slab.

Jinks whispered, 'She carved his name, she told me all about him.'

He looked up at her and smiled gently. She could see his eyes were brimming with tears. Sitting back on his heels he opened the urn, held the contents in his hand. He trickled the soft ashes between his fingers, spreading them over his dead son's grave, then rubbed them until they were part of the stone, part of the scratched name, 'Freedom'.

Jinks walked slowly to her father and stood behind him. He

turned, wrapping his arms around her, and cried like a child in his own child's embrace. He broke her heart as he said her mother's name over and over ... said it so softly, with such tenderness, that she knew he still loved her.

Jinks and Edward travelled back to London together on the fast morning train. He sat opposite her, and when she looked up from her book she found him scrutinizing her. 'You know, without those bloody glasses you'd be a smasher. Do you have to wear them? Take the damned things off and let's have a look at you.'

Jinks would not meet his eyes as he removed her spectacles. 'Shouldn't this be in a movie? "Good God, Miss Jones, you're beautiful ... "' She smiled at her own joke, but he saw the way she avoided his gaze, the embarrassed flush spreading up her cheeks.

'Untie your hair.'

'Oh, Daddy, please don't, people will start looking.'

'I don't care – it's about time someone took you in hand. It's all right, don't look so startled, I'm not saying it should be me. But you know,' he said reassuringly, 'you look terrible ... Your mother never had much dress sense, but one time she came back from Paris and my God did she look a cracker ... hair, outfits ... You got a boyfriend?'

'No I haven't, and please give me my glasses ...'

Edward held them away from her and peered through the lenses, then back at his daughter. 'Are you long- or short-sighted? Contact lenses would be better than these. Here, don't get all panic-stricken, put them on, go back into hiding.'

She put them on and looked around quickly to see if any of the passengers had noticed. Then she gazed out of the window and whispered, 'Got rather a long nose, and if that wasn't bad enough I'm cross-eyed, my left eye ...'

'You are not.'

'I am.'

'Look at my finger ... Come on, look at my finger and I'll

tell you if you're bloody cross-eyed or not – that was your mother . . . My God.'

'See, I told you.'

'No . . . you don't understand – Miss Jones, you are beautiful – you are beautiful!'

Jinks laughed, and he loved the deep, throaty sound of it. She put her hands up to cover her face . . . She needed to be cared for, given confidence in herself. Suddenly he knew who could do it . . . His daughter looked plain, dowdy, but with the right help she could make the best of herself . . .

Barbara replaced the telephone receiver and tapped it with her perfectly manicured nails. Edward had rarely, if ever, called her over the years. He had said little about why he had suddenly contacted her, just that his daughter needed her help. They would be driving past her house on the way to Greenwich, and Barbara could think of no reason to refuse. Jinks, on the other hand, had been furious with her father.

'What? Auntie Barbara? I'm not going! How could you, you know Mother detested her.'

'You don't have to like the woman, for Chrissakes, just use her. She knows just about everyone, and she's got great style.'

Jinks was waiting for her father outside the station as the car was brought up from the parking bay.

'Barbara's brought up two daughters of her own, and she has contacts. You'll like her, once you get over her duchess act.'

Jinks sat moodily at his side. 'She was always foul to Mother, didn't even come to her funeral, and now I'm supposed to go round and see her. Well, I won't. I don't need her, I don't need anybody.'

'No? Grow up, sweetheart. You look like a frump, and you could do with someone to give you a hand. Don't think because you've got brains life is going to be an easy ride.'

'Oh, I see! It's a bit late, isn't it?'

Edward braked sharply to a stop and turned towards the glowering, petulant girl. 'Maybe I am too late for you to care about what I think or feel, but it's not too late for you to make the best of yourself. Stop behaving like a spoiled brat, a stinking rich kid! You want to get out? Well? Yes or no?'

She turned away from him, shrugging her shoulders. Edward restarted the Rolls and it surged forward. She had one hell of a stubborn streak in her, and he could see the way she clenched her hands as she fought to control her temper. He reached over to pull her closer, but she resisted, and in the end they continued their journey to Mayfair in silence.

Barbara was waiting for them in the small drawing room. She looked as immaculate as ever, and viewed Jinks with a critical, almost professional, scrutiny.

'Dear God, you should have brought her to me before. My darling girl, don't you realize what most women would give to have a figure like yours? Clothes, darling, are designed for you – not that I could recommend the ones you have on, but with those long legs you'll be a dream to dress. Have you ever been to the Paris collections?'

Jinks wouldn't look at Barbara. She mumbled that she had been to Paris with her school; then, suddenly, she tossed her head back and squinted at Barbara through her glasses. 'Besides, I'll be going to university, not frightfully interested in Paris, or clothes.'

'Yes, darling, I can see that.' Barbara cocked her head to one side, then flicked a half-smile to Edward. 'God, she's like her mother . . . which university?'

Proudly, Edward told her that Jinks had gained coveted places at both Oxford and Cambridge. Barbara lit a cigarette, not impressed in the slightest. She let the smoke drift from her nostrils, still looking Jinks up and down.

'Ghastly places . . . why the hell don't you go to Vassar? At least you'd be out of this freezing country. English universities breed excellent, horsey frumps. If Evelyn had won a place I'd be over the moon, but females . . . No, no, I don't think you should go, darling. Big world out there – what do you want to do with your life? Bury it?'

Jinks blushed, tucking her size nine feet beneath her chair. She gave her father a helpless look, wanting to leave. Barbara took a large diary from her desk drawer and thumbed through it, making murmuring noises, then snapped it shut.

'I can start Thursday week, taking you around London, just to get a few outfits to travel to Paris in. I'm going anyway, I always go for the collections, and Jinks can travel with me. Darling, those glasses – why on earth don't you wear contact lenses? You'll regret it later in life – you'll get an awful mark across your nose and red lines under your eyes. If you'll be here at nine, I like to start early to avoid the crush of unwashed humanity. Edward, I'll call you with our itinerary, because I like to have everything arranged. It'll be expensive, but worth it.'

She rang a little gold bell on her desk, a signal that they were leaving. Edward picked up his coat and laughed. 'Thanks, duchess, I appreciate this and so does Jinks. She'll be here, and you call me or Miss Henderson for anything you need.'

In truth, Barbara did behave as if she was royalty, enjoying herself, almost flaunting herself in front of Edward. He shook her hand as they left, and Jinks said a polite 'thank you'.

As the butler closed the front door Jinks snorted, 'Oh, God, what does she think she's playing at? And the voice? She's coming on stronger than the Queen Mother.'

Edward held the car door open for his daughter and tapped her on the nose. 'Like I said, sweetheart, use her. She'll have every designer in Paris fighting to dress you.'

The Rolls surged into the Park Lane traffic. Jinks remained silent, chewing her nails, a habit she had picked up from her mother, and Edward pulled her hand from her mouth.

'Don't bite your nails. Your mother always chewed hers, bad habit.'

But Jinks paid no attention, thinking over what Barbara had said. 'What do you know of Vassar? My going there? Only, I was actually thinking about it myself . . . Maybe I should look into it before making a decision. The important thing is, is what they have on offer better than I could get from Oxford or Cambridge? Education-wise, I doubt it very much.'

'That's my girl. We can be on the first plane to New York if that's what you want.'

'What? And miss my shopping spree with her ladyship? No need to rush things. I'll get Miss Henderson to contact them, send me the details. I just want to get one thing straight, though – I've no intention of becoming some glorified debutante for you or Barbara. It's an out-of-date farce now anyway. But maybe I should travel, think seriously about Vassar. You think it would be a good training ground? I'm not really interested in the trappings of the English colleges.'

'All depends on what you want to do, sweetheart.'

'Oh, I know exactly what I want to do – go into business.'

'Oh, yes? Anything particular?'

'Well, banking, of course – didn't Mother tell you?'

Edward turned his head sharply. For a moment he thought she was joking. She wasn't – she gave him a direct look, then turned to gaze at the traffic. She smiled. 'One day I'll be taking over the Barkley Company, won't I? Stands to reason I should know what I am doing.'

He said nothing, concentrating on his driving. The thought had never entered his head that his daughter would consider entering the family business.

As if she was reading his mind, she said softly, 'You didn't expect me to want to, did you? I suppose it would be different if I was your son. If I was your son I would automatically presume I was going to work in the company. Evelyn ...' She turned and stared at him, and he kept his eyes on the road, wondering how much she knew.

'What about Evelyn?'

'I was just thinking ... he's in France, so if I go to Paris with his mother I will no doubt meet up with him. Did you know Uncle Alex sent him there? About the only place that would take him, so I hear.'

'And where did you hear all this?'

'Miss Henderson, of course. She and I are just like that.' She crossed her fingers. 'She's always taken care of me. She never forgets my birthday, she never forgets.'

Edward found her directness, her quietness, unsettling. He realized that, though his daughter might be gauche, there was a strength in her, an edge he hadn't bargained for and didn't quite understand.

'So you'll go to Paris with Barbara, will you?'

She shrugged her shoulders and then took off her glasses, polishing them with her fingers. 'I don't suppose there's any harm in it. As you said, use her – I don't have to like her, or her son.'

'What do you think of Evelyn?'

Her reply almost caused him to run into the car in front of them. 'Oh, him . . . he reminds me of a gypsy. Unfortunately, he behaves like one. He was expelled for stealing – pitiful when you consider the opportunities he has. Oh! Would you drop me at the corner? I think I'll go and see some friends. Dewint's packing all my bags for me. There's not a lot I want from the manor, anyway. I'm moving in with two girls, it's all arranged.'

Edward pulled the car over and she immediately reached into the back seat for her overnight case. He put his hand on her shoulder.

'I thought we could have dinner tonight?'

'Oh, I'm sorry, I've a previous engagement. Another time, maybe.'

He withdrew his hand as the car door swung open. She slammed it shut, then tapped on the window. 'If I decide I'm interested in Vassar, could we go to New York?'

'Yes, of course. I'll call you first thing in the morning.'

She strode off without saying goodbye. He had been wrong in thinking his daughter was nervous – there was an arrogance to her, a mannish quality. She was so tall, taller than most of the men she passed in the street. He realized he had no idea who her friends were, or where she was going. He sat drumming his fingers on the steering wheel . . . There was so much that he didn't know about his daughter, and it was strange, because he didn't feel a great deal of affection for her at that precise moment. If anything, she reminded him of Allard ... He slapped the wheel. 'Christ, that's it, that's who she's like – bloody Allard.'

Suddenly he felt old and tired, and he swung the car back into the traffic, heading for Victoria. He spent ages trapped in the rush hour, and by the time he reached Greenwich he was in a foul temper.

Dewint greeted him with brimming eyes, and for one moment Edward wondered what on earth was wrong with him. Then he realized it was only a few days since the funeral. Dewint asked if his flowers had arrived, and Edward said they were the best there, everyone had remarked on them. In actual fact he had no recollection of them. Heavy-hearted, he walked up the stairs to his room, pausing as the full realization struck him. She would never be coming home, he would never see her again. He felt helpless.

'You know, we would never have been divorced? I loved that crazy lady – I loved her, Norman, you know that?'

'I know you did, sah. I'll bring up some nice home-made soup.'

Edward loosened his tie and looked around. The place was in need of redecoration, it was tired like himself. The few family photographs around his dressing-table mirror caught his eye. One was of Evelyn that Christmas when he had arrived on their doorstep. It was the last time the house had felt lived in. He picked up the snapshot and lay on his bed, looked at the cheeky grin that stretched from ear to ear ... He muttered to himself, he should never have let him go, never let him leave the house that night. He stared at the picture until his hand flopped to his side. Evelyn belonged to him, he was his son ... He sat up, slammed his fist against his other palm. 'I'm going to get him back, I'm going to bring my son home.'

'Soup, sah,' said Dewint, carrying the loaded tray, and found the photograph thrust beneath his nose.

'This is my son, my son, and I'm going to bring him home ...'

Edward rushed from the room, knocking the tray from Dewint's trembling hands. As it crashed on the floor, he heard Edward's shout and the awful, thundering sound as he fell headlong down the stairs.

Dewint managed to get him on to the sofa in the lounge before he blacked out. He was streaming blood from a head wound, and the panic-stricken Dewint rushed to phone the doctor. When he got back, Edward was white as a sheet, and lay absolutely motionless.

The doctor wanted Edward to go into hospital for a checkup, but he refused. He did, however, agree to remain in bed for a few days. But he never got as far as his bedroom, preferring to lie on the sofa in front of the fire. He stared into the flames for hours on end, or at the photograph of Evelyn, which was always in his hand.

Although Dewint did his best to keep him from drinking, he started again. He tried to get Edward to eat, but met with nothing but abuse. He did allow Dewint to keep the fire built up, but would accept nothing else from him. In the end Dewint just brought trays every mealtime and left them on a side table. They were always there, untouched, when he returned.

He just did not know what to do. Edward had been drinking steadily for four days, and never left the room except to go to the bathroom. Then he would shamble straight back into the lounge. It was obvious to the old man that Edward was very sick. His eyes were sunken, he was unshaven, and bottles were strewn about the room. Late one night Dewint heard the familiar sound of rock 'n' roll music, the same record over and over again, until he hid his head under the pillow trying to block out the repetitious racket.

The music pounded through the house while Edward desperately sought oblivion. The more he drank, the more his mind reeled. Voices called to him, his head ached continuously. He sweated, his face dripping, so he threw open the french windows. No sooner had he done that than he felt chilled to the bone. Shivering with fever, his teeth chattering, he slammed the window shut and stoked the fire until it blazed, then wrapped a blanket around himself. The heat began to sweep over him again, so he rested his head on the cold, wet windowpane.

Gazing at the river, he saw a fire had been lit by the jetty at the end of the long, tangled garden. Vague, shadowy shapes huddled around it, hands held out to the flames. He was about to scream at them to get off his land when one of them started to sing. The words were distorted by the echo from the river, but soft, as though the singer sang only for himself. The song ripped through Edward's drunken mind . . .

> Can you rokka Romany,
> Can you play the bosh
> Can you jal adrey the staripen,
> Can you chin the cosh . . .

He pressed his face against the cold, damp window and began to sing the words, dredging them from his past. In the red glow of the flames, the singer turned towards him and smiled. Edward was rigid with fear as the man rose to his feet, still singing softly, but now looking at Edward. The man was Freedom.

'Come on, Eddie, don't be afeared, boy. Gimme yer hand, make a Romany of thee.'

Involuntarily, Edward made to move from the window, but pressed close again as he saw a small, naked child walk through the overgrown garden. The child lifted both arms to Freedom, and Edward knew he was watching himself. In slow motion, shimmering in the fireglow, he watched Freedom lift the boy and carry him to the flames . . . The voice whispered close; he could feel the warmth of the man's breath as he whispered over and over, telling him not to be afraid. A knife glinted and the child's eyes widened; he sobbed in fear, but Freedom was holding him safely, holding him with those deep black eyes, with gentleness, with such love it was overwhelming . . .

'Give me thy hand . . .'

The child held up his right hand, and Edward pressed his own flat against the window, wincing with pain as the knife cut clean down his thumb. A single, bright red tear of blood dripped down the child's hand, and Freedom knelt before him, licking at the blood ... then turned and spat into the fire. The flames rose higher and the coals burned brighter ...

Edward backed further and further from the brightness beyond the window, moving away from the memory, away from the sight of his father – moving away from the memory of himself as a boy, the long-forgotten memory of his initiation into the Romany clan. He didn't want to see any more.

The song started up again and repeated, over and over:

> Can you rokka Romany,
> Can you play the bosh ...

Edward was crazy with fear. Turning to run from the room he was caught by his own image in the mirror – but it wasn't his own face staring back at him, it was the face of his father. He screamed, 'Get away from me! Go away!' But still Freedom's face remained, and then the tears flowed down his cheeks, terrible, streaming tears. Edward closed his eyes to shut out the face of his father, but it remained as clear if not clearer than the image in the mirror. The tears continued dripping down the high, carved cheeks, falling on to naked shoulders while the eyes stared wide, unblinking.

Edward's chest heaved as the deeply buried memories surfaced, exploded, and he remembered killing his father, remembered every fragmented second ...

Once more he was screaming with rage. He was seventeen years old, shouting and punching out at Freedom, screeching that he was going to Cambridge, no one would hold him back – no failure, no has-been boxer, no pitiful loser like Freedom could stop him ...

Freedom began to undo the thick leather belt from his waist. Now Alex was there, little Alex weeping for them to stop, crying to them not to fight.

Edward put his arm over his face as if to block out the image that would appear next. He couldn't bear to face his mother, but she was there, standing at the kitchen door and begging for them to stop. He could see her clearly, her white pinafore, her dark red, coiled hair. She tried to come between them, but Edward pushed her aside and she fell backwards. The dog was barking – Rex, the white bull terrier, growling and yapping, scuttling between their feet, jumping up as if even he was afraid of what was going to happen. He yelped as Freedom tripped over him and lurched against the kitchen table . . .

Slowly, the inevitable happened again, so slowly . . . Edward opening the kitchen drawer. Edward taking out the sharp knife, the big knife Evelyne used to carve their Sunday roasts. He took out the knife as his father turned to him . . .

Edward's face was distorted with blind rage as he screamed, 'Come on, you bastard! I dare you to fight me now! Come on!'

Freedom seemed to relax. He no longer attempted to take his belt to his son – instead, he smiled, and lifted his arms in a gesture of love, opening his arms wider and wider, moving closer and closer to his son, closer to the knife.

Edward tried to stop the memory, tried to stop the memory continuing . . . Picking up a bottle, he smashed it against the fireplace . . . but the smiling face of his father would not go away. He moved closer, as if to embrace his son. Edward snatched up a poker from beside the fireplace and brought it crashing down between the open arms, crashing into the face that haunted him, the face that would not let him be in peace, would not let him forget. He smashed the face in the mirror into a thousand pieces, broke his own face into myriad jagged pieces . . . but Freedom was still there.

> Can you rokka Romany,
> Can you play the bosh . . .

Edward put his hands over his ears to cut out the sing-song voices – and suddenly there was silence. He felt his father's arms embrace him as the knife cut upwards into his heart, opening his chest. Freedom sighed, he sighed just as he had done on the day it happened . . .

Edward stepped back, looking at his blood-stained hands. Splinters of glass had cut his palms to shreds and he was covered in his own blood, but his mind was so confused and disorientated that he believed it was his father's.

Freedom was lying face down on the floor, lying where he had fallen, embedding the knife deeper into his heart. Evelyne knelt beside him, rocking him in her arms, as his blood spread like deep crimson flowers over the carpet, over her white apron . . . Edward's mother cradled Freedom until his body was stiff, until they had to prise his arms away from her.

Slowly the images faded, the song stopped, the fire outside the window was gone. Edward was left with his own blood still wet, still dripping from his cuts. Now he knew what he had done, and he felt the pain opening him up within; he felt his head draw back as if the pain was so great it was splitting him into two beings. And the howl, when it came, was so loud, inhuman, it sounded like the baying of a wounded animal.

At the top of the house, Dewint heard the howl. At first he thought it was an animal, something trapped. As he listened he realized it was coming from the sitting room below.

He crept down the stairs, fearful of what he would discover. The sound was quieter now, and he listened at the door. Gradually the howling subsided and was replaced by sobbing. Concerned, yet too afraid to go and see, he sat on the stairs and waited.

> Will walk in his shadow, bleed with his blood,
> Cry loud with his anguish and suffer his pain.

Edward lay face down on the sofa, his head buried in his hands. At long last he was able to ask his father's forgiveness for what he had done. When Dewint inched open the door, he saw the blood all over the floor, the broken mirror, and Edward's still figure. Above the fireplace, where the mirror had hung, a red spray of blood resembled a necklace, with small blood drops like pearls. The talisman.

Creeping closer, he saw that Edward was still breathing. He hurried to the telephone.

Alex arrived at the manor within the hour. Dewint let him in and ushered him towards the drawing room. This would be the first time Alex had seen Edward since that terrible Christmas, since the realization that Evelyn was in fact Edward's son. Any anger or hatred evaporated as soon as he saw his brother, his bloated body, his blotched, boozed-out face and his filthy clothes covered in bloodstains. Like a bum, he half sat, half lay slumped on the sofa staring vacantly at the wall. Aghast, Alex turned to Dewint.

'Dear God, how long has he been like this?'

'Ever since the funeral, sah, and I can't do anything with him. I think he's dying, sah. He's been in this room for days.'

Alex looked down into his brother's face, now hardly recognizable. Looking closely at him, the physical change was frightening. He must have weighed almost twenty stone, and was such a tragic figure that Alex knelt down beside him. 'Eddie, it's me, Alex. Can you hear me?'

Suddenly the ghost of Edward's old self flashed across his dazed face, he gave a sad half smile. 'Hello, old buddy. How ya doin'?'

'A helluva lot better than you, by the look of it.'

'You should have been at her funeral, Alex. She was very fond of you, always liked you. You should have given her that much respect, Alex. She hadn't a bad thought in her poor mind.'

Dewint carried in a bowl of hot water and a face cloth.

'It was eerie, sah. He sat at the kitchen table, even carved her name on it, he did. Then he went outside, stood by her tree and the phone rang to say she was gone. He seemed to know, sah, as if he'd come back to bury her ... and he's been this way since he returned from Yorkshire. I'm going to wash your face now, Mr Edward, just lean back. Shockin' mess you got your hands in.'

'I'll call a doctor,' said Alex. 'I think someone should be brought in to see him, get him checked over. All this extra weight can't be good for his heart.'

Alex looked around the dark bottle-strewn room and moved to open the curtains. Suddenly Edward's voice was strong, angry. 'Leave them closed, don't open them.'

Alex shrugged and let the dark velvet curtain fall into place. He moved back to Edward and sat on the edge of the worn sofa.

He tried not to let his anger show, but seeing Edward again and knowing the mayhem he had caused, the trouble he had been through just to get permission to let cheques leave the company without his brother's signature, the deals he had lost due to delays, constant enquiries about his whereabouts, and not one word . . . He sighed. 'Where the hell have you been, Edward, where?'

Slowly Edward turned to him and his bloodshot eyes blinked.'To hell and back, brother, but I hear you've been running things pretty smoothly without me, not made any gigantic steps forwards, but the company is still looking good, brother. But you can take a breather for a while, because I'm back . . . I'm still alive. How's Evelyn?'

Alex clenched his fists, and with all his will-power kept his voice quiet, even managed to keep the smile on his face as he answered, 'Evelyn is just fine. Well, if there's nothing I can do here, I'll leave you in Dewint's obviously capable hands, but I'll organize a doctor to give you a good check-up, all right? I'll show myself out.'

'Not going to say you're glad to have me back, eh? Aren't you glad to have me back?'

Alex slammed the door behind him. Edward let loose a deep shuddering sigh, shaking his head. 'Why do I do it? Norman? Why do I always have to goad him? Even now . . . Hell, I try so hard, even want to put out my hand to him, hold him, but instead I torment him, why?'

The old pixie face peered up at Edward. 'Well, sah, maybe because you know that you can. Straightaway you ask him about his son, knowing it'll be like a knife . . .'

Edward frowned, then leaned back. 'And you, you old faggot, know more than you should. Now, leave me alone and let me sleep.'

Dewint's knees cracked as he straightened up. He paused before he left the room. 'You carry on this way, sah, tormentin' him and you will be sorry. Leave his son alone. You can't always have what you want, that's the way life is.'

Edward looked at the man who had served him for so many years. He smiled. 'What did you want that you never got, Norman?'

Dewint cocked his head to one side. 'Well, I would have liked a round-the-world travel ticket.'

Edward laughed and held up his hand for Dewint to help him up from the sofa. Dewint buckled beneath his weight as Edward leaned heavily against him. 'Right, Norman, I think it's time for breakfast television.'

They staggered into the hall and began slowly to mount the stairs. The telephone rang and leaving Edward already out of breath only three steps up, Dewint went back to answer it.

'It's Skye Duval, Mr Barkley.'

Edward leaned over the banister to take the phone, and spoke into it briefly. 'Okay, I'll sort it out, leave it with me ...' He eased his bulk to sit on the stairs and hung up. 'Norman, if you get anyone asking for me, I am unobtainable, that clear?'

'Is it trouble, sah?'

'You could say that, there's a warrant out for my arrest.'

Alex decided to go straight to the office. He still had no idea where Edward had been for all that time, but he was back and Alex knew if he intended holding on to the reins, now was the perfect time to have Edward declared unfit to return as his part- ner. He called George Windsor to arrange for two independent Harley Street doctors to visit Edward that morning. He wanted proof of his alcoholism, proof he was incapable in his present condition of running the company.

At eleven-fifteen Miss Henderson rang through to say two

gentlemen had called to speak to Edward. She knew he had returned to London for the funeral, and wondered if he was coming into the office.

'Who are they?'

'They wouldn't give me their names.'

'Tell them Edward is indisposed and can't see anybody.'

Two hours later Miss Henderson entered his office. She appeared flustered and said that the two men had returned and were refusing to leave. Alex sighed and briskly told her to find out who the hell they were. She said they were customs officials and now wished to speak to him; they had said it was a very urgent matter. Alex checked his watch, he had already set up the board meeting to discuss his brother's return and subsequent dismissal, and had two appointments for that morning. Miss Henderson waited for his instructions.

Angrily, Alex said she was to show the men in but interrupt him in five minutes.

Alex knew instinctively something was up as the two men entered. Both wore ill-fitting grey suits with white shirts and silk ties, and carried identical leather briefcases. They were suntanned and very confident. Alex's hackles rose like those of an animal who could smell danger. These were no ordinary customs officials.

'Well, gentlemen, how can I help you?'

He glanced at their identification, and indicated two seats for them in front of his desk. They were from the South African Government. He continued, 'I'm afraid my brother is unobtainable, but if you would like to tell me how I can be of assistance . . .'

The two men were investigating the illegal exportation of semi-precious stones from South Africa. Their neat briefcases contained thick files on Skye Duval of Duval Limited.

'Do you have any knowledge of this company, Duval Limited, Mr Barkley?'

Warily Alex shook his head. How many times in the past had he heard that name? He wished he had checked more thoroughly. He could feel the sweat trickling down his spine, knowing that this must have been what his brother had been doing for the last six years. His hands were steady as he took the documents outlining the vast mining activities of Duval Limited. His eyes flew over the pages ...

'The Duval company has, over the past ten years, systematically bought up thousands of acres of perlite territory. The crosses indicate the exact locations of the productive mines. The mines close to rivers, marked with blue lines, have been producing semi-precious stones.'

Miss Henderson tapped on the door and entered, interrupting Alex as he had requested. He gave her a sharp, dismissive wave, then waited until the door closed behind her.

'You must forgive me, gentlemen, I am sure you have some reason for wanting to speak to my brother about this ... er, Duval organization, but for the life of me I cannot understand why. I am a very busy man, and my brother, as you have been informed, is unobtainable, so unless you have a very valid reason for taking up my time I must ask you to leave.'

He was handed an enlarged black-and-white photograph, and one of the men, in clipped tones, asked, 'You know this man?'

Alex stared at the photo and shook his head.

'But you can identify this man, can't you?' Alex was shown another photograph. He flicked a look at it.

'Yes, that is my brother. The other man I have no knowledge of.'

'That is Mr Skye Duval and, sir, we have reason to believe that Duval Limited is in fact owned by your brother, Mr Edward Barkley.'

'Then, gentlemen, I suggest you take this matter up directly with him, or with Mr Duval himself, surely he can assist you. I'm sorry I cannot be of any further help, but I do have another appointment, so if you will excuse me ...'

The two men took their time, carefully repacking the files and photographs in their briefcases.

'You are aware, sir, that the transportation of gems out of

South Africa without an export licence is a criminal offence? Perhaps you would inform your brother that we wish to speak to him, and that he must contact us as soon as possible. I think it would benefit all parties if we were to discuss this amicably. Thank you for your time, sir. Good day.'

Miss Henderson jumped to attention as Alex opened his office door. Before the two men had left the reception area, Alex had cancelled his next two appointments. He ordered his car to take him to Greenwich, and left instructions that the board members were to wait for his return if he should be late.

Edward was lying on his bed, watching television. The room was littered with used cartons from take-away food, and the stale smell of hamburgers, brandy and cigars sickened Alex. He stared at Edward, waiting for him to acknowledge his presence. Eventually he walked across to the TV, switched it off and stood in front of it. Edward made no move to stop him, but yawned and asked, 'What do you want?'

'Some facts ... about South Africa, about a man called Skye Duval ... you listening?'

Edward laughed, wagging his finger at Alex. 'Ahhh, and I thought for a second you were interested in my well-being. That'll be the day, huh? The day anyone gives a fuck about me, I'll be under the sod.'

Alex pulled up a chair and sat close to the bed. 'Two so-called customs officials were at the office this morning. They had photographs of you and this man, Duval.' He passed Edward their calling card, and waited as he turned it over. He looked at Alex with a bored expression, then sighed and lay back on the pillows.

'Well, haven't you got anything to say about it? Edward? They are making enquiries about illegal shipments of gems out of South Africa ...'.

'So what? Nothing to do with me.'

'No? So how come they have photographs of you and this Duval character? Are you behind this company or not?'

Edward shrugged his massive shoulders and yawned. Alex stared at him, then pushed his chair back in anger. 'Jesus, I might have known it, are you crazy? What in God's name do you think you're playing at?'

'It's got nothing to do with you.'

'Like hell it hasn't! I want to know what's going on and I want to know now. You're not dragging me down any sewer with you, you try it and I'll . . .'

Edward reached out and grabbed his brother's wrist. 'What, Alex? What'll you do? It's none of your business, I'll take care of it, all right? I'll take care of it just like I take care of everything else . . .'

Alex brought his wrist up so hard he caught Edward's face with his hand. Blazing with anger, he shouted, 'You do that, Edward. If this is trouble, then you take care of it because, as from today, I wash my hands of you and your stinking deals . . .'

Edward applauded him, smirking, 'That's my brother talking . . . You do that, Alex. You go and wash your hands of me, but don't come back with them held out begging when you fuck up!'

Alex slammed out of the room and hurried down the stairs. He brushed past Dewint, snatched his coat from him, and said, 'Make sure he sees the doctor. Start cleaning the place up and I'll sort someone out to give you a hand, all right?'

He hurried to his car.

Hearing a sound, Dewint looked up the stairs. Edward smiled down at him, then crooked his finger for him to go upstairs.

'Run me a bath, and see if there's anything in the wardrobe I can get into . . . now, Norman. Don't bother cleaning the place, you'll have plenty of time for that when I've gone.'

Alex strode back into his office. Miss Henderson scurried after him, telling him that the board members were all gathered and had been waiting for over half an hour.

By the end of the afternoon Alex was well pleased with his work. The board had discussed his taking over at length, and in the end it had been agreed that when medical certificates verified his brother's precarious mental state, there could be no foreseeable opposition to Alex heading the company. As it was, no one could deny the fact that it was Alex who fronted the vast organization, and it would therefore only be a matter of time before he had the company legally under his control.

George Windsor, waiting to drive Alex home, reported that Edward was no longer in residence, he had done yet another of his famous disappearing acts. The doctors had been told he had gone abroad – somehow he had managed to get himself together and slip the net. Alex's buoyant mood collapsed. Closing his eyes, he leaned back against the leather upholstery and spoke very softly, almost to himself.

'Well, the seeds are sown, give the bastard enough rope and he'll hang himself.'

Book Eight

Chapter Twenty-Nine

Jinks had half expected to hear from her father. Over the years she had been used to his broken promises, but after the funeral and the subsequent meeting with Barbara, she had thought their relationship had become closer. But he didn't contact her, and she made no effort to see him. In truth she had no need of him, her finances were always dealt with by Miss Henderson, and her allowance covered any expenditures she incurred.

She had flown to New York, returning after two weeks, having enrolled for the forthcoming term at Vassar. She also made her early morning appointment with Barbara, and they had bought a number of smart outfits in preparation for the trip to Paris. Barbara had already booked an appointment with an optician, and Jinks' glasses were unceremoniously dropped in the waste bin, Barbara ignoring her pleas that they helped disguise her problem.

'What problem? That you're a bit short-sighted, or what?'

'No, I have a lazy eye, my left one. Mother was always going on about it.'

Jinks could smell Barbara's heady perfume as she peered closely, then held Jinks at arm's length, scrutinizing her eyes. 'Absolute rubbish, there's not a sign of a squint, probably all in her imagination.'

She was positively smug with satisfaction when the optician

announced that Jinks did not need any kind of correction to her sight. 'You see? What did I tell you? All the years you've had those terrible things wrapped around your face and you never needed them. Typical! Once I asked your mother to be a guest at a Wild Life luncheon – you know, Save the Animals – my dear, she turned up with a silver fox fur dangling round her neck! It was frightful, all through the lunch I could see this wretched thing with its glass eyes glinting at me. She did it on purpose – typical! Your eyes, darling, are your best feature, and you must learn to make the most of them. In fact, you are going to learn to make the most of yourself . . .'

Jinks was paraded through beauty salons, her body massaged and creamed. Her hair was trimmed, but Barbara wouldn't hear of her having it cut short. She ran her fingers through Jinks' thick curls and instructed the hairdresser to simply thin and shape it. Jinks, beginning to trust Barbara's judgement, didn't argue. There was no particular warmth between them, and Barbara treated her neither like a daughter nor a friend. But if she felt it a chore to be Jinks' chaperone, she never showed it. She felt slightly sorry for Jinks in some way; the girl's helplessness and lack of social graces were a challenge to her. And unlike her own daughters, Jinks took her advice without question. Then, as the trip drew nearer, Barbara suggested to Jinks that she should stay overnight in Mayfair so they could travel to the airport together.

Jinks was given Evelyn's bedroom. The small room contained little or nothing of the boy, but she took a sneaky look through all the drawers and even read some of the stories he had written when he was a child. They dined very formally and Jinks said little, but noted the interaction between her uncle and his elegant wife. They appeared as formal with each other as they were to her.

Later, as she got ready for bed, she overheard them talking in Barbara's bedroom. When she realized they were discussing her father, she listened intentionally. Alex had been quiet at dinner, but obviously agitated. Jinks could hear Barbara asking him if

Jinks' presence in the house upset him. Alex replied that he really couldn't care less.

Jinks pressed her face against her door, eager not to miss a word of what was being said. Alex's voice rose in anger as he described Edward's total disregard for the company, for the amount of work Alex was doing . . . Jinks could hardly believe what she was hearing.

'That bastard will drag me down with him unless I do something drastic. This time I'm not taking it, this time I've had enough. At this afternoon's board meeting it was carried unanimously. I am taking over the company . . .'

'It's about time. I'm surprised you waited this long. If it's not drugs, it's drink; you should get him certified . . .'

'That is just what I am doing.'

Alex's laugh sounded hollow, humourless. The next moment, Jinks had to hurry across to her bed as she heard him in the corridor. Her door inched open, and he popped his head round.

'Jinks? You asleep? If I don't see you in the morning, have a good trip. Goodnight.'

'Goodnight, Uncle Alex, and thank you for letting me stay.'

'You're welcome any time, good night.'

He closed the door and went to his own room, leaving Jinks unable to sleep for hours, repeating over and over in her mind every word she had heard her uncle say. She wondered if it was really possible for Alex to take over the Barkley empire and, if so, where would that leave her?

Jinks had been a lonely child, often having to take care of her mother. Now the realization that she also had to take great care of her own future, that nothing could be depended upon, made her aware of just how valuable Barbara Barkley could be.

Jinks began to practise a subtle manipulation of her aunt. She wanted to cut corners, and she knew Barbara could show her exactly how; after all, as her father had said, 'You don't have to like the woman, just use her.' She began to see just what he had meant. The first-class travel was easily bought by anyone, but the extras that a VIP like Barbara Barkley could command were a revelation. She did indeed know everyone, and they moved their suites at the Hotel St George twice before Barbara was satisfied.

'Honey, you never accept the first room they offer. You want the best, you can pay for the best, you make damn sure you get it . . .'

Barbara swept through Paris. The season was in full swing, and before they had unpacked the telephone was ringing every two minutes. Invitations poured in, and Barbara acquired a personal maid, a chauffeur-driven stretch limo and a secretary, plus a PR agent to announce where Barbara Barkley would be and at what time. Jinks stood back and admired her, flattered her, and paid close attention to every detail. Barbara obviously loved it all, exuding energy and a zest for life that women half her age would covet. She delighted in having Jinks close at hand to whisper and giggle with, and often said the most outrageous things. She appeared to know who had had what lifted and by whom, and when Jinks asked how she knew so much she roared with laughter.

'Because, sweet thing, I have used their doctors myself. You don't remain thirty-eight for long without paying for it, and when it's in such good condition and all in working order, you bet your sweet arse I know who else has been having the same tucks . . .'

Together they moved with the élite, surrounded by film stars and Parisian society. Jinks soaked up everything she saw like a sponge. Barbara never let her down, and whisked her to one designer after another. She also took her protégée's wardrobe very seriously and introduced her to many young designers she thought more suitable than the named houses she herself preferred. After one show she insisted on taking Jinks backstage to meet Jerry Hall, a model as tall, and with feet as big as Jinks', to give her a good look at what she could do with herself if she tried.

Barbara received so many invitations that did not include Jinks that occasionally she would depart for luncheons or dinners without her. On one of these evenings Jinks was sitting alone, brushing her hair and trying on some of her new clothes. She had ordered room service, so when there was a knock on the door she called for them to come in to set up her dinner. But there were no sounds of a trolley or clinking of cutlery, so she walked through to the lounge.

Evelyn Barkley leaned against the door frame. For a moment she was afraid, not recognizing him, then he tilted his head and smiled at her.

'Well, hello, cousin, surprise, surprise! Expected Mother, where is she?'

Jinks felt herself flushing, and stammered that Barbara was out for the evening.

'Oh, she must have forgotten. Still, not to worry.'

There was a knock on the door and he opened it, standing aside for room service to enter. Jinks excused herself and returned to her bedroom to dress. By the time she came out, he was sitting down, pouring a glass of wine.

He was wearing the filthiest pair of leather trousers and an old leather jacket, a scarf knotted at his throat. His motorbike boots had so many straps and buckles he looked like a Hell's Angel, but he was perfectly at ease. Smiling, he told her he had ordered a steak for himself.

She could not meet his black, slanting eyes. His delicate bone structure was reminiscent of Barbara's finely chiselled features; and he was an exceptionally handsome boy, but his face, like his hands, was filthy. His hair was lank and greasy, and he wore an elaborate silver skull-and-crossbones earring. She accepted the glass of wine, and before she could offer a toast he had downed his full glass and was pouring another.

'So what's with you? What are you doing here with the duchess?'

'I'm here for the collections.'

He looked at her and laughed. 'Oh, we're here for the collections, are we? Christ, how tall are you? You must be nearly six feet.'

Jinks flushed bright pink and sat down quickly, picking up her napkin to cover her embarrassment. He leaned over and tugged her hair. 'You look better than you did last time. Christ, you used to wear those specs, and those pigtails ...'

Jinks could not think of anything to say, so she sipped her wine while he made himself at home, forking salad out of the bowl and then eating it with his fingers, filthy fingernails prodding at the tomatoes and then dipping them into the salad dressing.

'How's college, aren't you at college here?' Jinks finally managed.

Evelyn snorted. With his mouth full, he told her about his time at St Martin's of Pontoise. 'Place is, rather was, run by friggin' monks. We hadda call them Brother or Frère. Place was like a concentration camp – mass every day, bloody dormitories, fucking ice-cold showers ... Jesus, it was a shit-hole. I got out after my first term, not that the old lady knows, or the old man. They wouldn't know if I died of the clap over here, but they keep on sending the allowance, so who gives a fuck. Know what I mean?'

His steak arrived, and he sauntered to the door to let the waiter in, then kicked it shut. He proceeded to eat the steak with his hands, waving it around the room as he talked. Suddenly Jinks started to laugh. He was trying so hard to impress her or disgust her, she couldn't tell which, but it was just so ridiculous, and it was all the funnier to think that he was Barbara's son.

'Has your mother seen you in this get-up? Or have you bought it especially for tonight?'

He looked at her and licked his filthy fingers. Then, with an open-handed gesture, he enquired what was wrong with his gear ... but he was smiling, and his eyes were like a naughty boy's, wonderful, twinkling eyes with thick, long eyelashes. He threw himself on to the sofa, propped his boots on the satin cushions and unzipped one of his many pockets.

'I'd rather hoped the duchess would be here so I could hit her

for some cash. She coughs up fast when I look like this, especially if she's got company . . . you wanna smoke?'

Evelyn drew a rather squashed joint from his pocket, lit it, and
inhaled the smoke deeply. Jinks continued to sip her wine, leaving her food untouched.

'So you've left college?'

He nodded, then offered her the joint. She hesitated a
moment, then walked over to take it. He pulled her down to sit
next to him.

'So how's life, willow-legs? You look very affluent, what do
you do? You work, do you?'

Jinks puffed tentatively at the joint, but the end was soggy so
she handed it back. He took a deep drag, then stared at her.

'What does a little rich girl do in Paris, huh?'

'I'm going to college in America.'

'Oh, are we? Isn't that exciting . . .'

'If you are no longer at St Martin's, what do you do?'

'I live in a commune. My friends and I fight against the stinking capitalist shits who run this country.'

He watched her closely for a reaction, but receiving none
either way he continued, growing serious about his political
beliefs. He spoke in glowing terms of the Baader-Meinhof gang,
and spouted the Red Army jargon. Looking at her, he gestured
to her silk robe.

'Sitting in the lap of luxury I doubt if you could understand,
could feel any compassion for the injustices . . .'

Jinks had heard enough. His childish and irritating arrogance
annoyed her. 'On the contrary, I am more than aware of the
injustice in the world, but I doubt if joining some tin-pot terrorist organization can put it to rights. You are a typical recruit.
It's a fact that most terrorist organizations draw the offspring of
wealthy parents like magnets. Although, as far as I have discovered, there is usually an element of their own failure that
surpasses their hatred of their so-called capitalist parents' wealth.
I'm not saying that all the offshoots, all terrorist organizations,
are made up of rich kids, but they are essentially useful – if for

nothing else but finances. You had every opportunity to make something of yourself but you blew it. If you want my opinion you'd be better off going back to college, or better still, if you don't want to use the money that I presume is still being paid out for your education and is consequently being wasted, give it to some kid who wouldn't have the chance . . .'

He jumped to his feet in a fury, shouting at her, 'If I wanted a fucking lecture I'd go to my father, you mind your own damned business!'

'Fine! You started it, I didn't ask you to come in here spouting political dogma. In fact, I'd appreciate it if you left, you stink – doesn't this commune of yours possess a bath, or is it not the thing to do?'

They glared at each other, then suddenly he roared with laughter. 'Come to think of it, I wouldn't mind a bath, thanks . . . You know, I preferred you with your hair in pigtails and those weird glasses you used to wear. How's Aunt Harriet?'

Jinks had to turn away from him. 'She died, nearly nine months ago . . .'

Evelyn hesitated, and he suddenly dropped his act, became real, even appeared vulnerable. 'I'm sorry, I didn't know. She was nice . . . You sure it's okay for me to have a bath?'

Jinks turned to him, and they were totally at ease with each other. She nodded her head. For a moment he looked just like he had done at school, a cheeky grin flashed on his handsome face, then he disappeared into her bedroom.

She could hear him moving around, and then the sound of the bath running. After a moment he called out for her to come and talk to him. She hesitated . . . and opened the door.

He was stripping off his clothes in preparation for his bath, tipping bath salts and perfume into the steaming tub. She remained hovering in the doorway, and he looked over, laughing, as she flushed crimson and returned to the lounge. She rang for room service to clear dinner, and waited for fifteen minutes, listening to him singing and splashing in the bathroom.

Room service cleared the trolley and delivered fresh coffee.

She had just poured herself a cup when he reappeared, wrapped in bath towels. While she poured him the coffee he asked for, he stood very close to her, too close, and she was aware of his body. His hair, washed and drawn back from his face, dripped water down his naked back. In a genuinely friendly gesture he slipped an arm around her.

'Clean enough, Miss Juliana? Little Four-eyes?'

'Not any more. I don't even wear glasses, and your dear mother is showing me the ropes ... apparently I inherited my mother's appalling dress sense. How do you think I look?'

He stood back and looked her up and down. 'You look okay ... yeah, you look okay. Did Mother say when she would be back?'

'I don't know, she went to a dinner party.'

'Oh, so that's what she calls it nowadays? She screwin' anyone I would know of?'

'I'm sure I wouldn't know ...'

'How's your father? How's the Big Bad Wolf?'

'Apparently bigger and badder, you know the way he is.'

'I like him. You remember that Christmas I came over – best Christmas I ever had. I got this great car, a police car with sirens.'

They sat drinking their coffee. He seemed miles away, deep in thought. Jinks felt herself constantly wanting to look at him, his eyes, his hair, his delicate bone structure. He had always been a good-looking boy; now he was really exceptionally handsome. His eyes were as dark as her father's, but his lashes were thick and long as a girl's. As if he were reading her mind, he looked up to meet her gaze ... and he smiled, the sweetest of smiles.

'I couldn't hit you for a couple of hundred, could I? It's just I'm a bit desperate, you know the old man keeps me short, in the hope I'll behave, ha, ha, ha. I'll pay you back.'

As Jinks reached for her handbag, he leaned close and cupped her chin in his hand. She stared into his face, and it was over in a second ... he simply bent his head and kissed her lips. It was a gentle kiss, a simple 'thank you'. She blushed, and he touched her cheek with his hand, then watched as she counted out the notes. He kissed them as she held them out, then he walked into the bedroom, dropping the towel and reaching for his trousers just as Barbara walked in. She was a little tipsy, carrying a large bouquet of flowers and a magnum of champagne, calling out as she entered, 'Jinks, we have been invited by Count Emilio de . . .'

Barbara stared at her half-naked son, hopping into his trousers, then at Jinks. There was a moment when none of them said a word. The flowers were thrown aside, and Barbara snapped, 'What the hell has been going on here?'

Evelyn sauntered in from the bedroom. 'Just came round to see you. You weren't in, so we decided to have a fuck, so that's what's been going on, okay? No harm done, Mother.'

Evelyn ducked as Barbara went for him, grabbed him by the hair and slapped his face. She was screaming incoherently, and received in return a slap that sent her reeling across the room. He picked up his boots and jacket, backing away from his mother.

'You're sick, you know that? I need some cash, that's all I came for, the only reason I ever come to see you. So where's your bag?'

Jinks tried to intervene, but he pushed past her, picked up his mother's evening bag, tipped out the contents and took what money she had, stuffing it into his pocket. Jinks went and helped Barbara to her feet – she was shaking badly, and her cheek was inflamed where he had slapped her.

Evelyn finished dressing, stamping his feet into his boots, and Barbara never said a word. As if his mother weren't in the room, he smiled at Jinks, thanked her for a pleasant evening, and walked out.

Barbara examined her face in the mirror. She was calm, back in control. Patting her hair, she turned to Jinks. 'I think you had better tell me what's been going on.'

Jinks shrugged her shoulders and began picking up the flowers. 'Nothing, he just came round to see you, and you weren't here.'

'Oh, I'm sure! Don't treat me like an imbecile, darling, I'm not your mother, and I'm a damn sight sharper than you give me credit for, so give me the truth – just what has been going on between you two? Has he been sneaking in to see you while I've been out? Has he?'

Jinks felt faintly disgusted, and repeated that nothing had been going on, it was all a misunderstanding. Barbara whipped round on her; the fashion-plate-duchess act dropped, replaced by the old toughness she had spent so many years trying to disguise.

'Look, sweetheart, who do you think you're kidding? And don't think I like doing this, but I walk in to find my son fucking naked in your bedroom – what the hell do you think I'm gonna think is going on, you tell me?'

Jinks could feel her temper rising, and she faced Barbara. Her sweet 'butter wouldn't melt in my mouth' act dropping as fast as Barbara's. 'I don't think it's any of your business, but if you want to know, he came round to see you. You weren't here, he took a bath, and he was just getting dressed when you walked in ... And I don't like your attitude, or your assumption that I have, in your words, been fucking your son. That may be your style, or your daughters', but it isn't mine.'

'My, my, how the little mouse turns.'

'I've had a very good teacher.'

'So, are you going to see him again?'

'Oh, for goodness' sake, Barbara, does it matter?'

'Yes – he's no good, and don't think I don't know how attractive a little bastard he is. He's been putting himself about since he was fourteen years old, and I just wanna know if you are intending to see him again? Are you telling me you didn't find him attractive?'

Jinks took a deep breath and, keeping her voice calm, suggested that Barbara drop the subject. It had been a misunderstanding and it was best forgotten. Barbara took two brandy glasses from the cocktail cabinet and smiled. She was quieter, calmer now.

'Yeah, I guess that's what you call jumping the gun, to put it mildly. I guess that's down to my own promiscuous, ill-spent youth. I can't help it if I presume every girl's a woman after my own libido! Here, take it, you might need it.'

She handed Jinks a large brandy. Jinks wondered if Barbara was drunk; if she was about to divulge her past indiscretions she really didn't want to hear them. Quietly and firmly she refused the drink, sounding rather scathing even to herself.

Barbara smirked. 'Christ, you know, sometimes you are so like your father. Here, take it, it's good brandy . . . The cold, vocal put-down doesn't wash with me, but give you time, sweetheart. You have the killer instinct, I can feel it, and you know why I know? Because once he put me down, he did it just like that . . .'

Barbara snapped her fingers, drained her glass and refilled it immediately. Jinks could feel a strange sensation, as if she were stepping out of her body, protecting herself, moving away from a danger – but what, she couldn't grasp. Barbara lit a cigarette, allowed the smoke to drift out of her nostrils, and stared at Jinks through the haze.

'I married Alex before I met Edward, and it's obvious to anyone who meets them which one my type of woman would go for. Oh, they were both good-looking, but . . .'

Barbara was twisting the cigarette, her long, bright-red nails like talons. 'I would have left Alex, if he'd wanted me to, but he was using me like he uses everyone who walks into his life.' Suddenly she stubbed out the cigarette, grinding it, then looked directly at Jinks. 'Evelyn is his son. I'm surprised you couldn't tell just by looking at him. Apparently your mother knew, that Christmas, that time he came over to see you all. She knew, she must have realized then. Perhaps that was what made her go crazy . . . I know she'd been sick before, but that time sort of finished her off.'

Jinks closed her eyes. There was the nightmare of her mother cradling the doll, holding it to her naked breast . . . She could hear the pounding of her father running up the stairs, dragging the terrified Jinks away from the sight of her mother's madness.

Her voice betrayed nothing of her emotional state. 'Does Evelyn know?'

Barbara swayed slightly as she got up to fill her glass again.

'No, he thinks Alex is his father. Edward gave up any right to him before he was born, Alex's name is on the birth certificate. Alex found out, but he will never give him up – in a perverse way he has the only thing Edward, with all his money, can't buy.' She laughed a soft, slightly drunken laugh.

Jinks moved quickly across to her bedroom door, then turned to Barbara. Her face was set, impassive, giving no sign of the emotional turmoil raging inside her. 'I overheard Uncle Alex saying he was trying to take over the Barkley Company. I intend to become part of that company, and neither my uncle nor Evelyn will take what is rightly mine. I don't think I want to see you again, Barbara. You are a vain, egotistical woman without a shred of decency or compassion. You should never have treated my mother with such disrespect – perhaps if you had a grain of sensitivity you would have realized the anguish you must have caused her ... Goodnight.'

The bedroom door closed. There was an expression on Jinks' face that unnerved the older woman. A mask of complete unapproachability had fallen into place. Barbara had seen that mask before, when Edward ended their affair. Now she felt the same bitter anger, the betrayal, all over again. She slammed out of the suite, telling herself that when that little bitch came round needing her help she would tell her, just as she had told her father, to go to hell. She felt not the slightest twinge of guilt.

Barbara did not get the satisfaction she had hoped for. Jinks had already left Paris by the following morning, on her way to New York. Evelyn called his mother and, afraid he would turn up looking as wretched as he had on the previous night, she arranged for more money to be transferred to his account. She made no attempt to enquire if his studies were going well. She still seethed over the scene with Jinks, and as Evelyn had been more than a problem throughout his life she found it easier to pay him whatever it cost to keep him out of her sight.

Evelyn's so-called friends waited for him to return with the money. In some way the group replaced the family he had never been part of.

The money he had taken from Barbara was used to buy two .22 Birettas. Like children playing with new toys, they inspected the weapons. Evelyn practised loading the .22 short cartridge, and listened with awe as one of the boys, their self-designated leader Kurt Spanier, took it from him. Kurt was older than the rest of the group, and with great authority he told them the Israeli teams used the same weapons, although they were ballistically limited. However, the SOPS of the Massad 'Sayaret' teams liked them because they were fairly quiet.

Evelyn looked from Kurt to the gun and back again. 'Yeah, but we're not going to kill anyone . . . I mean, these are just for show.'

The gun was held to Evelyn's temple and his friend whispered in his ear, 'Best way is to pump the shots directly into the bastard's brain. That way, my rich friend, death is assured . . . and that is exactly what we'll be doing, if it should prove necessary. We're gonna hit the post office in two weeks, and we need more cash, 'cause we'll need explosives. So, we got a few hundred from mummy – why don't you tap that nice rich daddy of yours, he's a fuckin' capitalist tycoon, isn't he? Or has one visit with your bourgeois relatives changed your ideals?'

Evelyn was paying for the rent on the farmhouse, plus most of the food they consumed. Suddenly, with the talk of using the weapons, he wasn't sure that he wanted to get involved so deeply. The embrace of Spanier, hugging him close so that Evelyn could smell the garlic breath, made him afraid. His fear increased when Spanier whispered, 'You don't like it, my friend, you go out wrapped in the blankets the rifles came in, you understand? You, my friend, are in too deep to walk away, so don't even try it.'

Chapter Thirty

Skye Duval was speechless. He couldn't take it in, couldn't assimilate all the facts and figures in one sitting. Edward poured another glass of wine. His cigar smoke made the air, already thick and clammy, stifling.

Edward had arranged a complete buy-out with an American-based company. He wanted to retain nothing except the Fordesburg mine. That had been his only stipulation . . .

Skye picked up the thick folder of documents, then looked at Edward. Edward's face was jowelled, his once-slim, muscular frame so overweight that his suit and shirt flapped as if accentuating the flab beneath. He was also sweating profusely, and his breath hissed in his barrel-like chest.

Skye chewed on a matchstick, saying, 'But I can't see why! I mean, if those bastards are after you for exporting the stones, we pay 'em off as we've always done. But to sell off everything we've worked for all these years . . . I mean, don't you even want to retain any of the rights in the beds not yet mined?'

Edward sighed. 'I'm through, an' I got a feeling it's the right time. In a few years all hell will break loose over here. We sell now, I sell now, and the money is secure.'

Skye threw his hands in the air. 'Why? It's not as if you need the money . . . You tellin' me the Barkley Company's in shit? You tellin' me I don't know how many millions you've already got stashed away in Switzerland? God knows how many banks we've got all over the world? So what in hell is making you sell now, before we've opened a quarter of the mines . . .?'

'Maybe I wanna buy something.'

'You wanna buy something? You walk in, tell me to sign on the fucking dotted line, sign over my life's work, because you wanna buy something? What?'

Edward picked at the end of his cigar. 'None of your business, buddy. You've got a few hours, then, I'm afraid, whether you like it or not, I'm walking. You've been bleating on about want-ing out, having no time for yourself . . . Well, now I'm offering it, and you'll get more than your share.'

He puffed on his cigar until his face was almost obscured by the thick, heavily scented smoke, then tapped the ash off the end. Slowly he placed the documents in his briefcase. There was a finality in the gesture, and Skye put his head in his hands.

'Jesus Christ, you've already done it, haven't you?'

Edward snapped the briefcase closed and leaned on the table. 'Thanks for all you've done. If you want to stay on, there's a place for you, just a different man pulling the strings, so it's up to you. You want some advice, get the hell out . . .'

Skye reached over and gripped Edward's hand. 'You can't walk out on me. I want in on whatever you're so desperate to buy . . . Take me with you – whatever the deal, I want to be part of it.'

'Not this time, buddy.'

'But you an' me, we're partners! Even if you don't want me in on the deal. Just tell me, what, in God's name, costs so much?'

Edward released Skye's hand gently. His dark eyes looked into the desperate face, and then he pulled Skye close in a bear hug. His voice was gruff with emotion. 'My son . . .'

Edward Barkley walked out of Skye Duval's life just as he had walked into it all those years ago. He left his puppet a rich man, but without that powerful hand guiding him. Without his master pulling the strings, it would only be a matter of time before Duval would, as he had threatened years before, blow his brains out. There would be no tell-tale witness to Edward Barkley's illegal transactions in South Africa.

Edward's arrival in New York coincided with his daughter's birthday. He had not seen her since just after the funeral of Harriet. He had cabled her from Mexico, where he had been systematically selling off all his holdings and finalizing the sale of various companies.

He had booked a suite at the Plaza Hotel and ordered flowers and champagne. His gifts were wrapped and stacked on a coffee table. Miss Henderson had been called to double-check that Jinks had received his cable and would meet him as requested. Now he paced the room, checking the time, and called down to the desk to say his daughter was expected.

Juliana Barkley arrived in a chauffeur-driven limousine. She had been with her college friends, celebrating the honours passes she had gained in every subject, and would take this chance to discuss with her father her ambition to join the company. She was nervous and, purposely, fifteen minutes late. As she rode up in the lift Jinks checked her appearance. She had put Barbara's advice about clothes to good use, and was wearing Calvin Klein. She was still exceptionally thin, but had learned to wear her hair in a more flattering style, and had inherited her mother's flawless skin, so she required little make-up. Her mouth felt dry, and she licked her lips. She had virtually written herself a script for this meeting with Edward, rehearsing exactly what she would say to him. She was armed with the knowledge that Alex was intending to try to take over the Barkley Company, and that Evelyn was her father's illegitimate son.

Everything she had prepared to say, all her neat, rehearsed speeches, flew from her mind. Just as she was about to knock, her father opened the door and clasped her in his arms. He pulled her into the room and, like a little boy, proudly gestured to her birthday gifts. Then he held her at arm's length and swept her once more into his arms, hugging her close, telling her how wonderful she looked, insisting she open his gifts. As she slipped the ribbon from a large silver box, the telephone rang. Edward glared at it, apologized, and crossed the room.

She had a chance to look at him properly. She could see how much weight he had put on. He was like a giant. She continued to open her gifts, taking out a delicate nightdress. He covered the telephone mouthpiece and beamed.

'You like it? I chose it myself . . . open the small box on your left next . . . Hello? Edward Barkley here. What . . .?'

Jinks saw his manner change. Turning his back to her he listened intently to the caller. She saw his fists clench, and the small muscle at the side of his cheek twitched. It was as if she were forgotten, no longer in the room.

'You sure about this? I see . . . Well, I want a meeting straight away, can you come to my hotel? Good, 'bout fifteen minutes.'

She heard him murmur under his breath, then he carried the phone to the small desk and sat down. His bulk made the writing chair creak ominously. He began to thumb through a small notebook and promptly redialled, tapping his fingers on the desk.

'Is something wrong, father?'

Edward gave a brief nod, then spoke into the phone in a low voice. Jinks could not make out exactly what he was saying, but he was asking about shares in some company and what they were now standing at. Eventually he hung up, but made four more calls before turning to her. She still held the small box and he waved his hand for her to open it. At the same time he checked his watch.

'Sorry, sweetheart, something's come up. I had hoped we could spend some time together.'

'So had I.' Her mouth was a thin, tight line. She stood up, carefully folding the tissue paper from her gift box.

He stuck his hands in his pockets and sighed. 'It never works out with you and me, does it?'

She shrugged, picking up her handbag and gloves. 'No, I guess not, but then you've never really had time for me. I'm starting work with a bank on Wall Street to gain experience. I would like, when you have a spare moment, to see you about working for the Barkley Company.'

Edward retrieved his briefcase from the sofa and began to take out files. She waited for an answer: receiving none, she walked to the door.

'Don't go. Maybe you should sit in on this meeting. I own twenty-five per cent of a company called "Ming". The little Japanese bitch who owns it has tried unsuccessfully to get back that twenty-five per cent. Over the years she has skimmed and cheated, even threatening to try to cut me out of a business that I virtually handed to her on a plate. Now she's got Japanese part-ners, and they don't like having anyone else in the pond with them – in particular myself. So what she's done is form another company called "Lotus", specifically to deal with Japan.'

Jinks joined her father at the desk and started going through the files with him.

'Is this legal? I mean, can she do this?'

'Sure, she'll be competing against herself. She's going public with Ming, and obviously she'll push all the money back into the new company. I wouldn't be surprised if she intends letting it go into liquidation eventually. Easily done – she starts to bring in new lines that don't sell, and bingo, she gets liquidated, but still retains the secure new company – and my twenty-five per cent won't be worth a penny.'

'What are you going to do?'

'Put her out of business. I'm going to start buying more shares in Ming as soon as it goes public.'

'But you'd have to be named if you buy more than five per cent of shares in any company! They have to know the pur-chaser, that's the law.'

Edward smiled at his daughter's bid to show him she knew the business. He found it charming, and he pinched her cheek.

'But if I buy 4.99 per cent, the law's on my side. I'll use what is called the "concert party" system. I buy my quota, you buy, you get your friends to buy, they get their friends to buy . . . and when the show closes, they sell their shares straight back to me.

End result? I own the lion's share, and the first thing I do is knock Miss Takeda right off her perch and, second, we flatten Lotus and get the Japs coming straight to us.'

Edward laughed his deep, rumbling, infectious laugh. He strode over to her unwrapped gifts and began ripping the paper from them. 'See her new lines? All this stuff is from Lotus. It's Japanese and she's got French labels sewn in. She's sticking ridiculous prices on them. We'll expose it, get some great press. We'll buy the same stuff and undercut her by half . . . then when the company is back on its feet I sell, and guess who to?'

'The Japanese?'

'That's my daughter. Now, look over these contracts and . . .'

The phone rang again. Edward answered it, gave his name and just listened to the caller. Jinks looked at the 'gifts' – even those were connected with his business, and yet she couldn't feel any anger because she was genuinely interested. The garments were very delicate, in pale shades of pink and lilac, with fine handmade lace – and all with French designer labels.

Edward called her. He held his hand over the mouthpiece and told her to go down to reception and bring him all the English newspapers.

She returned to the suite to hear Edward instructing reception to get his car brought round as he was leaving for the airport immediately.

'You're leaving?'

Edward held out his hand for the papers and flipped them over. 'You had a look at them?'

'No. I just brought them straight up.'

He banged them down on the desk. His breath hissed as he flipped through them. 'Jesus Christ, the stupid kid, the stupid bastard!' He strode into the bedroom and began throwing his clothes into a suitcase.

Jinks looked at the papers. She picked up *The Times* and followed her father into the bedroom. There was a photograph of Alex halfway down the front page under the banner headline, 'TYCOON'S SON ARRESTED'.

'I'm getting the first flight to Paris. Stupid bastard's in real trouble; you read it?'

Jinks skimmed the article, which stated that Evelyn Barkley had been arrested among a group of French terrorists.

'What about the meeting? You said they were coming here?'

'Forget it, this is more important. You wait here, tell them I'll be in touch as soon as I can. I'll leave the documents, just hand them over.'

He swept into the lounge to pack his briefcase just as reception called to tell him his car was waiting.

'Who called you? Was it Alex?'

'No, Barbara. She's hysterical, has no idea what to do. Apparently the rags are having a field day, they've reporters hanging around the house. She can't contact Alex, doesn't know where he is . . .'

'Why do you have to go?'

'Because Alex couldn't squeeze a fart out, never mind get his son off this rap.'

'Don't you mean your son?'

Edward hesitated, then began stuffing papers into his briefcase. Jinks continued, her voice becoming shrill. 'You can find time for him but not for me, you've never had the time for me because I'm just your daughter. He's no good, he never was! Let him rot for a while, it'll do him good . . .'

'What the hell would you know about it?'

He checked his passport, and she moved closer to him, trying desperately to keep herself calm.

'Maybe before you go running to Evelyn and dear Uncle Alex, you should know that Alex is trying to get you thrown out of the Barkley Company. This is the first time you've seen me in months, and you never had the decency to even ask how I was doing. Happy birthday? You want to make it happy? Then you give me what I want, pay me off! Then you need never see me again — if you don't want me in your company, give me enough to start up a business of my own.'

Edward said nothing, but he removed from his case all the

documents relating to the Ming company. He tossed them on to the desk.

'Earn it, like I had to. Here, this is for starters.'

She watched him sign all the documents over to her. She was close to tears, desperate for him to hold her, comfort her, but he did nothing but flick through each page. Satisfied everything was in order, he replaced the top of his pen carefully, and picked up his cases. She still fought to keep her voice steady, fought not to cry.

'You don't care about me, just as you never cared for my mother. It was knowing about Evelyn, knowing about you and Barbara that killed her. I hate you, I hate you ... and I always have.'

He couldn't stand her harping voice, that vicious look on her face. Her words hit him hard and he felt sick to his stomach. She was looking at him with such loathing that he could say nothing, do nothing but walk out.

Jinks bathed her face, holding the cold cloth to her cheeks. She didn't cry, couldn't have cried now, it was too late. She returned to the lounge and looked once again through the papers.

Ten minutes later two men arrived, introducing themselves as her father's brokers. They listened attentively as she explained that she would be handling the business with the Ming company. Hesitantly, she enquired about her father's other interests. The two men looked at each other, and after a moment the younger one, Mike Doytch, was given the nod to speak. His blond, crew-cut head and chiselled features gave the impression of youth although he was in fact over forty. He coughed and loosened his collar.

'Your father made contact three, almost four, weeks ago. We have been instructed to sell all his shares and to deposit the money in Swiss bank accounts. The meeting today was simply to give him confirmation that this was all being done. However, this morning he asked us to retain his shares in the Ming company. Apparently Mr Barkley has been given some information that changed his mind. He had instructed us to sell to Miss Takeda.'

Jinks poured them drinks. She bit her lip. 'I hope, gentlemen, that whatever we discuss will be in the strictest confidence. The instructions to sell my father's interests, were they directly from the Barkley Company or from my father personally?'

Again the two men glanced at each other before Mike spoke. 'Your father's holdings in America and Mexico were private. The property and the land was, I believe, owned personally and were nothing to do with the Barkley Company. We have never done any business for them, only for Edward Barkley.'

Jinks sipped her Perrier water, the ice clinking in the glass. 'Have you ever had any dealings with Alex Barkley? My father's brother?'

Both men shook their heads. Jinks thought carefully before she spoke. She hinted that she would continue to use them if they could give her some idea as to how much they estimated her father had accumulated through his sell-out. She even smiled and told them confidentially, 'You see, my uncle has insinuated that my father's mental state is not . . . well, not one hundred per cent. He is an alcoholic, so if you could give me some idea, would that be possible? Just so I can report back to London.'

Jinks closed the door, thanking both men and telling them she would contact them within the week. Her knees were shaking, but she gave no outward hint of her nerves – quite the reverse, she was smiling and confident, and it was not until the lift gates closed that she dropped her act. She poured herself a stiff brandy and slumped on to the sofa.

The men had been very cagey, and it had taken a considerable amount of drink before they had more than hinted at Edward's personal wealth. Once they had told her they seemed strangely relieved, and then a trifle boastful of their own capabilities, Edward Barkley had made close to four hundred million. Jinks repeated it over and over in her mind, four hundred million . . .

She felt something hard digging in the small of her back, and moved the cushion. There was the tiny box her father had given her, the one she had not opened. She unwrapped it; it contained a gold bracelet similar to the one her mother had given her the afternoon before she died. Jinks turned it over in her palm, wondering for a moment if her father knew she already had the first present he had ever given Harriet. The difference was in the clasp, this bracelet was not broken. Four hundred million and this was her birthday gift. She weighed the gold in her hand, then hurled it across the room.

'You cheap bastard! I'll show you, and I'll do it without your bloody help!'

Alex had been called out of a meeting by Miss Henderson. He was tight-lipped with anger, demanding to know what was so important that it could not have waited. When he learned of his son's arrest he was on the next flight to Paris. Sitting on the plane Alex felt numb, unable to comprehend the mixed emotions that swept over him.

He sighed and leaned his head back against the seat rest. It was strange he should think of it now, all these years later, but instead of his son's trouble taking precedence, all he could think of was his own past. Memories that had been nothing but a blur became clear. He could see himself younger than Evelyn, his face twisted in fear arriving at the remand home, Rochester House. Long-forgotten memories came flooding back, and the grey curtain began drawing over him as it had done as a child lying weeping in his bed.

He turned to stare from the window, wanting to blank out the memory of his own frightened face. But the clouds reminded him of the dream, the dream he had been so desperate to hide behind, the dream of the rider on the black stallion, of his father and the mountain. The dream that gave him such nightmares. He felt as if he had been cursed. Why now? he asked himself, just as he was making headway, this time alone, without Edward. Just as he almost had the entire Barkley

Company within his grasp, why did he feel it was being taken from him, and why, when he had first been told of his son's arrest, had his first thought been to contact Edward? Was he always to be tied to him?

The stewardess made Alex jump, he hadn't even heard her asking if he would like a drink. He asked for a brandy.

Sipping it, Alex's hatred of his brother, his deep anger at everything Edward had done to him, rose up and gave him renewed energy. His head was clear again, and he was ready to fight for himself and for his son.

At the hotel Alex immediately contacted the lawyers allocated to Evelyn's case and asked for a meeting as soon as possible. He began to read the French news coverage. The headlines ran 'TYCOON'S SON HELD IN MASS TERRORIST ARREST'. The more he read the less likely seemed Evelyn's involvement. He realized that he would be away from London for longer than he had at first anticipated. He began to make numerous urgent business calls to cover for his absence. Alex was making sure his departure could not be compared with any of Edward's frequent disappearing acts. He instructed Miss Henderson to call every board member and make his personal apologies, but to say nothing regarding his son. Simply that there had been a family crisis. Should anyone require to talk to Alex urgently, they could contact him in Paris.

Alex was asking the lawyers for details before giving them time to remove their coats. He was told about the raid on the farmhouse Evelyn had rented. The police had found a veritable armoury, and it was obvious the boy was very much a part of the terrorist group. He had not attempted to deny it. He had been held in a local jail and then transferred to the Prison de la Santé in Paris.

Alex felt his initial energy and positive thinking slipping away. If anything, the newspaper articles had not suggested anywhere near the seriousness of Evelyn's involvement. Everything the lawyers told him made Evelyn's situation worse. After a long time, when he had digested it all, he asked quietly, painfully, how long they thought his son would get if he were convicted.

'There is no doubt whatsoever, Mr Barkley, that he will be sent to trial, even though there is no evidence as yet that he actually took part in the raids. One of the captured men has given evidence that your son was an active member of the gang, an offshoot of the Front de Libération de la Bretagne pour la Libération Nationale et Socialisme, and that he gave them his financial backing. Eleven of their members were arrested in '72 – they are small, and appear to be outside the mainstream of international terrorism. They don't have much in common with the other left-wing radical groups . . .'

'How long – for Chrissake, tell me what he's likely to get?'

'Ten to twelve years.'

Alex felt the breath rush from his body, and he had to be helped to a chair. Someone put a glass of water in his hand, which was shaking, and the glass rattled against his teeth when he tried to drink. 'Will I be allowed to see him? Tonight?'

'Yes, sir. I suggest you go to the jail immediately. They are moving them all to a top-security wing first thing in the morning. It's a prison forty kilometres outside Paris. I am very sorry, Mr Barkley, but we will use every moment we have, do everything we can. I have a car waiting if you would like to leave now . . .'

Alex was driven to the prison in a Mercedes. He leaned back and closed his eyes, saying over and over to himself what a fool his son was, what a fool . . . All he could picture in his mind was Evelyn on his fifth birthday, running to him, yelling at the top of his voice, 'Dad, Dad, I got a farmyard, I got a farmyard – I got cows and sheep and chickens . . .' Alex sighed – this farmyard was full of weapons.

Alex was searched, and questioned until his brain reeled, then he had to wait for over an hour before he was led into a small visiting room. Two guards were stationed at the door.

At last he heard footsteps and keys turning in locks. His mouth went dry and he couldn't get his breath. He half rose from his seat only to be ordered by the guards to sit down again.

Through the small glass window in the door he could see the top of his son's head. He swallowed hard to stop the tears welling up.

Evelyn was led into the room. He was wearing grey overalls and his hair had been cut very short. He was thin, almost gaunt. His wrists were handcuffed, his hands hanging loosely in front of him. He gave his father the ghost of a smile, but his eyes, his dark, wide eyes, were terrified. Alex had to sit back in his seat when he saw the guards push his son into the chair, ordering him to put his hands on the small, bare table.

'You all right? They treating you all right?'

'Yes . . .'

'I got here as soon as I could, I only heard this morning.'

Alex turned to one of the guards and asked if he could hold his son's hand. The man shrugged, and Alex reached over and gripped Evelyn's hands tightly with his own. The boy hung his head, ashamed.

'I've only got fifteen minutes, so I'll be as informative as possible. I've got the best lawyers there are, and they will be working around the clock. They have asked me to tell you to be completely honest with them, and not to hold anything back – you understand? I will stay here, and when they move you tomorrow, I shall come to see you as soon as possible. I think I can do more here in Paris, see the right people and try to sort this out.'

Evelyn clung to his father's hands, unable to look up, incapable of speech. The tears trickled down his cheeks. Alex swallowed again, trying to keep his own emotions in check.

'I can bring you some food, and shaving stuff. They said you will be allowed fruit, and a little money for cigarettes. You must keep yourself to yourself, don't mix. Don't, whatever you do, get into any fights. Evelyn? This is not the time to say what you did or didn't do, I just want you to know that I am here, I am with you, and I will stand by you . . . Look at me, son, look at me.'

Slowly, Evelyn raised his tear-streaked face. 'I'm sorry . . . Go back to England, there is nothing you can do. I was part of them, Dad, whether I wanted to be or not is immaterial. You'll only make it worse for me inside if you try to get me off.'

Alex gritted his teeth and held the boy's hand so hard he could feel the bones. 'Ask to be placed in solitary, keep away from the others, hear me? We may have a chance, but only if you are segregated. I don't want to hear you say again that you were part of them – you were not, hear me? You were not.'

'I was . . . I'll take whatever they hand out, it's the way it has to be.'

Alex could no longer hold his tears back, and his voice broke. 'I love you, I love you, and I'll be close, visit you whenever I can.'

The look on the boy's face made Alex reach over to take him in his arms, hold him tight. The bell rang, it was over, and the guard had to pull them apart.

They hauled Evelyn to his feet, marched him to the door. As they took him away he whispered he was sorry, sorry . . .

Alex heard the prison warders shouting at his son. He froze into a catatonic state, unable to make his limbs work. The sounds, the walls, the smell . . . He was back inside himself, he was suffocating . . . He clawed at the edge of the table, somehow managed to rise to his feet and leave, but he had no recollection of the journey back to his hotel. Just those sounds, those echoed voices, those keys . . . and those terrible locked doors.

There were messages waiting for Alex from his office and the lawyers, and there had been five telephone calls from Ming. He lay on the bed, unable even to wash himself or eat.

At last he roused himself to call Barbara, but the butler told him she was not at home. He called Miss Henderson, and noted down all the things he had to take care of. She began to tell him how sorry she was, and he cut her short, not wanting to discuss it. She told him she had given Ming his Paris number as she had been calling the office every hour on the hour. Whatever it was must be very urgent.

It was after midnight and he was still taking calls from the lawyers, arranging meetings. Every time he put the phone down it rang again with more messages, and top of the list was always Ming. He rang room service, then told the switchboard to block his calls while he took a shower. The water felt good, and he began to relax.

He rang down for his messages, and no sooner had he put the phone down than it rang again. This time it was Ming in person. Before he could say a word she berated him for not returning her calls. He let the phone rest on his shoulder, closed his eyes while she went on.

'Alex . . . are you there? Alex, will you answer me? I have just had a visit from Juliana Barkley, did Edward put her up to it? Alex, how can you, you of all people, treat me like this? I have trusted you . . . Alex? Are you there?'

He sighed and admitted he was, and Ming continued, 'This little bitch walked in as if she owned the building. I offered her more than her shares are worth, double, and she refused. She wants all the audited accounts, and the Japanese company is giving me hell . . . You told me to go ahead and agree there would be no third party involved . . . Alex . . .?'

Alex swung his legs down from the bed. 'Yes, I am here, and right now I couldn't give a tuppenny damn about your bloody tinpot company. I know nothing of Edward's daughter, and I haven't seen him for months . . . and I don't give a damn about it. Do you hear me? I don't give a fuck what you do from now on, just don't call me again.'

She screamed down the line, 'You had better get this thing sorted out, do you hear me? You have been paid a hell of a lot of money off the top, so don't start saying you don't give a damn. You said you were taking over the Barkley Company – well, Alex, are you? I have to know.'

Alex hung up on her, then told the switchboard he was not going to take any more calls from Miss Takeda. Ming had, as always, touched a chord inside him. His intentions of taking over were as strong as ever but, like the pattern that always formed in his life, every time he took a step forward something dragged him back. He had not given a thought to Edward, to the carefully laid plans for uprooting him. Nothing could be further from his mind, and in a strange way he almost wished his brother were with him.

The phone rang again, and he picked it up. Miss Henderson told him that the press was full of leaks on insider dealing, the Barkley Company could be in trouble, and she needed to contact Edward. Did Alex know where he was?

Sighing, he interrupted her. 'Will you not call me again unless it directly concerns my son, is that clear? Anything else will have to wait until my return. Just fend everyone off, do you understand me?'

There was a loud crackle on the phone, and Miss Henderson apologized for the intrusion, then the phone went dead.

Chapter Thirty-One

Edward's arrival in Paris coincided with the transfer of Evelyn to the top-security wing. He missed his son by a matter of hours. He contacted London and discovered Alex was in Paris, so he went directly to the hotel, only to find he had checked out and left no forwarding address.

Edward spent a considerable time asking questions of as many people as he could get to see. He sifted through the facts, those he managed to acquire, then tried once again to discover where Alex was staying, without success. He decided to make his way to where Evelyn was being held. Before he left, he paid a visit to the Foreign Office, then drove across Paris to the prison in the hope of seeing Evelyn.

Edward now knew it was far worse than he had anticipated. The main terrorist group were amateurs who had been making attacks on post offices, telephone exchanges, television transmitters, tax offices and banks since the late seventies. They had also destroyed an office at the Académie in Brittany. The new faction had not started causing real damage until three years ago, when they had bombed an officers' mess, two banks and a customs depot. The list made no sense, there was no logic to it. The only good thing from Evelyn's point of view was that no one had been killed or seriously injured.

But the police had found enough ammunition and explosives

at the farmhouse to give great cause for alarm. The terrorists' every movement had been monitored by the police, who had had them under surveillance for six months. Initially prepared to wait and catch them red-handed, they changed their minds when they discovered that the group had bought vast amounts of explosive. They decided to move in before anyone got killed, and had raided the farmhouse. One of the ringleaders, Kurt Spanier, was determined, if he and his friends went down, to take their little stool pigeon with them. He had given the police a long statement implicating Evelyn as the financier behind the organization.

Edward was refused permission to see Evelyn. He was standing outside the high prison walls wondering how to trace Alex, when he saw him driving out of the prison. He shouted and waved, chased the car. His brother's face was grey with worry, and he stared in panic at Edward for a moment, not recognizing him. Edward gasped for breath, 'I've been trying to contact you all day, lemme in the bloody car ... Hang on, I'll pay off my cab.'

Alex opened the door and Edward, wheezing and coughing, squeezed in beside him. The cigar smoke made Alex feel sick, and he opened the window as he drove away from the threatening brick walls topped with barbed wire.

The visits were a nightmare for Alex. Every time he entered the prison he went through agonies. He washed himself obsessively after each visit, unable to get the stench of disinfectant and urine out of his nostrils. The acrid cigar smoke had a similar effect on him, and he kept gasping for air, unable to talk. Edward was totally unaware of the mental strain Alex was undergoing every time he visited Evelyn. Attempts at conversation drew nothing but blank silence.

Alex's hotel room, though a double, was small. It was clean, but without any of the luxuries the two men had become used to. Alex splashed cold water on his face from the small handbasin, soaped and scrubbed his hands and nails. His brother's questions, fired at him one after another, made him feel worse.

Finally Edward blew his top, yelling, 'For God's sake, Alex, talk to me, talk to me.'

Edward's presence filled the room along with his cigar smoke. He lay down, the single bed creaking beneath his weight.

Alex was washing his hands yet again, and Edward threw his up in despair. 'You going to fucking talk this through with me or not? You tell me what you've got and I'll say what I've sniffed out – isn't there any room service in this dump?'

Alex loosened his tie and put his head into his hands. The headache still throbbed, but it was fading, the nausea subsiding. At last he spoke. 'Any way you look at it, he's going to get at the very least eight, they say more like ten years. The police were staking out the place, the farmhouse, for over six months. They watched him coming and going freely, so there's nothing to that angle we can try. They have cheques I sent which were signed over to one of them – a German, the one they call Kurt Spanier. The stupid bastard was part of it whether we like it or not.'

Edward took off his thick overcoat and threw it on to the only chair in the room. It fell to the floor in a heap. 'What about bribes, any joy in that area?'

'That what you're here for? What are you going to do, splash your money around? Grow up, money won't get him off this one – have you seen the list of things they've been trying to blow up?'

'Yeah, talk about arseholes . . . I dunno, but money gets everyone off everything, just that you're too dumb to know it . . . I want to talk to the lawyers. I've got contacts in the Foreign Office, maybe we can work something out, some kind of deal. If you ask me, it would maybe do the boy some good to spend a year or two behind bars getting his arse kicked . . . You never gave him the thrashing he deserved over that Harrow business.'

'Don't you start telling me how I should have treated my son . . .'

'He's my son, and you know it.'

'Wrong – you lost him when you kicked my wife out of your

bed. Now why don't you and your fat cigar get the hell out of here and leave me to try to sort out my son's problems.'

'Don't be a fucking crass idiot. Your son, my son, what difference does it make? Stupid git gets himself into trouble, surely the two of us can put our heads together and come up with something to get him out ...'

'I'm doing just that, and I don't need you ... I don't want you, nor does he – go on, get out!'

Edward took a massive wad of notes from his pocket and started to count them. 'That's exactly what I said to your wife when she came running round begging me to help. She had no idea where you were. Where have you been all these months, anyway? All hell's going to break loose in the City – you know that, don't you? So I've been cleaning up the back yard, so to speak, and keeping a very low profile. You know the Americans have started blabbing? Take one big guy down and the rest fall like a pack of cards. You know who they've got, don't you? Well, if he can cough up millions in fines, he's going to make sure he's got a deal and he will name names ... You hear what I'm saying, Alex?'

'Right now I'm not interested in the backhanded deals you have always persisted in, all right? I will straighten everything out as usual, when I get back. Just get your bulk out of here and leave me alone.'

Edward showed no inclination to get off the bed. He plumped up the pillow, lay back on it. 'Way I look at it, Alex, you are desperate to hold on to him as your son, because – and for this reason only – you know I want him.'

Alex flung open a window to clear the cigar smoke that billowed around his brother's head. 'Oh, yeah, what are you going to do? Offer me a deal, you get him off and he's yours, is that it? You're too late, you won't ever have him ...'

For a man his size, Edward moved incredibly fast, pinning his brother against the wall, pushing him so hard his head snapped back. 'This is the second time I've had to do this, first time was with your bitch wife, you know what she's worried about? That you won't get your fucking title! That's what she's worried about, so just listen, you stupid bastard ... I don't care if he knows who I am, what I am. I'm here to get him out, even if it means using a rope and scaling the wall. All right? I know I lost him, I know he's not "mine", and I have to live with it, here, inside me ...'

'All right, all right, I'm sorry ... I'm all strung up, it's the prison, it gets to me.'

'Yeah, well, it would ... You got to admit you did a bloody poor job of bringing him up.'

Alex pushed his brother away, went to lie on the other single bed. Even when Edward wasn't talking, his presence was an intrusion, and his heavy breathing was irritating Alex. He closed his eyes, sighed. 'You're right, maybe I did make a mess of bringing him up, but that was down to you. You destroyed everything I had going with him, did you know that? For a while I hated the poor kid, not because of what he had done, but because of what you had done. Barbara may be a bitch, but deep down inside that plastic body there is this guilt. Maybe it wouldn't have been so bad if he'd been a girl, but your son? Have you any idea what it felt like to find that out? The way I held him, when he was born – I was there, and to find out he wasn't ... wasn't ... Ah, shit ...'

Edward had a coughing fit while he thought of something to say. But, unusually for him, there wasn't anything, because he was actually trying to imagine what it must have been like for his brother.

Alex stared at the wall, then after a while he said, turning to Edward, 'See, I was blinded, because I thought he looked like Dad. But she, Barbara, never knew him, all she saw every time she looked at Lyn, as she calls him, all she ever saw was you ... When I found out, Christ, I felt such a prick, so dumb that I'd never even tumbled to it ... Jesus, what a cunt you have been, all my life you've been kicking me. So tell me, why did you go to bed with her? Why, Eddie? All the women you could have had, and it had to be her, why? Was it to get at me? Was that it?'

Edward coughed again, spat in the handbasin and ran the water. 'I didn't want her, Alex, she came of her own free will. I never set out to take her, I never set out to hurt you. And right now, if I said I was sorry, it would mean nothing, but if you want to hear it . . .'

'I don't – like everything to do with you, it's too late.'

Edward walked aimlessly around the room, searched his coat pocket for another cigar. He could remember Barbara's visit clearly, and that it had coincided with one of Harry's breakdowns. But there was no point bringing it up. He unwrapped the cellophane from the cigar, picked off the small gold band. He had screwed her, and had even enjoyed it for a while. He patted his pockets, looking for matches – he never could keep a lighter for more than a few weeks. Well, only one. He had kept the solid gold one he had been given in payment for the use of his body. He chuckled to himself – he wouldn't be paid so much as a matchstick for it now, the size he was. He puffed on the cigar, the smoke coiling in the air, then sat on the bed opposite his brother. He looked at Alex as he lay stretched out on the other bed, put out his big hand and squeezed his shoulder. No words could ever make up for the things he had done, and he knew it.

Alex put his arm across his face and began to cry. Between heart-rending sobs he described what Evelyn had looked like in jail, how he had gripped his father's hands and seemed so helpless.

Edward pulled out his silk, polka-dot handkerchief, leaned over and wiped his brother's face, just as he had done when they were kids. 'Listen, you and me both, we'll leave no stone unturned, we'll get this thing sorted out together, yeah? That's the deal, brother, okay?'

Alex blew his nose and wiped his eyes. 'I love him, Eddie, I love him, and you know something? He's just as stubborn a bastard as you always were. But he is my boy, and it wasn't until he clung to me, held me, that it meant so much. He needs me, and . . . I need him.'

Edward flopped back on to the bed, the springs creaking ominously. 'Look, I'll agree to anything, but will you stop calling me Eddie ...? Now then, I have a contact in the Foreign Office, and I shall have to spread a lot of jam. Maybe I can swing it, get it down to a couple of years ...? I'm not making promises ...'

Alex drew himself up to sit facing his brother. His blue eyes were troubled, his face twisted as he dredged up his past. 'Not good enough, Eddie, because you do that and I can tell you exactly what's going to happen to him. Believe me, I know – it doesn't matter if it's here in France or in England. Behind bars men all act the same way – he's a good-looking kid, they won't leave him alone.'

He reached for his case – the one with the Gucci monogram – and took out a bottle of duty-free Scotch. Unscrewing the cap he drank, and slowly, piece by piece, Edward learnt what Alex had been put through as a boy even younger than Evelyn. The bottle was half-empty by the time he had finished, and he had not once passed it to his brother. Holding it carefully by the neck he stood it on the table between the beds. Edward looked up at him, bereft of words, swamped by a terrible helplessness at his inability to ease his brother's anguish, so long kept hidden beneath the surface – so much pain. He reached up, offering his brother his hand in a gesture of submission, of understanding. If Alex did not take his hand, Edward did not know what he would do with himself.

Slowly, Alex reached out, threaded his fingers through his brother's. He spoke so softly Edward had to strain to hear him. 'Oh, Eddie, how I hated you ... and it went on and on, it never ended. Barbara, Evelyn – everything I had you took from me. You know where I've been all these weeks? With Skye Duval ... Yeah, you're surprised?'

Alex released his brother's hand, began to walk around the room. 'Eddie, I have letters back in England – that doctor I sent you to, when you were ill, remember? Well, there are other letters, and newspaper clippings, proving you are a drunkard and incapable of running the Barkley empire. I wanted it, I wanted all of it, and just in case you tried to fight the board, I got proof of your illegal transactions in South Africa. Plus your part in the murder of a woman called . . .?'

Edward said the name quietly, 'Julia.'

'Right . . . and the hit and run, the "accident" that killed Richard Van der Burge.'

Edward smiled, shaking his head, and then laughed. 'You son of a bitch, you son of a bitch, I'll take you on, Alex, any day, any time.'

Alex stuffed his hands in his pockets and kicked the end of his brother's bed. 'No, you won't, because when it comes down to it I don't think I could see it through. Oh, I'd like to think I could, but . . . you've always beaten me. In a way I'm just like that poor bastard Skye Duval. You pull his strings, just as you pull mine – we're your puppets.'

Edward picked up his heavy overcoat and walked to the door. He paused a moment, his back to Alex, then said, 'You know, you dumb bastard, you're wrong. From the moment I looked into your cradle – I was just tall enough to see over the edge – Ma said, "Come and see him, Edward, come and see Alex"; and there you were, smiling up at me with those big blue eyes. There was no jealousy, no envy, because I wanted to protect you, look out for you. You had me by the balls, my old son, even then. We're brothers, Alex, we got each other so tight by the nuts we're not much cop without each other. I love you, Alex, and I'll get our boy off, and maybe you'll be free of me for good. Everything I've got is yours. I guess it always was . . . Now get some rest, I'll be back.'

He walked out without another word, without waiting for a reply, without turning round.

Outside, a janitor watched the big, overweight man leaning against a dirty brick wall. He was punching the wall with his fists, hitting it time and time again until his knuckles bled. The janitor did not dare approach him – the man was too big, too crazy . . . He clanked his bucket and mop in his haste to get out of sight. He didn't see the massive frame hunch up, didn't see

Edward press his face against the dirty brick wall, nor did he hear the strange, strangled moan . . .

Edward did not return for two weeks, during which time Alex spent every possible moment with Evelyn. Somehow the relief of telling his brother everything had made it easier to cope with the prison.

The lawyers began to prepare their case. Through Edward, they had secured a total press blackout on the proceedings. The trial was to be held at the main court in Paris, Les Assises.

Evelyn's time in prison proved to be a period of growth for him. In some ways Edward had been right, solitary confinement gave him peace to review his life and come to terms with it. He realized what he had wasted, what he had abused, and he was ashamed. He discovered in Alex a loving tenderness that he had never hoped to find. The visits drew them closer together, and they talked about everything that had harmed their relationship and kept them apart.

Alex brought Evelyn many books to fill the time in his cell, and he read avidly. He was a model prisoner and took notice when Alex told him that at any cost he must keep himself segregated. Any trouble he got into would go against him. Alex was able to make him understand what confinement does to a man, the homosexual practices of which he could become the victim. He found his son's sense of humour touching when he said he had come across enough of that in school to be able to cope with it. Alex even worked out a fitness programme for him, so that he could keep his body strong. He showed Evelyn a couple of exercises, getting down on the visiting room floor to demonstrate. Whereas his visits used to cause him such mental anguish, now it was the partings that became more and more difficult. Their time was so precious, precious because looming over them both was the forthcoming trial. Just as freedom seemed so sweet, the possibility of not being granted it played on Evelyn's mind.

*

Edward started with the men and women arrested at the farm-house with Evelyn. He had already paid handsomely for having his messages carried into the jail via the lawyers, offer-ing vast sums of money, money their families would benefit from, if not themselves. One by one they altered their state-ments, claiming that Evelyn was just a rich young boy they had manipulated. Kurt Spanier was the most difficult to persuade, as he stood to be charged with kidnapping and holding Evelyn against his will. But money can bend minds, and Spanier nego-tiated for a deal.

Alex listened as Edward outlined the second part of his com-paign. He began to work on the press, arranging interviews, and bought witnesses prepared to swear on oath that Evelyn Barkley was held against his will at the farmhouse. Edward even had sworn affidavits from the frères at St Martin's. Alex could only guess at the cost of what his brother was doing, he knew it would have to be astronomical. But he obeyed his instructions and queried nothing. The days sped by, the trial drawing clos-ing and closer.

'I'm going to have to see him, Alex, he's got to give a per-formance, and he's going to need me to tell him exactly what to say . . . I want no one else there, no lawyers, not even you, and I give you my word I'll be there for exactly what I've told you, nothing more. Can you arrange it? Within the next two days?'

Alex agreed, and after discussion with the prison authorities Edward was given permission to visit Evelyn. Alex had a diffi-cult assignment himself – he was to give a full press interview as the distraught father. That would not require any acting ability, but it was vitally important that he give a display of total support for his son's innocence.

The two brothers shook hands. Edward knew he must make himself very scarce – no one must associate him with Alex or con-nect the two with any behind-the-scenes manipulation. There had been no violence, no threats – just the temptation of money.

Judge Grégoire Maréchal was the last man Edward had arranged to meet, the last link in his chain.

Edward was body-searched, then left waiting for more than two hours. The room smelt of stale body odour and tobacco.

At last he heard footsteps on the tiled floor, and a warder gestured for him to follow. He was shown into a small, stiflingly hot room. A thick glass barrier ran the length of the room, and a telephone hung on the wall. After a further ten minutes the door behind the barrier opened. The guards removed Evelyn's handcuffs and he sat down, rubbing his wrists.

It was a moment before Evelyn realized who Edward was. Edward started sweating – he licked his lips and reached for the telephone. Evelyn did the same.

'There's nothing wrong with Dad, is there? He's all right?'

Edward hesitated, finding the telephone system confusing. He wanted to be face to face with Evelyn, but he couldn't be heard unless he spoke directly into the telephone.

'Your father's fine. I'm here for the lawyers, I am with the law firm that's taking your case, do you understand?'

'I didn't recognize you at first, you look different.'

'Yep, we all change . . . You all right?'

Edward found it unnerving looking into the boy's face, seeing his dark eyes, his fine features, his beauty. The slender neck emerging from the rough prison shirt, the long tapering fingers as he held the phone. Even his voice sounded distorted through the receiver, almost surreal.

'Is this how Alex has to speak to you?'

'Yes. Put your hand against the glass, I'll show you how we touch.'

Evelyn pressed his palm against the glass partition, and Edward slowly lifted his own hand and pressed it against the glass on his own side. They 'touched' . . . after a moment the glass began to warm . . . Edward became more adept with the telephone, and he was now able to speak to Evelyn and remain looking at him. Evelyn lifted his hand from the glass.

'No, no . . . don't take your hand away, please . . .'

Evelyn complied, left his hand pressed close to Edward's. He found his uncle disturbing. The black eyes held him and he could see the huge man's body was shaking. But there was no tremor in the deep, husky voice. 'Keep looking at me, don't take your eyes off my face, Evelyn, and listen . . . It's very important for you to understand, take in everything I say.'

Edward kept his left hand pressed against the glass, against his son's. His voice was calm as he told Evelyn slowly that being kidnapped must have been a dreadful experience, to be dragged from the school gates . . .

Evelyn made to withdraw his hand, and Edward almost shouted, 'Keep your eyes on me, you must remember every word, understand me, every word.'

The minutes ticked by while the two of them sat with phones pressed to their ears, hands against the glass. Edward gave Evelyn dates, times, details, and he could tell by the expression on the boy's face that he was taking it all in.

When the bell rang, Edward kept talking, but Evelyn banged on the glass, shaking his head. The phone had been disconnected.

Edward dropped the receiver and put both hands against the glass. Evelyn pressed his face to the glass, mouthed 'thank you' as the door behind him opened.

It was over so fast – the handcuffs replaced, the two guards gripping Evelyn's elbows as they led him away. He looked back to see his uncle, his hands still raised to the window as if in contact with Evelyn's, his huge frame filling the entire soundproof cubicle. He was banging on the glass, shouting at his son, words Evelyn couldn't hear . . . and then the door was locked behind him.

Alone in his cell, Evelyn lay on his bunk. He had felt such power, such strength from the big man. He had been drawn close, just as if he were still the child who had run to him all those years ago. He recalled exactly what Edward had said when he had found the little boy crying at the big dining table, crying because he didn't want to leave the manor. Edward had whispered, 'We are blood to blood, put your hand on my heart, feel it, feel me . . . I am always here, don't ever be afraid.'

Evelyn placed his hand across his own heart. It had all gone so wrong and he had no one to blame but himself. He remembered not just the words but also what it had felt like all those years ago, slipping his tiny hand inside his uncle's jacket, pressing his palm against the big man's heart. In that brief moment he had felt an overwhelming and powerful bond, and he had felt it again today, even though he had been unable to touch him. He wasn't afraid any more – he knew he would be able to take whatever punishment was handed out to him, and he vowed that he would make it up to everyone, especially Alex. Calmly, he drifted into a deep sleep. It was strange because since his arrest he had been unable to, but now, as if another heart beat in rhythm with his own, he felt at peace.

There was nothing more Edward could do. He didn't even say goodbye to Alex, just threw his old case in the boot of his hired Citroën.

Driving out of Paris he felt, as ever, the desire to overtake every other vehicle on the road. Edward knew that Evelyn would more than likely be acquitted – a few months in jail, perhaps, and then he would be free.

Of late Edward had been drawn back into moments of his past, flashes of total recall. Now, as the sun broke through the clouds, he heard his father's voice. That soft, gentle voice as he sat Alex on his knee and explained to him about life and death. Edward had never sat on his father's knee, not that he could remember, it had always been Alex. What was it Freedom had said? Ahhhh, yes now he remembered – he had said, 'If you love something, set it free. If it comes back it is yours, if it doesn't then it never was.' Edward had promised his son to Alex, he would never again try to take him away. It would be the one promise in his life that he would keep. He would set them both free . . . He put his foot down harder on the accelerator, pushing it to the floor, and the car quickly picked up speed. He sang at the top of his voice, 'Can you rokka Romany, can you play the bosh . . .'

Driving at over a hundred miles an hour, he passed a police car. They switched on their siren and gave chase . . . Edward roared with laughter, and sang even louder, 'Can you jal adrey the staripen, can you chin the cosh . . .'

The Citroën began to trail thick, black smoke from its exhaust. Cars swerved, mounting the hard shoulder as the police car, siren wailing, gave chase . . .

The back tyre of the Citroën blew, and sparks mingled with thick, acrid smoke from the burning rubber . . . The car seemed to leap into the air, turned half over and skidded for more than fifty yards on its bonnet before crashing into a low brick wall. As if in slow motion, the car righted itself . . .

The police car that had chased Edward, followed by two others, pulled up, and uniformed gendarmes ran towards the wrecked Citroën.

An hysterical woman with her pet dog began to scream, a thin, high-pitched sound . . . In the pandemonium the dog broke free and began snarling and snapping at the car.

As the gendarmes came within yards of the car, Edward Barkley could clearly be seen, a calm half smile on his face. He raised a hand and waved them back. His gesture saved their lives. They paused for a moment, and in that split second the petrol tank exploded. The car became a mass of twisted metal and shattered glass . . . A thick, black, mushroom-shaped cloud rose from the wreck, spreading its choking fumes in the air . . .

Helpless and horrified, the watchers stood . . . It was eerie – there were no screams from the car – the man who was burning alive in front of their eyes was sitting looking at them, and smiling. The dog stopped howling, it slunk on its belly and whimpered as the terrible black smoke swirled . . .

There was a sudden, unreal silence, not a single sound, an unnatural, ominous quiet . . . All the witnesses seemed frozen as if held in time for a fraction of a second. They saw a black crow, black-eyed with glittering, silky wings . . . It flew overhead and hung poised above the charred car. It screamed, a single, sharp note, then flapped its wings and rose, straight through the smoke and into the clear sky beyond.

Jinks woke in the middle of the night, feeling as though her body was on fire . . . She screamed, the heat was suffocating her. She scrabbled at the bedclothes, ripping them away from her body, then started to cough, gasping for breath.

Her bedroom door was flung open and her flatmate switched on the light. Jinks was sitting bolt upright in bed, her eyes staring, still screaming. She stopped abruptly, opening and closing her mouth like a silent bird.

'Jinks . . . Jinks, wake up . . .'

Her friend shook her, but she seemed unaware of being touched. Eventually she lay back against the pillow, the sweat glistening on her forehead. Her friend quickly rinsed a face cloth and laid it gently across her brow. 'You were having a nightmare, are you all right now?'

Jinks took the cloth from her forehead and pressed it to her throat. The coolness soothed her, and she apologized for waking her. From a distance she heard her voice saying everything was fine, she was all right.

At last her bedroom door closed and she was alone. She didn't understand what was happening to her. All her senses were sharpened – the hairs on her arms and neck were tingling, and the tips of her fingers twitched of their own accord . . . She tried to regulate her breathing, stop the fluttering breathlessness, but to no avail . . .

Her head and body felt light, carrying her out on to the balcony, into the night, of their own accord. The shutters opened wide with one touch of her fingertips, the curtains billowed in the still night . . . Jinks knew, knew he was dead. In her dream she had seen the road, the blazing car, the smile on her father's handsome face . . . Edward Barkley was dead. Her chest heaved as a searing, scorching pain ripped through her, forcing the breath from her body. Something . . . something had flown out of her . . .

The tingling sensation subsided, and she returned to her room, struggling to close the heavy, unwieldy shutters. She started to pack her cases.

To her friend's astonishment, Jinks left first thing in the morning for New York. She had always tried to prepare herself for the death of her father, but it had come sooner than she anticipated. She felt no loss, but an excitement, a release . . . She felt free.

Evelyn Barkley had been sentenced to eighteen months' imprisonment, the judge accepting his innocence of the acts of terrorism. At the same time, however, Evelyn had voluntarily financed the terrorists' activities, and thus aided their cause.

He had already been in jail for five months, so he would, with good behaviour, be released in three to four months' time. But his lawyer's request for him to be allowed to serve the sentence in England was refused.

When he was led away to begin his sentence, he was told he would be allowed a few minutes alone with his father. He was coming to say goodbye before returning to England.

Alex had sat in court every day during the hearing. He had been supportive, attentive to Evelyn's every need, and in return his son gave him a warm but respectful show of affection. He wanted, needed, to give Alex his solemn oath that on his release he would prove to his father and his uncle that everything they had done for him was worthwhile.

Evelyn was shocked at his father's appearance. It was as though he had aged ten years in a matter of hours. Evelyn made an involuntary move towards him, but he stepped back. Knowing there was something terribly wrong, Evelyn placed a chair beside his father because he looked about to collapse.

'He's dead, I just got a call as I left the court. They want me to identify the body – I'm sorry, but I will have to go.'

Evelyn could not touch him. Alex seemed to recoil from any

physical contact. He was so shocked, at a loss, and his confusion had a helpless, childlike quality to it. He clutched his briefcase, half rose, then sat down again. 'Anything you need, the lawyer . . . er, the lawyer . . .'

'It's all right, father, you go and do what you have to. I'll write, and . . . I'll be home soon. Thank you for all you've done . . .'

'All I've done? It was Edward, Edward . . . Eddie? Eddie?'

Alex stared around the room, repeating his brother's name, then turned as his chauffeur appeared at the door. Evelyn watched as Alex slowly walked out, leaning heavily on the man's arm for support. When he turned back his eyes were brimming with tears.

'One time at school, this bully punched me and another kid. Eddie came in with fists flying, an' he got a right shiner. Ma found us and demanded to know what was going on. Eddie said . . . he said, "Eh, Ma, this bully punched me an' Alex and this kid, it's not our fault."' Alex said it softly, more to the room than his son. He gave a strange, sad smile, then abruptly walked out. Now that Edward was gone he was trying to find an excuse for him, but there was none. In the end he was still the Big Bad Wolf.

Chapter Thirty-Two

At the mortuary Alex was handed the gold medallion with the single word 'Stubbs' engraved on one side. He turned it over in the palm of his hand. He held it tight, afraid someone might take it from him. There were also Edward's charred wallet and papers, but he could not bring himself to touch them.

Barbara was waiting at the airport, and she too was shocked at her husband's appearance. She helped him into the Rolls, and instructed the chauffeur to take them straight home. They were being flooded with calls, and Barbara had hired a secretary to fend off all the enquiries.

The news stands carried posters, 'TYCOON DIES'. Evelyn's trial was no longer front-page news.

Edward Barkley's remains were flown back to England, and Barbara set about arranging the funeral. Alex wanted a small, quiet ceremony with only the family – Barbara could go to town on the memorial service if she wished. Barbara fully intended it to be unforgettable in the hope that it would cover her embarrassment at their son's imprisonment.

Jinks did not come to the funeral, but sent a small wreath. She telephoned to say she would arrive in time for the memorial service. Edward's ashes were left at the crematorium, with a small plaque saying simply, 'Edward Barkley, 1924–1987'.

Alex finally went to the office. Miss Henderson was wearing black, and was obviously distressed. Aware that she cared a great deal for his brother, Alex offered her as much time off as she wanted.

The building seemed empty, and everyone was shocked and uneasy. Suddenly there was no 'king'. Edward's death had left his throne empty and yet unattainable. Alex could not bear to look in the direction of Edward's office door, where his name still hung on a black plaque. It reminded Alex of Edward's grave, and Alex could not climb into that vacant throne.

Alex coped with the many necessary meetings, long overdue because of Alex's absence and the death of his brother. The French police had investigated the accident, even at one time hinting that Edward's car could have had explosives planted in it. Alex dismissed these far-fetched theories, as there were police witnesses to the fact that Edward had been driving at over a hundred miles an hour when he crashed. However, when he was alone he did consider the possibility. Edward had made contact with a lot of unsavoury people to enable him to bribe Evelyn's partners in crime. At one point he even made out a list – there were more people than he cared to think about who might want his brother dead. Even George Windsor had given him a look that seemed to say how fortuitous Edward's accident was. Alex made a conscious decision to forget the whole thing, but it still hung over him like a small, black cloud, whether he liked it or not. Edward had had many enemies – at one time Alex had numbered himself among them. But at the end he could honestly say they were friends, brothers once more.

Eventually Alex could no longer put off entering Edward's office. There were papers to be found, documents to be signed. The executors of the estate were in constant contact. The will would take a long time to sort out. They were having difficulty

tracing some of the many beneficiaries, and Edward had stipulated so many conditions. Alex was not overly concerned – he
did, after all, know exactly what his brother's will contained, or
the bulk of it. He was the sole heir, everything came to him,
and so the delay did not concern him over much. He had so
many other matters to deal with.

Edward's death also helped considerably over the allegations
of insider dealing. It enabled Alex to cover his tracks, and by the
time he had finished there was not one iota of proof against
him – any illegal transactions had been swept under the carpet,
or rather into Edward's grave. All the blame was down to his
brother – Alex was, and always had been, above reproach.

The portrait of Edward dominated the office. There was still
the old wooden panelling, the vast oak desk. When Alex
entered, he realized for the first time what Edward had meant
by power. It took his breath away, and he felt it from every
square inch of the room. Now it came home to him, now the
power was his, and his alone. It all belonged to him – at long
last, Alex had everything.

He experienced a tremendous surge of energy, and slowly
everyone began to notice – it was as if Alex had taken on
Edward's persona. He was more confident, more outgoing, and
now he began to take an interest in the arrangements for the
memorial service. He knew he was still on the current year's
Honours List, and began to like the sound of 'Sir Alex Barkley'.
The throne was no longer empty, the empire had a king, and
it was Alex. The company swung back into action under his
control.

Miss Henderson discovered Alex trying to open one of
Edward's locked drawers. 'There seem to be some keys missing,
I know Edward had a personal safe in here, is it in the desk?'

'No, sir, the entire office is computerized. You see, he had
a double security system installed.'

'What?'

'Every office has a camera, as you know, connected to the security room in the basement – but they are also connected to a bank of screens behind that wall, and the computer is built into the desk.'

'What?'

'It's very complicated, and I'm not sure how it works, no one but Mr Edward ever touched it.'

Alex glanced at his watch – he would be late if he didn't get a move on. He told Miss Henderson to get a representative from the security firm that installed the equipment into the office first thing in the morning.

Miss Henderson, still dressed from head to toe in black, was waiting anxiously for Alex to leave so she and the rest of the staff could go to the memorial service. Of course, they had not been invited to the Savoy for champagne afterwards with two hundred other guests.

She became agitated, looking at the clock. 'Mrs Barkley is waiting, sir. Shall I tell her you are just on your way? It's almost time.'

'Yes, yes, do that . . .'

Alex took another look round Edward's office. Now he had a damned good idea how his brother had kept tabs on every move the company made. As he left he looked into his own office, and sure enough there was another camera. He would never have known it was there if he hadn't known to look for it.

He sat at his desk, rang down for his car. The medallion was in a drawer, and he took it out, held it in the palm of his hand. Alex had been 'killed' in a car crash, his body identified by false dental evidence. For a moment he wondered, could Edward . . .? Would he have done it to himself? He turned the medallion over – 'Stubbs'. Barbara burst into the room.

'Alex, if we don't get a move on we will be late – it's your brother, for Chrissake! Really, I've been waiting for over half an hour, and we are in the front pew . . .'

'All right, all right . . . I'll be with you. Wait in the car.'

'Yes Alex, no Alex, you know you are beginning to sound like him? Just don't get like him, I don't think I could stand it.'

'No? You did once, more than liked him.'

'That was uncalled for.'

'Maybe, but if you don't like our present arrangement then you know what you can do, any time you want. Right, let's get this show on the road – has anyone had word from his wayward daughter?'

'She'll no doubt be at the memorial service . . .'

'No doubt.'

Alex replaced the medallion in the drawer and slammed it shut.

Miss Henderson was just leaving. As she hurried along the corridor, a tall figure, veiled and swathed in black, walked into reception.

'Hello, Hennie – recognize me?'

Slowly the figure lifted the mourning veil and smiled. Miss Henderson gasped. 'Why it's Miss Jinks . . .'

'I hate to be called that – Juliana, my name is Juliana.'

The memorial service was, as Barbara had planned, an ornate show of wealth and social contacts. Cars were parked along the Strand almost to Trafalgar Square. The small St Mark's Chapel was filled to capacity and press photographers clustered outside snapping politicians, film stars, actors . . . It was an elaborate but exceptionally well-organized circus.

Barbara had invited four well-known Shakespearian actors to read verses, and they stood in the small vestry rehearsing their lines as though getting ready for a theatrical première. In some ways it was – out in the pews were some very famous people, and one never knew when luck would strike. Why not at Edward Barkley's funeral?

Alex and Barbara were the last to arrive. Barbara's grandchildren were acting as ushers. Every pew was filled, and the rows of elegantly attired people looked around to see who was there. Two rows of exceptionally beautiful women, all dressed in black, sat in the centre of the chapel. No one knew who they were, but all eyes were upon them. They looked neither to left nor right. Jodie and her girls mourned Edward Barkley, some of the older ones more than the new young breed of girls. Jodie had brought them all from the still-flourishing Notting Hill Gate house. She was soon to own it outright – Edward Barkley had remembered her in his will.

Jinks sat well back, her hat pulled over her face to make sure she was not photographed or pressured into giving an interview. Jinks was not emotionally disturbed in any way by the showiness of the occasion – far from it. She took surreptitious glances at her watch, wondering how long it would go on.

A few seats in front of her Miss Henderson wiped the tears from her eyes. She turned and gave Juliana Barkley a small, intimate smile.

Alex was growing impatient. Yet another actor stepped up to the small, lily-bedecked rostrum. His voice rang out as he began Christina Rossetti's poem, 'Remember me when I am gone away, Gone far away into the silent land; When you can no more hold me by the hand ...'

Alex turned to Barbara in fury. 'Who chose this? Why this?'

Barbara looked round the chapel quickly, then glared at Alex. She whispered that it was Dewint's idea, apparently Edward had liked it. Alex bowed his head – it had been his mother's favourite poem, the one she had recited to him when he was a child. He gripped the edge of his seat, gritted his teeth. He could hear his mother's voice.

'Damn Barbara, damn her interfering bloody memorial service ...' he cursed silently. 'Damn you, Edward, for this charade.' He could feel himself ready to explode, 'I've got to get out of here ...'

Alex half rose from his seat, and was saved an embarrassing moment as the congregation stood to sing the final hymn.

Standing hidden in the shadows at the very back of the

church was Evelyn Barkley. He had only just made it. He had been released from prison ahead of time, his lawyers having requested for him to be present. He had watched Alex's face during the proceedings, and his mother, sitting there like royalty. Before the end of the service he left, feeling unable to cope with everyone at the Savoy, unable to return to the house in Mayfair . . . His good intentions were already fading. He didn't want to talk to his mother.

Evelyn arrived at the manor house, he had nowhere else to go and no money. Dewint came walking painfully up the over-grown gravel drive. He wore razor sharp creases in his trousers, his stiff-collared shirt and black tie, a thick black arm band around his jacket sleeve. He had to support himself with a stick, his arthritis was so bad. He had been allocated a seat at the very back of the church, and had wept through the entire service. When he saw the boy waiting, he couldn't walk another step, he recognized him immediately but couldn't speak.

'Hello, it's Dewint, isn't it? I hope you don't mind, I wondered if I could stay over for the night. It's Evelyn, Evelyn Barkley.'

'I know who you are – come in, sah, we'll go the back way, Mr Edward put a new-fangled lock on the front door and I'm blowed if I can fathom it out . . .' The pixie face crumpled, and he apologized as he took out a neatly pressed handkerchief. 'Oh, I'm sorry, sah, but I just can't get used to not having him come home.'

Evelyn helped the aged servant round to the back door, and they entered the kitchen. Having Evelyn there gave Dewint something to do, and he bustled around muttering about making up a bed, and that it would be best to use Mr Edward's as the spare rooms had not been slept in for years. He appeared not to need his walking stick, and fussed over Evelyn like an old woman.

Evelyn wandered around the house. It was in dreadful dis-repair, and creaked and groaned. Shutters banged, and it was obvious that Dewint had not dusted or cleaned for months.

Evelyn pushed open the door to what had once been Jinks' bedroom, the neat rows of toys still there, as if waiting for the child to return. Evelyn flushed as he remembered her – she was someone to whom he had to make amends, the funny little girl with the cross-eyes and lopsided pigtails . . . He had not seen her at the memorial service and he wondered how she had taken the death of her father.

Eventually he found his way to the master bedroom. The four-poster bed had been made up, and he touched the linen sheets. He noticed that his uncle's initials were embroidered on everything, sheets, towels, pillowcases, even his shirts in the wardrobe . . .

Dewint smiled at Evelyn's interest. 'Oh, that was Miss Harriet, she took a course in it. I've even got a few embroidered tea towels. She did it with a machine, very professionally . . . If you have everything you need, sah, then I'll say goodnight, sah.'

'Goodnight, Mr Dewint.'

'Will you be staying for the reading of the will, sah? The whole family's coming, Mr Edward stipulated it. It's to be read in the dining hall.'

'If it's all right with you?'

'Oh, yes, I would like it, it's good to have someone here.'

Evelyn waited until the old boy had gone up to his attic, then went back downstairs. The lounge was shuttered and dark. There were ashes left in the grate from the last fire . . . Then he realized there was something missing – he remembered there had been a large, ornate mirror over the fireplace.

He lifted the dusty lid of the old-fashioned record player, and twisted his neck to read the label of the record still on the turntable. He chuckled – it happened to be one of his favourite groups, The Doors, the lead singer long-since dead. He switched it on, settling back on the old, worn velvet sofa. Jim Morrison's voice boomed out.

This is the end, my beeeautiful friend,
This is the end, my only friend,

It hurts to see you free, but you'll never follow me.
This is the end of laughter and soft lies,
The end of summer nights we tried to die,
This is the eeennnddd . . .

Evelyn switched it off, scratching the record in his haste. The room was stuffy, and he pushed open the french windows looking over the river. He breathed in the cold night air, then noticed something was written in the dust on the window. He deciphered the scrawl: 'Evelyn . . . Evelyn . . . Evelyn MY SON . . . MY SON . . . MINE.'

Dewint tried to persuade Evelyn to contact his parents, but he refused. He remained in the manor house until the morning the will was due to be read.

Alex could not believe his eyes when Evelyn opened the door to him. 'When did you get here?'

'Just arrived, lawyers told me the will was to be read at the manor, so I came straight over.'

'I see – well, you could at least have called me. You all right?'

'Yes, yes – and you?'

'Well, I'm fine, but I could do without all this business. Still, it's typical. They'll all be arriving, so I came early to get the old fella sorted out. Few bottles in the car need putting on ice, want to give me a hand? Jesus, this place gives me the creeps, and it's not been dusted for months . . . It stinks! Dewint?'

Evelyn gestured for Alex to go into the kitchen ahead of him. Together they washed glasses and put three bottles of champagne on ice.

Some of the family arrived, and Alex bustled around giving orders for curtains to be drawn and windows opened to air the place. Barbara promptly followed him saying they should be closed as it was freezing. Evelyn hung back shyly, but Barbara swept him into her perfumed arms and said she was pleased to have him home. It almost made him laugh – like an outsider, he watched her daughters arriving with their husbands, saw the same sweeping gesture, heard the long drawn-out, 'Daaaahhhling . . .'

They all appeared more as if they were arriving for a party than the reading of a will. Evelyn noticed that his father took the throne-like chair at the head of the dining table. He looked very elegant, and smoked a cigar similar to those Edward always used to have clenched in his teeth.

Three lawyers arrived, carrying bulging briefcases. Someone remarked that they hoped luncheon had been ordered as it looked as though it was going to be a long day.

Evelyn found it difficult to answer his cousins' and aunts' questions. He avoided them as much as possible, growing quieter and quieter as the family grew louder. In the midst of laughter and funny stories, no one, not one of them, referred to the reason they were all there. Edward's name was not even mentioned.

Jinks had not yet arrived, and Evelyn kept one eye on the doors. Everyone else was there, and Alex began to get tetchy, checking his watch every minute or so. He asked the lawyers if they could begin as there was obviously a lot of paper to be got through.

Evelyn surveyed the members of his family. There was not a shred of feeling for Edward between the lot of them. Another dreadful portrait of him hung above Alex's head. It must have been painted when Edward was in his thirties, with coal-black hair. He positively glared into the room. Although it was not a good painting, it was so powerful it dominated the sitter in the throne before it. But Alex was unconscious of it, he was more interested in getting the business over and done with. Evelyn couldn't help but smile at the face in the painting, it was as though Edward knew exactly what was going on.

Just as the lawyers had agreed to begin, Dewint tapped on the door. 'Excuse me, sah, Miss Juliana has just driven up.'

Barbara muttered, 'About time too,' and like the rest of the family she turned to face the double doors. Dewint was holding one open, and swung the other wide. Both doors stood open, but the marble hall was empty.

Jinks had waited for this moment. She had been parked across the street, watching them all arrive, and had timed it to perfection. The looks on their faces made every second of the wait worthwhile.

No film star, no top model, could have made a better entrance. She was swathed in a mink coat that Barbara could tell with one glance had set her back at least twenty thousand pounds. Her slightly wavy, long hair was gleaming, and as she tossed her head it swung back from her face. A beautiful face, finely sculptured, with little or no trace of make-up. She took her time walking the entire length of the room, and offered her cheek for Alex to kiss.

'Uncle Alex.'

Alex rose to his feet – she was as tall as he was. She moved on to Barbara, bent and gave her the same non-committal cheek. She gave a languid handshake to the lawyers, two of whom bowed and scraped their chairs back, offering her their seats. One took her coat, the other seated her. At the same time she gave each of her cousins a soft, humourless smile. She said their names in turn – Annabelle, Selina, Lord Henry, Charles, James ... her eyes lingering for a fraction of a second on each face. She paused a moment longer when she looked at Lady Annabelle's daughters. The two teenage girls were open-mouthed with awe at their cousin. She hesitated over their names, not embarrassed, but amused by their gaping mouths ... Her eyes slowly roamed around the table until they rested on his face – the one person she had not seen arrive, the one she had been waiting for and wanting to see.

'Ahhh, Evelyn, how fortunate you were, being released from prison for this occasion. Well, isn't it something, I think maybe I am wrong, but isn't this the first time we have all been brought together? Oh, I am sorry, Uncle Alex – please, please don't let me delay the proceedings any longer. I am sure you were just about to begin.'

Alex nodded to the lawyers to begin and they started by naming all the beneficiaries. Edward had forgotten no one. Dewint had been left more than five hundred thousand pounds. There were names no one had ever heard of: Jodie, Sylvia, and all the girls from Notting Hill Gate had been left five or ten thousand pounds. Many employees, including Miss Henderson, were generously remembered, of course ... the list was endless.

Evelyn wanted it to go on, and on, and on – it gave him time to look at his cousin Jinks. He could not believe that this was the gawky, nervous girl from France. He continued to stare at her until she turned and gave him a look of total contempt. She pointed to a glass, and he filled it with champagne, passed it along to her.

At long last the lawyers turned to their last file. Alex puffed on his cigar. He couldn't help wondering what Edward had left to his now exceptionally glamorous niece.

The lawyer coughed and someone passed him a glass of water, which he sipped, then he licked his lips. 'We come now to the final section of the late Edward Barkley's will ...'

Alex leaned forward slightly, looking at the date on the will. He could see it quite clearly – 15 March 1987, shortly before Edward's death. This meant it could not possibly be the same document Alex had passed to the lawyers. He made an involuntary move towards the document, and the lawyer hesitated. He coughed again, pulled the will closer, and began to read ...

'To my daughter, Juliana Harriet Barkley, I leave three million pounds, to be signed over immediately. On her twenty-first birthday, a further one million ...'

The colour drained from her face. She waited for them to continue, her heart thudding ... The lawyer looked at Alex, and got as far as saying that Alex would retain his half-share in the Barkley Company and would receive a further two million when Alex snatched the will and read for himself what was written.

Edward Barkley had left to Evelyn, on condition that he publicly announced he was Edward's son, his entire fortune, plus all his shares in the Barkley Company. In other words, Evelyn was now Alex's partner. No cheque, not a single document, could be sent out from the Barkley Company without a double signature. The power, only just tasted, held for so short a time, slipped out of Alex's hands.

His initial shock subsided into a calm, deep rage. Edward had cheated him, even in death. With every ounce of control he possessed, Alex stood up and walked out of the room. He passed his son, Edward's son, with nothing more than a cursory glance. Evelyn lifted his hand as if to stop him, but Alex brushed past him. He was quickly followed by Barbara, who almost snapped her fingers to her daughters and their husbands to leave with her.

Evelyn was confused – they were looking at him with such hatred, such open loathing . . . He banged the table suddenly. 'What the hell is going on? What does he mean? What does this mean?'

Evelyn held up the will, and Barbara snatched it from him, threw it back to the lawyers. 'He wants you to announce that you are his bastard, don't you understand plain English? All your life he wanted you, tried to get you, but he couldn't . . . Now he's grabbed at you, making fools of us all, from his grave. Well, damn him, and damn you . . .'

Her family gathered around as she burst into tears. They left in a pack, and the roar of their powerful cars sounded like the start of a race . . .

Jinks turned to the lawyers, showing no emotion, showing nothing of what she was feeling. Quietly, she told them they could leave.

Evelyn, sitting with the will in his hands, offered it back to the lawyer, who nervously suggested he keep it, as it was only a copy.

Jinks remained in her seat, waiting until she heard the front door close behind them. She then turned to Evelyn as she picked up her fine, black kid gloves. She eased one on, pulling the fingers until they fitted snugly . . .

Evelyn moved closer, close enough to touch her. 'I don't want it, I don't want any of it.'

She brought her hand back and slapped him across the face. The leather hurt more than flesh . . . The slap was masculine, with so much force behind it that his neck cracked, and he gasped in shock. She then picked up her other glove.

Her voice was still low, husky, the same throaty sound he had teased her about as a little girl. She leaned close, and he could see the perfection of her skin.

'You will not get it, not a penny, it's mine . . .'

Alex paced his office like a wild animal. He walked into his brother's office, wanting to take a knife to the painting, slash Edward's face. But he didn't – he looked up at the portrait and laughed. He must have been out of his mind – the stupidity of his rage, his ridiculous behaviour . . . He could manipulate Evelyn, use him – he had brought him up, so what the hell did it matter if he announced he was Edward's son? Whoever he was, Alex would still be the controller. Evelyn knew nothing about banking, about the company, and Alex was his legal guardian. The Barkley empire had feet of clay, it was rotten to the core. This boy, this fool he had fought so hard for, was totally dependent on him, and now he would fight to bind Evelyn to him until he could make no move alone . . .

'You mind if I come in – Uncle?'

Alex had not heard her soft steps, and he turned, startled at her voice. 'No, no, Jinks, come in . . . I was just ticking myself off for my rather stupid show of temper this afternoon. Can I get you a drink?'

'No . . . I was here earlier, actually. Hennie – Miss Henderson – and I are old friends. I think I had better come clean . . . You see, I was just as, shall we say upset, as you were this afternoon. I am the legal heir, Alex, and I want my fair share. Now, I am sure whatever Evelyn wants or doesn't want will, as far as you are concerned, be of little importance – either way, you win – am I right?'

Alex side-stepped sharply. She had her finger right on the pulse. She was Edward's daughter, all right, and he shrugged, giving her a dazzling smile. 'Well, I suppose that would be Evelyn's decision, he is Edward's son . . . I've known about it for years, and now I suppose everyone else will. I'll just have to accept it.'

'But I am his daughter. I am his legitimate daughter – I could bind this company up in legal wrangles for years. You know I could fight that will – my father's drinking, and his mental state at the end of his life was rather . . . unsavoury, wasn't it? You and I know that. So don't let's play games. If I were to freeze this company's assets there would be years of litigation . . . I want to be your partner, Alex.'

'Well, sweetheart, what you want and what is legally left to you are two different things . . .'

'Whoever's son he is, it doesn't make him anything but a fool. You and I know what he is, and we can cut him out like that.' She snapped her fingers.

He stared at her, his eyes narrowed. 'What do you want? You have more than enough money, what do you want?'

She leaned against the desk, smiling. 'Well, I want what you thought had slipped right out of your hands when you heard your little boy had got the lion's share – I want this company.'

He smiled, believing she was joking. But her face was deadly serious. 'I sold Ming's – Miss Takeda's – shares back to her, for a very good price, but for less than they would have reached on the open market. In return she has given me information, Mr Stubbs. Make me your partner, or you will end up back in prison. I will make them open the grave of Alex Stubbs, East End gangster, club owner found dead in – I think it was a 1962 Jaguar, white, registration number 243 HJL. I will take over this office tomorrow morning. Perhaps you would like to know exactly what is on my father's computer? You made a mistake there, Alex, you should have got to it first ... Miss Henderson and I are just like that.'

Juliana 'Jinks' Barkley held up her crossed fingers. She gave Alex a small bow and walked out with a smile on her face, a smile so like Edward's that Alex's breath caught in his throat and left him speechless.

He sat down, incapable of coherent thought. After a long time he took off his tie and began to loosen his stiff white collar. His fingers touched the gold medallion. 'Game, set and match, Eddie, and by your own daughter.' Alex started to laugh, shaking his head at her audacity, and he let his laugh grow until he rocked back in the chair. His voice boomed out, roared with laughter. It had been years since he had laughed, actually laughed out loud. The brothers had fought for their son and, unnoticed, right under their noses, she had grown up. He knew she would be as ruthless as Edward and, just maybe, as mad as her mother. The game wasn't over, not yet, not by any means ... Only now, he was going to enjoy every minute.

The telephone rang, and he was given the tip-off that he was to be honoured, from now on he would be Sir Alexander Barkley. He laughed until the tears rolled down his cheeks. At last someone, somewhere, had beaten Edward, and it was fate, fate in the shape of his own daughter. And she was his daughter all right, no question about it. She was like an Amazon, a beautiful, red-haired Amazon.

The following morning, Alex discovered his Amazon had not stopped after her visit to him in his office. Among the mail left for his attention was a legal document requiring his signature for the transfer of all Evelyn Barkley's shares in the Barkley Company – transferring them to none other than Juliana Barkley. He now had a fight on his hands for his own survival. Juliana, he suspected, wanted more than a partnership.

*

Evelyn watched his father flip through the documents, spreading them out in his hand like a fan. He then threw them in Evelyn's face in fury.

'Why? Just tell me why?'

'You're better off without me, if you're honest you'd say it yourself.'

'Too damned right I'd be better off without you, so why didn't you sign them over to me? Why give your share to her – I sign this and you're out, you relinquish everything.'

'It makes you equal partners, that is what she wanted. It won't quite be everything, I still have a considerable amount to live on.'

Alex interrupted him, shouting, 'You said it, that little bitch wants the entire company! She's already got access to Edward's own transactions – she doesn't want a partnership, you idiot, she'll have the major share, don't you even understand what that means?'

Sighing, Evelyn stuffed his hands in his pockets and stared out across the river. It seemed he could never do anything to please his father.

'Maybe, maybe I did it for you. I don't want to fight, I don't want to be dragged through the law courts, I don't want to stand up publicly and make you a laughing stock. I give her what she wants, I don't have to make a statement, a public statement that Edward Barkley, your brother, was my father . . .'

Alex closed his eyes and seemed to deflate completely.

Juliana applauded, leaning on the jamb of the open sitting-room door. 'Well, isn't this cosy? Believe me, Alex, all I want is my inheritance, my share, my partnership, nothing more. It will save a lot of time if you sign here and now. I have no intention of taking over, we will continue the double signature, we will both run the Barkley Company.'

Alex spun round, loathing her smirking, beautiful face, but he was already unscrewing the top of his solid gold fountain pen. He snapped, 'You learn very fast.'

'I don't let the carpet get worn out under my feet, as my father would say.'

Evelyn watched Alex as he began signing the documents. Juliana, standing at his side, slowly eased off her soft leather gloves. She then signed alongside each one.

That done, she carefully replaced the cap on the pen and handed it to Alex. 'Well, partner, will you have lunch with me? I have a reservation at Le Caprice for one-thirty, and I'd like to discuss the data on Father's computer, it makes very interesting reading . . . in particular the South African companies. If you agree, I'd like to call a halt to the cloak-and-dagger tactics of my father, bring it all out in the open.'

Alex had to hand it to her, even though he would have liked to wring her neck. He stood back in admiration. 'I'll be there, one-thirty.'

She bent and kissed his cheek, taking him right off-guard. She seemed quiet and sincere, meeting his eyes with a warmth he had never seen before. She touched his cheek affectionately. 'I won't let you down, I'll make you see that this was the right, the only, decision to be made.' As she passed Evelyn on the way out, she gave him not one word of thanks, didn't even look in his direction.

Neither man spoke a word until they heard her car going away down the drive, then Alex sighed. He felt strangely awkward, even trying to make light of the situation.

'Well, that's that. I suppose I should thank you. If any scandal had broken I doubt I'd get my title . . . Did I tell you I made the Honours List?'

'Congratulations . . . Goodbye, Alex.'

Helplessly, Alex watched Evelyn walk from the room. He picked up his briefcase and followed his son into the hall. He had already reached the top of the staircase.

'What'll you do?'

Evelyn didn't look back. Mounting the stairs, he said, 'Don't know, not thought about it yet.'

'If you need me, you know where I am.'

Evelyn laughed softly, and his reply was almost inaudible. 'Yep, you'll be at the office with your partner.'

Neither of them was able to say what he felt, they could not even hold each other. The front door closed softly after Alex.

Evelyn lay down on Edward's bed. He felt drained, squeezed, wrung out. Dewint coughed politely.

'Excuse me, sah, but I was packing my possessions and, well, there's a few things Mr Edward left in 'ere . . . I found this.'

He handed Evelyn a small, brown envelope. Inside was a worn, flat book, stamped across the front. It was a Post Office Savings book, the copperplate handwriting faint over the stamp, looped and old-fashioned. It was dated May 1921, and bore the name of Evelyne Jones. Between the pages was a photograph that Evelyn remembered being taken the Christmas he had stayed at the manor.

'Who's Evelyne Jones?'

'I don't know who she is, sah, there was never anyone called Jones livin' 'ere. Will you be staying on? Only, I'm almost packed, be off in the morning. Goin' to Bermuda, sah, I've always fancied it.'

Evelyn smiled at the old man. 'Well, you have a good time . . . oh, and Dewint, if there's anything you want from the house, take it, take anything you like.'

Dewint gave one of his formal little nods, and paused at the door. 'Thank you very much, sah, an' may God bless you.' Evelyn's dark eyes and black hair made him want to weep, he was so like Edward. His high-pitched voice broke, and he swallowed. 'He loved you, sah, always loved you.'

Bowing out for the last time, Dewint went to finish his packing. Evelyn stared at the ceiling, unconsciously holding the small savings book. He turned it over, then opened it.

In Edward Barkley's handwriting was a neat list of bank account numbers. They belonged to his first-class Swiss accounts, and they were now made over to his son. The old legacy, left to his grandmother, Evelyne Stubbs, then passed to her son, Edward, still contained one pound, fifteen shillings and sixpence to be withdrawn. Evelyn Barkley held in his hands not only the original legacy, but also access to the vast personal fortune of his blood father. One billion in cash, no strings attached, no partnerships, no ties, just a short scrawled message:

'This is your freedom.'

Epilogue

One year after the death of Edward Barkley, the Barkley Company, with Juliana and Alex at the helm, was well respected and had moved into legitimate share-trading, reaping vast profits. But the nightmare of the City crash in October 1987 looked set to destroy all they had built.

Panic reigned in the City and within the Barkley organization. The pair worked frantically to salvage their tumbling shares. Alex poured his personal fortune into the failing company until he was at breaking point, but the slide continued until it became an avalanche of loss.

The Silver Cloud Rolls-Royce parked at the edge of the gypsy camp. A filthy, ramshackle, heartbreaking place, hemmed in by iron fences, it snuggled under the foul, fume-filled motorway without a single blade of grass in sight.

George Windsor had driven Alex to the camp on three consecutive nights. Each time, after driving slowly past, Alex had ordered him to take them home. But tonight Alex had made up his mind to go in, even though Windsor had warned him not to.

Threading his way among the broken-down cars, caravans and trailers, Alex finally reached the main semi-circle of wagons. From within could be heard the sounds of television sets and muffled voices. He stood in the darkness, unsure of what to do next.

A hand grabbed him by his fur collar and whipped him round. 'What the hell do you want, man?'

Two more surly-looking men appeared from the gloom. Shaking with fear, Alex put his hands up, thinking the man was about to hit him. 'Please, I mean no harm. I need to speak to a dukkerin.'

He was pushed roughly between them as they jeered and laughed at him, pushing him back and forth, their voices rising.

'Need a what? What the hell you want, man, eh? Eh?'

Lights came on, doors opened and voices yelled for the men to keep quiet as there were kids sleeping. 'Get out, man, go on, get out!' Hands touched him, patted his pockets, almost took his wallet. A woman's voice screeched, 'What you men doin'? Gerraway from him! You! Come here.'

The woman had an instant effect on the men, and they released Alex.

'What you want, mun? What you come here for?'

Alex moved nearer, his hands up in a gesture of submission. 'Please, I need to speak with a dukkerin, is there one among you? A fortune-teller?'

The men behind him laughed, mimicking his voice, but the old woman scrutinized him, sucking her lips into her toothless mouth.

'Please help me, my father was a Romany . . .'

'Bring him in, lads, then leave him be. An' if yer got his wallet, give it back.'

She sat in a creaking armchair and waved him to another. Her hands, with rings on every finger, were arthritic, gnarled, and she was more lined than any woman he had ever seen. Her holed stockings were as wrinkled as she was, but her eyes, black, small eyes, were bright and young in her strange wizened face.

'Dukkerin, eh? Where you learn the old language?'

'My father was Freedom Stubbs.'

She shrugged, and if she knew the name she gave no hint of recognition. 'Why you come here? What you want?'

Alex tried to explain, feeling helplessly inadequate and near to breaking point, the tears constantly prickling his eyes. In a halting voice he told her of his father, of Edward. Then he put his head in his hands and wept, unashamedly.

'I always believed Edward was a lucky man, just a lucky man, but now I don't know. It's as if he's still alive, but turning everything rotten. I don't know if it's his face I see or my father's, but I can't sleep . . .'

'He's haunting you, is that it?'

The relief that she said it so simply was astonishing, and he nodded, licking his lips. He reached out to hold her hand.

'Yes, yes, that's it exactly, but I can't tell anyone, they'd think me crazy. I feel him around me all the time . . . I'm a rich man, I'll give you anything you ask if you can help me.'

She held his hand, looking into his face, then she touched his forehead. 'You got the Romany blood in you. You get us a decent camp, mun. You get us moved to a decent place.'

'I'll do whatever is in my power to help you, I give you my word.'

She released his hand and settled back in her chair. 'You have something of his with you?'

He shook his head, then he remembered. He loosened his tie, unbuttoned his collar, and took off the gold medallion.

Evelyn Barkley returned to Wales to discover more of his background. When he learned of the Barkley Company's losses, he wrote to Juliana with permission to sell the manor and all its contents. The land alone would be worth a quarter of a million on the property market.

No one had entered the manor since the reading of the late Edward Barkley's will. The house was in a state of ruin; during the hurricane of November 1987, a tree had crashed through the south end of the roof.

Juliana began to check the house for items that could be auctioned. Intent on her work, she remained until evening. As it grew dark she tried the light switches, but the electricity had been cut off, so she fetched a candle from the kitchen.

As she passed through the hall she noticed the door to the dining room was slightly ajar, and she paused a moment, feeling drawn to the room.

Her father's portrait faced her. Water had seeped through the ceiling and run down the gilt frame. It had dripped down his cheeks, leaving stains that looked like tears. She stood looking up into her father's face, without fear, without hatred.

Putting the candle down, she made a note of the table and the ornate chairs, then opened a large Victorian dresser. She added the solid silver cutlery to the inventory and bent to open the lower drawers, where she found silver serving dishes, wrapped in damp newspaper that was yellow with age. At ten-fifteen she paused. The candle was burning low and she was uncertain whether or not to continue, but there was only the drawing room left.

Shielding the candle flame, she inched open the heavy double doors into the room. The room had been left untouched with the ashes of a fire still in the grate.

There was writing, still legible, scrawled on a window over-looking the river: 'My son, my son Evelyn'. The candle flame flickered and sputtered. Above the mantelpiece, in the centre of the dark-edged space where the mirror had hung, was a strange, red-brown stain that resembled a necklace. The room felt icy cold and Juliana shivered, almost dropping the candle in fright when she heard footsteps, slow footsteps ... She turned in terror as the door creaked open.

'Oh, God, Alex, you almost gave me a heart attack! Why didn't you call out? This is the last room, I've done all the others. I'm afraid there's not much worth selling, but at least we'll get a good price for the land. They can build a tower block of apart-ments, great view over the river. I reckon we can ask more than we ... Alex?'

He was standing directly in front of the fireplace, staring at the stain on the wall. Fishing a box of matches from his pocket he struck one, held it above his head. 'It's like my mother's necklace, the shape.'

'I suppose it must be water, every room's got water stains. Anything worth selling has been ruined.'

Alex still stared at the stained wall.

'He took it from her grave, he should never have done that. He had the medallions made from the gold. What did you do with Edward's?'

Juliana was bending to peer into a glass cabinet filled with ornaments. 'These are junk — what did you say?'

'The medallion I gave you, the gold medallion.'

'Well, funnily enough I wear it. You always said my father had the Midas touch, I thought it would bring me luck. How wrong can one be? Right now our luck's running out so fast . . .'

Alex took his own chain from his pocket and walked over to her. 'Give it to me, take the damned thing off. Take it off!'

She backed away from him, her hand to her throat. 'Don't be stupid, Alex . . . The candle, mind the candle!'

The stub of the candle rolled across the floor, spilling its wax, but he ignored it. He held out his hand for the medallion as she unclasped it from her neck. When he looked again, the candle was lying against the side of the sofa, still alight. He picked it up and walked out of the room, calling for her to follow.

In the hall were three cans of petrol. 'Start in the master bedroom, pour it over everything. I'll begin down here. We've got to set light to the place, it's got to burn down.'

'Are you crazy? What about the silver, the furniture?'

He had already opened one of the cans. 'Everything worth anything must burn.'

'Why? Insurance? Is that what all this is about, insurance?'

Alex was pouring petrol along the hallway. He pushed open the door to the dining room, splashing the strong-smelling liquid everywhere.

'Alex, answer me. Are you doing this for the insurance?'

'No, but the flames will take away his evil, and they'll scorch his pain . . . We're burying a curse. Think me crazy, think whatever you like, but don't try to stop me.'

She stood watching him, helplessly, as he emptied the can of petrol. Tossing the can aside, he held out his hand to her, looking up at Edward's portrait. 'Come here, it's all right. Look at his face, his eyes . . . Same eyes as my father, Romany eyes – black eyes that never let you know what's behind them, what they're thinking.'

Standing a little distance from Alex, she looked up at her father's face, then turned. Alex seemed transfixed by the painting, and she looked again. Her father's eyes seemed alive, the water-stain tears distorting his face. When Alex spoke she could barely hear him.

'I never noticed before, but you can see it in his face. He did a terrible thing, it wasn't premeditated, but it was done in terrible anger. Long, long ago he killed your grandfather, my father . . . His name was Freedom, Freedom Stubbs. The name engraved on the medallions is our real name. Edward changed it to Barkley, but Freedom wouldn't let him go – he couldn't, because the gold in the medallions was taken from the grave. I don't think he even knew what he had done – the gold was Freedom's talisman.' Alex paused, closed his eyes. 'We were brothers, but only Edward inherited the powers, and I believed he was haunting me, trying to destroy me from the grave. But I was wrong – he's warning me, for Evelyn's sake, for his son. Edward was cursed, and it will pass to Evelyn.' He held up the two gold medallions and repeated the last lines of the Romany curse:

> For who steals the charm of a dukkerin's son,
> Will walk in his shadow, bleed with his blood,
> Cry loud with his anguish and suffer his pain.
> His unquiet spirit will rise up again,
> His footsteps will echo unseen on the ground
> Until the curse is fulfilled, the talisman found.

They both stood close to the jetty, right at the water's edge. From there they watched, knowing that any moment the flames would begin to show. They could see the black, curling smoke; had seen it for almost ten minutes.

It exploded like a bomb. The boom! as it caught the heart of the house could be heard for miles around, but they did not leave until they were sure that the fire was unquenchable. Edward Barkley's soul burned.

Alex struck the wood of the coffin lid. From his pocket he took the two medallions – his own and Edward's. He laid them, with their chains, on the coffin in the sign of a cross. The gold talisman was given at last to the grave.

When he had shovelled back the earth, he knelt in prayer. 'Rest in peace, Freedom, peace be with you both. It's over, Edward, it's over now.'

As he walked away from the grave he felt the oppressive weight lift from his shoulders. It was as if it had always been there – but now he felt light, he was free.

Evelyn was waiting at the gates of his small, rented farmhouse. He had been waiting ever since Juliana had called, even though he knew it would take at least four or five hours for them to get to him, sitting impatiently on the five-barred gate.

The Rolls-Royce sparkled in the early morning sun as it came over the hilltop and along the small country lanes. Evelyn ran to meet it, shouting, arms held wide.

Alex stepped out of the car, hesitant at first, then sprinted the last few yards to his son and clasped him in his arms. Overcome with emotion he fumbled in his pocket for a handkerchief, then gave up and wiped his face with the back of his hand.

'Some tycoon, eh? Crying like a baby . . . You know, this is the first time I've ever wept because . . . because I'm happy. Will you come home?'

Juliana stepped from the car. There was such a gentleness about Evelyn, such a genuine warmth, that Juliana threw her arms around his neck and kissed him. His response was a little bemused, but then he tilted his head back and laughed his wonderful laugh . . .

Alex shouted, pointing across the fields between the hills. His delight showed in his face like a child's as he said, 'It's the mountain, it's the mountain . . . It's my mountain!'

Rising up against the brilliant dawn sky, lit by the bright sun, was the mountain from his dreams that had always been beyond his reach, that the black rider had leapt, passing by the outstretched hand of the young boy. Now it was before him, no longer a dream but tangible, real, waiting and beckoning him to climb to the very top. He turned to them, his face shining, more alive than either of them had ever seen him. The years seemed to drop away and his handsome face was youthful, vibrant, and his clear blue eyes were those of a young boy.

'I want to climb that, go right to the top.'

They stood together at the very top of the mountain, their arms linked. Alex gently brushed Juliana's cheek with his hand. She opened her eyes and they both looked at Evelyn.

He too held his face, as they had done, to the sky. They were transfixed, mesmerized by him – he was in a world of his own, his eyes closed, his long, dark lashes shadowing his cheeks. His hair flew in the wind . . . Slowly, he lifted his arms and breathed in the sweet, clear air and smiled, his perfect face softening as he whispered, 'Freedom . . .'

The whisper echoed round the mountain, and he opened his eyes and laughed.

Alex felt as though his heart would burst. He was at the top of his mountain and, even if Evelyn hadn't meant to say his grandfather's name, it was the culmination of his dream. It no longer mattered that the boy was of Edward's blood, because their blood was one. They were bound together, and at last had come together in peace. He reached out and took their hands, whispering joyously, 'I am a lucky man.' Then he lifted their arms high and shouted to the mountain, 'Freedom . . . Freedom . . . Freeeeeedooooooooommmmmm . . .'